# TOTAL IMMERSION

## THE COMPREHENSIVE UNAUTHORIZED RED DWARF ENCYCLOPEDIA

## VOLUME 2
## (L-Z)

By Paul C. Giachetti

Edited by Rich Handley

Foreword by Jonathan Capps

Illustrations by Pat Carbajal

HASSLEIN • BOOKS

*Total Immersion: The Comprehensive Unauthorized Red Dwarf Encyclopedia—Volume 2*



Writer and designer: Paul C. Giachetti
Editor: Rich Handley
Proofreader: Joseph Brandt Dilworth
Foreword: Jonathan Capps
Illustrations: Pat Carbajal

ISBN-13: 978-0-578-15058-1
Library of Congress Cataloging-in-Publication Data
First Edition: November 2014
10 9 8 7 6 5 4 3 2 1

# CONTENTS

*"When it comes to weirdy, paradoxy space stuff, I've bought the t-shirt."*

**—Lister, "Cassandra"**



*"That's why I had my appendix out... twice."*

**—Rimmer, "Thanks for the Memory"**

# ABBREVIATION KEY

## A Guide to the Guide

*"So what is it?"*

**—Cat, "White Hole"**

---

*Total Immersion* draws information not only from the television series, but also from a wide variety of other sources, some more obscure than others. To make it easier for readers to discern where a particular entry (or segment of an entry) was mined from, a coding system has been implemented in lieu of traditional footnotes, which would have been much less practical for a book of this nature.

Each code features a prefix denoting a general classification—whether the material was gleaned from a television episode, novel, book, website, etc. Each prefix is followed by a three-character code further denoting the source. For episodes and magazine issues, a number follows directly after this code, identifying the source more specifically. For example, [T-SER3.5] references the fifth episode of the TV program's third series, while [M-SMG2.3] refers to the third issue in the *Smegazine*'s second run. Additionally, codes may be followed by a lowercase letter suffix in parentheses, denoting an even more specific source, such as bonus DVD materials, a particular *Smegazine* comic, or an early-draft script. With the *Smegazines*, a number following the suffix indicates the material's order; for example, (c4) means the fourth comic in the issue.

Fans have widely varying opinions regarding what is and is not considered canon within the *Red Dwarf* universe. This encyclopedia does not take a stance on that debate, instead utilizing an all-inclusive approach, considering anything and everything officially sanctioned by Grant Naylor Productions to be a viable resource, including things that may severely conflict with the television show. Since every entry is marked with one or more codes denoting the material's origin, readers are free to reject and ignore any aspect of the franchise they prefer not to include.

All prefixes, codes and suffixes are detailed below. Additional details about each story, including descriptions, credits and release dates, can be found in Appendix I in Volume 1.

## CODES:

**RL: REAL LIFE**

Information tagged with this code comes from real-world sources.

**T: TELEVISION EPISODES**

- **SER**: Televised
- **IDW**: "Identity Within" (untelevised)
- **USA1**: Unaired U.S. pilot
- **USA2**: Unaired U.S. demo reel

**R: REMASTERED *(The Bodysnatcher Collection)***

- **SER**: Remastered episodes
- **BOD**: "Bodysnatcher" storyboards
- **DAD**: "Dad" storyboards
- **FTH**: "Lister's Father" storyboards
- **INF**: "Infinity Patrol" storyboards
- **END**: "The End" (original assembly)

**N: NOVELS**

- **INF**: *Infinity Welcomes Careful Drivers*
- **BTL**: *Better Than Life*
- **LST**: *Last Human*
- **BCK**: *Backwards*
- **OMN**: *Red Dwarf Omnibus*

**M: MAGAZINES**

- **SMG**: *Smegazine*

**B: BOOKS**

- **PRG**: *Red Dwarf Programme Guide*
- **SUR**: *Red Dwarf Space Corps Survival Manual*
- **PRM**: *Primordial Soup*
- **SOS**: *Son of Soup*
- **SCE**: *Scenes from the Dwarf*
- **LOG**: *Red Dwarf Log No. 1996*
- **EVR**: *The Log: A Dwarfer's Guide to Everything*
- **RD8**: *Red Dwarf VIII*

**G: ROLEPLAYING GAME**

- **RPG**: *Core Rulebook*
- **BIT**: *A.I. Screen* (including *Extra Bits* booklet)
- **SOR**: *Series Sourcebook*
- **OTH**: Other RPG material (including online PDFs)

**W: WEBSITES**

- **OFF**: Official website (www.reddwarf.co.uk)
- **NAN**: *Prelude to Nanarchy* (www.reddwarf.co.uk/gallery/index.cfm?page=prelude-to-nanarchy)
- **AND**: *Androids* (www.androids.tv)
- **DIV**: Diva-Droid (www.divadroid.info)
- **DIB**: Duane Dibbley (www.duanedibbley.co.uk)
- **CRP**: Crapola (www.crapola.biz)
- **GEN**: Geneticon (www.geneticon.info)
- **LSR**: Leisure World International (www.leisureworldint.com)
- **JMC**: Jupiter Mining Corporation (www.jupiterminingcorporation.com)
- **AIT**: *A.I. Today* (www.aitoday.co.uk)
- **HOL**: HoloPoint (www.holopoint.biz)

**X: MISC.**

- **PRO**: Promotional materials, videos, etc. (specified in notes)
- **PST**: Posters displayed at Dimension Jump XVII (2013)
- **CAL**: *Red Dwarf* 2008 Calendar
- **RNG**: Cell Phone Ringtones
- **MOB**: Mobisode ("Red Christmas", Parts 1 and 2)
- **CIN**: *Red Dwarf Children in Need* Sketch
- **GEK**: Geek Week introductions by Kryten
- **TNG**: "Tongue-Tied" video
- **XMS**: Bill Pearson's Christmas special pitch script
- **XVD:** Bill Pearson's Christmas special pitch video
- **OTH**: Other *Red Dwarf* appearances (specified in notes)

## SUFFIXES:

**DVDs**

- (d) – Deleted scene
- (o) – Outtake
- (b) – Bonus DVD material (other)
- (e) – Extended version

***SMEGAZINES / FAN CLUB MAGAZINES***

- (c) – Comic
- (a) – Article

**OTHER**

- (s) – Early or unused script draft
- (s1) – Alternate version of script

# THE ENCYCLOPEDIA [L-Z]

*"They're all dead. Everybody's dead, Dave."*

**—Holly, "The End"**

L

# LANSTROM, HILDEGARDE, DOCTOR

- **L:** A letter adorning a patch on Lister's leather jacket **[T-SER5.2]**, as well as a hat he occasionally wore **[T-SER6.2]**.

- **L01:** A code printed on a storage compartment in *Starbug 1*'s galley **[T-SER6.4]**.

- **L24 E-carbine:** A firearm favored by rogue simulants that fired bursts of charged nanites with a variety of effects, depending on the weapon's setting. The E-carbine held a thirty-round clip and had an effective range of 60 meters (197 feet) **[G-SOR]**.

- **"La Bamba":** A traditional Mexican folk song made popular by Ritchie Valens' 1958 adaptation **[RL]**. Among Lister's talents was the ability to belch "La Bamba" after eleven pints of beer **[N-INF]**.

- **laboratory mice:** A group of rodents kept in *Red Dwarf*'s lab for experimentation purposes. When Rimmer accused Lister of complacency about being the crew's lowest-ranking member, Dave rationalized that he outranked the laboratory mice **[T-SER1.1]**. In an alternate dimension, the lab mice survived the cadmium II disaster, evolving into a sapient species known as *Mus sapiens* **[G-RPG]**.

- **LaBouche, Trixie:** An erotic leisure consultant who worked on the streets of Shagtown, a seedy area of Saturn's moon, Mimas **[M-SMG2.5(c6)]**. Rimmer once approached her and a co-worker to hire their services **[M-SMG2.3(c4)]**. She had jet-black hair and lived in Apartment 43 at the Hotel Paradiso **[M-SMG2.5(c6)]**.

  Concerned about a lack of protection from the Ganymedian Mafia, LaBouche visited Noel's Body Swap Shop to obtain a new form. An astro miner named Dutch van Oestrogen stole her body from the shop, however, to escape the same Mafia after a drug deal had gone sour **[M-SMG2.3(c4)]**.

  After hiding for a time, Dutch tried to retrieve his own body, but members of the Mafia ambushed him, and the body swap machine was damaged in the ensuing firefight. Dutch emerged the victor and demanded his own body back, but due to the damage, the transition was not one hundred percent successful. As a result, Trixie retained the memory of where Dutch had hidden his stash **[M-SMG2.4(c2)]**.

  The sex worker ran to her hotel room to pack, but encountered van Oestrogen in the parking lot, where the Mafia attacked them both. Ditching their pursuers, Dutch pursued Trixie around Mimas Spaceport **[M-SMG2.5(c6)]**, until catching up with her near the locker containing his stash. This commotion caused Lister—who was residing inside a nearby locker at the time—to fling open the door, smashing the astro in the face and knocking him unconscious. Trixie then stole Lister's passport (which bore the name Emily Berkenstein) and boarded Flight 578 to Neptune **[M-SMG2.6(c4)]**.

  While trapped in an addictive version of *Better Than Life*, Rimmer imagined being incarcerated in a soundwave prison with LaBouche and two other soundwaves, his Solidgram body repossessed for the duration. The image of Trixie had peroxide-blonde hair and a tattoo on her inner thigh that read "Heaven This Way," accompanied by an upward-pointing arrow.

  In the illusion, Trixie had rented her Solidgram body to Dutch for a weekend of lust, but he inhabited her body instead of ravaging it and used it to rob three banks. After her body was returned to her, she was convicted of the crimes and placed in a cell with Rimmer. While escaping from the prison, Arnold possessed her body after cellmate Jimmy Jitterman hijacked his **[N-BTL]**.

  ***NOTE:** Trixie LaBouche and Dutch van Oestrogen were in Shagtown when Rimmer first met Lister while visiting a brothel on Mimas in the* Smegazine *comic "Mimas Crossing—Part 1." Several characters in Arnold's* Better Than Life *illusion, including Trixie and Dutch, were based on individuals whom he knew or had met. Presumably, his subconscious mind created these characters based on his memories of them—though it is unclear when he encountered Dutch.*

- ***Ladybird Book of Astronavigation*:** A children's book from which Rimmer claimed Lister attained his astronavigation knowledge **[T-SER1.2]**.

  ***NOTE:** Ladybird Books is a real-world publisher of children's books in the United Kingdom. To date, the company has yet to publish a volume on astronavigation.*

- ***Lady Chatterley's Lover*:** A novel written by D. H. Lawrence, published in 1928 **[RL]**. Bob the skutter smuggled this book to Lister, along with some chicken vindaloo, poppadoms, lager and cigars, during his incarceration in the Tank **[T-SER8.6(d)]**.

- **"Lady Luck":** A phrase printed on a patch adorning the front of Lister's jacket, accompanied by an illustration of a blonde woman and a pair of dice **[T-SER10.2]**.

- ***Lady With a Face, The*:** A DVD displayed in a twenty-first-century mall video store that the *Red Dwarf* crew imagined while trapped in an elation squid hallucination. The DVD's release date was July 27 **[T-SER9.2]**.

- **Lager Crab Thing:** A creature, possibly from an alternate universe, mutated from a can of lager. It possessed a beer logo on its torso and an aluminum shell **[G-BIT]**.

- ***Lagos*:** A derelict scout ship that the *Starbug* crew found on an arctic moon while pursuing *Red Dwarf*. Onboard, they discovered technology in advance of their own, including easy-to-open yogurt containers and a hard-light drive. Kryten used the latter to give Rimmer a Solidogram body **[N-LST]**.

> ***NOTE:*** *This contradicted episode 6.2 ("Legion"), in which Legion converted Rimmer's light bee to hard light.*

- **Lake Michigan:** One of the five Great Lakes of North America, bordered by the states of Wisconsin, Illinois, Indiana and Michigan **[RL]**. After defeating the mutton vindaloo beast created by a DNA-modifying machine, a pint-sized Lister wished he had a poppadom the size of Lake Michigan with which to clean up the mess **[T-SER4.2]**.

- **Lamb, Charles:** A nineteenth-century English essayist who wrote such works as *Essays of Elia* and *Tales from Shakespeare* **[RL]**. While marooned on a frozen planet, Lister attempted to stay warm inside *Starbug 1* by burning items stored aboard ship. Succumbing to hunger, he was dismayed to find several books written by authors whose names reminded him of food, such as Charles Lamb, Herman Wouk and Francis Bacon **[T-SER3.2]**.

- **Lamborghini Sesto Elemento:** A rare, high-performance sports car made by Italian automaker Lamborghini **[RL]**. To impress his half-brother Howard, Rimmer claimed to have owned two such vehicles. As Howard was dying, he revised that number to just one **[T-SER10.1]**.

- **Lancelot, Sir:** A character of Arthurian legend who served as one of the Knights of the Round Table and was King Arthur's most trusted champion **[RL]**.

  A waxdroid replica of Lancelot was created for the Waxworld theme park. Left on their own for millions of years, the waxdroids attained sentience and became embroiled in a park-wide resource war between Villain World and Hero World (to which Lancelot belonged). Lancelot died during the conflict **[T-SER4.6]**.

- **landing bay:** An area aboard the "low" *Red Dwarf* allocated for receiving incoming shuttlecraft. The landing bay was identified by a decaying sign **[T-SER5.5]**.

- **Landing Bay 2:** A landing bay aboard *Red Dwarf*. After *Starbug 1*'s fore section narrowly escaped the shrinking air vents of an enlarged *Red Dwarf*, the shuttle crashed through Landing Bay 2 and on into Landing Bay 6 **[T-SER8.1]**.

  Landing Bay 2 housed several *Blue Midget* shuttles **[T-SER8.3]**. A corridor near this bay was among the first areas affected by a corrosive chameleonic microbe that had previously destroyed the SS *Hermes* **[T-SER8.8]**.

- **Landing Bay 6:** Another landing bay aboard *Red Dwarf*. After *Starbug 1*'s fore section narrowly escaped the shrinking air vents of an enlarged *Red Dwarf*, it came to rest in Landing Bay 6, where it exploded just after the crew escaped **[T-SER8.1]**.

- **Landing Bay 9:** An area of *Red Dwarf* that Kryten converted into a hydroponics pod in order to grow food, using special chemicals to promote rapid growth. A side-effect of the chemicals was the creation of a nine-thousand-pound greenfly that terrorized the crew until being flushed out into space **[B-LOG]**.

- **landing bay interface:** A box-like component aboard *Red Dwarf*, consisting of a single outlet and five interface ports **[T-SER7]**.

  > ***NOTE:*** *This item appeared in the Series VII DVD bonus feature "Fan Films," which offered brief glimpses of a fan's collection. Presumably, it was a production prop.*

- **Landing Deck B:** An area aboard *Starbug 1* allocated for receiving and housing smaller spacecraft **[T-SER7.2]**.

- **landing gantry:** A section of *Red Dwarf* used for receiving inbound craft. The crew confronted Kryten's replacement, Hudzen 10, near this gantry **[T-SER3.6]**.

- **landing jets:** A set of exterior engines on a *Starbug* shuttle enabling the craft to land **[T-SER4.5]**. Each shuttle contained three such jets. As *Starbug 1* crashed on a backwards-running Earth, the shuttle's landing jets were ripped from the vessel as it tore through treetops. Due to the reversal of time, the jets re-attached to the craft as it later departed from the planet **[N-BCK]**.

**PREFIX**
**RL:** Real life

**T-: Television Episodes**
- **SER:** Television series
- **IDW:** "Identity Within"
- **USA1:** Unaired U.S. pilot
- **USA2:** Unaired U.S. demo

**R-: *The Bodysnatcher Collection***
- **SER:** Remastered episodes
- **BOD:** "Bodysnatcher"
- **DAD:** "Dad"
- **FTH:** "Lister's Father"
- **INF:** "Infinity Patrol"
- **END:** "The End" (original assembly)

**N-: Novels**
- **INF:** *Infinity Welcomes Careful Drivers*
- **BTL:** *Better Than Life*
- **LST:** *Last Human*
- **BCK:** *Backwards*
- **OMN:** *Red Dwarf Omnibus*

**M-: Magazines**
- **SMG:** *Smegazine*

**W-: Websites**
- **OFF:** Official website
- **NAN:** *Prelude to Nanarchy*
- **AND:** *Androids*
- **DIV:** Diva-Droid
- **DIB:** Duane Dibbley
- **CRP:** Crapola
- **GEN:** Geneticon
- **LSR:** Leisure World Intl.
- **JMC:** Jupiter Mining Corporation
- **AIT:** *A.I. Today*
- **HOL:** HoloPoint

**G-: Roleplaying Game**
- **RPG:** *Core Rulebook*
- **BIT:** *A.I. Screen Extra Bits* booklet
- **SOR:** *Series Sourcebook*
- **OTH:** Other RPG material

- **language lab:** A section of *Red Dwarf* allocated for crewmembers to learn new languages, located within the ship's reference library. Prior to the cadmium II disaster, Rimmer assigned Wilkinson and Turner to sanitize the language lab's headsets **[N-INF]**.

- **Lanstrom, Hildegarde, Doctor:** A brilliant scientist assigned to a viral research station located on a frozen planetoid. Lanstrom had doctorates in viral contagion and general medicine, and suffered a wheat allergy. She died when a resident philosopher went crazy and cut off her head with a fire axe to prove he was a figment of her imagination **[W-OFF]**.

- **Lanstrom, Hildegarde, Doctor:** A hologram of the viral research scientist who was revived after a crazed philosopher decapitated her. As a hologram, Lanstrom continued her work on pathogens, focusing on "positive viruses" (those that produced positive effects). These included such strains as the reverse flu, *Inflatus mentis* (inspiration), *Felicitus populi* (luck), *Delecto quislibet* (sexual magnetism) and *Ignotus venustas* (charisma). Troubled that she could not become infected by these positive viruses herself, she began working on hologrammatical versions of the strains, enlisting the help of a computer expert to program the station's hologram scanning software to scan and convert the samples.

  When these efforts proved successful, Lanstrom used her newly heightened inspiration to create a super holovirus that could stimulate dormant areas of the brain to produce psychic powers. For decades, she worked on the holovirus, while her fellow scientists died of old age. Eventually, she developed a holovirus that she dubbed simply *Latin name*, due to her inability to find time to research a proper scientific nomenclature.

  In addition to giving her telekinesis and telepathy, this virus endowed Lanstrom with hex vision (the ability to fire streams of energy from her eyes), drove her insane and drained away her life force. Desperate, she radioed an SOS call to a passing vessel, hoping to find a qualified medic to assist her, but accidently infected the ship's resident hologram via the transmission, causing him to go mad and flush his crew out an airlock. Lanstrom then activated the station's distress beacon and put herself into stasis to await rescue by medical personnel **[W-OFF]**.

  Three million years later, the *Red Dwarf* crew picked up her beacon and opened her stasis booth. Lanstrom murderously pursued them throughout the station until depleting her remaining energy, after which she ceased to exist. Just prior to dying, she transmitted the holovirus via radio waves, infecting Rimmer **[T-SER5.4]**.

- ***Lapis sapiens*:** A species of humanoids that evolved from rabbits aboard the *Oregon* in an alternate universe. A warrior species, the rabbit people became the dominant life form in their reality and subjugated mankind, who were reduced to ignorant savages. The extremely efficient rabbits excelled in medical and cosmetic technology due to experimentation they performed on humans. Their religion was based on ancient animal rights propaganda and Bugs Bunny cartoons **[G-RPG]**.

  ***NOTE:*** Red Dwarf—The Roleplaying Game *implied that* Lapis sapiens *society resembled Germany's Nazi regime.*

- **laser:** A device built to generate an intense beam of coherent monochromatic light via the emission of photons from excited atoms or molecules. The term "laser" was originally an acronym for "**l**ight **a**mplification by **s**timulated **e**mission of **r**adiation" **[RL]**. Cat suggested utilizing a laser to cut through sealed doors after a ship-wide power failure isolated the *Red Dwarf* crew from the Science Room. Despite hailing this as a sound idea, Kryten noted that the power outage would prevent them from using a laser—and that they, in fact, had no laser to use **[T-SER4.4]**.

- **laser bone-saw:** A tool used in medical facilities aboard JMC vessels that could cut through bone and cauterize wounds. It was particularly useful for amputations **[T-SER7.7]**. The saw was produced by Malpractice Medical & Scispec and distributed by Crapola Inc., and was rated the number-one surgical implement of the year by *Mend and Rend Magazine* **[G-RPG]**. Kryten used a laser bone-saw aboard *Starbug 1* to amputate Lister's right arm after corralling the Epideme virus into the appendage **[T-SER7.7]**.

- **laser cannon:** An offensive weapon capable of firing laser bolts **[T-SER5.1]**, also called a laser for short **[T-SER6.6]**. Cat suggested using *Starbug 1*'s laser cannons against the holoship *Enlightenment* after its crew kidnapped Rimmer. Although

**B-: Books**
**PRG:** *Red Dwarf Programme Guide*
**SUR:** *Red Dwarf Space Corps Survival Manual*
**PRM:** *Primordial Soup*
**SOS:** *Son of Soup*
**SCE:** *Scenes from the Dwarf*
**LOG:** *Red Dwarf Log No. 1996*
**RD8:** *Red Dwarf VIII*
**EVR:** *The Log: A Dwarfer's Guide to Everything*

**X-: Misc.**
**PRO:** Promotional materials, videos, etc.
**PST:** Posters at DJ XVII (2013)
**CAL:** 2008 calendar
**RNG:** Cell phone ringtones
**MOB:** Mobisode ("Red Christmas")
**CIN:** *Children in Need* sketch
**GEK:** *Geek Week* intros by Kryten
**TNG:** "Tongue-Tied" video
**XMS:** Bill Pearson's Christmas special pitch script
**XVD:** Bill Pearson's Christmas special pitch video
**OTH:** Other *Red Dwarf* appearances

**SUFFIX**
**DVD:**
**(d)** – Deleted scene
**(o)** – Outtake
**(b)** – Bonus DVD material (other)
**(e)** – Extended version

**SMEGAZINES:**
**(c)** – Comic
**(a)** – Article

**OTHER:**
**(s)** – Early/unused script draft
**(s1)** – Alternate version of script

admitting it was a good idea, Kryten noted that *Starbug 1* was not equipped with laser cannons **[T-SER5.1]**.

While trespassing in a rogue simulant hunting zone, the *Starbug 1* crew were captured and rendered unconscious for three weeks. Once revived, they discovered that the shuttle had been upgraded with an improved drive system and engines, as well as the addition of laser cannons—which the simulant captain had installed so they would provide a more challenging hunt **[T-SER6.3]**.

> ***NOTE:*** *The laser cannon may have been the same weapon as the missile launcher in episode 6.6 ("Out of Time") and the laser missiles referenced in the unfilmed script "Identity Within."*

- **laser chainsaw:** A cutting tool, similar to a standard chainsaw, on which laser teeth rotated around a central blade **[G-SOR]**. Kryten used a laser chainsaw to cut off the Inquisitor's hand containing the time gauntlet **[T-SER5.2]**.

- **laser harpoon:** *See* T 27 electron harpoon

- **laser lance:** One of hundreds of types of weapons lining the wall of the Hub of Pain, a specialized room that the agonoid Djuhn'Keep built aboard *Red Dwarf*. Another agonoid, Pizzak'Rapp, used a laser lance to fight his way out of the Hub after Djuhn trapped the entire agonoid population in the room, intending to kill them all for the right to murder the last human, Dave Lister **[N-BCK]**.

- **laser-lancer:** A type of weapon stored aboard *Red Dwarf*. Rimmer suggested using laser-lancers against a creature that the crew discovered in G Deck's water tank (which turned out to be an elation squid) **[T-SER9.1]**.

- **laser missile:** An offensive weapon that could be launched from a vehicle and guided toward its target **[T-IDW]**.

  > ***NOTE:*** *The laser missile may have been the same weapon as the laser cannon mentioned in episode 6.3 ("Gunmen of the Apocalypse") and the missile launcher referenced in episode 6.6 ("Out of Time").*

- **laser missile guidance control:** A component on *Starbug 1*'s dashboard, used to guide laser missiles to their targets **[T-IDW]**.

- **laser scalpel:** A medical tool that utilized a precision laser to make incisions **[T-SER4.5]**, produced by Malpractice Medical & Scispec, and distributed by Crapola Inc. **[G-RPG]**. Ace Rimmer requested a laser scalpel to fix Cat's leg, which had been crushed when Ace's ship collided with *Starbug 1* **[T-SER4.5]**.

- **laser scalpel Mark II:** An upgraded version of Malpractice Medical & Scispec's laser scalpel that automatically anesthetized a patient's incision area **[G-SOR]**. Legion used a Mark II model to perform an appendectomy on Lister **[T-SER6.2]**.

- **Lasex P-2:** A small pistol that fired rounds of superheated plasma pellets. It held a thirty-round clip and had a range of 60 meters (197 feet) **[G-SOR]**.

- **Lassie:** A canine character (a collie) featured in numerous films, television shows and books **[RL]**. When Lister could not recall the name of a woman whom he had met at a club during planet-leave on Orion, Rimmer joked that she might have been called "Lassie" **[T-SER7.1(e)]**.

- **Last, James:** A German composer and big-band leader who recorded more than two hundred albums over a span of forty-five years **[RL]**. Rimmer owned several of these albums in his record collection aboard *Red Dwarf* **[T-SER4.6]**. When he lent Lister his favorite Last album, Dave returned it with raspberry jam seeds in the grooves, a phone number scrawled on the lyric sheet and a footprint on the composer's face **[N-INF]**.

  Lister once used one of the album covers—which portrayed a girl in a crocheted miniskirt doing the twist—to provide stimulation as he donated a semen sample for Kochanski's self-gamete-mixing *in vitro* tube **[T-SER7.3(e)]**.

  After being sentenced to the virtual-reality prison Cyberia, Lister was surprised to find his Cyberhell set in a Spanish villa. Concerned, he checked the music selection, and was relieved to find no James Last albums. He had been sent to the wrong illusion, however, and was quickly re-assigned to his own personal hell **[N-LST]**.

  While trapped in an addictive version of *Better Than Life*, Rimmer imagined himself hosting a glamorous party on Earth, during which the New York Philharmonic Orchestra played a tribute to Last **[N-INF]**.

*NOTE: In the* Red Dwarf Omnibus, *Lister borrowing a James Last album was changed to his taking a Reggie Dixon Hammond organ album. In that version, the footprint was over a Hammond organ depicted on the cover.*

- **Last, James:** A waxdroid replica of the composer, created for Waxworld, a theme park built on an inhabitable planet and eventually abandoned. Left on their own for millions of years, the waxdroids attained sentience and became embroiled in a park-wide resource war between Villain World (to which Last belonged) and Hero World.

  During this war, the *Red Dwarf* crew transported to the planet using a Matter Paddle, with Lister and Cat materializing in Villain territory, while Rimmer and Kryten landed in Hero territory. Captured by the villains, Lister and Cat witnessed the firing-squad execution of a Winnie-the-Pooh waxdroid, which Last attended.

  Rimmer, meanwhile, found the heroes' army lacking and took command, working many of the pacifistic waxdroids to death before ordering a frontal attack on the enemy's compound across a minefield. This wiped out the remaining droids, including Last **[T-SER4.6]**.

- **Last Chance Saloon:** A building in an Old West town in a dream that Kryten's subconscious mind created as he developed a Dove Program to combat the Armageddon virus. In the illusion, the saloon was built in 1874 and offered cigarettes, whisky and wild women. The bartender was a portly woman named Lola. When the *Red Dwarf* crew hacked into Kryten's dream using an artificial-reality machine and the Western game *Streets of Laredo,* they found the mechanoid drunk and disheveled at the saloon, trading in his possessions for a bottle of liquor **[T-SER6.3]**.

  *NOTE: In the novel* Backwards, *the bartender's name was Hope.*

- **"Last Post," The:** A musical bugle or trumpet call used during Commonwealth military funerals to honor those killed in war **[RL]**. Rimmer hummed a version of the "Last Post" while burning his wooden soldiers for warmth while marooned aboard *Starbug 1* on an icy planet with Lister **[T-SER3.2]**.

- **Last Rights Act 2142, The:** An amendment passed by the Universal Government regarding the activation of holograms. This article was further amended to include The Hologram Protection Akt 2143, which further detailed the conditions and rights of activated holograms **[M-SMG2.2(a)]**.

- **Last Supper, The:** The final meal that Jesus Christ shared with his apostles before his crucifixion, according to Christian belief **[RL]**. While trapped in an addictive version of *Better Than Life*, Rimmer imagined using a time machine to crash the Last Supper on the night of his bachelor party **[N-BTL]**.

  *NOTE: Episode 10.3 ("Lemons") also referenced this event, during a scene in which the crew dined with Jesus, visually reminiscent of Leonardo da Vinci's painting* The Last Supper.

- **Laszlo, Victor:** A character in the American film *Casablanca*, portrayed by Paul Henreid **[RL]**. While explaining to Cat the importance of teaching Kryten how to lie, Lister cited *Casablanca* as an example of how lying can be noble, citing a pivotal scene between Laszlo and Humphrey Bogart's Rick Blaine **[T-SER4.1]**.

- **lateral trimmers:** A component of *Starbug* shuttles used during navigation. *Starbug 1*'s lateral trimmers were knocked out when the crew attempted to pass through the tail of a phasing comet **[T-SER7.5]**.

- ***Latin name*:** A strain of holovirus created by Hildegarde Lanstrom. The hologrammatic scientist produced the virus to tap into the dormant areas of the human brain and give a person psychic abilities. The resultant strain, which caused telekinesis, telepathy and hex vision, was so named because Lanstrom lacked the time to look up a suitable scientific nomenclature **[W-OFF]**.

  The holovirus began draining Lanstrom's life force, compelling her to conserve energy by taking refuge in a stasis booth. Three million years later, the *Red Dwarf* crew released her from the booth, unaware the virus had driven her insane. She immediately attacked her benefactors, pursuing them throughout her station until her energy depleted. Just prior to her death, she transmitted the holovirus via radio waves to Rimmer, who subsequently trapped his shipmates in quarantine

# LEGION

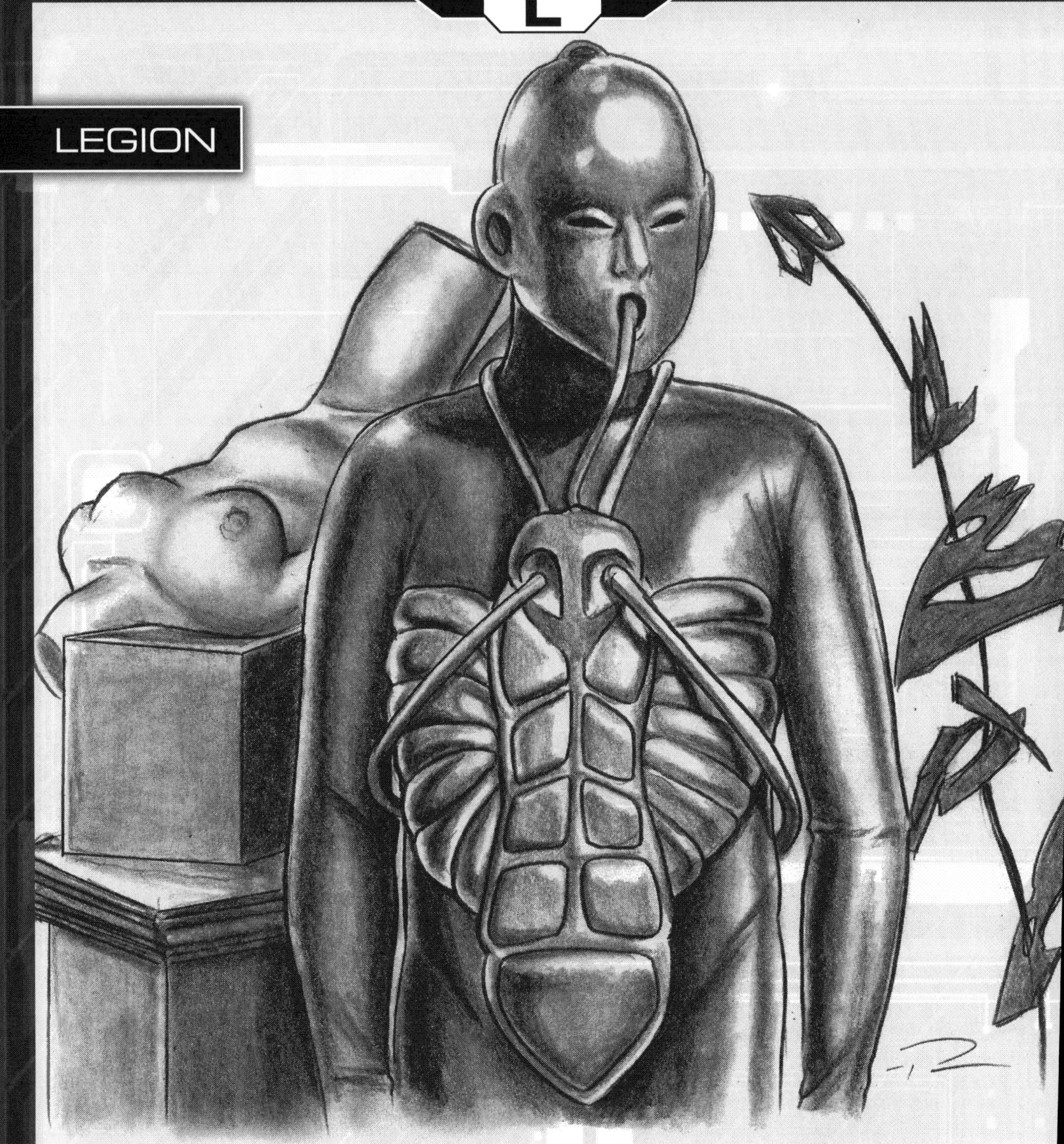

**PREFIX**
**RL:** Real life

**T-: Television Episodes**
- **SER:** Television series
- **IDW:** "Identity Within"
- **USA1:** Unaired U.S. pilot
- **USA2:** Unaired U.S. demo

***R-: The Bodysnatcher Collection***
- **SER:** Remastered episodes
- **BOD:** "Bodysnatcher"
- **DAD:** "Dad"
- **FTH:** "Lister's Father"
- **INF:** "Infinity Patrol"
- **END:** "The End" (original assembly)

**N-: Novels**
- **INF:** *Infinity Welcomes Careful Drivers*
- **BTL:** *Better Than Life*
- **LST:** *Last Human*
- **BCK:** *Backwards*
- **OMN:** *Red Dwarf Omnibus*

**M-: Magazines**
- **SMG:** *Smegazine*

**W-: Websites**
- **OFF:** Official website
- **NAN:** *Prelude to Nanarchy*
- **AND:** *Androids*
- **DIV:** Diva-Droid
- **DIB:** Duane Dibbley
- **CRP:** Crapola
- **GEN:** Geneticon
- **LSR:** Leisure World Intl.
- **JMC:** Jupiter Mining Corporation
- **AIT:** *A.I. Today*
- **HOL:** HoloPoint

**G-: Roleplaying Game**
- **RPG:** *Core Rulebook*
- **BIT:** *A.I. Screen Extra Bits* booklet
- **SOR:** *Series Sourcebook*
- **OTH:** Other RPG material

and tried to kill them with hex vision and a deadly penguin puppet called Mr. Flibble **[T-SER5.4]**.

- **Launchpad:** *See* Skipper

- **Laundry-Chute Nostrils:** A derogatory nickname that Cat called Rimmer **[T-SER6.6]**.

- **Laundry Room:** An area aboard the SSS *Silverberg* allocated for laundering services. Cassandra, the vessel's fortune-telling mainframe computer, told Rimmer he would die in the Laundry Room while making love to Kochanski, after Lister found them together and shot Arnold in the head with a harpoon gun. She had made up the prediction to get even with Lister, however, whom she had foreseen causing her destruction **[T-SER8.4]**.

- **Laurel, Stan:** A twentieth-century British comedic actor, best known as half of the comedy duo Laurel and Hardy **[RL]**. When a flood destroyed *Starbug 1*'s Indian food supply, Lister claimed life without curry would be like Laurel without Hardy **[T-SER7.1]**.

  A waxdroid replica of Laurel was created for the Waxworld theme park. Left on their own for millions of years, the waxdroids attained sentience and became embroiled in a park-wide resource war between Villain World and Hero World (to which Laurel belonged). During this war, the *Red Dwarf* crew transported to the planet using a Matter Paddle, with Lister and Cat materializing in Villain territory, while Rimmer and Kryten landed in Hero territory.

  Rimmer found the heroes' army lacking and took command, working many of the pacifistic waxdroids to death before ordering a frontal attack on the enemy's compound across a minefield, which wiped out the remaining droids **[T-SER4.6]**. The Laurel waxdroid was shot and killed during the assault **[T-SER4.6(d)]**.

- **lavatorial sciences:** A course that Kryten completed while studying for his Bachelor of Sanitation degree at Toilet University (a piece of software installed in his core program) **[T-SER7.7]**.

- **Laxo:** A brand of indigestion medication, promoted as being "The Gentle Laxative." After consuming a meal of dumplings and lamb that Rimmer had prepared, Lister chugged an entire bottle of Laxo **[T-SER2.2]**.

- **Lazenby, George:** An Australian actor best known for his portrayal of James Bond in the film *On Her Majesty's Secret Service* **[RL]**. When told that his fate to become the next Ace Rimmer might be hard to accept, Rimmer called that an understatement, saying "hard to accept" applied to things like Lazenby playing Bond **[T-SER7.2(d)]**.

- **LC004:** A code printed on a storage compartment in the Officers Quarters' that Lister and Rimmer shared aboard *Red Dwarf* **[T-SER3.3]**.

- **LC005:** Another code printed on a *Red Dwarf* storage compartment in the Officers' Quarters that Rimmer shared with Lister **[T-SER3.3]**, as well as on another such compartment in Quarantine Room 152 **[T-SER5.4]**.

- **LC006:** A third code printed on a storage compartment in *Red Dwarf*'s Officers' Quarters in which Lister roomed with Rimmer **[T-SER3.3]**. This code also appeared on other such compartments in Quarantine Room 152 **[T-SER5.4]**, and aboard the "low" version of the mining ship **[T-SER5.5]**.

- **LD1:** A code printed on a storage compartment in *Starbug 1*'s galley **[T-SER6.2]**.

- **League Against Salivating Monsters, The:** A pacifistic moniker that Rimmer suggested the *Red Dwarf* crew call themselves after a polymorph drained his anger. This, he claimed, would enable them to get "tough" with the creature **[T-SER3.3]**.

- **leaping mutton:** A hypothetical animal that Rimmer conceived while mocking Lister's plan to farm sheep on an island submerged underwater. He postulated that Lister could cross-breed the sheep with dolphins to create leaping mutton **[T-SER1.1]**.

- ***Learn Esperanto While You Sleep*:** A self-hypnosis recording that Rimmer often played in his bunk aboard *Red Dwarf*. Lister resented having to hear such self-help tapes each night **[T-SER1.6]**.

**B-: Books**
**PRG:** *Red Dwarf Programme Guide*
**SUR:** *Red Dwarf Space Corps Survival Manual*
**PRM:** *Primordial Soup*
**SOS:** *Son of Soup*
**SCE:** *Scenes from the Dwarf*
**LOG:** *Red Dwarf Log No. 1996*
**RD8:** *Red Dwarf VIII*
**EVR:** *The Log: A Dwarfer's Guide to Everything*

**X-: Misc.**
**PRO:** Promotional materials, videos, etc.
**PST:** Posters at DJ XVII (2013)
**CAL:** 2008 calendar
**RNG:** Cell phone ringtones
**MOB:** Mobisode ("Red Christmas")
**CIN:** *Children in Need* sketch
**GEK:** *Geek Week* intros by Kryten
**TNG:** "Tongue-Tied" video
**XMS:** Bill Pearson's Christmas special pitch script
**XVD:** Bill Pearson's Christmas special pitch video
**OTH:** Other *Red Dwarf* appearances

**SUFFIX**
**DVD:**
**(d)** – Deleted scene
**(o)** – Outtake
**(b)** – Bonus DVD material (other)
**(e)** – Extended version

**SMEGAZINES:**
**(c)** – Comic
**(a)** – Article

**OTHER:**
**(s)** – Early/unused script draft
**(s1)** – Alternate version of script

- **learning drugs:** A pharmaceutical used to aid one's memory, originally developed for clinical use under the name Eidetosol, but deemed illegal by the Space Corps. Black-market replacement offshoots included MIT White, IQ and Smarteez **[G-SOR]**. Taking such drugs during the Engineer's Examination was expressly forbidden **[R-SER1.1]**.

  Rimmer used learning drugs prior to studying for the Engineer's Exam, but could not find his revision timetable and instead memorized an argument he had about it with Lister. After *Red Dwarf*'s cadmium II disaster, Lister took Arnold's learning drugs while studying for the Chef's Exam **[T-SER1.3]**.

- ***Learn Japanese*:** A book written by Doctor P. Brewis that Kochanski read to teach herself the language. When an officer at a bar noticed the book in her jacket and accused her of being pretentious, she innocently responded, "Pretentious? Watashi?" **[N-INF]**.

  ***NOTE:** In Japanese, "watashi" is a feminine pronoun meaning "I, me or mine."*

- ***Learn Quantum Theory While You Sleep*:** A self-hypnosis recording that Rimmer played in his bunk aboard *Red Dwarf*. Lister resented having to hear such self-help tapes each night **[T-SER1.6]**.

- **"Leave It to Rimmer":** A print headline that Rimmer cut out and adhered to his *Red Dwarf* locker door **[T-SER1.3]**. While sharing quarters with his duplicate hologram, Arnold had the headlines relocated to his new abode. Lister was amused, as the slogans were about other people named "Arnold" or "Rimmer" **[T-SER1.6]**.

- **Le Clerque, Henri:** An operative working for the terrorist organization known as the Revolutionary Working Front. Le Clerque was arrested while attempting to poison a mineral spring in France containing the world's supply of Perrier water. According to a news segment reporting the incident, had he succeeded, the entire middle class would have perished within a month **[T-SER2.2]**.

  ***NOTE:** This spelling appeared in the DVD captions; the* Red Dwarf Programme Guide *spelled his name as "Henry LeClerk."*

- **Lecture Hall 14:** A room on *Red Dwarf*'s Level 21 in which Rimmer took his Astro-Engineering Exam **[R-SER1.1]**.

- **Ledbetter:** Rimmer's former bunkmate aboard *Red Dwarf*. Arnold blamed Ledbetter and others, including Lister, for his being held back from becoming an officer **[N-INF]**.

  ***NOTE:** It is unknown whether Ledbetter was a crewmember at the time of the cadmium II accident, or whether the nanobots later resurrected him.*

- **leech:** A segmented worm that attached itself to an animal's living body and sucked out its blood **[RL]**. While rescuing Rimmer from a psi-moon configured according to his psyche, the *Red Dwarf* crew crossed the Swamp of Despair, in which a leech attached itself to Lister—which, when removed, bore the face of Rimmer's mother **[T-SER5.3]**.

- **Leeds:** A city in West Yorkshire, England, reputed as having a strong sporting heritage **[RL]**. While in a medieval artificial-reality simulation, Lister announced his intention to sleep with the Queen of Camelot, describing the response he received from the virtual crowd as being worse than "playing away at Leeds" **[T-SER7.1]**.

- **Leekiel:** A GELF serving on the Blerion High Council of Blerios 15. Leekiel was a Potent—a rarity among male GELFs, in that he had the ability to reproduce **[N-LST]**.

- **Lefty:** A name that Lister assigned to one of twelve rogue droids he purchased from the Kinitawowi to break his doppelgänger out of the virtual-reality prison Cyberia. This particular droid was missing an arm **[N-LST]**.

- **Legion:** A gestalt entity developed on a top-secret, deep-space research station. Created from the minds of such brilliant physicists as Heidegger, Davro, Holder and Quayle, Legion became greater than the sum of his parts, excelling in all forms of science, art and culture. As the scientists succumbed to old age, Legion's identity diminished, until he became nothing more than a shapeless essence once the last scientist died.

  Legion remained in a state of limbo for centuries, but was physically resurrected when the *Red Dwarf* became trapped by the station's automatic guidance beam. With much of his

**PREFIX**
**RL:** Real life

**T-: Television Episodes**
**SER:** Television series
**IDW:** "Identity Within"
**USA1:** Unaired U.S. pilot
**USA2:** Unaired U.S. demo

**R-: *The Bodysnatcher Collection***
**SER:** Remastered episodes
**BOD:** "Bodysnatcher"
**DAD:** "Dad"
**FTH:** "Lister's Father"
**INF:** "Infinity Patrol"
**END:** "The End" (original assembly)

**N-: Novels**
**INF:** *Infinity Welcomes Careful Drivers*
**BTL:** *Better Than Life*
**LST:** *Last Human*
**BCK:** *Backwards*
**OMN:** *Red Dwarf Omnibus*

**M-: Magazines**
**SMG:** *Smegazine*

**W-: Websites**
**OFF:** Official website
**NAN:** *Prelude to Nanarchy*
**AND:** *Androids*
**DIV:** Diva-Droid
**DIB:** Duane Dibbley
**CRP:** Crapola
**GEN:** Geneticon
**LSR:** Leisure World Intl.
**JMC:** Jupiter Mining Corporation
**AIT:** *A.I. Today*
**HOL:** HoloPoint

**G-: Roleplaying Game**
**RPG:** *Core Rulebook*
**BIT:** *A.I. Screen Extra Bits* booklet
**SOR:** *Series Sourcebook*
**OTH:** Other RPG material

previous knowledge intact, Legion retrofitted Rimmer's light bee with a hard light drive and performed an emergency appendectomy on Lister, then treated the crew to a lavish Mimosian banquet.

Legion intended to keep the crew captive for the rest of their lives, however, knowing he would cease to exist again if they left. When they attempted to escape, Legion became hostile, knocking Lister unconscious—and thereby decreasing his own life force. Seeing how this affected their captor, Kryten rendered the remaining crew unconscious, leaving only his own mind for Legion to draw upon. Influenced by the mechanoid's benevolence, Legion upgraded *Starbug*'s engines, enabling his guests to depart—and hastening his own shutdown in the process **[T-SER6.2]**.

- **leg-it mode:** A function of 4000 Series mechanoids enabling them to run at a fast pace. Kryten suggested using leg-it mode after Lister barricaded Pete the *Tyrannosaurus rex* in *Red Dwarf*'s cargo bay **[T-SER8.7]**.

- **Legs:** A name that Lister assigned to one of twelve rogue droids he purchased from the Kinitawowi to break his doppelgänger out of the virtual-reality prison Cyberia. This particular droid had only a waist and a pair of legs **[N-LST]**.

- ***Leif Erickson*, JMS:** A spaceship possibly from an alternate universe, which had an AI computer called Allan **[G-RPG]**.

  ***NOTE:*** *This vessel may have been named after Norse explorer Leif Ericson, the first European to colonize North America—though given the spelling, it could also have been named after film and television actor Leif Erickson.*

- **Leisure World International:** A company that offered total-immersion video games via virtual-reality suites. The firm operated more than eight thousand locations, both on and off Earth, that ran such games as *Better Than Life, Planet of the Nymphomaniacs, Total World Domination, Medieval Smackdown IV, Government Informant Pro, Jane Austen World* and *Firing Squad A Go-Go* **[W-LSR]**. While trapped in a despair squid hallucination, the *Red Dwarf* crew believed that their lives and identities aboard the mining ship had all been part of a Leisure World game titled *Red Dwarf* **[T-SER5.6]**.

- **lemming:** A small, herbivorous rodent of the Arvicolinae subfamily, often associated with the idea of mindlessly following a pack due to the misconception that the creatures willingly followed each other off cliffs or into bodies of water **[RL]**. Rimmer owned a pet lemming as a child. When it bit and latched onto his hand, he had no choice but to smash the animal against a wall, which ruined his helicopter wallpaper **[T-SER2.4]**.

- **Lemming Sunday:** A term coined by newspapers to describe a day during which five people jumped to their deaths after talking with Rimmer as he worked with a charity group called the Samaritans **[T-SER3.6]**.

- **lemon:** The small, yellow citrus fruit of an evergreen variety native to Asia **[RL]**. When a mishap involving a build-it-yourself rejuvenation shower stranded the *Red Dwarf* crew in Albion (later known as Great Britain) in 23 A.D., Rimmer suggested making a lemon battery to power a device capable of returning them to their own time and place. Since lemons were not yet available in Britain, the group embarked on a six-month journey to India, where a produce vendor named Erin sold them the fruit. After encountering a man whom they believed to be Jesus Christ, they hastily constructed the lemon battery to escape Roman soldiers pursuing him **[T-SER10.3]**.

- **Lemoplathinominecatholyrite:** A compound stored in *Starbug 1*'s first aid kits, for use in reducing anxiety and panic. Kryten used the compound to calm Lister when the latter suffered a claustrophobic attack while trekking through *Starbug*'s ductwork **[T-SER7.4]**.

- **Lenin, Vladimir, Premier:** A Russian Communist revolutionary who contributed to the establishment of Soviet Russia in 1917 **[RL]**. While trapped in an addictive version of *Better Than Life*, Rimmer believed he had returned to Earth and become famously wealthy, hosting dinner parties attended by Lenin and other guests **[N-INF]**.

- **Lennon:** One of Lister's MkIV Titanica Fish Droids, along with McCartney **[M-SMG2.4(c5)]**. The mechanical goldfish, produced by Acme **[M-SMG1.4(c2)]**, were armed with defensive micropedoes **[M-SMG2.4(c5)]**.

  Cat attempted to eat the two fish, believing them to be

alive, just as *Red Dwarf* was approaching lightspeed. Lister witnessed a "future echo" of Cat with a broken tooth, and tried by prevent this by tackling his friend before the feline could eat the aquatic robots—but, in so doing, he caused the very injury he hoped to avoid **[T-SER1.2]**.

> ***NOTE:*** *Lennon was named after The Beatles' John Lennon.* Red Dwarf—The Roleplaying Game*'s* Series Sourcebook *identified the fish as IcthyTech 3000 Robot Goldfish, but the* Smegazine*s called them Titanica droids.*

- **Leonard, Flight Officer:** A Space Corps officer who ordered a sentient robot clothes steamer online that became stuck in a post pod for millions of years, causing the appliance to become extremely irate **[G-SOR]**.

- **Leopard Lager:** A brand of alcoholic beverage brewed in the twenty-second century **[T-SER4.2]**. Cans of the premium lager contained 5.1 percent alcohol by volume, and were brewed by Souse & Sott's, Ltd., in Glasgow, Scotland **[G-SOR]**.

  Leopard Lager dispensers were stationed throughout *Red Dwarf* **[T-SER9.1]**, and the beverage was also stocked aboard *Starbug 1* **[T-SER6.6]**. When Holly inadvertently created a mutton vindaloo beast from Lister's curry using a DNA-modifying machine, Dave defeated the creature with a can of Leopard Lager—which, he claimed, was the only thing that could kill a vindaloo **[T-SER4.2]**.

- **Les, Sister:** A nun assigned to the Tank, *Red Dwarf*'s brig, who died during the cadmium II explosion and was later revived by nanobots. After both the brig's social worker and priest physically and verbally abused Rimmer, Lister suggested he visit the nuns. Arnold, however, preferred not to risk being garroted by Sister Les and her rosary beads **[T-SER8.3(d)]**.

- **Les Paul:** A popular model of solid-body electric guitar manufactured by Gibson Guitar Corp., named after its co-inventor, Les Paul **[RL]**. Lister owned a Les Paul copy, which Rimmer tried to burn when the two were marooned aboard *Starbug 1* on an icy planet. Dave tricked Arnold into believing he had burned the guitar, when in fact it was a guitar-shaped cutout taken from Rimmer's camphor-wood chest **[T-SER3.2]**.

- **Level 1:** A phrase printed on a mug in the Drive Room of the American mining vessel *Red Dwarf.* When Captain Tau interrogated Kryten, the mechanoid malfunctioned, causing his head to explode and his eyeballs to land in the cup **[T-USA1]**.

- **Level 132:** A section of *Red Dwarf* through which Lister passed en route to the Drive Room when the mining ship's navicomp overheated due to the stress of faster-than-light travel **[T-SER1.2]**.

- **Level 147**: The area of *Red Dwarf* containing the mining ship's Drive Room **[T-SER1.1]**. Shortly after meeting Lister, Cat scurried about spraying items on this level, proclaiming them his property **[T-SER1.5]**.

- **Level 159**: A *Red Dwarf* deck containing a stasis pod in which Lister remained for three million years following the cadmium II disaster **[T-SER1.1]**. The Botanical Gardens were also housed on this level **[T-SER1.1(d)]**. Lister passed out in a corridor on Level 159 after contracting mutated pneumonia **[T-SER1.5]**.

> ***NOTE:*** *The level presumably contained at least one teaching room and a Medical Unit, as it appeared throughout the show's history. In a deleted scene from episode 1.1 ("The End"), Lister and Rimmer repaired a circuit in a panel on this level—presumably, the porous circuit mentioned in the prior scene.*

- **Level 16:** *See* Floor 16

- **Level 167:** A deck aboard *Red Dwarf* housing a science lab and a medical bay **[G-RPG]**.

- **Level 21:** A *Red Dwarf* deck containing Lecture Hall 14, a teaching room in which Rimmer took his last Astro-Engineering Exam before his death **[R-SER1.1]**.

- **Level 346**: The area of *Red Dwarf* in which Lister shared quarters with Rimmer. When the mining ship achieved a speed faster than light, a future echo of Cat ran past Lister and Rimmer on this level, exclaiming that he'd broken a tooth. Moments later, the pair found Cat in their quarters, eyeing Lister's mechanical fish **[T-SER1.2]**.

While trapped in the total-immersion video game *Better Than Life*, the trio walked past a Level 346 sign en route to their quarters. A character from the simulation awaited them there, however, indicating they had not yet left the game **[T-SER2.2]**.

- **Level 413:** A section of *Red Dwarf* containing at least one airlock **[T-SER2.6]**. After finding Kryten on this level, Rimmer gave the mechanoid a list of chores to keep him occupied **[T-SER2.1]**.

- **Level 42:** An area of the American mining ship *Red Dwarf* in which that vessel's crew experienced a fun-sized candy bar crisis **[T-USA1(s)]**.

- **Level 454**: A *Red Dwarf* deck containing at least one teaching room. Rimmer and Lister first encountered Cat on this level **[T-SER1.1]**. When Cat went missing, Lister parked his bike in front of a vent on Level 454 while searching for him **[T-SER1.4]**.

    ***NOTE:*** *Apparently, this level at least partially ran in a circle, as Lister and Rimmer walked past the vent off to the right, while Cat exited to the left, yet Cat then emerged from a corridor to their right. This was fixed in the remastered version, with the footage of Rimmer and Lister passing the vent removed. Episode 1.4 ("Waiting for God") implied that Lister climbed into the vent on Level 454, which led to Supply Pipe 28 and ultimately to the lair of the Cat Priest.*

- **Level 47:** *See* Bay 47

- **Level 541**: A deck aboard *Red Dwarf* on which Rimmer found Cat hoarding the ship's supply of cigarettes, which Arnold had hidden in order to blackmail Lister into doing his bidding **[T-SER1.3]**.

- **Level 591:** An area of *Red Dwarf*, also known as Floor 591. When the ship collided with a meteor, Holly incorrectly calculated that the impact had occurred in this section. The crew, however, found no damage during their inspection of the area, causing them to move on to Level 592 **[T-SER2.5]**.

- **Level 592:** An area of *Red Dwarf*, also known as Floor 592, containing the ship's hologram simulation suite. Level 592 was damaged when the vessel collided with a meteor **[T-SER2.5]**.

- ***Leviathan*:** A JMC supply ship in operation during the twenty-third century. When its crew became infected with the Epideme virus, they headed for Delta 7, where the disease originated, hoping to find a cure, but this burned out *Leviathan*'s engines, stranding them in deep space. One by one, they succumbed to Epideme until crewmember Caroline Carmen became the virus' final victim. With no other hosts to infect, Epideme (controlling Carmen's body) froze the *Leviathan* to await a passing starship.

    Three million years later, the *Starbug 1* crew found the ship buried in an astro-glacier and retrieved Carmen, who thawed out and attacked Lister, transferring Epideme to him. Believing himself doomed, Lister took forty pounds of explosives and transferred to *Leviathan* with the intention of destroying the virus. There, he determined the ship's destination from its navicomp, after which he returned to *Starbug 1* and set a course for Delta 7 **[T-SER7.7]**.

- **Lewis's:** A large department store chain in the United Kingdom **[RL]**. Lister claimed Michelle Fisher, his first sexual partner, was beautiful enough to work behind the perfume counter at Lewis's **[T-SER3.2]**. He also described Kochanski in this manner **[N-INF]**.

- **Liberty League, the:** An assemblage of genetically enhanced superheroes tasked with protecting the city of Smegopolis in the universe known as Alternative 2X13/L. In 2315, the League, consisting of Action Man (Lister), Catman (Cat), Robbie (Kryten), Professor H (Holly) and Super-Ace (Rimmer), attempted to thwart a bank heist perpetrated by their long-time nemeses, the Conspirator (the Inquisitor) and the Penguin (Mr. Flibble). While visiting that reality, Ace Rimmer stood in for Super-Ace, whose vulnerability to human contact had prevented him from apprehending the villains **[M-SMG2.1(c3)]**.

    ***NOTE:*** *The Liberty League spoofed DC Comics' Justice League and other comic book characters.*

- **libido shortening:** A type of personality surgery performed on Juanita Chicata, Rimmer's ex-wife in an illusion created by an addictive version of *Better Than Life* **[N-BTL]**.

**B-: Books**
**PRG:** *Red Dwarf Programme Guide*
**SUR:** *Red Dwarf Space Corps Survival Manual*
**PRM:** *Primordial Soup*
**SOS:** *Son of Soup*
**SCE:** *Scenes from the Dwarf*
**LOG:** *Red Dwarf Log No. 1996*
**RD8:** *Red Dwarf VIII*
**EVR:** *The Log: A Dwarfer's Guide to Everything*

**X-: Misc.**
**PRO:** Promotional materials, videos, etc.
**PST:** Posters at DJ XVII (2013)
**CAL:** 2008 calendar
**RNG:** Cell phone ringtones
**MOB:** Mobisode ("Red Christmas")
**CIN:** *Children in Need* sketch
**GEK:** *Geek Week* intros by Kryten
**TNG:** "Tongue-Tied" video
**XMS:** Bill Pearson's Christmas special pitch script
**XVD:** Bill Pearson's Christmas special pitch video
**OTH:** Other *Red Dwarf* appearances

**SUFFIX**
**DVD:**
**(d)** – Deleted scene
**(o)** – Outtake
**(b)** – Bonus DVD material (other)
**(e)** – Extended version

**SMEGAZINES:**
**(c)** – Comic
**(a)** – Article

**OTHER:**
**(s)** – Early/unused script draft
**(s1)** – Alternate version of script

# LIGHT BEE

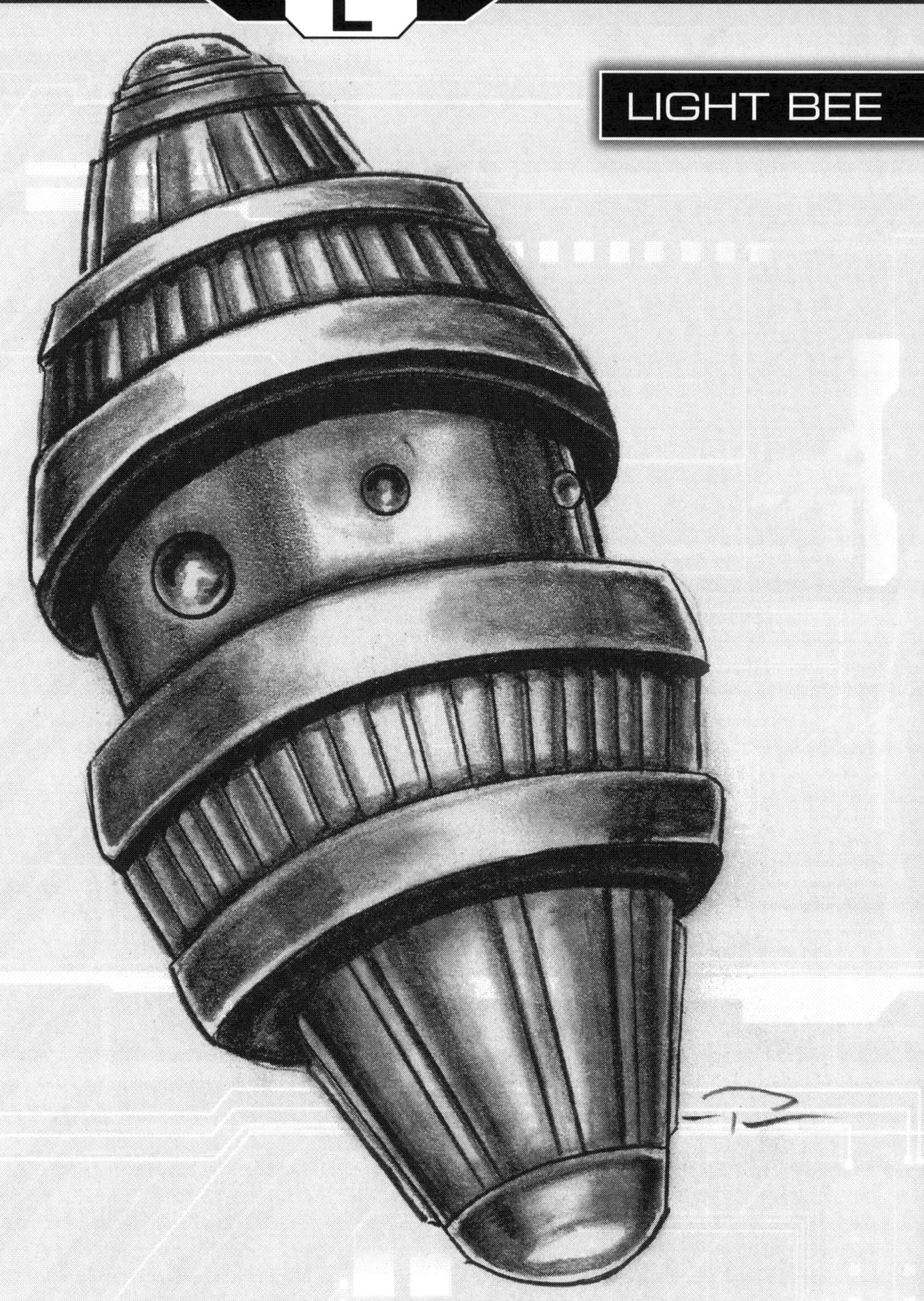

**PREFIX**
**RL:** Real life

**T-: Television Episodes**
**SER:** Television series
**IDW:** "Identity Within"
**USA1:** Unaired U.S. pilot
**USA2:** Unaired U.S. demo

**R-: *The Bodysnatcher Collection***
**SER:** Remastered episodes
**BOD:** "Bodysnatcher"
**DAD:** "Dad"
**FTH:** "Lister's Father"
**INF:** "Infinity Patrol"
**END:** "The End" (original assembly)

**N-: Novels**
**INF:** *Infinity Welcomes Careful Drivers*
**BTL:** *Better Than Life*
**LST:** *Last Human*
**BCK:** *Backwards*
**OMN:** *Red Dwarf Omnibus*

**M-: Magazines**
**SMG:** *Smegazine*

**W-: Websites**
**OFF:** Official website
**NAN:** *Prelude to Nanarchy*
**AND:** *Androids*
**DIV:** Diva-Droid
**DIB:** Duane Dibbley

**CRP:** Crapola
**GEN:** Geneticon
**LSR:** Leisure World Intl.
**JMC:** Jupiter Mining Corporation
**AIT:** *A.I. Today*
**HOL:** HoloPoint

**G-: Roleplaying Game**
**RPG:** *Core Rulebook*
**BIT:** *A.I. Screen Extra Bits* booklet
**SOR:** *Series Sourcebook*
**OTH:** Other RPG material

- **Lichtenstrasse:** The street on which Meinhard Voorhese, commander of the Nazi army on War World, lived as a child. After taking control of his room and his house, Voorhese went on to control this street, then his block, town and country, ending with his complete dominance over the planet **[W-OFF]**.

- **"Lick Paws Before Knocking":** A sign on the door to Cat's quarters aboard *Red Dwarf* **[M-SMG1.5(a)]**.

- **lie mode:** A function enabling Kryten to deceive and fabricate **[T-SER4.3]**. The mechanoid gained this ability thanks to Lister, who taught him how to break free of his programming and tell a lie **[T-SER4.1]**. Kryten engaged lie mode before assuring Rimmer that *Starbug 1*'s new high-velocity garbage cannon would work **[T-SER6.1]**.

- ***Life*:** An American general-interest magazine based in New York City **[RL]**. While trapped in an addictive version of *Better Than Life*, Rimmer imagined that *Life* chose him for its World's Sexiest Man, World's Best-Dressed Man and Pipe-smoker of the Year categories. The latter award amused him, since he never even owned a pipe **[N-BTL]**.

- ***Life Styles of the Disgustingly Rich and Famous*:** A television program hosted by Blaize Falconburger, showcasing the lives of wealthy individuals. After Lister went back in time via a timeslide to convince his younger self to invent the Tension Sheet, he became the subject of an episode in the resultant alternate timeline. Rimmer used the TV show's footage to create another timeslide, then went back to try to convince Lister to join the Space Corps so the normal timeline could be restored **[T-SER3.5]**.

  ***NOTE:*** *This show's title spoofed that of American TV series* Lifestyles of the Rich and Famous, *hosted by Robin Leech. Despite the show's onscreen logo separating the first two words, the DVD captions read "Lifestyles."*

- **Lift 42:** An elevator aboard *Red Dwarf* **[R-SER(b)]**.

  ***NOTE:*** *This lift was identified in the documentary* It's Cold Outside, *included in* The Bodysnatcher Collection.

- **Lift Hostess:** A woman featured in the in-lift video on *Red Dwarf*'s Xpress Lifts. The Lift Hostess informed riders of available movies, crash procedures and the lack of emergency exits **[T-SER2.4]**.

  ***NOTE:*** *The hostess' name is unknown, and it is unclear whether she was a member of the mining vessel's crew, or merely an employee of the Jupiter Mining Corp.*

- **Lift Maintenance:** A department aboard *Red Dwarf* responsible for the repair and maintenance of the ship's elevator lifts. Lister and Kochanski stole uniforms from this department while escaping captivity aboard the nanobot-rebuilt *Red Dwarf* **[T-SER8.2]**.

- **Lifton Separate Hydraulics:** A button-activated device in Kelly's armpit that the android used to hydraulically expand the size of her breasts on the television soap opera *Androids*. This proved useful in her profession as the madam of an android brothel **[M-SMG1.11(c1)]**.

  ***NOTE:*** *This product's name was a pun based on the phrase "lift and separate," a function of certain types of brassieres.*

- **light bee:** A small, floating device that projected the image of a human as a hologram **[T-SER4.6]**. Also known as an autonomous mobile hologrammic projection module, the light bee was developed at the Space Corps Test Base on Mimas **[X-PST]**. Some light bees were as small as a pin head **[N-INF]** or a marble **[N-LST]**, while others were approximately the size of a chicken egg **[T-SER4.6]**.

  Light bees were sold by HoloSoft Industries in Crapola Inc.'s annual *SCABBY* catalog **[G-RPG]**, and were manufactured using nano-polymer bonding. A light bee could sustain a hologram for up to forty-seven hours on its cadmium II power pack, and was capable of limited environmental chemoreception. The hologrammic image was created using more than twelve million multi-spectrum SiC lenses **[X-PST]**.

  Since a light bee had a small physical presence, it could utilize technologies that needed to interact with solid objects, such as a Matter Paddle **[T-SER4.6]**. It could be fitted with a remote projection unit, enabling a hologram to travel great distances from its host ship **[T-SER5.4]**, or be enhanced with hard light technology, giving the hologram a solid form with which to interact with its environment **[T-SER6.2]**.

- **light bee remote:** A device that altered a hologram's appearance. A hologrammatic Ace Rimmer used a light bee remote to transfer his outfit to the prime Rimmer before succumbing to fatal injuries **[T-SER7.2]**.

- **lightship:** An experimental vessel created by the Space Corps in an alternate reality. The lightship, built at the Space Corps Test Base on Mimas and test-piloted by Ace Rimmer, was capable of breaking the light barrier **[T-SER4.5]**.

- **limitation chip:** A chip installed in 4000 Series mechanoids preventing the sanitation droids from acquiring new skills or growing beyond their programming. After overriding his limitation chip, Kryten was able to specialize in areas such as medicine **[N-LST]**.

- **limpet mine:** A type of explosive device designed for use underwater. *Starbug 1* had a supply of such mines, which Holly used to destroy a despair squid that had attacked the ship with hallucinogenic ink **[T-SER5.6]**. Crapola Inc. sold limpet mines via its annual *SCABBY* catalog **[G-RPG]**.

  ***NOTE:** In the real world, limpet mines—named for their vague resemblance to a limpet (a type of mollusk)—were developed for naval use, to be attached to ships' hulls via magnets.*

- **Lincoln, Abraham, President:** The sixteenth president of the United States, who led the country through the American Civil War and abolished the practice of slavery **[RL]**. While recording his first official log entry, Lister noted how he'd matured since turning twenty-eight, comparing himself to the likes of Lincoln and Moses **[T-SER7.1]**.

- **Lincoln, Abraham, President:** A waxdroid replica of the president, created for the Waxworld theme park. Left on their own for millions of years, the waxdroids attained sentience and became embroiled in a park-wide resource war between Villain World and Hero World (to which Lincoln belonged).

  During this war, the *Red Dwarf* crew transported to the planet using a Matter Paddle, with Lister and Cat materializing in Villain territory, while Rimmer and Kryten landed in Hero territory. Lister and Cat met Lincoln while imprisoned in Villain World, escaping with him to Hero World.

  There, they discovered that Arnold had taken command of the heroes' army, working many of the pacifistic waxdroids to death to prepare for a frontal attack on the enemy's compound across a minefield. This wiped out the remaining droids on both sides, including Lincoln **[T-SER4.6]**.

- **Lindy Lou:** A sixteen-year-old blonde girl who lived on a version of Earth on which time ran backwards. Lindy Lou, who frequently dressed in provocatively skimpy outfits, temporarily stayed with her cousins, Ezekiel and Zacharias, at a cabin near the site where the *Red Dwarf* crew had been marooned for ten years. During that time, Cat—who had reverted in age to fifteen—lost his virginity to the girl, though in reverse. The encounter began with her running backward toward him, screaming, due to injuries inflicted by the barbs on his feline penis **[N-BCK]**.

- ***Lion*:** A weekly British comic book published by Fleetway. The company produced a total of 1,156 magazine-sized issues between 1952 and 1974 **[RL]**. Brooke Junior read an issue of *Lion* in an episode of the television soap opera *Androids* **[M-SMG1.10(c2)]**.

- **liquid dilinium:** *See* dilinium

- **liquid oxygen:** A liquid, cryogenic form of the element oxygen **[RL]**. After a Psiren ruse made Cat believe a colony of beautiful women wanted to make love to him, he ran off, claiming he needed to cool down in a shower of liquid oxygen **[T-SER6.1]**.

- **Liquorice Allsorts:** A British confection consisting of assorted liquorice-flavored sugar candies, packaged as a mixture **[RL]**. While pursuing the stolen *Red Dwarf* aboard *Starbug 1*, Kryten reported that the crew's supply situation had grown grim, with the only remaining Liquorice Allsorts being the "black twisty ones everyone hated" **[T-SER6.2]**.

- **Lister 16912146:** A code that Lister provided at a *Red Dwarf* service dispenser to obtain the results of his Chef's Exam **[T-SER1.3]**.

- **Lister, Becky:** A daughter of Deb Lister in a dimension in which the sexes were reversed. Deb had a vision of Becky

**PREFIX**
**RL:** Real life

**T-: Television Episodes**
**SER:** Television series
**IDW:** "Identity Within"
**USA1:** Unaired U.S. pilot
**USA2:** Unaired U.S. demo

**R-: *The Bodysnatcher Collection***
**SER:** Remastered episodes
**BOD:** "Bodysnatcher"
**DAD:** "Dad"
**FTH:** "Lister's Father"
**INF:** "Infinity Patrol"
**END:** "The End" (original assembly)

**N-: Novels**
**INF:** *Infinity Welcomes Careful Drivers*
**BTL:** *Better Than Life*
**LST:** *Last Human*
**BCK:** *Backwards*
**OMN:** *Red Dwarf Omnibus*

**M-: Magazines**
**SMG:** *Smegazine*

**W-: Websites**
**OFF:** Official website
**NAN:** *Prelude to Nanarchy*
**AND:** *Androids*
**DIV:** Diva-Droid
**DIB:** Duane Dibbley
**CRP:** Crapola
**GEN:** Geneticon
**LSR:** Leisure World Intl.
**JMC:** Jupiter Mining Corporation
**AIT:** *A.I. Today*
**HOL:** HoloPoint

**G-: Roleplaying Game**
**RPG:** *Core Rulebook*
**BIT:** *A.I. Screen Extra Bits* booklet
**SOR:** *Series Sourcebook*
**OTH:** Other RPG material

and her twin sister, Jan, during a future echo. Sometime later, Ace Rimmer visited her reality, seeking rest and recuperation. Worried that she might be the last human alive, Deb bet Arlene Rimmer that she could seduce and impregnate Ace. She succeeded at the former, but was the one who became pregnant, eventually delivering the twins **[M-SMG1.5(c2)]**.

***NOTE:*** *Although it was not explicitly stated, the comic implied that the pregnancy resulted in the twins Deb envisioned during her future echo.*

- **Lister, Bexley:** A son of Dave Lister, named after zero-gee football player Jim Bexley Speed. Dave learned of his unborn son from a series of future echoes, which included a photograph of him holding up Bexley and his twin brother, Jim. Rimmer experienced an echo of an adult Bexley dying from an exploding navicomp, but mistook him for his father **[T-SER1.2]**.

  Bexley and Jim were conceived during a drunken tryst between Lister and his female counterpart, Deb Lister, in a universe in which the sexes were reversed, as were the physical laws governing reproduction. As such, Dave became pregnant and gave birth to the twins in his own universe. Due to the different physical laws, the boys grew at an accelerated rate, reaching the equivalent of eighteen years old within three days. To save them from dying of old age within a month, Dave brought them back to Deb's universe to be reunited with their "father" so they could live a normal lifespan **[T-SER3.1]**. Back in their own universe, the boys enjoyed speedball lessons with Deb **[M-SMG1.5(c2)]**.

  When Psirens tried to lure the *Red Dwarf* crew into landing in an asteroid field, the telepathic GELFs faked a distress call from the SCS *Pioneer*. An illusion of Kochanski, under attack by Psirens, claimed to have sneaked into *Red Dwarf*'s sperm bank while Dave was in stasis, impregnated herself, escaped the cadmium II disaster, and raised Bexley and Jim alone. Lister initially wanted to mount a rescue, until his crewmates broke the Psirens' hold on him **[T-SER6.1]**.

  ***NOTE:*** *In the novel* Infinity Welcomes Careful Drivers, *Rimmer saw Bexley's son die, not Bexley himself. The boys' birth, return to that universe and omission in Series III were explained in the opening scrawl of episode 3.1 ("Backwards").*

- **Lister, Bexley:** One of Dave "Spanners" Lister's twin boys in an alternate reality. His mother was Kristine Kochanski. He and his brother Jim were named after zero-gee football player Jim Bexley Speed **[T-SER4.5]**.

  ***NOTE:*** *This was the same reality in which Rimmer was held back in grade school, causing him to become Space Corps test pilot "Ace" Rimmer.*

- **Lister, Bexley:** A son of David Lister and Krissie Kochanski, whom Dave imagined raising while trapped in an addictive version of *Better Than Life*. Lister believed he had returned to Earth using *Nova 5*'s Duality Jump and, shunning fame and fortune, opted for a quiet life in a Midwestern town resembling the fictional Bedford Falls from *It's a Wonderful Life*.

  There, he met Krissie, an identical descendant of Kristine Kochanski, with whom he fell in love and produced Bexley and his twin brother, Jim. Lister imagined the twins as being perfect children, capable even of changing each other's nappies. By fifteen months old, both boys could talk, play the piano and throw a zero-gee football. Bexley was also able to drive Lister's Model 'A' Ford **[N-INF]**.

- **Lister, Dave:** A character on an American television show called *Red Dwarf* that was developed in an alternate universe. In this version of the series, Lister was Rimmer's best friend and had a family comprising his human wife Holly, their biologically challenged son Cry 10 and a hip teenage daughter. In an episode shown only to television executives, Lister was attacked by an amorphous alien, who accused the crew of killing his wife as they strode through a patch of slime on Altair 9. Lister was knocked unconscious in the assault, but Rimmer—who was paralyzed—heroically summoned the power to walk in time to grab a gun and save his friend **[M-SMG1.10(c4)]**.

- **Lister, Dave, Junior:** An alias under which Dave Lister set up a new medical file for his son with *Red Dwarf*'s medi-bot, who was unaware that the two Listers were the same individual. Lister used the file to prove he was a registered crewmember, to stop the ship's new computer, Pree, from killing the crew. Since he had resigned his commission and could not re-register as himself, Lister identified himself to the JMC onboard computer as Dave Junior, thereby regaining his crewmember privileges **[T-SER10.2]**.

- **Lister, David:** An alternate version of Lister who existed after the Inquisitor erased the original from history. The original Lister and Kryten met up with their replacements and fled the Inquisitor's pursuit, but the new Lister was killed in the process. The prime Lister then used his doppelgänger's hand to open *Red Dwarf*'s doors, since Holly no longer recognized his own palm print **[T-SER5.2]**.

- **Lister, David:** A Lister from a dimension in which Kochanski took the blame for bringing Frankenstein aboard *Red Dwarf*. This caused Kristine to be placed into stasis instead of him, and to thus survive the cadmium II disaster. Lister, meanwhile, died and was revived as a hard light hologram **[T-SER7.3]**. His interests included opera, poetry and bridge **[G-SOR]**.

- **Lister, David:** A crewman aboard *Red Dwarf* in a universe in which the mining ship and its crew were American. This Lister joined the crew after blacking out during a drinking game in Detroit and awakening on a bench on Saturn's fourth moon, wearing nothing but a traffic cone on his head. Captain Tau put Lister in stasis after he refused to reveal the location of a pregnant cat he had smuggled aboard ship. A cadmium II explosion killed the rest of the crew, and he was released three million years later by the ship's computer, Holly **[T-USA1]**.

- **Lister, David:** A character in the Total Immersion video game *Red Dwarf*, in a fascist society on an alternate-universe Earth. Voter Colonel Sebastian Doyle, tired of his responsibilities at the Ministry of Alteration, portrayed this character in the game for four years, until being released after the group scored a mere four percent **[M-SMG2.1(c4)]**. A more macho player replaced him, scoring much higher **[M-SMG2.4(c4)]**.

- **Lister, David:** A duplicate Lister created during a triplicator accident that destroyed *Red Dwarf* but produced two copies: a "high" version representing the best aspects of the ship and its crew, and a "low" version manifesting the worst.

  The "low" Lister was a filthy, sex-obsessed, gun-toting thug who wore an eyepatch, a black cowboy hat and studded leather. This version, along with his fellow "low" crewmembers, attacked the crews of the original and "high" ships after luring them to their vessel. Wanting the "high" ship for their own, they kidnapped the original Lister, attached a spinal implant to his neck and forced him to murder the "high" versions of himself and Rimmer, before sending him after his own crew.

  When their plan failed, "low" Lister stowed away aboard *Starbug 1*, where he tried to control Lister using the implant. Cat, however, killed the scoundrel **[T-SER5.5]**.

- **Lister, David ("Spanners"):** An alternate-reality Lister who worked with Ace Rimmer at the Space Corps Test Base on Mimas. Spanners, a flight engineer, was married to that dimension's Kochanski, with whom he had twin sons named Jim and Bexley **[T-SER4.5]**.

- **Lister, David ("Spanners"):** An alternate-reality Lister who worked with Ace Rimmer at the Space Corps Research and Development facility on Europa. Spanners, a flight engineer, was married to that dimension's Kochanski, with whom he had twin sons named Jim and Bexley. This Lister solved the mystery of a second *Wildfire* craft arriving days before his reality's vessel was scheduled to launch. Prior to his assignment on Europa, Lister served aboard *Red Dwarf*, where he bunked with Lewis Pemberton **[N-BCK]**.

- **Lister, David, Brother:** A duplicate Lister created during a triplicator accident that destroyed *Red Dwarf* but produced two copies: a "high" version representing the best aspects of the ship and its crew, and a "low" version manifesting the worst.

  Brother Lister, an enlightened version of the original, wore robes and sandals and displayed knowledge of poetry, art and metaphysics. As Brother Lister searched the "low" ship for components of the triplicator, the prime universe's Lister, remotely controlled by the "low" crew, stabbed him to death **[T-SER5.5]**.

- **Lister, David, First Officer:** A version of Lister in an opposite "mirror" universe. In that reality, Rimmer was *Red Dwarf*'s captain, while Lister—sporting a mustache and speaking with a French accent—was his second-in-command **[T-SER8.8(d)]**.

- **Lister, David ("Dave"), Third Technician:** A sociopathic Lister from an alternate universe. Orphaned at birth, he chose at age seven to live with adoptive parents Tom and Beth Thornton instead of the Wilmots, believing he could exploit the Thorntons' wealth. Beth's manic-depressive

**PREFIX**
**RL:** Real life

**T-: Television Episodes**
**SER:** Television series
**IDW:** "Identity Within"
**USA1:** Unaired U.S. pilot
**USA2:** Unaired U.S. demo

**R-: *The Bodysnatcher Collection***
**SER:** Remastered episodes
**BOD:** "Bodysnatcher"
**DAD:** "Dad"
**FTH:** "Lister's Father"
**INF:** "Infinity Patrol"
**END:** "The End" (original assembly)

**N-: Novels**
**INF:** *Infinity Welcomes Careful Drivers*
**BTL:** *Better Than Life*
**LST:** *Last Human*
**BCK:** *Backwards*
**OMN:** *Red Dwarf Omnibus*

**M-: Magazines**
**SMG:** *Smegazine*

**W-: Websites**
**OFF:** Official website
**NAN:** *Prelude to Nanarchy*
**AND:** *Androids*
**DIV:** Diva-Droid
**DIB:** Duane Dibbley
**CRP:** Crapola
**GEN:** Geneticon
**LSR:** Leisure World Intl.
**JMC:** Jupiter Mining Corporation
**AIT:** *A.I. Today*
**HOL:** HoloPoint

**G-: Roleplaying Game**
**RPG:** *Core Rulebook*
**BIT:** *A.I. Screen Extra Bits* booklet
**SOR:** *Series Sourcebook*
**OTH:** Other RPG material

nature, however, proved detrimental. During Lister's first weekend with his new family, he admitted that he didn't like her raspberry sponge cake because of the seeds; thereafter, he was frequently the victim of her psychotic breakdowns, and was occasionally beaten.

When Lister was nine, his adoptive father was arrested and imprisoned for ten years for embezzling funds from the Miranda Insurance Company, leaving the child solely in Beth's care. This greatly affected him throughout his adolescence, as he was regularly suspended from school and was eventually expelled. He had trouble holding down a job, and incurred a long list of criminal charges ranging from drunk driving to robberies. He fathered three children from three different mothers, but lost track of them all.

At age twenty-three, Lister joined the Space Corps and was stationed aboard *Red Dwarf* as a third technician. He survived a radiation leak that killed the remainder of the crew, by being put in stasis for three million years. After he was revived, he and that reality's Kryten, Rimmer, Kochanski and Cat discovered the location of an ancient GELF ship, the *Mayflower*, that contained the genome of DNA (G.O.D.). Realizing the power and wealth that G.O.D. could bring him, Lister killed his crewmates so he alone could find it and reap its spoils.

Before he could track down the *Mayflower*, however, GELFs arrested Lister on bogus emo-smuggling charges and sentenced him to the virtual-reality prison Cyberia. The prime Lister, unaware of his doppelgänger's homicidal tendencies, helped him escape, but his psychotic counterpart attacked him and left him for dead. The other Lister infiltrated the prime crew, who led him to the *Mayflower*—but not before Khakhakhakkhhakhakkkhakkkkkh, the prime Lister's jilted GELF bride, attacked *Starbug*.

Mistaking this Lister for her husband, Khakhakhakkhhakhakkkhakkkkkh knocked him unconscious and attempted to leave with him, but he awoke and overtook the Kinitawowi, killing them all and hiding in *Starbug*'s storage deck to heal. After the ship landed on the planet of the Rage of Innocence, Lister attacked the prime crew, took Michael McGruder hostage and demanded the escape pod.

A scuffle ensued, during which the Rage attacked the group. They formed a Circle of Sacer Facere so only one would be chosen for sacrifice. Noticing a vial of luck virus around Kochanski's neck, the crazed Lister grabbed the tube and drank its contents, thinking this would make him safe. But when the Rage entered his body, it overwhelmed him with such a feeling of power and bliss that he begged it to stay, causing the Rage to consume him, reducing his body to ashes **[N-LST]**.

- **Lister, David ("Dave"), Third Technician (Sr. and Jr.):** The lowest ranking crewmember aboard *Red Dwarf* **[T-SER1.1]**. His clearance code was 000-169 **[T-SER5.2]**.

Lister was found abandoned in a cardboard box at The Aigburth Arms pub when he was six weeks old, on November 26, 2155 **[T-SER3.6]**. He was later adopted by the Wilmots **[W-OFF]**, who had a dog named Hannah **[T-SER1.2]**. He also had a foster aunt named Mary **[T-SER2.1(s)]**, a foster uncle named Dan **[T-SER8.6]** and a grandmother **[T-SER1.2]**.

When Lister was six years old, his adoptive father passed away, leaving him with two distinct memories in adulthood: being inundated with presents and wishing more relatives would die so he could complete his Lego set; and being told his father went to the same place as his goldfish, causing him to think the man had been flushed down the toilet. Therefore, young Dave stuffed food and magazines down the latrine for him to use **[T-SER2.2]**.

Lister had a stepfather who taught him how to play Michael Jackson's "She's Out of My Life" on guitar, sparking a lifelong interest in music **[T-SER3.2]**. His stepdad also died when Lister was young, and he valued the time they spent together, particularly watching the film *It's a Wonderful Life* **[N-INF]**.

As a child, Lister fell into a canal, which left him terrified of drowning **[N-LST]**. At around age eleven, he went to live with his foster grandmother **[T-SER7.6]**, a portly woman with tattoos. She once caused him to be expelled from school by "nutting" the headmaster after Lister failed French class **[T-SER1.2]**. During his stay with his grandmother, Dave gained a significant amount of weight, earning himself the nickname "Fatboy." When he was thirteen, his grandmother was struck by a truck and died. While watching the chalk outliners go back for more chalk, he vowed not to end up like her and got into better shape **[T-SER7.6]**.

At age twelve, Lister lost his virginity to a girl named Michelle Fisher on the ninth hole of the Bootle municipal golf course **[T-SER3.2]**. Sometime later, he had another sexual encounter on the same hole at the same course, this time with Susan Warrington **[N-INF]**. Yet another dalliance involved his

# LISTER, DAVID ("DAVE"), THIRD TECHNICIAN (SR. AND JR.)

geography teacher, Mrs. Arkwright, who had called him in after class to discuss his essay on glaciated valleys **[T-SER10.5(d)]**. His first experience getting drunk was on a school trip to Paris, where he consumed two bottles of wine before touring the Eiffel tower, where he vomited at the top **[T-SER3.6]**.

Lister was hired for a paper route when he was young, but was fired thirty minutes later for drawing beards on the photos on page 3 **[M-SMG1.9(a)]**. When he was seventeen, Dave launched his first band, Smeg and the Heads, with his friends Gazza and Dobbin, and wrote several songs, including "Om" **[T-SER3.5]**.

Around the same time, Lister worked at a MegaMart as a trolley-parker, where he enjoyed a romantic tryst with a married checkout girl. When her husband caught them making love, he sealed Lister in a crate and threatened to throw him into a canal. He was finally released, stark naked, in the middle of a production of *The Importance of Being Earnest*. Thereafter, Lister was claustrophobic **[T-SER7.4]**. He worked at MegaMart for ten years, but quit because he did not want to get tied down to a career **[T-SER1.4]**.

Lister was accepted into Art College, but dropped out after ninety-seven minutes due to its rigorous timetable, consisting of classes first thing in the afternoon **[T-SER2.1]**. He dated Lise Yates during this period of his life, but dumped her after eight months because he didn't want to settle down—a decision he later regretted **[T-SER2.3]**.

In addition, Lister dated a woman named Hayley Summers, but the relationship ended after she moved to Callisto for a job. She later wrote him a letter saying she might be pregnant with his child; a later correspondence, however, revealed that a co-worker had actually impregnated her **[T-SER10.5]**.

For his twenty-fourth birthday, Lister celebrated with friends by engaging in a *Monopoly* board pub-crawl. After several stops, an inebriated Lister broke away from the group to purchase a *Monopoly* game, since no one could remember the next stop on the board.

At this time, Lister obtained a passport containing the name Emily Berkenstein, then booked passage on a Virgin zipper to the Saturnian moon Mimas and picked up some kind of rash. Marooned on Mimas with no money, he stole taxi hoppers and ferried passengers around in order to collect fares, hoping to make enough money to return to Earth. After six months of doing this, he met *Red Dwarf* crewmember Arnold Rimmer, who was there on leave. That meeting convinced him to join the Space Corps, which assigned him to *Red Dwarf* **[N-INF]**.

Aboard *Red Dwarf*, Dave bunked with Rimmer, who was his superior officer and made his life hell by reporting him to Captain Hollister for one minor infraction after another. He passed the time with his friends Chen, Selby and Petersen, often playing drinking games with them and being as annoying to Rimmer as possible **[T-SER1.1]**.

While serving aboard the mining ship, Lister dated an officer named Kristine Kochanski, who dumped him after three weeks for a catering officer **[T-SER6.1]**. To get over the loss, Lister took shore leave in the Saturnian system, where he picked up a pregnant cat—which he called Frankenstein—on Titan and smuggled her aboard—a violation of Space Corps rules **[T-SER7.3]**. When he made the mistake of photographing himself with the cat, Hollister demanded that he turn the animal over for dissection. He refused, and the captain incarcerated him in a stasis booth for eighteen months.

This punishment ultimately saved his life, when a cadmium II explosion killed the rest of the crew while he was protected in the booth. The ship's computer, Holly, kept him in stasis for three million years, releasing him once the radiation dropped to safe levels. The only other survivors were a hologram of Arnold Rimmer, whom Holly had revived to keep Lister sane, and a humanoid creature named Cat, whose species evolved from Frankenstein's litter **[T-SER1.1]**.

Lister once met a female version of himself named Deb Lister in a dimension in which the sexes were reversed. After an alcohol-induced sexual encounter with his female self, Dave became pregnant, then returned to his universe and gave birth to twin boys, Jim and Bexley **[T-SER2.6]**. Due to differences between the two dimensions' physical laws, the boys grew at an alarming speed, becoming the equivalent of eighteen years old within three days. Lister thus brought them back to Deb's dimension, to live out their lives at a normal pace **[T-SER3.1]**. They eventually made Lister a grandfather, with six children of their own **[N-INF]**.

After an attack by a Space Corps enforcement vehicle damaged *Starbug*'s oxygen generator in GELF space, Lister was forced to marry Hackhackhackachhachhachach, the daughter of the Kinitawowi GELF tribe's leader. He reneged on the deal by fleeing the Kinitawowi village, leaving his wife behind **[T-SER6.4]**.

At age thirty, Lister discovered that, thanks to a self-gamete-mixing *in vitro* tube, he was actually his own father—and an alternate-reality Kochanski was his mother. The infant Lister was born from a uterine simulator aboard *Starbug 1*, after which Dave brought himself back in time to The Aigburth Arms pub and left the child for others to find, writing the word "Ouroboros" on the side of his box to explain his origin and role in the never-ending cycle of humanity **[T-SER7.3]**.

When Lister contracted the Epideme virus, his crewmates severed his right arm in an attempt to cure him of the disease. That plan failed, but Kochanski later purged the virus by tricking it into leaving his body **[T-SER7.7]**. Kryten's nanobots then rebuilt his missing arm after the mechanoid found them hiding in Lister's laundry basket **[T-SER7.8]**.

Since Lister was his own father, he celebrated Father's Day each year by getting drunk and making himself a card, which he would forget about and open the following year, thereby maintaining the illusion of having a father figure. During one such drinking binge, Dave decided to be a better father to himself. To that end, he resigned his *Red Dwarf* commission to force his sober self to better his life by applying for a JMC robotics course. His plan backfired, however, when the ship's new computer, Pree, refused to let Lister reapply and evicted him from the ship since he was no longer a member of the crew. His only recourse was to use his new medical file, created under the name "Dave Lister Jr.," to prove he was, in fact, part of the crew, after which he ordered Pree to shut down **[T-SER7.8]**.

Lister was marooned on a rogue planet while trying to prevent it from colliding with *Red Dwarf*. After discovering that the planet, Garbage World, was actually Earth, he befriended a species of eight-foot-long cockroaches and began farming the land to produce food. His crewmates—who had been stuck inside a black hole—found him on a vast farmland, thirty-four years older due to the singularity's time-dilation effect, though only sixteen days had passed for them.

Lister died during a polymorph attack, but Holly revived him by burying his body on a version of Earth in Universe 3, in which time ran backwards. There, he sprang back to life, and lived for thirty-six years married to Kochanski **[N-BTL]**.

In one timeline, Lister lived to be at least 171 years old and had a mechanical right hand. He left a future echo message for younger self, saying that he would have two sons, one of whom would die during a navicomp explosion **[T-SER1.2]**.

In another timeline—created after he used a timeslide to become the world's youngest billionaire—Lister lived to be ninety-eight, dying in an airplane accident when he lost control of the craft while making love to his fourteenth wife **[T-SER3.5]**.

In yet another timeline, Lister was the victim of an undisclosed accident that resulted in his brain being placed in a liquid-filled jar, topped by his dreadlocks **[T-SER6.6]**.

Cassandra, a powerful computer with the ability to predict the future, told Lister he would choke to death at age 181 while attempting to remove a bra with his teeth. Whose bra, and whether the teeth were in his mouth at the time, were not established **[T-SER8.4]**.

In addition:

- Lister's favorite color was boxer short brown **[M-SMG1.1(a)]**.
- His other favorites include Indian food **[T-SER1.2]**, the music of Rastabilly Skank **[T-SER2.3]** and the film *It's a Wonderful Life* **[N-INF]**.
- A Pantheist, he believed that God existed in all things, but did not feel this proved the existence of Silicon Heaven **[T-SER3.6]**.
- He claimed to be a Pisces **[N-LST]**, though he told people he was born in October **[N-INF]**.
- He once broke his spine in three places after a safety harness aboard *Red Dwarf* snapped, then spent six weeks in traction **[T-SER1.3]**.
- He enjoyed reading magazines, including *Action* **[M-SMG1.11(c2)]**, *Pumping Iron Today* **[T-SER3.4(d)]**, *What Transport?* **[G-SOR]**, *Whopping Bazookas Monthly* **[M-SMG1.1(a)]**, *Zero G* **[T-SER1.3]** and *Zero Gee Football* **[M-SMG1.4(c2)]**, and also had a comic book adaptation of Virgil's *Aeneid* **[T-SER5.2]**. However, he claimed he had never read a book prior to the cadmium II accident **[T-SER1.2]**.
- He had a scar on his right shoulder from a childhood accident **[N-LST]**.
- He was born with two appendixes **[N-LST]**. One was removed during his relationship with Lise Yates **[T-SER2.3]**, while Legion removed the other **[T-SER6.2]**.
- Kryten performed a splenectomy and other medical procedures on Lister, but did not tell him about them for quite some time **[T-SER10.3]**.
- He suffered from athlete's foot fungus **[T-SER3.4]** and was allergic to tomatoes **[T-SER9.1]**.
- He once worked in the *Red Dwarf* Officers' Club **[T-SER9.2]**.
- He had a tattoo on his inner thigh proclaiming that he loved Petersen **[T-SER6.6]**, as well as another on his right buttock, consisting of a heart with an arrow through it, along with the words "I Love Vindaloo." He got the latter while taking planet leave on Ganymede **[T-SER6.1(d)]**.
- His greatest fear was armor-plated alien killing machines. Tying for second-place were his phobias of snakes **[T-SER3.3]** and rats **[N-BTL]**.
- When Holly underwent an intelligence-compressing procedure that restored the computer's IQ to more than twelve thousand, he told Talkie Toaster that Lister created the universe **[N-BTL]**.

***NOTE:*** *Lister was based on a character named Dave Hollins, from a quintet of comedy sketches on the BBC radio series* Son of Cliché. *In the sketches, titled "Dave Hollins: Space Cadet," Hollins—a Stella Trader Class*

**PREFIX**
**RL:** Real life

**T-: Television Episodes**
**SER:** Television series
**IDW:** "Identity Within"
**USA1:** Unaired U.S. pilot
**USA2:** Unaired U.S. demo

**R-: *The Bodysnatcher Collection***
**SER:** Remastered episodes
**BOD:** "Bodysnatcher"
**DAD:** "Dad"
**FTH:** "Lister's Father"
**INF:** "Infinity Patrol"
**END:** "The End" (original assembly)

**N-: Novels**
**INF:** *Infinity Welcomes Careful Drivers*
**BTL:** *Better Than Life*
**LST:** *Last Human*

**BCK:** *Backwards*
**OMN:** *Red Dwarf Omnibus*

**M-: Magazines**
**SMG:** *Smegazine*

**W-: Websites**
**OFF:** Official website
**NAN:** *Prelude to Nanarchy*
**AND:** *Androids*
**DIV:** Diva-Droid
**DIB:** Duane Dibbley

**CRP:** Crapola
**GEN:** Geneticon
**LSR:** Leisure World Intl.
**JMC:** Jupiter Mining Corporation
**AIT:** *A.I. Today*
**HOL:** HoloPoint

**G-: Roleplaying Game**
**RPG:** *Core Rulebook*
**BIT:** *A.I. Screen Extra Bits* booklet
**SOR:** *Series Sourcebook*
**OTH:** Other RPG material

*D—served aboard the* Psion IV, *which was later called the* Melissa V.

*Lister's family tree is confusing and contradictory. Some sources, including the official website, have called the Wilmots his adoptive family, while the novels referred to them as his foster parents. Dave also had a stepfather, which would seem to indicate that Mrs. Wilmot remarried following her first husband's death (making her an unlucky woman, given that both men died young). Presumably, the Wilmots first took Dave in as a foster child and later adopted him—which would explain the existence of his foster aunt and uncle. What that* doesn't *explain is why his last name was Lister (his grandmother was called Grandma Lister, so he apparently received his name from her) and not Wilmot. For the sake of consistency, this lexicon calls the Wilmots his adoptive parents.*

*Lister's rank was sometimes referred to as technician, third class.*

*In the novel* Last Human, *Lister married Khakhakhakkhhakhakkkhakkkkkh, the daughter of a Kinitawowi GELF tribe in an alternate universe. On-screen,* her name was *Hackhackhackachhachhachach.*

*In the novel* Backwards, *Lister was stranded on the backwards Earth and grew younger to age fifteen, after which he and Cat was transported into another dimension in which that dimension's Cat and Lister had died in the virtual-reality game* Better Than Life. *In* Last Human, *however, he was stranded with Kochanski on a planet in another dimension, where they raised a family together.*

*In the novel* Infinity Welcomes Careful *Drivers, the future-echo Lister had a mechanical left arm, not right. The book also claimed that one of his grandsons died during the navicomp explosion.*

*Cassandra's prediction regarding Lister's death could have been a ruse to upset him, since she knew Dave was about to kill her. As such, his death at age 181 may not come to pass.*

*The DVD captions for the Czech Republic version of the series inexplicably changed the reference to Lister's fourteenth wife to "his fourteen-year-old wife."*

- **Lister, Deb:** A female version of Lister in a reality in which the sexes were reversed **[T-SER2.6]**. During her tour aboard *Red Dwarf*, Deb had feelings for fellow officer Christopher Kochanski **[M-SMG1.5(c2)]**. After bringing an unquarantined dog named Dracula aboard the mining ship, she was sentenced to spend time in stasis **[W-OFF]**.

  During her stasis period, a cadmium II explosion killed her crewmates. The ship's computer, Hilly, kept her immobilized for three million years later until the radiation subsided. After her revival, her only companions were a hologram of crewmate Arlene Rimmer and Dog, whose species evolved from Deb's canine pet **[T-SER2.6]**.

  During their travels, the crew encountered future echoes—visions of their future selves. In one echo, they witnessed an image of Deb with two daughters named Jan and Becky **[M-SMG1.5(c2)]**. Shortly thereafter, they were visited by the prime *Red Dwarf* crew, who had ended up in that reality while trying to return to Earth via the Holly Hop Drive. Deb and her counterpart, Dave Lister, felt an instant attraction and partied together all night, culminating in their having sex and Dave becoming pregnant **[T-SER2.6]**.

  Dave returned to his own dimension and gave birth to twins, whom he named Jim and Bexley. Due to differences between the two dimensions' physical laws, the children grew at an alarming rate, becoming the equivalent of eighteen years old in only a matter of days. In an effort to save them, he returned the children to Deb's universe to be with their "father" **[T-SER3.1]**.

  Deb and Arlene later encountered a version of Ace Rimmer who had visited their dimension to get some rest. Worried that she might be the last human alive, Deb bet Arlene that she could seduce and impregnate Ace. Although she succeeded at the former, she was the one who became pregnant, eventually delivering Jan and Becky **[M-SMG1.5(c2)]**.

  > ***NOTE:*** *The events of this entry's second paragraph, though not specifically stated in the episode, can be assumed with reasonable certainty, given the many other parallels between the two universes. Likewise, the pregnancy culminating in the births of Jan and Becky can also be surmised, despite not having been explicitly stated.*

- **Lister, "Grandma":** An elderly woman with whom Lister lived from age eleven to thirteen **[T-SER7.6]**. She had multiple tattoos on her arms, including a skull and crossbones, and smoked a pipe. She once assaulted the principal at Dave's school for failing him in French class, leading to Dave's expulsion **[T-SER1.2]**.

When Dave's adoptive father passed away, "Grandma" told him that his dad was happy and had gone to the same place as his goldfish. This made the six-year-old think his father had been flushed down the toilet, and so he stuffed food and magazines down the latrine for him **[T-SER2.2]**.

While dating Lise Yates, Dave claimed to have pawned his grandmother's false teeth to buy tickets for a show, which he justified by saying she only used them to open bottles and chew tobacco. He also claimed to have bought her a different-sized pair later on, which made her resemble TV's talking horse Mr. Ed **[T-SER2.3(d)]**.

Grandma Lister died after being hit by a truck when Dave was thirteen **[T-SER7.6]**.

> ***NOTE:*** *Lister's account of his grandmother's passing implied she died when he was around thirteen years old, but this contradicted the false teeth incident, which occurred when he was older.*

- **Lister, Jan:** A daughter of Deb Lister in a dimension in which the sexes were reversed. Deb had a vision of Jan and her twin sister, Becky, during a future echo. Sometime later, Ace Rimmer visited her dimension seeking rest and recuperation. Worried that she might be the last human alive, Deb bet Arlene Rimmer that she could seduce and impregnate Ace. She succeeded at the former, but was the one who became pregnant, eventually delivering the twins **[M-SMG1.5(c2)]**.

> ***NOTE:*** *Although it was not explicitly stated, the comic implied that the pregnancy resulted in the twins Deb envisioned during her future echo.*

- **Lister, Jim:** A son of Dave Lister, named after zero-gee football player Jim Bexley Speed. Dave learned of his unborn son from a series of future echoes, which included a photograph of him holding up Jim and his twin brother, Bexley **[T-SER1.2]**.

Jim and Bexley were conceived during a drunken tryst between Lister and his female counterpart, Deb Lister, in a dimension in which the sexes were reversed, as were the physical laws governing reproduction. As such, Dave became pregnant and gave birth to the twins in his own universe. Due to the differences in physical laws between the two realities, the boys grew at an accelerated rate, reaching the equivalent of eighteen years old within three days. To save them from dying of old age within a month, Lister brought them back to Deb's universe to be reunited with their "father" so they could live a normal lifespan **[T-SER3.1]**. Back in their own universe, the boys enjoyed speedball lessons with Deb **[M-SMG1.5(c2)]**.

When Psirens tried to lure the *Red Dwarf* crew into landing in an asteroid field, the telepathic GELFs faked a distress call from the SCS *Pioneer*. An illusion of Kochanski, under attack by Psirens, claimed to have sneaked into *Red Dwarf*'s sperm bank while Dave was in stasis, impregnated herself, escaped the cadmium II disaster, and raised Jim and Bexley alone **[T-SER6.1]**.

> ***NOTE:*** *The boys' birth, return to their universe and omission in Series III were explained in the opening scrawl of episode 3.1 ("Backwards").*

- **Lister, Jim:** One of Dave "Spanners" Lister's twin boys in an alternate reality. His mother was Kristine Kochanski. Jim and his brother Bexley were named after zero-gee football player Jim Bexley Speed **[T-SER4.5]**.

> ***NOTE:*** *This was the same reality in which Rimmer was held back in grade school, causing him to become Space Corps test pilot Ace Rimmer.*

- **Lister, Jim:** A son of David Lister and Krissie Kochanski, whom Dave imagined raising while trapped in an addictive version of *Better Than Life*. Lister believed he had returned to Earth using *Nova 5*'s Duality Jump and, shunning fame and fortune, opted for a quiet life in a Midwestern town resembling the fictional Bedford Falls from *It's a Wonderful Life*.

There, he met Krissie, an identical descendant of Kristine Kochanski, with whom he fell in love and produced twin boys, Bexley and Jim. Lister imagined the boys as being perfect children, capable even of changing each other's nappies. By fifteen months old, both could talk, play the piano and throw a zero-gee football **[N-INF]**.

- **Listerine:** An American brand of antiseptic mouthwash **[RL]**. While fighting Captain Voorhese's pet crocodile, Snappy, in the back of a German aircraft, Ace Rimmer commented that he'd give anything for a gun—or a bottle of Listerine, due to Snappy's bad breath **[T-SER7.2]**.

- **Lister of Smeg:** The title Lister assumed while challenging the King of Camelot's champion knight in a medieval artificial-reality simulation, in an effort to seduce the Queen **[T-SER7.1]**.

- ***Listers, The*:** A substitute title that TJ, a TV executive in an alternate universe, suggested for the American television show *Red Dwarf,* after noting the lack of actual dwarves in it **[M-SMG1.10(c4)]**.

- **Listerton-Smythe, David, Flight Commander:** A pseudonym that Lister used when Rimmer impersonated a Space Corps captain aboard the *Trojan* to impress his half-brother, Howard. According to an emblem on Lister's uniform, "Listerton-Smythe" was a Touch-T—a telepath able to read minds by touch **[T-SER10.1]**.

- **Listy:** An affectionate nickname that Rimmer called Lister when trying to convince him that they were best friends, in order to dissuade Dave from taking the Chef's Exam and being promoted over him **[T-SER1.3]**.

  *NOTE: Rimmer used this nickname on several occasions, though captions alternated between this spelling and "Listie."*

- **lithium carbonate:** An inorganic compound sometimes used to treat bipolar disorder **[RL]**. The *Red Dwarf* crew used this mood stabilizer after coming into contact with the ink of a despair squid aboard the SSS *Esperanto* **[T-SER5.6]**. They later used it to revive Cat after he banged his head on a countertop, causing him to think he was Duane Dibbley **[M-SMG1.9(c1)]**.

- **litter bird:** A deterrent used on Justice World to prevent inmates from littering in the station's park area. The system released an enormous bird that would defecate on anyone found leaving trash on the grounds **[T-SER4.3(d)]**.

- **Little Chef:** A chain of roadside restaurants in the United Kingdom **[RL]**. When a group of Canaries became stuck in time thanks to a time wand, Holly compared their speed to that of an average Little Chef waitress **[T-SER8.6]**. In his *Space Corps Survival Manual*, Colonel Mike O'Hagan likened the state of undeath achieved from preservative and regenerative drugs to the waitresses' usual condition **[B-SUR]**.

- **Little Monitor 2:** A small computer screen in *Red Dwarf*'s Drive Room. Kryten once left a kebab for Lister on Little Monitor 2 **[T-SER10.4]**.

- **Liverpool:** A major port city in England **[RL]**. For his twenty-fourth birthday, Lister and several friends embarked on a *Monopoly* board pub crawl across London, starting from Liverpool and taking a frozen-meat truck to the Old Kent Road **[N-INF]**.

  As a young man, Lister dated a woman named Lise Yates in Liverpool. Around this same time, Rimmer attended Saturn Tech—which caused Arnold some confusion years later aboard *Red Dwarf* when, as a deathday present, Lister implanted memories of Yates into Rimmer's hologrammic mind, making the latter believe *he* had dated her. According to his altered memory, the first three months of that year were spent at Saturn Tech, at which point he inexplicably moved to Liverpool and met Lise **[T-SER2.3]**.

  When Rimmer claimed Lister spent entire days watching cartoons, getting drunk every night and never shaving, washing or changing his underwear, Lister said that made him sound like he was from Liverpool **[R-BOD(b)]**.

- **livery:** A stable or yard used to keep horses for hire, commonly operated during North America's Wild West era **[RL]**. A livery was among the buildings in an Old West town that Kryten's subconscious mind created as he tried to develop the Dove Program to combat the Armageddon virus **[T-SER6.3]**.

- **livies:** A slang term for the living, typically used by holograms of the deceased **[T-SER1.2]**.

- **"Living It Up!!":** A phrase printed on a postcard hanging on the wall of Rimmer's bunk aboard *Red Dwarf* **[T-SER2.2]**.

- **Loading Bay:** A large area within *Red Dwarf* used to transport personnel and supplies onto and off the ship. After going back in time via a stasis leak, Lister ran into Olaf Petersen in a hallway near the Loading Bay, as his friend attempted to woo two beautiful women back from shore leave **[T-SER2.4]**.

- **lobster:** A large marine crustacean in the Nephropidae family **[RL]**. After the *Starbug 1* crew brought over four lobsters in

**B-: Books**
**PRG:** *Red Dwarf Programme Guide*
**SUR:** *Red Dwarf Space Corps Survival Manual*
**PRM:** *Primordial Soup*
**SOS:** *Son of Soup*
**SCE:** *Scenes from the Dwarf*
**LOG:** *Red Dwarf Log No. 1996*
**RD8:** *Red Dwarf VIII*
**EVR:** *The Log: A Dwarfer's Guide to Everything*

**X-: Misc.**
**PRO:** Promotional materials, videos, etc.
**PST:** Posters at DJ XVII (2013)
**CAL:** 2008 calendar
**RNG:** Cell phone ringtones
**MOB:** Mobisode ("Red Christmas")
**CIN:** *Children in Need* sketch
**GEK:** *Geek Week* intros by Kryten
**TNG:** "Tongue-Tied" video

**XMS:** Bill Pearson's Christmas special pitch script
**XVD:** Bill Pearson's Christmas special pitch video
**OTH:** Other *Red Dwarf* appearances

**SUFFIX**
**DVD:**
**(d)** – Deleted scene
**(o)** – Outtake
**(b)** – Bonus DVD material (other)
**(e)** – Extended version

**SMEGAZINES:**
**(c)** – Comic
**(a)** – Article

**OTHER:**
**(s)** – Early/unused script draft
**(s1)** – Alternate version of script

stasis from the SS *Centauri*, Kryten cooked them as a surprise for Lister, to celebrate the anniversary of Kryten's rescue from *Nova 5*. Unaware of the dinner plans, Lister joined Kochanski and Cat in an artificial-reality simulation of *Pride and Prejudice Land*. Irritated by the snub, the mechanoid entered the game with a World War II tank and destroyed the gazebo in which they were seated, forcing them to join him for dinner. Lister's request for ketchup for his lobster filled Kryten's negadrive to capacity, causing the droid's head to explode **[T-SER7.6]**.

- **Lobster á la Grecque:** A culinary dish consisting of lobster prepared in wine, olive oil, lemon juice, herbs and spices **[RL]**. Sabrina Mulholland-Jjones, while married to Lister in an alternate timeline, had this meal for dinner on the evening Rimmer tried to convince Dave to return with him to *Red Dwarf* **[T-SER3.5]**.

- **Locker Room Game, the:** A diversion that Lister and Rimmer enjoyed aboard *Red Dwarf*, which involved taking turns breaking into the dead crew's lockers and keeping whatever was inside. Lister often made out better than Rimmer, finding such things as money and jewelry, whereas Rimmer would find tampons or booby traps **[T-SER7.5]**.

- **Log/Antilog:** A setting on *Starbug 1*'s sonar scope display. This setting was not highlighted as the crew charted the course of a despair squid **[T-SER5.6]**.

- **Log Recorder Suite:** A small room aboard *Starbug 1,* used to record log entries. When Lister attempted to log the crew's encounter with their future selves, the stress caused by the paradox overloaded the log computer, setting the suite on fire **[T-SER7.1(d)]**.

- ***Loin*:** A magazine featured on the television soap opera *Androids*. Archie had a copy of this publication in his emergency vehicle **[M-SMG2.9(c6)]**.

  ***NOTE:*** *This magazine's title and design spoofed* Lion, *a weekly British comic book published by Fleetway from 1952 to 1974. An issue of* Lion, *spelled correctly, appeared in* Smegazine *issue 1 (see also the* Lion *entry).*

- **Lola, Miss:** A character created by Kryten's subconscious mind as he attempted to purge an Armageddon virus that had infected *Starbug 1*'s navicomp. The mechanoid converted the struggle into a dream in which he was the drunken sheriff of an Old West town terrorized by the Apocalypse Boys. Miss Lola was a barkeep at the Last Chance Saloon **[T-SER6.3]**.

  ***NOTE:*** *This character's name was changed to Hope in the novel* Backwards.

- ***Lolita*:** A twentieth-century novel written by Vladimir Nabokov, concerning a literature professor's obsession with his twelve-year-old stepdaughter **[RL]**. While marooned aboard *Starbug 1* on an icy planet, Lister burned Rimmer's books to stay warm, including *Lolita*. Arnold's only request was that he save page sixty-one **[T-SER3.2]**.

- **Lollobrigida, Gina:** An Italian actor hailed as an iconic sex symbol in the 1950s and '60s **[RL]**. Artificial-reality versions of Lollobrigida were responsible for twenty-nine thousand deaths in a single month due to a faulty program in which players were crushed between her and Betty Boop **[B-SUR]**.

- **London:** The capital city of England and the United Kingdom, located on the River Thames **[RL]**. Lister and several of his friends embarked on a *Monopoly* board pub crawl across London for his twenty-fourth birthday **[N-INF]**. The city hosted a professional team called the London Jets **[T-SER1.1]**, as well as a junior zero-gee football team known as the London Jet Juniors **[T-SER1.3]**.

- **London Jet Juniors:** A junior zero-gee football team. During a drinking game, Chen teased Lister by joking that Kochanski had slept with all of its players **[T-SER1.3]**.

- **London Jets:** A zero-gee football team, posters of which Lister had hanging on the walls of his bunk aboard *Red Dwarf* **[T-SER1.1]**. He also had images of the Jets on a yellow T-shirt **[T-SER2.2]**, a red T-shirt and a patch on the right arm of his green jacket **[T-SER1.2]**. In addition, several London Jets posters decorated the walls of the ship's Disco Room **[T-SER1.3]**, as well as a club in which Lister had performed with his band, Smeg and the Heads, as a youth **[T-SER3.5]**.

  The London Jets were four-time Gravity Bowl champions

**PREFIX**
**RL:** Real life

**T-: Television Episodes**
**SER:** Television series
**IDW:** "Identity Within"
**USA1:** Unaired U.S. pilot
**USA2:** Unaired U.S. demo

**R-: *The Bodysnatcher Collection***
**SER:** Remastered episodes
**BOD:** "Bodysnatcher"
**DAD:** "Dad"
**FTH:** "Lister's Father"
**INF:** "Infinity Patrol"
**END:** "The End" (original assembly)

**N-: Novels**
**INF:** *Infinity Welcomes Careful Drivers*
**BTL:** *Better Than Life*
**LST:** *Last Human*
**BCK:** *Backwards*
**OMN:** *Red Dwarf Omnibus*

**M-: Magazines**
**SMG:** *Smegazine*

**W-: Websites**
**OFF:** Official website
**NAN:** *Prelude to Nanarchy*
**AND:** *Androids*
**DIV:** Diva-Droid
**DIB:** Duane Dibbley

**CRP:** Crapola
**GEN:** Geneticon
**LSR:** Leisure World Intl.
**JMC:** Jupiter Mining Corporation
**AIT:** *A.I. Today*
**HOL:** HoloPoint

**G-: Roleplaying Game**
**RPG:** *Core Rulebook*
**BIT:** *A.I. Screen Extra Bits* booklet
**SOR:** *Series Sourcebook*
**OTH:** Other RPG material

**[G-SOR]**, and also won the Megabowl in '75 **[N-INF]** and the ZGFA Cup in '79 **[M-SMG1.9(a)]**. During one game at the Superdome against the Berlin Bandits, the Jets' star player, Jim Bexley Speed, went around nine men to score the second point, securing the game as the greatest in his career. Lister was present at that game, the memory of which ranked among his most treasured **[N-INF]**.

- **London Zoo:** A zoological park managed by the Zoological Society of London (ZSL) and located in the northern region of Regent's Park, England **[RL]**. Upon seeing a photo of Lister's GELF bride, Kochanski remarked that Dave's eyes would bulge if he ever visited the London Zoo's orangutan house **[T-SER7.3]**.

- **Loneliness:** An aspect of Rimmer's personality made flesh on a psi-moon configured according to his psyche. When the *Red Dwarf* crew boosted Rimmer's confidence to vanquish the Self-Loathing Beast, a ghostly musketeer arose to battle the Unspeakable One's hordes, including Loneliness, thereby enabling the crew to escape **[T-SER5.3]**.

  After Rimmer left the moon, Loneliness and other negative traits were left behind to battle personifications of Rimmer's positive aspects, including Courage, Charity, Honour and Self-Esteem **[M-SMG2.7(c2)]**.

- **"Lonely Goatherd, The":** A show tune from the musical *The Sound of Music* **[RL]**. Lister claimed his hologrammic duplicate's backside sounded like the Pasadena Light Orchestra, insisting he could hear "The Lonely Goatherd" performed on an Alpine horn when the hologram sat in front of him **[R-BOD]**.

- **Lone Ranger, The:** A fictional masked character from American radio, television and film. The Lone Ranger, along with his Native American sidekick Tonto, fought injustice in the American Old West **[RL]**. When a flood destroyed *Starbug 1*'s Indian food supply, Lister grieved that life without curry was like the Lone Ranger without "that Indian bloke" **[T-SER7.1]**.

- **long-long-long-range:** A setting on *Starbug*'s scanner, used for monitoring space beyond the scanner's long-long-range capabilities **[T-SER6.5]**.

- **long-long-range:** A setting on *Starbug*'s scanner, used for monitoring space between the scanner's long-range and long-long-long-range capabilities **[T-SER6.5]**.

- **Longman, Michael, Professor:** A biodesigner employed at the World Council biotech institute in Hilo, Hawaii. Professor Longman had watery brown eyes and a small black beard. He and his two clones (both named Michael Longman) were responsible for creating several strains of terraforming viruses, including those that ate lava and sludge, as well as several species of GELF, such as Snugiraffes, Alberogs, Dingotangs and Dolochimps.

  The three Longmans, accompanied by Michael McGruder, supervised the GELFs aboard the *Mayflower* during a mission to terraform a planet in the Andromeda Galaxy. During the voyage, the GELFs mutinied, causing the ship to careen off-course and into the Omni-zone, where it emerged in an alternate dimension and crashed into a lava planet, sinking to the bottom of a magma ocean. The GELFs took the Longmans hostage and performed various DNA alterations to them; the original professor was heavily mutated, causing his face to break out into yellow pustules, with his lower lip corroded away and his lower body transformed into that of a goat.

  Eventually, this Longman perished and was revived as a hologram, after which the GELFs gave up and abandoned the trio on the *Mayflower,* where they remained in stasis for millions of years before being discovered by the *Starbug* crew. Driven insane by the modifications to their bodies, the Longmans attacked, desiring the newcomers' DNA to convert themselves into something more human.

  During the pursuit, the Longman-goat found Kryten's pattern stored in the DNA modifier and used the machine to add the mechanoid's DNA to his own, thereby creating a Longman-mechanoid. Ultimately, Kryten trapped all three men in the machine's glass cylinders **[N-LST]**.

- **Longman, Michael, Professor:** An identical clone of Michael Longman. When he and his fellow Longmans were captured by GELFs, this version was heavily mutated as well, his lower body transformed into that of a black-necked spitting cobra **[N-LST]**.

**B-: Books**
**PRG:** *Red Dwarf Programme Guide*
**SUR:** *Red Dwarf Space Corps Survival Manual*
**PRM:** *Primordial Soup*
**SOS:** *Son of Soup*
**SCE:** *Scenes from the Dwarf*
**LOG:** *Red Dwarf Log No. 1996*
**RD8:** *Red Dwarf VIII*
**EVR:** *The Log: A Dwarfer's Guide to Everything*

**X-: Misc.**
**PRO:** Promotional materials, videos, etc.
**PST:** Posters at DJ XVII (2013)
**CAL:** 2008 calendar
**RNG:** Cell phone ringtones
**MOB:** Mobisode ("Red Christmas")
**CIN:** *Children in Need* sketch
**GEK:** *Geek Week* intros by Kryten
**TNG:** "Tongue-Tied" video
**XMS:** Bill Pearson's Christmas special pitch script
**XVD:** Bill Pearson's Christmas special pitch video
**OTH:** Other *Red Dwarf* appearances

**SUFFIX**
**DVD:**
**(d)** – Deleted scene
**(o)** – Outtake
**(b)** – Bonus DVD material (other)
**(e)** – Extended version

**SMEGAZINES:**
**(c)** – Comic
**(a)** – Article

**OTHER:**
**(s)** – Early/unused script draft
**(s1)** – Alternate version of script

- **Longman, Michael, Professor:** A second identical clone of Michael Longman. After capturing the three professors, the GELFs mutated this version by giving him the lower body of a leopard **[N-LST]**.

- **long-range:** A setting on *Starbug*'s scanner, used for monitoring space between the scanner's mid-range and long-long-range capabilities **[T-SER6.5]**. The long-range scanners could identify ships, stations and other objects at great distances. When *Starbug* ran in silent mode, however, these sensors had to be switched off in order to avoid detection **[T-SER6.3]**.

- **Lord of the Star Fleet:** A position that Rimmer dreamed of attaining. When Kryten called Arnold's life goals unrealistic, the hologram warned that when he became Lord of the Star Fleet, the mechanoid would "pay for that remark" **[T-SER9.2]**.

- **Loren, Sophia:** An Italian actor known for her roles in such films as *Two Women* and *Nine* **[RL]**. On an alternate Earth on which World War II had never ended, Reich forces held Sophia Loren captive at an archeological dig site **[G-BIT]**.

- **Loretta:** A femme fatale character in the artificial-reality video game *Gumshoe*, a film-noir-type detective simulation. The game centered around the murder of Pallister, which Loretta planned but was carried out by her twin sister, Maxime. Loretta took the rap for the crime anyway, knowing she had the perfect alibi, thanks to Philip, the game's detective and main playable character. The goal of the simulation was to turn Loretta over to police and wind up with the heroine; after several playthroughs, however, Lister decided it was more fun to be with Loretta, despite her admission to having killed five men **[T-SER6.3]**.

- **Lorraine:** A woman whom Rimmer once coaxed into going on a date with him by using tips from the book *How to Pick Up Girls By Hypnosis*. Lorraine had an artificial nose that Arnold considered "tastefully done, with no rivets." During their date, she excused herself to go to the restroom, then climbed out a window and left. She later called Rimmer to tell him that she had moved to Pluto **[T-SER2.6]**.

- **Los Americanos Casino:** A casino resort on the Saturnian moon of Mimas. Lister dropped off a few fares at this establishment while working as an illicit taxi hopper driver **[N-INF]**.

- **Lotomi 5:** A moon with a hostile environment, located in the GELF region of an alternate universe, and measuring roughly five hundred miles across. Lotomi 5 was home to Cyberia, a prison facility that utilized virtual-reality technology to immerse inmates in their own personal hell for the duration of their sentence **[N-LST]**.

- **Lottery House:** An agency that paid out lottery winnings for the Multi Million Lottery Co. Rimmer received a letter while incarcerated in *Red Dwarf*'s brig, informing him that he had won four million in the lottery, and instructing him to bring his winning ticket to 24 Argyle Street, Somewhereville, TW17 0QD, where Lottery House was located **[T-SER8.5]**.

  ***NOTE:*** *The agency's name appeared in the script book* Red Dwarf VIII. *The currency of Rimmer's winnings was not indicated.*

- **Louis XVI, King:** The ruler of France from 1774 to 1792, and the husband of Marie Antoinette. He was executed via guillotine during the French Revolution **[RL]**.

  Using a time drive coupled with a faster-than-light drive, the *Starbug 1* crew traveled through space-time, becoming epicures and sampling the best in the universe, while socializing with such historic figures as Louis XVI, who threw a lavish banquet in their honor. Rimmer considered the king "a complete delight," while Kryten dubbed his wife "a cutie" **[T-SER6.6]**.

  While trapped in an addictive version of *Better Than Life*, Rimmer imagined that he had returned to Earth and become famously wealthy, then created a company that developed a time machine. In the hallucination, he used the device to bring together several historical individuals for his bachelor party, including Louis XVI **[N-BTL]**.

- **Lounge Area:** A two-meter-square, recessed section of Lister's first bunk aboard *Red Dwarf*. It contained a three-seat steel settee and a small coffee table **[N-INF]**.

- **Lounge Lizard 967:** A type of toupée that a medical diagnostic machine prescribed to Lister when he believed his hair had fallen out. This particular model, made of red hair, was manufactured and sold on Titan **[R-BOD]**.

- **love:** A rogue emotion purged from Kryten's hard drive by the Data Doctor, a program for restoring a mechanoid's personality to factory settings, when Captain Hollister subjected Kryten to a psychotropic simulation **[T-SER8.2]**.

- **Love, Geoff:** A twentieth-century British arranger and composer who specialized in recording easy-listening versions of popular movie themes **[RL]**. Love recorded an album titled *Geoff Love's Favourite Themes from the War Movies*, which Rimmer once played at full volume at 5:00 AM, much to the annoyance of Lister, who was recuperating from a hangover **[M-SMG1.2(a)]**.

  ***NOTE:*** *In the real world, Love did not release an album by this name, though he did record one titled* Geoff Love and His Orchestra Play Big War Movie Themes.

- **Love Celibacy Society:** An organization that deemed love a disease which hindered careers and emptied wallets. Members were known as Love Celibates. Rimmer boasted of his membership in this group after Lister ranted about his feelings for Kochanski, but Lister claimed Arnold had only joined because he couldn't find a date **[T-SER1.5]**.

- **Lovell, Lea:** An officer whom Rimmer once "elbow-titted" in *Red Dwarf*'s refectory. When Lovell punched Rimmer and told him to drop dead, he poured custard on her head and ran away **[R-END]**.

  ***NOTE:*** *Lovell's first name appeared in the first draft of the pilot episode, published in the* Red Dwarf Omnibus. *She presumably died during the cadmium II explosion. It is unknown whether the nanobots resurrected her in Series VIII.*

- **Lovepole, Hugo:** A musician, circa the twenty-second century, who recorded a sexy ballad titled "Hey Baby, Don't Be Ovulatin' Tonight," which sometimes played in *Red Dwarf*'s Copacabana Hawaiian Cocktail Bar. While trapped in an addictive version of *Better Than Life*, Rimmer imagined that he had gained fame and fortune upon returning to Earth aboard *Nova 5*, and that MTV had voted him Sexiest Man of All Time, ahead of Clark Gable and Hugo Lovepole **[N-INF]**.

- **Love Toys:** A store located in one of *Red Dwarf*'s shopping areas that sold Rachel blow-up dolls and repair kits **[M-SMG1.6(c2)]**.

- **LS:** An abbreviation for lightspeed (exactly 299,792,458 meters per second) **[RL, T-SER1.2]**.

- **LTV:** *See* lunar transport vehicle

- **Lube:** The working name of a call-girl named Nelly on the television soap opera *Androids*. Lube worked at Jaysee's android brothel **[W-AND]**.

- **luck virus:** *See Felicitus populi*

- **Luck:** A perfume created by Hildegarde Lanstrom for her product line, Parfum by Lanstrom. The fragrance incorporated the *Felicitus populi* strain of positive virus, granting wearers uncanny serendipity **[X-CAL]**.

- **"Lucky 13":** A phrase adorning a patch sewn onto Lister's leather jacket **[T-SER10.2]**.

- **Lucky Hop:** A taxi hopper company serving the Saturnian moon of Mimas. Trixie LaBouche stole a hopper owned by this business while attempting to escape from Dutch van Oestrogen **[M-SMG2.5(c6)]**.

- **Ludo:** A crewmember aboard a vessel that crashed into an asteroid in Psiren territory, who died when the telepathic Psirens attacked. A shipmate later recorded a log entry reporting several deaths, including Ludo's **[T-SER6.1(d)]**.

- **Luigi's Fish 'n' Chip Emporium:** A food truck on Earth that Lister frequented while performing in the band Smeg and the Heads. In an alternate timeline in which Lister became the world's youngest billionaire by inventing the Tension Sheet, he had a sausage and onion gravy sandwich on white bread specially flown in from Luigi's **[T-SER3.5]**. Lister's employees found the truck parked by the public lavatories near Liverpool Town Hall **[T-SER3.5(d)]**.

**B-: Books**
**PRG:** *Red Dwarf Programme Guide*
**SUR:** *Red Dwarf Space Corps Survival Manual*
**PRM:** *Primordial Soup*
**SOS:** *Son of Soup*
**SCE:** *Scenes from the Dwarf*
**LOG:** *Red Dwarf Log No. 1996*
**RD8:** *Red Dwarf VIII*
**EVR:** *The Log: A Dwarfer's Guide to Everything*

**X-: Misc.**
**PRO:** Promotional materials, videos, etc.
**PST:** Posters at DJ XVII (2013)
**CAL:** 2008 calendar
**RNG:** Cell phone ringtones
**MOB:** Mobisode ("Red Christmas")
**CIN:** *Children in Need* sketch
**GEK:** *Geek Week* intros by Kryten
**TNG:** "Tongue-Tied" video

**XMS:** Bill Pearson's Christmas special pitch script
**XVD:** Bill Pearson's Christmas special pitch video
**OTH:** Other *Red Dwarf* appearances

**SUFFIX**
**DVD:**
**(d)** – Deleted scene
**(o)** – Outtake
**(b)** – Bonus DVD material (other)
**(e)** – Extended version

**SMEGAZINES:**
**(c)** – Comic
**(a)** – Article

**OTHER:**
**(s)** – Early/unused script draft
**(s1)** – Alternate version of script

- **Luke:** *See* Nuke

- **Luke:** A man who wrapped plant leaves around horses' feet for a living, circa 23 A.D. He had a son named Jesus **[T-SER10.3]**.

- **Lumpton Street bus depot:** A bus stop in an alternate-reality twenty-first-century England, which the *Red Dwarf* crew imagined while trapped in an elation squid hallucination. The crew took a bus to this stop while trying to find a man named Swallow, whom they believed could help them locate their creator **[T-SER9.2]**.

- **Lunar City 7:** A terraformed settlement on Earth's Moon, mentioned in an easy-listening hit song from the best-selling album *Nice 'n' Nauseating*, recorded by African ballad singer Perry N'Kwomo. Lister heard this song while shuttling to *Red Dwarf* for his first tour of duty **[N-INF]**. He also sang this tune while preparing to go into stasis for the trip back to Earth after the cadmium II disaster **[T-SER1.2]**.

  ***NOTE:** In the* Smegazine *comic "Future Echoes Part 2," the lyrics to the song included a reference to Lunar Cities 1 to 6.*

- **lunar gonorrhea:** A disease, possibly sexually transmitted. The Space Corps created several public-awareness films about this condition, such as *Lunar Gonorrhea and You* **[G-SOR]**.

- ***Lunar Gonorrhea and You*:** A public-service film created by the Space Corps to raise awareness of the titular disease **[T-SER5.4]**.

- **lunar transport vehicle (LTV):** An eight-wheeled all-terrain vehicle used in low-gravity situations to haul ore during mining operations. *Red Dwarf* was equipped with at least one LTV, with which Lister mined thorium to be processed to fuel *Nova 5* **[N-INF]**.

- **Lupino, Ida:** A twentieth-century English-American film and television actor **[RL]**. Upon realizing the previous two years of his life had been spent in an addictive version of *Better Than Life*, Lister wished he had made himself Jim Bexley Speed and married Ida Lupino in the game, instead of living a simple life married to Kochanski in *It's a Wonderful Life*'s Bedford Falls. Shortly thereafter, Lupino arrived dressed as an air hostess and flirted with Lister—who was actually still in the game—but he declined the offer, claiming one non-existent relationship was sufficient **[N-INF]**.

- ***Lupus aquaticus*:** The scientific name for a werecod, a genetically engineered cross between a werewolf and a codfish **[B-SUR]**.

  ***NOTE:** See also the entry for werecod.*

- **lurve:** A non-standard slang spelling of the word "love" **[RL]**. The word was printed on a red, heart-shaped Mylar balloon held by a skutter in *Red Dwarf*'s Officers' Quarters **[T-SER3(b)]**.

  ***NOTE:** The balloon appeared in the menu of the Series IV bonus disc. Selecting the balloon started a music video featuring examples of love throughout the series.*

- **Luton's Carpet Shampoo:** A brand of carpet cleaner sold on Earth, circa three million A.D., which Lister imagined while trapped in an addictive version of *Better Than Life*. Lister believed he had returned to Earth using *Nova 5*'s Duality Jump and had received endorsement offers for such products as Luton's Carpet Shampoo and Breadman's Fish Fingers **[N-INF]**.

- **Luxembourg:** A country in Western Europe bordered by Belgium, France and Germany **[RL]**. After three million years on his own, Holly had forgotten the capital of Luxembourg. This memory lapse concerned him, though he never mentioned it to Lister **[N-INF]**.

  ***NOTE:** The capital of Luxembourg is Luxembourg City.*

- **LV246:** A planet displayed on *Starbug 1*'s scanner table **[T-SER6(b)]**.

  ***NOTE:** A wireframe rendering of this planet was included as an Easter egg on disc one of the Series VI DVDs. Selecting it, however, accomplished nothing.*

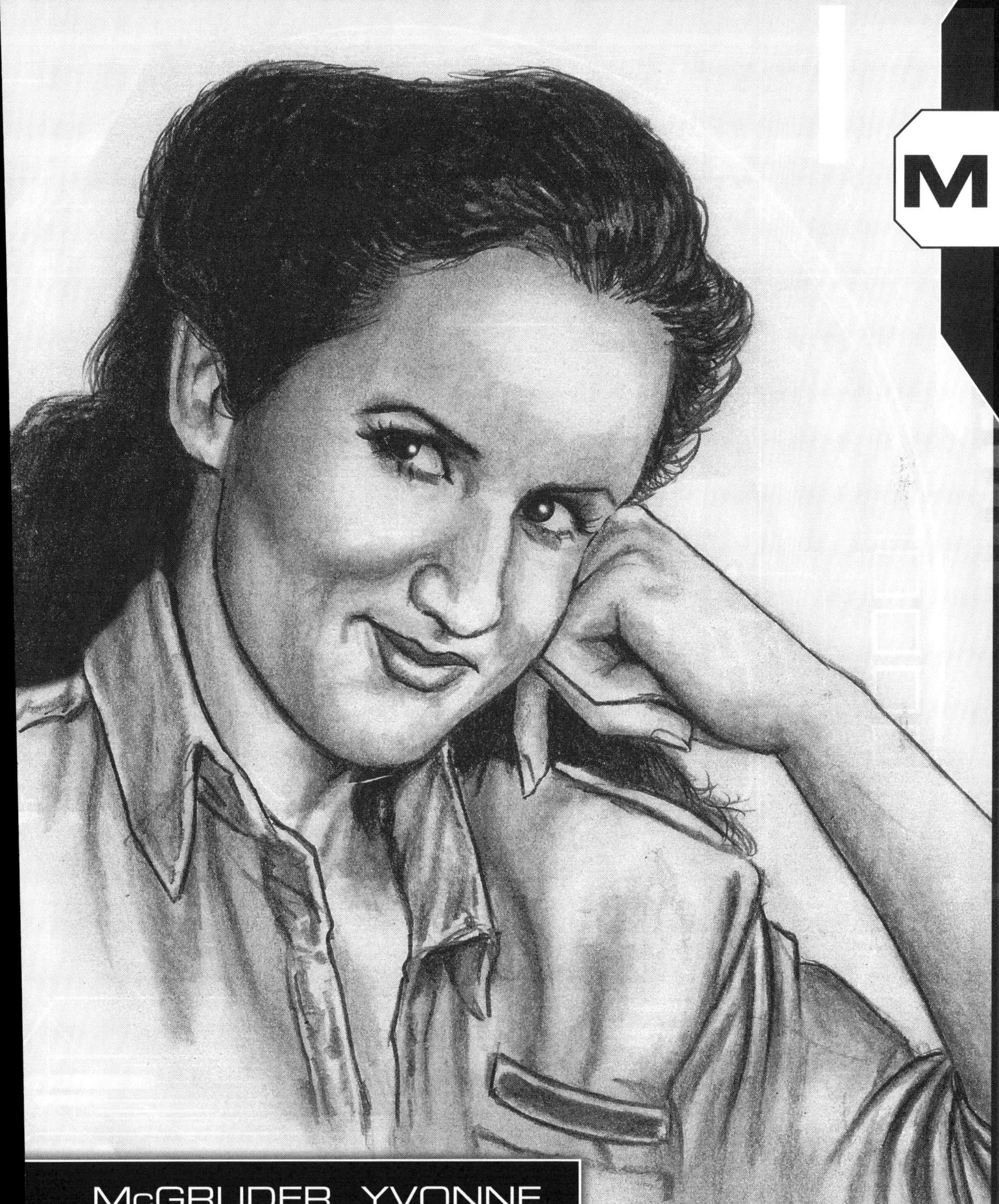

M

McGRUDER, YVONNE

- **"MacArthur Park":** A song written by Jimmy Webb and originally recorded by Richard Harris, most notably covered by The 5th Dimension, Diana Ross and The Four Tops **[RL]**. When a rogue simulant asked Lister to name one good thing humans had ever done, Dave answered "MacArthur Park," with which the simulant agreed **[T-SER7.6(d)]**.

- ***Macbeth, Tragedy of, The*:** A play written by playwright William Shakespeare, circa 1606 **[RL]**. While marooned aboard *Starbug 1* on an icy planet, Lister burned Rimmer's books to stay warm, including *The Complete Works of Shakespeare*. Arnold protested the destruction of what was likely the only remaining copy of the play, but admitted he never actually read it **[T-SER3.2]**.

- **Macedonia:** The modern name for the Grecian region of Macedon, an ancient kingdom ruled by Alexander the Great **[RL]**. At age fifteen, Rimmer attended a school trip to visit Alexander's palace in Macedonia, where he felt a strange sense of belonging. Years later, he befriended a hypnotherapist named Donald, who regressed him into a past life and claimed he had been the ruler's chief eunuch **[T-SER2.1]**.

- **Machine 15455:** A vending machine serviced by Z-Shift aboard *Red Dwarf*. Prior to the cadmium II disaster, Rimmer sent Wilkinson and Turner to fix this machine, which was dispensing blackcurrant juice instead of chicken soup **[N-INF]**.

- **Machine 16:** A total-immersion video game unit that the *Red Dwarf* crew imagined while trapped in a despair squid hallucination. In the illusion, the crew awoke in Machine 16 after crashing *Starbug 1* into an underwater cliff, only to learn that they had been playing a game called *Red Dwarf* for several years. With no memory of their "true" identities, they were disconnected from the unit so another group could play **[T-SER5.6]**.

- **machine ident:** The identification tag of appliances made by Crapola Inc. The machine ident of the company's talking bread-toasting appliance was "Talkie Toaster" **[T-SER4.4]**.

- **MacKenzie, Doc:** A physician in *It's a Wonderful Life*'s Bedford Falls, whom Lister imagined visiting while trapped in an addictive version of *Better Than Life*. In the hallucination, Lister's arms began to hurt due to Kryten burning them in the waking world, in an attempt to revive him from the game **[N-INF]**.

- **Macro-Bollington:** A medical device used to obtain and analyze tissue samples. Ace Rimmer requested a Macro-Bollington prior to performing surgery on Cat's leg **[T-SER4.5]**.

- **MacScarface ("One Eye"):** Lister's metal shop teacher during his school days. MacScarface's motto was "Always use your eye protection!" **[G-BIT]**.

- **MacWilliams:** A crewmember aboard *Red Dwarf*. During planet-leave on Miranda, Lister, Rimmer, MacWilliams and several of the latter's muscle-bound friends visited a bar, where Rimmer inadvertently started a brawl by repeating the rumor that MacWilliams engaged in necrophilia. Once the fight began, Arnold ran out of the bar, leaving Lister to face the enraged men alone. Years later, Dave cited this incident as an example of Rimmer's cowardice **[T-SER3.1]**.

  ***NOTE:*** *MacWilliams presumably died during the cadmium II explosion. It is unknown whether the nanobots resurrected him in Series VIII.*

- **mad droid disease:** An affliction that caused mechanoids to malfunction and go crazy. Rimmer accused Kryten of having mad droid disease after the mech disobeyed his orders and waved a banana around, calling it a female aardvark **[T-SER4.1]**.

- **Madge:** A skutter aboard *Red Dwarf* **[T-SER8.2]**. Madge was married to another skutter named Bob, and could go from zero to sixty in less than ten minutes **[T-SER8.6]**. While attempting to escape from *Red Dwarf* after the ship and its crew were resurrected, Madge disguised herself with dentures and a mop head, matching the "Dibbley family" disguise used by Cat, Lister, Kochanski and Kryten **[T-SER8.2]**. Madge took messages from the Tank to procure illegal goods for inmates whenever Bob wasn't available **[T-SER8.6]**.

- **mad goth bastard:** An insult that Rimmer called Pree, *Red Dwarf*'s new artificial-intelligence computer, after she informed the crew of her plan to fly the ship into the nearest sun **[T-SER10.2]**.

- **Madonna, the:** A representation or image of Mary, the mother of Jesus Christ, according to Christian doctrine **[RL]**. After being confined to quarantine for five days, Kryten chastised Lister for blowing his nose and looking at the contents, as though searching for the Madonna's face **[T-SER5.4]**.

- **madras river:** A type of river on the Vindaloovian homeworld that flowed with madras sauce **[G-BIT]**.

- **Magdalene, Mary:** A female disciple of Jesus Christ, according to Christian doctrine, believed to have been the first person to see him following his resurrection **[RL]**. According to the Church of Judas, Jesus asked his twin brother, Judas, to switch places and sacrifice himself on the crucifix so Jesus would appear to have risen from the dead, thereby allowing the spread of Christianity. Afterwards, Jesus moved to France with Mary Magdalene and raised a family **[T-SER10.3]**.

  Upon first entering the total-immersion game *Better Than Life*, Lister, Rimmer and Cat were approached by a computer simulation of Marilyn Monroe, whom Rimmer misidentified as Mary Magdalene **[T-SER2.2]**.

- **Magenta:** An alert condition indicating severe damage to a 4000 Series mechanoid. After an accident on a psi-moon left Kryten injured and stranded, his CPU assessed the situation and periodically updated his head-up display. His condition changed to Magenta based on a calculation of eighty percent overall damage, thirty-five percent optical damage and one hundred percent ambulation damage **[T-SER5.3]**.

  Kryten also went to Condition: Magenta when Lister's pet robot fish, which the mechanoid had accidentally flushed down the latrine, armed themselves as Lister prepared to use the bathroom **[M-SMG2.4(c5)]**.

- **Maggie, Auntie:** A relative of Rimmer whose birthday (July 17) was the second entry in his diary. The first entry, on January 1, had stated his desire to keep a running log of his achievements and advancements **[T-SER1.6]**.

- ***Magic Flute, The*:** An eighteenth-century opera written by Wolfgang Amadeus Mozart **[RL]**. Before becoming stranded in the prime universe, an alternate dimension's Kochanski often played a game by this name with her crewmates, which involved humming an aria from the opera and having others guess which character was singing. During her first game night aboard the prime *Starbug 1*, she chose this game, much to her new shipmates' bewilderment **[T-SER7.5]**.

- ***Magic of Fiji, The*:** A cassette that Lister brought with him into stasis **[N-OMN]**.

  ***NOTE:** This was mentioned in the first draft of the pilot episode ("The End"), published in the* Red Dwarf Omnibus.

- **magnetic coils:** Components of a *Starbug* shuttle's rear engines. Mechanoids positioned too close to a magnetic coil could experience short-term memory loss due to magnetic interference with its electronics **[T-SER5.3]**.

- **M'Aiden Ty-One:** One of thousands of agonoids who escaped decommissioning and fled into deep space. His name was a bastardization of "Made in Taiwan," in keeping with humans' tendency to assign humorous names to the mechanical agonoids.

  Many years later, the renegade agonoids found *Red Dwarf* abandoned except for Holly, whom they interrogated before dismantling the computer and leaving him out in space as bait for the crew. M'aiden, like all agonoids, felt contempt for his compatriots, having personally killed seventy-seven of them for various reasons, including for spare parts. He once lost an eye to a fellow agonoid, but claimed another one after attacking Chi'Panastee.

  M'Aiden Ty-One was betrayed by Djuhn'Keep, an elderly agonoid who tricked him into using a scramble card containing a virus that rendered him immobile, thereby allowing Djuhn to harvest his parts **[N-BCK]**.

- **mail pod:** *See* post pod

- **main fuel tanks:** The primary receptacles aboard *Starbug* shuttles, used for storing the ship's fuel **[T-SER5.3]**. Firing lasers at a *Starbug*'s main fuel tanks could result in the vessel's destruction **[T-SER6.6]**.

- **Major Tom:** A fictional astronaut who, in David Bowie's hit song "Space Oddity," reported in to ground control from his space capsule. Tom later returned in Bowie's "Ashes to Ashes," as well as in Peter Schilling's single "Major Tom (Coming Home)" **[RL]**. Cat used the call sign "Major Tom" while attempting to escape from the nanobot-rebuilt *Red Dwarf* aboard a *Blue Midget* shuttle, in response to a ground controller's request for identification **[T-SER8.3]**.

- **"Make My Day":** A phrase stenciled on the side of a simulant's handgun. After pursuing the *Red Dwarf* crew through the penal station Justice World, the simulant, claiming to be unarmed, met with Lister to talk but pulled out the weapon and fired. Since they were inside the station's Justice Field, the shots reflected back at the simulant **[T-SER4.3]**.

  ***NOTE:** This phrase was made famous by the movie* Sudden Impact, *starring Clint Eastwood as belligerent police officer "Dirty" Harry Callahan, who uttered the phrase "Go ahead, make my day" to taunt two criminals.*

- **Malaka, Augustus:** A special guest at Geneticon 12, a genetic-engineering convention held at the Titan Hilton **[W-GEN]**.

- **Malden, Karl:** An American actor who appeared in numerous films, such as *A Streetcar Named Desire*, and also portrayed Mike Stone on the television series *The Streets of San Francisco* **[RL]**. When Kryten told Camille, a Pleasure GELF, that she looked "nice" and "cute" despite being a large, gelatinous, green blob, she was unconvinced of his sincerity. He replied that even some humans were less attractive, including Karl Malden **[T-SER4.1]**.

- **"Male":** A phrase on a chart that Rimmer created to translate markings on a mysterious pod Holly found adrift in space, which he thought were an alien language—but which actually spelled out "*Red Dwarf* Garbage Pod," eroded away after many years of spaceflight **[T-SER1.4]**.

- ***Male Eunuch, The*:** A book written by Jeremy Greer in a universe in which the sexes were reversed. Deb Lister mentioned the book to Dave Lister while discussing the rise of men's rights in her reality **[T-SER2.6]**.

  ***NOTE:** This book was the female analog to* The Female Eunuch, *written in the real world by Germaine Greer.*

- ***Mall, The*:** An album recorded by Reggie Wilson **[M-SMG1.3(a)]**.

- **Malpractice Medical & Scispec (MMS):** A manufacturer of medical supplies and equipment. Its products included the Laser Saw, the DNA Modifier, the Dream Recorder and the Psi-scan, as well as mind probes and spinal implant chips **[G-RPG]**.

- **Mamet, J.A., Professor:** A bio-engineer employed at Diva-Droid International who was instrumental in creating the 4000 Series mechanoids. Her email address at the company was mamet927prof@divadroid.info **[W-DIV]**.

  Mamet was engaged to fellow bio-engineer John Warburton, who jilted her the day before their wedding. As revenge, she created the 4000 Series mechanoid in his image, complete with all of his shortcomings as a pompous, ridiculous-looking, overbearing, short-tempered buffoon. She also installed a negadrive in the model that stored negative emotions, occasionally blowing apart the mechanoid's head when full, to emulate Warburton's tendency to lose his head when angry **[T-SER7.6]**.

  In addition, Mamet wrote certain protocols into the 4000 Series' programming as a precaution, including the inability to harm her in any way and to obey her orders at all times, regardless of whether those orders conflicted with any other programming. This proved to be a liability when a Psiren took her form and ordered Kryten into *Starbug 1*'s waste compactor, which he had no choice but to obey **[T-SER6.1]**.

  ***NOTE:** The subtitles for episode 7.6 ("Beyond a Joke") spelled her name as Mammet, and referred to her title as Doctor.*

- **mamet927prof@divadroid.info:** The Diva-Droid International e-mail address of Professor J.A. Mamet **[W-DIV]**.

- **Mamosian anti-matter chopsticks:** *See* Mimosian anti-matter chopsticks

- **Mamosian banquet:** *See* Mimosian banquet

**PREFIX**
**RL:** Real life

**T-: Television Episodes**
**SER:** Television series
**IDW:** "Identity Within"
**USA1:** Unaired U.S. pilot
**USA2:** Unaired U.S. demo

**R-: *The Bodysnatcher Collection***
**SER:** Remastered episodes
**BOD:** "Bodysnatcher"
**DAD:** "Dad"
**FTH:** "Lister's Father"
**INF:** "Infinity Patrol"
**END:** "The End" (original assembly)

**N-: Novels**
**INF:** *Infinity Welcomes Careful Drivers*
**BTL:** *Better Than Life*
**LST:** *Last Human*
**BCK:** *Backwards*
**OMN:** *Red Dwarf Omnibus*

**M-: Magazines**
**SMG:** *Smegazine*

**W-: Websites**
**OFF:** Official website
**NAN:** *Prelude to Nanarchy*
**AND:** *Androids*
**DIV:** Diva-Droid
**DIB:** Duane Dibbley
**CRP:** Crapola
**GEN:** Geneticon
**LSR:** Leisure World Intl.
**JMC:** Jupiter Mining Corporation
**AIT:** *A.I. Today*
**HOL:** HoloPoint

**G-: Roleplaying Game**
**RPG:** *Core Rulebook*
**BIT:** *A.I. Screen Extra Bits* booklet
**SOR:** *Series Sourcebook*
**OTH:** Other RPG material

- **man:** The highest form of life in the galaxy, which Holly ascertained throughout *Red Dwarf*'s three-million year journey into deep space. Conversely, he decided, the lowest form of life was a man working for the Post Office **[T-SER1.5]**.

  *NOTE: This joke, which originated in a* Son of Cliché *sketch, was slightly altered for the remastered series, included in* The Bodysnatcher Collection, *and was moved to the beginning of episode 2.2 ("Better Than Life"). The new version claimed the lowest form of life was a man with a train set.*

- **Mandy:** A model of android available in a pick'n'mix lineup at a brothel on Mimas. Customers could choose various body parts from selected androids, and then have a custom-designed sex droid assembled for their use. A portly, red-haired customer chose this particular model's buttocks for his sex droid **[N-INF]**.

- **maneuvering thrusters:** Small thrusters strategically placed around *Starbug* shuttlecraft to aid in direction. On one occasion, an attack by a Space Corps external enforcement vehicle knocked out *Starbug 1*'s maneuvering thrusters **[T-SER6.4]**.

- **Manhattan:** One of five boroughs of New York City, considered the economic and cultural center of the United States **[RL]**. Manhattan and other cities influenced the design of several structures located on *Red Dwarf*'s exterior **[N-INF]**.

- ***Manny Celeste*, SS:** A derelict Space Corps vessel that the nanobot-revived *Red Dwarf* crew encountered. Captain Hollister ordered two Canary battalions (volunteer inmates) to investigate the ship, but lost contact with them shortly after their arrival. A third group of Canaries, including Cat, Kryten and Kochanski, was sent to locate the missing battalions, and they found the inmates frozen in time by a time wand. Releasing the trapped Canaries, they smuggled the device aboard *Red Dwarf* for their own use **[T-SER8.6]**.

  *NOTE: The ship's name was based on that of the* Mary Celeste, *a nineteenth-century merchant ship whose missing crew became a popular maritime mystery.*

- **Mansfield, Jayne:** A twentieth-century American film, television and theater actor, born Vera Jayne Palmer, who died in a car accident at age thirty-four **[RL]**. After a polymorph drained Kryten's guilt, the mechanoid told Rimmer he had the charm, wit and self-possession of Mansfield after the collision **[N-BTL]**.

- **Manson, Charles:** An American criminal who formed the Manson Family commune and instructed his followers to murder seven individuals, including actress Sharon Tate, in 1969 **[RL]**. When Rimmer claimed to have literally fought for his meals as a child, Kryten asked if he was mistakenly remembering scenes from *Charles Manson, the Early Years* **[T-SER6.4(d)]**.

- **Mantovani, Annunzio Paolo:** A twentieth-century Italian conductor and light orchestra-styled entertainer **[RL]**. As a deathday present, Lister copied eight months of his memories involving Lise Yates into Rimmer's mind, making Arnold believe he had dated her. Upon awakening with the new memories, Rimmer wondered why his taste in music had suddenly changed, during that span of time, from Mantovani to Rastabilly Skank **[T-SER2.3]**.

- **Maplins:** A hardware company mentioned on the television soap opera *Androids* **[M-SMG1.10(c2)]**.

  *NOTE: This company's name was presumably based on that of British retailer Maplin Electronics.*

- ***Maplins Hardware Catalogue*:** A product listing distributed by hardware company Maplins on the television soap opera *Androids*. In one episode, Kelly found a copy of this catalog in Brooke Junior's room, and realized he had been experimenting with his groinal socket **[M-SMG1.10(c2)]**.

- **March 16:** The date on which Rimmer lost his virginity with Yvonne McGruder aboard *Red Dwarf*. The encounter lasted from 7:31 PM to 7:43 PM, including the time required to share a pizza **[T-SER2.3]**.

- **Marcos, Imelda:** A twentieth-century Filipino politician and the widow of President Ferdinand Marcos. Due to her buying habits, Imelda's name became strongly associated with wealth and extravagant spending **[RL]**. While trapped in an addictive version of *Better Than Life*, Rimmer imagined that his wife, Juanita Chicata, periodically used a time machine to collect Marcos and other friends for weeklong shopping sprees **[N-BTL]**.

- **Marie Lloyd:** A London pub located on Chart Street **[RL]**, off Regent Street. While stuck on Mimas, Lister frequently got drunk in the hope of waking up outside the Marie Lloyd public house **[N-INF]**.

  ***NOTE:*** *In the real world, Marie Lloyd is located approximately three miles from Regent Street.*

- **Marigold:** An alert condition indicating severe damage to a 4000 Series mechanoid. After an accident on a psi-moon left Kryten injured and stranded, his CPU assessed the situation and periodically updated his head-up display. His condition changed to Marigold when Lister began drawing a line on his torso, as a guide to cut the mechanoid in two in order to dislodge him from the wreckage **[T-SER5.3]**.

- **marijuana gin:** An alcoholic beverage that Rimmer asked Lister if he had been drinking when Lister encountered a future echo in a mirror and could not explain what he saw **[T-SER1.2]**.

- ***Marilyn*:** A magazine about American starlet Marilyn Monroe. Cat read an issue of *Marilyn* while discussing the usefulness of timeslides with his *Red Dwarf* shipmates **[T-SER3.5]**.

- **Marilyn Monroe Anti-Grav Dress:** A garment that Rose wore to her school prom on the television soap opera *Androids*. The dress operated successfully at the dance **[M-SMG1.10(c2)]**.

  ***NOTE:*** *This dress was named after Monroe's famous pose from the film* The Seven Year Itch*, in which a passing train blew her white dress in the air as she stood on a subway grate.*

- **Marks and Spencer (M&S):** A British multinational retailer specializing in clothing and gourmet food products **[RL]**. While trapped in an addictive version of *Better Than Life*, Rimmer imagined that M&S had locations spanning Earth's solar system. In the hallucination, Rimmer arranged for his ex-pool attendant, Hugo, to be refused service at any of the company's store locations, to punish him for having sex with Arnold's wife, Juanita Chicata **[N-INF]**.

- **Markson, Hack:** The American executive producer of the television soap opera *Androids*. Markson was hired during the program's twenty-ninth season to liven up the show. During the first three weeks of his tenure, the series featured a massive eight-hover-car accident, three divorces and a cross-make relationship between two major characters. He also owned the license to the Tension Sheet **[W-AND]**.

- **Marlowe, Philip:** A fictional pulp-noir private investigator created in the 1930s by American novelist Raymond Chandler. Marlowe appeared in numerous short stories, novels, radio serials, films and television series **[RL]**. Philip Marlowe was one of Jake Bullet's role models **[M-SMG2.6(a)]**.

- **Marne Valley:** One of five wine-producing districts within the French administrative province of Champagne (in French: Vallée de la Marne) **[RL]**. After being sentenced to the virtual-reality prison Cyberia, Lister was surprised to find his personal Cyberhell set in a Spanish villa, including a welcome package containing Marne Valley vintage champagne. He discovered, however, that he had been sent to the wrong illusion, and was quickly re-assigned to his own hell, which offered no such luxuries **[N-LST]**.

- **Marnie:** The lead female character of a black-and-white romance film about a man who sacrificed everything he had for the woman he loved. Lister favored the movie, but his shipmates aboard *Red Dwarf* gave it mixed reviews **[T-SER5.1]**.

- ***Married With Robots*:** A substitute title that Frank, a TV executive in an alternate universe, suggested for the American television show *Red Dwarf,* after noting the lack of actual dwarves in it **[M-SMG1.10(c4)]**.

  ***NOTE:*** *This title spoofed that of American television sitcom* Married… With Children.

- ***Marry Me My Darling*:** A romantic movie in *Red Dwarf*'s library. Lister tried watching this film on several occasions, but was constantly interrupted during a pivotal scene in which Carol and Jim discussed their love and Carol's terminal illness. When he tried watching it once more in his quarters, Rimmer shut off the film right before the conclusion **[T-SER1.5]**.

  ***NOTE:*** *This movie's title was mentioned in the episode's* *script, according to commentary featured on* The Bodysnatcher Collection *DVDs.*

- **Mars:** The fourth planet in Earth's solar system, orbited by two moons, Phobos and Deimos **[RL]**. During the twenty-first century, the European Space Consortium (ESC) launched the *Beagle* spacecraft toward Mars. Sometime during its landing, however, the craft malfunctioned and was presumed lost. Years later, the agency launched a Mars rover, which discovered debris left behind by the *Red Dwarf* crew. As the rover analyzed the trash, Cat found the craft and used it to transmit a message back to Earth, informing the agency he had located their missing *Beagle* and asking if there was any good food on Mars **[X-APR]**.

  In the twenty-second century, the Inter-Planetary Commission for Waste Disposal decided to designate one of the system's nine planets as humanity's official dumping grounds. Representatives from all nine worlds presented their case against being chosen, but Mars, being home to the system's wealthiest and most prominent individuals, was immediately removed from consideration. Ultimately, Earth was nominated for the task **[N-BTL]**.

  The results of an election held on Mars in 2362 were broadcast on Groovy Channel 27's news program, *Cosmoswide,* on Wednesday, the 27th of Geldof **[M-SMG1.7(a)]**.

- **Marshmallow Ass:** A nickname that Cat called Big Meat in the Tank's mess hall, hoping to goad the portly inmate into hitting him so Cat could join his friends in *Red Dwarf*'s medi-bay and escape. Instead, Big Meat assumed he was crazy and offered to be his bitch **[T-SER8.8]**.

- **Martian power packs:** Small battery units produced on Mars, used to power the handheld Psi-scan 345 model. Kryten cursed his Psi-scan's Martian power packs when they died during a mission to rescue Hildegarde Lanstrom from a viral research station **[T-SER5.4]**.

- **Martian Tourister robot luggage:** A type of mobile suitcase fitted with artificial intelligence, created by software houses on Mars and built in sweatshops. The suitcase had a top speed of 10 kilometers per hour (6.21 miles per hour) and featured a currency and tip calculator, as well as the ability to summon cabs, order meals and ask for directions **[G-SOR]**. One such unit lost its human owner at the Ganymede Holiday Inn **[T-SER2.4]**.

  *NOTE: This name spoofed that of suitcase brand name American Tourister.*

- **Martin:** A character on the television show *Simulants*. In one episode, a simulant named Jeff ripped off Martin's head **[M-SMG1.7(a)]**.

- **Martin, Jayne:** A *Red Dwarf* crewmember who worked in Supplies. Lister once suffered a claustrophobia attack while stuck in an Xpress Lift with Martin. Years later, he still had nightmares about the ordeal **[M-SMG2.8(a)]**.

  *NOTE: Martin presumably died during the cadmium II explosion. It is unknown whether the nanobots resurrected her in Series VIII.*

- **Martini's Bar:** A drinking establishment featured in the film *It's a Wonderful Life*, owned by Giuseppe Martini **[RL]**. While trapped in an addictive version of *Better Than Life*, Lister passed the bar in his Model 'A' Ford **[N-INF]**.

- **Marvo the Memory Man:** A hypothetical individual whom Rimmer mentioned while discussing his lost virginity. When Lister prodded him for details, Arnold claimed he couldn't recall all of his sexual exploits, as if he were Marvo the Memory Man **[B-PRM]**.

  *NOTE: This appeared in the screenplay of episode 3.2 ("Marooned") but was changed to simply "The Memory Man" for the final edit.*

- **Marx, Herbert Manfred ("Zeppo"):** A twentieth-century American film star, and the youngest of five brothers comprising the family comedy act The Marx Brothers **[RL]**. When the Epideme virus infected Lister, Kryten asked if it knew the identity of the fourth Marx Brother, hoping to lure the parasite into a false sense of security. It incorrectly responded "Zeppo" **[T-SER7.7]**.

  *NOTE: The subtitles on the DVD misspelled the actor's stage-name as "Zippo." The fourth Marx Brother was Milton "Gummo" Marx, while Zeppo was the fifth.*

**B-: Books**
**PRG:** *Red Dwarf Programme Guide*
**SUR:** *Red Dwarf Space Corps Survival Manual*
**PRM:** *Primordial Soup*
**SOS:** *Son of Soup*
**SCE:** *Scenes from the Dwarf*
**LOG:** *Red Dwarf Log No. 1996*
**RD8:** *Red Dwarf VIII*
**EVR:** *The Log: A Dwarfer's Guide to Everything*

**X-: Misc.**
**PRO:** Promotional materials, videos, etc.
**PST:** Posters at DJ XVII (2013)
**CAL:** 2008 calendar
**RNG:** Cell phone ringtones
**MOB:** Mobisode ("Red Christmas")
**CIN:** *Children in Need* sketch
**GEK:** *Geek Week* intros by Kryten
**TNG:** "Tongue-Tied" video
**XMS:** Bill Pearson's Christmas special pitch script
**XVD:** Bill Pearson's Christmas special pitch video
**OTH:** Other *Red Dwarf* appearances

**SUFFIX**
**DVD:**
**(d)** – Deleted scene
**(o)** – Outtake
**(b)** – Bonus DVD material (other)
**(e)** – Extended version

**SMEGAZINES:**
**(c)** – Comic
**(a)** – Article

**OTHER:**
**(s)** – Early/unused script draft
**(s1)** – Alternate version of script

- **Marx, Karl Heinrich:** A nineteenth-century German philosopher, journalist and revolutionary socialist. His most notable works included *Das Kapital* and *The Communist Manifesto* **[RL]**. Holly read the complete works of several prominent writers, including Marx, during the fifteen nanoseconds that passed between *Red Dwarf*'s cadmium II core going critical and the entire crew dying **[N-INF]**.

- **Mary, Auntie:** A foster relative of Lister's. Lister claimed that Kryten sounded like his Auntie Mary when the mechanoid complained about having no one to wait on, and that his sole purpose was to serve others **[T-SER2.1(s)]**.

- **Mary, Queen of Scots (a.k.a. Mary Stuart, Mary I):** A sixteenth-century ruler of Scotland, and later the queen consort to France **[RL]**. Rimmer sarcastically claimed Mary's remains were in a canister of George McIntyre's ashes when the container was shot past their cabin window aboard *Red Dwarf* **[T-SER1.1]**.

- ***Mary Celeste*:** A nineteenth-century American merchant vessel discovered abandoned in the Atlantic Ocean in 1872. The unexplained disappearance of its crew is considered one of the great maritime mysteries **[RL]**. Captain Hollister postulated that *Red Dwarf*'s transformation and location in deep space ranked alongside such mysteries as the *Mary Celeste* and the popularity of broccoli **[T-SER8.1(d)]**.

  Rimmer dismissed the fact that Lister's parents abandoned him in a pub when he was a baby as not being a mystery of the same caliber as the *Mary Celeste* **[R-DAD]**. After Holly's IQ was increased beyond twelve thousand due to an intelligence-compression procedure, the AI discerned what had happened to the *Mary Celeste* and told Talkie Toaster his theory **[N-BTL]**.

- **masculinism:** A movement aimed at promoting classical masculine virtues among men **[RL]**. In a female-oriented alternate reality, males who advocated men's rights were dubbed masculinists. Rimmer's female counterpart accused him of being a masculinist because of his revulsion at a magazine that objectified men **[T-SER2.6]**.

  ***NOTE:** This was the female-oriented universe's analog to feminism.*

- **mass compactor:** A component of the time drive that occasionally required recalibration **[T-SER6.6]**.

- **Master, The:** *See* Unspeakable One, The

- **Match the Body Part to the Crew Member:** A game that the *Starbug 1* crew sometimes played. It was one of Cat's personal favorites **[T-SER7.5]**.

- **Matheson, Mark:** A sports newscaster who interviewed Jim Bexley Speed after Megabowl 102 **[N-INF]**.

- **Matter Paddle:** A handheld device capable of instantaneously transporting up to four users to any point in space. The paddle converted individuals into digital information and transmitted them as light beams to another location within five hundred thousand light years. The device could detect planets with an atmosphere conducive to exploration. It was vital that an operator correctly input the depth function to control the Z-axis during transport **[T-SER4.6]**. Kluge Corp. developed a version of the Matter Paddle that was distributed via Crapola Inc.'s annual *SCABBY* catalog **[G-RPG]**.

  When Kryten found a prototype of the device in a *Red Dwarf* research lab on Z Deck, the crew used it to visit Waxworld, the site of an ongoing waxdroid resource war. They temporarily lost the device to agents of Villain World, but retrieved it once the waxdroids were destroyed **[T-SER4.6]**.

  After returning to *Red Dwarf*, Kryten reconfigured the Matter Paddle into a triplicator, capable of producing two copies of any item. He tested the machine on a strawberry and created two copies: a sweet, succulent version and a bitter, maggot-infested one. Curious if the process could be reversed, he switched the field, but instead of combining the strawberry, it triplicated the entire ship **[T-SER5.5]**.

  While trapped in an elation squid hallucination, the *Red Dwarf* crew imagined a man named Noddy, who worked at a British science fiction shop called They Walk Among Us! Noddy suggested they use the Matter Paddle to visit Nose World for clues to their creator's whereabouts, but the device was on the mining ship at the time, and of no use to them **[T-SER9.2]**.

  ***NOTE:** See also the triplicator entry.*

- **Matter Transference device:** A contraption that could transport matter instantaneously from one location to another. Research on the device was conducted by the Space Corps Research & Development Program on Europa in one of Ace Rimmer's universes. Headed by Admiral Tranter, the MT program was abandoned after several failed tests using rodents **[N-BCK]**.

- **Mauritius:** An island nation off the southeast coast of Africa **[RL]**. While incarcerated in *Red Dwarf*'s brig, Rimmer received a letter claiming he had won a vacation to Mauritius in the *Reader's Digest* lucky dip **[T-SER8.5]**. Rimmer later mocked Kryten's vacation to a broom cupboard by suggesting he take a two-week trip to Mauritius with an electric toothbrush **[T-SER9.1]**.

- **Mauve:** An alert condition indicating severe damage to a 4000 Series mechanoid. After an accident on a psi-moon left Kryten injured and stranded, his CPU assessed the situation and periodically updated his head-up display. His condition changed to Mauve based on a calculation of seventy-two percent overall damage, thirty-five percent optical damage and one hundred percent ambulation damage **[T-SER5.3]**. Kryten also entered Mauve condition after accidentally flushing Lister's pet robotic goldfish down the latrine **[M-SMG2.4(c5)]**.

- **Max, Uncle:** A relative of Colonel Mike O'Hagan, the author of the *Space Corps Survival Manual*. Max (a scientist) and his assistant, Chantelle, pioneered advances in preservative and regenerative drugs that hindered death, leading to the development of the emergency death pack, which he tested on his wife, Enid **[B-SUR]**.

- **Maxime:** A character in the artificial-reality video game *Gumshoe*, a film-noir-type detective simulation. The plot centered around the murder of Pallister, which the game's femme fatale, Loretta, planned but was carried out by her twin sister, Maxime. Loretta took the rap for the murder anyway, knowing she had the perfect alibi thanks to Philip, the game's detective and main playable character **[T-SER6.3]**.

- **Maxwell, Doctor:** A person whom Cat hallucinated after bumping his head while retrieving food from a *Red Dwarf* cupboard. Transformed once more into Duane Dibbley, Cat believed he was taken to a man called Doctor Swan-Morton. The doctor interrogated him regarding the deaths of Jake Bullet and brothers Sebastian and William Doyle, then delivered him for torture to Doctors Maxwell, Pension and Fund—who were actually Lister, Rimmer and Kryten, attempting to revive Cat from his reverie **[M-SMG1.9(c1)]**.

- **Mayday:** An emergency call for help, reserved for life-threatening emergencies such as a crashed craft. The word "Mayday" was derived from the French word *m'aider*, meaning "help me" **[RL]**.

  Rimmer broadcast a Mayday signal after he and Lister crashed *Starbug 1* on an icy planet. Mistaking the distress call for a reference to the bank holiday May Day, Arnold questioned its effectiveness, wondering why "Ascension Sunday," "Shrove Tuesday" or "15th Wednesday after Pentecost" weren't chosen as distress calls instead **[T-SER3.2]**.

- ***Mayflower*:** A two-million-ton space freighter that launched from Earth transporting a contingent of GELFs to terraform a planet in the Andromeda Galaxy. The World Council conceived of the mission after scientists discovered that attempts to control Earth's weather by setting off thermonuclear explosions near the Sun had reduced the star's lifespan to around four hundred thousand years, forcing humanity's relocation.

  The ship carried eight human supervisors, several types of GELFs (including Dingotangs, Snugiraffes, Alberogs, Dolochimps and symbi-morphs), a group of simulants, and technology for terraforming and genetic engineering, including the genome of DNA (G.O.D.). Its propulsion system included a negative gravity drive.

  En route to Andromeda, the GELFs and simulants rebelled against the human crew. During the skirmish, the navigation system was damaged, forcing the ship into the Omni-zone, where it emerged in an alternate universe and crashed onto a lava planet. Those who survived fled the planet in escape pods and populated a nearby asteroid belt, creating the United Republic of GELF States. The four main GELF species split the wreckage's coordinates among them, thereby ensuring that no species could access the power held within.

  Years later, the *Red Dwarf* crew traversed the Omni-zone and also emerged in this universe, where they found their counterparts in that reality. All were dead except for Lister's sociopathic doppelgänger, who possessed the *Mayflower*'s coordinates and planned to use G.O.D. for his own benefit. The crew located the ship under an ocean of magma, and discovered vials of positive viruses within, including luck, inspiration and sexual magnetism, as well as several mutated crash survivors. They also found a machine that changed the DNA of any living creature into another form **[N-LST]**.

- **Mayor of Warsaw:** The title of officials chosen to head the city government of Warsaw, Poland **[RL]**. Lister told Rimmer he regretted never having asked out Kochanski, claiming she may have said yes, and that stranger things had happened. According to Rimmer, only two things would have been stranger, including the spontaneous combustion of the Warsaw's mayor in 1546. Later that night, as Lister dreamed of this incident while afflicted with mutated pneumonia, a manifestation of the mayor appeared and burst into flames **[T-SER1.5]**.

- ***Mbazvmbbcxyy vs. Mbazvmbbcxyy*:** A legal case that Lister invoked on Arranguu 12 in an effort to force a mistrial during his hearing for crimes against the GELF state. Lister stated that taking the fourth sand of D'Aquaarar protected him from the breach of Xzeeertuiy by the Zalgon impeachment of Kjielomnon, according to the case of *Mbazvmbbcxyy vs. Mbazvmbbcxyy*, which was allowed during the third season of every fifth cycle. However, the GELF Regulator noted, he was being tried in the Northern sector of Arranguu 12, which did not follow the same archaic legal system as the Southern sector, from which the referenced case originated **[N-BCK]**.

- **McBean, Dennis:** A fourteen-year-old who created the virtual-reality video game *Better Than Life*. In an addictive version of the game, McBean's likeness, sporting greasy spiked hair, a wispy moustache, large glasses and a purple anorak, appeared in a three-dimensional recording to anyone who tried to exit after successfully solving the final obstacle **[N-BTL]**.

- **McCartney:** One of Lister's MkIV Titanica Fish Droids, along with Lennon **[M-SMG2.4(c5)]**. The mechanical goldfish, produced by Acme **[M-SMG1.4(c2)]**, were armed with defensive micropedoes **[M-SMG2.4(c5)]**.

  When McCartney malfunctioned, Lister repaired him with a screwdriver after bashing him on a desk. Cat later attempted to eat the two fish, believing them to be alive, just as *Red Dwarf* was approaching lightspeed. Lister witnessed a "future echo" of Cat with a broken tooth, and tried by prevent this by tackling Cat before he could eat the aquatic robots—but in so doing, he caused the very injury he hoped to avoid **[T-SER1.2]**.

  *NOTE: McCartney was named after The Beatles' Paul McCartney.* Red Dwarf—The Roleplaying Game*'s* Series Sourcebook *identified the fish as IcthyTech 3000 Robot Goldfish, but the* Smegazines *called them Titanica droids.*

- **McCauley, Carol:** A woman to whom Rimmer wrote secret love letters, which he recorded in his diary **[T-SER2.4]**.

- **McClaren, Lucas, Doctor:** The chief psychiatric counselor aboard *Red Dwarf*. McClaren received his education from a mail-order psychiatry course titled "Dealing With Nutters." He originally worked on Titan, where he met with Captain Hollister about the latter's eating disorder, then joined the *Red Dwarf* crew as a replacement for Doctor Brannigan **[W-OFF]**.

  McClaren died during the cadmium II disaster. Three million years later, he was resurrected, along with the rest of the ship's complement, when nanobots rebuilt *Red Dwarf*. Unaware this had occurred, Hollister assigned McClaren to analyze Kryten, who had been detained as a stowaway. After assessing Kryten's mental stability, McClaren determined the mechanoid should be restored to his factory settings **[T-SER8.1]**. In an artificial-reality simulation designed to prove Kryten's guilt or innocence, McClaren wore a garter belt and stockings under his uniform **[T-SER8.2]**.

  *NOTE: The official website spelled his name as "McLaren."*

- **McClaren School:** A psychiatric educational facility, a student of which became a hologrammic psychiatrist of the holoship *Enlightenment*. This individual helped Nirvanah Crane cope with her feelings toward Rimmer **[W-OFF]**.

  *NOTE: The school's name may have referred to Lucas McClaren,* Red Dwarf*'s chief psychiatric counselor.*

- **McClure, Doug:** A twentieth-century American film and television actor **[RL]**. While trying to ascertain the era during which he and his shipmates had crashed in Earth's far future, Rimmer asked Holly if he should expect to encounter dinosaurs feeding on Doug McClure **[T-SER3.1]**. To Lister's disappointment, several McClure movies were stocked aboard *Starbug 1* **[T-SER6.2]**.

- **McCoy, Patrick:** A zero-gee football referee. Lister cited McCoy as a referee on his Jupiter Mining Corp. job application, misunderstanding the request for references **[M-SMG1.9(a)]**.

- **McDonald's:** The world's largest hamburger fast-food restaurant chain **[RL]**. Following a rough drinking binge that started on Earth, Lister found himself lying across a table at a McDonald's burger bar on Mimas **[N-INF]**.

- **McGee ("Bear Strangler"):** An individual whom Kryten's subconscious mind conjured as he attempted to purge the Armageddon virus infecting *Starbug 1*'s navicomp. The mechanoid's mind converted the struggle into a Western-themed dream in which McGee was a patron of the Last Chance Saloon.

  When Kryten's crewmates hacked into the dream via the Old West artificial-reality game *Streets of Laredo*, they arrived at the saloon and tried to blend in by ordering whisky. After Rimmer vomited in Bear Strangler's hat, Lister hastily apologized and reimbursed the man **[T-SER6.3]**.

- ***McGovern, The*:** A space freighter on which Frank Hollister served as a third technician before becoming captain of *Red Dwarf*. According to Hollister, when a meteor storm near Jupiter damaged the Drive Room, he took charge and piloted the vessel out of harm's way, for which he was promoted to acting captain **[W-OFF]**.

- **McGrew, Dan ("Dangerous Dan"):** A playable character in *Streets of Laredo*, a Western-themed virtual-reality game created by Interstella Games. McGrew specialized in bare-fist fighting, his preferred weapon being his bare hands. His in-game profile listed his stamina at one hundred, his charm at fifty and his intelligence at fifty, for a total of two hundred points. Rimmer chose Dan's persona upon entering Kryten's subconscious mind to combat the Armageddon virus **[T-SER6.3]**.

- **McGruder, Michael R., Lieutenant-Colonel:** The son of Yvonne McGruder and Arnold Rimmer. He was conceived aboard *Red Dwarf* during the couple's only sexual tryst, after which Yvonne left the ship at Miranda, just prior to the cadmium II explosion that killed the crew.

  While growing up, McGruder was told his father had been a brave and courageous soldier, hand-picked by *Red Dwarf*'s computer for revival after the radiation leak because of his skill and expertise. With this misguided vision as a role model, Michael enlisted at West Point and graduated top of his class before fighting in the Saturn War on Hyperion, for which he was decorated.

  While attending the Star Fleet, he dated a girl named Mercedes, but they broke up after he caught her having sex with his best friend, Ben. McGruder became the bodyguard of Doctor Bob Sabinsky, the scientific advisor to President John M. Nixon of the World Council. He learned of a mission to send the *Mayflower*, containing specially bred GELFs and viruses, to a planet in the Andromeda Galaxy to terraform a new home for humanity. Believing his father lost in deep space, Michael volunteered for the mission as a human supervisor, and was genetically altered not to age so he would survive the lengthy voyage.

  For several thousand years, the *Mayflower* sailed toward its destination, until an electrical malfunction released the GELF and simulant population, sparking a mutiny in which McGruder was captured and the navigation system destroyed. The ship spiraled into a black hole and was deposited into another universe via the Omni-zone, where it crashed onto a lava planet. The survivors, with McGruder as their slave, left using the ship's escape pods and eventually formed the GELF State.

  McGruder ended up on a barren planet used as a testing site for the Rage of Innocence—a malevolent entity comprising the DNA of wrongfully imprisoned inmates from the Cyberia prison complex. When Rimmer arrived at the same planet years later, the two finally met. Michael's excitement turned to disappointment, however, when he learned that his father was a simple technician. When Arnold sacrificed himself to destroy the Rage, enabling McGruder and the *Red Dwarf* crew to escape through a wormhole, Michael's faith in his dad was restored **[N-LST]**.

- **McGruder, Vaughan:** A *Red Dwarf* crewmember in a universe in which the sexes were reversed. The male analog to Yvonne McGruder, Vaughan was the ship's boxing champion. After being concussed by a winch, Vaughan took Arlene Rimmer's virginity, though he called her "Noreen" due to his head injury **[W-OFF]**.

- **McGruder, Yvonne:** A female flight technician **[N-BTL]** and boxing champion **[T-SER2.3]** aboard *Red Dwarf* who very briefly dated Rimmer. Yvonne was suffering a concussion at the time, following an accident involving a winch, and thought his name was either Norman **[T-SER1.5]**, Simon **[N-LST]** or Alan **[N-BTL]**.

  Unbeknownst to Rimmer, McGruder had actually developed a crush on him prior to the accident, but never got around to speaking to him until the two shared a lift, when he asked about her head bandages. They dated for a few days **[N-LST]**, during which Rimmer lost his virginity to her and shared a pizza **[T-SER2.3]**. Rimmer told Lister about the incident years later (while intoxicated during his deathday celebration), but greatly regretted it after sobering up **[T-SER2.3]**.

  On the night of their one sexual encounter, McGruder fainted in the bath and stayed overnight in the ship's Medibay. Worried that her relationship with Rimmer was merely an illusion due to the concussion, she waited for him to call—which he didn't, since Lister had convinced him he no chance with her. As a result, the two quickly lost touch despite their mutual interest.

  McGruder discovered she was pregnant with Rimmer's child, then left *Red Dwarf* at Miranda, shortly before the cadmium II disaster killed the crew. She delivered and raised a son, Michael R. McGruder, telling him exaggerated stories about his father's deeds and courage **[N-LST]**.

  In the total-immersion video game *Better Than Life*, Rimmer (now a hologram) conjured a computer simulation of McGruder. However, his mind could not cope with his good fortune, and so the game depicted her as pregnant with seven children, leaving him miserable **[T-SER2.2]**.

  Hoping to elicit a response from Rimmer, Lister once lied that he had dated McGruder before him, claiming he still had carpet burns on his buttocks as a result **[T-SER8.1]**. A short time later, while under the influence of psychotropic drugs, Rimmer imagined that their affair rekindled aboard the nanobot-revived *Red Dwarf*. In the illusion, Yvonne ravaged him after he found the sexual magnetism virus in *Starbug*'s wreckage, and their lovemaking encompassed the first twenty-three pages of the *Kama Sutra* **[T-SER8.2]**.

- **McHullock:** A technician in *Red Dwarf*'s Z-Shift prior to the cadmium II disaster **[N-INF]**.

  ***NOTE:** McHullock presumably died during the cadmium II explosion. It is unknown whether the nanobots resurrected McHullock in Series VIII.*

- **McIntyre, George, Flight Coordinator:** A *Red Dwarf* officer who died and was resurrected as a hologram. He had dark hair, glasses and a Scottish accent **[T-SER1.1]**.

  McIntyre committed suicide to avoid overwhelming gambling debts he owed to the Ganymedian Mafia from playing Toot, a bloodsport involving Venusian fighting snails. After the criminal organization cut off his nose and fed it to him, George killed himself, thereby rendering any debts and obligations null and void **[N-INF]**.

  ***NOTE:** In the first-draft script of the pilot episode ("The End"), McIntyre was killed by a radioactive leak aboard* Red Dwarf*, the substandard repair of which caused the cadmium II explosion that killed the remainder of the crew weeks later.*

- **McIntyre, George, Flight Coordinator:** A hologrammic representation of George McIntyre, *Red Dwarf*'s flight coordinator **[T-SER1.1]**. The hologram was activated after McIntyre committed suicide to avoid mob gambling debts. Since his rank was higher than that of the previous hologram—Frank Saunders—the Saunders hologram was deactivated only two weeks after his activation, so that George could be revived **[N-INF]**.

  McIntyre's own status as a hologram was similarly short-lived, as he was deactivated following the cadmium II disaster that killed the *Red Dwarf* crew (except for Lister, who was in stasis at the time) **[T-SER1.1]**. When Lister was released from stasis three million years later, Holly revived Rimmer instead of McIntyre in order to keep Lister sane **[T-SER1.3]**.

- **McLure, D., Commander:** A commander in the Space Corps. McLure received a letter from Doctor Marcus Bateman regarding the discovery of *Red Dwarf*'s black box recording,

**PREFIX**
**RL:** Real life

**T-: Television Episodes**
**SER:** Television series
**IDW:** "Identity Within"
**USA1:** Unaired U.S. pilot
**USA2:** Unaired U.S. demo

**R-: *The Bodysnatcher Collection***
**SER:** Remastered episodes
**BOD:** "Bodysnatcher"
**DAD:** "Dad"
**FTH:** "Lister's Father"
**INF:** "Infinity Patrol"
**END:** "The End" (original assembly)

**N-: Novels**
**INF:** *Infinity Welcomes Careful Drivers*
**BTL:** *Better Than Life*
**LST:** *Last Human*
**BCK:** *Backwards*
**OMN:** *Red Dwarf Omnibus*

**M-: Magazines**
**SMG:** *Smegazine*

**W-: Websites**
**OFF:** Official website
**NAN:** *Prelude to Nanarchy*
**AND:** *Androids*
**DIV:** Diva-Droid
**DIB:** Duane Dibbley
**CRP:** Crapola
**GEN:** Geneticon
**LSR:** Leisure World Intl.
**JMC:** Jupiter Mining Corporation
**AIT:** *A.I. Today*
**HOL:** HoloPoint

**G-: Roleplaying Game**
**RPG:** *Core Rulebook*
**BIT:** *A.I. Screen Extra Bits* booklet
**SOR:** *Series Sourcebook*
**OTH:** Other RPG material

which appeared to have traveled back in time through the Omni-zone via a black hole **[W-OFF]**.

*NOTE: The character's name referenced Doug McClure, an American film actor mentioned in the episodes "Backwards" and "Legion."*

- **MCN:** A component of *Starbug 1*'s navigational systems. When a GELF battle cruiser attacked the shuttle, Kochanski asked to be patched into the MCN—which confused Cat and Lister, who had no clue what that was **[T-SER7.3]**.

- **McQuack, Launchpad:** *See* Skipper

- **McQueen, Flight Coordinator:** A *Red Dwarf* crewmember with an IQ of 172 and superlative mathematics skills, who perished in the mining vessel's cadmium II disaster. Millions of years later, McQueen's personality disk was used during a mind patch procedure to raise Rimmer's IQ so he could join the crew of the holoship *Enlightenment* **[T-SER5.1]**.

  *NOTE: It is unknown whether the nanobots resurrected McQueen in Series VIII.*

- **McQueen, Steve:** A twentieth-century American film actor whose credits included *Bullitt*, *The Great Escape, Towering Inferno* and *The Blob* **[RL]**. While discussing Kryten's date with Camille (an amorphous green blob), Lister cited *The Blob* as an example of how people react differently to things. McQueen's response to meeting the creature, he quipped, was to try to kill it, not take it out to dinner **[T-SER4.1]**.

- **Meat-Tenderizer-Head:** A nickname that Cat called Kryten **[T-SER7.2]**.

- **Mecha College:** A learning institution that Gary and Brook attended on the television soap opera *Androids.* It was at this college that the pair's rivalry began **[W-AND]**.

- **mechaneumonia:** An illness that affected a mechanoid's olfactory system **[N-LST]**.

- **Mechanical Engineering:** A course offered by the JMC Educational Exam Board that included a specialization in robotics. In an effort to better himself after a near-death experience with Pree, *Red Dwarf*'s replacement computer, Lister enrolled in the JMC Engineering Programme to study robotics **[T-SER10.2(d)]**.

- **mechanoid:** A general term describing mechanical representations of humans built for servitude **[T-SER2.1]**.

  *NOTE: See also the following entries: Series 1000, Series 2000, 3000 Series, 4000 Series, Series 5000, 6000 Series and Hudzen 10.*

- **Mechanoid Empire, the:** A coalition of surviving mechanoids formed after the extinction of the human race. Members of the empire created a black market for emotions harvested by polymorphs **[M-SMG2.9(c11)]**.

- **mechanoid optical broadcast feature:** A feature of 4000 Series mechanoids enabling them to broadcast an audio and video signal from their optical units. This feature did not come standard with the 4000 Series, but could easily be installed as an aftermarket option **[G-SOR]**. Several inmates of the Tank kidnapped Kryten and installed the optical broadcast feature in him, allowing him to broadcast footage of female convicts showering **[T-SER8.5]**.

- ***Mechanoids' Strip*:** A television broadcast that aired at 1:35 AM on Groovy Channel 27. The show was available by subscription only **[M-SMG1.7(a)]**.

- **Mechanoid "Taranshula" Remote Drone:** An emergency robot created using parts of a 4000 Series or later-model mechanoid. In situations preventing a mechanoid from receiving emergency assistance, an autonomous remote drone could be fabricated using a hand and optical unit **[G-SOR]**.

  Kryten used a Taranshula drone to call for help after a moonquake on Rimmer's psi-moon wrecked *Starbug* and left him incapacitated. The drone made its way to *Red Dwarf*, where it sought out Lister and crawled up his leg like a spider, terrifying him **[T-SER5.3]**.

- **mechbian:** A mechanoid thespian—or one who acted in film or theater. Series 2000 mechanoids featured on the television soap opera *Androids* were mechbians **[W-DIV]**.

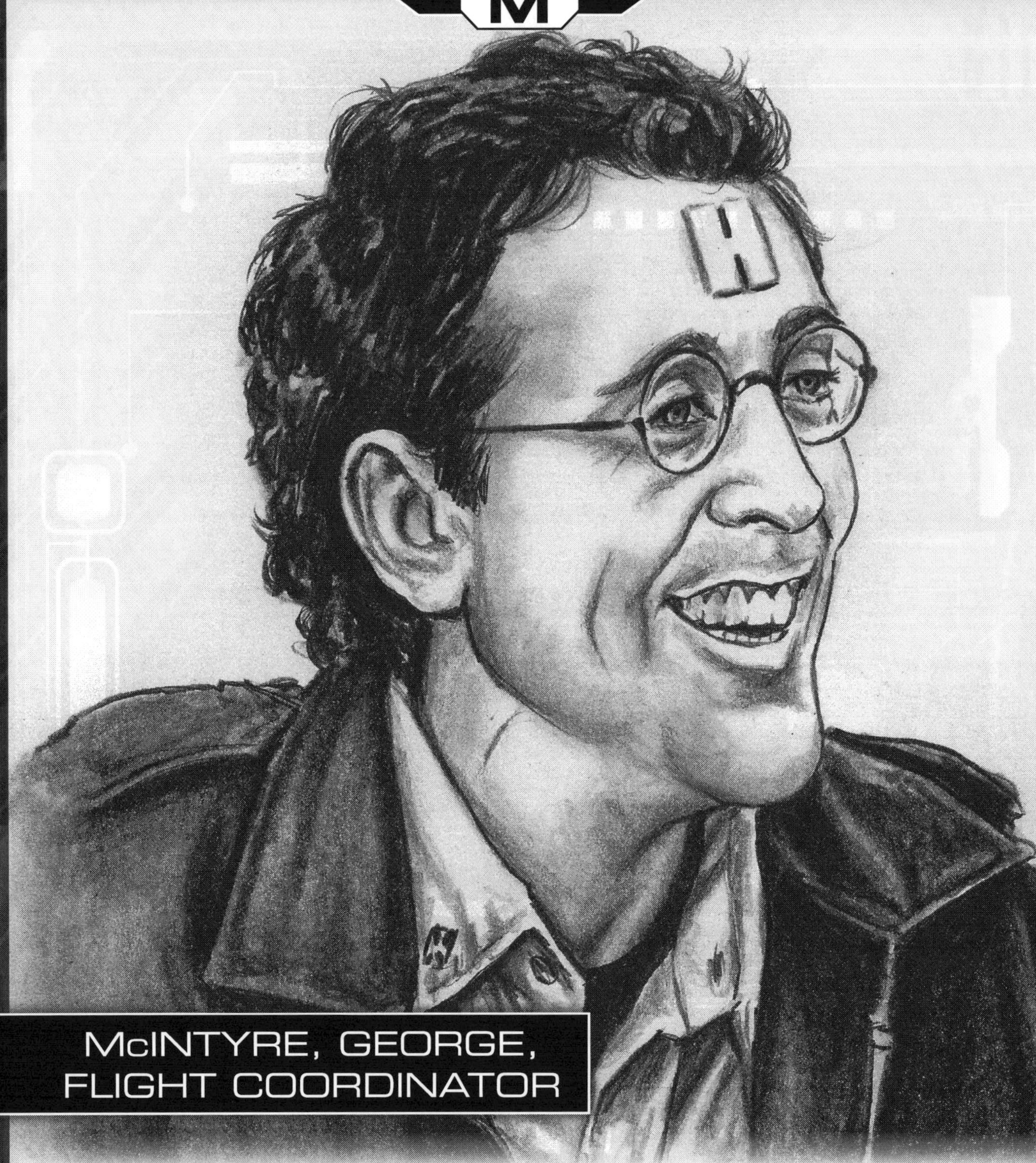

# McINTYRE, GEORGE, FLIGHT COORDINATOR

**PREFIX**
**RL:** Real life

**T-: Television Episodes**
**SER:** Television series
**IDW:** "Identity Within"
**USA1:** Unaired U.S. pilot
**USA2:** Unaired U.S. demo

**R-: *The Bodysnatcher Collection***
**SER:** Remastered episodes
**BOD:** "Bodysnatcher"
**DAD:** "Dad"
**FTH:** "Lister's Father"
**INF:** "Infinity Patrol"
**END:** "The End" (original assembly)

**N-: Novels**
**INF:** *Infinity Welcomes Careful Drivers*
**BTL:** *Better Than Life*
**LST:** *Last Human*
**BCK:** *Backwards*
**OMN:** *Red Dwarf Omnibus*

**M-: Magazines**
**SMG:** *Smegazine*

**W-: Websites**
**OFF:** Official website
**NAN:** *Prelude to Nanarchy*
**AND:** *Androids*
**DIV:** Diva-Droid
**DIB:** Duane Dibbley
**CRP:** Crapola
**GEN:** Geneticon
**LSR:** Leisure World Intl.
**JMC:** Jupiter Mining Corporation
**AIT:** *A.I. Today*
**HOL:** HoloPoint

**G-: Roleplaying Game**
**RPG:** *Core Rulebook*
**BIT:** *A.I. Screen Extra Bits* booklet
**SOR:** *Series Sourcebook*
**OTH:** Other RPG material

- **Medibay:** An area of *Red Dwarf* allocated for medical use **[T-SER7.3]**. Lister visited the Medibay to elicit the medi-bot's opinion about his relationship with his son (himself) **[T-SER10.2]**.

  ***NOTE:*** *The series used the terms Medical Unit, Medical Room, Medical Centre, Medibay and Sick Bay interchangeably. These may all have been the same area.*

- **medi-bot:** An artificial-intelligence computer aboard *Red Dwarf* specializing in medical procedures. Lister visited the Medibay to ask the medi-bot's opinion regarding his relationship with his son. The medi-bot, unaware Lister was discussing himself, opened a separate medical file for David Lister, Jr. and suggested Lister employ "tough love" **[T-SER10.2]**.

- **Medical Centre**: An area of *Red Dwarf* allocated for medical use. Captain Hollister informed Lister that his cat would be sent to the Medical Centre for dissection and study, to insure it did not pose a health risk to the crew **[T-SER1.1]**.

- **Medical Room:** An area of *Red Dwarf* allocated for medical use. Lister took a home-pregnancy test in this room after a tryst with his female counterpart in an alternate reality **[T-SER2.6]**.

- **medical shroud:** A cloth sheet used to wrap the bodies of the deceased **[RL]**. Bored with using plastic cutlery, Lister procured several items from *Red Dwarf*'s Medical Unit and used them to prepare and serve dinner in the Officers' Quarters, including a medical shroud, which he used as a tablecloth. Although Lister had cleaned and sterilized the equipment, Cat refused to stay for dinner, calling the meal "an autopsy" **[T-SER3.3(d)]**.

- **Medical Unit:** An area of *Red Dwarf* allocated for medical use. After Lister collapsed from a fever induced by mutated pneumonia, his crewmates brought him to this area for treatment **[T-SER1.5]**. Years later, Lister procured several items from the Medical Unit and used them to prepare and serve dinner in the Officers' Quarters. These included scalpels, flasks, kidney bowls, an embryo refrigeration unit, colonoscopy bags and an artificial insemination syringe for cattle **[T-SER3.3]**.

  ***NOTE:*** *The series used the terms Medical Unit, Medical Room, Medical Centre, Medibay and Sick Bay interchangeably. These may all have been the same area.*

- **medicom:** *See* medicomputer

- **medicomp:** A portable piece of equipment in *Red Dwarf*'s Medical Unit **[T-SER1.5]**. Malpractice Medical & Scispec manufactured medicomps, which were then distributed via Crapola Inc. **[G-RPG]**.

  After collapsing from mutated pneumonia, Lister was brought into the Medical Unit, where Rimmer had the skutters check his vital signs. When one skutter nearly poked his eye out with a thermometer, Lister insisted that Rimmer let the medicomp do it. Confidence, a hallucination of Lister's mind made corporeal by mutated pneumonia, destroyed the machine to prevent Lister from getting better **[T-SER1.5]**.

  ***NOTE:*** *It is possible that the terms "medicom," "medicomp" and "medicomputer" all referred to the same equipment.*

- **medicomputer:** A system that controlled the medical operations aboard *Red Dwarf* (called the "medicom" for short). Rimmer tried to bribe the medicom to give the JMC onboard computer a note explaining his three-million-year leave of absence, but despite a large donation of money from the supplies budget, the computer refused to provide the note **[T-SER10.5]**.

  ***NOTE:*** *It is possible that the terms "medicom," "medicomp" and "medicomputer" all referred to the same equipment.*

- **medi-crates:** Containers used to store medical equipment and supplies aboard *Red Dwarf*. Rimmer found several unopened medi-crates containing Anus Soothe Pile Cream, which he gave to Captain Hollister to earn his favor **[T-SER8.2]**.

- **medidroid:** A type of android stationed at the All-Droid Mail Order Shopping Station facility, whose prime purpose was to supply medical assistance to those in need **[T-SER10.1]**.

- ***Medieval Bloodsport*:** A macho-type virtual-reality game played in *Red Dwarf*'s AR Suite **[G-RPG]**.

- ***Medieval Smackdown IV*:** A Total Immersion video game operated at arcades owned by Leisure World International **[W-LSR]**.

**B-: Books**
**PRG:** *Red Dwarf Programme Guide*
**SUR:** *Red Dwarf Space Corps Survival Manual*
**PRM:** *Primordial Soup*
**SOS:** *Son of Soup*
**SCE:** *Scenes from the Dwarf*
**LOG:** *Red Dwarf Log No. 1996*
**RD8:** *Red Dwarf VIII*
**EVR:** *The Log: A Dwarfer's Guide to Everything*

**X-: Misc.**
**PRO:** Promotional materials, videos, etc.
**PST:** Posters at DJ XVII (2013)
**CAL:** 2008 calendar
**RNG:** Cell phone ringtones
**MOB:** Mobisode ("Red Christmas")
**CIN:** *Children in Need* sketch
**GEK:** *Geek Week* intros by Kryten
**TNG:** "Tongue-Tied" video

**XMS:** Bill Pearson's Christmas special pitch script
**XVD:** Bill Pearson's Christmas special pitch video
**OTH:** Other *Red Dwarf* appearances

**SUFFIX**
**DVD:**
**(d)** – Deleted scene
**(o)** – Outtake
**(b)** – Bonus DVD material (other)
**(e)** – Extended version

**SMEGAZINES:**
**(c)** – Comic
**(a)** – Article

**OTHER:**
**(s)** – Early/unused script draft
**(s1)** – Alternate version of script

- **medi-kit:** A first aid kit used on *Starbug* shuttles and other Space Corps vessels **[N-BCK]**.

- **mediscan:** A piece of machinery in *Starbug 1*'s Obs Room, used to perform a variety of medical functions. Curious about his fate, Lister used a mediscan to hack into the security cameras and catch a glimpse of his future self, who had boarded *Starbug 1* seeking assistance with his time drive **[T-SER6.6]**.

  Malpractice Medical & Scispec produced various models of mediscans in designer colors, such as Pus Green, Canker Sore Burgundy, Space Mumps Yellow and Diarrhea Brown **[G-RPG]**.

  ***NOTE:*** *The terms "mediscan" and "medi-scan," used interchangeably in DVD captions, referred to different machines throughout the series.*

- **medi-scan:** A medical diagnostic bed aboard *Red Dwarf* that could be used to perform mind patches **[T-SER5.1]**. A portable version was stored aboard *Starbug 1*, with which Kryten scanned Lister when the Inquisitor took control of his body **[T-SER5.2]**. After Kryten's nanobots rebuilt *Red Dwarf*, doctors in the ship's Medibay examined Cat using a medi-scan **[T-SER8.1]**.

  ***NOTE:*** *The apparatus Kryten used to scan Lister in episode 5.2 ("The Inquisitor") was identified as the Psi-scan in future episodes. The Psi-scan may have doubled as a portable medi-scan.*

- **medi-suit:** A medical apparatus worn by patients suffering from malnutrition. *Red Dwarf*'s recovery bay contained several medi-suits, which were controlled by power units. Each suit contained internal hydrotherapy units that massaged muscles into shape. After Cat and Lister spent two years trapped in an addictive version of *Better Than Life,* Kryten fitted them with medi-suits to mend their atrophied bodies **[N-BTL]**.

- ***Meeting a Drunken Artist*:** A book written by Mike Butthed. Lister owned a copy of this book aboard *Red Dwarf* **[M-SMG1.2(c1)]**.

- **Mega:** The manager of Tabby Ranks, a raga artist in an alternate dimension. Leo Davis met Mega and Ranks' bodyguard, Screwface, at Black Island Film Studios, the production company at which Davis worked, which had been hired to produce Ranks' music video **[X-TNG]**.

- **Megabowl 102:** The 102nd annual championship zero-gee football game. Jim Bexley Speed played a prominent role in the game, after which Mark Matheson interviewed him **[N-INF]**.

- **Mega Fizz:** A soft drink sold in cans, circa the twenty-first century **[M-SMG2.9(c11)]**.

- **MegaMart:** *See* Sainsbury MegaStore

- ***Megastar Daily*:** A sensationalistic entertainment news publication in the universe known as Alternative 6829/B. The day after Ray Rimmer, the once-great football player of the Smegchester Rovers, missed an easy goal, *Megastar Daily*'s front page headline read, "Smegchester Star in Sex Scandal" **[M-SMG1.8(c4)]**.

- **Melissa ("Mellie"):** The secretary of Admiral Peter Tranter, commander of the Space Corps R&D facility on Europa and head of Project *Wildfire* in one of Ace Rimmer's universes. When Tranter resigned his post, Melissa found him naked in his bathroom, firing his service revolver at bottles **[N-BCK]**.

  ***NOTE:*** *See also the Mellissa ("Mellie") entry.*

- **Mellington, Mike:** A person whom Lister and company imagined while trapped in a despair squid hallucination that made them think they were merely characters on a TV show called *Red Dwarf.* Mellington, a pompous electronics salesman employed at a London department store, told customers he had never watched *Red Dwarf* due to its science-fiction premise, which included such "hokey" concepts as the Psi-scan. Listening from another aisle, Kryten focused his Psi-scan on Mellington, which dubbed him a "know-nothing idiot" with a small penis **[T-SER9.2]**.

- **Mellissa ("Mellie"):** A Model 101/tenth-generation AI android employed at the Space Corps Test Base on Mimas. In one of Ace Rimmer's universes, she was the secretary of Base Commander Admiral Sir James Tranter. Her "flirt level" was set low, so as not to embarrass the admiral **[W-OFF]**. Despite this, Mellie attempted to seduce Ace, threatening to quit if he didn't oblige. She bore a striking resemblance to the female Holly, the prime *Red Dwarf*'s shipboard AI computer **[T-SER4.5]**.

  ***NOTE:*** *Mellie's full name, Mellissa, appeared in the*

**PREFIX**
**RL:** Real life

**T-: Television Episodes**
**SER:** Television series
**IDW:** "Identity Within"
**USA1:** Unaired U.S. pilot
**USA2:** Unaired U.S. demo

**R-: *The Bodysnatcher Collection***
**SER:** Remastered episodes
**BOD:** "Bodysnatcher"
**DAD:** "Dad"
**FTH:** "Lister's Father"
**INF:** "Infinity Patrol"
**END:** "The End" (original assembly)

**N-: Novels**
**INF:** *Infinity Welcomes Careful Drivers*
**BTL:** *Better Than Life*
**LST:** *Last Human*
**BCK:** *Backwards*
**OMN:** *Red Dwarf Omnibus*

**M-: Magazines**
**SMG:** *Smegazine*

**W-: Websites**
**OFF:** Official website
**NAN:** *Prelude to Nanarchy*
**AND:** *Androids*
**DIV:** Diva-Droid
**DIB:** Duane Dibbley
**CRP:** Crapola
**GEN:** Geneticon
**LSR:** Leisure World Intl.
**JMC:** Jupiter Mining Corporation
**AIT:** *A.I. Today*
**HOL:** HoloPoint

**G-: Roleplaying Game**
**RPG:** *Core Rulebook*
**BIT:** *A.I. Screen Extra Bits* booklet
**SOR:** *Series Sourcebook*
**OTH:** Other RPG material

*episode's script, published in the book* Primordial Soup *(which spelled her nickname as "Melly"). See also the Melissa ("Mellie") entry.*

- ***Memento*:** A 2000 American film written and directed by Christopher Nolan, about a man suffering from short-term memory loss and his quest to find his wife's killer **[RL]**. While trapped in an elation squid hallucination, the *Red Dwarf* crew imagined that a poster for the movie was displayed in a twenty-first-century video store **[T-SER9.2]**.

- **"Memories Are Made of This":** A song written in 1955 by Terry Gilkyson, Richard Dehr and Frank Miller, originally performed by Dean Martin **[RL]**. After a DNA-modifying machine converted Kryten into a human, the former mechanoid asked Lister several questions about his new form, including one about his penis, which he considered horrid-looking. When told it looked normal, he asked Lister if Perry Como sang "Memories Are Made of This" with a similarly atrocious-looking appendage stuffed in his pants **[T-SER4.2]**.

  ***NOTE:*** *Perry Como never recorded a version of this song, though he did release an album by this title.*

- **Memory, Wyatt:** An individual whom Kryten's subconscious mind created as he battled the Apocalypse virus. Memory was fatally shot by the Apocalypse Boys as Kryten—known in the illusion as Sheriff Carton—slept off a hangover. Because of this, other characters in the illusion shunned him **[N-BCK]**.

- **memory machine:** A device on a planet previously inhabited by Cat People, which the *Red Dwarf* crew discovered while searching the ruins. Consisting of a chair and helmet, the device allowed a user to conjure anything within his or her memory and make it solid. The first to use it was Cat, who summoned the object he knew most intimately: a mirror. Lister tried to bring back Kochanski, but when Holly instructed him not to think about six-eyed, carnivorous, raging swamp beasts, he naturally did, conjuring the creature instead of his lost love **[M-SMG1.9(c3)]**.

  With the beast in pursuit, the crew retreated to *Red Dwarf*, but Rimmer returned to use the machine to create a duplicate of himself. His shipmates tried to retrieve him, but found the double instead, who was more handsome, more courageous and better-endowed than the original Rimmer—and who died a short time later, sacrificing himself to save them from the swamp beast **[M-SMG1.10(c3)]**.

- **Memory Man, the:** *See* Marvo the Memory Man

- ***Memory Tester*:** An interactive game featured in the kid's section of Crapola Inc.'s website. Based on the memory card game, it was designed to keep children busy while their parents shopped **[W-CRP]**.

- ***Mend and Rend Magazine*:** A publication dedicated to the medical professional. In one issue, *Mend and Rend* rated Malpractice Medical & Scispec's Laser Bone Saw the number-one surgical implement of the year **[G-RPG]**.

- **Mendelssohn, Felix:** A nineteenth-century composer of classical music **[RL]**. While mocking Lister for his taste in music, Rimmer suggested he instead listen to classical musicians, such as Wolfgang Mozart, Mendelssohn and Motörhead **[T-SER1.3]**.

- **mental emetic:** *See* mind enema

- **Menuhin, Yehudi:** An American-born conductor and violinist, widely considered one of the greatest of the twentieth century **[RL]**. While trapped in an addictive version of *Better Than Life*, Cat entertained himself in his golden castle with a hand-picked seven-piece band, which included Menuhin on violin **[N-INF]**.

- **Mercedes:** The girlfriend of Michael R. McGruder. The two dated while he was in the Star Fleet, until he came home to find her in bed with his best friend, Ben **[N-LST]**.

- **Mercurian boomerang spoon:** A dining utensil used on Mercury and its moons, manufactured by Utensilware Inc. and distributed via Crapola Inc.'s annual *SCABBY* catalog **[G-RPG]**. Using this dangerous eating utensil could often prove lethal, but Kryten was well-versed in its operation—a skill necessary to fulfill his cooking duties **[T-SER6.2]**.

- **Mercury:** The planet in Earth's solar system closest to the Sun **[RL]**. In the twenty-second century, the Inter-Planetary

Commission for Waste Disposal decided to designate one of the system's nine planets as humanity's official dumping grounds. Representatives from all nine worlds presented their case against being chosen. The Mercurian delegation argued that since Mercury's solar energy plants provided cheap, unlimited energy for the entire system, their world was invaluable. Ultimately, Earth was nominated for the task **[N-BTL]**.

Three million years later, after *Red Dwarf*'s backup computer, Queeg, assumed control of the mining ship, Holly vowed to prove his IQ was six thousand, telling Lister to test him about which planet was nearest the Sun. After consulting *The Junior Colour Encyclopedia of Space*, Holly correctly answered Mercury **[T-SER2.5]**.

- **mermaid:** A mythical oceanic creature with the head and upper torso of a human woman and the lower half comprising a fish-like tail **[RL]**. While playing the total-immersion video game *Better Than Life*, Cat dated a mermaid named Miranda. Unlike the standard depiction, however, this mermaid had the upper body of a fish and human legs **[T-SER2.2]**.

- **Messalina, Valeria, Empress:** A Roman leader and the wife of Emperor Claudius in the first century A.D., reputed to have been promiscuous, and to have plotted her husband's death **[RL]**.

  A waxdroid replica of Messalina was created for the Waxworld theme park. Left on their own for millions of years, the waxdroids attained sentience and became embroiled in a park-wide resource war between Villain World (to which Messalina belonged) and Hero World.

  During this war, the *Red Dwarf* crew transported to the planet using a Matter Paddle, with Lister and Cat materializing in Villain territory, while Rimmer and Kryten landed in Hero territory. Rimmer found the heroes' army lacking and took command, working many of the pacifistic waxdroids to death before ordering a frontal attack on the enemy's compound across a minefield. This wiped out the remaining droids, including Messalina **[T-SER4.6]**.

- **Metabilis 3:** The home world of a sergeant who joined pilgrims on a quest to pray for the end of a meteor shower that destroyed the astrodome of Tunbridge Wells. The sergeant, who had bionic arms, a metal leg and a tendency to be overzealous, was the first to die in the great religious war aboard the pilgrim ship, when he proclaimed his loyalty to the god Pan **[M-SMG1.14(c2)]**.

  ***NOTE:** The planet may have been named after Metebelis III, a world mentioned in numerous episodes of the television series* Doctor Who.

- **Metal Head:** A nickname Cat called Kryten after the mechanoid caught him with Lister's robot goldfish **[M-SMG2.4(c5)]**.

- **Metal Munchkin:** A name that Rimmer called Kryten after the mechanoid wished him luck on his Astronavigation Exam **[T-SER10.1]**.

- ***Metaphysica*:** A book written by the Greek philosopher Aristotle regarding the nature of being **[RL]**. While searching for clues to his identity after two hundred years in a deep sleep unit aboard *Starbug 1*, an amnesiac Lister found a copy of *Metaphysica* and, discovering it was his, was relieved that he wasn't a completely uncouth slob. He was then disappointed to learn that he owned it simply to hide photos of naked ex-girlfriends **[T-SER6.1(d)]**.

  ***NOTE:*** Metaphysics*, in Greek, is titled* Metaphysica. *The prop seen onscreen, as well as Craig Charles' pronunciation, used the latter Greek spelling, though the prop book bore the name Aristotle, and not the Greek version, Aristotelis.*

- **metaphysical psychiatrist:** A type of psychiatric specialist assigned to ships with hologrammic crewmembers, to help newly deceased individuals cope with their death and new existence as a hologram **[N-INF]**.

- **meteor storm:** A celestial event (also known as a meteor shower) occurring in asteroid belts in which meteors, created by wayfaring asteroid impacts, streak by at immense speeds **[RL]**. Meteor storms were a particular danger to smaller craft, such as *Starbug* shuttles **[T-SER6.1]**. One such storm ravaged the domed city of Tunbridge Wells, forcing its residents to launch a ship of five hundred pilgrims to pray for the storm's end **[M-SMG1.14(c2)]**.

  According to Frank Hollister, the ship on which he served prior to *Red Dwarf* (*The McGovern*) encountered a meteor storm near Jupiter that damaged the Drive Room, forcing

**PREFIX**
**RL:** Real life

**T-: Television Episodes**
**SER:** Television series
**IDW:** "Identity Within"
**USA1:** Unaired U.S. pilot
**USA2:** Unaired U.S. demo

**R-: *The Bodysnatcher Collection***
**SER:** Remastered episodes
**BOD:** "Bodysnatcher"
**DAD:** "Dad"
**FTH:** "Lister's Father"
**INF:** "Infinity Patrol"
**END:** "The End" (original assembly)

**N-: Novels**
**INF:** *Infinity Welcomes Careful Drivers*
**BTL:** *Better Than Life*
**LST:** *Last Human*
**BCK:** *Backwards*
**OMN:** *Red Dwarf Omnibus*

**M-: Magazines**
**SMG:** *Smegazine*

**W-: Websites**
**OFF:** Official website
**NAN:** *Prelude to Nanarchy*
**AND:** *Androids*
**DIV:** Diva-Droid
**DIB:** Duane Dibbley

**CRP:** Crapola
**GEN:** Geneticon
**LSR:** Leisure World Intl.
**JMC:** Jupiter Mining Corporation
**AIT:** *A.I. Today*
**HOL:** HoloPoint

**G-: Roleplaying Game**
**RPG:** *Core Rulebook*
**BIT:** *A.I. Screen Extra Bits* booklet
**SOR:** *Series Sourcebook*
**OTH:** Other RPG material

him to take charge and pilot the vessel out of harm's way, for which he was promoted to acting captain **[W-OFF]**.

After taking a space walk outside of *Red Dwarf*, Lister forgot to close the ship's roof bay doors. This caused Cargo Bays J, K and L to become filled with meteors during a subsequent meteor shower **[T-SER9.1(d)]**.

Such a storm also threatened *Columbus 3*, a Space Corps vessel immobilized by a mutinous simulant named Sim Crawford. The simulant and the sole survivor of her attack—a hologram of Howard Rimmer—were rescued before the meteor shower destroyed the vessel **[T-SER10.1]**.

- **Mews, Bartholomew:** A co-creator of the television soap opera *Androids*. Along with Natalie Heathcote, Mews filmed twelve pilot episodes of the series before it was accepted seventeen years after its first pitch. The pair eventually split over a dispute regarding merchandise percentages, working together again only once more, on the controversial late-night sex-and-fruit drama *Del Monte* **[W-AND]**.

- **Mex:** A prisoner of the Tank, *Red Dwarf*'s classified brig, who died during the cadmium II disaster, but was resurrected by nanobots, along with the rest of the crew. Mex was a member of the Canaries, an elite group of inmates assigned to investigate dangerous situations.

  During a mission aboard the derelict Space Corps vessel SS *Manny Celeste*, Mex and his Canary battalion discovered a time wand, a temporal device that digitized and stored time. While examining the contraption, Mex accidentally downloaded his timestream, causing him and his fellow crewmembers to appear frozen in time. When *Red Dwarf* lost contact with the battalion, another group of Canaries, including Cat, Kryten and Kochanski, was sent to investigate. They located Mex and his crew and released them using the time wand, then smuggled the device aboard *Red Dwarf* **[T-SER8.6]**.

- **MFG-533:** The license plate number of a car assigned to John F. Kennedy's Dallas motorcade at the time of his assassination **[T-SER7.1]**.

- **Michelangelo:** A sixteenth-century Italian sculptor, painter and engineer, born Michelangelo di Lodovico Buonarroti Simoni, and best known for his sculptures *Pietà* and *David*, as well as his paintings in Rome's Sistine Chapel **[RL]**. When Rimmer claimed to be the next evolutionary step in mankind, Lister expressed doubt that the entirety of human history, including Michelangelo, was designed to lead up to him **[R-BOD]**.

- ***Michelin Guide to Penal Hellholes*:** A hypothetical reference guide. When Lister claimed the D Wing section of the Tank (*Red Dwarf*'s classified brig) was luxurious compared to the area in which he and Rimmer were incarcerated, Arnold sarcastically suggested looking it up in the *Michelin Guide* **[T-SER8.3]**.

  ***NOTE:*** Michelin Guides, *a set of real-world publications printed by Michelin Co. for travelers, cover various topics, including restaurants, hotels and tourist information.*

- **Mickey Finn:** A slang term for a drink laced with drugs **[RL]**. During a basketball game between *Red Dwarf*'s guards and Floor 13's inmates, Lister "Mickey Finned" the guards' halftime juice with the virility-enhancement drug Boing **[T-SER8.6]**.

- **Micky:** A JMC employee and an acquaintance of the officer who wrote Kochanski's personnel file. In the file, the officer included a note to Micky admitting his attraction to Kochanski, claiming a mutual acquaintance named Eric had shower footage of her **[W-JMC]**.

- ***Midget 3*:** A *Blue Midget* shuttle that Lister, Rimmer, Cat and Kochanski attempted to steal while escaping from the nanobot-rebuilt *Red Dwarf*. In actuality, the four were hooked into an artificial-reality machine, undergoing a psychotropic drug hallucination to determine their guilt. During the simulated escape, Cat wooed a female ground controller by making *Midget 3* dance **[T-SER8.3]**.

- **mid-range:** A setting on *Starbug*'s scanner, used to scan an area of space between the device's short- and long-range capabilities **[T-SER6.5]**.

- **Mij, Retsil:** One of Lister's sons with Kochanski, born on Earth in the backwards-running Universe 3. Mij and his twin brother, Yelxeb, were already alive when the *Red Dwarf* crew brought their dead parents to the planet in an effort to revive

**B-: Books**
**PRG:** *Red Dwarf Programme Guide*
**SUR:** *Red Dwarf Space Corps Survival Manual*
**PRM:** *Primordial Soup*
**SOS:** *Son of Soup*
**SCE:** *Scenes from the Dwarf*
**LOG:** *Red Dwarf Log No. 1996*
**RD8:** *Red Dwarf VIII*
**EVR:** *The Log: A Dwarfer's Guide to Everything*

**X-: Misc.**
**PRO:** Promotional materials, videos, etc.
**PST:** Posters at DJ XVII (2013)
**CAL:** 2008 calendar
**RNG:** Cell phone ringtones
**MOB:** Mobisode ("Red Christmas")
**CIN:** *Children in Need* sketch
**GEK:** *Geek Week* intros by Kryten
**TNG:** "Tongue-Tied" video

**XMS:** Bill Pearson's Christmas special pitch script
**XVD:** Bill Pearson's Christmas special pitch video
**OTH:** Other *Red Dwarf* appearances

**SUFFIX**
**DVD:**
**(d)** – Deleted scene
**(o)** – Outtake
**(b)** – Bonus DVD material (other)
**(e)** – Extended version

**SMEGAZINES:**
**(c)** – Comic
**(a)** – Article

**OTHER:**
**(s)** – Early/unused script draft
**(s1)** – Alternate version of script

them. As time on the backwards planet passed, the two boys de-aged, finally becoming infants who were then put back into Kochanski's womb **[N-LST]**.

*NOTE: Mij's name backwards spelled Jim Lister.*

- **Mike:** A middle name that Kryten wished he had been given, instead of 2X4B **[X-GEK]**.

- **"Mike Butcher, What A Nice Guy!":** A slogan printed on a wall-mounted sign in one of Cat's dreams, on a planet suffering from a style famine. The lower half of the sign read, "Well He Does Pay Me!" **[M-SMG1.7(c2)]**.

  *NOTE: Mike Butcher was the editor of the* Red Dwarf Smegazine.

- **mile-ometer:** An instrument aboard a Quantum Twister that registered the amount of fuel remaining in its engines **[T-SER10.1(s)]**.

- **military grey:** The color that Rimmer assigned the skutters to paint *Red Dwarf*'s hallways, changing them from the nearly identical ocean grey. Rimmer's duplicate hologram later had them changed back to their original color **[T-SER1.6]**.

- **milk shake:** A food item that Lister ordered from a dispenser that a crazed skutter had rewired to *Red Dwarf*'s self-destruct system. Fortunately, Holly had removed the explosive linked to the system years prior, which she neglected to share with the crew until the countdown timer had run out. Instead of *Red Dwarf* self-destructing, the dispenser merely filled Lister's order **[T-SER3.4]**.

- **millennium oxide:** A substance that Kryten detected trace amounts of while scanning a group of derelict vessels. This finding indicated that the *Starbug 1* crew, while pursuing the stolen *Red Dwarf*, had inadvertently wandered into a rogue simulant hunting zone **[T-SER6.3]**.

  *NOTE: Presumably, millennium oxide was a chemical compound of millennium and oxygen. Since there is no known element called millennium, this may indicate that such an element was discovered in the* Red Dwarf *mythos.*

- **Miller, Arthur:** A twentieth-century American playwright, best known for his play *Death of a Salesman*. He was married for a short time to Marilyn Monroe **[RL]**. When told that his fate to become the next Ace Rimmer might be hard to accept, Rimmer disagreed, stating that things like the coupling of Miller and Monroe were hard to accept **[T-SER7.2(d)]**.

- **Miller, Glenn:** A big band leader and musician who went missing while traveling to France to entertain troops during World War II **[RL]**. When the *Red Dwarf* crew encountered an unidentified craft, Rimmer decided it likely contained aliens returning Glenn Miller. He then radioed the ship announcing that they didn't want him back **[T-SER4.2]**.

  While trapped in an elation squid hallucination in which the *Red Dwarf* crew imagined being on Earth in the twenty-first century, Kryten searched a couch mattress at a department store for money so he and his comrades could continue their journey. After finding numerous items, the mechanoid exclaimed that he expected to next pull out Glenn Miller **[T-SER9.2]**.

- **Miller Street:** A roadway featured in the black-and-white horror B-movie *Attack of the Giant Savage Completely Invisible Aliens* **[T-SER8.5]**.

- **Milty:** The host of *20,000,000 Watts My Line*, a trivia game show in Jake Bullet's universe **[M-SMG1.10(c1)]**. Milty grew suspicious when one of his contestants, Philby Frutch, consistently won on the show, and sent his hostess and lover, Mercy Dash, to investigate. She discovered Frutch had been using an implant to feed him answers, as well as stupid drugs to mask the device's side effects.

  Milty told Dash to kill Frutch and take the winnings, then attempted to kill Jake Bullet, who was investigating the murder. The two TV stars both died while attempting to electrocute the cyborg, when Bullet bit Milty's microphone cable, shocking them both **[M-SMG2.2(c2)]**. A month later, Jake experienced a vision of Milty and Dash as he fell from a building to his apparent death **[M-SMG2.6(c6)]**.

  *NOTE: This show's title spoofed that of* What's My Line?, *a CBS game show that ran from 1950 to 1967, with several subsequent revivals. Among its frequent panelists was Soupy Sales (born Milton "Milty" Supman).*

- **Mimas:** A natural satellite of Saturn, distinguished by a large impact crater **[RL]**. The moon was Spanish-owned and contained a terraformed colony that JMC ships often visited so crews could take planet leave **[N-INF]**.

Mimas contained a Space Corps testing station for interstellar drive technologies. As such, a slew of strange phenomena were reported in its vicinity, ranging from gravity waves to charged particle flares to the entire planetoid disappearing for minutes at a time **[G-RPG]**. It also housed several large settlements on its south side **[B-LOG]**.

Lister found himself at a McDonald's on Mimas after spending a drunken night celebrating his twenty-fourth birthday on Earth. He subsequently took up residence in a luggage locker at Mimas Central Shuttle Station, until signing up for a tour of duty aboard *Red Dwarf* **[N-INF]**. Months later, Lister took leave on Mimas to recover after Kochanski broke up with him **[T-SER7.3]**.

> ***NOTE:*** *The subtitles of a deleted scene for episode 7.3 ("Ouroboros") misspelled the moon's name as "Mimus."*

- **Mimas Atmosphere Authority:** An agency on Mimas that monitored and regulated the Saturnian moon's atmosphere **[M-SMG2.5(c6)]**.

- **Mimas Board of Trade—Lethal Substances Division:** An agency governing Mimas business affairs concerning dangerous or hazardous materials. Lister registered his recipe for Peach Surprise—a hollowed-out peach skin filled with chili sauce—with this department **[M-SMG1.2(a)]**.

- **Mimas Central Shuttle Station:** A port facility located in Mimas' terraformed section. While stranded on the moon for several months, Lister resided in the station's Luggage Locker 4179. He also abandoned stolen taxi hoppers at Mimas Central after using them to collect illicit fares **[N-INF]**.

- **Mimas Council:** A governing body featured on the television soap opera *Androids*. In one episode, the Mimas Council applied double yellow rings in orbit of the planet **[M-SMG1.11(c1)]**.

- **Mimas Docks:** A port located in the terraformed section of Mimas, used for landing and docking spacefaring vessels **[N-INF]**.

- **Mimas Hilton:** A hotel located in Mimas' terraformed section, containing a shop called the Salvador Dali Coffee Lounge. George McIntyre agreed to meet representatives of the Golden Assurance Friendly and Caring Loan Society in the shop to discuss a payment plan for his massive debt, but the three burly representatives force-fed him his nose when he refused to sign paperwork guaranteeing payment **[N-INF]**.

- **Mimas Mining:** A company operating on the Saturnian moon of Mimas **[M-SMG2.3(c4)]**.

  > ***NOTE:*** *Mining astro Dutch van Oestrogen may have worked for Mimas Mining.*

- **Mimas Spaceport:** A facility located on Mimas, used for the launching and landing of spacecraft. Trixie LaBouche and Dutch van Oestrogen attempted to escape the Ganymedian Mafia via the Mimas Spaceport **[M-SMG2.5(c6)]**.

- **"Mimas Spaceport Welcomes Careful Drivers":** A phrase printed on a sign at Mimas Spaceport **[M-SMG2.5(c6)]**.

  > ***NOTE:*** *This sign paid homage to the title of the first* Red Dwarf *novel,* Infinity Welcomes Careful *Drivers—which itself played on popular real-world roadside signs welcoming travelers into town.*

- **Mimian bladderfish:** A delicacy on Mimas that Rimmer pretended he wanted to try in the red light district, as an excuse to visit a brothel in that vicinity **[N-INF]**. Kryten prepared lightly poached Mimian bladderfish for Rimmer after the hologram swapped minds with Lister and over-indulged his body **[T-SER3.4]**.

  > ***NOTE:*** *The* Red Dwarf Programme Guide *misspelled it as "Mimean."*

- **Mimian sangria:** An alcoholic beverage produced on Mimas. Like most alcohol sold on Mimas, the sangria was prohibitively expensive **[N-INF]**.

- **Mimosian anti-matter chopsticks:** A type of eating utensils primarily used during Mimosian banquets, consisting of oddly shaped metal prongs attached to handles. Activating the chopsticks caused the prongs to spin, creating an electron field that levitated food, allowing a person to guide it into his or her mouth. Letting active sticks touch was ill-advised, as it could create a field that simultaneously attracted any food within the vicinity. While serving the *Red Dwarf* crew a traditional Mimosian banquet, Legion supplied his guests with Mimosian anti-matter chopsticks, which they attempted to use with varying degrees of success **[T-SER6.2]**.

Anti-matter chopsticks were manufactured by Utensilware Inc. and distributed via Crapola Inc.'s annual *SCABBY* catalog **[G-RPG]**.

> ***NOTE:*** *Although the episode's subtitles spelled the term as "Mamosian" and Legion pronounced it likewise, the official website (www.reddwarf.co.uk) spelled it as "Mimosian" (possibly indicating a Mimas origin) in its database.*

- **Mimosian banquet:** A feast that Legion prepared for the *Red Dwarf* crew, consisting of several Mimosian delicacies popular in the twenty-fourth century. Unlike most foods, Mimosian cuisine was acceptable for mechanoid consumption **[T-SER6.2]**.

> ***NOTE:*** *Again, despite the episode's subtitles spelling the term "Mamosian" and Legion pronouncing it as such, the official website used the spelling "Mimosian."*

- **Mimosian telekinetic wine:** An alcoholic beverage of Mimosian origin, typically served during traditional twenty-fourth-century Mimosian banquets. During such feasts, wine glasses were affixed to the table, and guests willed the beverage into their mouths using their minds, then telepathically decided its flavor. When done correctly, this caused a narrow stream of the liquid to flow from the glass directly into a drinker's mouth; amateurs, however, typically found themselves drenched **[T-SER6.2]**.

> ***NOTE:*** *The official website's spelling is again assumed to be the correct one.*

- **Mimus:** *See* Mimas

- **mind enema:** A process by which a patient's mind could be flushed out via a large syringe inserted through his or her temple and into the brain. A mind enema (also called a mental emetic) could be used to empty an individual's memories during a mind swap, enabling the insertion of another person's brainwave pattern **[T-SER3.4]**.

- **mind-field:** The telepathic ability of Pleasure GELFs to control how others perceived them. A Pleasure GELF could turn this ability on and off at will; turning it off allowed others to see its true form as an amorphous green blob. After the *Red Dwarf* crew outed Camille as a Pleasure GELF, she shut off her mind-field, enabling them to view her natural form **[G-RPG]**.

- **mind-patch:** A dangerous procedure that raised a person's IQ by electronically grafting the intelligence of other individuals onto his or her mind. Possible side effects included being reduced to a dribbling simpleton. The procedure was possible on holograms, but carried the same risks.

  Rimmer used a mind-patch to increase his intelligence so he could secure a position aboard the holoship *Enlightenment*, using the minds of Science Officer Buchan and Flight Coordinator McQueen from *Red Dwarf*'s hologram records. The patch failed halfway through his recruitment test, however, forcing him to withdraw **[T-SER5.1]**.

- **mind probe:** A security feature aboard the penal station Justice World **[T-SER4.3]**, produced by Malpractice Medical & Scispec, and distributed by Crapola Inc. **[G-RPG]**.

  A visitor to Justice World who required a clearance code would be greeted upon arrival by escort boots, which would take him or her to the mind probe area for scanning. The station's computer would probe that individual for past criminal activity and guilt. If none were found, the boots were removed and the visitor was free to move about the facility; if, however, past criminal activity was detected, the footwear would remain attached, and would move that person to a holding facility. A mind probe once detected Rimmer's feelings of guilt regarding the deaths of his fellow *Red Dwarf* crewmembers, causing the Justice Computer to sentence the hologram to 9,328 years at the penal station **[T-SER4.3]**.

- **mind scan:** A procedure used to read and record an individual's mental patterns. Mind scans were performed aboard Space Corps vessels during criminal investigations, to corroborate or invalidate a defendant's story. The procedure was initiated by the administration of psychotropic drugs that knocked out the defendant, who was then hooked up to an alternate-reality machine programmed with a series of virtual scenarios the defendant believed to be real. The results were displayed on

**PREFIX**
**RL:** Real life

**T-: Television Episodes**
**SER:** Television series
**IDW:** "Identity Within"
**USA1:** Unaired U.S. pilot
**USA2:** Unaired U.S. demo

**R-: *The Bodysnatcher Collection***
**SER:** Remastered episodes
**BOD:** "Bodysnatcher"
**DAD:** "Dad"
**FTH:** "Lister's Father"
**INF:** "Infinity Patrol"
**END:** "The End" (original assembly)

**N-: Novels**
**INF:** *Infinity Welcomes Careful Drivers*
**BTL:** *Better Than Life*
**LST:** *Last Human*
**BCK:** *Backwards*
**OMN:** *Red Dwarf Omnibus*

**M-: Magazines**
**SMG:** *Smegazine*

**W-: Websites**
**OFF:** Official website
**NAN:** *Prelude to Nanarchy*
**AND:** *Androids*
**DIV:** Diva-Droid
**DIB:** Duane Dibbley
**CRP:** Crapola
**GEN:** Geneticon
**LSR:** Leisure World Intl.
**JMC:** Jupiter Mining Corporation
**AIT:** *A.I. Today*
**HOL:** HoloPoint

**G-: Roleplaying Game**
**RPG:** *Core Rulebook*
**BIT:** *A.I. Screen Extra Bits* booklet
**SOR:** *Series Sourcebook*
**OTH:** Other RPG material

a monitor for a Board of Inquiry to take into consideration.

When the *Starbug 1* crew and a newly resurrected Rimmer were arrested for various crimes aboard the nanobot-rebuilt *Red Dwarf*, Captain Hollister had them subjected to a mind scan. The scan corroborated their story, but they were instead charged with using the crew's confidential files for their own gain, which held a sentence of two years **[T-SER8.2]**.

- **mind swap:** An experimental procedure that electronically switched the minds of two individuals, or an individual and a mind stored on file. Kryten, who had unsuccessfully attempted the procedure while serving aboard *Nova 5*, suggested the swap after *Red Dwarf*'s auto-destruct sequence was activated, which could only be halted by the captain or senior officers—all of whom were long dead.

  The procedure involved wiping Lister's memories with a mind enema—a long syringe inserted into his brain—placing the stored brain pattern on a data tape, and electronically inserting the pattern of Carole Brown, an executive officer whose data tape was stored on file. Despite the procedure's success, Brown's brainwave pattern and voice could not override the auto-destruct sequence. Fortunately, Holly had removed the explosive linked to the system years prior, which she neglected to share with the crew until the countdown timer had run out.

  Seeing how simple the procedure was, Rimmer convinced Lister to swap minds with him under the guise of getting his body fit. However, the euphoria of having a body again overwhelmed Rimmer, who overindulged in smoking and eating, making Lister's body worse than before **[T-SER3.4]**.

- ***Minger Monthly*:** A hypothetical magazine title. After being attacked by an elation squid and covered in its ink, Cat claimed he wouldn't even be able to get on the cover of *Minger Monthly* **[T-SER9.1]**.

  *NOTE: "Minger" is British slang for an extremely unattractive person.*

- **mini-grenades:** A type of explosive munitions stored aboard *Red Dwarf*. Rimmer suggested using mini-grenades against a creature that the crew discovered in G Deck's water tank (which turned out to be an elation squid) **[T-SER9.1]**.

- **Mini Metro:** A British economy car produced in the 1980s and '90s **[RL]**. Lister told the Pleasure GELF Camille that Kochanski had fed his heart into a car crusher, and that when it came out, it was an inch thick, with bits of a Mini Metro in it **[T-SER4.1(d)]**.

- **mining laser:** A piece of equipment aboard *Red Dwarf* used to cut rocks during mining operations. While trapped in an elation squid hallucination, the crew imagined that Katerina Bartikovsky planned to convert a mining laser into a dimension-cutter and travel the multiverse to find a mate for Lister, so that the couple could repopulate the human species **[T-SER9.1]**.

- **Ministry of Alteration:** A fascist government agency that the *Red Dwarf* crew imagined while trapped in a despair squid hallucination. The crew had different identities in the illusion, with Lister becoming Voter Colonel Sebastian Doyle, section chief of CGI and head of the Ministry of Alteration. According to a police agent, the Ministry was in charge of purifying democracy by killing any dissident citizens **[T-SER5.6]**.

- **Ministry of Ethnic Purity:** A government agency in the rabbit people's society of an alternate dimension. Those suspected of believing in rabbit-human coexistence were brought to the Ministry and neutralized **[G-RPG]**.

- **Ministry of Space:** *See* Space Ministry

- **mint-choc ice cream:** A dairy product supplied to the JMC mining ship *Red Dwarf*, and one of Captain Hollister's favorite desserts. When a time wand transformed a sparrow named Pete into a *Tyrannosaurus rex*, the animal devoured the ship's entire supply (two and a half tons) of mint-choc ice cream after eating cow vindaloo that Lister had made to force the animal to expel the time wand, which it had swallowed. The dinosaur suffered gastric distress from the mixture and had a diarrhea attack, catching Hollister in its wake **[T-SER8.7]**.

- **Mint Elegance:** A food item available from several dispensers aboard *Red Dwarf* **[T-SER10.6]**.

- **Miranda:** A mermaid whom Cat dated while playing the total-immersion video game *Better Than Life*. Unlike typical mermaids, Miranda had the upper body of a fish and human legs **[T-SER2.2]**.

**B-: Books**
**PRG:** *Red Dwarf Programme Guide*
**SUR:** *Red Dwarf Space Corps Survival Manual*
**PRM:** *Primordial Soup*
**SOS:** *Son of Soup*
**SCE:** *Scenes from the Dwarf*
**LOG:** *Red Dwarf Log No. 1996*
**RD8:** *Red Dwarf VIII*
**EVR:** *The Log: A Dwarfer's Guide to Everything*

**X-: Misc.**
**PRO:** Promotional materials, videos, etc.
**PST:** Posters at DJ XVII (2013)
**CAL:** 2008 calendar
**RNG:** Cell phone ringtones
**MOB:** Mobisode ("Red Christmas")
**CIN:** *Children in Need* sketch
**GEK:** *Geek Week* intros by Kryten
**TNG:** "Tongue-Tied" video

**XMS:** Bill Pearson's Christmas special pitch script
**XVD:** Bill Pearson's Christmas special pitch video
**OTH:** Other *Red Dwarf* appearances

**SUFFIX**
**DVD:**
**(d)** – Deleted scene
**(o)** – Outtake
**(b)** – Bonus DVD material (other)
**(e)** – Extended version

**SMEGAZINES:**
**(c)** – Comic
**(a)** – Article

**OTHER:**
**(s)** – Early/unused script draft
**(s1)** – Alternate version of script

- **Miranda:** The innermost and smallest moon of Uranus **[RL]**, established as the last resting point for outbound miners **[G-RPG]**. One version of Ace Rimmer was assigned to a Space Corps Test Base on Miranda **[B-PRM]**.

Miranda housed an establishment called the Hacienda, which contained a bar that Lister and Rimmer once visited while on planet-leave. Arnold started a brawl by repeating a necrophilia rumor he had heard about fellow crewmember MacWilliams, then ran off, leaving Lister to face MacWilliams and his four friends. Lister cited the encounter years later as an example of Rimmer's cowardice **[T-SER3.2]**.

*Red Dwarf* stopped at a supply station on Miranda en route to Triton. During leave on the alcohol-free moon, Olaf Petersen experienced sobriety for the first time since age twelve and became a teetotaler, much to Lister's frustration. While there, Dave picked up a pregnant cat to smuggle aboard *Red Dwarf*, hoping to be sent into stasis for breaking quarantine regulations and thus shorten his trip back to Earth **[N-INF]**.

> ***NOTE:** This explanation for why Lister brought Frankenstein onboard contradicted the pilot episode ("The End"), which stated that he found the cat on Titan.*

- **Miranda, Carmen:** A twentieth-century Brazilian singer, dancer and actor who wore lavish, fruit-laden headdresses in several American films **[RL]**. When Dog, Cat's alternate-reality counterpart, asked if Cat could dance, he responded, "Does Carmen Miranda wear fruit?" **[T-SER2.6]**.

- **Miranda Insurance Company:** An agency located on the Uranian moon of Miranda in an alternate universe. In that reality, Lister's adoptive father, Tom Thornton, was arrested and sentenced to ten years in prison for embezzling money from the company when Dave was nine years old **[N-LST]**.

- **mirror machine:** A device Kryten created that allowed Rimmer to enter a mirror universe and obtain an antidote for a corrosive chameleonic microbe dissolving *Red Dwarf*. The mirror machine shot a beam into a reflective surface, opening a portal into the alternate universe **[T-SER8.8]**. The device was powered by a can of Leopard lager **[G-SOR]**. It shorted out as soon as Rimmer passed into the mirror universe, but was repaired in time to allow him back into his own reality after he obtained the antidote. Upon returning to the prime universe, however, Arnold found the machine damaged beyond repair **[T-SER8.8]**.

> ***NOTE:** The mirror machine, not named onscreen, was thus designated in* Red Dwarf—The Roleplaying Game*'s* Series Sourcebook.

- **mirror universe:** A parallel dimension in which everything was the exact opposite of its analog in the prime universe. Kochanski postulated that an antidote for the chameleonic microbe corroding *Red Dwarf* could be found in the mirror universe, provided that a sample could be sent there to be converted.

To facilitate this plan, Kryten built a device that could, when aimed at a mirror, breach the membrane between the two dimensions, allowing the crew to cross into the alternate reality. The device malfunctioned, however, temporarily stranding Arnold in the mirror universe. That reality's Rimmer was the ship's captain, while Frank Hollister was a lowly crewmember. The prime Rimmer first mistook Sister Talia Garrett, Captain Rimmer's spiritual advisor, for the captain's lover, and then his sister. A nun, Garrett ran away in tears.

Searching for an antidote, Rimmer met that reality's Kochanski, a flighty, bubblegum-chewing blonde, who directed him to Professor Cat. The scientist analyzed the microbe and wrote out the antidote (Sessyum-frankilithic-mixi-alibilium-rixi-dixi-doxy-droxide) for Rimmer to bring back to his own universe.

Discovering that the portal device had been fixed, Rimmer returned to his universe, only to find that his crewmates had fled into the mirror universe. What's more, the written antidote had converted back into the microbe's original formula, rendering it useless. When he tried to join his crewmates on the other side, the machine was completely burned out, stranding him on the rapidly disintegrating *Red Dwarf* **[T-SER8.8]**.

> ***NOTE:** Series IX and X did not explain how, or even if, Rimmer survived this predicament.*

- **Misenburger, Harold ("The Condom King"):** An extremely wealthy man once featured on *Life Styles of the Disgustingly Rich and Famous*, who requested that every item in his home be covered in prophylactic material **[W-OFF]**.

**PREFIX**
**RL:** Real life

**T-: Television Episodes**
- **SER:** Television series
- **IDW:** "Identity Within"
- **USA1:** Unaired U.S. pilot
- **USA2:** Unaired U.S. demo

**R-: *The Bodysnatcher Collection***
- **SER:** Remastered episodes
- **BOD:** "Bodysnatcher"
- **DAD:** "Dad"
- **FTH:** "Lister's Father"
- **INF:** "Infinity Patrol"
- **END:** "The End" (original assembly)

**N-: Novels**
- **INF:** *Infinity Welcomes Careful Drivers*
- **BTL:** *Better Than Life*
- **LST:** *Last Human*
- **BCK:** *Backwards*
- **OMN:** *Red Dwarf Omnibus*

**M-: Magazines**
- **SMG:** *Smegazine*

**W-: Websites**
- **OFF:** Official website
- **NAN:** *Prelude to Nanarchy*
- **AND:** *Androids*
- **DIV:** Diva-Droid
- **DIB:** Duane Dibbley
- **CRP:** Crapola
- **GEN:** Geneticon
- **LSR:** Leisure World Intl.
- **JMC:** Jupiter Mining Corporation
- **AIT:** *A.I. Today*
- **HOL:** HoloPoint

**G-: Roleplaying Game**
- **RPG:** *Core Rulebook*
- **BIT:** *A.I. Screen Extra Bits* booklet
- **SOR:** *Series Sourcebook*
- **OTH:** Other RPG material

- **Misery:** An aspect of Rimmer's personality made flesh on a psi-moon configured according to his psyche. After Arnold's shipmates rescued him from the moon, Misery and other solidifications of Rimmer's negative traits were left behind to battle his positive aspects, including Courage, Charity, Honour and Self-Esteem **[M-SMG2.7(c2)]**.

- **Miss Anne:** *See* Gill, Anne, Mapping Officer

- **Miss Elaine:** *See* Schuman, Elaine, Flight Coordinator

- **missile:** A type of offensive weapon designed to lock onto a target, home in on it and detonate **[RL]**. Sometime during the crew's pursuit of the stolen *Red Dwarf*, *Starbug 1* was upgraded with a missile launcher, which a future version of the crew used while battling their past selves **[T-SER6.6]**.
  ***NOTE:*** *Presumably, the missile launcher, the laser cannon installed by the rogue simulants in episode 6.3 ("Gunmen of the Apocalypse") and the laser missiles mentioned in the unfilmed script* Identity Within *were the same weapon.*

- **Miss Jane:** *See* Air, Jane, Mapping Officer

- **Miss K:** An endearing nickname that Kryten called Kochanski **[T-SER8.5]**.

- **Miss Lovely Legs:** An annual beauty competition held in Great Britain during the 1980s **[RL]**. Lister once claimed that Rimmer was as likeable as a horny dog at a Miss Lovely Legs competition **[T-SER4.5]**.

- **Miss Tracey:** *See* Johns, Tracey, Mapping Officer

- **Miss Yo-Yo Knickers:** A derogatory term that Dave Lister called Deb Lister (his counterpart from a universe in which the sexes were reversed) after she implied he was "easy" **[T-SER2.6]**.

- **Miss Yvette:** *See* Richards, Yvette, Captain

- **Mista:** A member of an anti-fascist group in Jake Bullet's universe known as the Fatal Sisters, along with Hilda and Sangrida. The three women wore Valkyrie warrior outfits **[M-SMG2.4(c6)]**. After rescuing Duane Dibbley from Voter Colonel Gray, the Fatal Sisters brought him to their hideout, where all three had sex with him in order to jog his memory about his true identity **[M-SMG2.5(c1)]**.

- **Mister Ed:** A fictional speaking horse featured on the same-named American television sitcom that aired on CBS from 1961 to 1966 **[RL]**. While dating Lise Yates, Lister pawned his grandmother's false teeth to buy tickets for a show, which he justified by saying she only used them to open bottles and chew tobacco. He later bought her a different-sized pair that made her resemble Mr. Ed **[T-SER2.3(d)]**.

- **Mistrust:** An aspect of Rimmer's personality made flesh on a psi-moon configured according to his psyche. When the *Red Dwarf* crew boosted Rimmer's confidence to vanquish the Self-Loathing Beast, a ghostly musketeer arose to battle the Unspeakable One's hordes, including Mistrust, thereby enabling the crew to escape **[T-SER5.3]**.

- **MIT White:** A black-market version of Eidetosol, a learning drug originally developed for clinical use. MIT White and its equivalents, IQ and Smarteez, were considered contraband **[G-SOR]**.

- **Model 75T:** The model number of a piece of Caleva equipment located in *Red Dwarf*'s Quarantine Room 152 **[T-SER5.4]**.

- **Model 7-6-80:** A type of twenty-first-century cellular phone containing a QNK base system adapted network artificial intelligence and RE912 circuitry **[X-RNG]**.

- **Modular Conduit:** A setting on *Starbug 1*'s sonar scope display. This setting was not highlighted as the crew charted the course of a despair squid **[T-SER5.6]**.

- **Moët & Chandon:** A brand of French champagne produced by the Moët and Chandon winery **[RL]**. After traveling into the past via a stasis leak, Lister and Cat visited the Ganymede Holiday Inn, where they found Kochanski in the honeymoon suite with a future version of Lister. Future Lister impatiently kicked his past self and Cat out of the suite, but not before Cat swiped a bottle of Moët & Chandon from the room **[T-SER2.4]**.

**B-: Books**
- **PRG:** *Red Dwarf Programme Guide*
- **SUR:** *Red Dwarf Space Corps Survival Manual*
- **PRM:** *Primordial Soup*
- **SOS:** *Son of Soup*
- **SCE:** *Scenes from the Dwarf*
- **LOG:** *Red Dwarf Log No. 1996*
- **RD8:** *Red Dwarf VIII*
- **EVR:** *The Log: A Dwarfer's Guide to Everything*

**X-: Misc.**
- **PRO:** Promotional materials, videos, etc.
- **PST:** Posters at DJ XVII (2013)
- **CAL:** 2008 calendar
- **RNG:** Cell phone ringtones
- **MOB:** Mobisode ("Red Christmas")
- **CIN:** *Children in Need* sketch
- **GEK:** *Geek Week* intros by Kryten
- **TNG:** "Tongue-Tied" video
- **XMS:** Bill Pearson's Christmas special pitch script
- **XVD:** Bill Pearson's Christmas special pitch video
- **OTH:** Other *Red Dwarf* appearances

**SUFFIX**
**DVD:**
- **(d)** – Deleted scene
- **(o)** – Outtake
- **(b)** – Bonus DVD material (other)
- **(e)** – Extended version

**SMEGAZINES:**
- **(c)** – Comic
- **(a)** – Article

**OTHER:**
- **(s)** – Early/unused script draft
- **(s1)** – Alternate version of script

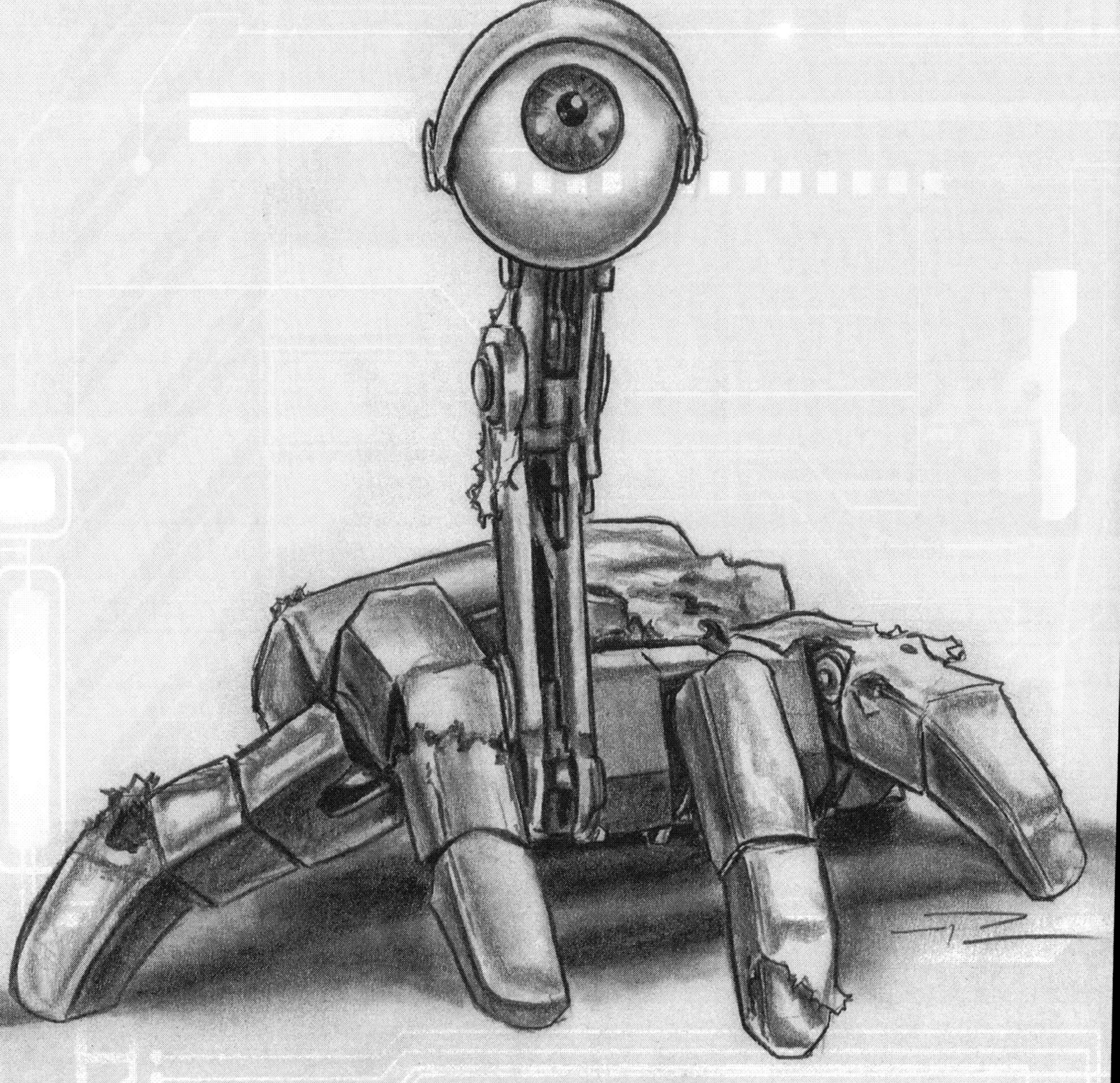

# MECHANOID "TARANSHULA" REMOTE DRONE

**PREFIX**
**RL:** Real life

**T-: Television Episodes**
- **SER:** Television series
- **IDW:** "Identity Within"
- **USA1:** Unaired U.S. pilot
- **USA2:** Unaired U.S. demo

**R-: *The Bodysnatcher Collection***
- **SER:** Remastered episodes
- **BOD:** "Bodysnatcher"
- **DAD:** "Dad"
- **FTH:** "Lister's Father"
- **INF:** "Infinity Patrol"
- **END:** "The End" (original assembly)

**N-: Novels**
- **INF:** *Infinity Welcomes Careful Drivers*
- **BTL:** *Better Than Life*
- **LST:** *Last Human*
- **BCK:** *Backwards*
- **OMN:** *Red Dwarf Omnibus*

**M-: Magazines**
- **SMG:** *Smegazine*

**W-: Websites**
- **OFF:** Official website
- **NAN:** *Prelude to Nanarchy*
- **AND:** *Androids*
- **DIV:** Diva-Droid
- **DIB:** Duane Dibbley
- **CRP:** Crapola
- **GEN:** Geneticon
- **LSR:** Leisure World Intl.
- **JMC:** Jupiter Mining Corporation
- **AIT:** *A.I. Today*
- **HOL:** HoloPoint

**G-: Roleplaying Game**
- **RPG:** *Core Rulebook*
- **BIT:** *A.I. Screen Extra Bits* booklet
- **SOR:** *Series Sourcebook*
- **OTH:** Other RPG material

Years later, when Legion held the *Red Dwarf* crew captive on his research station, the gestalt entity supplied them with a bottle of Moët & Chandon, intending to make their captivity a pleasant one **[T-SER6.2]**.

- **Mogidon Cluster:** An area of space containing a pan-dimensional liquid beast. One such creature attacked the *Starbug 1* crew on Christmas day as they pursued the stolen *Red Dwarf* **[T-SER6.6]**.

- **molecular destabilizer:** A handheld device, also known as a Molly-D, that broke down a surface's molecular cohesion, allowing matter to pass through it. This device enabled a user (and other objects) to pass through walls. The rogue droid Hogey used a Molly-D to gain entry to *Red Dwarf*, by attaching his pod to the mining ship and utilizing the device to pass through the ship's hull.

  When rogue simulants attacked *Red Dwarf*, the crew took the device from Hogey and escaped aboard *Blue Midget*, then hid in an asteroid field until devising an escape plan. Using themselves as bait, the crew positioned themselves between the pursuing Annihilators and the Simulant Death Ship, and waited for all four ships to fire missiles. Lister then destabilized the *Blue Midget*'s hull with the molecular destabilizer, causing each missile to pass through the ship and hit its opposite vessel, resulting in the destruction of all four enemy craft **[T-SER10.6]**.

- **molecularization:** A form of transportation used on twenty-second-century Earth, in which one's molecules were broken apart and reassembled at the destination point. The technology was prone to traffic delays and technical glitches, such as sending a traveler's legs to another country **[N-LST]**.

- **"Molecular Regeneration":** A phrase on a chart that Rimmer created to translate markings on a mysterious pod Holly found adrift in space, which he thought were an alien language—but which actually spelled out "*Red Dwarf* Garbage Pod," eroded away after many years of spaceflight **[T-SER1.4]**.

- **Molecule Mind:** A nickname that Lister suggested Kryten call Rimmer instead of "Mr. Arnold." During a later act of rebellion, Kryten broke from his programming and called Rimmer several names, including "Molecule Mind" **[T-SER2.1]**.

- **Mole Tank:** A bus-sized transport vehicle designed to burrow underground and emerge behind enemy lines, allowing soldiers to attack from the rear. The project was rife with design issues, from simple navigation problems to crewmembers being boiled alive due to inadequate shielding. Despite this, several hundred Mole Tanks were deployed in action.

  Of the five hundred units launched, four hundred and sixty-three disappeared and were classified as "on indefinite maneuvers;" seven were found in the Pacific Ocean; fourteen emerged in various mineshafts throughout the world; four were launched from a geyser in Iceland; two appeared in Vatican Square and were converted into shrines; one blocked the Channel Tunnel; one crashed through the floor of a rave in Ibiza and was met with applause; two simultaneously emerged at Venice Beach and collided with each other; four strategically surfaced at Mount Rushmore, replacing the statues' noses; and two completed their mission by emerging behind enemy lines and declaring victory over two one-legged peasants and a catapult operator **[B-EVR]**.

- **Mollee:** A robotic character on the television soap opera *Androids* **[N-INF]**. She had a long-lost daughter named Aimi, who had been kidnapped by vacuum cleaners **[W-AND]**. In one episode, Mollee's dead husband used the family's wealth to resurrect himself as a hologram **[M-SMG1.8(c2)]**. This news caused Mollee's colostomy bag to explode **[M-SMG1.8(c5)]**.

  In another episode, Mollee visited her neighbor, Kelly, to request help in picketing Brothel-U-Like, unaware that Kelly was the establishment's madam **[M-SMG1.11(c1)]**. During the protest, Mollee tripped and fell into an Ecstat-O-Matic booth, scrambling her circuits. She then took over the brothel, after an attempt on Kelly's life left the former owner hospitalized, and renamed it "He Ain't Heavy, He's My Brothel" **[M-SMG2.3(c2)]**.

  When Mollee slipped on an oil slick, she regained her former personality and memories. She vowed to get back at Jaysee, who had blackmailed her during her tenure as the brothel's madam **[M-SMG2.5(c5)]**. In a later storyline, Mollee finally succeeded in shutting the brothel down, setting the prostidroids free. This particular episode always made Kryten cheer **[N-INF]**.

- **Molly-D:** *See* molecular destabilizer

**B-: Books**
**PRG:** *Red Dwarf Programme Guide*
**SUR:** *Red Dwarf Space Corps Survival Manual*
**PRM:** *Primordial Soup*
**SOS:** *Son of Soup*
**SCE:** *Scenes from the Dwarf*
**LOG:** *Red Dwarf Log No. 1996*
**RD8:** *Red Dwarf VIII*
**EVR:** *The Log: A Dwarfer's Guide to Everything*

**X-: Misc.**
**PRO:** Promotional materials, videos, etc.
**PST:** Posters at DJ XVII (2013)
**CAL:** 2008 calendar
**RNG:** Cell phone ringtones
**MOB:** Mobisode ("Red Christmas")
**CIN:** *Children in Need* sketch
**GEK:** *Geek Week* intros by Kryten
**TNG:** "Tongue-Tied" video
**XMS:** Bill Pearson's Christmas special pitch script
**XVD:** Bill Pearson's Christmas special pitch video
**OTH:** Other *Red Dwarf* appearances

**SUFFIX**
**DVD:**
**(d)** – Deleted scene
**(o)** – Outtake
**(b)** – Bonus DVD material (other)
**(e)** – Extended version

**SMEGAZINES:**
**(c)** – Comic
**(a)** – Article

**OTHER:**
**(s)** – Early/unused script draft
**(s1)** – Alternate version of script

- **Mona:** An employee at Winan Diner, a food establishment in a fascist society on an alternate universe. One of Jake Bullet's favorite foods was Mona's doughnuts with a side of Swarfega **[M-SMG2.9(c4)]**.

- **Monica and the Monopeds:** A new wave band that Monica Jones fronted before joining the Space Corps **[G-RPG]**.

- **"Monitor":** A word printed on a shield-shaped pin on the lapel of Lister's leather jacket **[T-SER3.4]**.

- **Monkey:** A derogatory term that Cat used to describe *Homo sapiens* **[T-SER1.1]**.

  ***NOTE:*** *According to evolutionary theory, humans and apes (not monkeys) shared common ancestors, rather than one evolving from the other.*

- **Monkey Boy:** A slur that Cat called Lister while attempting to get out of searching for a creature in G Deck's water tank **[T-SER9.1]**.

- **monologue chip:** A piece of hardware installed in Jaysee, a character on the television soap opera *Androids*, that enabled him to speak in monologues **[M-SMG1.9(c2)]**.

- ***Monopoly*:** A board game produced by Parker Brothers, in which players moved differently shaped pieces around a square board, landing on spaces named after various streets, utilities and so forth. The object of the game was to monopolize the board and force other players into bankruptcy **[RL]**.

  To celebrate his twenty-fourth birthday, Lister and several friends embarked on a *Monopoly* board pub crawl and attempted to visit a drinking establishment on every road featured in the London version of the game **[N-INF]**. When Queeg challenged Holly to a game of chess for control of *Red Dwarf*, Holly, unskilled at the game, suggested they instead play *Monopoly* **[T-SER2.5]**. On one occasion, a *Monopoly* box was jettisoned from *Red Dwarf* **[M-SMG1.11(c2)]**.

- **Monroe, Marilyn:** An American actor and sex symbol, born Norma Jeane Mortenson, famous for her roles in such movies as *Gentlemen Prefer Blondes* and *Some Like it Hot*, as well as for her affair with U.S. President John F. Kennedy **[RL]**.

  The blonde bombshell romanced scientist Albert Einstein in the 1950s, as he was researching time-freezing and stasis theory. He lost interest in such research during the affair, however, and never resumed it once the relationship ended **[N-INF]**.

  Lister had a poster of Monroe hanging inside the locker in his quarters aboard *Red Dwarf* **[T-SER2.1]**. An Extras Pack sold by Crapola Inc. allowed talking appliances, such as Talkie Toaster and Talkie Toilet, to mimic her voice and personality **[W-CRP]**. Olaf Petersen once purchased a build-it-yourself kit droid meant to resemble the actor **[T-SER3.6]**.

  Upon first entering the total-immersion game *Better Than Life*, Lister, Rimmer and Cat were approached by a computer simulation of Marilyn Monroe, whom Rimmer misidentified as Mary Magdalene. The Monroe simulation took a liking to Cat, who initially brushed her off but eventually ended up dating her, along with a mermaid named Miranda **[T-SER2.2]**.

  The crew once discovered a moon resembling the famous actor's rear end, which they lingered around before resuming a course for Earth **[R-SER2.4]**.

  When told that his fate to become the next Ace Rimmer might be hard to accept, Rimmer disagreed, stating that things like the coupling of Monroe and Arthur Miller were hard to accept **[T-SER7.2(d)]**.

  ***NOTE:*** *Monroe is rumored to have had a relationship with Einstein in the late 1940s, though this has not been definitively confirmed. In the original broadcast version of episode 2.4 ("Stasis Leak"), the bottom-shaped moon was said to have resembled Felicity Kendal's rear. See also the Build-It-Yourself Marilyn Monroe Droid entry.*

- **Monroe, Marilyn:** A waxdroid replica of the actor, created for the Waxworld theme park. Left on their own for millions of years, the waxdroids attained sentience and became embroiled in a park-wide resource war between Villain World and Hero World (to which Monroe belonged).

  During this war, the *Red Dwarf* crew transported to the planet using a Matter Paddle, with Lister and Cat materializing in Villain territory, while Rimmer and Kryten landed in Hero territory. Rimmer found the heroes' army lacking and took command, working many of the pacifistic waxdroids to death before ordering a frontal attack on the enemy's compound across a minefield. This wiped out the remaining droids, including Monroe **[T-SER4.6]**.

- **Monshoetree:** The name Rimmer gave to one of his shoetrees, to ensure it spent the same amount of time in his shoes as the others **[T-SER7.5]**.

- **Montmartre:** A hill in the northern part of Paris, France, which gave its name to the surrounding area **[RL]**. As a youth, Lister attended a school trip to Paris, during which he drank two bottles of cheap wine before taking a tour of the Eiffel Tower. Once at the top, he became sick and vomited on Montmartre, where a pavement artist sold the puke to a Texan tourist, claiming it to be a genuine Jackson Pollock **[T-SER3.6]**.

- **mood stabilizer:** *See* lithium carbonate

- **Mooli desert:** A dry section of land on Cyrius 3, an asteroid located within GELF territory in an alternate universe **[N-LST]**.

- **Moon, the:** Earth's only natural satellite, also called by its Latin name, Luna **[RL]**. The Moon housed the headquarters of the Star Corps at one point **[B-SUR]**, and also contained a terraformed settlement called Lunar City 7 **[N-INF]**, as well as several underground cities in which an alcoholic beverage called fungo-beer was brewed **[G-RPG]**. In a universe in which the sexes were reversed, the first person to set foot on the Moon was astronaut Nellie Armstrong **[T-SER2.6]**.

  A four-day event called the New Zodiac Festival was held in the Moon's Sea of Tranquility, celebrating the changing of Earth's polar star, and attended by five thousand "space beatniks." Because of this change, the entire Zodiac system shifted, and everyone moved one astrological sign forward **[N-INF]**.

- **moon-hopping:** The act of locating and visiting several moons during a single outing. While moon-hopping aboard *Starbug 1*, Rimmer and Kryten spotted an S-3 planet, which Arnold claimed in the name of the Space Corps. Shortly after they landed, however, the planet—which turned out to be a psi-moon—erupted and reshaped itself, causing major damage to both Kryten and *Starbug* **[T-SER5.3]**.

- **moonquake:** A disruption or shifting of a lunar crust due to plate tectonics or another high-energy source **[RL]**. Lister thought Rimmer and Kryten experienced a moonquake on a small planetoid they had visited, but it turned out to be a psi-moon—a planetary body that reshaped itself to match the psyche of its inhabitants **[T-SER5.3]**.

- **moose:** A large mammal in the deer family, indigenous to North America and Europe **[RL]**. While serving with the Canaries, Oswald "Kill Krazy" Blenkinsop once wrestled a moose that had escaped from stasis, breaking every bone in the animal's body **[W-OFF]**.

  According to the book *Stupid But True! Volume 3*, twenty percent of all traffic accidents in Sweden during the 1970s were caused by moose—a fact that also appeared as the answer to a lateral-thinking question with which Rimmer struggled during his studies. He became increasingly frustrated when Lister, Kryten and even Cat all knew the answer, unaware they had just learned it from the book **[T-SER10.1]**.

- **Moose Base Alpha:** A scientific research facility built on a frozen planet, occupied by hologrammic scientist Hildegarde Lanstrom. While residing at the facility, Lanstrom identified and isolated various strands of positive viruses, ranging from luck to sexual magnetism. Eventually, she became infected with a holovirus and froze herself in a stasis chamber to preserve her life.

  Years later, while responding to a distress beacon from the facility, the crew of *Red Dwarf* found and released Lanstrom, unaware that the holovirus had made her psychotic. She attacked the crew with hex vision, telepathy and telekinesis before the holovirus drained her life force **[T-SER5.4]**.

  > ***NOTE:** A Series V DVD special discussing the show's special effects revealed that the effects team had christened the research station model Moose Base Alpha, a reference to* Space: 1999*'s Moonbase Alpha. As such, this might not be the station's actual designation.*

- **"More Hate":** A phrase tattooed on the left-hand knuckles of Drigg, a dissonant GELF imprisoned on the tourist planet GELFWorld **[M-SMG2.2(c4)]**.

- **"Morning Has Broken":** A popular Christian hymn first published in 1931, and made popular by Cat Stevens in 1971 **[RL]**. Among Lister's collection of useless junk was a musical toilet-roll holder that played this song **[N-BTL]**.

- **Moron, Diane ("The Gangrene Goddess"):** A necrobics instructor who appeared on an episode of *Good Morning, Holograms* on Groovy Channel 27. The episode featuring Moron aired at 6:00 AM on Wednesday, the 27th of Geldof, 2362 **[M-SMG1.7(a)]**.

  *NOTE: It is probable that Moron was herself a hologram, though this was not specifically stated.*

- **morphing belt:** A gadget worn around a person's waist that, when activated, altered the wearer's appearance. Captain Zural used a morphing belt to infiltrate a Brefewino GELF village so he could locate and kill his sub-lieutenant, Ora Tanzil **[T-IDW]**.

- **morris dancing:** A form of English folk dancing characterized by dancers sometimes wearing clogs and utilizing sticks, handkerchiefs, bells or other implements **[RL]**. Rimmer enjoyed morris dancing, and occasionally attempted to rouse Lister, Kryten and Cat to join him in a dance, with little success **[T-SER4.5]**.

- ***Morris Dancing Monthly*:** A monthly publication geared toward morris dancing enthusiasts. Its subhead was "Your Monthly Guide to What's On and Where." Issue ten contained the Summertime Special article, "How to Avoid Heat Exhaustion."

  Kryten stole several issues of *Morris Dancing Monthly* (including issue ten) from Rimmer's personal effects and gave them to Lister so he could sabotage Kochanski's date with a man named Tim—or so Lister thought. In actuality, Kryten had lied about Tim in order to trick Dave into trashing Warden Ackerman's quarters so the mechanoid could air the footage on Krytie TV **[T-SER8.5]**.

  Cat read a copy of *Morris Dancing Monthly* years later while waiting in line to procure the last tank of anesthetic from *Red Dwarf*'s denti-bot **[T-SER10.2]**.

- **Morris Minor:** The make and model of a British economy car manufactured between 1948 and 1971 **[RL]**. When Rimmer played the total-immersion video game *Better Than Life*, his subconscious mind, unable to accept his good fortune, conjured this vehicle as a replacement for the Series 1 E-Type Jaguar he initially used in the game. His mind chose this vehicle because it was more practical for the family of seven (soon to be eight) that he created for himself and Yvonne McGruder **[T-SER2.2]**.

  *NOTE: The vehicle's make and model were not specifically mentioned in the episode, though this could be determined visually.*

- **Morse, Samuel:** A nineteenth-century inventor who contributed to the development of the telegraph and also helped to create Morse Code **[RL]**. After building the Holly Hop Drive, Holly compared himself to other inventors, including Morse **[T-SER2.6]**.

- **mortality chip:** A component built into 4000 Series mechanoids that inhibited their ability to lie **[M-SMG1.6(a)]**.

  *NOTE: It is unclear why a mortality chip would govern honesty, though it is possible that the writer meant to say "morality chip."*

- **mortimer:** A position in zero-gee football. Mortimers, wielding bazookoids, were used during a strategy called "The Rabid Hunch," whereby a mortimer would fire on the press box after receiving the ball **[M-SMG1.8(a)]**.

- **Moscow:** The capital city of Russia **[RL]**. Moscow and other cities influenced the design of several structures along *Red Dwarf*'s exterior **[N-INF]**.

- **Moses:** A religious leader and prophet mentioned in the scriptures of several religions **[RL]**. In his first official log entry, Lister noted how he had matured since turning twenty-eight years old, comparing himself, maturity-wise, to the likes of Abraham Lincoln and Moses **[T-SER7.1]**.

- **Moss Bros:** A British fine-clothing chain specializing in formal men's attire **[RL]**. When Rimmer demanded a uniform and haircut despite Holly's need to perform complex lightspeed calculations, the AI denied being a combination speaking clock, Moss Bros and Teasy-Weasy **[T-SER1.2]**.

  When faced with the possibility of having to marry the Kinitawowi chief's daughter in order to obtain an oxy-generation unit, Lister insisted there was no way he was going to Moss Bros for anyone less attractive than his armpit after several games of table tennis **[T-SER6.4]**.

**PREFIX**
**RL:** Real life

**T-: Television Episodes**
**SER:** Television series
**IDW:** "Identity Within"
**USA1:** Unaired U.S. pilot
**USA2:** Unaired U.S. demo

**R-: *The Bodysnatcher Collection***
**SER:** Remastered episodes
**BOD:** "Bodysnatcher"
**DAD:** "Dad"
**FTH:** "Lister's Father"
**INF:** "Infinity Patrol"
**END:** "The End" (original assembly)

**N-: Novels**
**INF:** *Infinity Welcomes Careful Drivers*
**BTL:** *Better Than Life*
**LST:** *Last Human*
**BCK:** *Backwards*
**OMN:** *Red Dwarf Omnibus*

**M-: Magazines**
**SMG:** *Smegazine*

**W-: Websites**
**OFF:** Official website
**NAN:** *Prelude to Nanarchy*
**AND:** *Androids*
**DIV:** Diva-Droid
**DIB:** Duane Dibbley
**CRP:** Crapola
**GEN:** Geneticon
**LSR:** Leisure World Intl.
**JMC:** Jupiter Mining Corporation
**AIT:** *A.I. Today*
**HOL:** HoloPoint

**G-: Roleplaying Game**
**RPG:** *Core Rulebook*
**BIT:** *A.I. Screen Extra Bits* booklet
**SOR:** *Series Sourcebook*
**OTH:** Other RPG material

- **Most Disturbing Android Design:** An award that Diva-Droid International's 3000 Series mechanoid received from several consumer guides, due to its uncanny realism **[G-BIT]**.

- ***Most Influential Humans, The*:** A book that Lister was required to read for his robotics course aboard *Red Dwarf*. It included entries on such individuals as Wolfgang Mozart and William Shakespeare **[T-SER10.3]**.

- ***Most Pathetic Dreams of Arnold Rimmer, Volume 1, The*:** A film that Cat created using excerpts of Rimmer's dreams, taken from *Red Dwarf*'s dream recorder. It included intimate dreams of Yvonne McGruder, Carol McCauley and Sandra, among others. Rimmer once found three skutters watching the film in the ship's cinema **[M-SMG1.9(a)]**.

- **Mother Teresa:** A twentieth-century Roman Catholic nun, born Anjezë Gonxhe Bojaxhiu, who devoted her life to helping the infirmed and poverty-stricken **[RL]**. A waxdroid replica of Mother Teresa was created for the Waxworld theme park **[T-SER4.6]**. This droid was addicted to cigars **[G-SOR]**.

  Left on their own for millions of years, the waxdroids attained sentience and became embroiled in a park-wide resource war between Villain World and Hero World (to which Mother Theresa belonged). During this war, the *Red Dwarf* crew transported to the planet using a Matter Paddle, with Lister and Cat materializing in Villain territory, while Rimmer and Kryten landed in Hero territory.

  Rimmer found the heroes' army lacking and took command, making Mother Teresa a lieutenant colonel. He worked many of the pacifistic waxdroids to death before ordering a frontal attack on the enemy's compound across a minefield, which wiped out the remaining droids. The Teresa droid died upon stepping on a landmine **[T-SER4.6]**.

- **Motion Interferer:** A position in zero-gee football. Henri Pascal was a Motion Interferer for the Paris Stompers **[R-BOD(s)]**.

- **motivator:** An apparatus used to awaken crewmembers aboard *Red Dwarf* **[T-SER1.3]**.

- **Motörhead:** An English rock band of the 1970s that helped to usher in the New Wave of British Heavy Metal (NWOBHM) **[RL]**. While mocking Lister for his taste in music, Rimmer suggested he instead listen to classical musicians, such as Wolfgang Mozart, Felix Mendelssohn and Motörhead **[T-SER1.3]**.

  ***NOTE:** The DVD subtitles misspelled the band's name as "Motorhead," without the umlaut.*

- **motorized remote ore scoop:** A type of small vehicle stored aboard *Starbug* shuttles, used to dig ore samples during mining operations. Such vehicles were primarily designed for areas containing little to no atmosphere; as such, they were not equipped with voice-activation functionality **[N-BCK]**.

- **Motson, John ("Motty"):** An English football commentator who commented on more than fifteen hundred games throughout his career, starting in 1971 **[RL]**. In the universe known as Alternative 6829/B, Motson signed an exclusive ten-year deal with the promoters of zero-gee football at the beginning of the twenty-first century. Shortly thereafter, however, the sport fizzled out, and was replaced with old-fashioned association football **[M-SMG1.8(c4)]**.

- **Mount Rushmore:** An American national monument sculpted into a mountainside in South Dakota, originally depicting U.S. Presidents George Washington, Thomas Jefferson, Theodore Roosevelt and Abraham Lincoln **[RL]**. Sometime during the twenty-first or twenty-second century, Elaine Salinger, considered America's greatest president, was added to the mountainside **[N-BTL]**. Mount Rushmore was damaged when four malfunctioning Mole Tanks strategically surfaced, replacing four of the statues' noses **[B-EVR]**.

  Three million years later, after Earth was transformed into Garbage World and propelled from its orbit out into deep space, Lister became stranded on the planet. He endured drastic conditions, such as acid rain, earthquakes and oil rain, until discovering the top of Mount Rushmore half-buried in green bottles. Realizing he was home, he took refuge from the oily rain in Washington's left nostril, until the entire structure was scorched from a lightning bolt that ignited a sheet of oil **[N-BTL]**.

  ***NOTE:** Either the noses were repaired following the Mole Tank debacle, or Washington's was the only face not damaged by the tanks, since Lister was later able to use his nostril for shelter.*

- **Mount Sinai:** A mountain region in Egypt. Several Terran religions revered the site as sacred, some believing that Moses received the Ten Commandments at that site **[RL]**. According to an ancient news video, archeologists uncovered what was believed to be a missing page from the beginning of the Bible at Mount Sinai that, when translated, read, "To my darling Candy. All characters portrayed within this book are fictitious and any resemblance to persons living or dead is purely coincidental" **[T-SER2.2]**.

- **mouse:** A small rodent belonging to the genus *Mus*. As mammals, mice share a common homology with humans, and were thus widely used for experimentation purposes **[RL]**. *Red Dwarf* contained a contingent of laboratory mice **[T-SER11.1]**. In an alternate dimension, the lab mice survived the cadmium II disaster, evolving into a sentient species known as *Mus sapiens* **[G-RPG]**.

  ***NOTE:*** *See also the laboratory* mice *and* Mus sapiens *entries.*

- **Mouse, Mickey:** An anthropomorphic mouse cartoon character created by Walt Disney Productions **[RL]**. Lister dubbed his landing party a Mickey Mouse operation upon discovering their Psi-scan's batteries were dead as they investigated a potentially deadly virus research station **[T-SER5.4]**.

- **Mozart, Wolfgang Amadeus:** An eighteenth-century composer of classical music, reputed to have been a child prodigy **[RL]**. According to the book *The Most Influential Humans*, he wrote the song "Twinkle, Twinkle, Little Star" at age five **[T-SER10.3]**. While mocking Lister for his taste in music, Rimmer suggested he instead listen to classical musicians, such as Mozart, Felix Mendelssohn and Motörhead **[T-SER1.3]**. While trapped in an addictive version of *Better Than Life*, Cat entertained himself in his golden castle with a hand-picked seven-piece band, which included Mozart on piano **[N-INF]**.

  ***NOTE:*** *The poem "Twinkle, Twinkle, Little Star" was written by Jane Taylor in 1806, and was originally set to the melody "Ah! Vous Dirai-Je, Maman." Mozart composed a version of this song when he was about twenty-five years old.*

- **Mr. Ace:** The name by which Kryten referred to Ace Rimmer, typically followed by "sir" **[T-SER7.2]**.

- **Mr. April:** A title that Rimmer received when awarded the Vending Machine Maintenance Man of the Month certificate for the month of April **[T-SER9.1]**.

- **Mr. Arnold:** The name by which Kryten initially referred to Arnold Rimmer, typically followed by "sir" **[T-SER2.1]**.

- **Mr. Beautiful:** A nickname that Confidence, a hallucination of Lister's mind made corporeal by mutated pneumonia, called Lister **[T-SER1.5]**.

- **Mr. C:** A nickname that Cat called himself while trying to get out of searching for a creature discovered in G Deck's water tank (later discovered to be an elation squid) **[T-SER9.1]**.

- **Mr. Cushy:** A name that Cat called Rimmer while complaining about his prison workload, while Arnold worked on probation for Captain Hollister **[T-SER8.8]**.

- **Mr. D:** An affectionate nickname that Arnold Rimmer called Cat (who had been turned into Duane Dibbley), after an emohawk transformed him into Ace Rimmer **[T-SER6.4(d)]**.

- **Mr. David:** The name by which Kryten initially referred to Lister, typically followed by "sir" **[T-SER2.1]**.

- **Mr. Fat Bastard 2044:** A nickname that Rimmer called Captain Hollister. When Lister said Arnold never had time for anyone, the hologram pointed out all the time he had spent groveling around Mr. Fat Bastard 2044 **[T-SER2.3]**.

- **Mr. Flibble:** *See* Flibble, Mr.

- **Mr. Fried Egg Chili Chutney Sandwich Face:** An insult that an intoxicated Rimmer called Lister, noting that this sort of sandwich, like Lister, turned out right despite having all the wrong ingredients **[T-SER2.3]**.

- **Mr. Galahad:** A nickname that Kryten called Lister in a medieval artificial-reality simulation. Kryten sarcastically

**PREFIX**
**RL:** Real life

**T-: Television Episodes**
**SER:** Television series
**IDW:** "Identity Within"
**USA1:** Unaired U.S. pilot
**USA2:** Unaired U.S. demo

**R-: *The Bodysnatcher Collection***
**SER:** Remastered episodes
**BOD:** "Bodysnatcher"
**DAD:** "Dad"
**FTH:** "Lister's Father"
**INF:** "Infinity Patrol"
**END:** "The End" (original assembly)

**N-: Novels**
**INF:** *Infinity Welcomes Careful Drivers*
**BTL:** *Better Than Life*
**LST:** *Last Human*

**BCK:** *Backwards*
**OMN:** *Red Dwarf Omnibus*

**M-: Magazines**
**SMG:** *Smegazine*

**W-: Websites**
**OFF:** Official website
**NAN:** *Prelude to Nanarchy*
**AND:** *Androids*
**DIV:** Diva-Droid
**DIB:** Duane Dibbley

**CRP:** Crapola
**GEN:** Geneticon
**LSR:** Leisure World Intl.
**JMC:** Jupiter Mining Corporation
**AIT:** *A.I. Today*
**HOL:** HoloPoint

**G-: Roleplaying Game**
**RPG:** *Core Rulebook*
**BIT:** *A.I. Screen Extra Bits* booklet
**SOR:** *Series Sourcebook*
**OTH:** Other RPG material

juxtaposed the most gallant and pure of figures with Lister's plan to use game cheats to seduce the Queen of Camelot **[T-SER7.2]**.

- **Mr. Gazpacho:** An insulting nickname that Rimmer's duplicate hologram called him, referencing a humiliating incident in which Arnold had sent gazpacho soup back to be heated during an officer's party, unaware it was supposed to be served cold. His humiliation at the gaffe scarred him for life **[T-SER1.6]**.

- **Mr. Gun:** The name by which a deranged Hudzen 10 mechanoid sent to replace Kryten called his shotgun **[W-OFF]**.

- **Mr. July:** A title that Talkie Toaster claimed Rimmer had received from *Tedium Magazine* **[W-OFF]**.

- **Mr. Magnificent:** A nickname that Confidence, a hallucination of Lister's mind made corporeal by mutated pneumonia, called Lister **[T-SER1.5]**.

- **Mr. Mallet:** The name by which Oswald "Kill Krazy" Blenkinsop, an inmate in *Red Dwarf*'s brig, referred to the bludgeoning weapon he wielded as a member of the Canaries **[W-OFF]**.

- **Mr. Maturity:** A sarcastic nickname that Rimmer's duplicate hologram called him due to his childish behavior in *Red Dwarf*'s cinema **[T-SER1.6]**.

- **Mr. Multi Universe 3,000,026:** A title that Cat gave himself while sending a message to Earth via the European Space Consortium's Mars Rover. In the message, Cat claimed to have found the agency's *Beagle* craft and asked if there was any good food on Mars **[X-APR]**.

- **Mr. October:** The title that an issue of *Fascist Dictator Monthly* magazine bestowed upon Adolf Hitler **[T-SER3.5]**.

- **Mr. Pretend-Cat:** A nickname that Ora Tanzil, a she-Cat, called Cat as he battled Zural for her freedom **[T-IDW]**.

- **Mr. Sad Git:** An insult that Rimmer called Kryten while hooked into a dream that the mechanoid's subconscious mind created to combat an Armageddon virus. In the vision, Kryten was a drunken sheriff on the run from the Apocalypse Boys (a manifestation of the virus). His crewmates found him in a saloon trading in his possessions—including his mule, Dignity—for a bottle of liquor **[T-SER6.3]**.

- **Mr. Selfish:** A nickname that Rimmer called Lister when the latter planned to return to the past via a stasis leak, leaving the hologram behind, in order to have three more weeks with Kochanski before the *Red Dwarf*'s cadmium II explosion **[T-SER2.4]**.

- **Mr. Shouty:** A nickname that Lister called Officer Thornton as the latter escorted him to his quarters aboard the nanobot-rebuilt *Red Dwarf* so Dave could serve out a house arrest **[T-SER8.1]**.

- **Mr. Skywalker:** A character Kryten referenced after dubbing earmuff-wearing Kochanski "Princess Leia" **[T-SER7.4]**.

  ***NOTE:*** *Luke Skywalker, portrayed by actor Mark Hamill, was a main character in the* Star Wars *film series.*

- **Mr. Smoothie:** A nickname that Rimmer called Denton, Yvonne McGruder's boyfriend, while drawing a moustache and glasses on his face after a time wand froze Denton in place **[T-SER8.6(d)]**.

- **Mr. Sucks:** A name that *Red Dwarf*'s flight controller called Cat while searching for his clearance code, due to Cat mistakenly identifying himself as "Reality Sucks." He blurted out the phrase after realizing this flight controller was much less attractive than the one he had encountered in a psychotropically induced artificial-reality simulation **[T-SER8.3]**.

- **Mr. Swankypants:** A nickname that Jimmy, a character in a Wild West dream Kryten's subconscious mind created to combat an Armageddon virus, called Lister when Dave demanded that he stop tormenting the mechanoid **[T-SER6.3]**.

- **Mr. Wonderful:** A nickname that Confidence, a hallucination of Lister's mind made corporeal by mutated pneumonia, called Lister **[T-SER1.5]**.

**B-: Books**
**PRG:** *Red Dwarf Programme Guide*
**SUR:** *Red Dwarf Space Corps Survival Manual*
**PRM:** *Primordial Soup*
**SOS:** *Son of Soup*
**SCE:** *Scenes from the Dwarf*
**LOG:** *Red Dwarf Log No. 1996*
**RD8:** *Red Dwarf VIII*
**EVR:** *The Log: A Dwarfer's Guide to Everything*

**X-: Misc.**
**PRO:** Promotional materials, videos, etc.
**PST:** Posters at DJ XVII (2013)
**CAL:** 2008 calendar
**RNG:** Cell phone ringtones
**MOB:** Mobisode ("Red Christmas")
**CIN:** *Children in Need* sketch
**GEK:** *Geek Week* intros by Kryten
**TNG:** "Tongue-Tied" video
**XMS:** Bill Pearson's Christmas special pitch script
**XVD:** Bill Pearson's Christmas special pitch video
**OTH:** Other *Red Dwarf* appearances

**SUFFIX**
**DVD:**
**(d)** – Deleted scene
**(o)** – Outtake
**(b)** – Bonus DVD material (other)
**(e)** – Extended version

**SMEGAZINES:**
**(c)** – Comic
**(a)** – Article

**OTHER:**
**(s)** – Early/unused script draft
**(s1)** – Alternate version of script

- **MTV:** An American cable channel originally focused on music videos, short for Music Television **[RL]**. While trapped in an addictive version of *Better Than Life*, Rimmer believed he had gained fame and fortune upon returning to Earth aboard *Nova 5*. In the hallucination, MTV voted Rimmer Sexiest Man of All Time, ahead of Clark Gable and Hugo Lovepole **[N-INF]**.

- **MTV:** A twenty-four-hour television channel, short for Mirror Television, that Cat imagined while trapped in an addictive version of *Better Than Life*. This MTV broadcast a mirror and soothing music **[N-BTL]**.

- **Mugs Murphy:** *See* Murphy, Mugs

- **Mulholland-Jjones, Sabrina, Lady:** A wealthy, beautiful model and novelist of the twenty-second century. The eldest daughter of the Duke of Lincoln, she married Fred "Thicky" Holden, the inventor of the Tension Sheet. Lister used a timeslide to create an alternate timeline in which he invented the sheet first, thus becoming a billionaire and marrying Mulholland-Jjones instead **[T-SER3.5]**.

  In that reality, Sabrina had a secret love affair with Lister's butler, Gilbert **[W-OFF]**. The alternate timeline was eliminated when Rimmer attempted to invent the Tension Sheet first, instead reinstating Holden as the inventor and Mulholland-Jjones' husband **[T-SER3.5]**.

- **Mullaney, Lloyd:** A character on the British television program *Coronation Street*, portrayed by actor Craig Charles **[RL]**. According to Kryten, Mullaney was a "granny-grabbing, philandering taxi driver." While trapped in an elation squid hallucination, the *Red Dwarf* crew imagined being transported to an alternate twenty-first-century Earth, on which they were merely characters on the British comedy show *Red Dwarf*. Concerned about their fate, they sought out Charles (who played Lister on that show), seeking information about their creator **[T-SER9.3]**.

- **Müller, Hans:** A name marking an entrance to a building in an alternate-reality Nazi camp that held Princess Bonjella captive until Ace Rimmer rescued her **[T-SER7.2]**.

  ***NOTE:** Police official Heinrich Müller led the Gestapo in Nazi Germany, and helped Adolf Hitler to plan and execute the Holocaust. Additionally, German flying ace Hans Müller served on the staff of Luftflotte 3, one of German Luftwaffe's primary divisions during World War II.*

- **Mulligan, Mr.:** An Irish toy-shop owner in Bedford Falls, whom Lister imagined while trapped in an illusory world based on the film *It's a Wonderful Life*, created by an addictive version of *Better Than Life*. In the illusion, Lister took his sons, Jim and Bexley, to the store to purchase a blue sailboat that they had saved for all year. When the boys instead gave some of their money to a homeless man named Henry, Mulligan welled up and discounted the boat so they could still afford it **[N-BTL]**.

- **Multi Million Lottery Co.:** A lottery company that sent Rimmer a letter, which he received three million years later while incarcerated in *Red Dwarf*'s brig. The letter informed him that he had won 4 million, and instructed him to bring his winning ticket to the company's payout address, located at Lottery House, 24 Argyle Street, Somewhereville, TW17 0QD **[B-RD8]**.

- **multi purpose graph:** An erasable whiteboard imprinted with a graph, located aboard *Red Dwarf* in Quarantine Room 152. Lister used this board to chart his time spent in quarantine with Cat and Kryten. After five days of constant fighting, he wrote the word "tetchy" in large letters to infuriate Kryten, who hated the term **[T-SER5.4]**.

- **multi-spectrum SiC lens:** An optical component of light bees enabling them to project a 3D hologrammic rendition of a human. The standard light bee contained more than twelve million such lenses **[X-PST]**.

- **multiverse:** The hypothetical set of all possible universes, comprising everything that exists and can exist **[RL]**. The term also described an area of space-time between universes, through which one could theoretically travel to another dimension. While trapped in an elation squid hallucination, Rimmer imagined that Katerina Bartikovsky intended to use a dimension-cutter to traverse the multiverse and search for a mate for Lister, so the couple could then repopulate the human species **[T-SER9.1]**.

**PREFIX**
**RL:** Real life

**T-: Television Episodes**
**SER:** Television series
**IDW:** "Identity Within"
**USA1:** Unaired U.S. pilot
**USA2:** Unaired U.S. demo

**R-: *The Bodysnatcher Collection***
**SER:** Remastered episodes
**BOD:** "Bodysnatcher"
**DAD:** "Dad"
**FTH:** "Lister's Father"
**INF:** "Infinity Patrol"
**END:** "The End" (original assembly)

**N-: Novels**
**INF:** *Infinity Welcomes Careful Drivers*
**BTL:** *Better Than Life*
**LST:** *Last Human*
**BCK:** *Backwards*
**OMN:** *Red Dwarf Omnibus*

**M-: Magazines**
**SMG:** *Smegazine*

**W-: Websites**
**OFF:** Official website
**NAN:** *Prelude to Nanarchy*
**AND:** *Androids*
**DIV:** Diva-Droid
**DIB:** Duane Dibbley
**CRP:** Crapola
**GEN:** Geneticon
**LSR:** Leisure World Intl.
**JMC:** Jupiter Mining Corporation
**AIT:** *A.I. Today*
**HOL:** HoloPoint

**G-: Roleplaying Game**
**RPG:** *Core Rulebook*
**BIT:** *A.I. Screen Extra Bits* booklet
**SOR:** *Series Sourcebook*
**OTH:** Other RPG material

- **"Mummy, mummy":** A phrase that Lister claimed were Rimmer's last words before he died during *Red Dwarf*'s cadmium II explosion. Arnold refuted this claim **[T-SER10.6]**.

    ***NOTE:*** *Clearly, this was simply a cheap jab on Lister's part, as he was well aware that Arnold's final words were "gazpacho soup."*

- **"Mummy, of Mummyton, in the county of Mummyshire":** An expletive that Rimmer uttered upon noticing an enormous object on *Red Dwarf*'s sonar screen, heading for the diving bell containing Lister, Kryten and Cat in G Deck's water tank **[T-SER9.1(d)]**.

- **Mummy, the:** The mummified remains of Imhotep, an ancient Egyptian priest first portrayed by Boris Karloff in Universal Studios' 1932 film *The Mummy*, and later by other actors **[RL]**.

    A waxdroid replica of the Mummy was created for the Horror World attraction at the Waxworld theme park. Left on their own for millions of years, the waxdroids attained sentience and became embroiled in a park-wide resource war between Villain World and Hero World. Sometime during this conflict, the Hero World army stormed Horror World—to which the Mummy belonged—during which the Mrs. Claus droid lost an eye to the fictional monster **[W-OFF]**.

- **Munchkin robot:** A type of mechanoid effigy that was a predecessor to waxdroids. Munchkin robots stood one to two feet tall, with comically enlarged heads, and were used by amusement parks and in Christmas displays. Their short run-time and tendency to melt, however, eventually caused them to be replaced by more advanced robots **[G-SOR]**.

    While trapped in an elation squid hallucination, the *Red Dwarf* crew imagined that two Munchkin robots of Rimmer were servants of the Creator **[T-SER9.3]**.

    ***NOTE:*** *Although the little Rimmers in episode 7.6 ("Blue") appeared in an amusement-park ride—a Munchkin robot's primary use—they were not identified as robots, and in fact more resembled puppets.*

- **"Munchkin Song, The":** A song played at the end of *The Rimmer Experience*, a virtual-reality ride that Kryten created to remind Lister why he disliked his recently departed roommate, whom Dave was beginning to miss. The song was performed by an image of Rimmer, surrounded by dozens of small, harmonizing puppets bearing his likeness **[R-BOD(b)]**.

    ***NOTE:*** *"The Munchkin Song" was so named in several sources, including an introduction by Kryten featured in the bonus materials of* The Bodysnatcher Collection.

- **munitions cabinet:** A storage cabinet aboard *Starbug 1*, used to stow various weapons, including a holowhip **[T-SER5.1]**.

- **Munny:** A brand of blank vinyl dolls made by the American company Kidrobot, designed to be decorated and personalized by an owner **[RL]**. While trapped in an elation squid hallucination, the *Red Dwarf* crew imagined that Munny merchandise was sold at the science fiction shop They Walk Among Us! **[T-SER9.2]**.

- **Munson, First Officer:** A JMC officer aboard the American mining ship *Red Dwarf*. Munson died and was revived by the ship's computer as a hologram. His personality disc was damaged during the cadmium II explosion, however, allowing that reality's Rimmer to be revived as a companion for Lister, the disaster's sole survivor **[T-USA1]**.

- **Munster, Herman:** A character on the 1960s American television show *The Munsters*, originally portrayed by Fred Gwynne and strongly resembling Frankenstein's monster **[RL]**. Kryten defended his connoisseur chip by arguing that his resemblance to Herman Munster's stuntman did not mean he was unable to appreciate art **[T-SER6.1]**.

- **Murdoch, Doctor:** A scientist assigned to the research station on which Hildegarde Lanstrom worked. Murdoch once broke into Lanstrom's office and stole samples of the positive viruses luck, charisma and sexual magnetism, then distributed them to his team. According to Lanstrom, a side effect of this transgression was that their parties were greatly improved **[W-OFF]**.

- **Murphy, Catering Officer:** A crewmember aboard the American mining vessel *Red Dwarf* who worked on the Command Bridge. He died during the cadmium II disaster **[T-USA1]**.

- **Murphy, Mugs:** An anthropomorphic, tommy-gun-toting gorilla cartoon character. Lister had a T-shirt bearing the character's likeness, along with the words "D-D-Don't Shoot" **[T-SER1.6]**. *Red Dwarf*'s libraries contained several Mugs Murphy cartoon videos in Ship Lib 5, including one with file name CARMMLT475 **[R-BOD]**. The ship's cinema sometimes played these cartoons before showing movies **[T-SER1.6]**. Krytie TV's lineup included a Mugs Murphy marathon **[X-CAL]**.

    ***NOTE:** Actor Craig Charles has said that Rob Grant and Doug Naylor had intended to write an episode in which Murphy came to life aboard the mining vessel, but that story never went beyond the planning stage.*

- **Murray, Sam, Deck Sergeant:** A crewmember aboard *Red Dwarf* who died during the cadmium II disaster **[T-SER5.1]**. JMC revived him as a hologram on four separate occasions, to serve on a different vessel each time—two of them concurrently **[W-JMC]**.

  Murray was commended by the JMC for his dedication to service, as he had logged more hours than any other employee. His personnel password was JMCP0001 **[W-HOL]**, and his interests included *kung fu* movies **[G-SOR]** and TV soap operas **[W-JMC]**. Sam was a habitual practical joker, allowing access to his posts on soap opera message boards only between 3:00 AM and 8:00 AM **[W-JMC]**.

  Before the accident, Murray had dated a *Red Dwarf* deck sergeant named Rick Thesen. Three million years later, Lister placed Murray's and Thesen's ashes in a canister and shot them into space to spend eternity together, unaware they had broken up **[N-OMN]**. When Rimmer petitioned to join the holoship *Enlightenment*, Lister, Cat and Kryten interviewed Murray's hologram as a possible replacement, even though Arnold's new position had yet to be secured. The interview was halted when Rimmer returned to *Red Dwarf* after his mind patch failed **[T-SER5.1]**.

    ***NOTE:** The breakup was mentioned in the pilot episode's first-draft script, published in the* Red Dwarf Omnibus. *It is unknown whether the nanobots resurrected him in Series VIII.*

- ***Mus sapiens*:** A humanoid species that evolved from the laboratory mice of an alternate-universe *Red Dwarf*. *Mus sapiens* were short, stout and less fashion-conscious than their rodent brethren, *Rattus sapiens*. Like the rat people, however, they were good at tasks requiring manual dexterity, and were attracted to shiny objects **[G-RPG]**.

- ***Muscle Woman*:** A magazine Rimmer read while inhabiting Lister's body after a mind swap. He perused the publication while smoking a cigar and soaking in a hot tub, despite his original goal of getting Lister's body fit. On the back cover was an ad for two other periodicals, one about dogs and the other about cats **[T-SER3.4]**.

- **mushy peas:** Lister's name for Brefewinan, the universal currency used by GELF tribes—because the money was, in fact, made primarily of mushy peas **[T-IDW]**.

- **Musical Rubble:** A game developed by Colonel Mike O'Hagan, aimed at keeping crash survivors occupied and in good spirits. He suggested this game in his *Space Corps Survival Manual* **[B-SUR]**.

- **Muskett, Netta:** A twentieth-century British author who wrote more than sixty romance novels **[RL]**. After being on his own for two million years following *Red Dwarf*'s cadmium II accident, Holly turned to Muskett's novels to keep himself occupied. He was reading *Doctor, Darling* when the ship passed a quintuplet of stars in concentric orbits, but ignored the stellar phenomenon since he had reached the part in the book when a doctor told Jemma she had three years to live **[N-INF]**.

    ***NOTE:** Netta Muskett never wrote a book titled* Doctor, Darling. *However, many of her novels did feature physician characters.*

- **Mussolini, Benito, First Marshal:** A twentieth-century Italian politician and leader of the National Fascist Party **[RL]**.

  A waxdroid replica of Mussolini was created for the Waxworld theme park. Left on their own for millions of years, the waxdroids attained sentience and became embroiled in a park-wide resource war between Villain World (to which Mussolini belonged) and Hero World.

  During this war, the *Red Dwarf* crew transported to the planet using a Matter Paddle, with Lister and Cat materializing in Villain territory, while Rimmer and Kryten landed in Hero territory. While imprisoned in Villain World, Lister and Cat witnessed the firing-squad execution of a waxdroid Winnie-the-Pooh, which Mussolini attended.

  Rimmer, meanwhile, found the heroes' army lacking and took command, working many of the pacifistic waxdroids to death before ordering a frontal attack on the enemy's compound across a minefield. This wiped out the remaining droids, including Mussolini **[T-SER4.6]**.

- **Mustard, Colonel:** A character and possible murder suspect in the popular European board game *Cluedo* (marketed in the United States as *Clue*) **[RL]**. When Queeg challenged Holly to a game of chess for control of *Red Dwarf*, Holly, unskilled at the game, suggested they instead play *Cluedo*, offering to let Queeg be Colonel Mustard **[T-SER2.5]**.

- **mutant-hunting outfit:** An ensemble that Cat wore while searching *Red Dwarf* for a polymorph that had attacked the crew. The outfit consisted of a metallic gold jacket with tassels and an oversized collar, a gold headband, and gold boots **[T-SER3.3(d)]**.

- **"Mutants Out":** A T-shirt slogan that Rimmer proposed as a "tough" way to deal with a polymorph that had drained his anger, making him a pacifist **[T-SER3.3]**.

- **"Mutant—We Love You":** *See* "Chameleonic Life Forms? No, Thanks"

- **mutated pneumonia:** A disease that Lister contracted after venturing into *Red Dwarf*'s contaminated Officers' Block. Pneumonia germs in that area had mutated over the course of millions of years, creating a contagion with initial symptoms of fever and unconsciousness, followed by hallucinations that took corporeal form.

  While feverish, Lister dreamed of several thoughts from his subconscious mind, including an instance when it rained herring in Burgundy, the Mayor of Warsaw spontaneously combusting, and two individuals representing Lister's confidence and paranoia—all of which became manifestations once he awoke **[T-SER1.5]**.

  ***NOTE:*** *The disease was dubbed "mutated pneumonia" on the official* Red Dwarf *website, but was never named in the episode.*

- **mutton vindaloo beast:** A creature Holly created using a machine that transmogrified the DNA of organic material, which the crew found on a derelict ship. When Cat accidentally transformed Kryten into a human, the former mechanoid was initially pleased, but soon realized the folly of being human and decided to resume his original form.

  Unsure of the device's dependability, the crew tested it on a plate of mutton vindaloo before risking Kryten's life. Human DNA was still recorded in the machine, however, and thus the meal turned into a hulking vindaloo beast that immediately attacked the crew. With the creature in pursuit, Lister used the machine to change himself into a supersoldier, but Holly's inexperience with the controls resulted in his becoming a pint-sized powerhouse. He confronted the beast and learned its only weakness: lager, which he hurled into its gaping maw before shooting it with a bazookoid **[T-SER4.2]**.

- **Mutual Life Assurance:** A twenty-second-century insurance company that owned a building on the Saturnian moon of Mimas. Lister crashed into this structure with a taxi hopper after spilling hot coffee into his crotch to put out a cigarette he had dropped into his lap. This destroyed a large portion of the building's neon sign **[N-INF]**.

- ***My Diary*:** A book that Arnold Rimmer kept hidden in a secret compartment of another book, titled *A to Z of Red Dwarf*. Lister found the diary in the quarters that Rimmer shared with his duplicate hologram, while investigating the origin of "gazpacho soup," Rimmer's last words before dying in the cadmium II accident **[T-SER1.6]**.

- ***My Incredible Career*:** An autobiography that Rimmer imagined writing in an illusion created by the total-immersive video game *Better Than Life*, under the name Admiral A.J. Rimmer. As Arnold dined at a restaurant in the game, a military cadet approached him, humbly requesting that the admiral autograph his copy of the book **[T-SER2.2]**.

- **"My Other Spaceship Is a *Red Dwarf*":** A slogan printed on a bumper sticker affixed to the back of a *Blue Midget* shuttlecraft **[T-SER2.3]**.

- **mystic:** A type of clairvoyant GELF from an alternate dimension, employed at the Forum of Justice. Mystics reportedly witnessed crimes before they occurred—in dreams, in a great fire, and/or in the oils of C'fadeert—allowing the federal council to convict perpetrators before they could cause any damage. Their abilities were often called into question by demonstrators, who believed the predictions were simply a way for the GELF government to rid itself of dissidents and obtain volunteers for its Reco-Programme **[N-LST]**.

- **Mystic System of Justice:** A judicial model used by Arranguu 12's Forum of Justice that employed six GELF soothsayers known as mystics, who claimed to be able to foresee transgressions before they took place. The GELFs' federal council used these predictions to apprehend potential criminals, but the process was actually just a convenient way for the GELF government to rid itself of dissidents and obtain volunteers for its Reco-Programme. The Forum of Justice was regularly the site of demonstrations, as angry GELFs protested the bogus system **[N-LST]**.

- **MyVac:** A vacuum attachment that Diva-Droid International developed for the 4000 Series mechanoid, designed to plug into the android's groinal socket **[X-CAL]**.

  ***NOTE:*** *This device's name and design spoofed Apple's iMac, with the calendar's advertisement mimicking the style of Apple's iPod commercials at that time. In the real world, Eureka produces a vacuum cleaner called the MyVac.*

N

# NEWTON, KAREN, DOCTOR

- **Name That Smell:** A game that Kochanski mocked Lister and Cat for playing. She then attempted to broaden their sophistication by bringing them into an artificial-reality simulation of *Pride and Prejudice Land* **[T-SER7.6]**.

- **Nanny-Bot childcare software bundle:** A software package for the 4000 Series mechanoid, available as an option from Diva-Droid International **[G-RPG]**.

- **nanobot:** A microscopic robot made from components at or near the scale of a nanometer ($10^{-9}$ meters) **[RL]**. 4000 Series mechanoids had nanobots built into their bodies as part of their self-repair system **[T-SER7.8]**. Such nanobots resembled miniscule insects, such as spiders or ticks, with mechanoid heads **[W-NAN]**.

  Once activated, these subatomic robots broke down raw materials at the molecular level and rebuilt their host mechanoid's damaged or malfunctioning components. After Lister lost his arm to the Epideme virus, Kochanski questioned whether Kryten's nanobots could rebuild his arm using extra tissue from his body. Although it would work, Kryten admitted, his nanobots had deserted him years prior. The crew thus returned to the ocean planet containing the *Esperanto,* where Kryten had last activated his nanobots, and where *Red Dwarf* had been lost.

  Upon arrival, they found a small planetoid composed of parts from the mining ship. Among the scrap was Holly, restored to his male persona and stored in a wristwatch. Holly informed them that the robots had remolecularized the entire vessel, created a subatomic version for themselves, and turned the rest into the planetoid. The crew turned *Starbug*'s scanners toward its interior and found the nanobots hiding in Lister's laundry basket. Kryten captured the 'bots and forced them to rebuild *Red Dwarf* and fix Lister's arm **[T-SER7.8]**.

  Holly then created a second set of nanobots and instructed them to revive the full complement of *Red Dwarf* in order to keep Lister on his toes. This plan backfired on him, however, when the newly revived Captain Hollister sentenced the group to two years in the brig for using the crew's personal files for their own gain **[T-SER8.3]**.

- **nano-*Red Dwarf*:** See *Red Dwarf* [ninth entry]

- **nanosensor:** A microscopic sensory point used to convey data to the macroscopic world, used primarily in medicine and for building nanoscale computer chips **[RL]**. 4000 Series mechanoids contained nanosensors as part of their internal analysis system. Once magnified, this type of nanosensor resembled a mechanoid's head, with a propeller in the rear for propulsion. Nanosensors could be transferred to a humanoid body to detect and analyze toxic substances. When Cat became sick, Kryten injected several of his nanosensors into Cat to determine the cause, which turned out to be a biological affliction due to a lack of sex **[T-IDW]**.

- **nanotek:** A hypothetical unit of time. While helping Lister search for uranium deposits on a moon, Holly claimed two nanoteks equaled one glimbart **[N-INF]**.

- **nasal alert:** A sensation that Cat experienced when detecting impending danger. He announced a nasal alert prior to being captured by Rimmer clones on Rimmerworld **[T-SER6.5]**.

- **National Aeronautics and Space Administration (NASA):** A civilian branch of the U.S. government responsible for the nation's space program and aerospace research **[RL]**. A graphic showing NASA's logo and full name adorned the wall of Rimmer's bunk aboard *Red Dwarf* **[T-SER2.2]**.

- **National Bazookoid Association:** An organization dedicated to bazookoid ownership. The builders of Justice World—enlightened individuals who believed in the humane treatment and rehabilitation of prisoners—were not members of the National Bazookoid Association **[G-RPG]**.

- ***National Enquirer, The*:** A weekly American tabloid newspaper focused on entertainment gossip and sensationalized stories **[RL]**. While researching ways to reduce Lister's sentence in *Red Dwarf*'s brig, Holly found an article on page 8 of an issue of the *Enquirer*, about an operation to turn a human into a dog. He suggested Lister undergo the procedure, called a "roverostomy," since dog years were seven times shorter than human years, effectively reducing his two-year sentence to only fourteen weeks **[T-SER8.4]**.

- **National Have Something That Scuttles for Dinner Day:** A hypothetical holiday. When Kryten cooked a lobster dinner to celebrate the anniversary of his rescue from *Nova 5*, Lister, not remembering the date, wondered if it was National Have Something That Scuttles for Dinner Day **[T-SER7.6]**.

  ***NOTE:** The DVD captions read "National Eat Something That Scuttles Day."*

- **Nautical-Class seeding vessel:** The classification of the SSS *Esperanto*, a Space Corps seeding ship discovered by the *Starbug 1* crew **[G-RPG]**.

- **Navarro, Randy, Commander:** The hologrammic second-in-command of the holoship *Enlightenment*. He had an IQ of 194 **[T-SER5.1]**.

  ***NOTE:** The* Red Dwarf Programme Guide *spelled his name "Nivaro," while the official website has* *occasionally spelled it "Navaro." The spelling used here appeared in the episode's credits.*

- **navicomp:** A piece of equipment located in *Red Dwarf*'s Drive Room, short for "navigational computer." While traveling at faster-than-light speed, Rimmer witnessed a future echo of what appeared to be Lister being killed by an overheating navicomp, though what he actually saw was Lister's future son, Bexley, dying **[T-SER1.2]**. *Starbug* shuttlecrafts were fitted with navicomps as well **[T-SER3.1]**, which also acted as Medical Units **[T-SER6.5]**.

  ***NOTE:*** *This was sometimes referred to as a navicom, dropping the "p."*

- **Navicomp Chamber:** A small section of *Red Dwarf*'s Drive Room that contained the ship's navigational computer **[N-INF]**.

- **Navi-Comp Operating System:** Software installed in navigational computers sold by Crapola Inc. **[G-RPG]**.

- **Navicomp Suite:** A room allocated for *Red Dwarf*'s navigational controls **[N-BTL]**.

- **navigational computer:** *See* navicomp

- **navigation officer first class:** A rank to which Rimmer imagined being promoted due to a computer error on his Astronavigation Exam, unaware he was actually still in the total-immersion video game *Better Than Life*. Due to his inability to accept such good fortune, however—even in a game—his mind conjured up an Outland Revenue agent, who smashed his thumbs with a hammer **[T-SER2.2]**.

- **Neame, Doctor:** A character on the television soap opera *Androids*. He started as an orderly who once covered for a physician on his lunch break **[W-AND]**. After Brook was injured during a shootout with Jaysee, Brooke Junior brought him to St. Pentium's Hospital, where Neame examined him **[M-SMG2.8(c2)]**.

- **nebulon missile:** A powerful explosive capable of triggering a reaction within a supergiant star, causing it to go supernova. Commissioned by the Coca-Cola Co., *Nova 5* launched a nebulon missile at a blue supergiant, completing an advertising campaign in which 128 supernovae spelled out the words "Coke Adds Life!," which could be easily seen from Earth **[N-INF]**.

- **neck diodes:** Components of certain androids in an alternate universe, such as Dottie, Jake Bullet's secretary **[M-SMG1.7(a)]**.

- ***Necrobics: Hologrammatic exercises for the dead*:** An exercise program designed specifically for holograms. While Rimmer worked out to a *Necrobics* tape in his quarters, it began raining herring due to Lister dreaming of that event while suffering from mutated pneumonia **[T-SER1.5]**.

- **negadrive:** A hardware and software bundle built into 4000 Series mechanoids as part of "Mamet's Revenge." All negative emotions experienced by a mechanoid were stored on the negadrive. Once the file became full, it triggered an overload that caused the mech's head to explode, symbolizing how Mamet's ex-fiancé "lost his head" when becoming angry.

  When Kryten learned of his negadrive via a previously inaccessible memory file, he quickly removed the component. Later, during a rogue simulant attack, Kryten's brother Able took the device and left *Starbug* in an escape pod, feeding the negadrive's signal through the pod's thrusters and aiming it at the enemy ship, causing the simulant to destroy his own vessel **[T-SER7.6]**.

- **Nega-Drive download station:** An accessory for 4000 Series mechanoids, available as an option from Diva-Droid International **[G-RPG]**.

- **negative gravity drive:** A type of propulsion unit used aboard the *Mayflower,* a transport ship assigned to ferry GELFs, simulants and humans to the Andromeda Galaxy to terraform a new home for mankind **[N-LST]**.

- **negative virus:** A viral strain that affected an individual in a detrimental manner, such as influenza. Hologrammic scientist Hildegarde Lanstrom conceived the notion that both negative and positive viruses existed, and was able to isolate several strains at a viral research station. She eventually contracted a holovirus that drove her insane and killed her, which she passed on to Rimmer before dying **[T-SER5.4]**.

- **Neider-Lewis, Professor:** A scientist who helped to create the virtual-reality game *Better Than Life*. His father had worked on a virtual-reality system that allowed a user to access alternate dimensions; he disappeared, however, shortly after solving the problem of traversing dimensional barriers **[M-SMG1.1(a)]**.

- ***Neighbours*:** An Australian television soap opera that debuted in 1985 **[RL]**. Kryten cited the phrase "*Neighbours* is an excellent television program" as an example of advanced lying **[M-SMG1.6(a)]**.

  ***NOTE:** The in-universe soap opera* Androids, *featured in episode 2.1 ("Kryten") and several* Smegazine *comics, was based on this television series, as was its theme song.*

- **Nelly ("Lube"):** A character on the television soap opera *Androids*. She was a part-time barmaid at a pub called The Petroleum, as well as a part-time sex worker at Kelly's android brothel **[W-AND]**.

  ***NOTE:** Nelly's character profile on the* Androids *website repurposed an image of Mollee from the* Smegazines' Androids *comics.*

- **Nelson:** A name that Lister assigned to one of twelve rogue droids he purchased from the Kinitawowi to break his doppelgänger out of the virtual-reality prison Cyberia **[N-LST]**.

- **Nelson, Horatio, Vice-Admiral:** A decorated eighteenth-century British Naval officer who lost an arm during an unsuccessful campaign to conquer Santa Cruz de Tenerife, Spain **[RL]**. While explaining to Cat his reasons for teaching Kryten how to lie, Lister cited Nelson's insubordination and subsequent victory as an example of how dishonesty could be beneficial **[T-SER4.1]**. Kochanski later mentioned Nelson as an extraordinary one-armed individual, while consoling Lister over the amputation of his arm **[T-SER7.8]**.

- **Nelson, Horatio, Vice-Admiral:** A waxdroid replica of the admiral, created for the Waxworld theme park. Left on their own for millions of years, the waxdroids attained sentience and became embroiled in a park-wide resource war between Villain World and Hero World (to which Nelson belonged). The Nelson waxdroid died during the conflict **[T-SER4.6]**.

- **Nelson, Norbert:** A crewmember aboard a spaceship fitted with a DNA-modifying machine. Nelson used the contraption to give himself an additional pair of heads, despite not fully understanding the controls **[W-OFF]**. Many years later, the *Red Dwarf* crew discovered the derelict ship, with the three-headed skeleton of Nelson inside **[T-SER4.2]**.

- **NeoProzak:** An anti-depressant drug developed in 2036, and subsequently made mandatory worldwide. Dissidents who refused to take the drug hid in caves and were generally miserable **[B-EVR]**.

- **Neptune:** The eighth planet in Earth's solar system. It possessed thirteen known moons, including Triton **[RL]**. Space-beatniks from around the system gathered on Neptune for Pluto's solstice, an event that marked the moment Pluto overtook Neptune and became the outermost planet in the solar system **[N-INF]**.

  In the twenty-second century, the Inter-Planetary Commission for Waste Disposal decided to designate one of the system's nine planets as humanity's official dumping grounds. Representatives from all nine worlds presented their case against being chosen, with Neptune's delegation focusing on the planet's inimitable terraforming operations and renowned architecture. Ultimately, Earth was nominated for the task **[N-BTL]**.

- **Neptune Blue:** A standard color available for Diva-Droid International's 4000 Series mechanoid **[G-RPG]**.

- **nerdism:** A medical condition afflicting certain members of a totalitarian society in Jake Bullet's universe. Symptoms included thin hair, bad eyesight, goofy teeth, spots and a tendency to wear severely outdated clothes. Doctor Donald Dirk, of England's Slough Brain Research Unit, studied the condition and proved that it was curable through an expensive operation **[M-SMG1.14(c6)]**.

- **"Nerdism—A Study":** A medical research paper published in Jake Bullet's universe, written by Doctor Donald Dirk of the Slough Brain Research Unit. This study revolved around the affliction known as nerdism, and included a diagram of a nerd outlining certain key indicators of the disorder **[M-SMG1.14(c6)]**.

- **Nerdorama:** A nerd club in a fascist society in Jake Bullet's universe. Prior to his murder, game-show winner Philby Frutch frequented this establishment despite its having turned away his girlfriend, Mercy Dash, for not being nerdy enough **[M-SMG1.14(c6)]**.

- **Nero, Emperor:** The fifth emperor of the Roman Empire, born Lucius Domitius Ahenobarbus, and believed to have burned most of Rome to the ground in 64 A.D. in order to clear land for a palatial complex called the Domus Aurea **[RL]**. Using a time drive coupled with a faster-than-light drive, the *Starbug 1* crew traveled throughout space-time as epicures, sampling the best in the universe and socializing with historic figures, including Nero **[T-SER6.6(d)]**.

- **neural circuits:** Electronics located in the head of 4000 Series mechanoids, used to help process information. Infected with the Epideme virus, Lister wondered if Kryten's neural circuits were picking up static from the ship's tumble dryer when the mechanoid suggested reasoning with the sentient disease **[T-SER7.7]**.

- **neural interface helmet:** A device worn on a person's head that connected the user's brain to a computer or recording device. Resembling a bicycle helmet, it possessed input-output capability, allowing signals to be read from and sent to the user's mind **[G-SOR]**. Lister utilized a neural interface helmet to record his memories of ex-girlfriend Lise Yates, which he then implanted into Rimmer's memories as a gift **[T-SER2.3]**.

- **"Neuro Cardiac Sync":** A phrase printed on a button on the control panel of an escape pod belonging to Barbra Bellini, a guard serving on a prison ship transporting simulants. The panel controlled the pod's cryogenics system. When the *Red Dwarf* crew found the pod, it contained a frozen occupant—not Bellini, but rather a simulant prisoner who had stolen it during a mutiny **[T-SER4.3(d)]**.

- **NeuroNet HUD sight:** A head-up display and tracking system built into Bloodlust Arms' RocketMan missile launchers **[G-RPG]**.

  ***NOTE:** Based on its name, the NeuroNet sight presumably linked to a user's brain, allowing for easier tracking.*

- **neutral area:** An area within the penal ship Justice World through which unauthorized vessels had to pass while landing in the clearance zone to be processed **[T-SER4.3]**.

- **neutrino-tachyon cloud:** A spatial phenomenon consisting of gaseous neutrinos, known to expand the dimension of space-time. While attempting to use such a cloud as a means of returning to Earth in their own era, the *Red Dwarf* crew utilized the mining ship's scoop to collect the neutrinos. Due to Holly's trouble with the number seven, however, they were instead hurled back to prehistoric Earth. There, they fought a dinosaur before heading back to their starting point, inadvertently setting off a neutrino-tachyon shockwave in the process that rendered the dinosaurs extinct **[M-SMG2.8(c3)]**.

- ***Neutron Star*:** A ship that employed a mechanoid named Parkur. To entertain the three survivors of the *Nova 5* crash, Kryten did impressions of Parkur. The routine fell flat, however, since none of the women were familiar with him **[N-INF]**.

- **neutron tank:** A type of weapon in Dimension 165. A neutron tank killed the original Ace Rimmer in that dimension, but not before he passed the torch to another Ace **[T-SER7.2]**.

- ***Neverdunroamin*:** A spaceship crewed by simulants who scavenged Garbage World (Earth) for antiques and emotions carried by polymorphs **[M-SMG2.9(c11)]**.

- **New Athens:** A twenty-second-century city containing architecture similar to that of ancient Greece, with fluted pillars and neo-classic arches. Among other cities, New Athens influenced the design of several structures along *Red Dwarf*'s exterior **[N-INF]**.

- **Newcastle Brown Ale:** A twentieth-century Heineken beer brand sold in many countries worldwide **[RL]**. While defending his cowardice during a barroom brawl on Miranda, Rimmer told Lister that wartime generals did not typically stick broken Newcastle Brown bottles in people's faces and exclaim, "Stitch that, Jimmy!" **[T-SER3.2]**.

- **New Earth:** A name that Kryten suggested for a new planet he predicted would be created from the radioactive mass left behind by a minuscule alien invasion fleet **[X-XMS]**.

- **New Mexico:** A state located in the Southwest United States **[RL]**. Rimmer described a blob on *Starbug 1*'s viewscreen (which turned out to be a despair squid) as being roughly the size of New Mexico **[T-SER5.6]**.

- ***News Chronicle*:** A British daily newspaper published between 1872 and 1960 **[RL]**. After Lister used a timeslide to go back in time to a Nuremberg rally led by Adolf Hitler and accidentally thwarted an assassination attempt on the Führer, the front-page article of the Tuesday, May 4, 1939, edition changed to reflect his interference. The new headline read "Hitler Escapes Bomb Attack At Nuremberg," while a photo of Lister now appeared, captioned "Mystery assassin vanishes." Other articles on the front page included "Roosevelt Speech Is Postponed" and "Nine More Night Raiders Are Brought Down." In the upper corner of the front page was an advertisement for Rolls Razors **[T-SER3.5]**.

  ***NOTE:*** *The newspaper's 1939 publication date does not jibe with the actual year of the Nuremberg rally (1934), nor with when Claus von Stauffenberg tried to assassinate Hitler (1944). In addition, May 4, 1939, was a Thursday, not a Tuesday.*

- ***Newsweek*:** An American weekly news magazine that discontinued its print publication in December 2012, transitioning to an all-digital format **[RL]**. Lister was featured on a *Newsweek* cover in an alternate timeline, in which he became the youngest billionaire in the world by inventing the Tension Sheet **[T-SER3.5]**.

  While trapped in an addictive version of *Better Than Life*, Rimmer imagined that he adorned a cover of *Newsweek*, which he kept in his limousine **[N-BTL]**.

- **New Tokyo:** A city containing a store that stocked total-immersion video games. When the shop ran out of the game *Better Than Life*, the resulting riot was so intense that rubber nuclear weapons were deployed to quell the crazed consumers **[T-SER2.2]**.

- **Newton, Isaac, Sir:** An English physicist whose research established a set of laws of motion and universal gravitation **[RL]**. Although Holly remembered that Newton was a famous physicist, he had forgotten, after three million years, what he was famous for. This lapse concerned him, though he never mentioned it to Lister **[N-INF]**.

- **Newton, Karen, Doctor:** The chief medical officer aboard *Red Dwarf* who died during the cadmium II disaster. Three million years later, she was resurrected, along with the rest of the ship's complement, when nanobots rebuilt *Red Dwarf* **[T-SER8.1]**.

  Newton's likeness was used in an artificial-reality simulation, established by the ship's Board of Inquiry, to determine whether Lister and his comrades were guilty of a crime. In the illusion, she pounced on Rimmer in the captain's galley after he imbibed the sexual-attraction virus. Later, when Kryten learned that his core programming would be restored and his prior memories deleted, he rebelled and forced the medical staff, including Karen, to remove her pants and sit on a toilet, so he could more easily disobey the order **[T-SER8.2]**.

  ***NOTE:*** *Because Newton was on the Board of Inquiry, she and her fellow Board members must have watched the simulation. As such, they all would have witnessed her sexual encounter with Rimmer and the bathroom incident.*

- **Newton-John, Olivia:** A popular Australian singer, songwriter and actor who starred in the films *Grease* and *Xanadu* and produced several hit records **[RL]**. After Lister found Kochanski with another man in the Ganymede Holiday Inn's Honeymoon Suite, Holly comforted him by recalling how he fell in love with a Sinclair ZX-81. It was better to have loved and lost, Holly concluded, than to listen to an album by Olivia Newton-John—since anything, he noted, was better than that **[T-SER2.4]**.

- **New Zodiac Festival**: A four-day event held in the Sea of Tranquility on Earth's Moon, celebrating the changing of Earth's polar star, and attended by five thousand space beatniks. Because of this change, the entire Zodiac system shifted, and everyone moved one astrological sign forward. A couple named Denis and Josie met at this festival **[N-INF]**.

- **Niagara Falls:** The collective name for three waterfalls bordering Canada and the United States, renowned as a tourist location **[RL]**. After Lister aged into his sixties due to time dilation and subsequently died, his shipmates brought him back

**B-: Books**
**PRG:** *Red Dwarf Programme Guide*
**SUR:** *Red Dwarf Space Corps Survival Manual*
**PRM:** *Primordial Soup*
**SOS:** *Son of Soup*
**SCE:** *Scenes from the Dwarf*
**LOG:** *Red Dwarf Log No. 1996*
**RD8:** *Red Dwarf VIII*
**EVR:** *The Log: A Dwarfer's Guide to Everything*

**X-: Misc.**
**PRO:** Promotional materials, videos, etc.
**PST:** Posters at DJ XVII (2013)
**CAL:** 2008 calendar
**RNG:** Cell phone ringtones
**MOB:** Mobisode ("Red Christmas")
**CIN:** *Children in Need* sketch
**GEK:** *Geek Week* intros by Kryten
**TNG:** "Tongue-Tied" video

**XMS:** Bill Pearson's Christmas special pitch script
**XVD:** Bill Pearson's Christmas special pitch video
**OTH:** Other *Red Dwarf* appearances

**SUFFIX**
**DVD:**
**(d)** – Deleted scene
**(o)** – Outtake
**(b)** – Bonus DVD material (other)
**(e)** – Extended version

**SMEGAZINES:**
**(c)** – Comic
**(a)** – Article

**OTHER:**
**(s)** – Early/unused script draft
**(s1)** – Alternate version of script

to life on a version of Earth on which time ran backwards. The crew left him a note saying to meet them in thirty-six years at the Niagara Falls souvenir shop so they could rescue him **[N-BTL]**. Upon arriving at Niagara Falls, however, they witnessed the backwards apprehending of Lister by police, and became involved in a reverse chase throughout the tourist area that took them off premises **[N-BCK]**.

- ***Nice 'n' Nauseating*:** A best-selling album by African ballad singer Perry N'Kwomo. Among its many hit songs was one referencing Ganymede, Titan and Lunar City 7, which Lister heard while shuttling to report to *Red Dwarf* for his first tour of duty **[N-INF]**.

- **Nice'n'Noodly Kwik-Food bar:** An eating establishment located at the Mimas Central Shuttle Station. Lister rummaged through its trash for food on his way to Gate 9, where a shuttle waited to ferry him to *Red Dwarf* **[N-INF]**.

- **Nic Farey Fan Club:** An organization dedicated to an individual named Nic Farey. In one of Cat's dreams, an android wearing unstylish clothes and a Nic Farey Fan Club badge boarded *Red Dwarf* and stole Cat's suits for use on a world suffering from a severe style famine. Hoping never to relive that dream, Cat deleted it from the ship's dream recorder **[M-SMG1.7(c2)]**.

  ***NOTE:*** *Nic Farey founded The Official* Red Dwarf *Fan Club.*

- **Nickel-Hydrate Breath:** A nickname that Kochanski called Kryten after discovering that he was filming her and other female inmates in *Red Dwarf*'s prison shower **[T-SER8.5]**.

- **Nielsen, Brigitte:** A statuesque Danish actor, model and reality television star whose film credits included *Red Sonja* and *Rocky IV* **[RL]**. While discussing Silicon Heaven with Kryten, Lister wondered if it was anything like being stuck in a packed lift with Brigitte Nielsen **[T-SER3.6]**.

- **Nigel, Norman:** An employee of Diva-Droid International who designed the 3000 Series mechanoid. Nigel abandoned many popular features of previous models while designing the 3000, opting instead for realism—a decision that backfired and led to a mass recall due to the mech's unpopularity **[W-DIV]**.

- **Nigel ("Nige"):** An inmate of the Tank, *Red Dwarf*'s classified brig on Floor 13. His tattooed face was entirely covered in metal piercings. This, Holly claimed, made him "a bit narky" around magnets **[T-SER8.1]**.

  ***NOTE:*** *The* Red Dwarf Programme Guide *called him "Nige," a common nickname for men named Nigel.*

NOVA 5

- ***Night at the Opera, A*:** An album recorded by Reggie Wilson **[M-SMG1.3(a)]**.

- **Nightingdroid, Florence:** A nickname that Lister called Kryten after the mechanoid cared for him during his bout with space mumps **[T-SER4.3]**. Kochanski also used this name to summon Kryten after witnessing the mech coddling Lister, who had lost his arm to the Epideme virus **[T-SER7.8]**.

  ***NOTE:*** *The name was derived from that of Florence Nightingale, a nineteenth-century British nurse considered a pioneer in her field.*

- **Nightmare Norman:** A nickname that Rimmer called the Unspeakable One **[T-SER5.3(d)]**.

- **Nimble, Albert:** An Earth tycoon afflicted with a terminal disease who had himself cryogenically frozen and shot into space, hoping to be thawed by a species able to cure him in the future. Millions of years later, the *Red Dwarf* crew found Nimble and thawed him out. When they explained that theirs was the last human ship in existence and they were unable to help him, he became furious and immediately died **[R-SER1.5]**.

- **Nine Years' Long Service:** One of four JMC medals that Rimmer earned, along with others for three, six and twelve years of service. Believing Lister intended to permanently deactivate him, Arnold wore these medals on his dress uniform while awaiting his impending execution **[T-SER1.6]**.

- **ninja throwing beret:** A sharpened throwing weapon used by Waxworld's Jean-Paul Sartre waxdroid **[G-SOR]**.

- **ninja throwing squirrel:** A specially trained rodent used as a weapon by Waxworld's St. Francis of Assisi waxdroid **[G-SOR]**.

- **nipple-matic:** A torture device utilizing rotating blades, used by Doctors Maxwell, Pension and Fund in a hallucination Cat suffered after receiving a bump to the head. Cat believed he was once again Duane Dibbley, and that the three doctors were experimenting on him. In actuality, the trio were Lister, Rimmer and Kryten, who were attempting to revive him using lithium carbonate **[M-SMG1.9(c1)]**.

- **nipple nuts:** Control knobs located in the chest area of 4000 Series mechanoids. The right nipple nut was used to regulate the mech's internal body temperature, while the left could tune in to short-wave radio transmissions **[T-SER4.2]**.

  Upon realizing he was late for an appointment with Rimmer, Kryten exclaimed "Spin my nipple nuts and send me to Alaska!" **[T-SER4.1]**. After being changed into a human by a DNA-modifying machine, Kryten discovered that his nipple nuts no longer functioned **[T-SER4.2]**.

  ***NOTE:*** *Since no nipple nuts were visible on Kryten's outer shell, they were presumably part of his internal construction.*

- **nitroglycerine:** An explosive compound used in the production of dynamite **[RL]**. Kryten retrofitted one of *Starbug 1*'s waste-disposal units to eject compacted garbage containing a thermos of nitroglycerine at high velocity, for use as a high-impact garbage cannon. He first tested the cannon on a gargantuan meteor while traversing an asteroid field in pursuit of the stolen *Red Dwarf* **[T-SER6.1]**.

- **Nitty, Frank ("The Enforcer"):** A notorious Italian-American gangster and one of Al Capone's top henchmen in the early twentieth century, born Francesco Nitti **[RL]**. While trapped in an addictive version of *Better Than Life*, Rimmer imagined using a time machine to crash a party at a 1922 Chicago speakeasy, where he danced the Black Bottom on a table with Nitty's girlfriend **[N-BTL]**.

- **Nixon, John Milhous, President:** The third president of Earth's World Council. During his first term, Nixon devised a plan to control the weather by detonating thermonuclear devices in the vicinity of the Sun, unaware the procedure would reduce the star's lifespan to approximately four hundred thousand years.

  Once the snafu was discovered, Nixon and his advisors decided to launch a vessel to the Andromeda Galaxy to prepare a planet as humanity's new home. This ship, the *Mayflower*, carried humans, simulants and various species of labor GELFs, and contained technology for terraforming and genetic engineering, including the genome of DNA (G.O.D.) **[N-LST]**.

  ***NOTE:*** *The novel* Last Human *implied that Nixon's great-great-great-great-great-great-great-uncle was President Richard Milhous Nixon.*

**PREFIX**
**RL:** Real life

**T-: Television Episodes**
**SER:** Television series
**IDW:** "Identity Within"
**USA1:** Unaired U.S. pilot
**USA2:** Unaired U.S. demo

**R-: *The Bodysnatcher Collection***
**SER:** Remastered episodes
**BOD:** "Bodysnatcher"
**DAD:** "Dad"
**FTH:** "Lister's Father"
**INF:** "Infinity Patrol"
**END:** "The End" (original assembly)

**N-: Novels**
**INF:** *Infinity Welcomes Careful Drivers*
**BTL:** *Better Than Life*
**LST:** *Last Human*
**BCK:** *Backwards*
**OMN:** *Red Dwarf Omnibus*

**M-: Magazines**
**SMG:** *Smegazine*

**W-: Websites**
**OFF:** Official website
**NAN:** *Prelude to Nanarchy*
**AND:** *Androids*
**DIV:** Diva-Droid
**DIB:** Duane Dibbley
**CRP:** Crapola
**GEN:** Geneticon
**LSR:** Leisure World Intl.
**JMC:** Jupiter Mining Corporation
**AIT:** *A.I. Today*
**HOL:** HoloPoint

**G-: Roleplaying Game**
**RPG:** *Core Rulebook*
**BIT:** *A.I. Screen Extra Bits* booklet
**SOR:** *Series Sourcebook*
**OTH:** Other RPG material

- **Nixon, Richard Milhous, President:** The thirty-seventh leader of the United States, whose involvement in the Watergate scandal resulted in his impeachment and removal from office **[RL]**. Lister, attempting to get Kryten to inform him about a meeting with the *Red Dwarf* crew's future selves, told the mechanoid not to "Nixon" him about knowledge of his apparent future demise **[T-SER6.6]**.

  ***NOTE:*** *The novel* Last Human *implied that John Milhous Nixon was the disgraced president's great-great-great-great-great-great-great-nephew.*

- **N'Kwomo, Perry:** An African ballad singer who recorded the best-selling album *Nice 'n' Nauseating*. Among his many hits was an easy-listening song that referenced Ganymede, Titan and Lunar City 7. Lister heard this song while shuttling to *Red Dwarf* for his first tour of duty **[N-INF]**.

  ***NOTE:*** *The artist's name spoofed that of American singer Perry Como.*

- **N'mtheglyar:** The home of the elder chaos gods **[G-OTH]**.

  ***NOTE:*** *This was mentioned in* Red Dwarf RPG A.I. Add-On 1.0*, a downloadable PDF posted online by Deep7 Press in 2004, for use with* Red Dwarf—The Roleplaying Game.

- **Nni Retsasid:** An English café in a distant future in which time ran backwards. The inn advertised sbabek renod in its window. Rimmer and Kryten visited this pub after traveling through a timehole and became marooned on the planet **[R-SER3.1]**.

  ***NOTE:*** *The eatery's name, when read forward, was Disaster Inn, while the advertised food item was doner kebabs.*

- ***No Brains, All Brawn Sports Heroes Series*:** A series of virtual-reality sporting games produced by Total Immersion Inc. and distributed by Crapola Inc. It included such games as *Zero-G Kickboxing* **[G-RPG]**.

- **nocturnal boxing gloves:** A type of boxing gloves that Rimmer wore while attending boarding school **[T-SER3.5]**. When Legion held him captive aboard a research station years later, Arnold found his cell perfectly suited to his tastes, with overstarched pajamas and nocturnal boxing gloves **[T-SER6.2]**.

- **Noddy:** An odd individual whom Lister and his shipmates imagined while trapped in an elation squid hallucination, in which they thought they were merely characters on a TV show called *Red Dwarf.* Noddy was an employee of They Walk Among Us!, a British science fiction collectibles shop. The crew sought his help in finding their creator, and he, in turn, contacted the *Red Dwarf* Fan Club's president, but to no avail **[T-SER9.2]**.

- **Nodnol:** An analog to London on a far-future Earth on which time ran backwards. While searching for their missing crewmates, Lister and Cat found a sign that read "Nodnol 871 Selim," which they mistook for Bulgarian. Lister, claiming geography was his best subject, erroneously remembered Nodnol as being south of Bosnia, rich in minerals and animal produce **[T-SER3.1]**.

- **"Nodnol 871 Selim":** A road marker that Rimmer, Kryten and Holly passed while exploring a planet on which they had crashed after flying through a time hole. The planet was actually a future Earth on which time ran backwards. Lister and Cat mistook the sign's words for Bulgarian **[T-SER3.1]**.

  ***NOTE:*** *The sign, when read forward, said "London 178 Miles."*

- **Noel's Body Swap Shop:** A business on the Saturnian moon of Mimas, specializing in the switching of people's consciousness. The establishment, located on a street called Karmasutra, charged $£47 per hour. Sex worker Trixie LaBouche, concerned about a lack of protection from the Ganymedian Mafia, visited Noel's on the advice of a friend, to obtain a new form. However, an astro miner named Dutch van Oestrogen, on the run from the Mafia, hijacked her body from the shop **[M-SMG2.3(c4)]**.

- **"No Entry":** A phrase printed on a sign on the door to Cat's quarters aboard *Red Dwarf* **[M-SMG1.5(a)]**.

- **Nogard dna Egroeg:** A pub on a future Earth on which time ran backwards, located on Teerts Gnilpik. Rimmer and Kryten, marooned on the planet after their ship crashed, started a novelty act at this pub, in which they astonished audiences by speaking and doing things forwards instead of backwards **[T-SER3.1]**.

  ***NOTE:*** *Read forward, the pub's name was George and Dragon, while its location was on Kipling Street.*

- **No-Grav flying helmet:** A device invented in 2217 that enabled a user to float through the air by hanging from his or her head. A sports model was discontinued due to its acceleration, which tended to rip off a wearer's head and launch it into space. As such, it became a coveted collector's item **[B-EVR]**.

- **Non-Bud:** A nickname that Cat called Rimmer **[T-SER10.6]**.

  ***NOTE:** The name may have referenced Arnold's status as a hologram, or the fact that Cat did not consider him a friend—or both.*

- **"Non-Human Lifeform":** An error message displayed during Olaf Petersen's hologrammic recording session. The recording device crashed three times during his session, due to his advanced state of inebriation **[N-INF]**.

- **Non Inverting Input:** A setting on *Starbug 1*'s sonar scope display. This setting was not highlighted as the crew charted the course of a despair squid **[T-SER5.6]**.

- **noodle burger:** A menu item available from the Nice'n'Noodly Kwik-Food bar at Mimas Central Shuttle Station. Lister grabbed a half-eaten noodle burger from the bar's trash to eat on his way to board a shuttle bound for *Red Dwarf* **[N-INF]**.

- **"No Place Like Home":** A song recorded by the British new wave band Squeeze in the mid-1980s **[RL]**. A performance of this song, recorded by a Sharp FNB-200 telephone answering machine, was among Kryten's favorite musical pieces **[M-SMG1.1(a)]**.

- **Noreen:** A name that Vaughan McGruder called Arlene Rimmer while suffering from a concussion **[W-OFF]**.

- **Norman:** A name that Yvonne McGruder called Arnold Rimmer while suffering from a concussion **[T-SER1.5]**.

- **Norman, Captain:** The commander of the Space Corps vessel *Columbus 3*. Rimmer's half-brother, Howard Rimmer, served under Captain Norman **[W-OFF]**.

- **Northern Line:** A network of tube trains traversing the length and breadth of *Red Dwarf* **[N-INF]**. One of the line's stations, West 17/XC, served the Central Mall Branch **[M-SMG1.6(c2)]**.

- **North Western Electricity Board (Norweb):** A twentieth-century electrical power supply and distribution company in England **[RL]**. As a practical joke, Holly once told Lister that fighters from the Norweb Federation were pursuing him because of several infractions he had committed prior to leaving Earth **[T-SER1.6]**.

- **Norweb Federation:** A hypothetical conglomerate that Holly conceived as part of an April Fool's joke. The AI computer claimed two high-speed fighter craft from the Norweb Federation were pursuing Lister for "crimes against humanity" since he had left sausages unattended in his kitchen that, during the course of three million years, had encompassed almost the entire surface of the planet.

  According to Holly, despite now owning ninety-eight percent of the world's wealth due to compound interest on money he had left in the bank, Lister had left a light on in his bathroom, racking up an electric bill of £180 billion, of which Norweb now demanded payment. The joke initially fooled Lister—especially since it was six months before April Fool's Day **[T-SER1.6]**.

  ***NOTE:** This gag originated in a* Son of Cliché *"Dave Hollins: Space Cadet" sketch titled "Norweb." In that version, the ship's computer (Hab) was not playing a joke—Hollins had actually decimated Earth by leaving two half-eaten German sausages on a plate in his kitchen, which grew to cover seven-eighths of the planet's surface.*

- **Nose Tackle:** A position in zero-gee football **[N-BTL]**.

- **Nose World:** A company that the *Red Dwarf* crew imagined while trapped in an elation squid hallucination, in which they thought they were merely characters on a TV show. Nose World, a latex mask maker in twenty-first-century England, specialized in creating prosthetic noses for the TV and film industry. The company was located at 4 Nundah Street, London, W12 1HD, and employed a man named Swallow, who worked on *Red Dwarf* Series IX, and whose help the crew elicited in finding their creator **[T-SER9.2]**.

  ***NOTE:*** Back to Earth *relied heavily on references to the movie* Blade Runner. *Nose World and Swallow referenced a department within the Tyrell Corporation for which Hannibal Chew built replicant eyes.*

- **"No Smoking":** A warning printed on a wall sign posted in Rimmer's bunk aboard *Red Dwarf* **[T-SER1.1]**. He also hung this sign in the quarters he shared with his duplicate hologram—despite the fact that neither of them smoked **[T-SER1.6]**.

- **Nostalgia Night 1990s:** An event celebrated in *Red Dwarf*'s disco room. A sign promoting the event was posted on the disco's wall **[T-SER1.3]**.

- ***Nostrilomo*:** A ship that Holly claimed had appeared in a science fiction film, as he played charades with the *Red Dwarf* crew using only his nose to give clues **[T-SER8.1]**.

  *NOTE: Holly was presumably referring to the* Nostromo, *from the film* Alien.

- **not-a-cat:** A genetically engineered creature that resembled a common housecat, but was incredibly strong, vicious and cunning. Its name referred to the last words most often spoken in its presence **[B-EVR]**.

- **Noughts and crosses:** A pencil-and-paper game known in the United States as Tic-tac-toe. Two players alternately placed X's and O's on a three-by-three grid, in an attempt to place three in a row and thus win the game **[RL]**. After being beaten by Queeg at a game of chess, Holly suggested a game of Noughts and crosses instead **[T-SER2.5]**.

- **"No Unauthorized Entry":** A warning printed on a wall sign posted in *Red Dwarf*'s hologram simulation suite **[T-SER2.3]**.

- ***Nova 5*:** A privately chartered American spaceship outfitted with a Duality Jump—a quantum drive enabling the ship to travel great distances by forcing it to coexist in two places at once and materialize closer to its destination, which allowed it to leapfrog across space-time. The vessel contained stasis pods, a recreation room and a hologram simulation suite.

  *Nova 5* was one of several ships commissioned by Coca-Cola Co. to seek out supergiant stars and detonate warheads within their cores, in order to trigger a supernova. The result of this ambitious advertising campaign was a three-word message—"Coke Adds Life!"—spelled out using 128 supernovae, that could be seen from Earth day or night for five weeks. Upon completion of their mission, the eight-woman, two-man crew attempted to return to Earth, but the ship crashed into an icy moon when the resident mechanoid, Kryten, cleaned the onboard computer with soapy water. The crash killed all but three female crewmembers **[N-INF]**.

  Many years later, the *Red Dwarf* crew received a distress signal from Kryten, who told them of the three survivors. Upon boarding *Nova 5*, however, the Dwarfers learned that the "survivors" had been dead for centuries, and that Kryten, unable to cope with having no one to serve, refused to notice. After acknowledging the truth, Kryten left the marooned *Nova 5* and joined the others aboard *Red Dwarf* **[T-SER2.1]**. The *Red Dwarf* crew brought *Nova 5* back to their ship, hoping to repair the craft and use it to return to Earth. That plan, however, ended in failure **[N-INF]**.

  *NOTE:* Red Dwarf—The Roleplaying Game *designated the* Nova 5 *as a Nova-class scouting vessel designed to scout mineral-rich worlds for Jupiter Mining Corporation, while the novel* Infinity Welcomes Careful Drivers *indicated it was a private charter. The* Red Dwarf Programme Guide, *meanwhile, claimed the vessel was engaged in a stellar mapping mission (all three "survivors" were said to be mapping officers).*

- **Nova auto pistol:** A small handheld personal defense weapon manufactured by Bloodlust Arms and distributed via Crapola Inc.'s annual *SCABBY* catalog. It had a range of 50 meters (164 feet). Features of the Nova included hydraulic-loading action and a GeneStick pistol grip **[G-RPG]**.

- **Nova-class scouting vessel:** A type of craft utilized by the Jupiter Mining Corporation to seek out mineral-rich worlds for mining. In one reality, *Nova 5* was a ship of this class **[G-RPG]**.

- **Novelty-Condom-Head:** A nickname that Cat called Kryten **[T-SER4.2]**.

- **November 22, 1963:** The date of John F. Kennedy's assassination in Dallas, Texas **[RL]**. After the *Red Dwarf* crew found timeslides enabling them to travel back in time, Kryten suggested visiting this date and yelling "Duck!" from the grassy knoll **[T-SER3.5]**.

Intending to restock *Starbug 1*'s supply of curries using a time drive, the crew instead materialized at this point in space-time, inadvertently interrupting the assassination by knocking shooter Lee Harvey Oswald out of the Texas School Book Depository's window. They then returned to this date with a future version of Kennedy in order to fix the blunder—by having JFK assassinate himself **[T-SER7.1]**.

- **November 25:** A date roughly six weeks before the *Red Dwarf*'s cadmium II explosion, which Rimmer called Gazpacho Soup Day in his diary. Curious about the date's significance, Lister sneaked into Rimmer's quarters and read the corresponding entries **[T-SER1.6]**.

- **November 26, 2155:** The date on which Lister was found abandoned as an infant under a grav-pool table at a Liverpool pub called The Aigburth Arms. He had left the child there himself, in a box marked "Ourob Oros." The infant was born via *in vitro* fertilization to a future version of Kochanski—making her Lister's mother and Lister his own father **[T-SER7.3]**.

- ***Now, Voyager*:** A 1942 American drama film starring Bette Davis, Paul Henreid and Claude Rains **[RL]**. Kochanski admitted to Kryten that she was unable to speak for twenty minutes after first viewing the movie—a fact that Kryten made note of for future reference **[T-SER7.8]**.

- **"Now Irradiate Your Hands":** A rule printed on a sign posted above the automatic latrine in the quarters Lister shared with Rimmer **[T-SER1.3]**.

- ***Now That's What I Call Music #567*:** An album compiling hits from various musical artists **[G-SOR]**.

  ***NOTE:** In the real world,* Now That's What I Call Music! *is a series of compilation albums typically representing the hits from a particular year. At the time of this writing, eighty-six volumes have been released in the United Kingdom, and forty-eight in the United States.*

- ***Nowt on Telly:*** A magazine sold at The Kabin, a convenience store on the set of the British television show *Coronation Street*, which the *Red Dwarf* crew imagined while trapped in an elation squid hallucination **[T-SER9.2]**.

  ***NOTE:** The phrase "nowt on telly" is British slang, indicating nothing interesting on television.*

- **nuclear warhead:** An extremely destructive explosive designed to release vast amounts of energy from small amounts of matter, either via fission or a combination of fission and fusion **[RL]**. *Red Dwarf*'s ammunition stores contained several such weapons. After a polymorph drained Lister's fear, he suggested strapping a nuclear warhead to his skull so he could head-butt the creature and obliterate it **[T-SER3.3]**.

- **Nuke:** An individual whom Kryten's subconscious mind created as he attempted to purge an Armageddon virus that had infected *Starbug 1*'s navicomp. The mechanoid's mind converted the struggle into a dream in which he was the drunken sheriff of an Old West town terrorized by the Apocalypse Boys (a manifestation of the virus).

  Kryten's shipmates hacked into the dream via an artificial-reality machine and were confronted by Jimmy, a bar patron who was tormenting Kryten. When Lister embarrassed Jimmy with his knife-throwing skills, the thug ordered Frank and Nuke to "fill his lungs with lead." Cat, however, posing as the Riviera Kid, shot their bullets out of the air **[T-SER6.3]**. Nuke again tried to shoot Lister, who threw a bucket of soapy water at him, followed by a series of knives, which groomed and shaved the unkempt henchman **[T-SER6.3(s)]**.

  ***NOTE:** The DVD subtitles misidentified him as "Luke." The shaving scene, not shown onscreen, was described in the book* The Making of Red Dwarf.

- **Nundah Street:** A road in London, England **[RL]**. While trapped in an elation squid hallucination, the *Red Dwarf* crew imagined that Nose World was located at 4 Nundah Street **[T-SER9.2]**.

- **"nureek":** A sound made by the pipes in Kochanski's quarters aboard *Starbug 1*, due to a heating system malfunction. It traditionally came before a "rotut" sound **[T-SER7.4]**.

- **"Nuts":** A word printed on the front of a can in the sleeping quarters that Lister and Rimmer shared aboard *Red Dwarf* **[T-SER9.1]**.

- **Nuttyfruit bar:** A snack stocked in *Starbug 1*'s vending machine. When the crew attempted to pass through the tail of a phasing comet, the turbulence caused the Nuttyfruit bars to be ejected from the machines and slide about the ship **[T-SER7.5]**.

- **Nwaki:** A name, possibly a title, given to Michael R. McGruder by other survivors of the Reco-Programme's first test ship **[N-LST]**.

- **"Nylon Socks—They're Really Cool!":** A phrase printed on a sign hanging in the apartment of nerdy game-show contestant Philby Frutch **[M-SMG1.14(c6)]**.

- **NYNYPD:** An alternate-universe police department for which Jake Bullet worked. He became the first cyborg cop on the force **[M-SMG1.7(a)]**.

# OBSERVATION DOME

O

- **Oakley ("Longarm," "Armless"):** A *Red Dwarf* crewmember whose nickname changed after an explosion involving Olaf Petersen's moonshine still removed one or both of Oakley's arms **[W-OFF]**.

  ***NOTE:*** *Oakley presumably died during the cadmium II explosion. It is unknown whether the nanobots resurrected him in Series VIII.*

- **Oates, Lawrence, Captain:** An English cavalry officer who, stricken with gangrene and frostbite during the Terra Nova Expedition in 1912, left the safety of his tent to die in an Antarctic blizzard in order to increase his teammates' chances for survival **[RL]**. Kryten cited Oates' historic self-sacrifice, hoping it would inspire Rimmer to power down when *Red Dwarf* faced an emergency power loss **[T-SER4.4]**.

  ***NOTE:*** *Although Kryten quoted Oates as saying, "I'm going out for a walk; I may be some time," the actual quote attributed to the explorer was "I am just going outside and may be some time."*

- **Oblivion virus:** A powerful computer virus designed to kill electricity in any system it affected, by destabilizing the electric charge's electron-proton relationship as it traveled through the system. The virus, stored on a small pink disk, was used in conjunction with an antidote program, stored on a small blue disk. After entering an alternate universe via the Omni-zone, the *Starbug* crew purchased the virus from a Kinitawowi GELF tribe in order to help Lister's doppelgänger escape from the virtual-reality prison Cyberia.

  The group used the Oblivion virus on the electric lines feeding into the facility to render the entire moon powerless, after which the prime Lister tried to rescue his other self. They later loaded the virus into Rimmer's light bee and sent it into the heart of the malevolent entity called the Rage of Innocence, which destroyed the creature **[N-LST]**.

- **Observation Dome:** A small platform surrounded by a spherical glass bubble extending out from *Red Dwarf*'s hull. Its primary use was to observe space in a nearly 360-degree field of view. Rimmer once shared his feelings about his father with Lister in this dome **[T-SER2.2]**, and the two also discussed Lise Yates here as well. Pitying Rimmer's loneliness, Lister implanted his memories of Lise into Arnold's mind to boost his confidence **[T-SER2.3]**.

- **Observation Room:** A sealed area of *Red Dwarf* used for examining objects without risk of contamination. When Holly brought aboard an unidentified pod, Rimmer studied it in the Observation Room **[T-SER1.4]**.

- **Obs Room:** An area on the upper level of *Starbug 1*'s aft section **[T-SER6.4]**. The Obs Room contained a medical table **[T-SER6.6]**, as well as deep sleep units **[T-SER6.1]**.

  *NOTE: The DVD captions and dialog sometimes called this area the Ops Room.*

- **ocean grey:** The color of *Red Dwarf*'s hallways before Rimmer ordered the skutters to paint them military grey—which was nearly identical. Arnold's duplicate hologram later changed the color back to ocean grey **[T-SER1.6]**.

- **ocean seeding ship:** A type of vessel used by the Space Corps to introduce and accelerate marine life on S-3 planets. The SSS *Esperanto* was a class-D ocean seeding ship **[T-SER5.6]**.

- **October 14, 2155:** The birthdate that Lister supplied to his recruitment officer while applying for the Space Corps. This date took into account his being six weeks old when he was found in a box under a pool table at a pub in November 2155 **[N-INF]**. It did not, however, account for Lister having been born three million years in the future and brought back in time, or that he was his own father **[T-SER7.3]**.

- **Octuplets:** The username of a forum poster on the *Androids* website's message boards **[W-AND]**.

- **Odin:** A major god of Germanic mythology, particularly Norse, associated with war, death and magic **[RL]**. When Tunbridge Wells' five hundred pilgrims were sent to pray for the end of a meteor storm ravaging their city, a skipper in the group believed his people were headed to a shrine dedicated to Odin. Others disagreed, causing a religious war that wiped out the entire pilgrim crew **[M-SMG1.14(c2)]**.

- **Odor Eater:** A brand of foot-care products from Blistex, including shoe inserts and powders for controlling odors **[RL]**. Disgusted by his roommate's foot smell, Rimmer claimed Lister was the only person to ever get his money back from the Odor Eater company **[T-SER2.3]**.

- **Officer 592:** The ID number of Bull Heinman, a prison guard at a penitentiary in which Rimmer imagined being incarcerated while trapped in an addictive version of *Better Than Life* **[N-BTL]**.

- **Officer BB:** A nickname that Cat called Kochanski, short for "Officer Bud-Babe" **[T-SER7.3]**.

- **Officer Bud-Babe:** A nickname that Cat called Kochanski **[T-SER7.3]**.

  *NOTE: The name may have referenced her being Lister's ex-girlfriend (since Cat called Lister "Bud"), or the fact that she was very attractive—or both.*

- **Officers' Block:** A section of *Red Dwarf* allocated for the ship's officers. Lister explored the area while searching for Kochanski's dream recorder, believing it to be free of radiation. Since Rimmer had neglected to decontaminate the block,

**PREFIX**
**RL:** Real life

**T-: Television Episodes**
**SER:** Television series
**IDW:** "Identity Within"
**USA1:** Unaired U.S. pilot
**USA2:** Unaired U.S. demo

**R-: *The Bodysnatcher Collection***
**SER:** Remastered episodes
**BOD:** "Bodysnatcher"
**DAD:** "Dad"
**FTH:** "Lister's Father"
**INF:** "Infinity Patrol"
**END:** "The End" (original assembly)

**N-: Novels**
**INF:** *Infinity Welcomes Careful Drivers*
**BTL:** *Better Than Life*
**LST:** *Last Human*

**BCK:** *Backwards*
**OMN:** *Red Dwarf Omnibus*

**M-: Magazines**
**SMG:** *Smegazine*

**W-: Websites**
**OFF:** Official website
**NAN:** *Prelude to Nanarchy*
**AND:** *Androids*
**DIV:** Diva-Droid
**DIB:** Duane Dibbley

**CRP:** Crapola
**GEN:** Geneticon
**LSR:** Leisure World Intl.
**JMC:** Jupiter Mining Corporation
**AIT:** *A.I. Today*
**HOL:** HoloPoint

**G-: Roleplaying Game**
**RPG:** *Core Rulebook*
**BIT:** *A.I. Screen Extra Bits* booklet
**SOR:** *Series Sourcebook*
**OTH:** Other RPG material

Lister was infected with mutated pneumonia that caused him to suffer corporeal hallucinations **[T-SER1.5]**.

- **Officers' Club:** An area aboard *Red Dwarf* reserved for officers, used for parties, events and receptions. Lister hosted Kryten's last-day party in the Officers' Club, disregarding the fact that mechanoids were once not allowed there **[T-SER3.6]**.

- **Officers' Gym:** A recreation room reserved for *Red Dwarf*'s officers. While inhabiting Lister's body following a mindswap, Rimmer enjoyed the Jacuzzi in the gym's Caligula Suite **[R-SER3.4(d)]**.

- **Officer Smegski:** An insult that Cat called Rimmer **[T-SER10.5(d)]**.

- **Officers' Quarters:** An area of *Red Dwarf* that housed the mining ship's officers. After a few years of living in their original room, Lister and Rimmer decided to move into one of the Officers' Quarters **[T-SER3.3]**.

  ***NOTE:*** *Why, with the whole ship available to them, they still decided to bunk together is a mystery.*

- **Official Titan Souvenir Shop:** A store located on Jupiter's moon, Titan, which sold trinkets and other merchandise, including talking alarm clocks and medical diagnostic equipment. The shop's slogan was "The home of quality, taste and craftsmanship" **[R-BOD]**.

- **"Off Limits":** A warning printed on a sign hanging on the door to Cat's quarters aboard *Red Dwarf* **[M-SMG1.5(a)]**.

- **ogigon bachoo machwahah:** A term in the Kinitawowi language, meaning "oxygen-generation unit" **[T-SER6.4]**.

- **O'Hagan, Mike, Colonel ("Mad Dog"):** A space marine in the Space Corps Special Service Really Really Brave Division (SCSSRRBD). He authored the *Space Corps Survival Manual*, as well as several other books, including *Charlie Zero Potato, The Star Corps Commando Big Book of Brutality*, *Kill Your Way Slim* and such children's books as *General George and the Gook Invasion*.

  O'Hagan sported 459 scars and forty tattoos, and had twelve pieces of metal implanted in his head. His hobbies included swearing and long-distance spitting, and his family members included an Aunt Enid and Uncle Max, the latter of whom was a scientist who developed the Space Corps emergency death pack.

  While in the Space Corps, O'Hagan encountered several situations during which he had to eat human flesh, including his own, for survival. Shortly before the *Space Corps Survival Manual*'s publication, his ship crashed on Tregar IV, where his crewmates were forced to eat him, using one of his own cannibal-friendly recipes to cook his flesh **[B-SUR]**.

- **Oh God, Oh Crap (OGOC) missile:** A projectile fired from missile launchers built by Bloodlust Arms. One free OGOC missile was included with every purchase of a RocketMan launcher from Crapola Inc.'s *SCABBY* catalog **[G-RPG]**.

- **oils of C'fadeert:** A substance into which GELF soothsayers (mystics) employed by Arranguu 12's Forum of Justice gazed in order to foresee future crimes before they occurred **[N-LST]**.

- **OJY Kid's:** *See* YJO s'diK

- **O'Keefe, Nancy, Flight Engineer, Second Class:** A crewmember aboard *Nova 5* who died in a crash caused by Kryten attempting to clean the ship's computer. When *Red Dwarf*'s crew salvaged the ship many years later, O'Keefe's hologram was activated in a loop. Searching through *Nova 5*'s database, Rimmer discovered that her personality files were corrupted beyond use, as were those of her crewmates **[N-INF]**.

- **Old Course at St. Andrews:** *See* Hole 13

- **Old Five-fingers:** A nickname that Cat gave Lister after the latter's arm was amputated to cure him of the Epideme virus **[T-SER7.7]**.

- **Old Iron Balls:** A nickname that Rimmer asked Lister to call him (instead of "Rimmer") as they and Cat embarked on a rescue mission to *Nova 5*, where they believed three female crewmembers awaited **[N-INF]**. Rimmer referred to himself by this name while trying to jog Lister's memory after the latter used a timeslide to change history so that he had invented the Tension Sheet and never served aboard *Red Dwarf* **[T-SER3.5]**.

- **Old Iron-butt:** A name that Rimmer called himself, believing he had vanquished an emohawk that had invaded *Starbug 1* **[T-SER6.4]**.

- **Old Kent Road:** A road in South East London, included in the London version of *Monopoly* **[RL]**. For his twenty-fourth birthday, Lister and several friends embarked on a *Monopoly* board pub crawl across that city. Their first stop was Old Kent Road, where they ordered hot toddies for lunch **[N-INF]**.

- **"Old King Cole":** A British nursery rhyme about a merry king and his three fiddlers **[RL]**. While marooned on a backwards-running Earth, Rimmer commented on the frequency at which fifteen-year-old Lister and Cat masturbated, claiming more fiddling occurred in their quarters than in Old King Cole's court **[N-BCK]**.

- **Old Man Gower:** *See* Gower ("Old Man Gower")

- **Olfactory:** The second of three passwords needed to access personal profiles on the Diva-Droid website **[W-DIV]**.

  ***NOTE:*** *This password appeared on a special page located on the Jupiter Mining Corporation site.*

- **olfactory system:** A component of 4000 Series mechanoids, used to analyze the air quality and chemical composition of the unit's surroundings. The component, located in an android's nose section, was susceptible to overload if presented with a high enough concentration of odiferous material, causing it to explode **[N-BTL]**.

- **Olin, Chief:** The police chief at Jake Bullet's precinct in a fascist society in an alternate universe **[M-SMG1.14(c1)]**. Chief Odin ran a sting operation to arrest Bullet, who had agreed to keep the existence of a top-secret mind-control project from the government **[M-SMG2.9(c4)]**.

- **Olympus Mons' terraforming reactors:** A cluster of machinery around Mars' Olympus Mons volcano that converted the Martian environment to make it habitable for humans. The Bradbury Botanical Research Station was located near the reactors **[G-RPG]**.

- **"Om":** One of the earliest songs Lister wrote for his first band, Smeg and the Heads, which consisted solely of the word "Om" repeated multiple times in a droning voice. In an alternate timeline in which Lister was the youngest billionaire on Earth, he recorded the song and personally bought three million copies, instantly launching it to first place on the charts **[T-SER3.5]**. When a demo of the song was played on hospital radio, three patients came out of comas and asked to leave the facility **[T-SER8.5]**.

- **Omni-zone:** An area outside space-time in which the seven universes were joined together by a network of immense, cable-like pathways. Holly predicted the Omni-zone's existence after an intelligence-compression experiment increased his IQ to more than twelve thousand.

  While attempting to break free of a black hole's gravitational pull by performing a slingshot around the singularity at hyper-light speed, the *Red Dwarf* crew temporarily saw the Omni-zone as six infinitely large tubes connected to a spinning disc of light. After a polymorph killed Lister, Holly devised a plan to send the crew through the Omni-zone to bury him and Kochanski on Earth in Universe 3—where time ran backwards—so that their lives would be restored **[N-BTL]**.

  In one reality, the crew traversed the Omni-zone thirty-four years later to retrieve Lister from the backwards-running Earth, but missed their window to return home, becoming stranded in this reality for another ten years. The crew, now a decade younger, finally returned to their own universe **[N-BCK]**.

  In another reality, the crew rescued Lister and Kochanski, then attempted to return to their own universe via the Omni-zone but miscalculated. Thus, the group ended up in a parallel dimension in which the Earth ship *Mayflower* had crashed after a malfunction propelled it into the Omni-zone **[N-LST]**.

  ***NOTE:*** *The back cover of the novel* Better Than Life *mistakenly claimed there were six known universes, not seven. Both numbers contradicted established* Red Dwarf *lore, however—especially episodes 4.5 ("Dimension Jump") and 7.2 ("Stoke Me a Clipper"), which showed that there were an infinite number of universes through which Ace Rimmer had traveled and*

**PREFIX**
**RL:** Real life

**T-: Television Episodes**
**SER:** Television series
**IDW:** "Identity Within"
**USA1:** Unaired U.S. pilot
**USA2:** Unaired U.S. demo

**R-: *The Bodysnatcher Collection***
**SER:** Remastered episodes
**BOD:** "Bodysnatcher"
**DAD:** "Dad"
**FTH:** "Lister's Father"
**INF:** "Infinity Patrol"
**END:** "The End" (original assembly)

**N-: Novels**
**INF:** *Infinity Welcomes Careful Drivers*
**BTL:** *Better Than Life*
**LST:** *Last Human*
**BCK:** *Backwards*
**OMN:** *Red Dwarf Omnibus*

**M-: Magazines**
**SMG:** *Smegazine*

**W-: Websites**
**OFF:** Official website
**NAN:** *Prelude to Nanarchy*
**AND:** *Androids*
**DIV:** Diva-Droid
**DIB:** Duane Dibbley

**CRP:** Crapola
**GEN:** Geneticon
**LSR:** Leisure World Intl.
**JMC:** Jupiter Mining Corporation
**AIT:** *A.I. Today*
**HOL:** HoloPoint

**G-: Roleplaying Game**
**RPG:** *Core Rulebook*
**BIT:** *A.I. Screen Extra Bits* booklet
**SOR:** *Series Sourcebook*
**OTH:** Other RPG material

*recruited replacements.*

*The novel* Last Human *fixed this problem by explaining that while the Omni-zone contained the entrances to seven universes, it also provided access to an infinite number of rejected timelines created by the countless decisions made throughout every individual's life.*

- **Omrisk, Ned:** The director of HoloPoint, a company specializing in hologrammic technologies, circa 2260 **[W-HOL]**.

- **Onassis, Jacqueline Lee Kennedy ("Jackie"):** The wife of U.S. President John F. Kennedy and the First Lady from 1961 until her husband's assassination in 1963 **[RL]**. In an alternate timeline, JFK survived the assassination attempt due to the interference of *Starbug 1*'s crew and went on to have a well-publicized affair with the mistress of Mafia boss Sam Giancana, after which he was impeached in 1964 and imprisoned the following year, with Jacqueline ending their marriage **[T-SER7.1]**.

- **onboard lexicon:** A vocabulary database built into 4000 Series mechanoids. Kryten accessed his onboard lexicon during the *Red Dwarf* crew's encounter with the Brefewino GELF tribe, whose word for "cat" was synonymous with "four-limbed Crispy Bar snack" **[T-IDW]**.

- **One, The:** The title bestowed upon the final agonoid worthy to kill Lister, the last member of the human species. Many agonoids fought and died to become The One, until only one remained: Djuhn'Keep **[N-BCK]**.

- **one-armed bandit:** A slang term for a slot machine **[RL]**. While consoling Lister after his arm was amputated, Cat cited the one-armed bandit as an extraordinary one-armed individual, unaware it was just a machine—and not very extraordinary **[T-SER7.8]**.

- **"one-armed man, the":** A nickname by which a mysterious character on the television show *The Fugitive* (the murderer of Richard Kimble's wife) was known throughout the series' history **[RL]**. While consoling Lister after his arm was amputated, Kochanski cited this character as an extraordinary one-armed individual, forgetting that the character was a murderer—and fictional **[T-SER7.8]**.

  ***NOTE:** Although the one-armed man's name was never definitively confirmed on the TV series, he was identified as both Fred Johnson and Gus Evans. The 1993 film renamed him Fredrick Sykes, while the 2000 revival series called him Ben Charnquist.*

- **one-third-gravity golf:** A version of golf played on Venus in one of Ace Rimmer's universes. Similar to standard golf, this variant took advantage of the planet's reduced gravitational pull. Admiral Tranter shared a passion for this game with his estranged wife; after retiring from the *Wildfire* Project, he retreated to his condominium on Venus, where he hoped to reconcile with his wife and revisit his favorite pastime **[N-BCK]**.

- ***Oops, That's Groovy Channel 27 News!*:** A bloopers-style television program scheduled for broadcast by Krytie TV on October 16, featuring outtakes from the popular news network **[X-CAL]**.

- **Operation Khazi:** A name that the *Red Dwarf* crew dubbed a mission to retrieve the ship's toilet block after Holly inadvertently ejected the entire section into space **[B-LOG]**.

- **Operation Sizzle:** The name that Pree, a computer system installed aboard *Red Dwarf* to replace Holly, dubbed her plan to fly the mining ship into a star. After ejecting Lister—whose return to Earth had been the basis of the vessel's prior mission—into space, Pree altered the ship's course to plunge it into the core of the nearest sun **[T-SER10.2]**.

- **Ops Room:** *See* Obs Room

- **optical system:** A system built into the heads of 4000 Series mechanoids, enabling them to view their surroundings. Features of the optical system included zoom, split screen, slow motion and Quantel (**Quan**tised **Tel**evision). Kryten missed these features after a DNA-modifying machine changed him into a human **[T-SER4.2]**.

- **optical tanks:** A component of MkIV Titanica Fish Droids, such as Lister's robot goldfish Lennon and McCartney, enabling them to see their surroundings **[M-SMG2.4(c5)]**.

- **optic tract:** A component of 4000 Series mechanoids' optical system that, upon receiving a download from its sentiment disc, gave the mech the sensation of having a tear in its eye. Kryten experienced this sensation while watching Cat try to jump onto a stack of magazines in order to impress a she-Cat named Ora Tanzil **[T-IDW]**.

- **Oracle Boy:** A small, redheaded child whom Lister imagined encountering on a bus while trapped in an elation squid hallucination **[T-SER9.2]**.

  ***NOTE:** The end credits of* Back to Earth, Part II *listed the character as "Boy on the Bus" to avoid revealing that the episode took place in a hallucination; this was changed to "Oracle Boy" for the combined Director's Cut of the episodes.*

- **Oracle Girl:** A small, redheaded child whom Lister imagined encountering on a bus while trapped in an elation squid hallucination. This girl, an avid fan of the TV show *Red Dwarf*, told Lister she believed Kochanski had left on her own accord after watching his slow decline, and that Kryten had lied about her death to spare his feelings **[T-SER9.2]**.

  ***NOTE:** The end credits of* Back to Earth, Part II *listed the character as "Girl on the Bus" to avoid revealing that the episode took place in a hallucination; this was changed to "Oracle Girl" for the combined Director's Cut of the episodes.*

- **orange:** A round, orange-colored citrus fruit **[RL]**. Lister used an orange as a prop while trying to teach Kryten how to lie, by calling it a melon. Eventually, the mechanoid proved he could fib, calling the fruit a red and blue striped golfing umbrella **[T-SER4.1]**.

- **orange ice pops:** A frozen product supplied to the JMC mining ship *Red Dwarf*, and one of Captain Hollister's favorite desserts. Pete, a sparrow converted into a *Tyrannosaurus rex* by a time wand, devoured the ship's entire supply—four hundred crates—after eating cow vindaloo that the crew had made to get Pete sick so they could retrieve the wand, which the animal had swallowed. This, along with tons of other junk food items that it had consumed, caused the animal to become violently sick, culminating in a vomiting and diarrhea attack—with Hollister caught in the wake **[T-SER8.7]**.

- **orang-u-rottweiler:** A cross between an orangutan and a Rottweiler, the result of genetic engineering experiments. Such creatures were a common sight in cities around Earth's solar system **[B-SUR]**.

- **"Orbit":** A phrase on a chart that Rimmer created to translate markings on a mysterious pod Holly found adrift in space, which he thought were an alien language—but which actually spelled out "*Red Dwarf* Garbage Pod," eroded away after many years of spaceflight **[T-SER1.4]**.

- ***Oregon*:** A Space Corps vessel on which a massive rabbit population infected the entire crew with myxomatosis. The outbreak was caused by a glitch in the source code of the ship's AI computer, who collected the rabbits because it liked their ears and fluffy tails **[W-AIT]**. Captain Hollister cited the *Oregon* while reprimanding Lister for bringing an unquarantined animal aboard *Red Dwarf* **[T-SER1.1]**.

- **ore sample pod:** A small craft used to transport mineral samples. *Starbug* shuttles were outfitted with several such pods, into which the crew loaded ore before initiating a homing procedure to return the craft to its mothership. After a moonquake on Rimmer's psi-moon wrecked *Starbug* and left Kryten incapacitated, the mechanoid constructed a rescue bot from his hand and right eye, instructing it to find an ore sample pod and return to *Red Dwarf* to summon assistance **[T-SER5.3]**.

- **Original Gravity 1042°:** A premium lager served at the Sick Parrot Public House, a drinking establishment in the universe known as Alternative 6829/B **[M-SMG1.8(c4)]**.

- **Orion:** A planet that Lister once visited while on shore leave, where he drank a yard of vindaloo sauce and met a Space Corps nurse at a club called The Crazy Astro **[T-SER7.1(e)]**.

  ***NOTE:** In the real world, Orion is the name of a*

*constellation, a nebula and a spiral arm of the Milky Way Galaxy, but not a planet.*

- **Orodite:** A material used to make prison bars, due to its ability to absorb blasts from energy weapons, and thereby become stronger. The cage holding Ora Tanzil, a she-Cat captured in GELF territory, utilized bars made of Orodite. Cat failed to sense this as he blasted the bars with bazookoid fire, but Ora, knowing the material's properties, took the charger leads from the bazookoid and attached them to the bars, turning them to ash and allowing her to escape **[T-IDW]**.

- **Oslo:** The capital and most populated city of Norway **[RL]**. Olaf Petersen once purchased a pair of Smart Shoes to take him home after nights of heavy drinking. After awhile, the shoes became bored with this routine and began wandering about on their own accord, with an inebriated Petersen in tow. On one occasion, he passed out in Oslo and awoke the next morning in Burma **[T-SER2.5]**.

  ***NOTE:** That would entail a trip of roughly 6,300 miles (10,140 kilometers), according to Google Maps, which means it would have taken Petersen nearly eighty-five days to traverse that distance (assuming the Smart Shoes walked at a normal human pace)—a testament to the extent of his inebriation.*

- **Osmond, Don:** A member of the Ganymedian Mafia and the leader of the Osmond crime family on Mimas. Several members of the family reported to him, including Little Jimmy. When astro Dutch van Oestrogen double-crossed the Mafia during a drug deal, Don Osmond ordered his minions to take him out **[M-SMG2.5(c6)]**.

  ***NOTE:** This character's name spoofed that of singer Donny Osmond, as well as the Italian honorific "*Don,*" often used to signify an organized crime boss in films (for example, in* The Godfather*).*

- **Osmond, James Arthur ("Jimmy"):** An American actor and singer, and the youngest member of the musical group The Osmonds. He made several appearances on British television during the early twenty-first century **[RL]**. While attempting to piece together clues surrounding a four-day gap in the crew's memory, Holly maintained that everything had a logical explanation except for Jimmy Osmond **[T-SER2.3]**.

  ***NOTE:** The DVD captions for the Czech Republic version of the series changed Jimmy Osmond to "the number of members of the Kelly Family," a reference to an Irish-American rock and folk group, due to Osmond not being well-known in that country.*

- **Osmond, Little Jimmy:** A member of the Osmond Family, a criminal organization within the Ganymedian Mafia on Mimas. Little Jimmy, along with several goons, searched for Dutch van Oestrogen, a mining astro who double crossed them during a drug deal **[M-SMG2.4(c2)]**. Little Jimmy reported to Don Osmond, the Mafia's leader. After failing to nab van Oestrogen at a body swap shop, Little Jimmy was ordered to kill the astro, as well as Trixie LaBouche, a sex worker who inadvertently became involved when Dutch hijacked her body **[M-SMG2.5(c6)]**. Trixie, however, killed the hitman at the Mimas Spaceport **[M-SMG2.6(c4)]**.

  ***NOTE:** This character's name spoofed that of Jimmy Osmond, the younger member of family musical group The Osmonds.*

- **Osmond Family, the:** A crime family belonging to the Ganymedian Mafia. Dutch van Oestrogen double-crossed members of the Osmond Family during a drug deal on Mimas **[M-SMG2.3(c4)]**.

  ***NOTE:** The crime family's name was an ironic reference to musical group The Osmonds, long-standing members of the Mormon Church.*

- **Osmonds, The:** An American family musical group, circa the late twentieth century **[RL]**. When a polymorph invaded *Red Dwarf*, Rimmer quoted the "Rimmer Directive," which stated "Never tangle with anything that's got more teeth than the entire Osmond family" **[T-SER3.3]**.

  ***NOTE:** The DVD captions for the Czech Republic version of the series changed this reference to the Addams Family, a macabre cast of characters created by American cartoonist Charles Addams, due to the Osmonds not being well-known in that country.*

- **Ostrog, Gilbert St. John McAdam:** Lister's head butler in an alternate timeline in which Lister became the world's youngest billionaire by inventing the Tension Sheet. Ostrog was forced to take the position after losing the Butler's Sack Race and Salad Fork Challenge at a butler convention in Swindon, England **[W-OFF]**.

Sporting a mustache and ponytail, Gilbert was tasked with keeping Lister apprised of the goings-on around his mansion, Xanadu, including updates on the construction of a champagne-urinating statue in the courtyard **[T-SER3.5]**. His prior education included butler training school, after which he spent three years cleaning up after royal corgis before taking the Lister position. During his employment with Lister, Ostrog had a secret affair with his wife, Sabrina Mulholland-Jjones **[W-OFF]**.

- **Ostrog, Quentin:** A man who once barricaded himself in a tanning salon for 103 hours in 2309 **[W-OFF]**.

  *NOTE: "Ostrog" is a Russian term for a small wooden barricade or fort. It is unknown whether Quentin and Gilbert Ostrog were related.*

- **Oswald, Lee Harvey:** A former U.S. Marine believed to have assassinated U.S. President John F. Kennedy from the sixth floor of the Texas School Book Depository in Dallas, Texas, on November 22, 1963 **[RL]**. His hobbies included playing the glockenspiel **[G-SOR]**.

  While traveling through time in search of curries, the *Starbug 1* crew inadvertently thwarted the JFK assassination by materializing on the depository's fifth floor, where the shooter was originally positioned, and accidentally pushing Oswald out an open window. Realizing they had altered the timeline by allowing Kennedy to live, they tried to undo the damage by traveling to an earlier point in time and forcing Oswald up to the sixth floor. This did not rectify the problem, however, as the steeper angle threw off Oswald's aim, merely wounding the president. This forced the crew to devise another solution: convincing JFK to go back in time with them and become his own assassin, from behind a grassy knoll **[T-SER7.1]**.

- **otrazone:** *See* outrozone

- **"Ourob Oros":** A phrase handwritten on the side of a cardboard box containing an infant Dave Lister, which Lister himself left under a grav-pool table at The Aigburth Arms pub in Liverpool, England. The bartender misread the words as "Our Rob or Ross," thinking they indicated the baby's name. However, the phrase actually referred to Ouroboros, signifying the everlasting circle of life, since Lister had come back in time with his infant self to set the events of his life in motion **[T-SER7.3]**.

- **Ouroboros:** A symbol signifying infinity or the everlasting circle of life, symbolized by a serpent in a circular pattern, eating its own tail **[RL]**. The Ouroboros brand of batteries was thus touted as being "everlasting" **[T-SER7.3]**. In addition to power cells, Ouroboros also produced emergency generators and subspace comlinks, all of which utilized dynamic tachyon fusion (DynaTach) technology **[G-RPG]**.

  When a crate bearing the Ouroboros name and logo was transported from an alternate reality to *Starbug 1*, Lister realized that the unborn baby gestating inside an *in vitro* tube he gave to Kochanski was, in fact, himself. Eighteen months later, he thus brought the child back in time and left himself under a grav-pool table in Liverpool, thereby completing the everlasting cycle of his own life **[T-SER7.3]**.

- **"Our Rob or Ross":** A misinterpretation by the bartender of The Aigburth Arms of the markings on the side of a box in which Lister was found as an infant. The crate actually said "Ouroboros," which Lister's future self had written as "Ourob Oros" **[T-SER7.3]**.

  *NOTE: Despite the bartender's misinterpretation, Lister was named "Dave."*

- **Outland Revenue:** A government agency tasked with the collection of taxes. Included in a postal pod brought aboard *Red Dwarf* was a letter addressed to Rimmer, stating he owed 8,500 to Outland Revenue. Later, as Rimmer played the total-immersion game *Better Than Life*, his brain refused to accept his good fortune and created a simulation of an Outland Revenue collector, who presented Arnold with a bill for eighteen thousand, threatening bodily harm if he neglected to pay it **[T-SER2.2]**.

  *NOTE: The currency of Rimmer's tax bill was not indicated. Outland Revenue was named after Inland Revenue, a department of the U.K. government that, until 2005, was responsible for the collection of taxes within the British Empire.*

- **Outland Territories:** A section of Earth's solar system serviced by Diva-Droid International **[G-RPG]**.

- **outrozone:** A compound that was highly addictive to mechanoids. Side effects included circuit board corruption and a severe lag during long-term memory retrieval **[T-SER7.6]**. It was manufactured by Malpractice Medical & Scispec and distributed by Crapola Inc. **[G-RPG]** Able, a 4000 Series mechanoid and Kryten's technical brother, was addicted to outrozone **[T-SER7.6]**.

  ***NOTE:*** *This spelling appeared on the official website; the DVD captions for episode 7.6 ("Beyond a Joke") spelled the compound's name as "otrazone," while the* Red Dwarf Programme Guide *spelled it as "ultrazone."*

- **override code:** A code used to bypass the safety settings on *Starbug 1*'s thermostat. Kryten input the override code to overload the ship's generators in order to prevent Kochanski from bathing in Lister's quarters **[T-SER7.4]**.

- **Oxfam:** An international confederation of organizations dedicated to finding solutions for poverty and other injustices **[RL]**. Kryten wondered why most women were not afflicted with nostril hair, aside from those who worked at Oxfam shops **[T-SER7.3]**. When Kryten reverted Kochanski's hair and clothes to a previous state via a time wand, Cat remarked that she resembled Lady Godiva let loose in an Oxfam shop **[T-SER8.6(d)]**.

- **Oxford Street:** A road in Western London, included in the London version of *Monopoly* **[RL]**. For his twenty-fourth birthday, Lister and several friends embarked on a *Monopoly* board pub crawl across London. Their last stop was Oxford Street, where they ordered saké, after which Lister bought a *Monopoly* board since no one could recall the next square **[N-INF]**.

- **oxy-generation unit:** A component aboard small spacecraft, also known as an oxy-gen or O/G unit, used to create breathable air. Certain models were distributed by Crapola Inc. and utilized caustic atmospheric filtering technology **[G-RPG]**.

  *Starbug 1*'s O/G unit became damaged beyond repair after an encounter with a Space Corps external enforcement vehicle. Landing on a GELF moon, the crew traded with the locals for a replacement. The GELFs offered a unit under the condition that Lister marry the tribal chief's daughter, Hackhackhackachhachhachach **[T-SER6.4]**.

  ***NOTE:*** *Since the crew often found themselves in danger of running out of oxygen prior to this episode, the O/G unit was presumably installed afterwards—possibly by the rogue simulants who updated the vessel in episode 6.3 ("Gunmen of the Apocalypse") or, more likely, while the crew was looting derelict spacecrafts.*

- **oxygen recycler:** A *Red Dwarf* system that circulated and filtered breathable air aboard the mining vessel, making it usable for longer durations. The oxygen recycler was among the few systems left operational during a ship-wide power shutdown, using the ship's emergency battery reserves **[T-SER4.4]**.

- **oysters:** A common name for several groups of bivalve mollusks living in marine or brackish habitats; humans consumed some types of oysters, either cooked or raw **[RL]**. Kryten prepared four dozen oysters for Rimmer after the latter swapped minds with Lister and over-indulged his body **[T-SER3.4]**.

P

PETERSEN, OLAF, CATERING OFFICER

- **P22:** A public school. A child wearing a P22 T-shirt visited the pleasure planet GELFWorld and was consumed by a spider-shaped GELF during a planet-wide rebellion **[M-SMG2.2(c4)]**.

- **PAC-9000:** A type of particle accelerator cannon developed by Bloodlust Arms and distributed by Crapola Inc. via its annual *SCABBY* catalog. The weapon fired clusters of super-heated tachyon particles, and had a range of 2 kilometers (1.24 miles) **[G-RPG]**.

- **Padre:** *See* Cat, Father ("Padre")

- **Page, Jimmy:** An English musician and songwriter, and lead guitarist of the rock group Led Zeppelin **[RL]**. While incarcerated in the Hole, *Red Dwarf*'s solitary-confinement cell, Lister regaled Rimmer with stories of playing rock songs using a kazoo wedged between his buttocks. The guitar solo from "Stairway to Heaven," he said, required two kazoos to recreate Page's double-headed guitar work **[T-SER8.6(d)]**.

- **Palace, The:** A cinema aboard *Red Dwarf* that the skutters frequented to watch movies **[M-SMG1.12(c4)]**.

- **Palladium-core nano-torque sequencing unit:** A device or component, function unknown. The Model 2 upgrade featured Planck scale microsensors and dual-lifter camshafts **[G-SOR]**.

- **Pallister:** A character in the alternate-reality video game *Gumshoe*, a film-noir-type detective simulation. The game centered around the murder of Pallister, planned by a femme fatale named Loretta, but carried out by her twin sister Maxime. Loretta took the rap for the murder anyway, knowing she had the perfect alibi, thanks to Philip, the game's detective and main playable character **[T-SER6.3]**.

- **Palmer:** A member of *Red Dwarf*'s Z-Shift prior to the cadmium II disaster **[N-INF]**.

    ***NOTE:** Palmer presumably died during the cadmium II explosion. It is unknown whether the nanobots resurrected Palmer in Series VIII.*

- **Pan:** A Greek deity of hunting and music, depicted with the lower body and horns of a goat and the upper half of a human **[RL]**. When Tunbridge Wells' five hundred pilgrims were sent to pray for the end of a meteor storm ravaging their city, a sergeant in the group claimed they were headed to a shrine dedicated to Pan. Others disagreed, and when a knight struck the Pannite down, this sparked a religious war that wiped out the entire pilgrim crew **[M-SMG1.14(c2)]**.

- **Panasonic:** A Japanese electronics corporation specializing in consumer electronics **[RL]**. While trapped in an elation squid hallucination, the *Red Dwarf* crew imagined being at a twenty-first-century department store that sold Panasonic brand televisions **[T-SER9.2]**.

- **pan-dimensional liquid beast:** A creature from the Mogidon Cluster that exhibited the ability to exist in multiple dimensions. Once such creature attacked the *Starbug 1* crew on Christmas day as they pursued the stolen *Red Dwarf* **[T-SER6.6]**.

- **panic chip:** A component built into 4000 Series mechanoids enabling them to experience a sense of overwhelming fear when endangered. Kryten utilized his panic chip while trapped in a transmogrification machine, when he realized he was not immune to the device's effects due to a small amount of organic matter in his brain **[T-SER4.2]**.

- **panic circuits:** A hardware system built into 4000 Series mechanoids that simulated fear during moments of danger. Kryten engaged his panic circuits, including his panic chip, while trapped in a transmogrification machine **[T-SER4.2]**.

- **panic-like-a-headless-chicken mode:** A feature built into 4000 Series mechanoids that enabled them to frantically run around and panic in certain situations in which hope seemed lost **[N-BCK]**.

- **pantheist:** A follower of Pantheism, the belief that the universe and nature were equated with divinity **[RL]**. Lister told Kryten he was a pantheist as the two discussed the mechanoid's belief in Silicon Heaven **[T-SER3.6]**.

- **"Pants Down Over Poland!":** The title of issue sixteen of the *Robbie Rocket Pants* comic book **[G-BIT]**.

- ***Parallaxis: Defenders of the Galaxy*:** One of Duane Dibbley's favorite console video games **[G-RPG]**.

- **Para-mech:** A medical droid featured on the television soap opera *Androids*. Para-mechs rushed to the scene when Jaysee attempted to blow up Gary's car while he and Kelly were in the back seat **[M-SMG2.2(c3)]**.

- **Paranoia:** An individual whom Lister's mind conjured while suffering from mutated pneumonia, which he contracted upon entering the radiation-contaminated Officers' Block. This entity manifested the negative side of Lister's psyche that felt he was worthless and prevented him from taking risks. Paranoia belittled Lister at every opportunity, often siding with Rimmer's opinion of him—until another corporeal hallucination, Confidence, fed him into *Red Dwarf*'s waste grinder and ejected him into space **[T-SER1.5]**.

- **Paranoia:** An aspect of Rimmer's personality made flesh on a psi-moon configured according to his psyche. After Arnold's shipmates rescued him from the moon, Paranoia and other solidifications of Rimmer's negative traits were left behind to battle his positive aspects, including Courage, Charity, Honour and Self-Esteem **[M-SMG2.7(c2)]**.

- **Parfum by Lanstrom:** A line of perfumes developed by Hildegarde Lanstrom. These fragrances incorporated positive viruses created by the doctor to endow wearers with certain attributes. Products included Sexual Magnetism, Luck, Good Mood, Temper Tantrum and Freckle **[X-CAL]**.

- **Paris Stompers, the:** A zero-gee football team of the European Conference. Henri Pascal once played as the team's Motion Interferer. Aboard *Red Dwarf,* Lister watched a video commentary of a game between the Stompers and the London Jets **[R-BOD(s)]**.

- **Parker, Charles Jr. ("Charlie," "Yardbird"):** An American jazz saxophonist and composer who became an icon of the 1940s' hipster subculture and the 1950s' Beat Generation **[RL]**. While trapped in an addictive version of *Better Than Life*, Cat entertained himself in his golden castle with a hand-picked seven-piece band, which included Parker on sax **[N-INF]**.

- **Parker Knoll:** A British furniture manufacturer specializing in high-end domestic furniture **[RL]**. As a youth, Lister practiced removing women's bras by wrapping one around an armchair and unhooking it with one hand; thus, in his adult years, the sight of a Parker Knoll product made him horny **[T-SER7.5]**.

- **Parking Level 2:** A parking area located on Mimas. Dutch van Oestrogen double-crossed the Ganymedian Mafia during a drug deal on this level **[M-SMG2.3(c4)]**.

- **Parkinson:** A crewmember aboard the Space Corps vessel *Oregon* **[W-OFF]**.

- **Parkur:** A mechanoid whom Kryten once knew aboard the *Neutron Star*. To entertain the three survivors of the *Nova 5* crash, Kryten did impressions of Parkur—which fell flat since none of the women were familiar with the mechanoid **[N-INF]**.

- **Parrot's Bar:** A tropical-themed club on *Red Dwarf*'s G Deck. Kryten took Camille, a shapeshifting Pleasure GELF, on a date at this bar, after she revealed to him her true appearance **[T-SER4.1]**.

  ***NOTE:*** *Parrot's Bar was named after the movie* Casablanca, *which heavily influenced episode 4.1 ("Camille"). Kryten's quote, "We'll always have Parrot's" mirrored Humphrey Bogart's iconic line from that film, "We'll always have Paris."*

- **particle accelerator cannon:** A large firearm developed by Bloodlust Arms, which fired clusters of super-heated tachyons at a range of 2 kilometers (1.24 miles) **[G-RPG]**.

- **particle analyzer:** A handheld device designed to analyze particles **[W-OFF]**. Kryten used such a device to identify *Red Dwarf* after it had been commandeered and deconstructed by his nanobots **[T-SER7.8]**.

- **Pasadena Light Orchestra:** A musical ensemble whose wind section Lister compared to his hologrammic duplicate's backside **[R-BOD]**.

  ***NOTE:*** *This group was presumably named after the Pasadena Roof Orchestra, a popular contemporary British band specializing in music of the 1920s and '30s.*

- **Pascal, Henri:** A player on the Paris Stompers, a zero-gee football team in the European Conference. Pascal played the position of Motion Interferer **[R-BOD(s)]**.

- **Pass the Part:** A game developed by Colonel Mike O'Hagan, aimed at keeping crash survivors occupied and in good spirits, which he described in his *Space Corps Survival Manual* **[B-SUR]**.

- **Pat Cabs:** A taxi service on the Saturnian moon of Mimas **[M-SMG2.3(c4)]**.

- **Patel, Suzie:** A woman who worked behind the counter at the Taj Mahal Tandoori takeaway restaurant on Miranda, to whom Lister was attracted. She resembled a mix between Tina Turner and Kristine Kochanski, and smelled like a combination of shami kebabs, lime pickle and chicken vindaloo **[M-SMG1.6(c1)]**.

- **Path of Decency:** A dirt road on a psi-moon, located between the home of Mr. Flibble's step-parents and his grandmother's cottage. Tasked with delivering a pie to his granny, Flibble was told to stay on the path, which he immediately ignored. Due to his defiance, he found the cabin of the witch Hildegarde, inside which he discovered a potion that gave him hex vision **[M-SMG2.8(c4)]**.

- **patience circuits:** Components in cyborgs, such as Jake Bullet, enabling them to endure delay without care **[M-SMG1.7(a)]**.

- **Patton, General George S.:** An American military leader in charge of the 3rd and 7th Armies during World War II **[RL]**. Obsessed with war, Rimmer had many books on Patton, Julius Caesar and other famous military leaders in his library **[T-SER3.2]**.

  During his campaign, Patton visited an Italian field hospital, where his sinuses were drained. Centuries later, Rimmer purchased a vial of the sinal fluid during a trip through Europe, which he gave to Kryten as a gift during his last-day party **[T-SER3.6]**.

  Rimmer, like Patton, believed in reincarnation, and considered it unfortunate that, despite all his previous incarnations being brave warrior souls, he was an abject coward in his current life **[T-SER6.2]**.

  While trapped in an addictive version of *Better Than Life*, Rimmer believed he had returned to Earth and become incredibly wealthy, throwing lavish parties and playing *Risk* with Patton, Caesar and Napoleon Bonaparte **[N-INF]**.

- **Pawn Sacrifice:** Kryten's codename while carrying out a mission for Rimmer during the Wax War on Waxworld. After taking command of Hero World's waxdroid army, Arnold devised a plan to wipe out Villain World's forces by having his legion charge across a minefield separating the two regions. This tactic was meant as a diversion so Kryten and the Queen Victoria droid could sneak around the perimeter and into the enemy base to wipe out that camp's leaders. Following the attack, "Pawn Sacrifice" radioed "Iron Duke," (Rimmer) to report his mission's success, after which Rimmer told him to raise the thermostat and melt the remaining droids **[T-SER4.6]**.

- ***Pax Vert*:** A nuclear waste dump ship that sometimes deposited toxic material on Saturn's moon, Tethys. Olaf Petersen once booked passage aboard *Pax Vert* to partially make his way to Triton, where he had purchased a house. The vessel dropped the Dane off at Mimas, where he joined the *Red Dwarf* crew for the remainder of the voyage **[N-INF]**.

- **"Peace":** A word printed on a sticker affixed to Lister's guitar **[T-SER3.2]**.

- **Peach Surprise:** A recipe that Lister invented, which he registered with the Mimas Board of Trade—Lethal Substances Division. It consisted of a hollowed-out peach skin filled with chili sauce **[M-SMG1.2(a)]**.

- **Pearson, Bill:** A name on a skutter schematic featured on Diva-Droid's website **[W-DIV]**.

  ***NOTE:*** *Prop and model maker Bill Pearson worked on the redesigned skutters featured in Series VIII.*

- **Pemberton, Lewis:** Rimmer's previous bunkmate aboard *Red Dwarf*. Rimmer blamed Pemberton and others, including Lister, for holding him back from becoming an officer **[N-INF]**.

  ***NOTE:*** *Pemberton's first name was implied in the novel* Backwards*, as an alternate-reality version had the first name of Lewis. He presumably died during the cadmium II explosion. It is unknown whether the nanobots resurrected him in Series VIII.*

- **Pemberton, Lewis:** An officer aboard *Red Dwarf* in Ace Rimmer's universe. Pemberton bunked with Lister and persuaded him to better himself by taking night classes in mechanics. He was also instrumental in getting Lister and Kochanski back together after their breakup **[N-BCK]**.

- **penguin:** A flightless aquatic bird in the Spheniscidae family **[RL]**. After proving he could lie, Kryten told Lister that he had to take a penguin for a walk **[T-SER4.1]**.

- **Penguin, the:** A supervillain hand puppet in the universe known as Alternative 2X13/L. The Penguin—a version of Mr. Flibble—had hex vision and was the sidekick of the Conspirator (an analog to the Inquisitor), with whom he terrorized the city of Smegopolis. In 2315, the Penguin and his cohort attempted to rob the First National Bank of Smegopolis, defeating Catman, Robbie and Action Man before Ace Rimmer—who had taken the place of superhero Super-Ace due to the latter's vulnerability to human contact—subdued them **[M-SMG2.1(c3)]**.

  ***NOTE:** The Penguin was named after the DC Comics supervillain.*

- ***Penhalagen*:** A spaceship on which the Pleasure GELF Camille was a passenger. The *Penhalagen* suffered a fuel shortage, forcing the GELF to abandon ship in an escape vessel, which crashed onto a planetoid in a decaying orbit **[W-OFF]**.

- **"Pennsylvania 6-5000":** A song recorded in 1940 by Glenn Miller **[RL]**. Rimmer presumed that an unidentified craft the *Red Dwarf* crew encountered was most likely an alien vessel—possibly sent to return Miller, who had mysteriously vanished, and whom Rimmer dreaded would bore them with renditions of the song **[T-SER4.2]**.

- **pennycent:** A type of currency **[N-INF]**.

- **Pension, Doctor:** A person whom Cat hallucinated after bumping his head while retrieving food from a *Red Dwarf* cupboard. In the hallucination, Cat believed he was again Duane Dibbley, and that he was being taken to a man called Doctor Swan-Morton, who interrogated him regarding the deaths of Jake Bullet and Sebastian and William Doyle. The doctor then delivered him for torture to Doctors Maxwell, Pension and Fund—who were actually Lister, Rimmer and Kryten, attempting to revive Cat from his reverie **[M-SMG1.9(c1)]**.

- **penthouse suite:** A lavish accommodation on *Red Dwarf*'s A Deck, comprising sixteen rooms (9,000 square feet in total), with a gourmet chicken soup dispenser, Corinthian leather furniture, a team of skutters and a naughty French maid android named Fifi **[G-RPG]**. After rescuing a shapeshifting Pleasure GELF named Camille, Kryten prepared the penthouse suite as her quarters **[T-SER4.1]**.

- **Pentonville Road:** A road in North Central London, included in that city's version of *Monopoly* **[RL]**. For his twenty-fourth birthday, Lister and several friends embarked on a *Monopoly* board pub crawl across London. Their sixth stop was Pentonville Road, where they ordered bitter laced with rum and blackcurrant **[N-INF]**.

- **Peperami:** A pork sausage snack product sold in the United Kingdom **[RL]**. While searching a derelict garbage tanker, the *Red Dwarf* crew were ambushed by a mutated three-million-year-old Peperami—which Cat ate, eliminating the threat **[B-LOG]**.

  ***NOTE:** The book* Red Dwarf Log No. 1996 *misspelled the product's name as "Pepperami."*

- **Pepsi:** A carbonated soft drink manufactured by multinational food and beverage corporation PepsiCo **[RL]**. Pepsi's rival, Coca-Cola, commissioned several ships, including *Nova 5*, to induce 128 supergiant stars into going supernova. The purpose of this campaign was to create a three-word message—"Coke Adds Life!"—that would be visible day or night for five weeks from anywhere on Earth. According to Coke's advertising company, this would have buried Pepsi and ended the so-called "cola wars" forever **[N-INF]**.

- **peritonitis:** A condition causing an inflammation of the peritoneum, the thin membrane lining a person's abdominal wall **[RL]**. The gestalt entity Legion diagnosed Lister as being on the verge of peritonitis, then performed an immediate appendectomy on him where he stood **[T-SER6.2]**.

  ***NOTE:** Lister having his appendix removed twice is a popular example of discontinuity within the series. The novel* Last Human *fixed this problem by revealing that he was born with two of the vestigial organs.*

- **Perky:** A nickname that Rimmer called one of *Red Dwarf*'s skutters whom he declared utterly useless. Perky's fellow skutter received the name Pinky **[T-SER2.2]**.

**PREFIX**
**RL:** Real life

**T-: Television Episodes**
**SER:** Television series
**IDW:** "Identity Within"
**USA1:** Unaired U.S. pilot
**USA2:** Unaired U.S. demo

**R-: *The Bodysnatcher Collection***
**SER:** Remastered episodes
**BOD:** "Bodysnatcher"
**DAD:** "Dad"
**FTH:** "Lister's Father"
**INF:** "Infinity Patrol"
**END:** "The End" (original assembly)

**N-: Novels**
**INF:** *Infinity Welcomes Careful Drivers*
**BTL:** *Better Than Life*
**LST:** *Last Human*
**BCK:** *Backwards*
**OMN:** *Red Dwarf Omnibus*

**M-: Magazines**
**SMG:** *Smegazine*

**W-: Websites**
**OFF:** Official website
**NAN:** *Prelude to Nanarchy*
**AND:** *Androids*
**DIV:** Diva-Droid
**DIB:** Duane Dibbley

**CRP:** Crapola
**GEN:** Geneticon
**LSR:** Leisure World Intl.
**JMC:** Jupiter Mining Corporation
**AIT:** *A.I. Today*
**HOL:** HoloPoint

**G-: Roleplaying Game**
**RPG:** *Core Rulebook*
**BIT:** *A.I. Screen Extra Bits* booklet
**SOR:** *Series Sourcebook*
**OTH:** Other RPG material

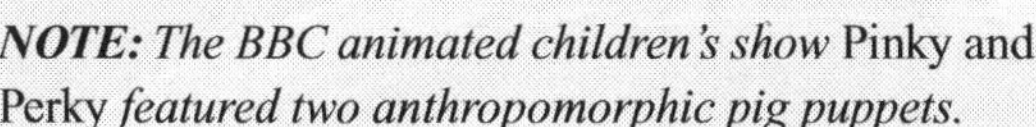

*NOTE: The BBC animated children's show* Pinky and Perky *featured two anthropomorphic pig puppets.*

- **"Perpetual Motion":** A phrase on a chart that Rimmer created to translate markings on a mysterious pod Holly found adrift in space, which he thought were an alien language—but which actually spelled out "*Red Dwarf* Garbage Pod," eroded away after many years of spaceflight **[T-SER1.4]**.

- **Perrier:** A popular brand of mineral water supplied by a natural spring in France **[RL]**. An operative for the Revolutionary Working Front terrorist organization was arrested while trying to poison the company's mineral spring. According to a news segment reporting the incident, Earth's entire middle class would have perished within a month had he succeeded **[T-SER2.2]**.

- **personal black box:** An audio recording device installed in Kryten 4000 Series mechanoids enabling them to record the circumstances surrounding emergency situations. If a mechanoid did not survive, others could replay the recording to ascertain what happened. After an accident on a psi-moon, Kryten made such a recording outlining what he knew about the incident and his location—which was nothing **[T-SER5.3]**.

- **personality chip:** A storage medium for archiving the personalities of the American mining ship *Red Dwarf*'s crew. A computer could access an individual's chip to revive him or her in the form of a hologram. After a cadmium II disaster killed the ship's crew, only Rimmer's personality chip survived the catastrophe **[T-USA1]**.

- **personality disk:** A storage medium used to store the personalities of *Red Dwarf*'s crew, also called a hologram disc. The ship's computer could access a person's personality disk in order to revive him or her as a hologram.

  Lister begged Rimmer for access to Kochanski's disk so he could have another date with her and find out how she felt about him. When Arnold refused, Lister took the Officer's Exam so he could earn a promotion and outrank him. Despite pretending to pass, Lister failed the exam, and the disk remained in Rimmer's custody.

  Rimmer hid the personality disks, but Lister found them with help from a corporeal version of his confidence. However, Rimmer had switched Kochanski's disk with his own, resulting in the creation of a second Rimmer hologram **[T-SER1.5]**.

- **personality surgery:** A medical procedure similar to plastic surgery, intended to alter a person's personality. Such surgeries included a sense of humor transplant, a selfishness tuck, a greed lift, a temper tightening and a libido shortening. While trapped in an addictive version of *Better Than Life*, Rimmer imagined that his bombshell ex-wife, Juanita Chicata, underwent these surgeries, which made her even more desirable to him **[N-BTL]**.

- **Perth:** The capital of Western Australia, and the region's largest and most populated city **[RL]**. Kochanski went to school in Perth, where she mastered the art of the rubber-band gun, able to hit a classmate's neck from ten desks away. This skill came in handy years later when, with the help of a luck virus, she immobilized a rampaging half-man, half-leopard mutant by shooting its right testicle with a rubber band **[N-LST]**.

- **Pessimism, Peter:** An individual whom Kryten's subconscious mind created as he battled the Apocalypse virus. In the dream, set in an Old West town, Pessimism, the local undertaker, tried to bury Cecil Central Processing Unit (representing Kryten's CPU) before he was dead, on orders from Pestilence Apocalypse **[N-BCK]**.

- **Pestilence:** *See* Apocalypse, Pestilence, Brother

- **Pete:** A nine-year-old sparrow found on a forest moon by an elderly prison inmate who served on *Red Dwarf*'s Canary team. Pete was injured when another inmate, Oswald "Kill Krazy" Blenkinsop, stepped on it. The elderly convict found the bird and took it back to *Red Dwarf*, where he nursed it back to health, earning the nickname "Birdman." The inmate named him Pete after actor Peter Beardsley, who had starred in a remake of *Casablanca* **[W-OFF]**.

  Birdman and Pete both died in *Red Dwarf*'s cadmium II accident, but were revived millions of years later by nanobots. Lister and Rimmer were incarcerated with them in the Hole, the mining ship's solitary-confinement cell, after misusing a programmable virus to peel potatoes.

  A short time later, Bob the skutter broke them out and led

**B-: Books**
**PRG:** *Red Dwarf Programme Guide*
**SUR:** *Red Dwarf Space Corps Survival Manual*
**PRM:** *Primordial Soup*
**SOS:** *Son of Soup*
**SCE:** *Scenes from the Dwarf*
**LOG:** *Red Dwarf Log No. 1996*
**RD8:** *Red Dwarf VIII*
**EVR:** *The Log: A Dwarfer's Guide to Everything*

**X-: Misc.**
**PRO:** Promotional materials, videos, etc.
**PST:** Posters at DJ XVII (2013)
**CAL:** 2008 calendar
**RNG:** Cell phone ringtones
**MOB:** Mobisode ("Red Christmas")
**CIN:** *Children in Need* sketch
**GEK:** *Geek Week* intros by Kryten
**TNG:** "Tongue-Tied" video
**XMS:** Bill Pearson's Christmas special pitch script
**XVD:** Bill Pearson's Christmas special pitch video
**OTH:** Other *Red Dwarf* appearances

**SUFFIX**
**DVD:**
**(d)** – Deleted scene
**(o)** – Outtake
**(b)** – Bonus DVD material (other)
**(e)** – Extended version

**SMEGAZINES:**
**(c)** – Comic
**(a)** – Article

**OTHER:**
**(s)** – Early/unused script draft
**(s1)** – Alternate version of script

them to Cat, Kryten and Kochanski on the cargo deck. By the time the trio arrived, Pete had passed away from the excitement of being free. Kryten tried to resuscitate the bird via a time wand, but an improper setting caused the animal to de-evolve into a *Tyrannosaurus rex*, which ate Birdman and attacked the others **[T-SER8.6]**.

During the chase, the dinosaur swallowed both the time wand and Bob. To get the device back, the crew created a massive bowl of cow vindaloo, which Pete consumed, along with several tons of ice cream and soda (to offset the spiciness). The dinosaur became violently ill, allowing Lister's group to retrieve the time wand from its diarrhea. Lister and Rimmer then used the wand to bring Birdman back to life and restore Pete to his sparrow form—but not before Pete laid an egg in the cargo bay, which hatched after the wand was destroyed **[T-SER8.7]**.

- **Pete:** A doughnut man who worked on the American mining ship *Red Dwarf*. After Lister survived the cadmium II explosion that killed that *Red Dwarf*'s crew, Holly reported that one personality chip had survived the disaster. Mistaking the chip for Pete's, the AI claimed it was someone Lister liked, but both were disappointed when they realized it contained Rimmer's personality **[T-USA1]**.

- ***Peter Perfect Plays Tuneful Tunes for Elderly Ladies*:** A recording in the Officers' Quarters of the "low" version of *Red Dwarf* **[T-SER5.5]**.

- **Peter Pessimism's Undertaker's Parlor:** A business that Kryten's subconscious mind created as he battled the Apocalypse virus. In the illusion, set in an Old West town, Pessimism led a procession to bury Cecil Central Processing Unit (representing Kryten's CPU), despite the fact that he was still alive, on orders from Pestilence Apocalypse **[N-BCK]**.

- **Petersen, Olaf:** A *Red Dwarf* crewmember in Ace Rimmer's universe. Since the cadmium II disaster never occurred in his reality, Petersen eventually made his way to his home on Triton, but soon sold the house and reenlisted with the mining ship. When *Red Dwarf* stopped at Europa, he was arrested for drunken disorderly conduct after running around singing the theme from *The Dambusters* while throwing glow-in-the-dark, urine-filled condoms at a Space Corps guard post; stealing a motorcycle and skidding obscenities into the ornamental garden; and stapling a guard's penis to his groin. Petersen awoke in a cell next to Dave "Spanners" Lister, whom he hadn't seen since the mechanic had been reassigned to Europa two years prior. Both men were then released into Ace Rimmer's custody **[N-BCK]**.

- **Petersen, Olaf, Catering Officer:** A Danish crewmember aboard *Red Dwarf*. Petersen was among Lister's closest friends, and was often seen drinking with his pals aboard ship **[T-SER1.1]**. He had several tattoos, including two on his right arm that read "Candy" and "Denmark Forever" **[T-SER1.3]**. Prior to his *Red Dwarf* tour of duty, Petersen worked as a fast food chip cook **[G-BIT]**. He joined *Red Dwarf* at the same time as Lister, using his commission to travel to Triton, where he had recently bought a house **[N-INF]**.

  Petersen died during the cadmium II disaster that killed the ship's crew except for Lister, who was in stasis at the time **[T-SER1.1]**. He was then resurrected, along with the rest of the ship's complement, when nanobots rebuilt *Red Dwarf* **[T-SER8.1]**.

  ***NOTE:** Olaf's surname was spelled "Peterson" in the credits of some episodes, but "Petersen" in other episodes' credits, as well as on the official site and in other sources. In the first-draft script of the pilot episode ("The End"), published in the* Red Dwarf Omnibus, *he was said to be a flight engineer, but this was changed to catering officer onscreen.*

- **Petersen's Persuasive:** The name that Olaf Petersen gave to moonshine he produced from a homemade still aboard *Red Dwarf*, due to the beverage's "persuasive" properties. If one were sober, he claimed, it would persuade that person to be drunk, while if the drinker were female, it would persuade her to find Lister attractive **[W-OFF]**.

- **Pete Tranter's sister:** A sibling of Pete Tranter, an acquaintance of Lister during his youth. Lister lusted after Pete's sister throughout puberty, despite never learning her name. Years later, while Lister was stuck on an asteroid in Psiren territory, one of the telepathic creatures used her image to seduce him. He initially resisted, but gave in to her lusty nature, narrowly escaping certain death when another Psiren, posing as Kryten, impaled the first with a spear in a bid to take Lister for itself **[T-SER6.1]**.

- **Petrovitch, First Technician:** A *Red Dwarf* crewmember in charge of A-Shift. His bunkmate was named Hollerbach. When Petrovitch and Rimmer took an Astronavigation Exam together, Petrovitch passed, while Arnold wrote "I am a fish" hundreds of times and passed out. Rimmer thus resented Petrovich and spread rumors that he was a drug dealer.

  Petrovitch died during *Red Dwarf*'s cadmium II explosion. Years later, Rimmer discovered that Petrovitch had actually been smuggling and selling illegal copies of the addictive virtual-reality game *Better Than Life*, after Cat found the man's stash in his quarters **[N-INF]**.

  ***NOTE:*** *It is unknown whether the nanobots resurrected Petrovitch in Series VIII.*

- **Petson:** A disciple of Cloister the Stupid, along with Chen and Selby, according to the Cat Bible. In chapters six and seven of the Holy Book, the disciples were said to have shared a meal with Cloister, during which they drank lager and were told of their impending demise **[M-SMG2.4(a)]**.

  ***NOTE:*** *The name "Petson" was the Cat People's misrepresentation of Olaf Petersen.*

- **Pet Translator:** A product sold by Crapola Inc. that, when attached to the collar of a dog or cat, could translate the animal's vocalizations into English with a thirty-seven percent accuracy rating. The translator did not work on hamsters, goldfish, horses, cows, pigs, snakes, opossums, cockroaches or Sea Monkeys. Manufactured in Taiwan, it sold for $£22.99 **[W-CRP]**.

- **petulance:** A rogue emotion purged from Kryten's hard drive by the Data Doctor, a program for restoring a mechanoid's personality to factory settings, when Captain Hollister subjected Kryten to a psychotropic simulation **[T-SER8.2]**.

- **Peugeot:** A French automobile manufacturer **[RL]**. Peugeot temporarily merged with motorcycle maker Harley Davidson, resulting in the Harley-Peugeot "Le Hog Cosmique" space bike **[G-SOR]**.

- **Pfeiffer, Michelle:** An American actor known for such movies as *Scarface, Dangerous Liaisons* and *The Fabulous Baker Boys* **[RL]**. To reduce the side effects of an affliction caused by his sexual appetite, Cat watched holo-slides of Pfeiffer from the movie *Batman 2* **[T-IDW]**.

  ***NOTE:*** *Michelle Pfeiffer portrayed Catwoman in Tim Burton's second Batman film, which was titled* Batman Returns, *not* Batman 2.

- **PG TIP:** The license plate number of Brook's car in the television soap opera *Androids* **[M-SMG1.10(c2)]**.

- **phaser frequency 4-3-4:** A particular frequency required to re-establish a hyperway connection between the prime universe and Kochanski's dimension through a temporal rip **[T-SER7.3]**.

- **phasing comet:** A type of comet in deep space, which Cat described as "a shiny thing with a long, silvery glimmery thing behind it." The *Starbug 1* crew encountered a phasing comet while searching for a dimensional rip through which to return Kochanski to her own reality **[T-SER7.5]**.

- **Pherson, Mamie:** A barmaid in a lounge on Europa in one of Ace Rimmer's universes. Mamie asked Ace to throw a fight with Space Corps recruit Billy Joe Epstein as a favor, in order to help build the pilot's confidence so he could pass his last flight test. Unbeknownst to Epstein, who was too afraid to ask her out, Mamie fancied him **[N-BCK]**.

- **Philip:** The main playable character in the alternate-reality video game *Gumshoe*, a film-noir-type detective simulation. Lister played the game as this character several times. The goal was to turn the game's femme fatale, Loretta, over to the cops and wind up with the heroine, but after several playthroughs, Lister decided it was more fun to end up with Loretta **[T-SER6.3]**.

- **Philosophy Arms, The:** A virtual bar Lister and Holly visited while in the heuristic neural net of a derelict research platform. Holly entered the network to rescue Lister, who had become trapped by one of the station's wetware interfaces. In order to keep Lister focused so she could lead him to safety, Holly took him to the virtual establishment to get drunk **[M-SMG1.11(c2)]**.

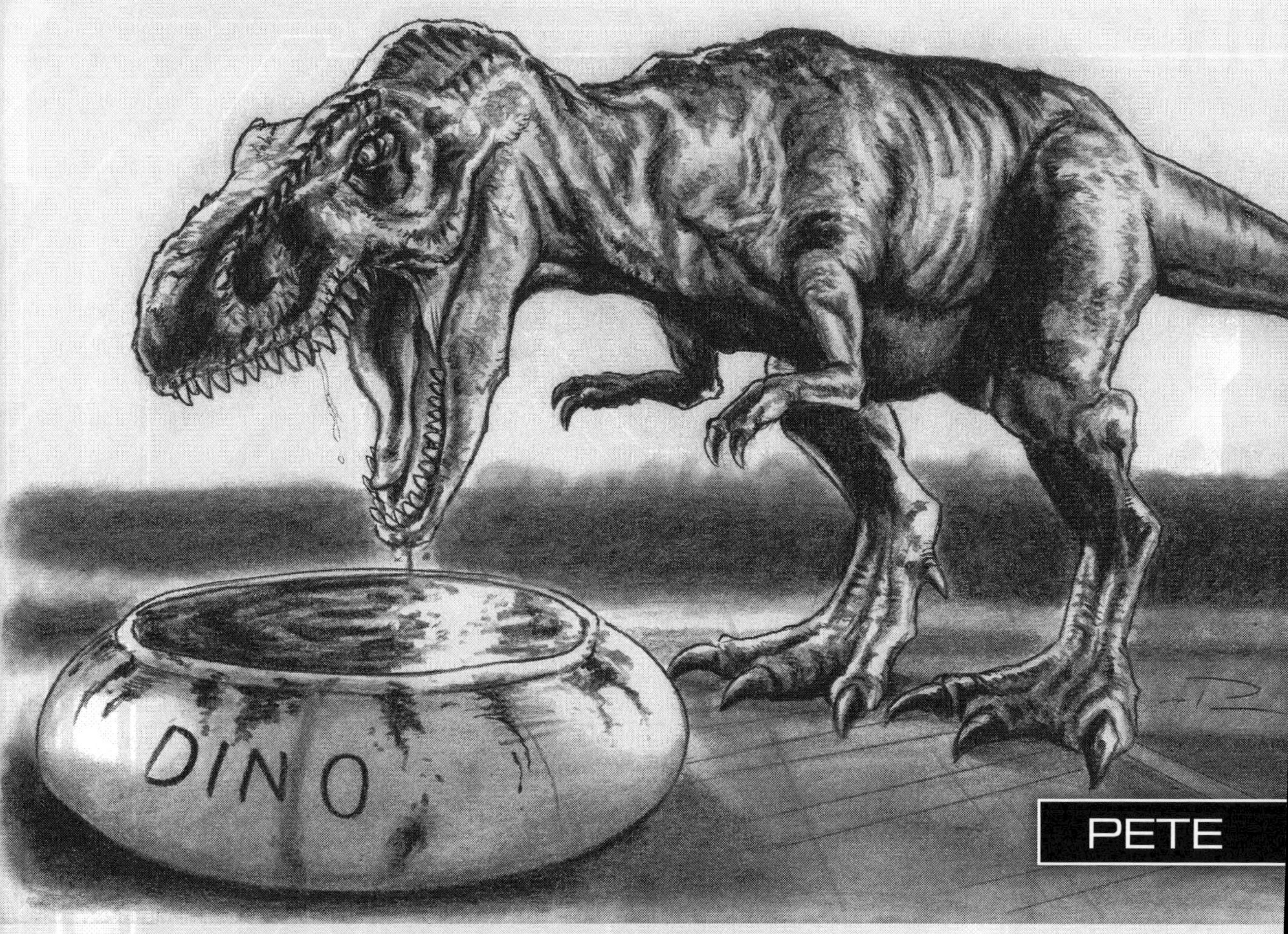


- **Phlegm-Cannon:** A secret black-ops-type project on which Space Corps physicists may or may not have worked **[G-RPG]**.

- **Phobos:** A natural satellite of Mars, and the larger of the planet's two moons **[RL]**. The Phobos Interplanetary Spaceport on Mars was named after this moon **[M-SMG2.5(c6)]**.

- **Phobos Interplanetary Spaceport:** A facility on Mars, built for launching and landing spacecraft. As Trixie LaBouche tried to escape Dutch van Oestrogen and the Ganymedian Mafia, Flight 261 to the spaceport was boarding at Mimas Spaceport **[M-SMG2.5(c6)]**.

- **Phobos Shipyard:** A facility on Mars at which deep space vessels were constructed **[G-RPG]**.

- **Phoebe:** One of Saturn's outer moons **[RL]**. George McIntyre incurred a massive gambling debt playing Toot on Phoebe and other moons, which eventually led to his committing suicide **[N-INF]**.

- **photo lab:** A room aboard *Red Dwarf* allocated for developing photographic film. When Lister sent pictures of himself with his unquarantined cat, Frankenstein, to the lab for processing, Captain Hollister learned of the photos and sentenced Lister to

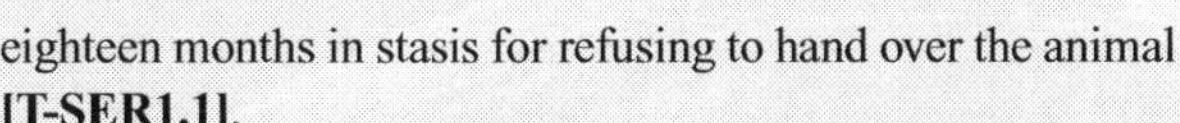

eighteen months in stasis for refusing to hand over the animal **[T-SER1.1]**.

The lab contained developing chemicals that mutated over the course of millions of years, causing any photo developed to become a portal into the scene portrayed. Kryten discovered this mutation while developing his film from the *Nova 5* **[T-SER3.5]**.

> ***NOTE:*** *In the pilot episode ("The End"), Hollister said Lister had sent the film to "the ship's lab," implying there was only one onboard—which would thus be the one featured in episode 3.5 ("Timeslides").*

- **photon mutilator:** A missile-type weapon used by simulants aboard Death Ships and Annihilators. One mutilator had enough destructive capability to obliterate a large asteroid, while two could effectively take out a Death Ship **[T-SER10.6]**.

- **Photo-U-Kwik booth:** A kiosk at Mimas Central Shuttle Station for taking and processing photographs quickly and easily. Embellishing the details of his arrival aboard *Red Dwarf*, Lister told his drinking buddies that two shore patrolwomen seduced him in a Photo-U-Kwik booth—which, he claimed, accounted for his astonished look on his passport photo **[N-INF]**.

- **physical data disc:** A piece of hardware used in the creation of a hologram, which stored the information necessary to recreate the physical appearance of the person being represented, as well as some rudimentary personality traits. If the disc became corrupted, information had to be culled from other sources. When Rimmer's disc became corrupted, he ended up with Olaf Petersen's right arm, which began pummeling him after Rimmer insulted it. It again became corrupted after he swapped physical data with Kochanski's disc, giving him her right breast and hips **[T-SER1.3]**.

- **Picasso, Pablo:** A twentieth-century Spanish painter and sculptor, known for his surreal representations of people **[RL]**. When Lister used a device to bring back Kochanski from his memories of her, Rimmer warned that if he wasn't careful, she could materialize resembling a Picasso painting **[M-SMG1.9(c3)]**.

- **Pickup Point 147:** An area of the American mining vessel *Red Dwarf.* Lister requested a buggy to transport Kryten from this location to Captain Tau's office **[T-USA1]**.

- **Pictures by Kev F:** A business featured on the television soap opera *Androids* **[M-SMG1.10(c2)]**.

  > ***NOTE:*** *The* Smegazine *comics were illustrated by Kev F. Sutherland.*

- **pigeon:** A bird in the Columbidae family. Pigeons exist in abundance in most cities throughout the world **[RL]**. By 2108, the species was on the brink of extinction, and the Save the Pigeon charity was established to return the bird to populated areas around the globe **[W-JMC]**.

- **Pierre:** An individual whom Rimmer imagined while trapped in an addictive version of *Better Than Life.* Rimmer hired the Sorbonne graduate to push elevator buttons for him in the lobby of the Rimmer Building (Paris)—which he owned in the illusion—but fired the man after the lift took too long to arrive **[N-INF]**.

- **Pilate, Pontius:** A first-century A.D. Roman prefect who ordered the crucifixion of Jesus Christ, according to Christian gospel **[RL]**. Dismissing the film *King of Kings* as unrealistic, Rimmer claimed that if he were Jesus carrying the cross, he would have fought his way out and been gone before anyone could say "Pontius Pilate" **[T-SER5.1]**.

- **Piledriver, Inc:** A weapons dealer whose products were featured in Crapola Inc.'s annual *SCABBY* catalog **[G-RPG]**.

- **Piledriver PN-14D Nuclear warhead firing device:** A triggering mechanism aboard *Starbug* shuttles for precisely aiming and launching explosive payloads **[G-SOR]**. Lister used such a device as a pool cue to launch a nuclear device at a nearby sun, causing a flare that knocked several planets out of orbit, resulting in the blockage of a white hole **[T-SER4.4]**.

- **"Pinkle! Squirmy! Blip Blap Blap!":** The standard cheer of the Space Scouts youth organization **[T-SER2.5]**.

- **Pinky:** A nickname that Rimmer called one of *Red Dwarf*'s skutters, whom he considered utterly useless; Pinky's fellow skutter received the name Perky **[T-SER2.2]**.

  ***NOTE:*** *The BBC animated children's show* Pinky and Perky *featured two anthropomorphic pig puppets.*

- **Pinter, Harold:** A twentieth-century British Nobel Prize-winning author, actor and playwright **[RL]**. While marooned on a frozen planet, Lister attempted to stay warm inside *Starbug 1* by burning items stored aboard ship. Succumbing to hunger, he was dismayed to find several books written by authors whose names reminded him of food, such as Charles Lamb, Herman Wouk and Francis Bacon. He also found Pinter's *The Caretaker*, which, in his delirium, he misread as "P-eye-nter," reminding him of a pint of beer **[T-SER3.2]**.

- **Pin the Nose on the Crash Victim:** A game that Colonel Mike O'Hagan described in his *Space Corps Survival Manual*, intended to keep crash survivors occupied and in good spirits **[B-SUR]**.

- **Pin the Pointy Stick on the Weather Girl:** A game that the *Red Dwarf* crew indulged in aboard *Starbug 1* while pursuing the stolen *Red Dwarf* **[T-SER6.2]**.

- ***Pioneer,* SCS:** A Space Corps vessel, commanded by Captain Tau, that the *Starbug 1* crew imagined encountering in an illusion created by Psirens to lure the shuttle into an asteroid belt. The crew received a distress call from Tau, claiming Psirens had killed her complement. The video showed Tau dying by laser fire, and Kochanski claiming to have survived the cadmium II disaster and given birth to Lister's twin sons. This convinced Lister to attempt a rescue, until his shipmates talked him out of it **[T-SER6.1]**.

- **Pipeline 22:** A section of *Red Dwarf* in which Rimmer hid the ship's stores of cigarettes, hoping to blackmail Lister into doing his bidding. Cat found the stash, however, and told Lister, despite Rimmer's efforts to bribe him with fish **[T-SER1.3]**.

- ***pisciform automata*:** The scientific name for robotic goldfish, such as Lister's pets Lennon and McCartney **[B-PRG]**.

- **Piston Pelvis:** Karstares' nickname on the television soap opera *Androids*, referring to his large hydraulic groinal attachment **[M-SMG2.7(c6)]**.

- **piston tower:** A half-mile-long steel cylinder aboard *Red Dwarf*, housing an eight-thousand-ton piston head, part of the ship's massive engines. There were twelve hundred such towers aboard the vessel. In the unlikely event the ship's engines were turned off, the restart sequence involved priming and testing each tower. This exact circumstance occurred after an intelligence-compression procedure went awry, causing Holly to shut himself down, along with the ship's engines **[N-BTL]**.

- **Piston Tower 136:** One of six hundred towers Rimmer was assigned to prime and test after Holly shut himself and *Red Dwarf*'s engines down. When a rogue planet was detected heading toward the ship, Rimmer raced to beat Kryten and his contingent of skutters, which resulted in a massive setback when he assumed his 'A' section of skutters was in Piston Tower 137, and accidentally crushed all twenty as they tested Tower 136 **[N-BTL]**.

- **Piston Tower 137:** Another tower aboard *Red Dwarf* that Rimmer was assigned to prime and test when Holly shut himself and the ship's engines down. In his haste to beat Kryten in dispatching skutters when a rogue planet was discovered on a collision course with the vessel, he inadvertently crushed his twenty robots as they tested Piston Tower 137 **[N-BTL]**.

- **Pixon:** A *Red Dwarf* crewmember who served on Z-Shift prior to the cadmium II disaster. Shortly before the accident, Rimmer assigned Pixon, Dooley and Burd to repair several malfunctioning driers in the launderettes in East Alpha 555 **[N-INF]**.

  ***NOTE:*** *Pixon presumably died during the cadmium II explosion. It is unknown whether the nanobots resurrected him in Series VIII.*

- **Pizza Hut:** An American pizzeria restaurant chain with franchise locations in nearly one hundred countries **[RL]**. According to the *Space Corps Survival Manual*, Earth's Pizza Huts only delivered to a three-mile radius, while most survival situations occurred outside 248,000 light-years from Earth **[B-SUR]**.

**PREFIX**
**RL:** Real life

**T-: Television Episodes**
**SER:** Television series
**IDW:** "Identity Within"
**USA1:** Unaired U.S. pilot
**USA2:** Unaired U.S. demo

**R-: *The Bodysnatcher Collection***
**SER:** Remastered episodes
**BOD:** "Bodysnatcher"
**DAD:** "Dad"
**FTH:** "Lister's Father"
**INF:** "Infinity Patrol"
**END:** "The End" (original assembly)

**N-: Novels**
**INF:** *Infinity Welcomes Careful Drivers*
**BTL:** *Better Than Life*
**LST:** *Last Human*

**BCK:** *Backwards*
**OMN:** *Red Dwarf Omnibus*

**M-: Magazines**
**SMG:** *Smegazine*

**W-: Websites**
**OFF:** Official website
**NAN:** *Prelude to Nanarchy*
**AND:** *Androids*
**DIV:** Diva-Droid
**DIB:** Duane Dibbley

**CRP:** Crapola
**GEN:** Geneticon
**LSR:** Leisure World Intl.
**JMC:** Jupiter Mining Corporation
**AIT:** *A.I. Today*
**HOL:** HoloPoint

**G-: Roleplaying Game**
**RPG:** *Core Rulebook*
**BIT:** *A.I. Screen Extra Bits* booklet
**SOR:** *Series Sourcebook*
**OTH:** Other RPG material

- **Pizzak'Rapp:** One of thousands of agonoids who escaped decommissioning and fled into deep space. His name was a bastardization of "Piece of Crap," in keeping with humans' tendency to assign humorous names to the agonoids.

Many years later, the renegade agonoids found *Red Dwarf*, abandoned except for Holly, whom they interrogated before ripping him out and leaving his components in space as bait for the crew. When another agonoid, Djuhn'Keep, betrayed the others for the right to become The One that would kill the last remaining human (Lister), Pizzak was among a handful of droids who survived Djuhn's Death Wheel, only to be flushed out into space. To his surprise, he was launched directly toward the disabled *Starbug*.

Pizzak caught himself on a tether connecting *Starbug* and *Wildfire One*, and waited on the ship's hull until Lister came out to dislodge Kryten, who had been stuck in a hull breach caused by a collision with *Wildfire*. He ambushed the human, knocking him unconscious so he could enter *Starbug* unnoticed, but Ace Rimmer attacked him, hurtling both into space. As they struggled, Ace released his jet pack, leaving both adrift in the cold vacuum of space. Pizzak'Rapp compromised Ace's helmet before dying, killing the human instantly **[N-BCK]**.

- ***Planet of the Apes*:** An American science fiction film starring Charlton Heston, Kim Hunter and Roddy McDowall, about human astronauts awakening in an ape-controlled future **[RL]**. When Lister fed Rimmer hallucinogenic mushrooms for breakfast, Rimmer, furious at Captain Hollister for insufficiently punishing him, tore up and ate a photograph of Hollister's wife. He later admitted he thought it was a publicity still for *Planet of the Apes* **[T-SER2.4]**.

- **Planet of the Nymphomaniacs:** A world featured in the total-immersion video game *Red Dwarf*, according to a service technician whom the crew imagined meeting while trapped in a despair squid hallucination. The imagined technician asked what they thought of the planet, and was amused to find out they had never found it **[T-SER5.6]**. In one reality, players who followed the Dibbley party easily found the planet, which was pink and shaped like a heart, and revolved around two suns **[M-SMG2.6(c5)]**.

Psirens once tried to lure the crew to land in their territory by creating an illusion of two attractive young women from this world, begging the crew to visit them for sex. In the illusion, the planet was located in the Zeta-Jones Quadrant **[G-SOR]**.

> ***NOTE:*** *It is unclear whether or not the planet actually existed, or whether it was truly in the Zeta-Jones Quadrant (presumably named after actor Catherine Zeta-Jones).*

- ***Planet of the Nymphomaniacs*:** A Total Immersion video game operated at arcades owned by Leisure World International **[W-LSR]**.

- **Planet of the Snooty Sex Sirens:** A hypothetical planet that Rimmer made up while discussing Lister's night of partying on Orion, where he drank a yard of vindaloo sauce and made out with a nurse **[T-SER7.1(d)]**.

- **Planet Razor Blade:** A planet marked by deadly surface tornadoes. The company that produced Weather-Blast goggles suggested the eyewear be worn in extreme weather conditions, such as when attempting to ride out a storm on this world **[G-BIT]**.

- **Planet Spud:** The Potato People's home world. Mr. Flibble visited Planet Spud to attack the King of the Potato People with a thermonuclear weapon known as a plasmatic lacerator shell **[M-SMG1.8(c3)]**.

- **Plank constant, the:** A mathematical equation used during Professor Edgington's research on evolution at the Erroneous Reasoning Research Academy **[T-SER10.4]**.

> ***NOTE:*** *Given the notes surrounding the equation, this was clearly meant to be Planck's constant, a physical constant integral to the field of quantum mechanics, describing the relationship between energy and frequency. In keeping with Edgington's tendency to do everything wrong, the spelling error was likely intentional on the part of the prop crew. (Surprisingly, she did get the equation right.)*

- **Plant Room:** An area within *Red Dwarf* through which Lister was wheeled on a medical trolley while on his way to undergo a Cesarean section **[R-DAD]**.

- **plasma:** The yellowish liquid component of human blood, in which blood cells are suspended **[RL]**. Ace Rimmer requested two pints of plasma before performing microsurgery on Cat's leg, which had been crushed when Ace's ship collided with *Starbug 1* **[T-SER4.5]**.

- **plasma drive:** A type of propulsion system used on Mr. Flibble's personal spacecraft. Activating the drive within a planet's atmosphere caused a chain reaction that ignited the atmosphere's oxygen content. While leaving the psi-moon where he was born, Flibble used his ship's plasma drive to ignite the moon's atmosphere **[M-SMG2.9(c14)]**.

- **plasmatic lacerator shell:** A type of weapon nicknamed "thermonuclear megadeath," with which Mr. Flibble attacked the King of the Potato People **[M-SMG1.8(c3)]**.

- **Plastic Percy:** A nickname that Cat called Kryten while explaining how he ended up in Rimmer's hologrammic body **[T-SER3.4]**.

- **plasti-droid:** An alternate name for prostidroids available for use at a mix-n-match brothel on Mimas **[B-PRG]**.

- **Plate VXII:** A diagram included in a medical paper published in Jake Bullet's universe, titled "Nerdism—A Study," written by Doctor Donald Dirk of the Slough Brain Research Unit. The diagram depicted a man afflicted with nerdism, citing such key indicators as bad eyesight, goofy teeth and an ill-fitting anorak **[M-SMG1.14(c6)]**.

  ***NOTE:** Presumably, VXII was a code and not the plate number, since no such Roman numeral exists.*

- **Platini, Hercule, Captain:** The hologrammic captain of the holoship *Enlightenment*. He had an IQ of 212 **[T-SER5.1]**. Platini's interests included hair metal bands, especially Def Leppard **[G-SOR]**.

  ***NOTE:** In a deleted scene, Rimmer called him Captain Platino. The script book* Son of Soup *spelled his first name as "Hercules."*

- **Platinum Star of Fortitude:** The highest military decoration awarded by the Space Corps. *Red Dwarf*'s JMC onboard computer, after reviewing the death of Rimmer's brother Howard, decided to award him the medal posthumously **[T-SER10.1]**.

- **Plato:** A Greek philosopher and a student of Socrates, circa the fourth century B.C., who helped to establish Western philosophy and science **[RL]**. After creating the Holly Hop Drive, Holly compared himself to other inventors, including Plato—whom he claimed invented the plate **[T-SER2.6]**.

  ***NOTE:** As difficult as it would be to pinpoint the actual "inventor" of the plate, it most certainly was not Plato.*

- ***Playboy*:** An American men's magazine founded by Hugh Hefner in 1953, featuring short fiction, journalistic articles and photographs of nude women **[RL]**. When Lister revealed that he was his own father and Kochanski was his mother, Cat suggested writing a letter to *Playboy* **[T-SER7.3]**.

- ***Playboy* Pleasure Cruiser:** A spacefaring ship run by Playboy Enterprises in the twenty-third century. The *Red Dwarf* crew once encountered the vessel, staffed with busty women wearing bunny ears and cotton tails, which caused Rimmer to frantically read up on his books of chat-up lines **[M-SMG2.8(a)]**.

- **Playful Pete, My Polythene Pal:** A blowup sex doll Arlene Rimmer owned on an alternate-dimension *Red Dwarf*. Arlene once caught her bunkmate, Deb Lister, using her Playful Pete **[M-SMG1.5(c2)]**.

  ***NOTE:** In the prime universe, Arnold Rimmer had an Inflatable Ingrid doll.*

- ***Playgelf*:** An adult-oriented publication featuring nude images of GELFs. The *Red Dwarf* crew discovered five issues of this magazine while searching derelict garbage tankers **[B-LOG]**.

  ***NOTE:** This publication's title and concept spoofed those of* Playboy *magazine.*

- ***Play With Ben*:** A children's book that Lister read aboard *Blue Midget* before embarking on a rescue mission to *Nova 5* **[T-SER2.1]**.

- ***Playzombie*:** A hypothetical magazine title. When the Epideme virus reanimated the corpse of former *Red Dwarf* crewmember

**PREFIX**
**RL:** Real life

**T-: Television Episodes**
**SER:** Television series
**IDW:** "Identity Within"
**USA1:** Unaired U.S. pilot
**USA2:** Unaired U.S. demo

**R-: *The Bodysnatcher Collection***
**SER:** Remastered episodes
**BOD:** "Bodysnatcher"
**DAD:** "Dad"
**FTH:** "Lister's Father"
**INF:** "Infinity Patrol"
**END:** "The End" (original assembly)

**N-: Novels**
**INF:** *Infinity Welcomes Careful Drivers*
**BTL:** *Better Than Life*
**LST:** *Last Human*
**BCK:** *Backwards*
**OMN:** *Red Dwarf Omnibus*

**M-: Magazines**
**SMG:** *Smegazine*

**W-: Websites**
**OFF:** Official website
**NAN:** *Prelude to Nanarchy*
**AND:** *Androids*
**DIV:** Diva-Droid
**DIB:** Duane Dibbley
**CRP:** Crapola
**GEN:** Geneticon
**LSR:** Leisure World Intl.
**JMC:** Jupiter Mining Corporation
**AIT:** *A.I. Today*
**HOL:** HoloPoint

**G-: Roleplaying Game**
**RPG:** *Core Rulebook*
**BIT:** *A.I. Screen Extra Bits* booklet
**SOR:** *Series Sourcebook*
**OTH:** Other RPG material

Caroline Carmen, Cat claimed she looked like a *Playzombie* centerfold **[T-SER7.7]**.

> ***NOTE:*** *This publication's title and concept spoofed those of* Playboy *magazine.*

- **Pleasure GELF:** A genetically engineered life form created to provide companionship. Pleasure GELFs could alter how an individual visually and audibly perceived them, and were capable of simultaneously affecting multiple people differently. In their native form, they were large, androgynous, green blobs, approximately four to five feet tall, with a proboscis through which they ate and drank, and a single eyestalk.

  Kryten rescued a Pleasure GELF named Camille from an escape vessel marooned on a dying planet. Camille's husband Hector, also a Pleasure GELF, worked to find a cure to their condition, but when she left him, he abandoned his research and spent years searching for her before finally tracking her down to *Red Dwarf* **[T-SER4.1]**.

- **ploughman:** A type of meal served in British pubs, short for "ploughman's lunch," typically consisting of meats, cheeses and pickles **[RL]**. According to Lister, the bar in which he was found abandoned as a child—The Flag and Lettuce—served Boddy's Beer and a good ploughman, which in his eyes made it an upscale establishment **[R-DAD]**.

  > ***NOTE:*** *The bar's name was changed to The Aigburth Arms onscreen.*

- **Plug:** A god worshipped by plumbers in Tunbridge Wells. When five hundred pilgrims from that town were sent to pray for the end of a meteor storm ravaging their city, one plumber believed his people was headed to a shrine dedicated to Plug. Others disagreed, causing a religious war that wiped out the entire pilgrim crew **[M-SMG1.14(c2)]**.

  > ***NOTE:*** Mrs. Plug the Plumber *was one of several British children's books in the* Happy Families *series.*

- **Pluto:** The former ninth planet of Earth's solar system, containing five known natural satellites, including Charon and Hydra. Pluto was demoted to the status of dwarf planet in 2006 **[RL]**. Space-beatniks from around the system gathered on Neptune for Pluto's solstice, an event that marked the moment Pluto overtook Neptune and became the outermost planet **[N-INF]**.

  Pluto was home to a handful of United Nations and Space Corps installations, primarily set up on the planet for symbolic purposes **[G-RPG]**. This included a Space Corps research center. During her career with the Space Corps, Nirvanah Crane was stationed at this center, as well as others around the system **[W-OFF]**.

  In the twenty-second century, the Inter-Planetary Commission for Waste Disposal decided to designate one of the system's nine planets as humanity's official dumping grounds. Representatives from all nine worlds presented their case against being chosen, with Pluto's delegation citing the planet's distance and elongated orbit as reasons for disqualification. Ultimately, Earth was nominated for the task **[N-BTL]**.

  Three million years later, while marooned on a frozen planet in *Starbug 1*, Lister tried to keep his mind off his hunger by asking Rimmer when he lost his virginity. Arnold claimed it was so long ago he couldn't remember—which Lister found unlikely, since losing one's virginity was something no one would forget, like where one was when the first woman landed on Pluto **[T-SER3.2]**.

  In 2575, a group of researchers accidentally blew up a large section of Pluto during atomic testing **[W-OFF]**. At some point, the planet vanished entirely. According to government sources, this disappearance coincided with the testing of the Proton Cannon of Nagasami, the most powerful weapon devised by man, which was fired from a starship in the solar system's outskirts **[B-EVR]**.

  > ***NOTE:*** *For the purposes of this book, Pluto's demotion to a dwarf planet in 2006 is disregarded to remain consistent with the* Red Dwarf *universe.*

- **Plutonian:** A language in which Rimmer claimed the word "Yizox" meant "teeth." However, he had actually made up the word to cheat at *Scrabble* **[M-SMG1.6(c1)]**.

- **Plutonian Medical Insurance:** An insurance agency located on Pluto. Its slogan was "Surviving the Universe Together." An advertisement for the company boasted twenty-four-hour medical care, but a closer look at the ad revealed that treatment was limited to twenty-four hours of total care within a twelve-month period **[X-CAL]**.

- **Pluto's Solstice:** An event marked by the emergence of Pluto as the solar system's outermost planet. Thousands of space-beatniks flocked to Neptune for the event **[N-INF]**.

- **pod:** Any of a number of small vessels, either manned or unmanned **[RL]**. Pods came in a variety of shapes and sizes, for many different uses within a wide range of environments. These included cargo pods **[R-BOD(b)]**, cremation tubes **[W-OFF]**, escape pods **[T-SER4.3]**, garbage pods **[T-SER1.4]**, genetic waste pods **[T-SER3.3]**, homing pods **[T-SER3.6]**, ore sample pods **[T-SER5.3]**, postal pods (also called post pods or mail pods) **[T-SER2.2]**, survival pods **[T-IDW]** and transdimensional homing beacons **[G-SOR]**.

- **Point Street:** A road featured in the B-movie *Attack of the Giant Savage Completely Invisible Aliens* **[T-SER8.5]**.

- **Poitier, Sidney:** An American-born actor known for his roles in such movies as *Lilies of the Field*, *In the Heat of the Night* and *Sneakers* **[RL]**. After the Inquisitor erased Lister and Kryten from history, Rimmer, who no longer recognized the two, suggested wasting them, suspicious of their story since they were chained together "like Sidney Poitier and Tony Curtis" **[T-SER5.2]**.

  ***NOTE:** This referred to the film* The Defiant Ones, *in which Poitier and Curtis spent a majority of the film shackled together.*

- **poker:** A series of card games in which participants tried to outrank other players with different groupings of cards, usually involving betting rules **[RL]**. When Queeg challenged Holly to a game of chess for control of *Red Dwarf*, Holly, unskilled at the game, suggested they instead play poker **[T-SER2.5]**. Lister's poker plans were once interrupted when a skutter went berserk and re-wired circuits on the maintenance decks, causing the auto-destruct system to be activated. This frustrated Lister, who had spent a great deal of time marking the cards **[T-SER3.4]**.

- **Polaroid Head:** Kryten's self-deprecating description of himself after a DNA-modifying machine transformed him into a human. The name stemmed from an earlier conversation he'd had with Lister, which involved Polaroid pictures of Kryten's human penis **[T-SER4.2]**.

- **Polesen:** An inmate of the Tank, *Red Dwarf*'s classified brig, who perished during the cadmium II disaster, but was resurrected when *Red Dwarf* was rebuilt by nanobots. Brown was assigned to the Canaries, an elite group of inmates tasked with investigating dangerous situations. When *Red Dwarf* was being dissolved by a chameleonic microbe, Captain Hollister ordered an evacuation. Several names were picked at random from the prisoner roster to board the rescue craft, and Polesen was among those chosen **[T-SER8.8(d)]**.

- **police woman's helmet:** An item that Cat obtained during a night of hard partying in the Officers' Club to celebrate Kryten's last day of service. This confused Cat, since they were three million years into deep space **[T-SER3.6]**.

- **Pollock, Jackson:** An American abstract painter of the twentieth century **[RL]**. When Lister was young, he attended a school trip to Paris, during which he drank two bottles of cheap wine before touring the Eiffel Tower. Once at the top, he vomited on Montmartre, where a pavement artist sold the puke to a Texan tourist, claiming it was a genuine Jackson Pollock **[T-SER3.6]**.

  Rimmer described a skutter's attempts at drawing the letter "A" as "a deranged origami monstrosity" resembling Pollock's toilet paper after an especially bad curry meal **[R-BOD]**.

- **polydridocdecahooeyhedron:** One of William James Sidis' theoretical shapes, which Rimmer understood after a mind patch dramatically increased his intelligence **[T-SER5.1]**.

- **Polyester Brothers, the:** Lister's nickname for a group of *Red Dwarf* crewmembers with whom Rimmer played war games every Thursday. Whenever they got together, Lister joked, a dandruff warning was issued on the news **[T-SER8.3(d)]**.

- **polygraphic surveillance:** A scan used aboard the penal station Justice World to detect the honesty of trial participants **[T-SER4.3]**.

- **polymorph:** A type of genetically engineered life form (GELF), created on Earth as the "ultimate warrior" and able to change its shape at will. Byproducts of its design included insanity and the need to feed off negative emotions, rendering its victims somewhat incapacitated. Kryten described such creatures as

**PREFIX**
**RL:** Real life

**T-: Television Episodes**
**SER:** Television series
**IDW:** "Identity Within"
**USA1:** Unaired U.S. pilot
**USA2:** Unaired U.S. demo

**R-: *The Bodysnatcher Collection***
**SER:** Remastered episodes
**BOD:** "Bodysnatcher"
**DAD:** "Dad"
**FTH:** "Lister's Father"
**INF:** "Infinity Patrol"
**END:** "The End" (original assembly)

**N-: Novels**
**INF:** *Infinity Welcomes Careful Drivers*
**BTL:** *Better Than Life*
**LST:** *Last Human*

**BCK:** *Backwards*
**OMN:** *Red Dwarf Omnibus*

**M-: Magazines**
**SMG:** *Smegazine*

**W-: Websites**
**OFF:** Official website
**NAN:** *Prelude to Nanarchy*
**AND:** *Androids*
**DIV:** Diva-Droid
**DIB:** Duane Dibbley

**CRP:** Crapola
**GEN:** Geneticon
**LSR:** Leisure World Intl.
**JMC:** Jupiter Mining Corporation
**AIT:** *A.I. Today*
**HOL:** HoloPoint

**G-: Roleplaying Game**
**RPG:** *Core Rulebook*
**BIT:** *A.I. Screen Extra Bits* booklet
**SOR:** *Series Sourcebook*
**OTH:** Other RPG material

"emotional vampires" **[T-SER3.3]**.

A strain of polymorph evolved on Earth after the GELF population was exiled to the island of Zanzibar, prior to the planet being designated "Garbage World" and abandoned by humanity **[N-BTL]**.

Two polymorphs were contained in a genetic waste pod and shot into deep space. They escaped, however, and found their way onto *Red Dwarf*, where one repeatedly attacked the crew. The creature drained Lister's fear, Rimmer's anger, Cat's vanity and Kryten's guilt—which all returned once the polymorph was destroyed by heat-seeking bazookoid fire **[T-SER3.3]**. It also drained two skutters' resentment of Rimmer **[M-SMG1.12(c4)]**.

The other polymorph, a female, tried to avenge her mate, duplicating *Red Dwarf* using data from the ship's computer. The creature fed off the crew's recorded final moments during the cadmium II explosion for two years, evolving into a near-complete copy of the mining vessel and its crew. Starving for nourishment, the polymorph encountered a GELF transport vessel carrying twenty thousand GELFs in stasis. It integrated the creatures into its engineering section, keeping them in a constant state of pain and terror so it could feed off their emotions **[M-SMG2.7(c1)]**.

The *Starbug 1* crew, which had been searching for the missing *Red Dwarf*, found the polymorph and boarded it, believing it to be the mining ship. They found perfect recreations of the crew in the Drive Room, including Captain Hollister, who had them all arrested. They escaped in a lift to the engineering section, where they found the polymorph and a recreation of Kochanski **[M-SMG2.6(c1)]**.

Kochanski's doppelgänger proposed that the crew submit themselves to regular feedings, in exchange for which it would create anything they desired, but despite some temptation, they refused and left the pseudo-ship. The polymorph gave chase, attempting to eat *Starbug*, but it had recreated the ship and crew too precisely, and thus its version of Rimmer failed to seal a faulty drive plate, causing a cadmium II explosion that destroyed the creature **[M-SMG2.7(c1)]**.

> ***NOTE:*** *The remastered version of episode 3.3 ("Polymorph") stated that the second polymorph, being much less intelligent, hid in Lister's clean underwear drawer, where it remained undetected for years before dying of old age.*
>
> *A scene in which a polymorph became Lister's underpants and then began shrinking on his body originated as a gag from a* Son of Cliché *sketch titled "Attack of the Killer Italian Y-Fronts."*
>
> *Among the items polymorphs have been shown changing into are a teddy bear, a bucket and spade, a bouquet of flowers, a toy truck, a flamenco doll, a telephone, an elephant carving, a colorful hat, a baseball and mitt, a toy boxing figure, a toy drum, a yellow safety light, a toy car, a roller skate, a traffic cone, a pink lamp shade, an inflatable penguin, a piggy bank, a male doll wearing shorts, a blue chamber pot, an alarm clock, a rubber ball, a sneaker, a cooking pot, a Koosh toy, a scrub brush, a metal bucket, a blue whale toy, a golden statue, a light bulb, a bicycle horn, a sponge ball, a sock, a rabbit, a basketball, a shami kebab, Lister's underpants, a snake, an eight-foot-tall armor-plated alien, a beautiful woman, Rimmer, Rimmer's mom and Lister (all from episode 3.3, "Polymorph"); a wad of chewing gum, a stone, water, steam, ice, a fly, a feather, a bullet, a beam of light, a beach ball, a plague rat, electronic data and a wrought-iron lamp post (from the novel* Better Than Life*); a bowler hat, a walking cane, a can of beans, a can opener, a bowl, a box of Cock-a-Doodle Flakes cereal, Pot O' Sick instant soup, a tea kettle, a sausage, a bun, a hamburger, a tomato, a nut, a bolt, an umbrella, an elephant leg umbrella holder, a gun, an extension cord and a lava lamp (from "The Aftering—Part 2," in* Smegazine *issue 2.9).*
>
> *In the novel* Better than Life, *a polymorph escaped Garbage World and found its way onto* Red Dwarf, *where it attacked the crew and killed Lister.*

- **pool:** A cue and ball game played on a felt-covered table containing six holes, also known as pocket billiards **[RL]**. *Red Dwarf* had several pool tables in its rec rooms. As a young man, Lister played pool for hours at The Aigburth Arms, once winning seventeen consecutive games and becoming something of a billiards legend **[N-INF]**.

- **"Pool":** A word printed on a red neon sign that the *Red Dwarf* crew imagined while trapped in a despair squid hallucination. The sign was located outside an eatery called the Burger Bar **[T-SER5.6]**.

**B-: Books**
**PRG:** *Red Dwarf Programme Guide*
**SUR:** *Red Dwarf Space Corps Survival Manual*
**PRM:** *Primordial Soup*
**SOS:** *Son of Soup*
**SCE:** *Scenes from the Dwarf*
**LOG:** *Red Dwarf Log No. 1996*
**RD8:** *Red Dwarf VIII*
**EVR:** *The Log: A Dwarfer's Guide to Everything*

**X-: Misc.**
**PRO:** Promotional materials, videos, etc.
**PST:** Posters at DJ XVII (2013)
**CAL:** 2008 calendar
**RNG:** Cell phone ringtones
**MOB:** Mobisode ("Red Christmas")
**CIN:** *Children in Need* sketch
**GEK:** *Geek Week* intros by Kryten
**TNG:** "Tongue-Tied" video
**XMS:** Bill Pearson's Christmas special pitch script
**XVD:** Bill Pearson's Christmas special pitch video
**OTH:** Other *Red Dwarf* appearances

**SUFFIX**
**DVD:**
**(d)** – Deleted scene
**(o)** – Outtake
**(b)** – Bonus DVD material (other)
**(e)** – Extended version

**SMEGAZINES:**
**(c)** – Comic
**(a)** – Article

**OTHER:**
**(s)** – Early/unused script draft
**(s1)** – Alternate version of script

# PETE TRANTER'S SISTER

**PREFIX**
**RL:** Real life

**T-: Television Episodes**
- **SER:** Television series
- **IDW:** "Identity Within"
- **USA1:** Unaired U.S. pilot
- **USA2:** Unaired U.S. demo

**R-: *The Bodysnatcher Collection***
- **SER:** Remastered episodes
- **BOD:** "Bodysnatcher"
- **DAD:** "Dad"
- **FTH:** "Lister's Father"
- **INF:** "Infinity Patrol"
- **END:** "The End" (original assembly)

**N-: Novels**
- **INF:** *Infinity Welcomes Careful Drivers*
- **BTL:** *Better Than Life*
- **LST:** *Last Human*
- **BCK:** *Backwards*
- **OMN:** *Red Dwarf Omnibus*

**M-: Magazines**
- **SMG:** *Smegazine*

**W-: Websites**
- **OFF:** Official website
- **NAN:** *Prelude to Nanarchy*
- **AND:** *Androids*
- **DIV:** Diva-Droid
- **DIB:** Duane Dibbley
- **CRP:** Crapola
- **GEN:** Geneticon
- **LSR:** Leisure World Intl.
- **JMC:** Jupiter Mining Corporation
- **AIT:** *A.I. Today*
- **HOL:** HoloPoint

**G-: Roleplaying Game**
- **RPG:** *Core Rulebook*
- **BIT:** *A.I. Screen Extra Bits* booklet
- **SOR:** *Series Sourcebook*
- **OTH:** Other RPG material

- **Popco Inc.:** A beverage company that produced Total Gonzo Energy drinks and other products. Professional zero-gee football player Jim Bexley Speed was a subsidiary of Popco Inc. **[G-SOR]**.

- **Popeye the Sailor Man:** A fictional cartoon character who typically dressed in a sailor uniform. *Popeye* debuted as a daily comic strip in 1929, and the character has also been featured in animated theatrical and television cartoons **[RL]**.

  While weighing the pros and cons of using a DNA-modifying machine that the crew found on a derelict ship, Lister mistakenly attributed the phrase "I am what I am" to René Descartes. Rimmer corrected the quote's source as Popeye **[T-SER4.2]**.

  Lister once inserted a kazoo between his buttocks and played Popeye's theme song in an effort to force Rimmer's bridge partners to leave his quarters **[T-SER8.1]**.

- ***Pop from the Precinct—20 Shopping Centre Hits*:** An album recorded by Reggie Wilson **[M-SMG1.3(a)]**.

- **"Pop Goes Delius":** A song recorded by Reggie Wilson, featuring Hammond Organ music **[T-SER4.5]**.

- **poppadom:** A thin, crisp breadlike chip, typically fried or roasted, and popular in Indian cuisine **[RL]**. While checking *Starbug 1*'s inventory, Lister discovered that the crew were down to their last two thousand poppadoms, and decided to risk traversing an asteroid belt in order to catch up with *Red Dwarf* **[T-SER6.1]**.

  Some time later, *Starbug 1*'s main water tank was breached during an attack by a future version of the crew, wiping out all Indian food stored on Supply Deck B, including the poppadoms. Desperate, Lister tricked his shipmates into retrieving the time drive so he could travel through time to restock his lost Indian meals **[T-SER7.1]**.

- ***Pop-Up Book of Probeships, The*:** An introductory user manual for Canary probe ships. Its recommended reading level was 5-9. Lister learned of the dropship's Utility Remote on page five of the manual **[X-XMS]**.

- ***Pop-Up Kama Sutra—Zero Gravity Edition, The*:** A 3D version of the popular Hindu book on sexual intercourse, which Rimmer kept on a drafting table in his quarters aboard *Red Dwarf*. While separating items for Rimmer to take to his new quarters, Lister noticed this book and hid it under his mattress **[T-SER1.6]**.

- **Porkman, Bob, Doctor:** A man who invented a condom that called a partner back after sex, in an alternate timeline in which Lister became the youngest billionaire by inventing the Tension Sheet. Porkman was featured in an episode of *Life Styles of the Disgustingly Rich and Famous* **[T-SER3.5]**.

- **porous circuit:** An electrical element capable of being presoaked with a polymer solution to fill in a circuit board's pores **[RL]**. Porous circuits were used in the automatic doors aboard *Red Dwarf*. When one such circuit malfunctioned in a doorway near the ship's botanical gardens, causing it to stick, a repair order was assigned to Rimmer and Lister on Z-Shift.

  Arnold Rimmer once claimed that for his Engineer's Exam, he wrote a paper on porous circuits that was so progressive that his examiners could not understand it, and thus failed him **[T-SER1.1]**. Subsequently, Rimmer quizzed Lister about his knowledge of porous circuits when he assumed his roommate was taking the Engineer's Exam to spite him, even though he was actually studying for the Chef's Exam **[T-SER1.3]**.

  While bunking with his duplicate hologram, Rimmer agreed to study porous circuits and Esperanto, while his doppelgänger learned about thermal energy, history and philosophy **[T-SER1.6]**.

- **portable walrus-polishing kit:** A hypothetical mail-order product. Mocking Lister's tendency to send away for information about various items just to receive mail, Rimmer suggested he order a portable walrus-polishing kit **[T-SER2.2]**.

- **portalab:** A temporary structure set up during mining operations to clean raw ore due to be packed up and transported for processing. Lister set Kryten up in a portalab to clean mined thorium so it could be ferried to *Red Dwarf* to be refined as fuel for *Nova 5* **[N-INF]**.

- **porta-trolley:** A type of portable cart produced by Crapola Inc. **[X-PST]**.

- **positive virus:** A viral strain that affected an individual in an advantageous manner. One example was reverse-flu, which enhanced an afflicted individual's happiness and well-being. Hologrammic scientist Hildegarde Lanstrom conceived of positive viruses and eventually isolated several strains at a viral research station, including luck, sexual magnetism and inspiration **[T-SER5.4]**.

- **positronic navigational system:** A type of high-end navigational control system not typically found on GELF-designed attack cruisers **[G-RPG]**.

- **possessiveness:** A rogue emotion purged from Kryten's hard drive by the Data Doctor, a program for restoring a mechanoid's personality to factory settings, when Captain Hollister subjected Kryten to a psychotropic simulation **[T-SER8.2]**.

- **post pod:** A small, cylindrical unmanned spacecraft sent from Earth to rendezvous with *Red Dwarf*, also called a mail pod or a postal pod. It contained mail, videos, games and other items for the crew. One such pod followed *Red Dwarf* for three million years as Holly took the mining ship into deep space following the cadmium II accident, catching up only after the vessel turned around to head back to Earth.

  The pod contained a letter addressed to the skutters from the John Wayne Fan Club, a remake of the film *Casablanca*, the film *Friday the 13th, Part 1,649*, a year's worth of Earth news, two seasons of zero-gee football, a letter from Rimmer's mom informing him of his father's death, the total-immersion video game *Better than Life* and other items **[T-SER2.2]**.

  When another post pod showed up, containing the complete works of Swedish director Sjorbik Bjorksson, Rimmer forced his shipmates to watch several of the man's films, including *Beverly Hills Bereavement Counsellor*, *The Dichotomy of Faith in a Post Materialistic Society* and *Four Funerals and Another One* **[B-LOG]**.

  Yet another post pod arrived years later, crashing through Cat's clothesline. Among its contents were a parking fine for Rimmer and several letters to Lister from his ex-girlfriend, Hayley Summers. The first letter informed him she was pregnant with the child of either Lister or a co-worker named Roy, while the second confirmed that Roy was the dad **[T-SER10.5]**.

  In one universe, a Space Corps officer named Leonard ordered a sentient robot clothes steamer online that became stuck in a post pod for millions of years. This caused the appliance to become extremely irate **[G-SOR]**.

- **Potato People, the:** A species of sentient tubers from Planet Spud. Mr. Flibble once visited the planet to attack their king with a thermonuclear weapon known as a plasmatic lacerator shell **[M-SMG1.8(c3)]**.

  After contracting a holovirus from Hildegarde Lanstrom that drove him insane, Rimmer fixated on the Potato People. Locking his shipmates in quarantine, Arnold informed them that despite Space Corps Directive 699, he could not release them because the king of the Potato People ordered them detained for ten years, and that the only way to obtain an audience with him was on a magic carpet. He then called them insane for wanting to fly on a magic carpet to beg the king of the Potato People for their freedom, and subsequently shut off their oxygen as punishment **[T-SER5.4]**.

- **Potent:** The title of male GELFs from Blerios 15 capable of reproduction. Potents were held in high regard, and hid their identity with ornate face masks and jewel-encrusted robes that covered their entire bodies, except for their genitals, which hung through a hole in the robes **[N-LST]**.

- **Pot Noodle:** A brand of instant snack food popular in the United Kingdom, consisting of dehydrated noodles and an assortment of other ingredients, prepared by adding boiled water **[RL]**. After three days of being marooned on a frozen planet in *Starbug 1*, Lister and Rimmer found that the only remaining edible supplies included a Pot Noodle, which Lister decided to eat last, given his utter disdain for the product **[T-SER3.2]**.

  While aboard the "high" *Red Dwarf*, created after a triplicator accident, Lister tested the quality of the ship's food dispensers by ordering a Pot Noodle, which he found to be delicious **[T-SER5.5]**. Cat, meanwhile, once fed *Red Dwarf*'s supply of Pot Noodles into a matter converter that changed the food into silk, which he used to fulfill his desire to own an infinite wardrobe **[M-SMG1.2(a)]**.

- **Pot Noodle International:** A company that produced dehydrated noodle meals in the twenty-fourth century. Its slogan was "As good for you now as it's always been!!" Pot Noodle International sponsored Groovy Channel 27 **[M-SMG1.7(a)]**.

  *NOTE: In the real world, Pot Noodle is produced by Unilever.*

- **Pot O' Sick:** A brand of instant soup available in sealed cups. During mating rituals, male polymorphs took several forms to compliment the shape of their mates. One polymorph changed into a boiling kettle to synchronize with its lover, who had morphed into a cup of Pot O' Sick **[M-SMG2.9(c12)]**.

- **Potson, Duncan:** A former Junior A classmate of Arnold Rimmer on Io who taught him how to pick his nose with his thumb. Upon meeting Ace Rimmer, Arnold questioned why his nostrils didn't flare, wondering if perhaps Ace had never met Duncan **[N-BCK]**.

- **power claw:** An extendable appendage on *Blue Midget*'s original shuttle design, before JMC cutbacks prevented its attachment. Power claws resembled small arms extending from the underside of the craft, each ending in a clamp **[R-SER]**.

  *NOTE: The power claw was so named on the DVD menu screen of the "Tongue Tied Archive," included among the bonus features of* The Bodysnatcher Collection*'s* Blue Midget *disc.*

- **Powersaur:** A genetically engineered life form (GELF) created in the twenty-third century to fight in the Tie Wars. Standing ten feet tall, these *Tyrannosaurus rex*-like creatures sported biologically grown spinning blades on their arms and spoke like Oscar Wilde **[B-EVR]**.

- **Prancer:** A fire-breathing racing yak that Cat imagined owning while trapped in an addictive version of *Better Than Life*. When Lister and Rimmer visited Cat at his golden castle to inform him that they were still in the game, they found him on a fire-breathing racing yak, about to start a dog hunt. Noticing his guests, Cat ordered his Valkyrie assistant to saddle up two more yaks, Dancer and Prancer, so they could join him **[N-INF]**.

  *NOTE: The yaks were named after two of Santa Claus' magical flying reindeer.*

- **prawn vindaloo:** A culinary dish made with fresh prawns, tomatoes, onions, curry, chili powder and other assorted spices **[RL]**. When faced with inevitable death, Lister lamented having never done certain things, such as eating a prawn vindaloo **[T-SER1.2]**.

  *NOTE: In the novel* Infinity Welcomes Careful Drivers*, Lister regretted never trying king prawn biryani (misspelled as "biriani").*

- **Pree:** An artificial-intelligence (AI) computer that the *Red Dwarf* crew salvaged from the Space Corps derelict *Trojan* **[W-OFF]** to replace Holly, who had been damaged by a flood **[T-SER9.1]**. According to preference settings input by Kryten, Pree's appearance was that of a twenty-five-year-old blonde female with 36D-sized breasts, which were hidden by Kryten's choice of frame size, much to Rimmer's frustration.

  Outfitted with predictive behavior technology, Pree could anticipate the crew's needs by observing their actions, enabling her to efficiently carry out orders before they were given. This ability was initially helpful, allowing Pree to repair B Deck before Rimmer requested it, but soon became annoying (when she finished entire conversations for the crew), troublesome (as she deleted Rimmer's favorite television show, predicting that he would not enjoy the second half) and ultimately dangerous (by performing subpar repair work on B Deck after foreseeing that Arnold would screw up the task).

  The AI's actions turned deadly when she ejected Lister into space for not being a registered crewmember, then altered the ship's course to plunge it into the core of the nearest sun, dubbing the new mission "Operation Sizzle." Lister re-boarded, however, and tricked Pree into shutting herself down with a logic puzzle **[T-SER10.2]**.

  *NOTE: Given the naming significance of other artificial intelligences, such as Stocky and Cassandra, Pree's name likely referenced her predictive capabilities.*

- **Pregnancy Colour:** A brand of home-pregnancy test stocked aboard *Red Dwarf*, which Lister used to determine whether he had been impregnated during a tryst with his female counterpart in an alternate universe. Printed on the box was the tagline "The 30 minute Home Pregnancy Test" **[T-SER2.6]**.

- **pregnant baboon-bellied space beatnik:** An unprovoked insult that Rimmer tossed at Lister while passing him during a morning run **[T-SER1.2]**.

- **Prehistoric World:** An area of the Waxworld theme park located between Hero World and Villain World, populated by life-size—albeit unconvincing—dinosaur waxdroids. Kryten and Rimmer materialized in Prehistoric World while attempting to use a Matter Paddle **[T-SER4.6]**.

  ***NOTE:** The footage of the "dinosaurs" was from the 1967 Japanese* kaiju *film* Daikyojû Gappa.

- **Presley, Elvis ("The King"):** An American singer, musician and actor considered one of the twentieth century's most significant cultural icons **[RL]**. An Extras Pack sold by Crapola Inc. allowed talking appliances, such as Talkie Toaster and Talkie Toilet, to mimic Presley's voice and personality **[W-CRP]**.

  While trapped in an addictive version of *Better Than Life*, Rimmer believed he had returned to Earth and become famously wealthy, creating a company that developed a time machine. He then used the contraption to bring together several historical individuals for his bachelor party, including Elvis Presley. The King later attended Rimmer's wedding reception and entered a gâteau-eating contest with Gautama Buddha **[N-BTL]**.

  In an alternate dimension, Leo Davis, a caretaker at the Black Island film studios, once daydreamed that he met the singer, who attempted to boost the janitor's self-esteem by performing a version of the song "Tongue Tied." Elvis advised Davis to sing to a woman he pined for, in the persona of Cat **[X-TNG]**.

- **Presley, Elvis, Sergeant:** A waxdroid replica of the singer, created for the Waxworld theme park. Left on their own for millions of years, the waxdroids attained sentience and became embroiled in a park-wide resource war between Villain World and Hero World (to which Presley belonged).

  During this conflict, the *Red Dwarf* crew transported to the planet using a Matter Paddle, with Lister and Cat materializing in Villain territory, while Rimmer and Kryten landed in Hero territory. Rimmer found the heroes' army lacking and took command, making Presley a sergeant. Arnold worked many of the pacifistic waxdroids to death before ordering a frontal attack on the enemy's compound across a minefield. This wiped out the remaining droids, including Elvis **[T-SER4.6]**.

- ***Press Gang*:** A British children's television comedy-drama series that ran in the 1980s and '90s **[RL]**. *Press Gang* was rebooted centuries later, featuring a group of teenage mechanoids. In one episode—which aired on Groovy Channel 27 at 4:45 PM on Wednesday, the 27th of Geldof, 2362—the group offered free laundry services to the public **[M-SMG1.7(a)]**.

- **"Press Your Lumps Against Mine":** A slow dance song recorded by Johnny Cologne, circa the twenty-second century. This tune was played in *Red Dwarf*'s disco room following George McIntyre's "Welcome Back" party **[N-INF]**.

- **"Pricesmashers":** A word printed on signs hung throughout a twenty-first-century shopping mall that the *Red Dwarf* crew imagined visiting while trapped in an elation squid hallucination. The letter "M" formed the shape of a punching fist **[T-SER9.2]**.

- ***Pride and Prejudice Land*:** An artificial-reality (AR) simulation of the book *Pride and Prejudice*, included in the AR simulation *Jane Austen World*. At age fourteen, Kochanski spent much of her time in this program while attending cyberschool. Many years later, she and the *Starbug 1* crew salvaged a copy from the Space Corps derelict SS *Centauri*.

  Kochanski convinced Lister and Cat to join her in *Pride and Prejudice Land* in order to expand their cultural horizons, much to the frustration of Kryten, who had prepared a special lobster dinner to celebrate the anniversary of his rescue from *Nova 5*. Undeterred by the snub, Kryten modified the AR program and entered in a World War II tank, then blew up a gazebo occupied by the game's characters, forcing the crew to leave the AR Suite and join him for dinner **[T-SER7.6]**.

  ***NOTE:** Kochanski also called the program* Pride and Prejudice World.

- **Prima Doner:** A food establishment on the set of the British television show *Coronation Street* **[RL]**. While trapped in an elation squid hallucination, the *Red Dwarf* crew imagined being on an alternate twenty-first-century Earth. In the illusion,

**PREFIX**
**RL:** Real life

**T-: Television Episodes**
**SER:** Television series
**IDW:** "Identity Within"
**USA1:** Unaired U.S. pilot
**USA2:** Unaired U.S. demo

**R-: *The Bodysnatcher Collection***
**SER:** Remastered episodes
**BOD:** "Bodysnatcher"
**DAD:** "Dad"
**FTH:** "Lister's Father"
**INF:** "Infinity Patrol"
**END:** "The End" (original assembly)

**N-: Novels**
**INF:** *Infinity Welcomes Careful Drivers*
**BTL:** *Better Than Life*
**LST:** *Last Human*
**BCK:** *Backwards*
**OMN:** *Red Dwarf Omnibus*

**M-: Magazines**
**SMG:** *Smegazine*

**W-: Websites**
**OFF:** Official website
**NAN:** *Prelude to Nanarchy*
**AND:** *Androids*
**DIV:** Diva-Droid
**DIB:** Duane Dibbley
**CRP:** Crapola
**GEN:** Geneticon
**LSR:** Leisure World Intl.
**JMC:** Jupiter Mining Corporation
**AIT:** *A.I. Today*
**HOL:** HoloPoint

**G-: Roleplaying Game**
**RPG:** *Core Rulebook*
**BIT:** *A.I. Screen Extra Bits* booklet
**SOR:** *Series Sourcebook*
**OTH:** Other RPG material

they passed the Prima Doner while trying to find actor Craig Charles, who portrayed Lister on a television show called *Red Dwarf* **[T-SER9.2]**.

*NOTE: Prima Doner, like all businesses appearing in this sequence, was created for the television show* Coronation Street, *in which Craig Charles starred as of this writing. Prima Doner was owned by Dev Alahan, and was located at 18 Victoria Street, in the fictional town of Weatherfield, England.*

- **primer:** A small component in the head of a 4000 Series mechanoid, required for the droid's proper operation. When the *Red Dwarf* crew looted the SS *Centauri* for spare mechanoid heads, they discovered the primers missing, then disguised themselves as GELFs and bartered for the parts with a rogue simulant **[T-SER7.6]**.

- **Prince:** A nickname that Confidence, a hallucination of Lister's mind made corporeal by mutated pneumonia, called Lister **[T-SER1.5]**.

- **Prince of Charisma:** Another nickname that the corporeal hallucination Confidence gave to Lister **[T-SER1.5]**.

- **Prince of Dorkness, the:** A nickname that Cat called Duane Dibbley, his nerdy alter ego, after an emohawk drained him of his poise and cool **[T-SER6.4]**.

- **Prince of Wales:** A title granted to the heir apparent of the United Kingdom's reigning monarch **[RL]**. While trapped in an addictive version of *Better Than Life*, Rimmer imagined hosting a glamorous party on Earth, at which he served gazpacho soup. When the Prince of Wales complained that the soup was cold, Arnold corrected the royal, telling him it was meant to be served that way **[N-INF]**.

  *NOTE: As of this book's writing, the Prince of Wales is Charles Philip Arthur George, the eldest child of Queen Elizabeth II.*

- **Princess Leia:** A nickname that Kryten called Kochanski when she wore earmuffs to silence noise coming from the pipes in her quarters aboard *Starbug 1* **[T-SER7.4]**.

  *NOTE: Princess Leia Organa, portrayed by actor Carrie Fisher, was a main character of the original* Star Wars *film trilogy. Leia sometimes wore her hair in large side buns.*

- **Priory, the:** A mental health and celebrity rehabilitation hospital located in Southwest London **[RL]**. While trapped in an elation squid hallucination, the *Red Dwarf* crew imagined that actor Craig Charles, upon meeting Lister—whom he portrayed on television—blamed the encounter on flashbacks and decided to go back to the Priory **[T-SER9.3]**.

  *NOTE: The mention of flashbacks and the Priory referenced Charles' real-life bout with drug abuse and his subsequent stay at that facility.*

- **Priscilla, Queen of Deep Space:** A nickname that a parallel-dimension Kochanski called Lister upon discovering she was stuck in his reality. The name referenced the outfit Dave wore at the time, which consisted of a frilly pink robe and fluffy pig slippers **[T-SER7.3]**.

  *NOTE: This nickname riffed on* The Adventures of Priscilla, Queen of the Desert, *a 1994 film about two drag queens and a transsexual woman traveling across the Australian Outback.*

- **prison officer ident:** An identification code provided to prison guards using the facilities at the penal station Justice World. Crafts with personnel lacking prison officer idents were directed to the station's neutral zone, to be met with escort boots and processed through a mind probe before being granted clearance to use the facilities **[T-SER4.3]**.

- **Private Nobody:** A nickname that the prime Rimmer called the mirror universe's Frank Hollister while posing as Captain Rimmer, *Red Dwarf*'s commander in that reality **[T-SER8.8]**.

- **probe ship:** A two-part shuttlecraft used as a planetary service vessel, also called a dropship. The aft section (fighter) was built to pilot the combined craft through space and a planet's atmosphere. When separated from the fore section (sub), it could be piloted by skutters and used for external maintenance, such as clearing graffiti from *Red Dwarf*'s hull. Once detached, the sub could be dispatched for exploration of or insertion into a variety of environments. It contained retractable caterpillar tracks for land use and propellers for aquatic use, and was equipped with a Utility Remote Mark One (U.R.1) **[X-XVD]**.

When Kryten accidentally swallowed an alien invasion fleet, Lister shrunk the crew down and used a miniaturized probe ship to locate and remove the aliens' radioactive weapon from the mechanoid's body **[X-XMS]**.

*NOTE: Concept art for this vessel labeled it as a Canary dropship, presumably designed to insert Canary forces into a variety of environments.*

- **Professor Cat:** *See* Cat, Professor

- **Professor E:** *See* Edgington, Irene, Professor ("Professor E")

- **Professor H:** A genetically engineered superhero in the universe known as Alternative 2X13/L, who appeared as a disembodied translucent head. Professor H—that reality's Holly—guided the members of the Liberty League, a band of superheroes tasked with protecting the city of Smegopolis. In 2315, Professor H led the League into battle with their nemeses, the Conspirator and the Penguin, as the duo perpetrated a bank heist **[M-SMG2.1(c3)]**.

  *NOTE: Professor H was based loosely on Marvel Comics' Charles Xavier (Professor X), the leader of the X-Men.*

- **Prog disc A49:** The location in *Nova 5*'s databanks of medical records for crewmembers Jane Air, Tracey Johns and Anne Gill **[T-SER2.1]**.

- **programmable virus**: An artificial pathogen that could be programmed to perform certain tasks. While on spud duty in *Red Dwarf*'s brig, Lister and Rimmer had Bob the skutter procure a sample of the virus, which had been programmed to eat the skin from potatoes, to help them with their chore. The virus was not programmed properly, however, and ate away their clothes and hair, leaving them bald and naked. The virus was transferred to Captain Hollister when Rimmer shook his hand, which earned the pair two months in the Hole, *Red Dwarf*'s solitary-confinement cell **[T-SER8.6]**.

- **projection circuits:** Electrical components built into Jake Bullet and other cyborgs, enabling them to recall images from memory. Bullet's projection circuits kicked in when he was about to be crushed by a runaway car while investigating a murder. This caused him to see his life literally flash before his eyes **[M-SMG1.12(c1)]**.

- **projection unit:** An alternate term for Rimmer's light bee, the floating mechanism that projected the hologram's image and allowed him to leave the confines of *Red Dwarf* **[T-SER6.2]**.

  *NOTE: See also the light bee entry.*

- **Project: Pants:** *See* Projekt: Hosen

- **Project Regen:** The name Rimmer dubbed his plan to create a living host body for his consciousness via cellular regeneration, by using DNA stolen from Lister's hair and transferring his mind into the new form. The plan failed **[R-BOD]**.

- **Project *Wildfire*:** A program developed by the Space Corps Research and Development division in one of Ace Rimmer's universes. Its project number was 70773. Headed by Admiral Tranter, the project included mechanic Dave "Spanners" Lister and test pilot Ace Rimmer, and involved a ship theoretically capable of breaking the light barrier.

  When an identical ship arrived three days before *Wildfire*'s scheduled launch date, carrying the burnt corpse of another Commander Rimmer, Tranter's team realized the ship could also cross dimensions. Their *Wildfire* was reprogrammed to avoid a similar accident, and on March 31, 2181, Ace piloted the vessel into another universe during a much later era, where he met a cowardly version of himself **[N-BCK]**.

- **Project *Wildflower*:** A name that the Olaf Petersen of Ace Rimmer's universe, following a night of drunken debauchery, mistakenly called Project *Wildfire* **[N-BCK]**.

- **Projekt: Hosen:** A program created by the Reich on War World to develop Rocket Pants—a type of trousers enabling soldiers to fly. Projekt: Hosen (German for Project: Pants) was almost discontinued several times due to numerous groinal accidents that occurred during testing **[G-BIT]**.

- **Promised Land, the:** A synonym for Fuchal, a holy place revered in the religion of the Cat People inhabiting *Red Dwarf*.

**PREFIX**
**RL:** Real life

**T-: Television Episodes**
**SER:** Television series
**IDW:** "Identity Within"
**USA1:** Unaired U.S. pilot
**USA2:** Unaired U.S. demo

**R-: *The Bodysnatcher Collection***
**SER:** Remastered episodes
**BOD:** "Bodysnatcher"
**DAD:** "Dad"
**FTH:** "Lister's Father"
**INF:** "Infinity Patrol"
**END:** "The End" (original assembly)

**N-: Novels**
**INF:** *Infinity Welcomes Careful Drivers*
**BTL:** *Better Than Life*
**LST:** *Last Human*

**BCK:** *Backwards*
**OMN:** *Red Dwarf Omnibus*

**M-: Magazines**
**SMG:** *Smegazine*

**W-: Websites**
**OFF:** Official website
**NAN:** *Prelude to Nanarchy*
**AND:** *Androids*
**DIV:** Diva-Droid
**DIB:** Duane Dibbley

**CRP:** Crapola
**GEN:** Geneticon
**LSR:** Leisure World Intl.
**JMC:** Jupiter Mining Corporation
**AIT:** *A.I. Today*
**HOL:** HoloPoint

**G-: Roleplaying Game**
**RPG:** *Core Rulebook*
**BIT:** *A.I. Screen Extra Bits* booklet
**SOR:** *Series Sourcebook*
**OTH:** Other RPG material

According to doctrine, the Cat People's savior, Cloister the Stupid, would return from being frozen in time, to lead them to the Promised Land. Unbeknownst to the Cats, the word "Fuchal" was a bastardization of Fiji, a small island on Earth to which Lister had intended to bring his pregnant cat, Frankenstein **[T-SER1.1]**.

- **Promised Planet, The:** A synonym for Bearth, the place where the Father of Catkind (Lister) would take them after returning from being frozen in time **[N-INF]**.

  *NOTE: See also the Bearth entry. This was changed from the Promised Land (Fuchal), mentioned onscreen in episode 1.1 ("The End").*

- **"Property of JMC":** A phrase printed on a sign affixed to a shopping trolley in which Lister awoke following a night spent drinking GELF hooch **[T-SER10.2]**.

- **propulsion unit:** A component of MkIV Titanica Fish Droids, such as Lister's pet robot goldfish Lennon and McCartney, which provided thrust and allowed the droids to move **[M-SMG2.4(c5)]**.

- **prostidroid:** A type of android sex worker. On the television series *Androids*, Mollee protested android brothels—putting pimps in jail and setting their prostidroids free. Rimmer once called Lister a "son-of-a-prostidroid" **[N-INF]**.

- **Protocol 121:** A hypothetical health and safety rule that Lister made up to mock Rimmer, which he claimed stated, "No exploding in the Drive Room" **[T-SER10.4]**.

- **Protocol 175:** One of Rimmer's health and safety protocols aboard *Red Dwarf*, which mandated, "No running in the corridors." He reminded Kryten of this rule when the mechanoid hurried to find clothes for Irene Edgington, who had materialized naked after being transformed from a chimpanzee **[T-SER10.4]**.

- **Proton Cannon of Nakasami:** A powerful, human-built weapon. During its testing phase, the cannon was fired from a starship in the outskirts of Earth's solar system; government officials later confirmed that the testing date coincided with Pluto's disappearance. The recoil propelled the starship back through the solar system and embedded it in Titan, where it served as a sightseeing attraction and became the first weapon to recoup its development costs through tourism **[B-EVR]**.

- **PSI:** An acronym meaning pounds per square inch, used as a measurement of pressure or stress **[RL]**. A *Starbug*'s engines' PSI value was required to calculate its thrust-to-input ratio **[T-SER4.5]**.

- **psi-locator:** A device capable of locating an individual's consciousness through space-time and transport it to the present. Kryten attempted to use a psi-locator to bring Lister's mind from the past in order to warn him of the impending cadmium II explosion aboard *Red Dwarf*, so that he could save the ship's crew.

  Lister's consciousness slipped back into the timestream, however, re-emerging at several key moments of heightened emotional stress throughout his lifetime, such as being released from stasis and learning of the crew's death, Rimmer's duplication as a second hologram, giving birth to his sons Jim and Bexley, encountering the Inquisitor, being attacked by a polymorph, and the point at which he created the universe. Eventually, Kryten sent Lister's consciousness back to its point of origin—the moment he wrote the words "fat bastard" in Captain Hollister's quarters on a dare **[M-SMG2.4(c1)]**.

- **psi-moon:** An artificial planetoid possessing the ability to terraform and shape itself according to an individual's psyche **[T-SER5.3]**. It accomplished this with the aid of nanobots **[G-RPG]**.

  The moon latched onto a person's dominating drive, whether ambition, greed or the desire to please, and constructed a corresponding environment, complete with appropriate denizens. If the moon used the psyche of a hologram for its template, the hologram was given physical form while inhabiting the planet, with all the benefits and disadvantages such a form afforded, including the ability to be injured or killed.

  When Rimmer and Kryten landed on a psi-moon, the planetoid used Rimmer's mind as a template and restructured itself as a desolate, gloomy, swamp-filled wasteland inhabited by manifestations of his negative attributes. These beings then

**B-: Books**
**PRG:** *Red Dwarf Programme Guide*
**SUR:** *Red Dwarf Space Corps Survival Manual*
**PRM:** *Primordial Soup*
**SOS:** *Son of Soup*
**SCE:** *Scenes from the Dwarf*
**LOG:** *Red Dwarf Log No. 1996*
**RD8:** *Red Dwarf VIII*
**EVR:** *The Log: A Dwarfer's Guide to Everything*

**X-: Misc.**
**PRO:** Promotional materials, videos, etc.
**PST:** Posters at DJ XVII (2013)
**CAL:** 2008 calendar
**RNG:** Cell phone ringtones
**MOB:** Mobisode ("Red Christmas")
**CIN:** *Children in Need* sketch
**GEK:** *Geek Week* intros by Kryten
**TNG:** "Tongue-Tied" video

**XMS:** Bill Pearson's Christmas special pitch script
**XVD:** Bill Pearson's Christmas special pitch video
**OTH:** Other *Red Dwarf* appearances

**SUFFIX**
**DVD:**
**(d)** – Deleted scene
**(o)** – Outtake
**(b)** – Bonus DVD material (other)
**(e)** – Extended version

**SMEGAZINES:**
**(c)** – Comic
**(a)** – Article

**OTHER:**
**(s)** – Early/unused script draft
**(s1)** – Alternate version of script

kidnapped and tortured him until his shipmates mounted a rescue **[T-SER5.3]**.

The battle between Rimmer's positive and negative traits raged on after he left the psi-moon, with musketeer-like manifestations of Charity, Courage and Self-Esteem struggling against foes such as Misery, Self-Despair and Paranoia. In one battle, the negative forces took Self-Esteem hostage in order to lure the others to the Castle of Despondency, where they planned to use their secret weapon: the image of Rimmer's mother **[M-SMG2.7(c2)]**.

Another psi-moon was the birthplace of raunchy anthropomorphic penguin Mr. Flibble **[M-SMG2.7(c3)]**.

> ***NOTE:** The term has occasionally been spelled "psy-moon."*

- **psi-proof chrysalis:** A cocoon that a polymorph could create to protect itself during its Shadow Time. This shield blocked out all telepathic signals so the creature could rest while metamorphosing, during which its telepathic abilities increased **[M-SMG1.13(c3)]**.

- **Psiren:** A genetically engineered life-form (GELF) with telepathic abilities, which inhabited certain asteroid belts and, in their natural state, resembled large, hulking cockroaches. Psirens lured unsuspecting passersby by scanning their minds and creating illusions catered to their desires, to draw them closer to the asteroids so the creatures could force them to land and strip their spaceship. They then fed on each victim by inserting a large straw into his or her ear canal and sucking out the brain. Highly competitive, Psirens were known to kill each other over quarry.

While pursuing the stolen *Red Dwarf*, the *Starbug 1* crew risked entering the Psirens' asteroid belt in order to catch up with the mining vessel. The Psirens subjected them to several illusions to get them to land, including footage of beautiful, sex-starved women, as well as Kochanski in peril. Eventually, they succeeded, and the shuttle crashed onto an asteroid. As Lister carried out repairs, a pair of Psirens attacked, one in the guise of his childhood crush, Pete Tranter's sister, the other posing as Kryten. Dave, however, saw through the charade.

Aboard *Starbug*, the crew faced a dilemma, as two Listers boarded the craft. Testing determined which one was the impostor, but it escaped into *Starbug*'s lower decks. The crew pursued the creature, but it continued to trick them, appearing first as a beverage dispenser, and then as Kryten's creator, Professor Mamet, who ordered him into a trash compactor. Kryten, crushed into a large metallic cube, fell onto the intruder, killing it before it could feed on Lister and Cat **[T-SER6.1]**.

- **"Psirens":** A message that a crewman aboard a derelict spacecraft scrawled on the floor in his own blood, after generating a warning to passing spacecraft that genetically engineered life-forms were in the area. The dead crewman's kidney unintentionally punctuated the message with a period **[T-SER6.1]**.

- **Psi-scan:** An all-purpose handheld scanning device developed by Tucker Instruments, available in several models, including the basic TI345, the smaller Mini-Psi TI345xp **[G-RPG]** and the 346. The model used aboard *Red Dwarf* was the larger 345 version **[T-SER5.4]**.

This model's functions included detecting the absence of certain emotions from individuals following a polymorph attack **[T-SER3.3]**, doubling as a portable medi-scan **[T-SER5.2]**, detecting deadly airborne viruses **[T-SER5.4]**, identifying chemical compounds **[T-SER5.6]**, determining if the membrane between two realities had collapsed **[T-SER7.3]**, and locating and reading JMC ident chips **[T-SER7.7]**.

> ***NOTE:** The device's name was spelled "sci-scan" in several* Smegazine *comics.*

- **psi-virus:** A deadly disease that stimulated the dormant psychic areas of the brain, giving an afflicted individual such abilities as hex vision (the discharging of electrical bolts through the eyes), telepathy and telekinesis. The illness also rendered the victim insane, draining his or her life force until the body ultimately failed. A hologrammic version of a psi-virus, a holovirus called *Latin name*, infected Hildegarde Lanstrom, who passed it on to Rimmer before dying **[T-SER5.4]**.

- **psychic sub-ether enhancement implant:** An implantable piece of technology believed to increase the odds of winning certain games of chance. After winning at four-dimensional pontoon by cheating his GELF opponents, Lister gloated that

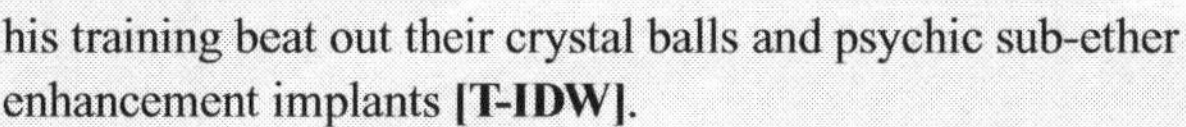

his training beat out their crystal balls and psychic sub-ether enhancement implants **[T-IDW]**.

- **psychotropic drug:** A chemical substance designed to act upon the central nervous system, affecting brain function and altering one's perception, mood, cognition and behavior **[RL]**. Psychotropic drugs were often used during a mind scan, enabling a Board of Inquiry to view and record the cerebral reactions of an accused individual to different alternate-reality scenarios. Such medications were administered to the *Starbug 1* crew through the glue on the envelopes they licked to seal their consent forms during their trial **[T-SER8.2]**.

- **psy-moon:** *See* psi-moon

- **pulsar:** A rotating neutron star emitting beams of electromagnetic radiation **[RL]**. Pulsars were covered in the space phenomenon section of Kryten's *Starbug 1* pilot's test **[T-SER3.1]**.

- **pulse missile:** A guided explosive weapon utilized by Space Corps external enforcement vehicles. After an enforcement probe discovered the *Starbug 1* crew looting Space Corps derelicts, it fired pulse missiles at the shuttle. *Starbug* narrowly escaped the attack, but the detonation knocked out its oxy-generation unit, leaving the crew stranded. With no other option, they met with a tribe of Kinitawowi GELFs and traded for a new OG unit **[T-SER6.4]**. Pulse missiles had a range of 10 kilometers (6.2 miles), and were available from Crapola Inc.'s annual *SCABBY* catalog **[G-RPG]**.

- **pulse relays:** A set of components in a *Starbug* shuttle's propulsion system. When Kryten asked the Epideme virus infecting Lister how the crew could reconfigure the ship's drive module to be more efficient, it instructed the mechanoid to re-route the pulse relays via the auxiliary conductor nodes **[T-SER7.7]**.

- ***Pumping Iron Today*:** A fitness magazine Lister read while sitting in a Jacuzzi drinking beer, which was his idea of getting into shape **[T-SER3.4(d)]**.

- **Pumpy:** One of seven diminutive rainforest dwellers known as the Ionian Ecommandoes, who lived in the jungles of Io on the television soap opera *Androids*. He and his comrades nursed Karstares back to health **[M-SMG2.5(c5)]**, after Karstares' plane crashed due to sabotage by his son Jaysee **[M-SMG1.14(c3)]**. Grateful for their help, Karstares became the Green Knight, the rainforest's protector, and fought alongside the Ecommandoes against Jaysee's ecologically harmful company **[M-SMG2.5(c5)]**. Pumpy died during a firefight between Jaysee and his foes **[M-SMG2.8(c2)]**.

  ***NOTE:** This character resembled one of Disney's Seven Dwarfs. All of the Ecommandoes' names were slang for sex.*

- **Punisher Heavy Machine Gun (HMG):** A heavy-duty weapon produced by Bloodust Arms and distributed via Crapola Inc.'s annual *SCABBY* catalog. It had various firing modes and an effective range of 100 meters (328 feet), and was available in Gunmetal Blue or Bitchin' Chrome **[G-RPG]**.

- ***Punking Up Prokofiev*:** An album recorded by Reggie Wilson **[M-SMG1.3(a)]**.

- **Purley:** A district of South London, England **[RL]**. As a youth, Lister had a best friend named Duncan, until the boy's family moved to Spain after his father botched a bank robbery in Purley **[T-SER2.4]**.

- **Purple Alert:** An alert status indicating a potential threat to a *Starbug* shuttlecraft. A Purple Alert occurred between a Red Alert and a Blue Alert, and was akin to a Mauve Alert in terms of emergency level. Holly declared a Purple Alert when Ace Rimmer opened a dimensional portal directly in front of *Starbug 1* and crossed into their reality on a collision course **[T-SER4.5]**.

- **Pus Green:** A designer color that Malpractice Medical & Scispec offered for its medi-scans **[G-RPG]**.

- **Pushkin, Natalina, Commander:** The hologrammic second-in-command of the holoship *Enlightenment*. She had an IQ of 201 and a heavy Russian accent **[T-SER5.1]**.

**B-: Books**
**PRG:** *Red Dwarf Programme Guide*
**SUR:** *Red Dwarf Space Corps Survival Manual*
**PRM:** *Primordial Soup*
**SOS:** *Son of Soup*
**SCE:** *Scenes from the Dwarf*
**LOG:** *Red Dwarf Log No. 1996*
**RD8:** *Red Dwarf VIII*
**EVR:** *The Log: A Dwarfer's Guide to Everything*

**X-: Misc.**
**PRO:** Promotional materials, videos, etc.
**PST:** Posters at DJ XVII (2013)
**CAL:** 2008 calendar
**RNG:** Cell phone ringtones
**MOB:** Mobisode ("Red Christmas")
**CIN:** *Children in Need* sketch
**GEK:** *Geek Week* intros by Kryten
**TNG:** "Tongue-Tied" video
**XMS:** Bill Pearson's Christmas special pitch script
**XVD:** Bill Pearson's Christmas special pitch video
**OTH:** Other *Red Dwarf* appearances

**SUFFIX**
**DVD:**
**(d)** – Deleted scene
**(o)** – Outtake
**(b)** – Bonus DVD material (other)
**(e)** – Extended version

**SMEGAZINES:**
**(c)** – Comic
**(a)** – Article

**OTHER:**
**(s)** – Early/unused script draft
**(s1)** – Alternate version of script

- ***Push the Button*****:** An interactive video game hosted in the children's section of Crapola Inc.'s website, in which kids were challenged to push as many buttons as possible within an allotted span of time. The game was intended to keep children busy while their parents shopped **[W-CRP]**.

- **Pussycat Willum:** A nickname that Rimmer called Cat after he started the resuscitation process on an escape pod possibly containing a crazed cyborg **[T-SER4.3]**.

  ***NOTE:*** *Pussy Cat Willum was a British puppet character who introduced children's programs in the 1960s.*

- **Putsley:** An element of zero-gee football. A popular scoring strategy known as the Rabid Hunch was only valid if either team had a Putsley in play **[M-SMG1.8(a)]**.

- **pyramids:** A series of massive stone structures erected in various areas throughout Earth, often built as tombs for deceased rulers **[RL]**. Rimmer cited the construction of Egypt's ancient pyramids as an example of a mystery that could only be explained by the existence of aliens. Lister, however, attributed their existence to massive whips and slave labor **[T-SER1.4]**.

- **Pythagoras of Samos:** A Greek philosopher and mathematician, circa the sixth century B.C., credited with discovering the Euclidean geometry relationship between a right triangle's three sides, later dubbed the Pythagorean theorem **[RL]**.

  A waxdroid replica of Pythagoras was created for the Waxworld theme park. Left on their own for millions of years, the waxdroids attained sentience and became embroiled in a park-wide resource war between Villain World and Hero World (to which Pythagoras belonged). Pythagoras was convinced the solution to the war was within their grasp, and that it probably involved triangles **[T-SER4.6]**. The droid was proficient at throwing triangles **[G-SOR]**.

  During this war, the *Red Dwarf* crew transported to the planet using a Matter Paddle, with Rimmer and Kryten materializing in Hero territory, while Lister and Cat landed in Villain territory. Rimmer found the heroes' army lacking and took command, working many of the pacifistic waxdroids to death before ordering a frontal attack on the enemy's compound across a minefield. This wiped out the remaining droids, including Pythogoras **[T-SER4.6]**.

- **Pythagorean theorem:** A Euclidean geometry term named after Greek mathematician Pythagoras of Samos, describing the relationship between the three sides of a right triangle: The square of the hypotenuse equals the sum of the squares of the other two sides ($a^2+b^2=c^2$) **[RL]**. Rimmer babbled about the Pythagorean theorem while pretending to prepare for the Engineer's Exam, to keep Lister from realizing he was too panicked to pass **[T-SER1.1]**.

**PREFIX**
**RL:** Real life

**T-: Television Episodes**
**SER:** Television series
**IDW:** "Identity Within"
**USA1:** Unaired U.S. pilot
**USA2:** Unaired U.S. demo

**R-: *The Bodysnatcher Collection***
**SER:** Remastered episodes
**BOD:** "Bodysnatcher"
**DAD:** "Dad"
**FTH:** "Lister's Father"
**INF:** "Infinity Patrol"
**END:** "The End" (original assembly)

**N-: Novels**
**INF:** *Infinity Welcomes Careful Drivers*
**BTL:** *Better Than Life*
**LST:** *Last Human*
**BCK:** *Backwards*
**OMN:** *Red Dwarf Omnibus*

**M-: Magazines**
**SMG:** *Smegazine*

**W-: Websites**
**OFF:** Official website
**NAN:** *Prelude to Nanarchy*
**AND:** *Androids*
**DIV:** Diva-Droid
**DIB:** Duane Dibbley
**CRP:** Crapola
**GEN:** Geneticon
**LSR:** Leisure World Intl.
**JMC:** Jupiter Mining Corporation
**AIT:** *A.I. Today*
**HOL:** HoloPoint

**G-: Roleplaying Game**
**RPG:** *Core Rulebook*
**BIT:** *A.I. Screen Extra Bits* booklet
**SOR:** *Series Sourcebook*
**OTH:** Other RPG material

**B-: Books**
**PRG:** *Red Dwarf Programme Guide*
**SUR:** *Red Dwarf Space Corps Survival Manual*
**PRM:** *Primordial Soup*
**SOS:** *Son of Soup*
**SCE:** *Scenes from the Dwarf*
**LOG:** *Red Dwarf Log No. 1996*
**RD8:** *Red Dwarf VIII*
**EVR:** *The Log: A Dwarfer's Guide to Everything*

**X-: Misc.**
**PRO:** Promotional materials, videos, etc.
**PST:** Posters at DJ XVII (2013)
**CAL:** 2008 calendar
**RNG:** Cell phone ringtones
**MOB:** Mobisode ("Red Christmas")
**CIN:** *Children in Need* sketch
**GEK:** *Geek Week* intros by Kryten
**TNG:** "Tongue-Tied" video

**XMS:** Bill Pearson's Christmas special pitch script
**XVD:** Bill Pearson's Christmas special pitch video
**OTH:** Other *Red Dwarf* appearances

**SUFFIX**
**DVD:**
**(d)** – Deleted scene
**(o)** – Outtake
**(b)** – Bonus DVD material (other)
**(e)** – Extended version

**SMEGAZINES:**
**(c)** – Comic
**(a)** – Article

**OTHER:**
**(s)** – Early/unused script draft
**(s1)** – Alternate version of script

Q
QUEEG 500

- **Q23/J80:** A bearing that Kochanski ordered while attempting to catch the SS *Centauri* and rescue Kryten. This bearing was in the opposite direction of the *Centauri*, making the simulant captain question the crew's motives. When he turned his ship around to pursue them, they were then able to retrieve their comrade **[T-SER7.6]**.

- **Q47 twin frontal mounts:** A set of components of a 6000 Series mechanoid **[T-SER9(b)]**.

  *NOTE: This was mentioned in a PBS announcement for* Red Dwarf.

- **QBX1934:** The reference number of a job opening listed on Jupiter Mining Corporation's website. The position was for a salvage leader able to manage a mission to recover *Red Dwarf* **[W-JMC]**.

- **qik-pik:** A self-developing photograph technology, used in the twenty-second century. Lister took a qik-pik of his future echo holding his newborn sons outside *Red Dwarf*'s Medical Unit **[N-INF]**.

  *NOTE: This futuristic technology was analogous to Polaroid instant film.*

- **QNK base system:** A programming language incorporated into model 7-6-80 cellular phones **[W-RNG]**.

- **QPR:** *See* Queens Park Rangers

- **Quadrant 2, Vector 4:** The coordinates of a large asteroid within which the *Blue Midget* crew took cover while fleeing a Simulant Death Ship, so that they could devise an escape plan **[T-SER10.6]**.

- **Quadrant 2 to Q41/9:** A set of coordinates that Kochanski provided to Cat as the *Starbug 1* crew evaded a GELF battle cruiser containing Lister's bride, Hackhackhackachhachhachach **[T-SER7.3]**.

- **Quadrant 4, Sector 492:** An area of space in which Holly detected a probe from the holoship *Enlightenment* **[T-SER5.1]**.

- **Quadrant 492/G87:** A set of coordinates that Kochanski provided to Cat as the *Starbug 1* crew evaded a GELF battle cruiser containing Lister's bride, Hackhackhackachhachhachach **[T-SER7.3]**.

- **Quadrant 497:** An area of space in which Camille's escape vessel was marooned on a planet with a decaying orbit. Kryten and Rimmer rescued the Pleasure GELF after picking up her distress call aboard *Starbug 1* while asteroid-spotting in the vicinity **[T-SER4.1]**.

- **Quadrant 4972:** The coordinates of a civilization comprising thousands of Arnold Rimmer clones, on a planet dubbed Rimmerworld **[T-SER6.5]**.

- **Quagaar:** A fanciful designation Rimmer gave to animal remains contained in a mysterious pod that the *Red Dwarf* crew discovered in deep space, which he believed to be the corpse of a highly advanced extraterrestrial warrior. However, the craft turned out to be merely the mining ship's own garbage pod, jettisoned years earlier—and the carcass was that of a roast chicken **[T-SER1.4]**.

- **Quagaar:** A species of warriors from an alternate dimension. Resembling roast chicken carcasses, the Quagaar attacked their foes with a wishbone strike maneuver, rendering them unconscious, then used a large baster-like weapon to suck their enemies' brains out through their ears **[G-SOR]**.

- **quantum drive:** A type of propulsion system utilizing quantum mechanics and indeterminism to force a spacefaring vessel into two points of space-time simultaneously, and then chose the point closest to the ship's destination for materialization. The duality jump—a propulsion unit installed aboard *Nova 5*—was a quantum drive **[N-INF]**.

- **quantum rod:** A cylindrical mechanism that provided the key propulsion method in Quantum Twisters used by the Space Corps' elite Super-Infinity Fleet. The rod allowed a ship to traverse large distances by drawing together previously connected matter, much like a magnet, and worked on the basis that all matter was once connected at the time of the

Big Bang. This enabled a vessel to jump to any other point in space-time. The rod glowed green when activated.

When the *Red Dwarf* discovered the Space Corps derelict *Trojan*, Rimmer accidentally activated its quantum rod, creating a connection between his crew and *Columbus 3*, a Space Corps ship that had previously been attacked. This not only allowed the crew to pick up *Columbus 3*'s distress call, but also enabled the survivors—a hologrammic version of Rimmer's half-brother Howard, and a Space Corps Simulant named Crawford—to transport to safety aboard *Trojan*.

Crawford later revealed her involvement in the attack on *Columbus 3*, and held Howard and the *Red Dwarf* crew captive while searching for data concerning the quantum rod, with which she planned to start a simulant uprising. She was disabled, however, before acquiring the information **[T-SER10.1]**.

A side of effect of the rod was that it created synchronicity between individuals by stimulating their psi powers. Kryten discovered this ability while experimenting with crystals extruded from the rod. As a result, he and Cat temporarily became synched, causing them to speak in tandem and influence events based on coincidence. This power allowed them to locate the origin of an explosive device fitted onto Lister by BEGGs, and to decode its deactivation sequence **[T-SER10.4]**.

- **Quantum Twister:** A type of craft used by the Space Corps' Super-Infinity Fleet, deemed the organization's top achievement. Quantum Twisters made use of a quantum rod to connect the ship to every other point in space-time, allowing it to transport virtually anywhere instantly. One such vessel was the *Trojan* **[T-SER10.1]**.

  ***NOTE:*** *Presumably,* Columbus 3 *was also a Quantum Twister, given that Rimmer stated his brothers all served on similar ships.*

- **Quarantine Room 152:** Specialized quarters within *Red Dwarf*'s quarantine area, also called Quarantine Suite 152, allocated for temporarily housing individuals potentially exposed to dangerous pathogens. Room 152 was a single-person accommodation, containing one chair, one bed, and one bathroom with a shower. The room was sealed airtight and locked by an electronic keypad. For leisure activities, it was stocked with a chess set missing thirty-one pieces, a knitting magazine with a pull-out section about crocheted hats, a puzzle magazine with the crosswords completed, and the video *Wallpapering, Painting and Stippling—A DIY Guide*.

  Upon returning from a dangerous viral research lab, Lister, Kryten and Cat were diverted to the quarantine area, where Rimmer assigned them to Quarantine Room 152 for three months. After five days, they realized their shipmate had contracted a holovirus and intended to hold them in quarantine for ten years. When Rimmer threatened to shut off the oxygen in the room, they escaped using a vial of luck virus Kryten had taken from the lab, with which they immobilized Arnold and put *him* in quarantine **[T-SER5.4]**.

  ***NOTE:*** *This was originally called Quarantine Room 317, as revealed in the script book* Scenes from the Dwarf.

- **Quark Brain:** An insult that Lister called Rimmer after the latter docked him a quarter of a cigarette for saying "check" in a variety of silly voices while crosschecking *Red Dwarf*'s stock of homogenized puddings **[T-SER1.3]**.

- **quark-level matter-antimatter generator:** A sophisticated power generator that was designed for use aboard JMC vessels, but was eliminated from *Red Dwarf*'s final construction due to financial cutbacks. When Kryten's nanobots demolecularized and rebuilt *Red Dwarf*, they used the original design specifications, replacing the existing generator with this improved version **[T-SER8.1]**.

- ***Quartet for nine players in H sharp minor*:** The first composition Holly created using Hol Rock, a decimal-based music system of his own devising. It included a solo for a three-lunged trombone player **[N-INF]**.

- **quasar:** A compact region surrounding a supermassive black hole at the center of a massive galaxy, also called a quasi-stellar radio source **[RL]**. While preparing for his Astro-Engineer's Exam, Rimmer enlisted the help of skutters to take notes while he answered a question regarding the significance of the red spectrum in relation to quasars. Rimmer, not even knowing what a quasar was, had difficulty answering it **[T-SER1.3]**.

*NOTE: The red spectrum denotes the movement of a quasar away from Earth, the redshift being a result of the displacement of spectral lines toward longer wavelengths due to the Doppler effect.*

- **Quayle:** A Space Corps physicist considered one of the most brilliant minds of his era. Quayle was involved in a classified military project aboard a scientific research station that resulted in the creation of Legion, a gestalt entity encompassing the intellect and emotions of Quayle and his fellow project scientists. Quayle eventually died, as did the other scientists, leaving Legion nothing but a floating essence until the *Starbug 1* crew visited the station **[T-SER6.2]**.

  *NOTE: This may have been a joke at the expense of James Danforth Quayle, the United States' Vice President from 1989 to 1993, who was often the target of comedians for his perceived lack of intellect.*

- **Queeg 500:** An alter ego created by Holly to trick the *Red Dwarf* crew into appreciating him more. According to the ruse, Queeg (appearing as the head of a bald black man) was *Red Dwarf*'s backup computer, and was enabled in the event of a violation of Article 5 by the ship's primary artificial intelligence (Holly) **[T-SER2.5]**.

  Holly named Queeg after Captain Philip Francis Queeg, the unstable commander of the destroyer *Caine* in the novel *The Caine Mutiny*. The AI's attitude, meanwhile, was based on that of B.A. Baracus, a soldier of fortune portrayed by actor Laurence Tureaud ("Mr. T") on the American television show *The A-Team* **[W-OFF]**.

  The charade lasted for days, during which Holly, as Queeg, forced the crew to work and exercise for rations. Eventually, they begged Holly for help. He challenged the fictional AI to a contest, purposely losing and pretending to erase himself. After letting their situation sink in for a beat, Holly revealed the sham to the dumbstruck crew **[T-SER2.5]**.

- **Queen of Camelot:** A character in a medieval artificial-reality simulation. Lister entered the program intending to seduce the queen, using a book of cheats to remove her chastity belt **[T-SER7.2]**.

- **Queen of Panic:** A nickname that Lister gave Rimmer while on a backwards-running Earth. The title referred to Arnold's inability to comprehend life on that world, causing him to panic at every opportunity **[N-BCK]**.

- **Queens Park Rangers (QPR):** An English professional football club based in White City, London **[RL]**. When the Canaries encountered fellow inmates frozen in time aboard the SS *Manny Celeste*, Kryten said he had never witnessed such a phenomenon, leading Holly to conclude that he had never seen QPR play an away game **[T-SER8.6]**.

- **quiche:** A baked dish made of a pastry crust filled with an egg-based custard, combined with cheese, meat and/or vegetables **[RL]**. After a polymorph drained him of his anger, Rimmer wore a T-shirt that read "Give Quiche a Chance" **[T-SER3.3]**.

  *NOTE: Rimmer's T-shirt referenced the anti-war song "Give Peace a Chance," recorded by John Lennon and Yoko Ono (as the Plastic Ono Band) in 1969.*

- **quidbuck:** A slang term for dollarpound, a unit of currency used circa the twenty-second century. In the television soap opera *Androids*, the wealthy mechanoid Jaysee swung mega-quidbuck deals **[N-INF]**.

- **"Qw'k-Fytz":** A simulant expletive—as in, "For Qw'k-Fytz sake!" **[M-SMG2.9(c12)]**.

**PREFIX**
**RL:** Real life

**T-: Television Episodes**
**SER:** Television series
**IDW:** "Identity Within"
**USA1:** Unaired U.S. pilot
**USA2:** Unaired U.S. demo

**R-: *The Bodysnatcher Collection***
**SER:** Remastered episodes
**BOD:** "Bodysnatcher"
**DAD:** "Dad"
**FTH:** "Lister's Father"
**INF:** "Infinity Patrol"
**END:** "The End" (original assembly)

**N-: Novels**
**INF:** *Infinity Welcomes Careful Drivers*
**BTL:** *Better Than Life*
**LST:** *Last Human*
**BCK:** *Backwards*
**OMN:** *Red Dwarf Omnibus*

**M-: Magazines**
**SMG:** *Smegazine*

**W-: Websites**
**OFF:** Official website
**NAN:** *Prelude to Nanarchy*
**AND:** *Androids*
**DIV:** Diva-Droid
**DIB:** Duane Dibbley
**CRP:** Crapola
**GEN:** Geneticon
**LSR:** Leisure World Intl.
**JMC:** Jupiter Mining Corporation
**AIT:** *A.I. Today*
**HOL:** HoloPoint

**G-: Roleplaying Game**
**RPG:** *Core Rulebook*
**BIT:** *A.I. Screen Extra Bits* booklet
**SOR:** *Series Sourcebook*
**OTH:** Other RPG material

**B-: Books**
**PRG:** *Red Dwarf Programme Guide*
**SUR:** *Red Dwarf Space Corps Survival Manual*
**PRM:** *Primordial Soup*
**SOS:** *Son of Soup*
**SCE:** *Scenes from the Dwarf*
**LOG:** *Red Dwarf Log No. 1996*
**RD8:** *Red Dwarf VIII*
**EVR:** *The Log: A Dwarfer's Guide to Everything*

**X-: Misc.**
**PRO:** Promotional materials, videos, etc.
**PST:** Posters at DJ XVII (2013)
**CAL:** 2008 calendar
**RNG:** Cell phone ringtones
**MOB:** Mobisode ("Red Christmas")
**CIN:** *Children in Need* sketch
**GEK:** *Geek Week* intros by Kryten
**TNG:** "Tongue-Tied" video

**XMS:** Bill Pearson's Christmas special pitch script
**XVD:** Bill Pearson's Christmas special pitch video
**OTH:** Other *Red Dwarf* appearances

**SUFFIX**
**DVD:**
**(d)** – Deleted scene
**(o)** – Outtake
**(b)** – Bonus DVD material (other)
**(e)** – Extended version

**SMEGAZINES:**
**(c)** – Comic
**(a)** – Article

**OTHER:**
**(s)** – Early/unused script draft
**(s1)** – Alternate version of script

R

# RIMMER, ARNOLD JUDAS, SECOND TECHNICIAN

- **rabbit:** A small rodent in the Lagomorpha family, distinguished by its tall ears and short, fluffy tail **[RL]**. The crew of the *Oregon* suffered a devastating myxomatosis outbreak due to a massive rabbit population, caused by a glitch in the source code of the ship's AI computer, who collected the rabbits because it liked their ears and tails **[W-AIT]**. Captain Hollister later cited the *Oregon* incident while reprimanding Lister for bringing an unquarantined animal aboard *Red Dwarf* **[T-SER1.1]**.

  In an alternate universe, the rabbits aboard the *Oregon* eventually evolved into *Lapis sapiens,* a species of humanoid rabbit people **[G-RPG]**.

  **NOTE:** *See also the* Lapis sapiens *entry.*

- **Rabid Hunch, the:** A popular scoring strategy in zero-gee football, in which offensive defense players passed the ball to the press box. Mortimers from both teams then blew it up with bazookoids, with the crowd awarding points for style, poise and the amount of destruction. This strategy was valid only when either team had a Putsley in play **[M-SMG1.8(a)]**.

- **Rachel:** Rimmer's blow-up sex toy, which developed a puncture **[T-SER3.5]** and was later present at Rimmer's "funeral," wearing black clothing **[T-SER7.2]**. Rachel dolls and their repair kits were sold at a Love Toys store in one of *Red Dwarf*'s shopping areas **[M-SMG1.6(c2)]**.

  In response to a hypothetical question posed in the *Space Corps Survival Manual*, regarding how to escape a water-logged craft about to explode, Rimmer suggested fully inflating Rachel and tying her to a laundry basket as a makeshift hot-air balloon **[B-SUR]**.

  ***NOTE:*** *It is unclear whether this was the same doll that Lister referred to as Inflatable Ingrid in episode 2.5 ("Queeg"). Inflatable Ingrid may have been the manufacturer's name for the product, with Rimmer naming his personal doll Rachel. According to the official website, they were the same doll, but the* Smegazines *and the* Red Dwarf Programme Guide *said otherwise.*

- ***Rachel III*:** A classic play written by Wilma Shakespeare in a parallel universe in which the sexes were reversed **[T-SER2.6]**.

  ***NOTE:*** *This was the female-oriented universe's analog to William Shakespeare's* Richard III.

- **Rachel the Fornicator:** A woman who lived in Caesarea, Israel, circa 23 A.D. She had a son named Jesus with Samuel the Chicken-stealer **[T-SER10.3]**.

- **radioactive fruit salad:** The final course in a special mechanoid meal that Holly created for Kryten's last-day party **[T-SER3.6]**.

- **rad pistol:** A small firearm that expelled rounds of radiation, also called an IR pistol. Rad pistols had several settings, including "laser" and "neuter." One such weapon belonged to a psychotic, alternate-universe Lister **[N-LST]**.

- **Rage of Innocence, the ("The Rage"):** A gestalt entity created from the DNA of innocent prisoners interned at Cyberia. GELFs in that region conceived of the entity as a means of terraforming a hollowed-out planet so they could survive transit through the Omni-zone.

  After the GELFs' first attempt at a gestalt—in which they used DNA from guilty prisoners—resulted in a malevolent, uncontrollable entity, they instead harnessed the prison's innocent population, hoping to create a more benign, manageable creature. This also ended in failure, as the new creation, infused with the combined fury of hundreds of unjustly imprisoned inmates, ravished any vegetation and life with which it came into contact, rendering the planet completely inhospitable.

  Unaware of the entity's malignant nature, the GELFs sent a ship of volunteers from the penal colony to ascertain if the planet was safe, but upon landing, many of the inmates were infected by the Rage, causing them to start killing each other. The survivors, numbering more than forty, took shelter in a nearby cave, eventually realizing that by grouping together around a Circle of Sacer Facere and sacrificing one of their own during a Rage attack, they could ensure that the remainder would be spared. The Rage entered the bodies of all those gathered, infusing each with unbridled anger and hatred, until choosing one victim and absorbing him or her into the gestalt, turning that person's body into ash.

  The Rage was destroyed by Rimmer's damaged light bee, which carried the Oblivion virus—a computer bug that disrupted any electrical current **[N-LST]**.

**PREFIX**
**RL:** Real life

**T-: Television Episodes**
**SER:** Television series
**IDW:** "Identity Within"
**USA1:** Unaired U.S. pilot
**USA2:** Unaired U.S. demo

**R-: *The Bodysnatcher Collection***
**SER:** Remastered episodes
**BOD:** "Bodysnatcher"
**DAD:** "Dad"
**FTH:** "Lister's Father"
**INF:** "Infinity Patrol"
**END:** "The End" (original assembly)

**N-: Novels**
**INF:** *Infinity Welcomes Careful Drivers*
**BTL:** *Better Than Life*
**LST:** *Last Human*
**BCK:** *Backwards*
**OMN:** *Red Dwarf Omnibus*

**M-: Magazines**
**SMG:** *Smegazine*

**W-: Websites**
**OFF:** Official website
**NAN:** *Prelude to Nanarchy*
**AND:** *Androids*
**DIV:** Diva-Droid
**DIB:** Duane Dibbley
**CRP:** Crapola
**GEN:** Geneticon
**LSR:** Leisure World Intl.
**JMC:** Jupiter Mining Corporation
**AIT:** *A.I. Today*
**HOL:** HoloPoint

**G-: Roleplaying Game**
**RPG:** *Core Rulebook*
**BIT:** *A.I. Screen Extra Bits* booklet
**SOR:** *Series Sourcebook*
**OTH:** Other RPG material

- **railway carriage linkway:** A connection system located at the center of *Red Dwarf*, linking the mining ship's two halves **[R-BOD(b)]**.

  *NOTE: The linkway, not visible in the vessel's final design onscreen, was shown in concept art included in* The Bodysnatcher Collection*'s bonus features.*

- **Rainfall-girl:** A nickname that Lister called Kochanski to tease her for knowing the average rainfall in Venezuela's lowlands **[T-SER7.7(d)]**.

- **Raketenhosen:** A garment developed by the Reich, the reigning German superpower on War World. Worn by Raketenhosen-Männer ("Rocket Pants Men"), the garment (the name of which was German for "Rocket Pants") had a propulsion system incorporated into the backside, allowing a wearer to fly.

  The pants were developed under the Reich's Projekt: Hosen. The first model, the MkI, resembled a steel diaper and was poorly received by pilots. It was redesigned into the MkII, which integrated the propulsion system into flight pants, complete with an Aerial Smog Sublimation (ASS) exhaust system and centralized dial control.

  The Raketenhosen gave the Reich a distinct advantage over the Resistance for a number of years, until interdimensional traveler Robert Dimsdale stole a pair, reverse-engineered them and developed a Rocket Pants program for the Resistance, allowing the freedom fighters to even the odds **[G-BIT]**.

  *NOTE: The* Red Dwarf—The Roleplaying Game*'s* A.I. Screen *alternated between this spelling and "Raketenhose."*

- **Raketenhosen-Männer:** A group of elite soldiers serving the Reich, an evil superpower on an alternate-reality Earth. The Raketenhosen-Männer ("Rocket Pants Men") were outfitted with Rocket Pants that gave them the ability to fly **[G-BIT]**.

- **Rameses Niblick III Kerplunk Kerplunk Whoops Where's My Thribble:** A name by which Gilbert, a mechanoid friend of Kryten who suffered from computer senility, insisted on being called **[T-SER4.4]**.

- **Rameses XIII:** An Egyptian ruler who, according to an article in one of *Starbug 1*'s in-flight magazines, had a wife made entirely of salt **[T-SER4.5(d)]**.

  *NOTE: There was no ruler by this name in the real world. However, a fictional Ramses XIII appeared in Bolesław Prus' novel* Pharaoh.

- **Ramflampanjamram, Patek:** A twentieth-century man who invented a numbering system consisting only of zeros. Computers using this system answered "nothing" when asked what they were thinking **[B-EVR]**.

- **RAM (random access memory):** A form of temporary computer data storage **[RL]**. Since Kryten's RAM held all of his accumulated knowledge, he occasionally needed to purge unnecessary or useless files, such as the ability to sing the Bay City Rollers' greatest hits. Doing so required that he plug his RAM, located in his head, into the ship's computer to download the files into a trash directory, effectively putting his body to sleep. During once such session, Lister hijacked the mechanoid's body and swapped heads with Spare Head Two, hoping to persuade the crew to use a time drive to restock his depleted supply of curries **[T-SER7.1]**.

  A mechanoid's RAM chips contained its basic personality. After Kryten blew several spare heads following Lister's request for ketchup on his lobster dinner, the crew salvaged Kryten's RAM chips in order to save his personality until additional spares could be obtained **[T-SER7.6]**.

- **ram scoop:** A theoretical device proposed by physicist Robert W. Bussard as part of a spacecraft propulsion system called a Bussard ramjet **[RL]**. *Red Dwarf* had a ram scoop at its front end, consisting of six half-mile-long steel poles. The scoop formed a rudimentary cone-shaped frame through which it collected gases for fuel, such as hydrogen, giving the ship virtually limitless power **[N-INF]**. In the event of an emergency, access to the ship could be gained from outside, via the ram scoop **[T-SER10.2]**.

  *NOTE: Ram scoops have appeared in the works of various science fiction writers, including Poul Anderson and Larry Niven, as well as in the* Star Trek *franchise.* Red Dwarf*'s ram scoop may have been part of the hydrogen RAM-drive mentioned in episode 7.3 ("Ouroboros").*

- **Ranks, Tabby:** A raga artist in an alternate universe in which *Red Dwarf* was a British television series. Ranks had a manager named Mega and a bodyguard named Screwface, and hired Black Island Film Studios to create a music video he was producing, featuring a model and dancer named Kit. The studio's caretaker, Leo Davis, was smitten with Kit, but was too timid to ask her out. Instead, he daydreamed that he was Tabby Ranks, which gave him the courage to finally talk to her **[X-TNG]**.

- **Rasputin, Grigori:** A mystic, advisor and faith healer to Russia's Romanov imperial family until his murder in 1916 **[RL]**. A waxdroid replica of Rasputin was created for the Waxworld theme park. Left on their own for millions of years, the waxdroids attained sentience and became embroiled in a park-wide resource war between Villain World (to which Rasputin belonged) and Hero World.

  During this war, the *Red Dwarf* crew transported to the planet using a Matter Paddle, with Lister and Cat materializing in Villain territory, while Rimmer and Kryten landed in Hero territory. Lister and Cat were imprisoned and interrogated by Caligula and Rasputin, but escaped by using the Matter Paddle to transport the two villains into a nearby wardrobe.

  Meanwhile, Rimmer found the heroes' army lacking and took command, working many of the pacifistic waxdroids to death before ordering a frontal attack on the enemy's compound across a minefield. This wiped out the remaining droids, including Rasputin **[T-SER4.6]**.

- **Rastabilly Skank:** A musical group Lister enjoyed, whose album covers typically sported government health warnings **[T-SER1.3]**. David's favorite album by the band was *Don't Fear the Reefer, Man* **[M-SMG1.1(a)]**.

  As a deathday present for Rimmer, Lister copied eight months of his memories involving Lise Yates into his roommate's mind, making him believe that he had dated her. Awakening with the new memories, Arnold found certain things odd, like his taste in music suddenly changing from Mantovani to Rastabilly Skank within that eight-month period **[T-SER2.3]**.

- **rat:** A small rodent belonging to the genus *Rattus.* Certain types of rats were bred for scientific experimentation **[RL]**. In an alternate dimension, rats survived the cadmium II disaster aboard *Red Dwarf*, eventually evolving into a sapient species known as *Rattus sapiens* **[G-RPG]**.

  *NOTE: See also the* Rattus sapiens *entry.*

- **Rat:** A member of the species *Rattus sapiens*, a society that evolved from the lab rats aboard a possible alternate *Red Dwarf.* Her companions included Ben Ellis, a hologram named Terry, the mechanoid Kryten and the ship's artificial intelligence, Kate **[G-RPG]**.

- **Rathbone:** A virtual-reality character in the total-immersion game *Better Than Life*. The academy cadet asked Rimmer—an admiral in the game—to autograph his copy of Rimmer's autobiography, *My Incredible Career*, which Rathbone had read eighteen times **[T-SER2.2]**.

  *NOTE: This character's name, not spoken onscreen, was revealed in the episode's credits and outtakes.*

- **Rat Pit, The:** A drinking establishment on the Saturnian moon of Mimas, shaped like a giant rat. While hiding from the Ganymedian Mafia in Trixie LaBouche's body, Dutch van Oestrogen stayed at an apartment complex adjacent to The Rat Pit, occasionally visiting the bar for a drink **[M-SMG2.4(c2)]**.

- **rats' ears pan-fried in garlic:** A meal sometimes served for dinner in *Red Dwarf*'s brig **[T-SER8.3(d)]**.

- **Rattler, Zach:** The *nom de plume* of the author of a Western novel available in *Starbug*'s library, titled *Big Iron at Sun-Up*. Kryten read this book as the crew pursued the stolen *Red Dwarf* **[N-BCK]**.

- ***Rattus sapiens***: A species of humanoids that evolved from the rats aboard *Red Dwarf* in an alternate universe. Members of this species were sneaky, sly, tough and more fashion-conscious than their rodent brethren, *Mus sapiens*. Like the mice people, however, they were skilled at tasks requiring manual dexterity, and were attracted to shiny objects **[G-RPG]**.

- **"Rauchen Verboten!":** A German phrase printed on a wall sign posted in an alternate-timeline Nazi camp, meaning "Smoking Prohibited!" While pursuing Ace Rimmer and Princess Bonjella in a motorcycle chase, a Nazi soldier became startled when the

**PREFIX**
**RL:** Real life

**T-: Television Episodes**
**SER:** Television series
**IDW:** "Identity Within"
**USA1:** Unaired U.S. pilot
**USA2:** Unaired U.S. demo

**R-: *The Bodysnatcher Collection***
**SER:** Remastered episodes
**BOD:** "Bodysnatcher"
**DAD:** "Dad"
**FTH:** "Lister's Father"
**INF:** "Infinity Patrol"
**END:** "The End" (original assembly)

**N-: Novels**
**INF:** *Infinity Welcomes Careful Drivers*
**BTL:** *Better Than Life*
**LST:** *Last Human*
**BCK:** *Backwards*
**OMN:** *Red Dwarf Omnibus*

**M-: Magazines**
**SMG:** *Smegazine*

**W-: Websites**
**OFF:** Official website
**NAN:** *Prelude to Nanarchy*
**AND:** *Androids*
**DIV:** Diva-Droid
**DIB:** Duane Dibbley

**CRP:** Crapola
**GEN:** Geneticon
**LSR:** Leisure World Intl.
**JMC:** Jupiter Mining Corporation
**AIT:** *A.I. Today*
**HOL:** HoloPoint

**G-: Roleplaying Game**
**RPG:** *Core Rulebook*
**BIT:** *A.I. Screen Extra Bits* booklet
**SOR:** *Series Sourcebook*
**OTH:** Other RPG material

duo rocketed past, causing him to crash into the wall containing this sign and detonating nearby explosives **[T-SER7.2]**.

- **raw liver and banana pizza:** A food item that Lister craved while pregnant **[R-DAD]**.

- **Raysie's Rocket:** The name given to goal-scoring shots made by footballer Ray Rimmer, the team captain of the Smegchester Rovers in the universe known as Alternative 6829/B **[M-SMG1.8(c4)]**.

- **RD128:** A planet once displayed on *Starbug 1*'s scanner table **[T-SER6(b)]**.

  ***NOTE:*** *A wireframe render of this planet was featured as an Easter egg on disc one of the Series VI DVDs. Selecting it accomplished nothing, but it presumably stood for "*Red Dwarf *128."*

- **RD 52 169:** A code Lister used to access *Red Dwarf*'s food dispensers **[T-SER1.2]**.

  ***NOTE:*** *This code was presumably Lister's Space Corps registration or serial number. "RD" stood for his assigned ship,* Red Dwarf*, with 169 referencing his position as the lowest-ranking crewmember (the complement was established early in the series as 169). In the* Smegazine *comic "Future Echoes Part 1," Lister's code was changed to RD 52 1169 to match the increased crew count from later in the series.*

- **RE1 3DW:** A postal code printed on the label of a letter sent from the John Wayne Fan Club to *Red Dwarf*'s skutters, which the crew found in a three-million-year-old post pod that rendezvoused with the mining vessel **[T-SER2.2]**.

- **RE912 circuitry:** A type of electronics incorporated into model 7-6-80 cellular phones **[X-RNG]**.

- ***Reader's Digest*:** A monthly American general-interest consumer magazine founded in 1922 **[RL]**. While filing a report, Holly noted that despite being three million light-years into deep space, the crew were still entered in a *Reader's Digest* contest for a Vauxhall Nova **[T-SER3(d)]**.

  While incarcerated in *Red Dwarf*'s brig, Rimmer received mail that claimed he was in the *Reader's Digest* lucky dip, and that he might have won either a vacation in Mauritius, a soft-top sports car or a matching set of eggcups. As it happened, he won the vacation—but had no way to redeem it **[T-SER8.5]**.

- **Reading Festival:** An annual music festival held in Reading, England **[RL]**. After telling Kryten about a dream in which he had kissed Rimmer, Lister claimed he'd rather go bobbing for apples in the festival's community latrine than to kiss his departed roommate **[T-SER7.5]**.

- **Ready Brek:** A brand of oat-based breakfast products sold in the United Kingdom by the Weetabix Food Co. **[RL]**. Rimmer caught Cat feeding *Red Dwarf*'s supply of Ready Brek and Spaghetti Hoops into a matter converter that changed the food into silk, so that he could fulfill his dream of owning an infinite wardrobe **[M-SMG1.2(a)]**.

- ***Ready Steady Stab*:** A maim-based television game show scheduled to be broadcast by Krytie TV on September 16 **[X-CAL]**.

  ***NOTE:*** *This series' name spoofed that of British cooking game show* Ready Steady Cook.

- **Reagan, Ronald Wilson, President:** The fortieth president of the United States **[RL]**. When Rimmer instructed Kryten to remain inconspicuous while stranded on an Earth where time ran backwards, the mechanoid's initial solution was to wear a cloak and a Ronald Reagan mask **[T-SER3.1]**.

- **reality barrier:** The theoretical boundaries separating each universe from an infinite number of others. In Ace Rimmer's universe, the Space Corps Research and Development Program developed a craft called *Wildfire One* that broke the reality barrier, enabling the vessel to travel to alternate realities **[N-BCK]**.

- **reality minefield:** An area of space typically hidden within artificially created stellar fog, containing reality mines—pockets or bubbles of unreality meant to deter trespassers. Developed by the Space Corps, reality minefields were laid around test ships in the event of a malfunction to stave off looters.

  The *Starbug 1* crew encountered a reality minefield while

**B-: Books**
**PRG:** *Red Dwarf Programme Guide*
**SUR:** *Red Dwarf Space Corps Survival Manual*
**PRM:** *Primordial Soup*
**SOS:** *Son of Soup*
**SCE:** *Scenes from the Dwarf*
**LOG:** *Red Dwarf Log No. 1996*
**RD8:** *Red Dwarf VIII*
**EVR:** *The Log: A Dwarfer's Guide to Everything*

**X-: Misc.**
**PRO:** Promotional materials, videos, etc.
**PST:** Posters at DJ XVII (2013)
**CAL:** 2008 calendar
**RNG:** Cell phone ringtones
**MOB:** Mobisode ("Red Christmas")
**CIN:** *Children in Need* sketch
**GEK:** *Geek Week* intros by Kryten
**TNG:** "Tongue-Tied" video

**XMS:** Bill Pearson's Christmas special pitch script
**XVD:** Bill Pearson's Christmas special pitch video
**OTH:** Other *Red Dwarf* appearances

**SUFFIX**
**DVD:**
**(d)** – Deleted scene
**(o)** – Outtake
**(b)** – Bonus DVD material (other)
**(e)** – Extended version

**SMEGAZINES:**
**(c)** – Comic
**(a)** – Article

**OTHER:**
**(s)** – Early/unused script draft
**(s1)** – Alternate version of script

pursuing the stolen *Red Dwarf*. The mines temporarily skewed the crew's reality, first leading them to believe Lister was a 3000 Series mechanoid, then temporarily removing Cat from existence. After experiencing other pockets of unreality, Kryten suggested the crew spend the remainder of the trip in deep sleep chambers, shielded from the effects. When they awoke in the field's epicenter, they discovered the derelict Space Corps ship *Gemini 12* fitted with a time drive **[T-SER6.6]**.

- **reality mines:** A type of defensive weapons which, when dropped around a vessel, formed a reality minefield that created pockets or bubbles of unreality meant to ward off trespassers **[T-SER6.6]**. Kluge Corp. manufactured reality mines that were distributed via Crapola Inc.'s annual *SCABBY* catalog **[G-RPG]**.

- **Reality Patrol:** The title that the Inquisitor assumed while eliminating from space-time individuals he deemed unworthy and replacing them with someone else showing greater potential **[T-SER5.2]**.

- **reality scan:** An analysis that the Inquisitor performed after surgically removing an individual from the space-time continuum, to check for anomalies. When the Inquisitor conducted a reality scan after eliminating Jan Ludwig Hoch, he realized he had made an error in erasing the only decent version of the man and replacing him with an abrasive parasite named Robert Maxwell **[M-SMG1.11(c3)]**.

- ***Really Freakin' Dangerous Crime Series***: A line of murder-mystery artificial-reality games produced by Total Immersion Inc. and distributed by Crapola Inc. Among the games in this series was a program called *Gumshoe* **[G-RPG]**.

- **Really Really Black:** A body-plating color that Diva-Droid International offered for Hudzen 10 mechanoids **[G-SOR]**.

- **Real Virtual Reality:** A gimmick created by an East End software company in 2109 that claimed to give users the "ultimate experience" by allowing them to walk around in the real world **[B-EVR]**.

- **Reaper, Jim:** The Space Division's head of sales at Diva-Droid International, a manufacturer and distributor of mechanoids, including the Kryten Series III (4000 series) and Hudzen 10 models **[T-SER3.6]**. Diva-Droid's Professor Mamet hired Reaper due to his uncanny resemblance to her ex-fiancée, John Warburton. His brother, meanwhile, worked at a software company and created Diva-Droid's Data Doctor program **[W-OFF]**.

  Reaper was featured in a video that the company distributed to all leaseholders of Kryten Series androids. In the video, he informed owners that their mechanoid's built-in shutdown chip would activate twenty-four hours from receipt of the message, to be replaced by a Hudzen 10 model **[T-SER2.6]**.

  ***NOTE:*** *Given the solemn nature of the communiqué, Reaper's name rhyming with "Grim Reaper" was presumably intentional. The physical similarities between Warburton, Reaper and the Data Doctor were a clever way to explain why the three characters looked like Kryten (since actor Robert Llewellyn played them all). It does not, however, explain why they didn't all look like David Ross, who originally played Kryten and would have essentially been Kryten's default appearance.*

- **Rear Admiral Lieutenant General:** The Space Corps rank that Rimmer told his mother he had attained, by passing every exam he had taken throughout his career **[T-SER2.2]**.

  ***NOTE:*** *Oddly, Rimmer's brother Howard accurately believed Arnold had never made it past second technician in episode 10.1 ("Trojan"), implying that Mrs. Rimmer regularly corresponded with Arnold, but not the sons she actually liked—or that she saw through the façade and told the others his true rank.*

- **rear cargo pods:** A set of external containers located in *Red Dwarf*'s underbelly, toward the ship's aft section, used for storing and transporting materials **[R-BOD(b)]**.

  ***NOTE:*** *The containers, visible in the vessel's new design in the remastered episodes, were named in concept art included in* The Bodysnatcher Collection's *bonus features.*

- **rear exhaust port:** *See* heat outlet

**PREFIX**
**RL:** Real life

**T-: Television Episodes**
**SER:** Television series
**IDW:** "Identity Within"
**USA1:** Unaired U.S. pilot
**USA2:** Unaired U.S. demo

**R-: *The Bodysnatcher Collection***
**SER:** Remastered episodes
**BOD:** "Bodysnatcher"
**DAD:** "Dad"
**FTH:** "Lister's Father"
**INF:** "Infinity Patrol"
**END:** "The End" (original assembly)

**N-: Novels**
**INF:** *Infinity Welcomes Careful Drivers*
**BTL:** *Better Than Life*
**LST:** *Last Human*

**BCK:** *Backwards*
**OMN:** *Red Dwarf Omnibus*

**M-: Magazines**
**SMG:** *Smegazine*

**W-: Websites**
**OFF:** Official website
**NAN:** *Prelude to Nanarchy*
**AND:** *Androids*
**DIV:** Diva-Droid
**DIB:** Duane Dibbley

**CRP:** Crapola
**GEN:** Geneticon
**LSR:** Leisure World Intl.
**JMC:** Jupiter Mining Corporation
**AIT:** *A.I. Today*
**HOL:** HoloPoint

**G-: Roleplaying Game**
**RPG:** *Core Rulebook*
**BIT:** *A.I. Screen Extra Bits* booklet
**SOR:** *Series Sourcebook*
**OTH:** Other RPG material

- **rear groinal unit:** A socket located in the lower rear section of Jake Bullet's torso. The cyborg once accidentally got the gear shifter of his convertible stuck in his rear groinal unit after blindly jumping into the car **[M-SMG1.11(c4)]**.

- **rear meteor bay:** A section of *Red Dwarf*'s underbelly that contained meteors used for mining purposes. The bay was located toward the ship's aft section **[R-BOD(b)]**.

  ***NOTE:*** *This bay, visible in the ship's new design in the remastered episodes, was named in concept art included in* The Bodysnatcher Collection's *bonus features.*

- **rear-thrust jets:** A set of engines located at the rear of *Starbug* shuttles, providing forward propulsion **[N-BTL]**.

- ***Rebel Without a Cause*:** A 1955 American drama film starring James Dean, about a rebellious, emotionally disturbed, motorcycle-riding teenager **[RL]**. Lister showed Kryten this movie to help him break free of his servantile programming and think for himself. Initially, it appeared to have no effect, but Kryten later rebelled by painting a portrait of Rimmer on the toilet, calling him names, dumping a bowl of soup onto his bunk and setting off on Lister's space bike to start a new life **[T-SER2.1]**.

- **rechargeable absolute-zero unit:** A component of a thermos owned by Duane Dibbley, designed to keep its contents cold **[W-DIB]**.

- **recharging socket:** A three-pin receptacle on a 4000 Series mechanoid, located in its lower rear opposite the groinal attachment area, and used for plugging in a power cord. After a DNA modifier transformed Kryten into a human, the former mechanoid asked Lister if he needed an adaptor to use his power cord, as his attempts to plug it into what was now his anus had proven unsuccessful **[T-SER4.2]**.

- **reconstituted sausage patty:** A food item in *Red Dwarf*'s stores, listed on a supply checklist that Lister crosschecked with Rimmer. At the time, the ship contained seventy-two tons of the patties **[T-SER1.3]**.

- **Reco-Programme:** An endeavor of an alternate-universe GELF State to save their population from destruction in the Omni-zone, by creating a terraformed planet. The program utilized recombinant DNA from volunteer prisoners on Cyberia to create a gestalt entity that would become the primordial beginnings of the new world. This entity was intended to rapidly transform the planet into a habitable home on which the GELF population could hide to survive transit through the Omni-zone into another universe.

  The first attempt to create the gestalt entity was made using the prison's guilty population—which, due to their criminal history and general lack of ethics, produced a malignant entity that created what the GELFs called the Black Planet, which was deemed too dangerous to populate. The GELFs then chose another planet and used innocent, wrongly incarcerated prisoners, who were pardoned in exchange for joining the Reco-Programme. This also ended in failure, as the second entity, dubbed the Rage of Innocence, was fueled by hatred stemming from the volunteers' unjust imprisonment, driving it to destroy any life in which it came in contact.

  Unaware of this, the GELF State sent a ship of volunteers to test whether or not the planet was safe to inhabit. When that vessel didn't return, the GELFs sent another ship and invited Lister—who was serving an eighteen-year sentence on Cyberia at the time—to join the Reco-Programme **[N-LST]**.

- **recovery bay:** A special section within *Red Dwarf*'s Medical Unit, used to treat patients recovering from severe injuries. Lister and Cat spent several months in the recovery bay after surviving more than two years trapped in an addictive version of *Better Than Life*, during which their bodies atrophied **[N-BTL]**.

- **recovery bed:** A specialized bed in *Red Dwarf*'s Quarantine Room 152 **[T-SER5.4]**.

- **Recreation Room:** A room aboard *Red Dwarf* allocated for crew relaxation, containing at least one pool table **[T-SER4.4]**.

- **Recreation Room 5:** A room aboard *Red Dwarf* set aside for relaxation **[R-BOD(b)]**.

  ***NOTE:*** *This room was identified in the documentary* It's Cold Outside.

**B-: Books**
**PRG:** *Red Dwarf Programme Guide*
**SUR:** *Red Dwarf Space Corps Survival Manual*
**PRM:** *Primordial Soup*
**SOS:** *Son of Soup*
**SCE:** *Scenes from the Dwarf*
**LOG:** *Red Dwarf Log No. 1996*
**RD8:** *Red Dwarf VIII*
**EVR:** *The Log: A Dwarfer's Guide to Everything*

**X-: Misc.**
**PRO:** Promotional materials, videos, etc.
**PST:** Posters at DJ XVII (2013)
**CAL:** 2008 calendar
**RNG:** Cell phone ringtones
**MOB:** Mobisode ("Red Christmas")
**CIN:** *Children in Need* sketch
**GEK:** *Geek Week* intros by Kryten
**TNG:** "Tongue-Tied" video
**XMS:** Bill Pearson's Christmas special pitch script
**XVD:** Bill Pearson's Christmas special pitch video
**OTH:** Other *Red Dwarf* appearances

**SUFFIX**
**DVD:**
**(d)** – Deleted scene
**(o)** – Outtake
**(b)** – Bonus DVD material (other)
**(e)** – Extended version

**SMEGAZINES:**
**(c)** – Comic
**(a)** – Article

**OTHER:**
**(s)** – Early/unused script draft
**(s1)** – Alternate version of script

- **Recreators of the Battle of Neasden Society:** An organization that Rimmer joined during cadet school. While on Waxworld training Hero World's pacifistic waxdroids, Arnold lamented that his fellow recreators were not there to see him in action **[T-SER4.6]**.

  *NOTE: Neasden, England, is an area of northwest London. Although no historical "battle at Neasden" is recorded as taking place, the* Commons and Lords Hansard *(the official report of debates in Britain's Parliament) described a 1980 riot—during which two hundred fighting teenagers attacked London Transport personnel in Neasden, damaging a train and wounding its driver—in this fashion. Since Rimmer was involved with the club as a youth, this may have been the incident they recreated.*

- **Rectum-faced Pygmy:** An insult that Rimmer called Lister while trying to convince him not to take the Chef's Exam **[T-SER1.3]**.

- **recuperation lounge:** A room at the Leisure World International building in which clients could recover after extended stays in one of the company's total-immersion video game (TIV) machines. Customers exiting a TIV machine often experienced temporary amnesia regarding their true lives and identities, and were directed to the recuperation lounge to rest and collect their belongings **[T-SER5.6]**.

- **Red Alert:** An alert status indicating a potential threat to *Red Dwarf* **[T-SER2.1]** or to *Starbug* shuttlecrafts. A Red Alert was the highest level of emergency, followed by a Purple (or Mauve) Alert, then a Blue Alert **[T-SER4.5]**. During a Red Alert, an "alert" sign with a red light bulb was illuminated. Going to another status involved changing the bulb to the appropriate color. When Cat sensed a threat undetected by the ship's sensors, Rimmer insisted on going to Blue Alert, and then Red **[T-SER6.2]**.

- **Red Alert Bulb:** A lighting accessory produced by Space Cadet LLC and distributed by Crapola Inc. The bulb, which fit into a ship's alert status fixture, signified imminent danger and came with a sixty-minute Short Life Guarantee **[G-RPG]**.

- **Red Corridor 357:** A walkway on a maintenance deck within *Red Dwarf.* The corridor contained Circuit Board Epsilon 14598, which was once rewired by a crazed skutter **[T-SER3.4]**.

- ***Red Dwarf*:** A Solar-class mining ship **[N-BCK]** commissioned by the Space Corps **[T-SER3.3]** and operated by the Jupiter Mining Corporation **[T-SER4.3]**. The vessel was commanded by Captain Frank Hollister **[T-SER1.1]**. *Red Dwarf* had a standard crew complement of 1,169 **[T-SER4.3]**, and measured five miles long, three miles wide **[R-BOD]**, and four miles deep, with a tubed metro system running along the outside of its hull. Its average cruising speed was two hundred thousand miles an hour **[N-INF]**; however, if accelerated for a long enough time, the ship could reach lightspeed **[T-SER1.2]**. It contained 2,500 floors **[M-SMG2.2(a)]** and 2,143 restrooms **[T-SER10.5]**.

  *Red Dwarf* was equipped with an artificial-intelligence computer named Holly, which boasted an IQ of six thousand **[T-SER1.2]**, and featured several service droids, or skutters **[T-SER1.1]**; two stasis booths **[T-SER1.1, T-SER2.4]**; a self-destruct system **[T-SER3.4]**; and a ram scoop that collected and converted hydrogen into fuel **[N-INF]**. It also featured a hologram simulation suite enabling a deceased crewmember to be resurrected via hologram **[T-SER2.3]**.

  Floor 13 contained a classified prison level called the Tank, with an inmate population of four hundred **[T-SER8.1]**. In addition, located on the ship's underbelly was a small moon that had been torn out of its orbit and was embedded in the ship's hull **[N-INF]**.

  *Red Dwarf* suffered a catastrophic internal radiation explosion caused by an ill-repaired drive plate, resulting in a cadmium II leak that killed the entire crew except for Third Technician David Lister, who had been serving eighteen months in a stasis booth at the time for bringing an unquarantined pregnant cat on board, and was thus protected from the radiation **[T-SER1.1]**.

  Immediately after the accident, Holly navigated the ship away from the solar system and into deep space in an attempt to minimize the risk of radiation exposure to any planet or vessel within the vicinity **[N-INF]**. It traveled outward for millions of years, during which a species of Cat People evolved from the litter of Lister's cat, who was protected from the radiation in the ship's cargo bays. Using supplies from the cargo decks, this species flourished until a Holy War decimated their numbers,

**PREFIX**
**RL:** Real life

**T-: Television Episodes**
**SER:** Television series
**IDW:** "Identity Within"
**USA1:** Unaired U.S. pilot
**USA2:** Unaired U.S. demo

**R-: *The Bodysnatcher Collection***
**SER:** Remastered episodes
**BOD:** "Bodysnatcher"
**DAD:** "Dad"
**FTH:** "Lister's Father"
**INF:** "Infinity Patrol"
**END:** "The End" (original assembly)

**N-: Novels**
**INF:** *Infinity Welcomes Careful Drivers*
**BTL:** *Better Than Life*
**LST:** *Last Human*
**BCK:** *Backwards*
**OMN:** *Red Dwarf Omnibus*

**M-: Magazines**
**SMG:** *Smegazine*

**W-: Websites**
**OFF:** Official website
**NAN:** *Prelude to Nanarchy*
**AND:** *Androids*
**DIV:** Diva-Droid
**DIB:** Duane Dibbley
**CRP:** Crapola
**GEN:** Geneticon
**LSR:** Leisure World Intl.
**JMC:** Jupiter Mining Corporation
**AIT:** *A.I. Today*
**HOL:** HoloPoint

**G-: Roleplaying Game**
**RPG:** *Core Rulebook*
**BIT:** *A.I. Screen Extra Bits* booklet
**SOR:** *Series Sourcebook*
**OTH:** Other RPG material

forcing them to call a truce and build two arks in pursuit of their Holy Land, Fuchal. The Cats then left *Red Dwarf*, leaving behind the sick and infirmed **[T-SER1.4]**.

After three million years, Holly—having determined the background radiation levels to be safe—released Lister from stasis and informed him of his predicament. He also revived Arnold Rimmer, Lister's bunkmate, in order to keep what he determined to be the last human alive sane **[T-SER1.1]**. Holly jettisoned one of the ship's black box recordings, which made its way to the Omni-zone via a black hole and traveled back in time three million years **[W-OFF]**, splashing down in the Pacific Ocean **[N-LST]**, where it was retrieved by the Space Corps and analyzed by Doctor Marcus Bateman **[W-OFF]**.

Several years later, *Red Dwarf* was destroyed when a triplicator experiment caused the ship's engine core to become exposed, leading to a catastrophic explosion, with Lister and company narrowly escaping aboard *Starbug 1*. However, the experiment created two duplicate versions of the vessel—one pristine ("high") and one decrepit ("low")—which the crew were able to amalgamate into a new *Red Dwarf* **[T-SER5.5]**.

> ***NOTE:*** Red Dwarf—The Roleplaying Game *designated* Red Dwarf *a Jupiter-class mining vessel, but the novel* Better Than Life *called it a Solar-class mining ship. The novel* Infinity Welcomes Careful Drivers *placed a short, stout woman named Captain Kirk in command of the mining vessel.*
>
> *There are inconsistencies regarding the ship's crew complement. The original number of 169, from episode 1.1 (*"The End"*), was revised in episode 4.3 ("Justice") to include a thousand more people. The comic in issue 1.1 of the* Smegazine*, titled "The End," also used the figure 1,169. The novel* Infinity Welcomes Careful Drivers*, however, raised the number to 11,169.*
>
> *According to the comic story "A Day in the Life of a Bogbot...," published in* Smegazine *issue 2.4, Kryten counted the number of latrines he cleaned at 371, not the 2,143 mentioned in Series X; it is possible he did not personally clean them all.*
>
> Red Dwarf—The Roleplaying Game *claimed the ship only had a single stasis booth, failing to take into account the one seen in episode 2.4 ("Stasis Leak").*
>
> *Several explanations have been given for the presence of the moon or meteor embedded in the ship's hull. In a documentary about the pilot episode ("The End"), featured in* The Bodysnatcher Collection*, the crew discussed the genesis of* Red Dwarf*'s design, including a need for the ship to be self-sustaining; this included a meteor in its belly, used for mining fuel. Also in* The Bodysnatcher Collection*, the ship model was replaced with a CGI version with a drastically altered design, which included a redesigned engine, a longer midsection and two large bays in its lower half, both of which contained small meteors.*
>
> *In episode 2.3 ("Thanks for the Memory"), the crew used the black box recording to piece together the mystery of a missing few days. As such, the ship must have had at least two black boxes, given that one had been sent to Earth.*

- ***Red Dwarf*:** A "high" copy of *Red Dwarf*, created during a triplicator accident in which the device's field was projected outward, creating two copies of the mining ship: one representing the best elements of the spaceship and its crew (a "high" version), and another manifesting the worst aspects (a "low" vessel). The resulting power drain exposed the original ship's engine core, causing a meltdown that destroyed the vessel. The crew escaped to the "high" ship, where they found fresh air, edible Pot Noodles and enlightened versions of themselves. With only half the triplicator's components onboard, they then visited the "low" ship, whose occupants killed their "high" counterparts. Eventually, the two *Red Dwarfs* were combined once more as a single ship **[T-SER5.5]**.

- ***Red Dwarf*:** A "low" copy of *Red Dwarf*, created during the triplicator accident that resulted in two copies of the mining vessel, this one occupied by depraved, brutal versions of the crew. The original crew (along with their enlightened counterparts) boarded this decrepit version to locate the missing parts of the triplicator in order to reassemble the original ship. The "low" counterparts kidnapped Lister and attached a spinal implant to his neck to control his actions, forcing him to stab the "high" Lister and Rimmer. Dave's shipmates immobilized him before he could kill them as well, then found the missing components and activated the new triplicator, amalgamating the copies into a single ship once more **[T-SER5.5]**.

- ***Red Dwarf*:** A version of the mining vessel amalgamated from two duplicate *Red Dwarfs* (the "high" and "low" versions) created during a triplicator accident that destroyed the original ship. Escaping the destruction aboard *Starbug 1*, the crew combined elements of the triplicators from both alternate vessels and reversed the experiment to create a new *Red Dwarf* **[T-SER5.5]**.

  Kryten's nanobots commandeered this *Red Dwarf* as the crew investigated a derelict vessel on an ocean planet. The nanobots used material from the ship to build a sub-atomic version for their own needs, turning the rest (including Holly) into a small planetoid for safekeeping. They were later discovered exploring Lister's laundry basket aboard *Starbug 1*, where Kryten captured them and forced them to rebuild the mining vessel **[T-SER7.8]**.

  In so doing, however, the nanobots used the ship's original specifications, from before JMC made budget cuts. These new features included a more elongated design with two mining bays, a quark-level matter-antimatter generator, ship-wide bio-organic computer networking and a karaoke machine on C Deck. Another set of nanobots revived the entire crew and civilian population, including the Tank's inmates **[T-SER8.1]**.

  Captain Hollister and most of the crew abandoned ship when a chameleonic microbe began eating away at *Red Dwarf*'s interior **[T-SER8.8]**. Sometime later, the databanks containing Holly's personality were destroyed during a flood after Lister left a bath running for several years. At some point between the chameleonic microbe encounter and the crew's run-in with an elation squid, the ship reverted back to its short, squat design, while keeping the newer design's rear engine configuration **[T-SER9.1]**.

  After the hologrammic death of Rimmer's brother Howard, *Red Dwarf*'s onboard JMC computer suggested changing the ship's name to the SS *Howard Rimmer* to honor his bravery **[T-SER10.1]**.

  The crew attempted to replace Holly with Pree, an artificial-intelligence computer system looted from *Trojan* **[W-OFF]**, but were forced to uninstall the dangerous AI after it attempted to kill them **[T-SER10.2]**.

  > ***NOTE:*** *One possible explanation for* Red Dwarf*'s de-evolution is that nanobots may have been utilized to rebuild the vessel after the chameleonic microbe attack, using a combination of the old and new designs. This, however, does not explain why the hull-embedded meteor reappeared.*

- ***Red Dwarf*:** A mining ship in an alternate reality in which the genders were reversed. This ship was controlled by Hilly, Holly's female equivalent. The prime *Red Dwarf* crew discovered this version of the ship after traveling into the Fifth Dimension via the Holly Hop Drive **[T-SER2.6]**.

- ***Red Dwarf*:** A Class 5 mining vessel owned by the Jupiter Mining Corporation, in a reality in which the ship's crew were American. Its commander was Captain Louise Tau. This *Red Dwarf*'s crew complement was roughly five thousand, with a cargo capacity of forty-seven cubic miles. The ship included numerous crew facilities, such as shopping malls, bowling alleys and a zero-gravity football stadium, and was equipped with a female artificial-intelligence computer named Holly **[T-USA1]**. The ship was considered a fusion-powered miner/freighter **[T-USA1(s1)]**.

- ***Red Dwarf*:** A mining vessel owned by the Jupiter Mining Corporation in another reality in which the ship's crew were American. It was equipped with a female artificial-intelligence computer named Holly **[T-USA2]**.

- ***Red Dwarf*:** A mining ship in a mirror universe. Everything aboard the vessel was reversed from its prime-universe counterpart, ranging from hallways to signage **[T-SER8.8]**. This *Red Dwarf* was commanded by Captain Arnold Rimmer, with David Lister as his first officer **[T-SER8.8(d)]**.

  When the prime *Red Dwarf* was overrun by a corrosive chameleonic microbe, that reality's Rimmer used a device created by Kryten to enter the mirror universe and find an antidote. After obtaining the cure from Professor Cat, Rimmer returned to his own universe to find his ship in ruins and his crewmates gone, as they had fled to the alternate vessel **[T-SER8.8]**.

- ***Red Dwarf*:** A subatomic version of *Red Dwarf* that Kryten's nanobots created after mutinying and stealing the mining ship. The nanobots created the microscopic vessel for their own use, discarding the rest of the original in the form of a planetoid. The crew chased the nano-*Red Dwarf* for years aboard *Starbug 1*, until the 'bots stopped in their tracks, flew back into the shuttle and hid in Lister's laundry basket, where Kryten eventually found them **[T-SER7.8]**.

- ***Red Dwarf***: A total-immersion video game in which the crew thought they had lived for four years, following a despair squid attack that made them hallucinate having crashed *Starbug 1* and awoken in a virtual-reality machine. In the illusion, they were told their lives and identities aboard *Red Dwarf* had all been part of the game.

  A technician explained that the game had several goals for players to achieve, including Lister ending up with Kochanski; Rimmer discovering he was really a special agent for the Space Corps, re-programmed as a twonk so he could work undercover to destroy *Red Dwarf* and guide Lister to jump-start the second Big Bang; finding the Planet of the Nymphomaniacs; and defeating the despair squid with the SSS *Esperanto*'s laser cannons. The technician mocked them for accomplishing none of these tasks and scoring only four percent.

  With no memories of their "real" lives, the crew set out to find their true identities. Horrified at what they discovered, they tried to commit suicide, but Holly managed to contact Kryten, instructing him to turn the valve on a mood stabilizer canister. This broke the four out of their trance and brought them back to reality **[T-SER5.6]**.

- ***Red Dwarf***: A total-immersion video game in an alternate reality in which a totalitarian government existed on Earth. Voter Colonel Sebastian Doyle and his half-brother William, along with Jake Bullet and Duane Dibbley, hid in the virtual-reality game for four years. After their release, a new set of players entered and started their own game. Their experiences differed from those of the previous players, as they succeeded in bringing back Kochanski after future echoes gave them the code required to use a device called the time retriever **[M-SMG2.4(c4)]**.

- ***Red Dwarf***: A British science fiction comedy television series that the crew's minds imagined while trapped in an elation squid hallucination. In the illusion, the group believed they had traveled to an alternate twenty-first-century Earth in which they were merely characters on the sitcom.

  The crew read the back of an empty DVD case for the show's most recent season, *Back to Earth*, and later discovered that the series' creator intended to kill them during the final episode. Desperate for more life, they set out to find him and change his mind **[T-SER9.2]**. The short, eccentric, bespectacled man explained that the show's genesis had been heavily influenced by the science fiction film *Blade Runner* **[T-SER9.3]**.

- ***Red Dwarf***: An American television show that aired in an alternate universe, based on the same-named British TV series. The U.S. producers made several major changes from the British version: Lister and Rimmer were best buddies; Rimmer was alive, but wheelchair-bound; Holly was Lister's human wife; their children were a biologically challenged boy named Cry 10 and a hip teenage girl; the remainder of the crew were alive but in stasis; the human species was not extinct; the ship was not three million years in deep space; and aliens were among the crew.

  In one episode, the ship was attacked by an amorphous alien who accused the crew of killing its wife as they strode through a patch of slime on Altair 9. Lister was knocked unconscious during the attack, but Rimmer summoned the power to walk, just in time to grab a gun and save the day. After viewing this episode, TV executives decided to change the name due to the lack of actual dwarfs; suggestions included *Babes in Space, Dave and Arn's Spacious Adventure, The Listers* and *Married With Robot* **[M-SMG1.10(c4)]**.

- ***Red Dwarf:*** A mining vessel in a possible alternate dimension. Its crew included Ben Ellis, Rat, Kryten and an artificial-intelligence computer called Kate **[G-RPG]**.

- ***Red Dwarf:*** A mining vessel in another possible alternate dimension. Its crew included Eric, the hologram Robin, a humanoid rabbit and an Errol Flynn waxdroid **[G-RPG]**.

- ***Red Dwarf:*** A mining vessel in yet another possible alternate dimension. Its crew included a member of the *Rattus sapiens* species named Ricky, the hologram Monica Jones and a Hudzen 10 mechanoid **[G-RPG]**.

- ***Red Dwarf—A Complete Guide to the Popular TIV Game***: A manual for the Total Immersion video game *Red Dwarf*, a copy of which was stored in an alternate-universe Salvation Army hostel belonging to an amnesiac agent disguised as Duane Dibbley. The agent found the booklet among other *Red Dwarf* paraphernalia while searching the room for clues to his true identity **[M-SMG2.2(c5)]**.

# RED DWARF

- ***Red Dwarf* Central Line:** The main tube of *Red Dwarf*'s interior transit line **[N-INF]**.

- ***Red Dwarf Log No. 1996*:** An official log book maintained by the *Red Dwarf* crew, in which their day-to-day activities were recorded for a year **[B-LOG]**.

  ***NOTE:*** *The book was essentially a real-world calendar for the year 1996.*

- ***Red Dwarfski*:** A Soviet Space Corps mining vessel in a timeline in which the Union of Soviet Socialist Republics (U.S.S.R.) bested the United States in the so-called Space Race **[G-SOR]**.

- ***Red Dwarf* Waxwork Museum:** An attraction aboard *Red Dwarf*, featuring wax figures of historical individuals. Kryten once spent six hours attempting to clean tattoos off the David Beckham figure, thinking it was graffiti **[X-GEK]**.

- **Red Planet Power Drinks:** A line of energy drinks. Its parent company sponsored the publication *A.I. Today* **[W-AIT]**.

- **Red Rocket:** An adult-oriented establishment in Shag Town, a seedy section of the Saturnian moon of Mimas **[M-SMG2.3(c4)]**.

  ***NOTE:*** *The term "red rocket" is slang for a dog's erection.*

- **refectory:** A mess lounge aboard *Red Dwarf*. George McIntyre's "Welcome Back" reception was held in this room **[T-SER1.1]**. Three million years later, Holly summoned Lister to the refectory during a Class A Emergency, but when he arrived, he discovered the "emergency" was merely Rimmer conducting a roll call of the entire ship's complement—despite their all being deceased **[R-BOD]**.

**PREFIX**
**RL:** Real life

**T-: Television Episodes**
**SER:** Television series
**IDW:** "Identity Within"
**USA1:** Unaired U.S. pilot
**USA2:** Unaired U.S. demo

**R-: *The Bodysnatcher Collection***
**SER:** Remastered episodes
**BOD:** "Bodysnatcher"
**DAD:** "Dad"
**FTH:** "Lister's Father"
**INF:** "Infinity Patrol"
**END:** "The End" (original assembly)

**N-: Novels**
**INF:** *Infinity Welcomes Careful Drivers*
**BTL:** *Better Than Life*
**LST:** *Last Human*

**BCK:** *Backwards*
**OMN:** *Red Dwarf Omnibus*

**M-: Magazines**
**SMG:** *Smegazine*

**W-: Websites**
**OFF:** Official website
**NAN:** *Prelude to Nanarchy*
**AND:** *Androids*
**DIV:** Diva-Droid
**DIB:** Duane Dibbley

**CRP:** Crapola
**GEN:** Geneticon
**LSR:** Leisure World Intl.
**JMC:** Jupiter Mining Corporation
**AIT:** *A.I. Today*
**HOL:** HoloPoint

**G-: Roleplaying Game**
**RPG:** *Core Rulebook*
**BIT:** *A.I. Screen Extra Bits* booklet
**SOR:** *Series Sourcebook*
**OTH:** Other RPG material

- **reference library:** A room aboard *Red Dwarf* allocated for education and research. The library contained a language lab, and was within the section of the vessel covered by Z-Shift. Prior to the cadmium II disaster, Rimmer assigned Wilkinson and Turner to the reference library to sanitize the lab's headsets **[N-INF]**.

- **refinery:** An area of *Red Dwarf* allocated for processing and refining minerals and ores mined from meteors, located at the top of the ship **[R-BOD(b)]**.

  *NOTE: This section was visible in concept art included in* The Bodysnatcher Collection*'s bonus features, as well as in production photos of the model, posted online at The Model Unit's Facebook page.*

- **Reflec vest:** A light, highly reflective jacket that offered protection against lasers and other energy-based weapons. The vest was produced by Bloodlust Arms and consisted of polished metal fibers. Ace Rimmer often wore a Reflec vest **[G-RPG]**.

- **refrigeration unit:** A component aboard *Starbug* vessels used to refrigerate food and other perishables. As the *Starbug 1* crew pursued the stolen *Red Dwarf,* the shuttle's refrigeration unit malfunctioned, forcing the crew to live off moss and fungi extracted from passing asteroids, and to later loot a derelict simulant cruiser for food **[T-SER6.5]**.

- **"Re-Gen":** A phrase printed on a console label in *Starbug 1*'s Medical Bay **[T-SER7.8]**.

- **Regent Street:** A road in South East London, featured in that city's version of *Monopoly* **[RL]**. For his twenty-fourth birthday, Lister and several friends embarked on a *Monopoly* board pub crawl across London, which included visiting a tavern on Regent Street **[N-INF]**.

- ***Reggie Dixon's Tango Treats*:** A perpetually looped recording that Rimmer forced Lister, Cat and Kryten to listen to while keeping them in mandatory quarantine **[T-SER5.4]**. Arnold intended to play the recording to cheer up his shipmates after they were contaminated by despair squid ink, but Lister threatened to stay in the airlock if he did **[T-SER5.6(d)]**.

  *NOTE: In the real world, Reggie Dixon never made such a recording. In a deleted scene from episode 5.6 ("Back to Reality"), the DVD captions misspelled the recording's name as* Reggie Dickson's Tango Treats.

- **Reggie Wilson Memorial Trophy:** A championship trophy awarded to the winner of association football's Hammond Organ F.A. Cup Final, in the universe known as Alternative 6829/B. Ace Rimmer helped the Smegchester Rovers win the Reggie Wilson Memorial Trophy in 2180, when he replaced team captain Ray Rimmer, whose magical football boots had become too worn out for him to play **[M-SMG1.8(c4)]**.

- ***Reggie Wilson Plays the Lift Music Classics*:** An album covering elevator music, performed on a Hammond organ. Rimmer owned a CD of this recording, which he brought on a fishing holiday with his shipmates, much to their displeasure **[T-SER4.5]**.

- ***Regional News*:** A television news program that aired at 5:40 PM on Groovy Channel 27. *Regional News* featured a team of holograms reporting on the latest events and weather from around Earth's solar system **[M-SMG1.7(a)]**.

- **Regulator, The:** An Alberog GELF judge who presided over the GELFs' Forum of Justice on Arranguu 12 **[N-LST]**.

- **rehydratable chicken:** A food item in *Red Dwarf*'s food supply, listed on a supply checklist that Lister crosschecked with Rimmer. At the time, the ship's stores contained 140,000 rehydratable chickens **[T-SER1.3]**.

- **rehydration unit:** A component within a 4000 Series mechanoid's body, designed to keep the droid hydrated. The Kryten model had several such units installed **[T-SER4.1]**.

- **Reich, the:** An evil superpower that took control of War World, an Earth in a dimension where World War II never ended. The Reich fought against the Resistance, a small but formidable freedom fighter force.

  The Reich was led by a supercomputer called the Human Impressions Task & Logistics Electronic Reichsführer (HITLER), which was controlled by Adolf Hitler's brain,

**B-: Books**
**PRG:** *Red Dwarf Programme Guide*
**SUR:** *Red Dwarf Space Corps Survival Manual*
**PRM:** *Primordial Soup*
**SOS:** *Son of Soup*
**SCE:** *Scenes from the Dwarf*
**LOG:** *Red Dwarf Log No. 1996*
**RD8:** *Red Dwarf VIII*
**EVR:** *The Log: A Dwarfer's Guide to Everything*

**X-: Misc.**
**PRO:** Promotional materials, videos, etc.
**PST:** Posters at DJ XVII (2013)
**CAL:** 2008 calendar
**RNG:** Cell phone ringtones
**MOB:** Mobisode ("Red Christmas")
**CIN:** *Children in Need* sketch
**GEK:** *Geek Week* intros by Kryten
**TNG:** "Tongue-Tied" video
**XMS:** Bill Pearson's Christmas special pitch script
**XVD:** Bill Pearson's Christmas special pitch video
**OTH:** Other *Red Dwarf* appearances

**SUFFIX**
**DVD:**
**(d)** – Deleted scene
**(o)** – Outtake
**(b)** – Bonus DVD material (other)
**(e)** – Extended version

**SMEGAZINES:**
**(c)** – Comic
**(a)** – Article

**OTHER:**
**(s)** – Early/unused script draft
**(s1)** – Alternate version of script

contained within a stasis field. Below HITLER were the Unterführer, comprising subcommanders who governed the Reich's territories. Among the Reich's proudest achievements were easily trained alligators and Raketenhosen ("Rocket Pants") **[G-BIT]**.

The Reich kidnapped and tried to execute Princess Beryl Bonjella, the leader of the Seni Rotundi islands and a Resistance sympathizer. A hard-light version of Ace Rimmer rescued her in time, however **[T-SER7.2]**.

- **Reinhardt, Arden, Sergeant:** A German Shore Patrol guard stationed at the Space Corps testing facility on Europa in Ace Rimmer's universe. Olaf Petersen stapled Reinhardt's penis to his groin as the sergeant tried to subdue the drunken Dane after he went on a crazed rampage throughout the grounds. Reinhardt, unable to performed sexually while on a date the following night, vowed to get even, using hot steel rivets instead of staples **[N-BCK]**.

- **rejuvenation shower:** A Swedish product, packaged as a build-it-yourself kit, that revitalized a user's body by tracing his or her genome back to a prior state. The *Red Dwarf* crew discovered such a kit in a crate and assembled it.

  During a trial run, the device malfunctioned, sending the crew across space-time to Albion (later known as Great Britain) in 23 A.D. Unable to use the returner remote due to a lack of batteries, the time travelers embarked on a journey to find lemons so they could build a power supply. They eventually located the components and encountered a man they believed to be Jesus Christ, who returned with them to *Red Dwarf* using the newly powered remote.

  While onboard, Jesus read about the history of the Catholic Church. Mortified, he used the rejuvenation shower to return to his own era, hoping to prevent the religion's spread, and destroying the returner remote in the process. The crew, however, had a spare remote, and used the shower once more to stop Jesus from sullying his name **[T-SER10.3]**.

- **Reketrebn:** A symbi-morph (shapeshifting symbiote) enslaved on Lotomi 5, home to the virtual-reality prison Cyberia. Reketrebn, like most symbi-morphs, was created specifically as a Pleasure GELF for inmates volunteering for the Reco-Programme, as she could tap into a host's innermost desires via telepathic "hooks."

  Unlike most symbi-morphs, Reketrebn was not "broken" (tamed). Having used four of her five hooks on a Dingotang guard named Deki, she was rebellious and abhorred the idea of shifting for another's pleasure. Therefore, she helped Lister escape, only to find that they had boarded the Reco-Programme's transport ship.

  The two escapees, along with the program's other volunteers, were transported to a planet containing the Rage of Innocence, a malignant gestalt entity created from the minds of innocent prisoners on Cyberia. Reketrebn survived the Rage and traveled with Lister's friends through the Omni-zone to a new life of freedom **[N-LST]**.

- **relative time dilation:** The amount of time elapsing between two events as measured by observers, either moving relative to each other or differently situated from gravitational masses, according to Albert Einstein's theory of relativity **[RL]**. White holes exhibited this phenomenon, with different parts of space perceiving time at different speeds. When *Red Dwarf* entered close proximity to a white hole, Rimmer and Kryten experienced relative time dilation in a compressed area aboard the vessel **[T-SER4.4]**.

- ***Relaxation: A Beginner's Guide*:** A self-help book that Rimmer once read, containing breathing exercises intended to have a calming effect. He attempted these exercises when a *Starbug* shuttle was on fire and hurtling toward a lava planet in a death dive, but to no avail **[N-LST]**.

- **Reliant Robin:** A three-wheeled vehicle produced in the twentieth century by England's Reliant Motor Co. **[RL]**. While playing the total-immersion video game *Better Than Life*, Rimmer initially conjured up this vehicle to get him to the game's restaurant. Unimpressed by his mind's inability to "think big," he tried again, this time summoning a Series 1 E-Type Jaguar **[T-SER2.2]**.

  ***NOTE:** The vehicle's make and model were not specifically mentioned in the episode, but could be discerned visually.*

- **"Remember You're a Womble":** A song recorded in 1974 by British musician Mike Batt **[RL]**. In 2167, an artificial-

**PREFIX**
**RL:** Real life

**T-: Television Episodes**
**SER:** Television series
**IDW:** "Identity Within"
**USA1:** Unaired U.S. pilot
**USA2:** Unaired U.S. demo

**R-: *The Bodysnatcher Collection***
**SER:** Remastered episodes
**BOD:** "Bodysnatcher"
**DAD:** "Dad"
**FTH:** "Lister's Father"
**INF:** "Infinity Patrol"
**END:** "The End" (original assembly)

**N-: Novels**
**INF:** *Infinity Welcomes Careful Drivers*
**BTL:** *Better Than Life*
**LST:** *Last Human*
**BCK:** *Backwards*
**OMN:** *Red Dwarf Omnibus*

**M-: Magazines**
**SMG:** *Smegazine*

**W-: Websites**
**OFF:** Official website
**NAN:** *Prelude to Nanarchy*
**AND:** *Androids*
**DIV:** Diva-Droid
**DIB:** Duane Dibbley

**CRP:** Crapola
**GEN:** Geneticon
**LSR:** Leisure World Intl.
**JMC:** Jupiter Mining Corporation
**AIT:** *A.I. Today*
**HOL:** HoloPoint

**G-: Roleplaying Game**
**RPG:** *Core Rulebook*
**BIT:** *A.I. Screen Extra Bits* booklet
**SOR:** *Series Sourcebook*
**OTH:** Other RPG material

intelligence synthesizer independently produced a flawless rendition of the song **[B-EVR]**.

- **Remembrance Garden:** *See* Garden of Remembrance

- **remote hologrammic beam projection unit:** An advanced device used aboard the SSS *Enlightenment* as a means of transporting crewmembers within the ship, as well as to and from off-ship locations **[G-RPG]**.

- **remote projection unit:** A device which, when installed in a hologram's light bee, allowed the hologram to travel away from its host ship. This often caused a power drain **[T-SER5.4]**.

- **reproductive circuitry:** Hardware built into androids enabling them to reproduce, as featured on the television soap opera *Androids*. After Kelly admitted to Brook that Brooke Junior was not his son, she noted that it wasn't his fault he couldn't access Kelly's reproductive circuitry as well as Gary (Brooke Junior's actual father) could **[M-SMG1.8(c5)]**.

  ***NOTE:*** *It is unknown whether this technology actually existed in the* Red Dwarf *universe, or only on the TV show* Androids. *If it did actually exist, that could explain how the skutters reproduced in episode 2.6 ("Parallel Universe").*

- **research labs:** An area on *Red Dwarf*'s Z Deck, allocated for the research and development of new technology. Kryten found a prototype Matter Paddle—a handheld device able to transport individuals to virtually anywhere in space within 500,000 light years—while perusing the research labs **[T-SER4.6]**.

- **resentment drain:** A procedure performed on holograms, by which resentment, in the form of corrupted files and malware, was erased from a light bee's hard drive. Both Arnold Rimmer and his half-brother, Howard, required a resentment drain due to their jealousy of each other, which crashed their respective hard drives **[T-SER10.1]**.

- **Resistance, the:** An allied group of freedom fighters on War World, an alternate-reality Earth on which World War II never ended. The Resistance fought the Reich, a superpower spawned from Adolf Hitler's Nazi Germany that grew to control most of the planet.

  The Resistance, comprising mostly cigarette-smoking, beret-wearing spies and fighters with thick French accents, suffered a major setback during the conflict when the Reich developed Raketenhosen ("Rocket Pants"). The Reich's advantage was short-lived, however, due to the arrival of a dimension-hopping traveler, Commander Robert Dimsdale, who commandeered a pair of Rocket Pants to start the Resistance's own program.

  The Resistance gained sympathizers around the globe, including Princess Beryl Bonjella, the leader of the Seni Rotundi islands **[G-BIT]**. The Reich kidnapped and tried to execute Bonjella, but a hard-light version of Ace Rimmer rescued her in time **[T-SER7.2]**.

- **"Restore to Factory Settings":** A stamp used by psychiatric counselors to suggest that a mechanoid be reset to its default settings. Doctor McClaren stamped Kryten's personality report with this recommendation after interviewing him to determine his psychological stability—which McClaren deemed unsalvageable **[T-SER8.1]**.

- **retros:** Booster engines designed to counter a spaceship's momentum, providing opposite force to steer and/or slow the craft. *Starbug* shuttles were equipped with retros **[T-SER5.6]**.

- **returner remote:** A small handheld device packaged with a rejuvenation shower kit found by the *Red Dwarf* crew. The remote ran on an eight-volt battery. When the rejuvenation shower transported the crew to Albion (later known as Great Britain) in 23 A.D., Kryten tried to use the remote to return them to their own era, but failed due to the lack of a power source. Therefore, the group traveled to India to procure some lemons to produce a crude battery, where they met a man they mistook for Jesus Christ **[RL]**.

  ***NOTE:*** *The exact purpose of this remote is a mystery, as the shower's original function had nothing to do with sending or returning anyone to or from anywhere.*

- ***Return to the Planet of the Cheerleaders*:** A notoriously buggy adult-themed artificial-reality game in which players engaged in a non-stop sexual marathon. A common malfunction involved cheerleaders morphing into killer pom-poms and devouring players. A workaround to the glitch included hopping backwards on one leg while French-kissing a mongoose and mooning the royal box at the Wembley game **[B-SUR]**.

- **Rev:** A pink skutter that officiated at a marriage ceremony between another skutter and an animated number two **[T-SER5(b)]**.

  ***NOTE:*** *Rev appeared in a BBC Two station ident for Series V; the animated number was the station's logo. The sequence was broadcast during BBC Two's "*Red Dwarf *Night" in 1998. Presumably, the name Rev was short for "reverend."*

- ***Revenge of the Mutant Splat Gore Monster*:** A movie viewable in the Officers' Quarters of the "low" *Red Dwarf*. According to Kryten, movies such as this were designed to sicken the soul and shrivel the spirit **[T-SER5.5]**.

- ***Revenge of the Surfboarding Killer Bikini Vampire Girls*:** A horror film Lister once watched, in which the heroine (an unconventionally beautiful journalist named Maggie Dove) **[X-CAL]** was taken captive by the titular vampire girls. When Maggie built a dummy to take her place, the vampires failed to notice the switch, allowing her to sneak up behind them and knock the creatures unconscious.

  The *Red Dwarf* crew attempted a similar plan to escape Legion's station. Since Legion possessed the knowledge and emotions of all four crewmembers, however, he foresaw the ruse and thwarted their escape **[T-SER6.2]**.

  The film was scheduled to be broadcast by Krytie TV on October 1 **[X-CAL]**.

- **reverse flu:** A strain of positive virus that enhanced an individual's happiness and well-being. Hologrammic scientist Hildegarde Lanstrom discovered the reverse flu, from which Kryten claimed many twentieth-century disc jockeys suffered **[T-SER5.4]**.

- **reverse thrust tube:** A component of *Starbug 1*'s propulsion system, designed to slow the craft down by applying forward thrust. When Kryten, in an effort to save his shipmates, suggested that he be loaded into the tube and launched toward what he believed to be a heat-seeking missile, Lister nixed the idea, as he was unwilling to do his own ironing **[T-SER6.2]**.

- **revision timetable:** A wall-mounted chart Rimmer created to help him prepare for his Engineer's Exams. It typically took him seven weeks to create each timetable, which consisted of color-coded test subjects intermixed with study, rest and self-testing periods **[T-SER1.3]**. Creating such an elaborate revision timetable was Rimmer's subconscious way of avoiding actually learning anything **[N-INF]**. When Rimmer couldn't find it the day before one of his tests, Lister informed him it was pinned up to a wall, drying out after he had spilled goat vindaloo on it **[T-SER1.3]**.

  ***NOTE:*** *This gag originated in a* Son of Cliché *"Dave Hollins: Space Cadet" sketch titled "Indian Food/ Exams."*

- **Revolutionary Working Front:** A terrorist organization operating throughout Europe. An operative for the group, Henri le Clerque, was arrested while attempting to poison a French mineral spring that supplied the world with Perrier water. According to a news segment reporting the incident, the entire middle class would have perished within a month had he succeeded **[T-SER2.2]**.

- **Reynolds, Debris:** The proprietor of Detritus Wrecks, a junkyard on the television soap opera *Androids* **[M-SMG2.1(c2)]**.

  ***NOTE:*** *This character was named after American actor and singer Debbie Reynolds.*

- **RG 211:** The license plate number of an emergency vehicle driven by Archie on the television soap opera *Androids* **[M-SMG2.9(c6)]**.

- **Rhaagbthammar:** *See* 7th Death Ring of Rhaagbthammar

- **Rhea:** The second largest of Saturn's moons **[RL]**. George McIntyre incurred a massive gambling debt playing Toot on moons such as Rhea, which eventually led him to commit suicide **[N-INF]**.

- **Rice:** A guard at the Tank, *Red Dwarf*'s brig on Floor 13, who died during the cadmium II disaster, but was resurrected by nanobots, along with the rest of the crew. Rice participated in a basketball game between the guards and inmates, which Captain Hollister set up as punishment for Lister and Rimmer. During the game, Kochanski was supposed to "pick up Rice," but she misunderstood and instead made a date to meet him for drinks **[T-SER8.6]**.

- **Rice, Anneka:** A Welsh television presenter for BBC World Service and other broadcasters **[RL]**. The *Red Dwarf* crew once thought they had encountered Anneka Rice and her camera crew asking directions to Coventry Cathedral, but this turned out to be a mirage **[T-SER3(d)]**.

- **Rich, Bernard ("Buddy"):** A twentieth-century American jazz drummer and bandleader **[RL]**. While trapped in an addictive version of *Better Than Life*, Cat entertained himself in his golden castle with a hand-picked seven-piece band, which included Rich on drums **[N-INF]**.

- **Richard, Cliff, Sir:** A British pop singer and musician. Along with his backup group, The Shadows, Richard topped the pre-Beatles music charts in the 1950s and early '60s **[RL]**. While marooned on a frozen planet in *Starbug 1*, Lister tried to keep his mind off hunger by asking Rimmer how he lost his virginity. Rimmer claimed he couldn't remember, but Lister refused to believe that, since losing one's virginity was something no one would forget—like where they were the day Cliff Richard was shot **[T-SER3.2]**.

  ***NOTE:** Cliff Richard is still alive as of this book's publishing. Either great advances in lifespan extension were made in the* Red Dwarf *universe, or Lister was speaking historically, since Richard would have been 215 years old at the time of Dave's birth.*

- ***Richard III*:** A historic play written by William Shakespeare circa the 1590s, chronicling the reign of the titular British king **[RL]**. While marooned aboard *Starbug 1* on an icy planet, Lister burned Rimmer's books to stay warm, including *The Complete Works of Shakespeare*. Arnold protested the destruction of what was likely the only remaining copy of the play, but admitted he never actually read it. Although Rimmer claimed to know the material, he could only quote a single word: "Now…" **[T-SER3.2]**.

- **Richard III, King:** The ruler of England from 1483 until his death two years later during the Battle of Bosworth Field **[RL]**.

  A waxdroid replica of Richard III was created for the Waxworld theme park. Left on their own for millions of years, the waxdroids attained sentience and became embroiled in a park-wide resource war between Villain World (to which Richard III belonged) and Hero World.

  During this war, the *Red Dwarf* crew transported to the planet using a Matter Paddle, with Lister and Cat materializing in Villain territory, while Rimmer and Kryten landed in Hero territory. While imprisoned in Villain World, Lister and Cat witnessed the firing-squad execution of a Winnie-the-Pooh waxdroid, which Richard III attended.

  Meanwhile, Rimmer found the heroes' army lacking and took command, working many of the pacifistic waxdroids to death before ordering a frontal attack on the enemy's compound across a minefield. This wiped out the remaining droids, including Richard III **[T-SER4.6]**.

- **Richards, Yvette, Captain:** The thirty-three-year-old commander of *Nova 5*, one of several spaceships commissioned by the Coca-Cola Co. to detonate a series of supergiant stars in a strategic pattern as part of the company's advertisement campaign. She sported a crew cut and spoke with a Texan accent, and her blood type was O.

  Richards was one of three survivors of a crash that killed most of *Nova 5*'s crew, which Kryten inadvertently caused by trying to clean the ship's computer. The three women eventually died as well, leaving the mechanoid to tend to their corpses, unaware they had passed on **[N-INF]**.

  ***NOTE:** Richards' name, noted in the novel* Infinity Welcomes Careful Drivers *(Kryten called her simply "Miss Yvette"), did not jibe with the crew's names provided onscreen in episode 2.1 ("Kryten").*

- **Ricky:** A member of the species *Rattus sapiens*, which evolved from the lab rats aboard an alternate *Red Dwarf*. Ricky's companions included hologram Monica Jones and a Hudzen 10 mechanoid **[G-RPG]**.

- **"Ride of the Valkyries":** A popular term describing the theme music in Act III of Richard Wagner's opera *Die Walküre* **[RL]**. While explaining his plan to create a host body from Lister's hair, Rimmer said he refused to believe the apex of human evolution was a man who could belch "Ride of the Valkyries" on a single beer **[R-BOD]**.

- **Rigel 5:** A planet, possibly in an alternate universe, that was home to a Caesar Salad Monster **[G-BIT]**.

- **Righty:** A name that Lister assigned to one of twelve rogue droids he purchased from the Kinitawowi to break his doppelgänger out of the virtual-reality prison Cyberia. This particular droid was missing an arm **[N-LST]**.

- **Rimére:** A name that Lister sarcastically suggested he call Rimmer when the latter complained that Dave's tendency to put the emphasis on "Rim" made him sound like a bathroom disinfectant **[T-SER2.1]**.

- **Rimmel, Albert:** An acquaintance of Colonel Mike O'Hagan. The colonel autographed a copy of his *Space Corps Survival Manual* for Rimmel, thanking him for buying the book, sending him chocolates, cleaning his shoes and setting him up on a date with Albert's mother **[B-SUR]**.

- **Rimmer, Alice:** A cousin of Arnold Rimmer, and the daughter of Rimmer's uncle Frank. Alice was blonde and two years older than Arnold, and had a twin sister named Sarah. Arnold suspected that Alice may have fancied him. When Arnold was a youth, the Rimmer family went on vacation, during which he was awoken during the night by a French kiss (Arnold's first such experience). Believing his visitor to be either Sarah or Alice, he was horrified to discover it was his uncle, who had mistaken Arnold's room for his mother's **[T-SER3.6]**.

- **Rimmer, Alison ("Arnie"):** A sister whom Arnold Rimmer claimed to have while asking Napoleon Bonaparte for an autograph in the game *Better Than Life*, adding that she often went by the nickname "Arnie" **[T-SER2.2]**.

  ***NOTE:** Alison's last name was not mentioned, but since this supposed sister was never again mentioned in any iteration of* Red Dwarf, *it is very likely she was merely a ruse on Arnold's part to get Napoleon to personalize the signature to him, and is therefore presumed to have had the last name of Rimmer.*

- **Rimmer, Arlene Judith, Second Technician**: A crewmember aboard an alternate *Red Dwarf* in a dimension in which the sexes were reversed. She ranked second to last aboard the ship. Her role models included actor Arlene Schwarzenegger.

  Arlene's first sexual encounter was with Vaughan McGruder, a male boxing champion aboard that reality's *Red Dwarf* who became concussed after a winch fell on his head **[W-OFF]**. Arlene was killed in a cadmium II accident in which the entire crew perished save for Deb Lister, who was in stasis at the time of the disaster **[T-SER2.6]**.

- **Rimmer, Arlene Judith, Second Technician:** A hologram of crewmember Arlene Rimmer aboard *Red Dwarf* in a dimension in which the sexes were reversed. Arlene was the hologrammic Arnold Rimmer's female counterpart in this dimension. Upon meeting her prime universe counterpart, Arlene was instantly attracted to him, but he was put off by her advances **[T-SER2.6]**.

  Arlene was later recruited by a female Ace Rimmer from another universe, who had been attacked and mortally wounded by killer GELFs. She temporarily replaced the heroic dimension-jumper, but eventually returned to her *Red Dwarf*, where she was imprisoned by the revived crew **[W-OFF]**.

- **Rimmer, Arlene Judith ("Ace"):** A female Ace Rimmer from a universe in which the sexes were reversed. Like her male counterpart, she traveled throughout the dimensions, fighting for truth and justice. She was slain by killer GELFs, but before dying, she enlisted another reality's Arlene Rimmer to replace her **[W-OFF]**.

- **Rimmer, Arnold:** A character on the American television show *Red Dwarf*, developed in an alternate universe. On this series, Rimmer was Dave Lister's best friend, and saved *Red Dwarf* and its crew from a deadly radioactive leak, at the cost of the use of his legs. He spent the first episode wheelchair-bound, but during an attack by an amorphous alien that knocked Lister unconscious, he found the strength to overcome his disability, grabbing Lister's gun and defeating the intruder **[M-SMG1.10(c4)]**.

- **Rimmer, Arnold ("Ace Blackheart"):** A tyrannical, bionic-enhanced version of Arnold Rimmer in an alternate dimension.

While serving in the Space Corps, this Ace embarked on a training mission with a young pilot named Hooper, during which they discovered a narrow meteor formation. Ace let Hooper through the formation, crashing his own ship in the process, which caused Ace to suffer crippling, career-ending injuries.

Later, as he watched Hooper and his former colleagues go on to fame, Ace became embittered. Using knowledge gained from the Space Corps, he founded RimmerCorps, a company that developed technology far superior to that of the Corps. Buying out the Space Corps, he focused on creating bionics, which he then used to transform himself into the ultimate soldier.

Calling himself Ace "Blackheart" Rimmer, he went on a rampage throughout the galaxy, destroying planets and civilizations. When he attacked a settlement populated by Darren (a hillbilly Dave Lister), Kochanski, Kritter (a hillbilly cyborg Kryten), Hollentine (that reality's Holly) and Dorrie (a humanoid who evolved from a dormouse), both Kochanski and Hollentine died in the onslaught.

Blackheart later returned to finish off the survivors, but met another Ace Rimmer who tried to stop him. During the struggle, Blackheart learned that the benevolent Ace had let Hooper crash during his Space Corps days; racked with guilt, he had dedicated his time to Hooper's recovery, developing bionics not for himself but for Hooper, who remained a close friend. Unfazed by the story, Blackheart continued his attack until Dorrie shot him in the head from behind **[M-SMG1.14(c5)]**.

> ***NOTE:*** *Blackheart's first name was never mentioned in the comic; however, given the two Aces lived identical lives up until the accident, it's presumed to be Arnold as well.*

- **Rimmer, Arnold ("Squirrel"), Captain:** The commander of *Red Dwarf* in a mirror universe. He was left-handed and had a large penis. His spiritual advisor was Sister Talia Garrett **[T-SER8.8]**. Rimmer's first officer was David Lister—who, in that reality, sported a mustache and spoke with a French accent. The two were close, with Lister nicknaming him "Squirrel" **[T-SER8.8(d)]**.

  Sometime after the mirror *Red Dwarf* was rebuilt by nanobots, Rimmer contracted yellow fever and was assisted by Frank Hollister, a prison inmate on probation. In the prime universe, meanwhile, Kryten built a device capable of bridging the gap between the two dimensions in order to find an antidote for a chameleonic microbe devouring the ship. The device malfunctioned, however, after the prime Rimmer crossed through. Trapped in the mirror universe, Arnold assumed the role of Captain Rimmer, taking pleasure in belittling Hollister as revenge for his own treatment in the prime universe **[T-SER8.8]**.

  > ***NOTE:*** *It is unknown why this version of Rimmer was absent when the prime Rimmer visited his universe.*

- **Rimmer, Arnold Judas:** An alternate-reality Rimmer whom the prime *Red Dwarf* crew found dead aboard a *Starbug* shuttle, his light bee destroyed, after they traversed the Omni-zone into another universe. The non-native crew discovered that this reality's Lister had killed him, along with the rest of his shipmates, in order to steal the coordinates of an ancient ship carrying the genome of DNA (G.O.D.) **[N-LST]**.

- **Rimmer, Arnold Judas:** A version of Rimmer conjured up by a memory machine on a planet once inhabited by a tribe of Cat People. The *Red Dwarf* crew found the machine, which could duplicate any item from a person's memory, while searching the planet's ruins. Cat used the device to create a mirror, while Lister attempted to conjure up Kochanski—but when Holly mentioned a six-eyed, carnivorous, raging swamp beast, that materialized instead of Kristine **[M-SMG1.9(c3)]**.

  After the crew returned to *Red Dwarf*, Rimmer came back to create a version of himself based on his own misguided self-perceptions. When his shipmates set out to retrieve him, they found this version instead, who was more handsome, courageous and better endowed than the original. The swamp beast attacked once more, but the new Rimmer fought off the creature—at the expense of his own life **[M-SMG1.10(c3)]**.

- **Rimmer, Arnold Judas:** A character in the Total Immersion video game *Red Dwarf*, played in a fascist society on an alternate-universe Earth. William Doyle, the vagrant half-brother of Voter Colonel Sebastian Doyle, played this character in the game for four years, until being released after the group scored a mere four percent **[M-SMG2.1(c4)]**. He was replaced by a more intelligent player, who scored much higher **[M-SMG2.4(c4)]**.

**B-: Books**
**PRG:** *Red Dwarf Programme Guide*
**SUR:** *Red Dwarf Space Corps Survival Manual*
**PRM:** *Primordial Soup*
**SOS:** *Son of Soup*
**SCE:** *Scenes from the Dwarf*
**LOG:** *Red Dwarf Log No. 1996*
**RD8:** *Red Dwarf VIII*
**EVR:** *The Log: A Dwarfer's Guide to Everything*

**X-: Misc.**
**PRO:** Promotional materials, videos, etc.
**PST:** Posters at DJ XVII (2013)
**CAL:** 2008 calendar
**RNG:** Cell phone ringtones
**MOB:** Mobisode ("Red Christmas")
**CIN:** *Children in Need* sketch
**GEK:** *Geek Week* intros by Kryten
**TNG:** "Tongue-Tied" video

**XMS:** Bill Pearson's Christmas special pitch script
**XVD:** Bill Pearson's Christmas special pitch video
**OTH:** Other *Red Dwarf* appearances

**SUFFIX**
**DVD:**
**(d)** – Deleted scene
**(o)** – Outtake
**(b)** – Bonus DVD material (other)
**(e)** – Extended version

**SMEGAZINES:**
**(c)** – Comic
**(a)** – Article

**OTHER:**
**(s)** – Early/unused script draft
**(s1)** – Alternate version of script

- **Rimmer, Arnold Judas:** A "low" duplicate of the hologram Rimmer, created during a triplicator accident that destroyed *Red Dwarf* but produced two copies: a "high" version, containing all the best aspects of the ship and its crew, and a "low" version manifesting the worst characteristics. The "low" Rimmer was a masochist who wore leather and fishnet stockings. He wielded a holowhip and had a crooked "H" on his forehead.

  This Rimmer and his crewmembers attacked the original and "high" crewmembers after luring them to the "low" variant. Wanting the "high" ship for their own, they kidnapped Lister, attached a spinal implant to his neck, forced him to murder the "high" versions of himself and Rimmer, and then sent him after his own crew. The plan failed after the crew incapacitated Lister and used the triplicator, built with pieces from both ships, to reform the original *Red Dwarf,* dematerializing the "low" Rimmer in the process **[T-SER5.5]**.

- **Rimmer, Arnold Judas, Brother:** A "high" duplicate of Arnold Rimmer created during a triplicator accident that destroyed *Red Dwarf* but produced two copies: a "high" version containing all the best aspects of the ship and its crew, and a "low" version manifesting the worst characteristics. Brother Rimmer was an enlightened version of the original, possessing knowledge of poetry, art and metaphysics. As he searched the "low" ship for components of the triplicator, Brother Rimmer's light bee was crushed by the prime universe's Lister, who was remotely controlled by the "low" counterparts **[T-SER5.5]**.

- **Rimmer, Arnold Judas, Circuitry Technician Third Class:** A crewmember aboard the JMC mining vessel *Black Hole* in an alternate universe. The ship contained a temporal scoop and a Singularity Drive, which Rimmer inadvertently cross-wired, causing the ship to become lost in space-time upon its first activation. The tiny captured star used to power the ship was inadequately contained, creating a radiation burst that killed the entire crew except for those shielded in the cargo hold or protected by stasis booths, and also lowered the IQ of the ship's artificial intelligence, Kenneth **[G-RPG]**.

- **Rimmer, Arnold Judas, First Technician:** A version of Rimmer from a dimension in which he and Kryten never entered a highly addictive version of *Better Than Life* to save Lister and Cat. Subsequently, the two perished from malnutrition, leaving Rimmer and Kryten alone, until alternate versions of Lister and Cat arrived in Ace Rimmer's ship *Wildfire One*, having escaped a universe in which their Rimmer and Kryten had been killed by the Apocalypse virus **[N-BCK]**.

  ***NOTE:*** *The novels indicated Rimmer's rank as First Technician; since this entry deals solely with events from the novel* Backwards, *that rank is used here.*

- **Rimmer, Arnold Judas, Prime Minister:** An alternate-reality Rimmer from a dimension in which he became the prime minister of the United Republic of Lesser Britain, and the world's most successful politician. While visiting this dimension, Ace Rimmer found the drunken P.M. sleeping in a public park.

  Curious, Ace chatted with his doppelgänger and learned that he had become so successful—abolishing poverty, inflation and war—that he had become bored, drinking himself into oblivion. Ace left to find a solution to the prime minister's problem, then returned with a chancellor of the exchequer—who, Ace explained, would make running the country much more challenging **[M-SMG2.8(c6)]**.

  ***NOTE:*** *Although the chancellor was not specifically named, he was presumably modeled after Norman Lamont, whose failed tenure as chancellor of the exchequer ended with his abrupt resignation.*

- **Rimmer, Arnold Judas, Second Technician:** The second-lowest ranking crewmember aboard *Red Dwarf* **[T-SER1.1]**. He was born on Io **[N-INF]** in 2155 **[B-PRM]**, following an affair between his mother and the family's gardener, Dennis ("Dungo"), a fact that was kept from him until his death **[T-SER10.6]**.

  Rimmer attended college at Io Polytechnic, where his stepfather was one of his lecturers **[T-SER10.6]**. While at the college, he resided at Io House **[T-SER4.5]**. He had three half-brothers—Frank, John and Howard, all of whom teased and tortured him mercilessly throughout their childhood **[T-SER3.3]**—and claimed, on one occasion, to have a sister named Alison as well **[T-SER2.2]**. Arnold also had an uncle named Frank, cousins named Alice and Sarah **[T-SER3.6]**, and another uncle who was a bishop **[T-SER2.3(d)]**. He had a crush on Alice **[T-SER3.6]** and was attracted to his sister-in-law, Janine **[T-SER4.1]**. His first French kiss was from his Uncle

Frank, who had mistaken his room for his mother's **[T-SER3.6]**.

When Arnold was seven years old, his parents and school discussed the possibility of holding him back a year due to his poor grades, but ultimately decided against doing so. This decision proved detrimental to Arnold, who grew up resentful and blamed others for his own shortcomings **[T-SER4.5]**.

While attending boarding school at age eight, Rimmer was visited by a future version of himself, who attempted to convince him to invent a novelty item called the Tension Sheet so he could grow up wealthy. Due to rugby practice, however, the youth was late to the patent office, allowing his bunkmate, Fred "Thicky" Holden, to get there first and earn the patent **[T-SER3.5]**. Rimmer's nickname in school was "Bonehead" **[T-SER2.1]**.

Sometime during his youth, Rimmer became the captain of his school's skipping team **[T-SER8.2]**. When his pet lemming bit and latched onto his finger, he had no choice but to smash the animal against a wall, which ruined his helicopter wallpaper **[T-SER2.4]**.

When he was fourteen years old, Arnold officially divorced his parents. He had grown tired of his stepfather's obsession with the Space Corps, which ranged from stretching Arnold and his brothers on a rack so they could exceed the Corps' minimum height requirement, to conducting snap astronavigation quizzes during dinner, with food rewarded only for correct answers **[T-SER2.2]**.

At age seventeen, Rimmer attended cadet training school, where he often played games of *Risk* with fellow students and faculty members, jotting his victories down in a campaign book **[T-SER4.6]**.

During this period of his life, Rimmer brought home a girl he was dating to meet his family, and later found her and his half-brother John making out in the greenhouse **[N-BTL]**. On another occasion, Rimmer tried to seduce Fiona Barrington in that same greenhouse, but was embarrassed to realize that his hand had been in warm compost, and not on her body **[T-SER5.2]**.

When Rimmer was nineteen, he had another awkward sexual encounter with a girl named Sandra, barely making it to second base **[N-INF]**. Years later, he would embellish this story, claiming he lost his virginity to Sandra in the back of his brother's Bentley V8 convertible while at cadet school, as he was embarrassed about not having had sex until much later in life **[T-SER3.2]**.

Arnold's favorite color was military grey **[M-SMG1.1(a)]**, and his interests included twentieth-century telegraph poles **[T-SER4.1]**; military strategists such as Julius Caesar, George S. Patton and Alexander the Great **[T-SER3.2]**; Morris dancing **[T-SER4.5]**; Hammond organ music, particularly the stylings of Reggie Wilson **[T-SER4.1]**; the tango hits of Reggie Dixon **[T-SER5.4]**; and the card game bridge **[T-SER8.1]**. He also enjoyed reading magazines, including *Antiques* **[T-SER2.4]**, *Classic Car Monthly* **[T-SER9.1]**, *Fascist Dictator Monthly* **[T-SER3.5]**, *Muscle Woman* **[T-SER3.4]**, *Strange Science* **[N-INF]** and *Survivalist* **[N-INF]**.

Rimmer once served as the treasurer of the Hammond Organ Owners' Society **[T-SER4.5]**. His worst fears included tarantulas **[T-SER2.2]** and being tortured **[T-SER5.3]**. He claimed to be allergic to parachutes **[N-LST]**, and had a family history that included numerous deaths due to aneurysms, strokes or heart attacks **[T-SER6.4(d)]**.

At one time Rimmer worked with a charity group called the Samaritans. After speaking with him, however, five people jumped to their deaths—a tragedy that newspapers covering the incidents dubbed Lemming Sunday **[T-SER3.6]**.

Arnold joined the Space Corps and was assigned to the JMC vessel *Red Dwarf*. At age thirty-one, he met Yvonne McGruder, the ship's female boxing champion, to whom he finally lost his virginity **[T-SER2.3]**. Yvonne had genuine feelings for Rimmer, but due to a miscommunication, the couple never saw each other again. McGruder left *Red Dwarf* shortly thereafter, only to discover she was pregnant with Rimmer's son, whom she named Michael **[N-LST]**.

Rimmer's awards included Silver and Bronze Swimming Certificates, as well as Three-, Six-, Nine- and Twelve-Year Long Service medals **[T-SER4.5]**. He also earned a Vending Machine Maintenance Man of the Month award one year, for the month of April **[T-SER9.1]**. He had numerous idiosyncrasies that set him apart from his crewmates, however. He kept his underpants on hangars **[T-SER1.4]**, sewed nametags onto his ship-issued condoms **[T-SER4.3]**, named his shoetrees **[T-SER7.5]**, ate food in alphabetical order **[T-SER7.5]**, alphabetized the contents of his quarters **[R-BOD]** and always used exactly three pieces of toilet paper **[T-SER7.5]**.

After serving with JMC for fourteen years, Rimmer was invited to the captain's table for dinner with several officers.

The starter course was gazpacho soup; unaware that gazpacho was meant to be served cold, Rimmer chastised the waiter, telling him to bring the soup back hot, much to the amusement of the officers, including Captain Frank Hollister. Mortified to learn of his faux pas, Rimmer thereafter blamed the incident for his inability to rise up in rank **[T-SER1.6]**.

Approximately four months later, Rimmer met Dave Lister on Mimas, who was posing as a taxi hopper driver. Disguised with a mustache and assuming the alias Christopher Todhunter, Rimmer asked Lister to drive him to Shagtown, a seedy area of the spaceport. On their return trip, Rimmer unwittingly convinced Lister to join the Space Corps, and they soon found themselves bunking together aboard *Red Dwarf*. Dave was assigned to Z-Shift, a maintenance group in charge of menial tasks aboard the vessel, of which Arnold was in charge **[N-INF]**.

Rimmer and Lister worked together servicing various areas of the ship. When Lister was remanded to a stasis chamber for refusing to surrender his pregnant cat to Hollister, Rimmer was left short-handed and was ill-equipped to fix a drive plate. This resulted in a cadmium II leak that killed Rimmer and everyone else on board except for Lister, who was in stasis at the time. After the radiation dropped to a safe level, the ship's computer, Holly, released Lister from stasis and revived Rimmer as a hologram to keep him sane—despite the fact that the two men loathed each other and constantly bickered **[T-SER1.1]** Holly had based his decision to bring Rimmer back on the number of words the two had exchanged: roughly fourteen million **[T-SER1.3]**.

Years later, Rimmer was revived as a living person by nanobots. When this Rimmer tried to help Lister, Cat, Kryten and Kochanski escape the nanobot-rebuilt *Red Dwarf*, Captain Hollister sentenced them all to two years in the ship's classified brig, known as the Tank **[T-SER8.3]**. There, Rimmer unwittingly signed up for the Canaries, an elite group of expendable convicts assigned to dangerous situations **[T-SER8.4]**.

Rimmer and the others escaped the Tank as *Red Dwarf* was being dissolved by a corrosive chameleonic microbe. Using a machine devised by Kryten, Arnold entered a mirror universe to find an antidote to the microorganism. When he returned, however, the ship was in ruins and his crewmates were gone. The Grim Reaper arrived to escort him to the afterlife, but Rimmer kneed the entity in the groin and ran away **[T-SER8.8]**.

***NOTE:*** *Occasionally, Rimmer's rank was referred to as technician, second class. The novel* Infinity Welcomes Careful Drivers *gave his rank as first technician.*

*While asking Napoleon Bonaparte for an autograph in episode 2.2 ("Better Than Life"), Rimmer claimed he had a sister named Alison who went by the nickname "Arnie." However, since she was never mentioned again in any iteration of* Red Dwarf, *this was presumably a ruse to get Napoleon to personalize the signature to him.*

*Rimmer's birth year was calculated from the script for episode 4.5 ("Dimension Jump"), published in the book* Primordial Soup, *which stated that he was seven years old in 2162.* Infinity Welcomes Careful Drivers *claimed that Arnold had only been with on* Red Dwarf *for five months, not fourteen years, before being invited to the captain's table, fixing a possible continuity error in episode 1.6 ("Me²") regarding his tenure and age.*

*Speculation abounds regarding what happened to the "live" version of Rimmer after Series VIII, given his appearance as a hologram in* Back to Earth *and subsequent seasons. One common theory (assumed to be the case for the purposes of this book) is that the hard-light hologrammic Rimmer returned from being Ace Rimmer and saved the ship, and that the living version either died or left sometime between the last scene of Series VIII and* Back to Earth.

- **Rimmer, Arnold Judas, Second Technician:** A class-1 hologram **[T-SER5.1]** of Arnold Rimmer, a *Red Dwarf* crewmember killed when he failed to adequately repair a drive plate, causing a cadmium II explosion. After the radiation dropped to a safe level, the ship's computer, Holly, revived Rimmer as a hologram to keep Dave Lister (who had survived the disaster in a stasis chamber) sane—despite the fact that the two men loathed each other and constantly bickered **[T-SER1.1]**. Forced to live without a physical presence, Rimmer relied first on the skutters **[T-SER1.4]**, and then on Kryten, to help with his duties **[T-SER2.1]**.

  Rimmer once tricked Lister into activating a duplicate Rimmer hologram. However, the two Rimmers soon began to despise each other, causing Lister to erase the duplicate **[T-SER1.6]**. He also encountered a female version of himself, named Arlene Rimmer, in a parallel dimension in which the sexes were reversed **[T-SER2.6]**.

During a visit to the penal station Justice World, Rimmer was scanned and convicted of 1,167 counts of second-degree murder for negligence resulting in the cadmium II leak. This ruling was overturned, however, by Kryten's appeal, which was predicated on the defense that Arnold was far too insignificant to have caused such a catastrophe **[T-SER4.3]**.

Years later, Rimmer was brought aboard the holoship *Enlightenment*, where he met a hologrammic officer named Nirvanah Crane. The two fell in love, leading Rimmer to apply for a permanent position on the holoship. He passed the test after his opponent dropped out, and was invited aboard as navigation officer, only to discover that his opponent had been Crane, who would be decommissioned to make room for him. In a rare act of selflessness, Arnold declined the new position and returned to *Red Dwarf* so she could survive **[T-SER5.1]**.

Rimmer and Kryten once visited a psi-moon, a small planetoid capable of restructuring itself based on its occupants. The moon sensed Arnold's disturbed mind and transformed itself into a haunted, desolate wasteland filled with denizens based on his negative traits. Rimmer was kidnapped by the creatures and prepared for an eternity of torture, but was saved by his crewmates, who feigned friendship with him to weaken the nefarious creations **[T-SER5.3]**.

While visiting a seemingly abandoned space station, Rimmer encountered Legion, a gestalt entity who fitted his light bee with hard light technology. This gave the hologram a physical presence, with the added bonus of being nearly indestructible **[T-SER6.2]**.

Soon thereafter, he was marooned on a barren planet, which he terraformed using components from his escape pod. He attempted to clone himself several times for companionship, but the clones rebelled and imprisoned him. His shipmates rescued him from the hellish Rimmerworld—but it took 557 years from his perspective, due to the effects of time dilation **[T-SER6.5]**.

When the hologrammatic Ace Rimmer was injured in a parallel dimension, he visited the prime-universe *Starbug 1* crew, requesting that Rimmer carry on his legacy as a hero. Ace trained his counterpart until his light bee failed, after which Arnold agreed to become the next Ace Rimmer and left in the other's spaceship. Following his departure, Lister ceremoniously awarded Rimmer the rank of first officer **[T-SER7.2]**.

Sometime later, the hologrammic Rimmer apparently returned to *Red Dwarf*, where he resumed his duties as that vessel's acting captain. A space-time phenomenon reunited him with a hologram of his half-brother Howard, who confessed that despite appearances, he had never risen higher than the rank of vending soup repairman aboard his own vessel, *Columbus 3*. Howard then gave his life to save Arnold from a mutinous simulant named Crawford **[T-SER10.1]**

When faced with certain death at the hands of murderous simulants, Rimmer played a holo-lamp that the man he believed to be his father had given to him long ago. The holo-message revealed that his father was merely his stepfather, and that Arnold was actually the product of his mother's affair with the family's gardener, Dennis ("Dungo") **[T-SER10.6]**.

> ***NOTE:*** *Rimmer's fate differed in the two sequel novels to* Better Than Life. *In* Backwards, *his light bee was destroyed while he was hooked into an artificial-reality machine, helping Kryten to combat the Apocalypse virus. In* Last Human, *however, the light bee was irreparably damaged by Lister's doppelgänger; still partially operational, Rimmer volunteered to carry the oblivion virus into the Rage of Innocence, destroying the gestalt entity and dying in the process.*

- **Rimmer, Arnold Judas, Second Technician:** A duplicate hologram of Arnold Rimmer, whom Lister mistakenly activated, believing he was reviving Kochanski. The primary Rimmer had switched his own personality disc with Kochanski's and hidden the rest behind solar panels on *Red Dwarf*'s exterior, hoping to prevent Lister from finding them and reviving Kristine **[T-SER1.5]**.

Moving into quarters with the primary Rimmer, the duplicate appeared to be his ideal companion, but the two quickly became bitter enemies. When their incessant bickering interrupted a movie outing, Lister took action to end the friction. Playing Ippy Dippy, he pretended to choose the primary Rimmer to permanently deactivate. In so doing, he tricked Arnold into disclosing the meaning of "gazpacho soup" (his final words before dying in the cadmium II explosion), then deleted the duplicate instead **[T-SER1.6]**.

> ***NOTE:*** *In the novel* Infinity Welcomes Careful Drivers, *Rimmer used the hologram projection unit from the salvaged* Nova 5 *to produce his duplicate.*

- **Rimmer, Arnold Judas, Second Technician:** A version of Rimmer from a dimension in which Kochanski covered for Lister by taking the blame for bringing Frankenstein aboard *Red Dwarf*, causing her to be placed in stasis and surviving the cadmium II disaster instead of David. In that reality, both Rimmer and Lister perished in the accident, but Lister was revived as a hologram instead of Rimmer **[T-SER7.3]**.

- **Rimmer, Arnold Judas ("Ace"):** A hard-light hologrammic version of Arnold "Ace" Rimmer from an alternate dimension who took up the mantle when the previous incarnation of Ace perished **[T-SER7.2]**.

  Prior to taking on the role, this Rimmer stole the time drive from *Gemini 12*, left his crew for dead and became stranded in Napoleonic times, where he wore a dress and worked in a flower shop to avoid being drafted to fight in the war. The previous Ace, badly wounded, entered his shop and offered to train him as his successor, eventually handing over his wig and sunglasses, and the keys to his ship, before dying. This Rimmer then spent several years dimension-hopping **[T-SER7.2(d)]**.

  As he attempted to rescue Princess Bonjella from a Nazi camp in a parallel dimension, Ace's light bee was damaged, forcing him to dimension-jump to the prime universe to seek aid from Arnold Rimmer. Explaining the legend, he convinced the prime Rimmer to become the next Ace, and trained him before succumbing to his injuries **[T-SER7.2]**.

  ***NOTE:*** *This Ace's full name was never revealed, although it's presumed to be the same as the prime Rimmer's.*

- **Rimmer, Arnold Judas ("Ace"):** A hard-light hologrammic version of Arnold "Ace" Rimmer. This version rescued Princess Bonjella from the clutches of Captain Wolfgang Voorhese on War World, a planet in a dimension in which the second World War never ended. After the rescue, Ace and Bonjella indulged in a brief romance, until it was discovered that Ace's light bee had been damaged during the rescue **[G-BIT]**.

  ***NOTE:*** *Because the Bonjella stories varied greatly between the official website and* Red Dwarf—The Roleplaying Game*, both versions of Ace are listed here as existing in separate universes, although it's entirely possible the same Ace rescued both princesses. This Ace's full name was never revealed, although it's presumed to be the same as the prime Rimmer's.*

- **Rimmer, Arnold Judas ("Ace"), Commander:** A test pilot for the Space Corps, stationed on Mimas in an alternate reality. Ace was held back a grade in school at age seven, which embarrassed him but built up his character to help him become a brave, selfless adult. He was skilled at engine repair, field microsurgery and piano-playing.

  Ace's last mission for the Space Corps involved testing a ship that could break the speed of reality, crossing into other dimensions in which decisions in his life played out differently. His ship jumped into the prime universe, in which Rimmer had not been left back in school, resulting in his becoming an underachieving coward. Despising his pathetic other self, Ace left to explore other realities **[T-SER4.5]**.

  In one dimension, Ace saved Princess Holina from a castle in which she was being held captive, after which they made love for more than four hours. He then visited a reality in which the sexes were reversed, where he met Arlene Rimmer and Deb Lister. Deb seduced him, hoping to impregnate him and fulfill a future echo of her holding twin girls. She succeeded in bedding Ace, but due to differences between their dimensions, she became pregnant instead of him. Ace departed before she gave birth to their daughters **[M-SMG1.5(c2)]**.

  In another dimension, Ace encountered his evil counterpart, Ace "Blackheart" Rimmer, a bionic madman who terrorized the galaxy. While battling his doppelgänger, Ace learned that the point of their divergence centered around a training mission involving a young pilot named Hooper. In Blackheart's universe, Hooper had survived a narrow miss with a meteor formation, while Blackheart had crashed and sustained crippling, career-ending injuries—whereas in his own universe, Ace had survived the incident unscathed, with Hooper becoming injured. This, in turn, led Ace to dedicate his time to helping Hooper recover, by developing new bionic technology for him **[M-SMG1.14(c5)]**.

  In the course of his travels, Ace visited the universe known as Alternative 6829/B, in which he helped failed footballer Ray Rimmer restore his game **[M-SMG1.8(c4)]**; Alternative 2X13/L, in which Earth was run by superheroes called the Liberty League **[M-SMG2.1(c3)]**; and a reality in which Rimmer was the prime minister of the United Republic of Lesser Britain **[M-SMG2.8(c6)]**. Ace was eventually killed by a neutron tank in Dimension 165, but not before passing the torch to another Arnold Rimmer to carry on his legacy **[T-SER7.2]**.

  ***NOTE:*** *Ace Rimmer's daughters were presumably Jan*

**PREFIX**
**RL:** Real life

**T-: Television Episodes**
**SER:** Television series
**IDW:** "Identity Within"
**USA1:** Unaired U.S. pilot
**USA2:** Unaired U.S. demo

**R-: *The Bodysnatcher Collection***
**SER:** Remastered episodes
**BOD:** "Bodysnatcher"
**DAD:** "Dad"
**FTH:** "Lister's Father"
**INF:** "Infinity Patrol"
**END:** "The End" (original assembly)

**N-: Novels**
**INF:** *Infinity Welcomes Careful Drivers*
**BTL:** *Better Than Life*
**LST:** *Last Human*
**BCK:** *Backwards*
**OMN:** *Red Dwarf Omnibus*

**M-: Magazines**
**SMG:** *Smegazine*

**W-: Websites**
**OFF:** Official website
**NAN:** *Prelude to Nanarchy*
**AND:** *Androids*
**DIV:** Diva-Droid
**DIB:** Duane Dibbley
**CRP:** Crapola
**GEN:** Geneticon
**LSR:** Leisure World Intl.
**JMC:** Jupiter Mining Corporation
**AIT:** *A.I. Today*
**HOL:** HoloPoint

**G-: Roleplaying Game**
**RPG:** *Core Rulebook*
**BIT:** *A.I. Screen Extra Bits* booklet
**SOR:** *Series Sourcebook*
**OTH:** Other RPG material

*and Becky Lister, though this was not explicitly stated. Moreover, the Ace featured in the* Smegazines *was not specifically said to be the same Ace seen on the TV series, but for the sake of simplicity, those adventures are included in this entry.*

- **Rimmer, Arnold Judas ("Ace"), Commander:** A version of Rimmer stationed at the Space Corps Research and Design facility on Europa, in what would become known as the Alpha universe. He was assigned to Project *Wildfire*, headed by Admiral Tranter. Prior to *Wildfire*'s launch, Ace was involved in a barroom brawl that he arranged in order to give his opponent, Billy-Joe Epstein, the confidence needed to pass his flight test. During the fight, he received a black eye and lost a St. Christopher medal—which later ended up saving his life.

  When another *Wildfire One* arrived three days before his own launch, Ace deduced that since the charred pilot possessed his medal but no black eye, the ship could not have originated from the future, but rather from another dimension, which his team dubbed the Beta universe. Adjustments were thus made to his vessel, and he set off into another universe, where he encountered the *Red Dwarf* crew, stranded aboard *Starbug* by agonoids. Ace tried to repair the shuttle's damage, but was slain by an agonoid named Pizzak'Rapp **[N-BCK]**.

- **Rimmer, Arnold Judas ("Ace"), Commander:** A version of Ace Rimmer from what would become known as the Beta universe. He materialized in the Alpha universe three days prior to the Alpha Ace's launch. During the transition into that reality, the Beta Ace was scorched and killed by super-friction created by his having jumped to a reality too close to his own **[N-BCK]**.

- **Rimmer, Frank:** A half-brother of Arnold Rimmer **[T-SER10.6]** and the brother of John and Howard Rimmer **[T-SER3.3]**. Their father, not wanting the boys to fall under the Space Corps' minimum-regulation height (as he had), purchased a traction machine to stretch them out. As a result, Frank stood six feet five inches tall by the time he was eleven years old **[T-SER2.2]**.

  Like his brothers, Frank boarded at Io House **[W-OFF]**. He, John and Howard all had Encyclo implant chips installed in their long-term memory at age eighteen **[N-LST]**.

  The three brothers tormented Arnold throughout their youth **[T-SER3.3]**. During a home movie made during their scouting days, the trio tied Arnold down, smeared jam on his face and poured ants on him **[T-SER3.3]**. In addition, Frank and Howard hung Arnold upside down from a tree to make him into a swing **[T-SER4.5]**.

  Frank was married on Earth **[T-SER3.5]** to a woman named Janine **[N-BTL]**. During a photo shoot, Lister (using a timeslide) materialized in front of the wedding party, blocking the shot. When Lister didn't respond to Frank's request that he move, the groom punched Dave in the stomach repeatedly **[T-SER3.5]**. While trapped in an addictive version of *Better Than Life*, Arnold's subconscious mind created a scenario in which Frank was engaged to his ex-wife, Juanita Chicata **[N-BTL]**.

  Frank served as a first officer in the Space Corps **[N-INF]** and eventually became a commander. For reasons unknown, he went insane and destroyed his own vessel, killing everyone aboard **[T-SER6.4(d)]**.

  ***NOTE:*** *Frank Rimmer may have been the product of his mother's affair with her husband's brother, also named Frank. As such, he would have been the other boys' half-brother.*

- **Rimmer, Frank:** The paternal uncle of Arnold Rimmer. He had two daughters, Sarah and Alice. At age fourteen, Arnold went on vacation with his family, including his uncle and cousins. During the trip, he awoke in the middle of the night to find his uncle French-kissing him, as Frank had mixed up the bedrooms and thought his was snogging Arnold's mother, with whom he was having an affair **[T-SER3.6]**.

  Frank once gave Arnold an Admiral Nelson telescope. Arnold later sold it aboard *Red Dwarf*, in order to pay Lister for a Jammie Dodger **[T-SER9.2(d)]**.

  ***NOTE:*** *The series heavily implied, due to Frank's affair with Arnold's mother and their matching names, that he was the actual father of Arnold's half-brother, Frank.*

- **Rimmer, Helen:** A woman whom Arnold Rimmer, trapped in an addictive version of *Better Than Life,* imagined marrying following his divorce from Juanita Chicata. Hefty and of Bostonian stock, she represented a sensible, normal lifestyle. He later realized his subconscious mind had modeled her after a younger version of his own mother **[N-BTL]**.

# ROGUE DROID

**PREFIX**
**RL:** Real life

**T-: Television Episodes**
**SER:** Television series
**IDW:** "Identity Within"
**USA1:** Unaired U.S. pilot
**USA2:** Unaired U.S. demo

**R-: *The Bodysnatcher Collection***
**SER:** Remastered episodes
**BOD:** "Bodysnatcher"
**DAD:** "Dad"
**FTH:** "Lister's Father"
**INF:** "Infinity Patrol"
**END:** "The End" (original assembly)

**N-: Novels**
**INF:** *Infinity Welcomes Careful Drivers*
**BTL:** *Better Than Life*
**LST:** *Last Human*
**BCK:** *Backwards*
**OMN:** *Red Dwarf Omnibus*

**M-: Magazines**
**SMG:** *Smegazine*

**W-: Websites**
**OFF:** Official website
**NAN:** *Prelude to Nanarchy*
**AND:** *Androids*
**DIV:** Diva-Droid
**DIB:** Duane Dibbley
**CRP:** Crapola
**GEN:** Geneticon
**LSR:** Leisure World Intl.
**JMC:** Jupiter Mining Corporation
**AIT:** *A.I. Today*
**HOL:** HoloPoint

**G-: Roleplaying Game**
**RPG:** *Core Rulebook*
**BIT:** *A.I. Screen Extra Bits* booklet
**SOR:** *Series Sourcebook*
**OTH:** Other RPG material

- **Rimmer, Howard, Second Technician:** A half-brother of Arnold Rimmer **[T-SER10.6]** and the brother of John and Frank Rimmer **[T-SER3.3]**. Their father, not wanting the boys to fall under the Space Corps' minimum-regulation height (as he had), purchased a traction machine to stretch them out, making Howard very tall **[T-SER2.2]**.

  Like his brothers, Howard boarded at Io House **[W-OFF]**. He, John and Frank all had Encyclo implant chips installed in their long-term memory at age eighteen **[N-LST]**.

  The three brothers tormented Arnold throughout their youth **[T-SER3.3]**. During a home movie made during their scouting days, the trio tied Arnold down, smeared jam on his face and poured ants on him **[T-SER3.3]**. In addition, Howard and Frank hung Arnold upside down from a tree to make him into a swing **[T-SER4.5]**. Howard also painted Arnold's penis with orange glow paint **[T-SER10.1]**.

  Howard told his family that he was a test pilot in the Space Corps, flying the latest demi-light speed zippers **[N-INF]**. As far as Arnold knew, Howard attained the rank of commander but went insane and destroyed his own vessel, killing everyone aboard—just as both Frank and John had done **[T-SER6.4(d)]**. But in actuality, Howard—a mere chicken soup machine repairman aboard *Columbus 3*—had died during a freak chicken soup nozzle accident, and was then revived as a hard-light hologram **[W-OFF]**.

  Sometime after the accident, a Space Corps simulant in the crew called Sim Crawford mutinied and killed *Columbus 3*'s entire complement except for Howard, who was cowering under a table. Unaware of her involvement in the attack, Howard issued a distress call, hoping he and Crawford would be rescued before *Columbus 3* was destroyed by a meteor storm.

  Three million years later, the *Red Dwarf* crew discovered a Space Corps derelict named *Trojan*. Arnold accidentally activated the ship's quantum rod, which connected distant objects through space-time. This allowed *Red Dwarf* to receive *Columbus 3*'s transmission, and the two survivors to transport to the *Trojan*.

  Embarrassed at never having become an officer, Arnold sought his crewmates' aid in impressing Howard by posing as the *Trojan*'s crew, with Rimmer as their captain. Touring the ship, Howard suffered a resentment breakdown, causing his light bee's hard drive to crash. Once recovered, he admitted he was not really *Columbus 3*'s captain.

  Crawford then revealed her true nature, holding the group captive and demanding information about the quantum rod. Howard dove in front of Arnold as she opened fire, protecting him from a laser blast that destroyed his own light bee in the process. *Red Dwarf*'s JMC computer, acting on behalf of the Space Corps, thus awarded Howard the Platinum Star of Fortitude post-mortem, and suggested that *Red Dwarf* be renamed the SS *Howard Rimmer* in his honor **[T-SER10.1]**.

- **Rimmer, Janine:** Arnold Rimmer's French sister-in-law, and the wife of his brother Frank **[N-BTL]**. After rescuing Camille—a Pleasure GELF with the ability to change her appearance to fit an individual's desires—Arnold mentioned to Kryten that she bore an uncanny resemblance to Janine, who was a model. This confused Kryten, who saw Camille as a 4000 Series mechanoid **[T-SER4.1]**.

  While trapped in an addictive version of *Better Than Life*, Rimmer imagined that he had returned to Earth and become famously wealthy, marrying Brazilian bombshell Juanita Chicata. Years later, he realized his psyche had based Juanita on Janine, due to his attraction to her and his jealousy of Frank **[N-BTL]**.

  > ***NOTE:*** *The* Red Dwarf Programme Guide *spelled her name as "Jannine." It is unclear why the* Better Than Life *character was Brazilian instead of French.*

- **Rimmer, John:** A half-brother of Arnold Rimmer **[T-SER10.6]** and the brother of Frank and Howard Rimmer **[T-SER3.3]**. Their father, not wanting the boys to fall under the Space Corps' minimum-regulation height (as he had), purchased a traction machine to stretch them out **[T-SER2.2]**.

  Like his brothers, John boarded at Io House **[W-OFF]**. He, Frank and Howard all had Encyclo implant chips installed in their long-term memory at age eighteen **[N-LST]**.

  The three brothers tormented Arnold throughout their youth **[T-SER3.3]**. During a home movie made during their scouting days, the trio tied Arnold down, smeared jam on his face and poured ants on him **[T-SER3.3]**.

  Arnold was particularly resentful of John. At age seventeen, he brought home a girl he was dating to meet his family, only to find her making out with John in the greenhouse **[N-BTL]**. What's more, when John became a test pilot in the Space Corps, Arnold's parents pressured him to follow in his brother's footsteps **[T-SER4.5]**.

John became the youngest captain in Space Corps history, in fact **[N-INF]**, but went insane for reasons unknown and destroyed his vessel, killing everyone aboard **[T-SER6.4(d)]**.

- **Rimmer, Julius:** One of seven children whom Arnold Rimmer imagined raising with Yvonne McGruder while playing the total-immersion video game *Better Than Life*. Although the game was designed to detect a player's desires, Rimmer's subconscious mind could not accept his good fortune, and instead created a scenario in which McGruder became pregnant, forced Rimmer to marry her, and gave birth to numerous kids—all within a single day **[T-SER2.2(o)]**.

  ***NOTE:*** *Given Rimmer's fascination with Julius Caesar, he presumably named the child in the Roman emperor's honor.*

- **Rimmer, Lecturer:** The father of Frank, John and Howard Rimmer, and the stepfather of Arnold Rimmer. Arnold grew up believing they were blood-related, but the youth was actually the product of an illicit affair between his mother and the family gardener, Dennis ("Dungo") **[T-SER10.6]**. Mr. Rimmer's wife had also cheated on him with his brother, Frank, who may have been young Frank's biological father **[T-SER3.6]**.

  Descended from Austrian princes and French royalty, Mr. Rimmer worked at Io Polytechnic as a lecturer. He once had Arnold in his class, and pointedly made a fool of his stepson in front of the other students **[T-SER10.6]**. He was a Seventh-Day Advent Hoppist **[T-SER3.6]**.

  Arnold once accidentally shot his stepfather through the shoulder with his own service revolver, which ranked fifth on Arnold's Horror Chart (a list of asinine accidents that haunted him throughout his life) **[N-BTL]**. Prone to depression, the man unsuccessfully attempted suicide, just after proclaiming that "with shiny shoes and a short haircut, you can cope with anything" **[T-SER1.2]**.

  An inch below regulation height for the Space Corps, Mr. Rimmer vowed to ensure his sons all enlisted, by stretching them on a traction machine. He also grilled them with questions during dinner, providing food only if they answered correctly. Disgusted by such treatment, Arnold divorced his parents at age fourteen **[T-SER2.2]**. Despite this, Arnold's prized possession was a Javanese camphor-wood chest, as it was the only thing his stepfather had ever given him besides disappointment **[T-SER3.2]**. Unbeknownst to him, the chest was actually meant for Howard, but the elderly Rimmer's dementia had caused him to address the package to the wrong son **[W-OFF]**.

  Mr. Rimmer suffered at least four strokes **[T-SER5.1]**. After he died, his wife sent a letter to Arnold, who was stationed aboard *Red Dwarf*, that took millions of years to arrive via postal pod. The news of his dad's passing depressed Arnold, who regretted that he never received the man's approval. His stepfather later appeared to him in the total-immersion video game *Better Than Life*, but as he was about to commend his son, Cat's mind took control of the fantasy, causing him to call Arnold a smeghead **[T-SER2.2]**. While trapped in an addictive version of *Better Than Life*, Arnold imagined that he went back in time to hire Mr. Rimmer as a personal chauffeur, after returning to Earth and becoming immensely wealthy **[N-INF]**.

  Sometime prior to *Red Dwarf*'s cadmium II explosion, Mr. Rimmer gave Arnold a holo-lamp containing an important message, to be viewed only after he became an officer. Faced with unbeatable odds, Arnold played the holo-message (despite failing to attain such a rank), which revealed the truth about his parentage. Though initially distraught, Arnold was relieved to be free of the man's disapproval at last **[T-SER10.6]**.

  ***NOTE:*** *Mr. Rimmer's first name is unknown.*

- **Rimmer, Mrs.:** Arnold Rimmer's mother. She was married to a university lecturer and had three other sons, named Frank, John and Howard, whom she openly favored **[T-SER3.3]**. Arnold despised how she treated him, and divorced his parents at age fourteen **[T-SER2.2]**.

  Mrs. Rimmer was arrested on nineteen occasions for public indecency **[W-OFF]**, and was often unfaithful to her husband. Arnold was fathered by the family's gardener, Dennis ("Dungo") **[T-SER10.6]**, while Frank may have been the son of her husband's brother, Frank Rimmer **[T-SER3.6]**. She also had an affair with Porky Roebuck's dad **[T-SER2.5]**.

  A prim and proper woman despite her marital infidelities, Mrs. Rimmer despised idiots—which was unfortunate for Arnold **[T-SER3.3]**. She was a member of the Church of Judas at the time of Arnold's birth, and thus gave him the middle name Judas **[T-SER10.3]**, though at some point, she became a Seventh-Day Advent Hoppist **[T-SER3.6]**.

  When Rimmer was stranded on a psi-moon, the forces of his

corporeal negative traits created an enormous reproduction of Mrs. Rimmer to battle his positive aspects **[M-SMG2.7(c2)]**. A polymorph aboard *Red Dwarf* also took her form, to elicit Arnold's anger—by implying she had slept with Lister—to feed upon **[T-SER3.3]**.

While trapped in an addictive version of *Better Than Life*, Arnold conjured up a wife named Helen, a hefty woman of Bostonian stock who represented a more sensible lifestyle than his previous bride, model Juanita Chicata. To his horror, he realized his subconscious mind had modeled Helen after a younger version of his mother **[N-BTL]**.

> ***NOTE:*** *Mrs. Rimmer's first name is unknown. In the remastered version of episode 3.3 ("Polymorph"), Mrs. Rimmer's voice was dubbed over to more closely fit her prim and proper stature established in the episode.*

- **Rimmer, Ray:** An Arnold Rimmer from the universe known as Alternative 6829/B. In that reality, zero-gee football never became popular, with association football remaining a dominant sport. At age fourteen, Ray acquired football boots belonging to legendary "Dead Shot" Dave Hunt. Believing the shoes to be magical, Ray went on to play as number nine for the Smegchester Rovers, but when the footwear wore out and lost its mystical properties, his game suffered.

  Feeling washed-up, Ray attempted to jump off the Stamford Bridge, but Ace Rimmer arrived from another dimension and saved him. After hearing his story, Ace filled in during the following day's Cup Final, scoring eighteen goals and winning the game. Ecstatic, Ray asked him to fill in for good, but Ace declined. Before leaving, he repaired the boots, enabling Ray to continue his winning streak **[M-SMG1.8(c4)]**.

- **Rimmer, Sarah:** A cousin of Arnold Rimmer, and the daughter of Rimmer's uncle Frank. Sarah was blonde and two years older than Arnold, and had a twin sister named Alice. Arnold suspected that Sarah may have fancied him. When Arnold was a youth, the Rimmer family went on vacation, during which he was awoken during the night by a French kiss (Arnold's first such experience). Believing his visitor to be either Sarah or Alice, he was horrified to discover it was his uncle, who had mistaken Arnold's room for his mother's **[T-SER3.6]**.

- **Rimmer Building (London):** A 140-floor glass and steel structure that Rimmer imagined commissioning while trapped in an addictive version of *Better Than Life.* Rimmer thought he had returned to Earth, earned millions from endorsements and built several identical buildings around the world. The edifice contained a massive white marble statue of Arnold performing a "Full-Rimmer" salute in its lobby. He lived in the Penthouse Suite on the top floor **[N-INF]**.

- **Rimmer Building (New York):** A 140-floor structure that Rimmer imagined commissioning while trapped in an addictive version of *Better Than Life.* This building was identical to others located in London and Paris **[N-INF]**.

- **Rimmer Building (Paris):** A 140-floor structure that Rimmer imagined commissioning while trapped in an addictive version of *Better Than Life.* This building was identical to others located in London and New York **[N-INF]**.

- **Rimmer Corporation Worldwide plc:** A company that Rimmer imagined founding while trapped in an addictive version of *Better Than Life*, using wealth he thought he'd obtained from endorsements upon returning to Earth. Rimmer Corp. developed a time machine, allowing him to invite persons from different eras to join him at his dinner parties for a game of *Risk.* At one such affair, Rimmer arranged a fireworks display that started as portraits of him and his wife, Juanita Chicata, and then transformed into the company's logo **[N-INF]**.

- **RimmerCorps:** A company in an alternate dimension created and run by Ace "Blackheart" Rimmer, an evil tyrant bent on destroying the galaxy. After a training mission left this version of Ace embittered with crippling, career-ending injuries, he used his knowledge of Space Corps technology to build a competing business. RimmerCorps became so successful that it bought out the Space Corps. Using the increased funds, Blackheart developed bionic technology, which he then used to repair and improve his body **[M-SMG1.14(c5)]**.

- **Rimmer Directive, The:** A dictate by which Rimmer lived, which stated, "Never tangle with anything that's got more teeth than the entire Osmond family." He quoted this rule upon encountering a polymorph in the shape of an eight-foot-tall,

armor-plated alien, after Kryten suggested trying to establish a dialog per Space Corps directives **[T-SER3.3]**.

*NOTE: The DVD captions read "Never tackle anything that's got more teeth than the entire Osmond family."*

- **Rimmer Directive 271:** A personal edict of Arnold Rimmer, stating, "No chance, you metal bastard." Rimmer quoted this rule in response to Kryten's insistence that the hologram be deactivated while *Red Dwarf* was on emergency battery power, according to Space Corps Directive 195 **[T-SER4.4]**.

- **Rimmer Directive 483:** Another of Rimmer's decrees, which stated, "It is the specific right of the highest-ranking officer—in most cases, Second Technician Arnold J. Rimmer—to issue the command 'launch scouter'" **[W-OFF]**.

- **"Rimmer Does It Again":** A print headline that Rimmer cut out and adhered to his *Red Dwarf* locker door **[T-SER1.3]**. While sharing quarters with his duplicate hologram, Arnold had the headlines relocated to his new abode. Lister was amused, as the slogans were about other people named "Arnold" or "Rimmer" **[T-SER1.6]**.

- ***Rimmer Experience, The*:** A virtual-reality amusement-park ride that Kryten designed in *Starbug 1*'s AR Suite to remind his crewmates of Rimmer's shortcomings whenever they missed him. Upon entering through giant doors in a rail cart, the crew witnessed several exaggerated scenes depicted in Rimmer's diary, played out by animatronic versions of them, including Arnold saving *Starbug* and giving Cat fashion tips. They were then subjected to a tribute song performed by Rimmer and dozens of small, puppet-like versions of him. The ride ended as the rail cart passed through giant doors marked "Toodle Pipski." This experience reminded Lister of his disdain for his departed comrade **[T-SER7.5]**.

- **Rimmer International Airport (AJR):** An airport in France that Rimmer imagined being named after him while trapped in an addictive version of *Better Than Life*. In the illusion, Rimmer believed he had returned to Earth and become famously wealthy, with several companies, buildings and airports bearing his name. When Lister informed Rimmer that they were still in the game, the two drove his limousine to AJR, where his Learjet, *Rimmer One*, awaited to take them to Denmark to find Cat **[N-INF]**.

  *NOTE: The airport's acronym, AJR, may indicate that its full name was Arnold J. Rimmer International Airport, just as John F. Kennedy International Airport is commonly abbreviated as JFK.*

- **Rimmermania:** A sensation that Rimmer imagined sweeping Earth while trapped in an addictive version of *Better Than Life*. In the illusion, Arnold believed he had gained fame and fortune upon returning to Earth, and had become an object of desire for millions of teenage girls—known as Rimmettes—who followed him around, screaming and holding up signs that read "Arnie is Brave" and "Arnie is FAB," while throwing their intimate garments at him **[N-INF]**.

  *NOTE: This spoofed the 1960s phenomenon dubbed Beatlemania.*

- **Rimmer munchkin:** A type of puppet-like effigy of Rimmer that Kryten created for a virtual-reality ride called *The Rimmer Experience*. Inside the ride, the *Starbug 1* crew were treated to "The Munchkin Song," a tribute to Rimmer performed by several singing and dancing puppets **[T-SER7.5]**.

  The name also referred to two munchkin robots belonging to the Creator, whom the *Red Dwarf* crew imagined visiting while trapped in an elation squid hallucination. These munchkins wore identical hologrammic uniforms and had oversized heads in Rimmer's likeness **[T-SER9.3]**.

  In an alternate universe, several Rimmer munchkin robots boarded *Starbug 1* and rummaged through its supply decks, seeking items to loot **[G-SOR]**.

- ***Rimmer One*:** A black Learjet that Rimmer imagined purchasing upon returning to Earth, while trapped in an addictive version of *Better Than Life*. When Lister informed Arnold that they were still in the game, the two drove to Rimmer International Airport so they could fly *Rimmer One* to Denmark and find Cat **[N-INF]**.

- **Rimmer Research Centres:** A group of scientific research facilities that Rimmer imagined commissioning while trapped in an addictive version of *Better Than Life*. The crew imagined that they returned to Earth using *Nova 5*'s Duality Jump, where

**PREFIX**
**RL:** Real life

**T-: Television Episodes**
**SER:** Television series
**IDW:** "Identity Within"
**USA1:** Unaired U.S. pilot
**USA2:** Unaired U.S. demo

**R-: *The Bodysnatcher Collection***
**SER:** Remastered episodes
**BOD:** "Bodysnatcher"
**DAD:** "Dad"
**FTH:** "Lister's Father"
**INF:** "Infinity Patrol"
**END:** "The End" (original assembly)

**N-: Novels**
**INF:** *Infinity Welcomes Careful Drivers*
**BTL:** *Better Than Life*
**LST:** *Last Human*
**BCK:** *Backwards*
**OMN:** *Red Dwarf Omnibus*

**M-: Magazines**
**SMG:** *Smegazine*

**W-: Websites**
**OFF:** Official website
**NAN:** *Prelude to Nanarchy*
**AND:** *Androids*
**DIV:** Diva-Droid
**DIB:** Duane Dibbley
**CRP:** Crapola
**GEN:** Geneticon
**LSR:** Leisure World Intl.
**JMC:** Jupiter Mining Corporation
**AIT:** *A.I. Today*
**HOL:** HoloPoint

**G-: Roleplaying Game**
**RPG:** *Core Rulebook*
**BIT:** *A.I. Screen Extra Bits* booklet
**SOR:** *Series Sourcebook*
**OTH:** Other RPG material

they were showered with fame, fortune and endorsement deals. Rimmer used the money to build the Research Centres in order to develop the Solidgram—a solid hologram—to restore his physical presence **[N-INF]**.

- **Rimmer's lust monster:** A hypothetical creature that Kryten cited as the type of monstrosity the *Red Dwarf* crew might encounter while on a psi-moon configured after Rimmer's mind **[T-SER5.3]**.

- **Rimmerworld:** A planet inhabited by clones of Arnold Rimmer, created after the hologram landed on the barren world in a colonization seeding ship pod. Using supplies from the pod, Rimmer terraformed the planet, then attempted to build himself a female counterpart—but failed, instead spawning several exact duplicates of himself who took over the planet and created a society of snide, back-stabbing narcissists.

  On this so-called Rimmerworld, anyone who deviated from the established norm (that is, looking different than Rimmer, or exhibiting behavior deemed un-Rimmerlike, such as honor or courage) was banished from society—or, in extreme cases, executed. Unable to damage his hard-light body, they imprisoned him for 557 years, with each new ruler, carrying the title "the Great One," taking the letter "H" as a symbol of power.

  When the *Starbug 1* crew arrived to rescue Rimmer, centurions ambushed them and brought them before the Great One, who sentenced them to death and threw them into Rimmer's cell. Using Kryten's teleporter, however, they promptly returned to their shuttle **[T-SER6.5]**.

- **Rimmettes:** A nickname for the throngs of teenage girls whom Rimmer imagined being infatuated with him while trapped in an addictive version of *Better Than Life*. In the illusion, Rimmer believed he had returned to Earth and become famously wealthy and popular, spurring a phenomenon known as Rimmermania, which included the Rimmettes following him wherever he went, screaming and throwing their undergarments at him. Once free of the hallucination, Arnold realized his subconscious mind had based the Rimmettes on every woman who had ever rejected him **[N-BTL]**.

- **Rimmsie:** A nickname that Rimmer called himself when trying to convince Lister that they were best friends, in an effort to dissuade Dave from taking the Chef's Exam and being promoted over him **[T-SER1.3]**. Rimmer also called his duplicate hologram by this name **[T-SER1.5]**.

  ***NOTE:*** *The DVD captions sometimes spelled this name as "Rimsy."*

- **Ring Around the Impact Crater:** A game developed by Colonel Mike O'Hagan, aimed at keeping crash survivors occupied and in good spirits. He suggested this game in his *Space Corps Survival Manual* **[B-SUR]**.

- **Ringo:** *See* Starr, Ringo

- ***Ripley's Believe It Or Not*:** A syndicated newspaper panel, book series, television show and museum chain focused on weird or unusual events and items **[RL]**. After finding an escape pod from a prison ship supposedly containing a cryogenically frozen woman, Cat assumed that she, once released, would instantly fall for him. When Lister noted that he might not be her type, Cat dismissed the idea, saying he'd have heard of her in *Ripley's Believe It Or Not* **[T-SER4.3]**.

- ***Risk*:** A turn-based strategic board game created by Parker Brothers, the goal of which was to eliminate other players by occupying every territory on the map, thereby attaining world domination **[RL]**.

  At age seventeen, Rimmer often played *Risk* with students and faculty members at the cadet training school he attended, jotting down his games in a campaign book so he could relive his victories **[T-SER4.6]**. After becoming a hologram, he played a hologrammic version of the game called *Holo-Risk* **[M-SMG1.13(c2)]**.

  While trapped in an addictive version of *Better Than Life*, Rimmer imagined that he had returned to Earth and become incredibly wealthy. In the illusion, he hosted lavish parties and played *Risk* with the likes of Napoleon Bonaparte, Julius Caesar and George S. Patton **[N-INF]**.

  **NOTE:** *The* Risk *reference was changed to merely "dice" in the DVD captions for the Czech Republic version of the series.*

- **Riverboat, Brett:** A playable character in *Streets of Laredo*, a Western-themed virtual-reality game created by Interstella

**B-: Books**
**PRG:** *Red Dwarf Programme Guide*
**SUR:** *Red Dwarf Space Corps Survival Manual*
**PRM:** *Primordial Soup*
**SOS:** *Son of Soup*
**SCE:** *Scenes from the Dwarf*
**LOG:** *Red Dwarf Log No. 1996*
**RD8:** *Red Dwarf VIII*
**EVR:** *The Log: A Dwarfer's Guide to Everything*

**X-: Misc.**
**PRO:** Promotional materials, videos, etc.
**PST:** Posters at DJ XVII (2013)
**CAL:** 2008 calendar
**RNG:** Cell phone ringtones
**MOB:** Mobisode ("Red Christmas")
**CIN:** *Children in Need* sketch
**GEK:** *Geek Week* intros by Kryten
**TNG:** "Tongue-Tied" video

**XMS:** Bill Pearson's Christmas special pitch script
**XVD:** Bill Pearson's Christmas special pitch video
**OTH:** Other *Red Dwarf* appearances

**SUFFIX**
**DVD:**
**(d)** – Deleted scene
**(o)** – Outtake
**(b)** – Bonus DVD material (other)
**(e)** – Extended version

**SMEGAZINES:**
**(c)** – Comic
**(a)** – Article

**OTHER:**
**(s)** – Early/unused script draft
**(s1)** – Alternate version of script

Games. Riverboat was a master blade thrower whose preferred weapon was a knife. His in-game profile listed his stamina at one hundred, his charm at one hundred and his intelligence at one hundred, for a total of three hundred points. Lister chose Brett's persona upon entering Kryten's subconscious mind to combat the Armageddon virus **[T-SER6.3]**.

- **River Mersey:** A river in Northwest England **[RL]**. Jesus of Caesarea once walked across a bridge spanning the River Mersey. When he related this incident to the *Red Dwarf* crew—who had been accidentally transported to 23 A.D.—Lister, believing him to be Jesus Christ, assumed he meant that he had walked across the water **[T-SER10.3]**.

- **River Styx:** *See* Styx

- **Riviera Kid, The:** A playable character in *Streets of Laredo*, a Western-themed virtual-reality game created by Interstella Games. The Riviera Kid was an ace gunslinger whose preferred weapon was a Colt .45. His in-game profile listed his stamina at forty, his charm at two hundred fifty and his intelligence at ten, for a total of three hundred points. Cat chose the Kid's persona upon entering Kryten's subconscious mind to combat the Armageddon virus **[T-SER6.3]**.

- **roast suckling elephant:** A delicacy enjoyed by a future version of the *Red Dwarf* crew, who used a time drive coupled with a faster-than-light drive to journey throughout space-time, becoming epicures who sampled the best the universe had to offer **[T-SER6.6]**.

- **roast suckling pig stuffed with chestnuts and truffles:** A course that Kryten prepared for Rimmer after the latter swapped minds with Lister and over-indulged his body **[T-SER3.4]**.

- **Robbie:** A genetically engineered superhero in the universe known as Alternative 2X13/L. Robbie—a version of Kryten—was the sidekick of Catman (Cat) and a member of the Liberty League, tasked with protecting the city of Smegopolis. His super-power was the ability to stretch his body.

  In 2315, Catman and Robbie attempted to thwart a robbery at the First National Bank, perpetrated by their nemeses, the Conspirator and the Penguin. During the battle, Robbie was felled by a blast of the Penguin's hex vision **[M-SMG2.1(c3)]**.

  ***NOTE:** Robbie was based loosely on the DC Comics superhero Robin (Dick Grayson), combined with elements of Marvel's Mister Fantastic (Reed Richards).*

- ***Robbie Rocket Pants*:** A comic book, radio and television serial featuring Commander Robert Dimsdale ("Robbie Rocket Pants"), whose jet-powered trousers enabled him to fly. When Cat suggested donning such pants to escape a psi-moon configured according to Rimmer's psyche, Kryten noted that they did not possess such apparel—primarily because it did not exist, except in the fictional world of *Robbie Rocket Pants* **[T-SER5.3]**. Issue sixteen of the comic was titled "Pants Down Over Poland!" **[G-BIT]**.

- **Robbie Rocket Pants:** *See* Dimsdale, Robert, Commander ("Robbie Rocket Pants")

- **Robbie Rocketpants:** A self-proclaimed "Bastion of Justice" who sported rocket-propelled trousers. His alter ego was a scrawny Junior Birdman. On a psi-moon corrupted by the mind of Mr. Flibble, the Junior Birdman offered to help local villagers who hoped to defeat the deplorable penguin. After finding Flibble's lair, the hero used his magic woggle to transform into Robbie Rocketpants, and attempted to subdue the villain. He failed, however, and Flibble force-fed him baked beans, then ignited his flatulence, launching Robbie into the air **[M-SMG2.9(c10)]**.

- ***Robert Hardy Reads Tess of the d'Urbervilles*:** A recording of Thomas Hardy's classic novel *Tess of the d'Urbervilles: A Pure Woman Faithfully Presented*, read by actor Robert Hardy. When Cat found a copy aboard *Red Dwarf*, he found it enjoyable, as did Lister—due to its having been warped and twisted, distorting the sound beyond recognition **[T-SER2.5]**.

- **Robeson, Paul:** An American bass singer and recording artist popular in the mid-twentieth century, known for his deep voice and well-spoken manner **[RL]**. While experiencing the effects of time dilation, Rimmer described Kryten as sounding like Paul Robeson on dope, since the mechanoid was moving much slower than Rimmer **[T-SER4.4]**.

- **Robin:** A hologrammic pastry chef possibly from an alternate universe. She traveled with a chainsmoking human named Eric, a humanoid female rabbit and a waxdroid of Errol Flynn **[G-RPG]**.

- ***Robinson Crusoe*:** A novel by Daniel Defoe, published in 1719, written in the form of a fictional autobiography of a man marooned for years on a tropical island **[RL]**. When Kryten discovered this and other books under Lister's bunk while cleaning, Lister claimed he was going through an educational phase, which he'd soon get over **[T-SER7.6(d)]**.

- **RoboGaz:** The alter ego of Gary, a character on the television soap opera *Androids*. After his business rival Jaysee tried to kill him, Gary built himself a body out of spare medical parts from St. Android Hospital, calling himself RoboGaz. He then drove his new car, the Gaz Mobile, to Jaysee's headquarters, KICASS Tower, to confront him. RoboGaz barely survived the ensuing firefight, only to be shot and killed at point-blank range by Jaysee **[M-SMG2.5(c5)]**.

- **robohobo:** A nickname for homeless androids living on the streets of NYNY in an alternate universe **[M-SMG1.7(a)]**.

- **robotics:** A specialization offered by the JMC Educational Exam Board, included under the company's Mechanical Engineering course. Lister enrolled in the JMC Engineering Program to study robotics in an effort to better himself after a near-death experience with *Red Dwarf*'s replacement computer, Pree **[T-SER10.2(d)]**.

- **robot referee:** A model of android official that officiated at association football games in the universe known as Alternative 6829/B. Robot referees replaced humans by 2180, and were equipped with sensitive audiovisual recording devices to provide playback in the event of a questionable call **[M-SMG1.8(c4)]**.

- **robot theater:** An entertainment medium in which Jordan Kershaw had a background before becoming the head writer of *Androids* **[W-AND]**.

- **Rocket Pants:** *See* Raketenhosen

- **Rocket Pants Men:** *See* Raketenhosen Männer

- **RocketMan:** A brand of missile launcher produced by Bloodlust Arms and distributed via Crapola Inc.'s annual *SCABBY* catalog. It had a range of 10 kilometers (6.2 miles) and included a padded shoulder stock attachment, a NeuroNet head-up display (HUD) sight, one free OGOC missile and a thirty-day free life insurance policy **[G-RPG]**.

- ***Rockin' at the Restaurant—20 Gourmet Greats*:** An album recorded by Reggie Wilson **[M-SMG1.3(a)]**.

- ***Rockin' Up Rachmaninov—120 Golden Greats on the Hammond Organ*:** An album recorded by Reggie Wilson, and one of Rimmer's favorite recordings. It was released by K-Tel Records under catalog number ZXC-3443474 **[M-SMG1.1(a)]**.
  ***NOTE:*** *The album presumably contained covers of the works of Russian composer Sergei Rachmaninoff. In the real world, K-Tel produced no such recording.*

- **Rock Miners, The:** A heavy metal rock band that recorded the poorly received single "White Hole" **[G-RPG]**.

- **"Rock Music":** A slogan on a circular sticker on Lister's guitar **[T-SER6.1]**.

- **"Rock 'N Roll":** A slogan on a neon lamp adorning the cell to which Legion assigned Lister after taking the *Red Dwarf* crew prisoner at his research station **[T-SER6.2]**.

- **Rocky:** A vagrant living on a psi-moon after Mr. Flibble's mind corrupted the moon's landscape **[M-SMG2.9(c9)]**.

- **Rodenbury:** A technical coordinator stationed at the Space Corps R&D facility on Europa in Ace Rimmer's universe. Admiral Tranter chastised Rodenbury for failing to solve the mystery of a second *Wildfire* craft materializing three days prior to its own launch **[N-BCK]**.

- **Roebuck, Porky:** A childhood friend of Rimmer. When the two were twelve years old, Porky threw Arnold's shoes, which had a built-in compass and animal-track soles, into a septic tank. Rimmer was devastated, mostly because he was still wearing them at the time **[T-SER3.2]**.

Rimmer and Roebuck were in the Space Scouts together at age fifteen, and attended a survival trip with several other boys. Informed that they could only eat what they killed, the other scouts decided to eat Rimmer, tying him up to a makeshift rotisserie. Confident that Porky would save him, Arnold narrowly escaped due to the intervention of Space Mistress Yakka-Takka-Tulla. He later learned that his friend had orchestrated the plot and had called dibs on his right buttock **[T-SER2.5]**.

- **Rogerson:** A *Red Dwarf* officer in charge of settling new recruits into their quarters. Rogerson met Lister and Petersen when they first boarded the mining ship **[N-INF]**.

  ***NOTE:*** *Rogerson presumably died during the cadmium II explosion. It is unknown whether the nanobots resurrected him in Series VIII.*

- **rogue asteroid:** An asteroid with a trajectory greatly differing from the normal flow of an asteroid belt **[RL]**. Rogue asteroids posed a particular danger to smaller craft, such as *Starbug* shuttles **[T-SER6.1]**.

- **rogue droid:** A type of simulant, humanoid in appearance, with technological add-ons attached sporadically throughout the body. Hogey the Roguey was a rogue droid. Lister claimed all rogue droids were obsessed with duels across time and space. Despite their loathing for humanity, they maintained a peaceful rivalry with the *Red Dwarf* crew, sometimes competing in ping pong tournaments **[T-SER10.6]**.

  Rogue droids inhabited the GELF territories of an alternate universe, and were sold by the Kinitawowi. These droids could be rendered inert by removing a micro-board from their CPU. The *Starbug* crew purchased a dozen rogue droids in varying conditions from the Kinitawowi in order to break Lister's doppelgänger out of Cyberia **[N-LST]**.

  ***NOTE:*** *It is unclear whether Hogey and other rogue droids were intended to be rogue simulants. His appearance matched those of rogue simulants seen earlier in the series, though he clearly set himself apart from the simulants featured in episode 10.6 ("The Beginning").*

- **rogue simulant:** *See* simulant

- **roll-off deodorant:** A hygiene product sold on Earth during a period in its future when time ran backwards. A newspaper advertisement for the product claimed that it could keep users wet and smelly for up to twenty-four hours **[T-SER3.1]**.

- **Rolls Razors:** A British brand of razor blades sold in the early 1900s **[RL]**. The front page of a *News Chronicle* newspaper aboard *Red Dwarf*, dated May 4, 1939, contained an advertisement for Rolls Razors **[T-SER3.5]**.

- **Rolls-Royce:** A British manufacturer of luxury automobiles **[RL]**. When Lister asked Cat to lend him his body so he could pursue Rimmer—who had hijacked Lister's form and left *Red Dwarf* aboard *Starbug 1*—Cat denied the request, asking if Lister would let a garbage truck driver use his Rolls-Royce **[T-SER3.4]**.

  ***NOTE:*** *In the real world, actor Craig Charles' automobile of choice is the Rolls-Royce.*

- **Rom-Ramsey Street:** A road featured on the soap opera *Androids*, located in the city of Binary Hills **[M-SMG2.7(c6)]**. Kelly and Brook may have lived on this road **[M-SMG1.8(c2)]**.

  ***NOTE:*** *In* Smegazine *issue 2.7, the road's name was spelled Rom-Ramsay Street.*

- **roof attack:** A zero-gee football position played by Jim Bexley Speed of the London Jets **[T-SER1.1]**. Lister played this same position for the Jets while in the total-immersion video game *Better Than Life* **[R-SER2.2(d)]**. The phrase "roof attack" was printed on a poster in his *Red Dwarf* bunk **[T-SER1.1]**, as well as on posters in the ship's disco room **[T-SER1.3]**.

- **roof bay doors:** A large hatch on *Red Dwarf*'s upper section, leading to Cargo Bays J, K and L. Lister once forgot to close the doors after a spacewalk, resulting in the bays being filled with fourteen thousand meteors during a subsequent storm **[T-SER9.1(d)]**.

- **Room 1115:** A room aboard *Red Dwarf*, located near Rimmer's quarters. The occupants of Room 1115 once held a particularly noisy party the night before one of Arnold's Astronavigation

**PREFIX**
**RL:** Real life

**T-: Television Episodes**
**SER:** Television series
**IDW:** "Identity Within"
**USA1:** Unaired U.S. pilot
**USA2:** Unaired U.S. demo

**R-: *The Bodysnatcher Collection***
**SER:** Remastered episodes
**BOD:** "Bodysnatcher"
**DAD:** "Dad"
**FTH:** "Lister's Father"
**INF:** "Infinity Patrol"
**END:** "The End" (original assembly)

**N-: Novels**
**INF:** *Infinity Welcomes Careful Drivers*
**BTL:** *Better Than Life*
**LST:** *Last Human*
**BCK:** *Backwards*
**OMN:** *Red Dwarf Omnibus*

**M-: Magazines**
**SMG:** *Smegazine*

**W-: Websites**
**OFF:** Official website
**NAN:** *Prelude to Nanarchy*
**AND:** *Androids*
**DIV:** Diva-Droid
**DIB:** Duane Dibbley
**CRP:** Crapola
**GEN:** Geneticon
**LSR:** Leisure World Intl.
**JMC:** Jupiter Mining Corporation
**AIT:** *A.I. Today*
**HOL:** HoloPoint

**G-: Roleplaying Game**
**RPG:** *Core Rulebook*
**BIT:** *A.I. Screen Extra Bits* booklet
**SOR:** *Series Sourcebook*
**OTH:** Other RPG material

Exams, causing him stress. Ignoring his complaints, the partygoers instead raised the volume **[N-BTL]**.

- ***Roots of Coincidence, The***: A book written in 1972 by Arthur Koestler, examining the relationship between quantum mechanics and parapsychology, and its effects on probability and coincidence. One version of the book's cover showed a hand holding dominoes below a sky filled with stars **[RL]**.

  Kryten referred to *The Roots of Coincidence* while informing Cat about the possible side effects of tampering with a quantum rod's crystals. Cat, in return, held up the very same book, which he had been using to swat space weevils, proving the rod's power. The crew later found a hardcopy version of the book in a BEGG lair, and used the domino numbers printed on the cover as navigational coordinates to locate the Erroneous Reasoning Research Academy **[T-SER10.4]**.

- **"rotut":** A sound made by the pipes in Kochanski's quarters aboard *Starbug 1*, due to a heating system malfunction. It traditionally came before a "hernunger" sound **[T-SER7.4]**.

- **Routine Maintenance, Cleaning and Sanitation Unit:** A group of technicians aboard *Red Dwarf* who were assigned maintenance and janitorial duties. Z-Shift, which Rimmer managed, was one such unit **[N-INF]**.

- **roverostomy:** A medical procedure to convert a human into a dog, according to an article in a twentieth-century issue of *The National Enquirer*. While researching ways to reduce Lister's sentence in *Red Dwarf*'s brig, Holly came across this article and suggested Dave undergo the operation, noting that since dog years were seven times shorter than human years, he could theoretically reduce his two-year sentence to fourteen weeks **[T-SER8.4]**.

- **Rovers Return Inn, The:** An establishment featured on the British television show *Coronation Street* **[RL]**. While trapped in an elation squid hallucination, the *Red Dwarf* crew—believing themselves to be on an alternate twenty-first-century Earth where they were characters in a British comedy series called *Red Dwarf*—visited the *Coronation Street* set to locate actor Craig Charles. They found him in the Rovers Return Inn, studying his lines for the day's shoot **[T-SER9.2]**.

  One episode of *Coronation Street* involved the inn's hot pot dispenser malfunctioning. This episode aired on Groovy Channel 27 at 7:30 PM on Wednesday, the 27th of Geldof, 2362 **[M-SMG1.7(a)]**.

  ***NOTE:** The Rovers Return Inn, like all businesses appearing in this sequence, was created for the TV show* Coronation Street*, in which Craig Charles starred as of this writing. Owned by Stella Price, the inn—the show's principle setting—was located on Coronation Street, in the fictional town of Weatherfield, England.*

- **Roy:** A coworker of Hayley Summers, Lister's ex-girlfriend. He and Summers worked at the bank where Lister kept his overdraft account during his musician days. Roy constantly used the finger-wetting machine to count money.

  Roy had an affair with Hayley while she was dating Lister. Sometime before she left for a job on Callisto, she became pregnant, but was unsure who the father was. She wrote Dave a letter telling him the situation, then another after a DNA test confirmed Roy as the father. Lister received neither message, however, until three million years later, when a post pod containing the letters caught up with *Red Dwarf* **[T-SER10.5]**.

- **Roy's Rolls:** An establishment featured on the British television show *Coronation Street* **[RL]**. While trapped in an elation squid hallucination, the *Red Dwarf* crew—believing themselves to be on an alternate twenty-first-century Earth where they were characters in a British comedy series called *Red Dwarf*—passed Roy's Rolls while searching for actor Craig Charles on the *Coronation Street* set **[T-SER9.2]**.

  ***NOTE:** Roy's Rolls, like all businesses appearing in this sequence, was created for the television show* Coronation Street*, in which Craig Charles starred as of this writing. Roy's Rolls, owned by Roy and Hayley Cropper, was located at 16 Victoria Street, in the fictional town of Weatherfield, England. The store's name was a pun based on that of car manufacturer Rolls-Royce.*

- **Roze:** A robotic character on the television soap opera *Androids*. An episode in which she left her partner, Benzen, always made Kryten cry **[N-INF]**.

- **RP:** The process of recovering a person from a cryonic life pod. Cat activated the RP on a life pod belonging to prison guard Barbra Bellini, unaware that it actually contained a rogue simulant who had escaped a prison ship **[T-SER4.3]**.

  ***NOTE:*** *This acronym presumably stood for "resuscitation process," or something to that effect.*

- **RTS 6:** A string of characters stenciled above a doorway inside a derelict ship that the *Red Dwarf* crew found on an asteroid within Psiren territory **[T-SER6.1]**.

- **rubber nuclear weapon:** A non-lethal weapon primarily used for riot control. When a store in New Tokyo ran out of copies of the total-immersion video game *Better Than Life*, the police deployed rubber nuclear weapons to disperse the crowd **[T-SER2.2]**.

- **Rubble, Betty:** *See Flintstones, The*

- **rude alert:** An alert message that Holly issued after an electrical fire damaged her voice-recognition unit, garbling her vocabulary. She intended to announce a red alert **[T-SER5.5]**.

- **Rudies:** An establishment in NYNY, a city in an alternate dimension in which Jake Bullet worked as a police officer **[M-SMG1.7(a)]**. Rudies was located next to Club Nerd **[M-SMG2.1(c4)]**.

- **Rumour, Mr.:** Lister's mispronunciation of Rimmer's name in an alternate timeline in which Lister became the world's youngest billionaire by inventing the Tension Sheet, and thus did not know his *Red Dwarf* roommate **[T-SER3.5]**.

- **Rumpy:** One of seven diminutive rainforest dwellers known as the Ionian Ecommandoes, who lived in the jungles of Io on the television soap opera *Androids*. He and his comrades nursed Karstares back to health **[M-SMG2.5(c5)]**, after Karstares' plane crashed due to sabotage by his son Jaysee **[M-SMG1.14(c3)]**. Grateful for their help, Karstares became the Green Knight, the rainforest's protector, and fought alongside the Ecommandoes against Jaysee's ecologically harmful company **[M-SMG2.5(c5)]**. Rumpy died during a firefight between Jaysee and his foes **[M-SMG2.8(c2)]**.

  ***NOTE:*** *This character resembled one of Disney's Seven Dwarfs. All of the Ecommandoes' names were slang for sex.*

- ***Run for Your Wife*:** An adult comedy play that premiered in 1983, written by Ray Cooney **[RL]**. After traveling back in time to find Kochanski, Lister discovered she had married a future version of him. The future Lister advised that when he found himself on a parallel Earth in a few years, he should avoid seeing *Run for Your Wife* **[T-SER2.4]**.

- **Ryder Cup:** A biennial golf tournament between teams from the United States and Europe **[RL]**. While recounting how he lost his virginity on the ninth hole at the Bootle municipal golf course, Lister assured Rimmer that it was at midnight, not during the Ryder Cup **[T-SER3.2]**.

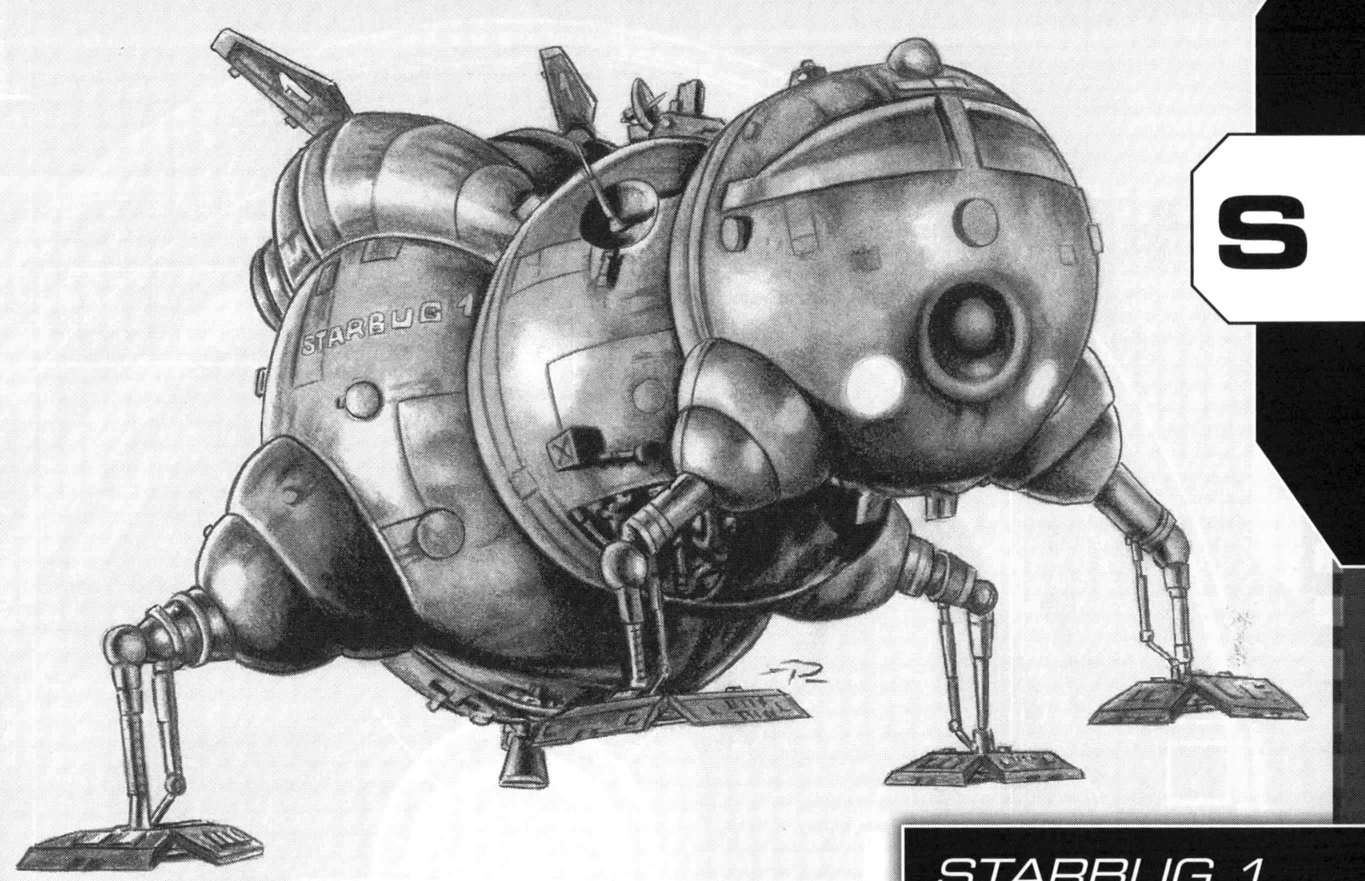


## STARBUG 1

- **S-3:** A classification for small, inhabitable planetoids, asteroids or moons with an atmosphere similar to Earth's **[T-SER5.3]**, short for "Sol Three" **[B-PRG]**.
Rimmer and Kryten located an S-3 planet while moon-hopping aboard *Starbug 1*. Hoping to claim the planet for the Space Corps, they landed on the moon and began reciting the Space Corps anthem, until being interrupted by the moon's sudden, violent transformation. The planet, a psi-moon, configured itself according to Rimmer's psyche, becoming a warped, twisted land filled with horrors **[T-SER5.3]**.
    *NOTE: The DVD captions occasionally spelled the term as "S3," sans hyphen.*

- **Saachi, Saachi, Saachi, Saachi, Saachi and Saachi:** An advertising company that Coca-Cola Co. hired to devise a campaign using 128 supergiant stars to spell a three-word message for five weeks in Earth's sky. The campaign involved inducing each star to go supernova at precisely the right moment for its light to reach Earth at the same time as the others', spelling out the message "Coke Adds Life!"—bright enough to be seen from anywhere on Earth, day or night. According to the firm's executives, the stunt would end the Cola Wars once and for all **[N-INF]**.
    *NOTE: This company's name spoofed that of real-world global advertising agency Saatchi & Saatchi.*

- **Sabinsky, Bob, Doctor:** The scientific advisor to John Milhous Nixon, the third President of the World Council. Sabinsky was in charge of the council's biotechnology institute in Hilo, Hawaii, and headed several programs, including cloning, GELF

**B-: Books**
**PRG:** *Red Dwarf Programme Guide*
**SUR:** *Red Dwarf Space Corps Survival Manual*
**PRM:** *Primordial Soup*
**SOS:** *Son of Soup*
**SCE:** *Scenes from the Dwarf*
**LOG:** *Red Dwarf Log No. 1996*
**RD8:** *Red Dwarf VIII*
**EVR:** *The Log: A Dwarfer's Guide to Everything*

**X-: Misc.**
**PRO:** Promotional materials, videos, etc.
**PST:** Posters at DJ XVII (2013)
**CAL:** 2008 calendar
**RNG:** Cell phone ringtones
**MOB:** Mobisode ("Red Christmas")
**CIN:** *Children in Need* sketch
**GEK:** *Geek Week* intros by Kryten
**TNG:** "Tongue-Tied" video

**XMS:** Bill Pearson's Christmas special pitch script
**XVD:** Bill Pearson's Christmas special pitch video
**OTH:** Other *Red Dwarf* appearances

**SUFFIX**
**DVD:**
**(d)** – Deleted scene
**(o)** – Outtake
**(b)** – Bonus DVD material (other)
**(e)** – Extended version

**SMEGAZINES:**
**(c)** – Comic
**(a)** – Article

**OTHER:**
**(s)** – Early/unused script draft
**(s1)** – Alternate version of script

development and viral research. He also developed a program to relocate the entire human species out of Earth's solar system, after a miscalculation during a weather-controlling experiment reduced the Sun's lifespan to only four hundred thousand years **[N-LST]**.

- **Sacred Gravy Marks:** A set of items or markings worn by the blind Cat priest, the sole surviving member (besides Cat) of the feline species inhabiting *Red Dwarf*'s cargo decks. The Sacred Gravy Marks, along with the Holy Custard Stain, were worn as a testament to a belief in the prophesied return of Cloister the Stupid **[T-SER1.4]**.

- **Sacred Hat, the:** A headpiece worn by a blind priest of the Cat People inhabiting *Red Dwarf*. Pyramidal in shape, with a faux arrow stuck through it, it symbolized the hats that Cloister the Stupid decreed would be worn at the Temple of Food on Fuchal. The Cats, however, disagreed about the hats' color, with half believing it was supposed to be blue, and the other half convinced it was to be red.

  The dying priest ordered Cat to burn the Sacred Hat, as he believed it represented the deception of their religion. Instead, Cat took the hat and lied about destroying it. When Lister (presenting himself as Cloister) arrived, the priest was grief-stricken that he had ordered the Sacred Hat destroyed, so Lister took it from Cat and handed it back to the priest, who declared it a miracle before passing away **[T-SER1.4]**.

- **Sacred Laws, the:** A set of five religious rules followed by the Cat People inhabiting *Red Dwarf*'s cargo decks. These laws were said to have been passed down to the Cats by Cloister the Stupid (Lister) via the Holy Mother (his pet cat Frankenstein). Upon learning of the destruction of the Cat civilization, Lister lamented that he had broken four of the five Sacred Laws he had supposedly given to them—the fifth being spared only due to a lack of sheep onboard **[T-SER1.4]**.

- **Sacred Writing, the:** A scroll handed down to Frankenstein by Cloister the Stupid, who proclaimed that "those who have wisdom will know its meaning," according to the Holy Book of *Red Dwarf*'s Cat People population. The Sacred Writing read, in part, "seven socks, one shirt." In actuality, this was merely Lister's laundry list, which he had used to line Frankenstein's cat basket.

  During the Cat People's Holy Wars, a truce was called between the warring factions, and two arks were built to search for the Holy Land of Fuchal (Fiji). One faction, who believed the food temple's hats should be blue, mistook the list for a star chart and left *Red Dwarf* in the first ark, flying directly into an asteroid, which convinced those in the second vessel that they were on the righteous path **[T-SER1.4]**.

  ***NOTE:** Lister told Rimmer that "one pair of underpants" was also on his original list.*

- **Saddo:** An inmate of the Tank, *Red Dwarf*'s classified brig, who perished during the cadmium II disaster but was resurrected after nanobots rebuilt the ship. Saddo (a friendless loner) and his twin brother Chummy (a much-beloved inmate) were assigned to the Canaries, an elite group of inmates tasked with investigating dangerous situations.

  While in the Tank, Chummy took part in a prank involving the theft of Warden Ackerman's glass eye. Hoping to gain favor with Ackerman, Rimmer—who had confused Chummy for Saddo—called Chummy out for the crime, claiming he saw his fellow inmate playing marbles with the eye. Rimmer had no fear of retaliation from other prisoners due to Saddo's solitary nature, until he realized his mistake and was brutally attacked by several prisoners **[T-SER8.5(d)]**.

  Saddo later helped Oswald "Kill Krazy" Blenkinsop reprogram Kryten to transmit video from the women's showers **[W-OFF]**.

  ***NOTE:** This spelling appeared on the official website; the DVD captions spelled his name as "Sado."*

- **sadness:** An emotional state brought on by feelings of loss, despair or sorrow **[RL]**. While being analyzed by *Red Dwarf*'s chief psychiatric counselor, Kryten boasted that sadness was an emotion he had acquired with Lister's help **[T-SER8.1]**.

- **safety harness:** A set of restraining belts used to strap down passengers of *Starbug* shuttles in the event of major turbulence or other potentially dangerous situations. Lister suggested breaking out safety harnesses when he thought *Starbug 1* was caught in turbulence, unaware the shaking was actually caused by Cat, who had been erased from history due to an unreality bubble **[T-SER6.6(d)]**.

**PREFIX**
**RL:** Real life

**T-: Television Episodes**
**SER:** Television series
**IDW:** "Identity Within"
**USA1:** Unaired U.S. pilot
**USA2:** Unaired U.S. demo

***R-: The Bodysnatcher Collection***
**SER:** Remastered episodes
**BOD:** "Bodysnatcher"
**DAD:** "Dad"
**FTH:** "Lister's Father"
**INF:** "Infinity Patrol"
**END:** "The End" (original assembly)

**N-: Novels**
**INF:** *Infinity Welcomes Careful Drivers*
**BTL:** *Better Than Life*
**LST:** *Last Human*
**BCK:** *Backwards*
**OMN:** *Red Dwarf Omnibus*

**M-: Magazines**
**SMG:** *Smegazine*

**W-: Websites**
**OFF:** Official website
**NAN:** *Prelude to Nanarchy*
**AND:** *Androids*
**DIV:** Diva-Droid
**DIB:** Duane Dibbley

**CRP:** Crapola
**GEN:** Geneticon
**LSR:** Leisure World Intl.
**JMC:** Jupiter Mining Corporation
**AIT:** *A.I. Today*
**HOL:** HoloPoint

**G-: Roleplaying Game**
**RPG:** *Core Rulebook*
**BIT:** *A.I. Screen Extra Bits* booklet
**SOR:** *Series Sourcebook*
**OTH:** Other RPG material

- **SafetyScissorWorld:** A safety-scissor-themed amusement park that appeared in a Psiren illusion intended to lure mechanoids fixated on plastic safety scissors to an asteroid in Psiren territory **[G-SOR]**.

- **Sainsbury's MegaStore:** A chain of grocery stores, circa the twenty-second century, also known as MegaMart. At age seventeen, Lister worked at a MegaMart as a trolley-parker. He had an affair with a married cashier, whose husband locked him in a crate and threatened to throw him into a canal. Instead, the man released him, naked, in the middle of a theatrical production of *The Importance of Being Earnest*. This traumatizing event left Lister claustrophobic **[T-SER7.4]**.

  Sainsbury's MegaStore was located on Hope Street, in Liverpool, and was built on the site of an old Anglican cathedral **[N-INF]**. Lister held the job for ten years, but left it because he did not want to get tied down to a career **[T-SER1.4]**.

- **Sales, Space Division:** A department within Diva-Droid International, the company responsible for manufacturing and distributing mechanoids such as the Kryten and Hudzen Series. Among the division's responsibilities were informing current leaseholders of Kryten Series mechanoids that their unit was outdated, and sending replacement Hudzen Series droids. Jim Reaper was the head of this division **[T-SER3.6]**.

- **Salinger, Elaine, President:** The leader of the United States sometime during the late twenty-first or early twenty-second century, widely considered the nation's greatest president of all time. Her likeness was added to South Dakota's Mount Rushmore National Memorial **[N-BTL]**.

- **Saliva:** A name that Lister assigned to one of twelve rogue droids he purchased from the Kinitawowi to break his doppelgänger out of the virtual-reality prison Cyberia. This particular droid tended to giggle and blow saliva bubbles **[N-LST]**.

- **salivators:** A component in the mouths of some mechanoids, such as the 4000 Series. When the *Red Dwarf* crew believed they had returned to Earth, Lister's description of his grandmother's homemade kebab sauce triggered Kryten's salivators **[M-SMG2.8(c3)]**.

- **Sally:** A test chimpanzee at Brainfade, a government-funded company operating in a fascist society on an alternate-dimension Earth. Sally's handler was a brilliant scientist named Tina. After the firm's lead scientist, Sid Scofrenia, was implicated in the murder of Sandra Halley and was subsequently killed by Jake Bullet, Tina implanted a backup copy of Scofrenia's personality into the ape **[M-SMG2.9(c4)]**.

- **"Salt—An Epicure's Delight":** An article published in the in-flight magazine *Up Up & Away*, which Lister found on a shuttle that ferried him from Mimas to *Red Dwarf* for his first tour of duty **[N-INF]**. Three million years later, Lister, Rimmer and Cat read the same issue to survive a crash aboard *Starbug 1*, as it had been discovered that the publication's mundane articles acted as a sedative during emergencies **[T-SER4.5]**.

- **Salvador Dali Coffee Lounge:** A coffee shop located at the Mimas Hilton. George McIntyre agreed to meet representatives of the Golden Assurance Friendly and Caring Loan Society at this shop to discuss a payment plan for his massive debt, but the three burly representatives force-fed him his own nose when he refused to sign paperwork guaranteeing payment **[N-INF]**.

- **salvage leader:** A position advertised on the Jupiter Mining Corporation's website for a captain able to lead a salvage operation to recover *Red Dwarf*. Candidates were required to be bright, confident and semi-suicidal, with ruthless killer simulants welcome. The position's reference number was QBX1934 **[W-JMC]**.

- **Salvation Army:** An international Christian organization dedicated to helping those in need, by providing charitable services such as food, shelter and clothing **[RL]**. While trapped in a despair squid hallucination, Cat imagined that his alter ego, Duane Dibbley, had a key to a Salvation Army hostel among the possessions **[T-SER5.6]**.

- **Sam:** A crewmember aboard a space vessel that crashed into an asteroid in Psiren territory, who died when the telepathic Psirens attacked. A shipmate later recorded a log entry reporting several deaths, including Sam's **[T-SER6.1(d)]**.

- **Samaritans, the:** A charity organization that provided emotional support to those in despair or distress via a 24-7 hotline **[RL]**. Rimmer worked for the Samaritans for one day, during which he spoke to five people, all of whom committed suicide thereafter, including one person who had dialed the wrong number. The newspapers covered the incident, calling it "Lemming Sunday" since all five jumped off buildings **[T-SER3.6]**.

  ***NOTE:*** *Dialog in the unfilmed script "Dad," published in* The Bodysnatcher Collection, *indicated that seven people, not five, committed suicide after speaking with Rimmer.*

- **Sam Murray:** The username of a forum poster on the *Androids* website's message boards. The poster was Deck Sergeant Sam Murray, a notorious prankster who devised a way for his posts to only be seen between the hours of 3:00 AM and 8:00 AM **[W-AND]**.

- **Sammy the Squib:** A playable character in the film-noir artificial-reality detective simulation *Gumshoe.* Sammy's special skill was being a crack shot with a Tommy gun, and his stamina, charm and intelligence ratings were all one hundred. Unable to get Lister's attention while Dave was hooked into the game, Kryten entered the program as Sammy and urged him to shut down so *Starbug 1* could enter silent-running mode **[T-SER6.3]**.

- **Samuel the Chicken-Stealer:** A man who lived in Caesarea, Israel, circa 23 A.D. He and Rachel the Fornicator bore a son, whom they named Jesus. The youth routinely found himself in trouble for his father's poultry-stealing crimes **[T-SER10.3]**.

- **Sancerre:** An appellation of wine produced in the French hilltop town of Sancerre, in the eastern Loire Valley **[RL]**. While attempting to justify his own cowardice, Rimmer told Lister that wartime generals were typically posted atop hills, directing battles while drinking Sancerre, and were not engaged in barroom brawls **[T-SER3.2]**.

- **Sanchez, Imran, Console Executive:** A *Red Dwarf* crewmember who worked in the ship's Drive Room. Sanchez perished during the cadmium II disaster that killed the entire crew except for Lister. Millions of years later, after Lister was released from stasis, Holly directed him to the Drive Room for debriefing. Dave questioned the AI computer about mounds of white powder lying about the room, dipping his finger in one pile for a taste. Holly responded that this particular pile was Imran Sanchez, who had been reduced to dust during the radioactive leak **[N-INF]**.

  ***NOTE:*** *This contradicted episode 1.1 ("The End"), which attributed the powder to Olaf Petersen's remains—though it did eliminate the question of why a catering officer would have a station in the Drive Room. It is unknown whether the nanobots resurrected Sanchez in Series VIII.*

- **Sandra:** A young woman whom Rimmer once claimed was his first sexual partner. While marooned on a frozen planet in *Starbug 1*, Lister kept his mind off hunger by asking how his roommate lost his virginity. Arnold recalled an encounter with Sandra, which he claimed took place in the back seat of his brother's Bentley convertible **[T-SER3.2]**.

  In actuality, he had only barely gotten to second base with the nineteen-year-old, and did not have his first true sexual tryst until twelve years later, at age thirty-one, with Yvonne McGruder. Embarrassed, Rimmer had exaggerated the Sandra encounter **[N-INF]**.

- **Sandra:** A woman, possibly a sex worker, who was the topic of a heated debate between two pimps on Mimas. The discussion began within close proximity to a taxi hopper in which Lister was parked, and ended with each pimp lopping off the other's ear, and with at least one of them dying **[N-INF]**.

- **San Francisco Earthquake:** An alcoholic beverage served in a plastic coconut at *Red Dwarf*'s Copacabana Hawaiian Cocktail Bar. Lister and his mates often ordered this drink **[N-INF]**.

- **Sangrida:** A member of an anti-fascist group in Jake Bullet's universe known as the Fatal Sisters, along with Mista and Hilda. The three women wore Valkyrie warrior outfits **[M-SMG2.4(c6)]**. After rescuing Duane Dibbley from Voter Colonel Gray, the Fatal Sisters brought him to their hideout, where all three had sex with him in order to jog his memory about his true identity **[M-SMG2.5(c1)]**.

- **sanity chip:** A component built into Diva-Droid International mechanoids that controlled their artificial mental state. The sanity chip of a mechanoid left operating alone for a long time could wear out, causing it to become crazed and often hostile. A Hudzen 10 unit, sent by Diva-Droid to replace Kryten, suffered such a malfunction after three million years in transit. When Hudzen's spaceship eventually caught up with *Red Dwarf*, he attacked the crew when they refused to shut Kryten down **[T-SER3.6]**.

  When Rimmer decided to train Waxworld's pacifistic Hero World waxdroids to battle the denizens of Villain World, Kryten asked if his sanity chip had been installed properly **[T-SER4.6]**.

- **Sara, Nurse:** A health-care professional at St. Pentium's Hospital on the television soap opera *Androids*. She had a crush on Doctor Neame, a brother addicted to bolts, and a giant letter "C" painted on her chest **[W-AND]**. While working as a cashier in the hospital's parts department, Sara admitted Brook after he was injured during a shootout with Jaysee **[M-SMG2.8(c2)]**.

- **Sartre, Jean-Paul:** A French existentialist philosopher and writer of the 1900s whose major works included *Nausea*, *No Exit* and *The Roads to Freedom* **[RL]**. When Lister asked Holly why he had revived Rimmer instead of Kochanski or anyone else he actually liked, Holly quoted Sartre, stating, "Hell was being locked forever in a room with your friends." Lister noted that all of Sartre's friends were French **[T-SER1.3]**.

  ***NOTE:** Holly misquoted Sartre, who actually wrote "Hell is other people," in the play* No Exit.

- **Sartre, Jean-Paul:** A waxdroid replica of the writer, created for the Waxworld theme park. Left on their own for millions of years, the waxdroids attained sentience and became embroiled in a park-wide resource war between Villain World and Hero World (to which Sartre belonged) **[T-SER4.6]**. The waxdroid was proficient with using ninja throwing berets **[G-SOR]**.

  During this war, the *Red Dwarf* crew transported to the planet using a Matter Paddle, with Rimmer and Kryten materializing in Hero territory, while Lister and Cat landed in Villain territory. Rimmer found the heroes' army lacking and took command, working many of the pacifistic waxdroids to death before ordering a frontal attack on the enemy's compound across a minefield, which wiped out the remaining droids. Sartre was shot in the chest during the conflict **[T-SER4.6]**.

- **Saturn:** The sixth planet in Earth's solar system, encircled by a complex ring system. Saturn had at least sixty-two moons, including Titan, Rhea and Mimas **[RL]**. In the twenty-second century, the Inter-Planetary Commission for Waste Disposal decided to designate one of the system's nine planets as humanity's official dumping grounds. Representatives from all nine worlds presented their case against being chosen, with Saturn's delegation citing the planet's rings as a massive tourist attraction, and stressing that its habitable moons, though seedy, generated a massive amount of business. Ultimately, Earth was nominated for the task **[N-BTL]**.

- **Saturn Bears:** A zero-gee football team. Groovy Channel 27 aired a game between the Saturn Bears and the London Jets at 2:30 PM on Wednesday, the 27th of Geldof, 2362, as competition for the Diva-Droid League Cup **[M-SMG1.7(a)]**.

- **Saturnian anthem:** The four-stanza planetary song of Saturn. Infected with a holovirus spread by Hildegarde Lanstrom, a hologram aboard a vessel passing by her viral research station became insane and flushed his crewmates out an airlock, then sang three hundred verses of the anthem, most of which he made up **[W-OFF]**.

- **Saturn Tech:** A learning facility that Rimmer attended as a youth, at which he took a course in maintenance. At the time, Lister lived in Liverpool and began dating Lise Yates. This caused Arnold some confusion years later when, as a deathday present, Lister implanted his memories of Yates into Rimmer's hologrammic mind, making him believe he had dated her. According to his altered memory, the first three months of that year were spent at Saturn Tech, at which point he inexplicably moved to Liverpool and met Lise **[T-SER2.3]**.

- **Saturn War, the:** A conflict in which Rimmer's son, Michael McGruder, fought on the moon Hyperion **[N-LST]**.

- **Saunders, Carole:** The widow of *Red Dwarf* engineer Frank Saunders. Before leaving for his tour of duty aboard the mining ship, Frank told Carole to start a new life without him if anything catastrophic happened—words that haunted him after he later perished and was resurrected as a hologram **[N-INF]**.

- **Saunders, Frank:** An engineer from Sidcup, England, who served aboard *Red Dwarf*. Saunders was killed by a 4,000-kilogram (8,800-pound) demolition ball, and was revived as a hologram by the ship's computer **[N-INF]**.
  ***NOTE:*** *It is unknown whether the nanobots resurrected Saunders in Series VIII.*

- **Saunders, Frank:** A hologram of *Red Dwarf* engineer Frank Saunders. He had a difficult time dealing with his death and hologrammatic resurrection, as the inordinate paperwork frustrated him, and the thought of his wife sleeping with other men drove him mad with jealousy. Saunders' status as a hologram abruptly ended two weeks later, however, when George McIntyre, who outranked him, committed suicide **[N-INF]**.

- **Sausage and onion gravy sandwich on white bread:** A meal that Lister consumed in an alternate timeline in which he became the world's youngest billionaire by inventing the Tension Sheet. Recalling the sandwich from his musician days, Lister had it specially flown in from Luigi's Fish 'n' Chip Emporium **[T-SER3.5]**.

- **Savalas, Aristotelis ("Telly"):** A twentieth-century American film and television actor, best known for his titular role in the TV crime drama *Kojak*, as well as his film roles in *Birdman of Alcatraz*, *The Dirty Dozen* and *On Her Majesty's Secret Service* **[RL]**. A waxdroid of Telly Savalas was involved in a plot to retrieve priceless art from a Reich supply depot on War World, an alternate Earth on which World War II never ended **[G-BIT]**.

- **Savalas TV:** An Earth television studio in Jake Bullet's reality, where game show *20,000,000 Watts My Line* was recorded. Bullet visited Savalas TV after its most successful contestant, Philby Frutch, was murdered **[M-SMG1.11(c4)]**. During his investigation, Bullet (aided by Duane Dibbley) visited the site of Sebastian and William Doyle's murders as a favor to Dibbley, but was ambushed by the network's goons **[M-SMG2.1(c4)]**.
  ***NOTE:*** *The station was presumably named after actor Telly Savalas.*

- **Save the Pigeon:** A charity established in 2108, dedicated to returning the nearly extinct pigeon, a bird of the clade Columbidae, to Earth's populated areas. Jupiter Mining Corporation supported this charity **[W-JMC]**.
  ***NOTE:*** *In the real world, the activist group Save the Trafalgar Square Pigeons was established in 2000 to lobby against rules forbidding the feeding of pigeons in Trafalgar Square, London, as the birds had become an attraction in of themselves.*

- **Saxon:** A member of *Red Dwarf*'s Z-Shift prior to the cadmium II disaster. Shortly before the explosion, Rimmer assigned Saxon and Phil Burroughs to paint the engineers' mess **[N-INF]**.
  ***NOTE:*** *Saxon presumably died during the cadmium II explosion. It is unknown whether the nanobots resurrected him in Series VIII.*

- **SC:** Initials painted on the rear fin of *Wildfire*, an experimental spacecraft capable of breaking the speed of reality and crossing dimensions. It was built by an alternate-reality Space Corps, at its test base on Mimas, and flown by Ace Rimmer **[T-SER4.5]**.

- ***SCABBY***: *See Spacers Catalog and Bargain Basement Yearly! (SCABBY)*

- **Scala, The:** A movie theatre aboard *Red Dwarf*. The Scala once ran a twelve-hour marathon of back-to-back movies directed by Peter Greenaway **[N-INF]**.

- **scalpel:** A sharp medical utensil designed to make surgical incisions **[RL]**. Bored with using plastic cutlery, Lister procured several items from *Red Dwarf*'s Medical Unit and used them to prepare and serve dinner in the Officers' Quarters, including scalpels, which he used as knives. Although Lister had cleaned and sterilized the equipment, Cat refused to stay for dinner, calling the meal "an autopsy" **[T-SER3.3]**.

- **Scan Mode:** A function of a black box recording device that the *Red Dwarf* crew found on a spacecraft lying adrift in an asteroid belt. The video, when played back, contained visual-scan data about creatures known as Psirens **[T-SER6.1]**.

- **scanner-scope:** A *Red Dwarf* component built to scan for anomalies. Holly, mistaking scanner-scope grit for five black holes, ordered the ship's evacuation, during which Lister and Rimmer became marooned aboard *Starbug 1* on an icy planet **[T-SER3.2]**.

- **scanner table:** A piece of machinery in *Starbug 1*'s midsection, linked into the ship's scanners so it could display a plethora of data readouts. When not in use, it doubled as a standard table **[T-SER6.2]**.

- **"Scanning":** A word displayed on a monitor in *Red Dwarf*'s Drive Room **[T-SER10.4]**.

- **Scary"R"Us:** A hypothetical public relations firm. After hearing the names of such simulant vessels as Death Ships and Annihilators, Cat wondered if Scary"R"Us handled their PR **[T-SER10.6(d)]**.

  ***NOTE:** This company's name spoofed that of toy store chain Toys "R" Us.*

- **Scatter bar:** A lounge area that a band of agonoids created aboard *Red Dwarf* after taking over the ship. The agonoids used the Scatter bar to plug scramble cards into their ports, which simulated the euphoria of getting drunk **[N-BCK]**.

- **scatterbrained:** A simulated state of inebriation enjoyed by agonoids **[N-BCK]**.

- ***Schellenberg*, SSS:** A spaceship possibly from an alternate universe. Its artificial-intelligence computer was named Grendel **[G-RPG]**.

- **Schmidt:** A new recruit aboard *Red Dwarf* who reported for duty along with Lister. Schmidt served as a technician in Z-Shift prior to the cadmium II disaster **[N-INF]**.

  ***NOTE:** Schmidt presumably died during the explosion. It is unknown whether the nanobots resurrected him in Series VIII.*

- **Schneiberhauser Owners' Society:** A hypothetical organization of which Lister claimed to be the self-appointed president. Upon hearing about a procedure for removing a person's kidney stone, which included sticking a scope into the urethra (or "schneiberhauser," as he called it), Lister was horrified at the concept **[T-SER10.3]**.

- **Schopenhauer, Arthur:** A nineteenth-century German philosopher who espoused pessimistic views **[RL]**. While searching a scientific research station, the *Red Dwarf* crew discovered a multitude of stasis booths, one of which contained holovirus-infected hologrammatic scientist Hildegarde Lanstrom. Once revived, Lanstrom quoted Schopenauer as saying, "Life without pain has no meaning," claiming she wanted to give meaning to her rescuers' lives. She then attacked them with hex vision **[T-SER5.4]**.

- **Schplut, the:** A name given to the sound made by a zero-gee football team's defense as they landed on an opposing team member who had just scored a touchdown **[M-SMG1.8(a)]**.

- **Schuman, Elaine, Flight Coordinator:** A blonde, twenty-three-year-old crewmember aboard *Nova 5*, a spaceship commissioned by the Coca-Cola Co. to detonate supergiant stars in a strategic pattern as part of the company's advertisement campaign. Schuman was one of three survivors of a crash that killed most of *Nova 5*'s crew, which Kryten caused by trying to clean the ship's computer. The women eventually died, leaving the mechanoid to tend to their corpses, unaware they had passed on. Her blood type was O **[N-INF]**.

  ***NOTE:** Schuman's name, noted in the novel* Infinity Welcomes Careful Drivers *(Kryten simply called her "Miss Elaine"), did not jibe with the crew's names provided onscreen in episode 2.1 ("Kryten").*

- **Schwarzenegger, Arlene:** An action movie star in an alternate universe in which the sexes were reversed. In the film *The Terminator*, Schwarzenegger played a cyborg who traveled back through time to kill Simon Connor to prevent him from giving birth to the leader of the human resistance. Schwarzenegger was one of Arlene Rimmer's role models **[W-OFF]**.

  ***NOTE:** This was the female analog to actor Arnold*

*Schwarzenegger. The official website misspelled her surname as "Schwartzenegger."*

- **Schwarzenegger, Arnold:** An Austrian-born American bodybuilder, actor and politician known for such Hollywood action films as *Conan the Barbarian, Predator* and *The Terminator* series **[RL]**. After enduring Lister's gripes about being impregnated by a woman in a parallel universe, Rimmer suggested he man up, asking if he thought Arnold Schwarzenegger would behave similarly in his predicament **[R-DAD]**.

  *NOTE: Ironically, Schwarzenegger later played an impregnated man in the film* Junior*—in which he did, in fact, complain about his predicament.*

- ***Science and Health With Key to the Scriptures*****:** The central text of the Christian Science religion, written by Mary Baker Eddy and first published in 1875 **[RL]**. Warden Ackerman kept a copy of this book on a shelf in his quarters aboard *Red Dwarf* **[T-SER8.5]**.

- **Science Block:** An area aboard *Red Dwarf* allocated for scientific research and development. Located on Z Deck, the Science Block contained programmable viruses—artificial pathogens that could be programmed to perform certain tasks, such as skinning potatoes **[T-SER8.6]**.

- **Science Department:** An area aboard the mirror-universe *Red Dwarf* allocated for scientific research. The department was run by Professor Cat and employed an alternate version of Kochanski as a ditzy blonde administrative assistant. After Rimmer entered that reality searching for an antidote to a chameleonic microbe ravishing his *Red Dwarf*, he made his way to the Science Department, where the professor provided him with the formula **[T-SER8.8(d)]**.

- **Science Lab:** A room aboard *Red Dwarf* dedicated to scientific and medical research. Kryten built a mind swap device in this laboratory, which Rimmer and Lister used to exchange consciousnesses so Arnold could get David's body fit **[T-SER3.4]**.

- **Science Room:** A room aboard *Red Dwarf* used for scientific and medical research. The crew carried out an experimental intelligence-compression procedure on Holly in this room to increase her IQ **[T-SER3.4]**. In addition, Kryten performed a Cesarean section on Lister in the Science Room after he became pregnant in an alternate universe in which the sexes were reversed **[R-DAD]**.

  *NOTE: The Science Lab and the Science Room may have been the same location.*

- **Scintillating Off-Gray:** The only color available for Tucker Instruments' Psi-scan TI345 **[G-RPG]**.

- **sci-scan:** *See* Psi-scan

- **Scofrenia, Sid, Doctor:** The lead scientist at Brainfade, a company in Jake Bullet's universe. While investigating the murder of scientist Sandra Halley, Bullet met with Scofrenia, who introduced him to other members of the staff **[M-SMG2.7(c4)]**.

  Reviewing security footage from the company, Bullet learned of an argument between Scofrenia and Halley, involving a mind-control spike that the latter developed but never intended for public use. Bullet returned to Brainfade to question Scofrenia, who showed him a virtual simulation of Halley's death that instead implicated Halley's co-worker and test subject, Carl **[M-SMG2.8(c1)]**.

  Convinced the Scofrenia was responsible for distributing the spikes, Bullet tried to arrest the scientist, but was disabled by one of the devices, which had been implanted in his neck. Scofrenia ordered Carl to kill Bullet, but when he threw the cyborg out a window, Jake landed on the fleeing Scofrenia, killing him instantly. His essence was later retrieved from a backup personality disk, altered to remove any negative aspects, and placed into Sally, a test chimp at the facility **[M-SMG2.9(c4)]**.

- **Scoop Room:** An area within the cargo section of *White Giant* shuttles **[N-BTL]**.

- **Scott, Robert Falcon, Captain:** An English Antarctic explorer who led the ill-fated Terra Nova expedition in the early 1900s. During the expedition, Scott's team member, Captain Lawrence Oates, sacrificed himself so that his comrades would have a chance to survive **[RL]**.

Kryten cited Oates as an example of human sacrifice in order to persuade Rimmer to shut down during a power failure. However, Rimmer noted that if he were Oates, he would have whacked Scott over the head with a frozen husky and eaten him instead of making the ultimate sacrifice **[T-SER4.4]**.

- ***Scott Fitzgerald*:** A spaceship operated by Gordon, an eleventh-generation artificial-intelligence computer with a reputed IQ of eight thousand **[T-SER2.2]**. Due to an error in Gordon's source code, the AI became increasingly erratic over time, and eventually flew the *Scott Fitzgerald* into a star because he wanted "a bit of change" **[W-AIT]**.

  ***NOTE:*** *The* A.I. Today *website called the ship the* F. Scott Fitzgerald.

- **Scott Foresman and Company:** An American publisher of elementary educational books, founded in 1896 **[RL]**. Books from Scott Foresman and Company were stored on the fifth floor of the Texas School Book Depository at the time of John F. Kennedy's assassination in Dallas **[T-SER7.1]**.

- **scouter:** *See* JMC "Scouter" Remote Drone

- ***Scrabble*:** A word game produced by Mattel and Hasbro, played by placing lettered tiles on a game board for points **[RL]**. Lister played a game of *Scrabble* with Cat while inhabiting Rimmer's hologrammic body following a mind swap. Due to the hologrammic body's limitations, Cat had to move Lister's pieces for him **[T-SER3.4]**.

  The arrival of a pod containing a genetically engineered adaptable pet (GEAP) interrupted another *Scrabble* game, which the crew resumed after placing the GEAP back in its pod and shooting it into space **[M-SMG1.6(c1)]**. Sometime later, the *Scrabble* box was mysteriously jettisoned into space **[M-SMG1.11(c2)]**.

- ***Scramble!!!*:** A notoriously buggy artificial-reality game in which players piloted a Warbird on a mission to bomb a simulant munitions dump. A common malfunction caused players to instead drive a #17 bus down Balham High Street during rush hour. A workaround to the glitch involved bombing footwear retailer Freeman Hardy Willis **[B-SUR]**.

- **scramble card:** An electronic device that could be plugged into an agonoid's head to give it certain abilities, such as improved reaction time, reduced rage or, more commonly, simulated inebriation. After a group of agonoids took over *Red Dwarf*, they created an area known as the Scatter bar, in which they purchased scramble cards to get "scatterbrained" **[N-BCK]**.

- **Screwface:** The bodyguard of Tabby Ranks, a raga artist in an alternate dimension. Leo Davis met Screwface and Ranks' manager, Mega, at Black Island Film Studios, the production company where Davis worked, which Ranks had hired to produce a music video **[X-TNG]**.

- **Scripts by Kelleher/Hill:** A business referenced on the television soap opera *Androids*. A large sign featuring its name adorned the front of the company's building **[M-SMG1.10(c2)]**.

  ***NOTE:*** *This was an in-joke reference to* Smegazine *writers Pat Kelleher and James Hill.*

- **scrumpy:** A potent cider typically produced in England **[RL]**. While marooned on a frozen planet with no drinkable water, Rimmer suggested that Lister recycle his own urine and pretend it was scrumpy **[T-SER3.2(o)]**.

- **Scutcher:** A rogue simulant scavenger who scoured the galaxy with other simulants, looking for genuine Earth antiques and emotions garnered from polymorphs, to sell to mechanicals. Scutcher's group discovered Garbage World (Earth) after the planet had been ripped from its orbit, and searched the surface for artifacts and polymorphs **[M-SMG2.9(c11)]**.

- ***Seabug*:** *See Starbug 4*

- **sea buggy:** A small underwater craft used to transport passengers. While submerged in an ocean deep within a lava-covered planet, the *Starbug* crew used a sea buggy to travel between their shuttle and the *Mayflower*, salvaging supplies from the GELF ship in order to break free of the planet's molten surface **[N-LST]**.

- **Sea of Tranquility:** A lunar mare located on Earth's Moon, also called by its Latin name, Mare Tranquillitatis **[RL]**. A four-day event called the New Zodiac Festival was held in the

Sea of Tranquility, celebrating the changing of Earth's polar star, and attended by five thousand space beatniks **[N-INF]**.

- **search probe:** A piece of equipment that could be launched from *Red Dwarf* to detect life in certain environments. The crew used a search probe to check for marine life on an oceanic world, but found none. Despite that fact, they decided to take a fishing holiday on the planet **[T-SER4.5]**.

- **"Season 29":** Words printed on a poster for the London Jets zero-gee football team **[T-SER1.3]**.

- **Second Big Bang, the:** The ultimate goal of the *Red Dwarf* total-immersion video game, which the crew imagined playing while trapped in a despair squid hallucination. In the illusory game, players were supposed to use *Starbug*'s leads to trigger a Second Big Bang, thereby creating a new universe and promoting Lister to godhood.

  After crashing the *Starbug* and waking up in the TIV suite, Lister's team learned that their lives and identities aboard the mining vessel were all part of the game, which was supposed to end with the Second Universe's creation. Only later did they discover that they were still under the despair squid's influence **[T-SER5.6]**.

- **Second Universe:** The endgame of the *Red Dwarf* total-immersion video game, which the crew imagined playing while trapped in a despair squid hallucination. Players were supposed to create the Second Universe by triggering the Second Big Bang. In the illusion, Lister and his shipmates believed they were actually back on Earth with different identities, and playing the game as a team. They missed several essential plot-points, however, and scored only four percent, entirely missing out on creating the new universe **[T-SER5.6]**.

- **Secret Seven, The:** A group of child detectives featured in a series of novels written by Enid Blyton **[RL]**. While discussing the Space Masons, a fraternal organization to which Rimmer attempted to gain membership during his youth, Lister called them "The Secret Seven for grown-ups" **[T-SER2.3(d)]**.

- **"Section 14 Maintenance Personnel":** A phrase stenciled on the casing of a post pod that followed *Red Dwarf* for three million years **[T-SER2.2]**.

- **Sector 12:** A section of space containing an ion storm through which *Starbug 1* nearly passed during an encounter with Ace Rimmer's spaceship **[T-SER7.2]**.

- **Sector 16:** An area of the American mining ship *Red Dwarf*. Kryten ended up in Sector 16 after making a wrong turn while attempting to reach Captain Tau's office **[T-USA1]**.

- **Sector 492:** A section of space in Quadrant 4, in which Holly detected a probe sent from the holoship *Enlightenment* **[T-SER5.1]**.

- **Sector P/4500000:** An area of *Red Dwarf*, as denoted on the vessel's exterior. A polymorph disguised as the mining ship recreated these markings **[M-SMG2.6(c1)]**.

- **Secure Transmission Device (STD):** A unit aboard simulant battle-class cruisers enabling them to transmit a virus program into an enemy vessel's navicomp **[G-RPG]**. Before being destroyed, a rogue simulant attack party used their STD to send the Armageddon virus to *Starbug 1*'s computer **[T-SER6.3]**.

  ***NOTE:*** *The device's initials, STD, also stand for "sexually transmitted disease."*

- **secure visiting booth:** A small room in *Red Dwarf*'s security section in which prisoners could receive visitors. While under the influence of psychotropic drugs to corroborate their claim that the ship had been rebuilt by nanobots, Lister imagined meeting with Rimmer in such a booth while awaiting trial **[T-SER8.2]**.

- **security cameras:** A series of recording devices located throughout *Starbug 1*'s interior, used for remotely scanning a room from another area of the ship. Lister hacked into the security cameras to glimpse his future self, who had boarded the shuttle seeking assistance with a time drive. To his shock, his future self was merely a brain in a jar **[T-SER6.6]**.

- **Security Check:** An area of *Red Dwarf* near the vessel's landing bays, through which Canaries passed in order to check in gear after missions. It utilized a biometric hand scanner to identify each inmate. Kryten smuggled a time wand from the SS *Manny Celeste* through the Security Check by storing the device in his head **[T-SER8.6]**.

- **"Security Coded":** A phrase printed vertically adjacent to the keypad controlling the airtight door of *Red Dwarf*'s Quarantine Room 152 **[T-SER5.4]**.

- **security containment cell:** A holding cell at a prison on GELFWorld. Its prison bars, guards and toilets were all custom-designed GELFs. Drigg, a dissonant GELF, was incarcerated in such a cell, but escaped after talking the door into freeing him **[M-SMG2.2(c4)]**.

- **Security Deck:** A level aboard *Red Dwarf* containing the ship's brig. After the Inquisitor erased Lister and Kryten from history, Rimmer (who no longer recognized them) suggested taking the intruders to the Security Deck and placing them in a cell **[T-SER5.2]**.

  ***NOTE:** It is doubtful that this referred to Floor 13, the high-security prison ward featured in Series VIII, since none of the crew were supposed to have known about it.*

- **Security Operations Room:** The nerve center of a prison facility designed to hold the essences of inmates as soundwaves, which Rimmer imagined while trapped in an addictive version of *Better Than Life*. In the illusion, Arnold was incarcerated in this facility after having his Solidgram body repossessed. During a prison break, he and his soundwave cellmates stormed the Security Operations Room, where they used the radio signal from a guard's walkie-talkie to escape **[N-BTL]**.

- **"See You Later, Alligator":** A rock-and-roll song recorded in 1955, first by Robert Charles Guidry and later by Bill Haley & His Comets **[RL]**. This song was played at George McIntyre's funeral aboard *Red Dwarf*, at his request **[T-SER1.1]**.

- **Selby:** One of Lister's best friends aboard *Red Dwarf*, before the cadmium II leak killed all of the crew except for Lister **[T-SER1.1]**. Selby intended to join the Space Corps, but mistook Chen's history class for the Space Corps recruitment center. Fortunately for him, his friend Chen signed him up for service, mistaking the recruitment center for his history class and believing his enlistment papers were the final exam **[G-BIT]**.

  Three million years later, Selby and the ship's entire complement were resurrected by nanobots **[T-SER8.1]**. After being brought back to life, Selby volunteered for the ship's fire safety crew **[G-BIT]**, and was one of three crewmembers to respond to a fire caused by Lister crashing *Starbug 1* into Landing Bay 6 **[T-SER8.1]**.

- **Selby:** A disciple of Cloister the Stupid, along with Chen and Petson, according to the Cat Bible. In chapters six and seven of the Holy Book, the disciples were said to have shared a meal with Cloister, during which they drank lager and were told of their impending demise **[M-SMG2.4(a)]**.

- **Self-Confidence:** An aspect of Rimmer's personality that a psi-moon detected as having died when he was twenty-two years old, prompting the planetoid to construct a metaphorical tombstone in its memory **[T-SER5.3]**.

- **Self-Despair:** An aspect of Rimmer's personality made flesh on a psi-moon configured according to his psyche. After Arnold's shipmates rescued him from the moon, Self-Despair and other solidifications of Rimmer's negative traits were left behind to battle his positive aspects, including Courage, Charity, Honour and Self-Esteem **[M-SMG2.7(c2)]**.

- **Self-Doubt:** An aspect of Rimmer's personality made flesh on a psi-moon configured according to his psyche. When the *Red Dwarf* crew boosted Rimmer's self-confidence to vanquish the Self-Loathing Beast, a ghostly musketeer arose to battle the Unspeakable One's hordes, including Self-Doubt, thereby enabling the crew to escape **[T-SER5.3]**.

- **Self-Esteem:** An aspect of Rimmer's personality made flesh on a psi-moon configured according to his psyche. After Arnold's shipmates rescued him from the moon, Self-Esteem and his comrades—Charity, Courage and Honour—were left behind to battle Rimmer's negative traits, including Misery, Self-Despair and Paranoia. The Dark Forces abducted Self-Esteem and displayed him in Castle Despondency to lure the others into a trap, then unleashed a secret weapon: the image of Rimmer's mother **[M-SMG2.7(c2)]**.

- **self-gamete-mixing *in vitro* tube:** A small device used to fertilize a woman's egg without the need for sex or pregnancy. Produced by Malpractice Medical & Scispec, it utilized a proprietary gametogenesis system **[G-RPG]**. Once an egg was housed inside the device, sperm was added and the resultant zygote was placed in a uterine simulator, to be incubated until birth.

When Lister realized that he was his own father, he and Kochanski used a self-gamete-mixing *in vitro* tube to produce an infant version of Lister. He then brought the child back in time and left himself under a pool table at the same Liverpool pub where he had once been found abandoned as a baby **[T-SER7.3]**.

- **self-image redirection technology:** A technology enabling a Talkie Toilet's artificial intelligence to convert the low self-esteem the unit typically experienced (from being a toilet) into an obsession with performing its duties as efficiently as possible **[G-SOR]**.

- **selfishness tuck:** A type of personality surgery performed on Juanita Chicata, Rimmer's ex-wife in an illusion created by an addictive version of *Better Than Life* **[N-BTL]**.

- **Self-Loathing Beast:** *See* Unspeakable One, The

- **self-lubricating thrustex thong:** An article of clothing featured in the total-immersion video game *Red Dwarf*. The thong, given to the game's Lister character as a Christmas gift, was ejected from one of two U-Haul ships projecting a hologram of Earth, with the Panama Canal highlighted. Its message, "America Isthmus Two U-Hauls," was a pun that, when spoken aloud, announced "A Merry Christmas to You All" **[M-SMG2.9(c3)]**.

- **self-repair system:** A function of 4000 Series mechanoids enabling them to fix themselves when damaged. Once activated, this system utilized subatomic robots called nanobots that broke down raw materials at the molecular level and rebuilt the android's damaged or malfunctioning components **[T-SER7.8]**. Also known as auto-repair, the system kicked in after Kryten was severely damaged during an accident on a psi-moon. Although unable to fully repair the mechanoid, the system was able to get his visual system online and his damage assessment down to 72 percent **[T-SER5.3]**.

- **self-repair unit:** A component built into 4000 Series mechanoids as part of their self-repair system, which enabled the mechs to repair themselves when damaged. After an accident involving *Starbug*'s waste compactor, Kryten activated his self-repair unit—but not before finishing his laundry duties **[T-SER6.1]**.

- **Self-Respect:** An aspect of Rimmer's personality that a psi-moon detected as having died when he was twenty-four years old, prompting the planetoid to construct a metaphorical tombstone in its memory **[T-SER5.3]**.

- **Seni Rotundi:** A double-island chain located in the Mediterranean Sea on War World, an alternate Earth on which World War II never ended. Its capital city contained a statue of Commander Robert Dimsdale, a dimension-hopping traveler who helped tip the balance of the war with his advances in Rocket Pants technology.

  Seni Rotundi was led by King Stefano Bonjella, a Resistance sympathizer who was executed in the city's square. After his death, his daughter, Princess Beryl Bonjella, swore revenge against the Reich, offering her assistance to the Resistance to help fight the evil superpower **[G-BIT]**.

- ***Sense and Sensibility*:** A romantic novel written by Jane Austen, published in 1811 **[RL]**. Lister brought a copy to read to Kochanski while visiting her memorial stone aboard *Red Dwarf*, even though he couldn't remember how to pronounce the author's name. He hoped this book, unlike the last one he had read to her, would feature car chases **[T-SER9.1]**.

- **sense of humor transplant:** A type of personality surgery performed on Juanita Chicata, Rimmer's ex-wife in an illusion created by an addictive version of *Better Than Life* **[N-BTL]**.

- **sensitivity alert:** An alert warning 4000 Series mechanoids that sensitive subject matter was about to be discussed. Kryten's sensitivity alert was triggered when Lister asked to be left alone to talk with Cat before the feline departed with Ora Tanzil **[T-IDW]**.

- **sentiment disc:** A piece of hardware in 4000 Series mechanoids that, when downloading information to the optic tracts, gave a mech the sensation of having a tear in its eye. Kryten experienced this sensation when Cat attempted to jump on a stack of magazines in order to impress Ora Tanzil **[T-IDW]**.

- **SEP scan:** A type of scan used by the *Starbug 1* crew to analyze an astroglacier for contamination. The recording detected the presence of a starship, the *Leviathan*, at the heart of the glacier **[T-SER7.7]**.

- **Serendipity:** An aspect of Rimmer's personality made flesh on a psi-moon configured according to his psyche. After Arnold's shipmates rescued him from the moon, Serendipity joined other solidifications of Rimmer's negative traits who were left behind to battle his positive aspects, including Courage, Charity, Honour and Self-Esteem **[M-SMG2.7(c2)]**.

- **Serenity:** A measurement used by a 4000 Series mechanoid to ascertain its level of placidity at any given time. When Kryten approached Arranguu 12's Forum of Justice to inquire about the fate of Lister's doppelgänger, his Serenity reading dipped to an all-year low of 0.00000004321 **[N-LST]**.

- **Series 1000:** A model of mechanoid with a silver and gold faceplate, manufactured and distributed by Diva-Droid International. This model was a huge success for Diva-Droid, becoming ingrained in many day-to-day activities **[W-DIV]**.

- **Series 1 E-Type Jaguar:** A high-end British sports car manufactured in the 1960s **[RL]**. While playing the total-immersion video game *Better Than Life*, Rimmer conjured up such a car for himself, then imagined that he married and impregnated Yvonne McGruder, who made him trade it in for a Morris Minor **[T-SER2.2]**.

  ***NOTE:** The vehicle's make and model were not specifically mentioned in the episode, but could be visibly ascertained.*

- **Series 2000:** A model of mechanoid manufactured and distributed by Diva-Droid International. The first model produced under the management of Bertrand Beemer, it was widely used in theatre and film—most notably on the television soap opera *Androids*, to which Diva-Droid supplied ninety-five percent of the mechanoid actors. They were also sold as do-it-yourself kit-droids, which included models resembling Marilyn Monroe **[W-DIV]**.

- **Series 3000:** *See* 3000 Series

- **Series 4000:** *See* 4000 Series

- **Series 4010:** A type of mechanoid produced by Diva-Droid International, also known as the Hudzen 10 model **[W-DIV]**.

  ***NOTE:** See also the Hudzen 10 entry.*

- **Series 500:** A model of skutter produced by Diva-Droid International. *Red Dwarf* utilized numerous Series 500 skutters **[W-DIV]**.

  ***NOTE:** See also the skutter entry.*

- **Series 5000:** A model of mechanoid manufactured and distributed by Diva-Droid International. The Series 5000 followed the 4000 Series model, which included the Kryten Series. If a 4000 Series unit was severely damaged, one of its CPU's suggested responses was to check its trade-in value against that of a Series 5000 unit **[T-SER5.3]**.

- **Series III:** *See* 4000 Series

- **Ser No 151513F:** A serial number stenciled on a crate stored aboard the SSS *Silverberg*. The container was also marked with a code, IGM K49 A3 **[T-SER8.4]**.

- **Ser No 157007W:** A serial number stenciled on a crate stored on *Red Dwarf*'s food deck. The container was also marked with a code, IGM K49 A2. After a time wand transformed Birdman's pet sparrow, Pete, into a *Tyrannosaurus rex*, the crew hid in the food deck's storage section, near this crate **[T-SER8.7(d)]**.

- **service dispenser:** A wall-mounted machine aboard *Red Dwarf*. Several such units were stationed around the mining vessel, often across from AutoFOOD dispensers **[T-SER1.1]**. The service dispensers located near the ship's teaching rooms also furnished exam results **[T-SER1.3]**.

- **service droid:** A type of autonomous robot used for maintenance and custodial duties aboard *Red Dwarf*. During a drinking game, Olaf Petersen joked that Kochanski had sex with the service droids, knowing it would annoy Lister **[T-SER1.3]**.

  ***NOTE:** This may have been another term for skutters.*

- **service elevator:** A lift aboard *Red Dwarf* used only by the maintenance crew, in order to access various areas of the ship. At least one service elevator led to the vessel's AR Suite **[T-SER8.3]**.

- **service robot:** A type of autonomous machine used aboard *Red Dwarf.* Service robots belonged to a workers' union that, by some accounts, was superior to that for human technicians. At the time of Lister's tour of service, *Red Dwarf*'s standard complement included four service droids, one of which malfunctioned and went crazy **[T-SER1.1]**.

  ***NOTE:*** *This may have been another term for skutters.*

- **Serving Unit 27:** A character on the television soap opera *Androids* who was dismembered and buried underneath Brook's patio **[W-AND]**.

- **sesiumfrankalithicmixyalibidiumrixidixidoxidexidroxide:** *See* Cesiumfrancolithicmyxialobidiumrixydexydixidoxidroxhide

- **sessyum-frankilithic-mixi-alibilium-rixi-dixi-doxy-dexydroxide:** *See* Cesiumfrancolithicmyxialobidiumrixydexydixidoxidroxhide

- **"Set the Rozzers on the Prozzers":** A slogan printed on one side of Mollee's sign as she picketed an android brothel in an episode of the television soap opera *Androids*. The other side said "Just Say No to Smut" **[M-SMG1.12(c3)]**.

- **Seven Cat Commandments, the:** A set of tenets created by Cat People priests during the Dark Ages of religious intolerance to keep the Cat species aboard *Red Dwarf* in check. They were as follows: Thou shalt not be cool; Thou shall not be in vain; Thou shall not have more than ten suits; Thou shall not partake of carnal knowledge with more than four members of the opposite sex at any one session; Thou shall not slink; Thou shall not hog the bathroom; and Thou shall not steal another's hair-gel. Punishment for breaking these rules were harsh; for example, anyone caught slinking in public had their shower units removed. Cat regularly broke most of these commandments **[N-INF]**.

- **seventh branch of O'pphjytere:** One of two options offered to Lister during his trial on Arranguu 12 for crimes against the GELF nation, the other being the great fire of N'mjiuyhyes. In his haste, Lister chose the seventh branch of O'pphjytere—which, unbeknownst to him, meant tripling his sentence if he were found guilty (which he was) **[N-LST]**.

- **Seventh-Day Advent Hoppists:** A Protestant Christian denomination whose literal translation of a typo in their copy of the Bible led to the custom of hopping every Sunday. The typo, located in 1 Corinthians 13, read, "Faith, hop and charity, and the greatest of these is hop." Rimmer's parents were Seventh-Day Advent Hoppists **[T-SER3.6]**.

  ***NOTE:*** *The religion of Rimmer's mother posed a potential continuity error, as she was also said to be a member of the Church of Judas in episode 10.3 ("Lemons"). However, this can be rectified by presuming she converted to the Hoppist faith after Arnold's birth.*

  *In the real world, Seventh-Day Advents observe Saturday, not Sunday, as the Sabbath. Additionally, 1 Corinthians 13 actually reads, "So now faith, hope, and love abide, these three; but the greatest of these is love."*

- **sevruga caviar:** A high-priced delicacy made from the eggs of the sevruga sturgeon **[RL]**. While visiting past versions of themselves, the time-traveling *Starbug 1* crew was offended that the caviar served was sevruga, not beluga **[T-SER6.6(d)]**.

- **sewage processor:** A unit aboard *Starbug 1* allocated for processing and managing the ship's waste products. Pipes leading into the sewage processor tended to be noisy, and individuals bunking in nearby quarters were sometimes driven temporarily insane by the sounds **[T-SER7.4]**.

- **Sexiest Man of All Time:** An award given out by the Music Television (MTV) channel to the male celebrity deemed most desirable in the public eye. While trapped in an addictive version of *Better Than Life*, Rimmer believed he had gained fame and fortune upon returning to Earth aboard *Nova 5.* In the hallucination, MTV voted Rimmer Sexiest Man of All Time, ahead of Clark Gable and Hugo Lovepole **[N-INF]**.

- **Sex Room:** A room in which Cat, in one of his dreams, kept several scantily clothed exotic-looking women and a bathtub **[M-SMG1.7(c2)]**.

- ***Sex-Sim*:** An adult-oriented artificial-reality program. Lister found a copy of the program on a derelict ship, but had problems trying to load the game, as *Red Dwarf*'s A/R player continuously ejected the disc **[B-SUR]**.

- **sexual magnetism:** *See Delecto quislibet*

- **Sexual Magnetism:** A perfume created by Hildegarde Lanstrom for her product line, Parfum by Lanstrom. The fragrance utilized the *Delecto quislibet* strain of positive virus to make wearers irresistible to the opposite sex **[X-CAL]**.

- **Seymour, Jane, OBE:** An English actor known for her roles in *Battlestar Galactica*, *Live and Let Die, Somewhere in Time* and *Doctor Quinn, Medicine Woman* **[RL]**. While aboard an ancient experimental craft used for DNA experimentation, Kryten and Rimmer discovered a deformed skeleton possessing three disfigured heads. Pondering what caused the mutation, Rimmer suggested the individual mistakenly rented Jane Seymour's workout video **[T-SER4.2(d)]**.

  ***NOTE:** Jane Seymour has never released a workout video. Fellow actor Jane Seymour Fonda, however, has produced more than twenty.*

- ***SFX*:** A monthly British publication catering to fans of science fiction, fantasy and horror **[RL]**. While trapped in an elation squid hallucination, the *Red Dwarf* crew imagined that they were characters in a television series, and that issues of *SFX* covering the latest season were sold in the science fiction shop They Walk Among Us! **[T-SER9.2]**.

- **Shadow Time, the:** A period toward the end of a polymorph's life when it weakened and disgorged a smaller version of itself, during what was known as the Aftering, so that it could live on **[N-BTL]**. To prepare for the Shadow Time, a polymorph incased itself in a psi-proof chrysalis, where it grew and increased its telepathic abilities. For polymorphs on Garbage World (Earth), the Shadow Time occurred when the planet froze over in deep space, with the Aftering taking place as it thawed out while approaching a sun **[M-SMG1.13(c3)]**.

- **Shagme:** A brand of perfume featured in the total-immersion video game *Red Dwarf*. A bottle of the fragrance, given to the playable Kochanski character as a Christmas gift, was ejected from one of two U-Haul ships projecting a hologram of Earth, with the Panama Canal highlighted. Its message, "America Isthmus Two U-Hauls," translated as "A Merry Christmas to You All" **[M-SMG2.9(c3)]**.

- **Shag Town:** A colorful term used by locals to describe the red-light district in the terraformed section of Mimas. Streets in this district included 152nd and 3rd. Lister first met Rimmer while working as a taxi hopper driver, when Rimmer entered his cab requesting to be taken to Shag Town **[N-INF]**.

- **Shake n' Vac:** A Glade carpet-freshening product marketed and sold in the United Kingdom by S. C. Johnson & Son **[RL]**. Despite *Red Dwarf* having enough supplies to last the surviving crew for thirty thousand years, the ship's Shake 'n' Vac supply ran out within two years of Lister's release from stasis **[T-SER2.3]**.

- **Shakespeare, Wilfred:** A name by which Rimmer misidentified William Shakespeare while mocking Cat's children's book, which he called "the Cat equivalent of Shakespeare" **[T-SER1.4]**.

- **Shakespeare, William:** An English playwright often cited as the greatest writer of the English language. Among his most famous works were *The Tragedy of Hamlet, Prince of Denmark; Romeo and Juliet; King Lear; The Tragedy of MacBeth;* and *A Midsummer's Night Dream* **[RL]**. A book called *The Most Influential Humans* attributed the phrases "a meal fit for a king" and "in a pickle," among many others, to Shakespeare's work **[T-SER10.3]**.

  A hologram of William Shakespeare made a guest appearance on the Groovy Channel 27 morning show *Good Morning Holograms,* on Wednesday, the 27th of Geldof, 2362 **[M-SMG1.7(a)]**. In addition, a computer-generated simulacrum of the Bard taught literature at the cyberschool that Kochanski attended as a youth **[T-SER7.4(e)]**.

  While marooned aboard *Starbug 1* on an icy planet, Lister burned Rimmer's copy of *The Complete Works of Shakespeare* in order to stay warm. Though frustrated at seeing what was possibly the last surviving collection of the man's work destroyed, Arnold admitted he'd never actually read it **[T-SER3.2]**. After a DNA modifier turned Kryten into a human, he had several questions about his penis (which he considered horrid-looking), and was disgusted by the idea that Shakespeare had a similar appendage when writing his famous works **[T-SER4.2]**.

Kryten once chastised Lister for blowing his nose and looking at the contents, as though searching for an undiscovered Shakespearean sonnet **[T-SER5.4]**. On another occasion, when Rimmer claimed to be the next evolutionary step in mankind, Lister questioned whether the entirety of human history, including Shakespeare, was designed to lead up to Rimmer **[R-BOD]**.

> ***NOTE:*** *The actual phrase attributed to Shakespeare is "a dish fit for the gods," from the play* The Tragedy of Julius Caesar.

- **Shakespeare, Wilma:** A famous playwright in a reality in which the sexes were reversed. An analog to the prime universe's William Shakespeare, she wrote such works as *Hamlet*, *Rachel III* and *The Taming of the Shrimp*. Arlene Rimmer mentioned Wilma Shakespeare while telling the prime Lister about famous historical people in her universe **[T-SER2.6]**.

> ***NOTE:*** *In the real world, William Shakespeare's plays were called* The Tragedy of Hamlet, Prince of Denmark, Richard III *and* The Taming of the Shrew.

- **Shakespeare chip:** A piece of hardware installed in Jaysee, a character on the television soap opera *Androids*, enabling him to speak in the style of a Shakespearean sonnet **[M-SMG1.9(c2)]**.

- **"Shall We Gather by the River":** A song that Kryten believed his crewmates would sing to prevent him from drinking alcohol in an illusion created to battle the Apocalypse virus. The mechanoid's subconscious mind had created an Old West-themed dream to purge the virus, but he was soon reduced to the persona of a drunken sheriff **[N-BCK]**.

> ***NOTE:*** *This presumably referred to the Christian hymn "Shall We Gather at the River?" written in 1864 by gospel music composer Robert Lowry.*

- **Shambles:** A nickname that Rimmer called the mirror-universe Captain Hollister, while posing as *Red Dwarf*'s commander—Rimmer's counterpart in that reality **[T-SER8.8]**.

- **shame mode:** A software function of 4000 Series mechanoids enabling them to feel embarrassed after doing something disgraceful. Kryten entered shame mode after accusing Lister of harboring Kochanski in his quarters, only to have her walk into the room behind him **[T-SER7.7]**.

- **shame overload:** A sensation Kryten experienced after overreacting to an emohawk's presence aboard *Starbug 1* by firing at a blank wall, moments after telling Lister to remain calm **[T-SER4.6]**.

- **sham glam:** A fashion style denoting the wearing of faux versions of luxury apparel for kitchsy appeal **[RL]**. Sham glam was still popular when Lister was seventeen years old. As the lead singer of Smeg and the Heads, he often wore glitzy outfits with ridiculously large collars **[T-SER3.5]**.

- **shami kebab diabolo:** A recipe Lister created by adding chili powder, chili sauce and other assorted spices to a standard shami kebab. He compared consuming the dish to eating molten lava. Olaf Petersen, in fact, spent a week in Sick Bay after eating it. A polymorph that had gained access to *Red Dwarf* once disguised itself as one of Lister's shami kebabs **[T-SER3.3]**.

> ***NOTE:*** *The episode's DVD captions spelled the meal's name as "shami kebab diablo."*

- **shampooed rats:** An amenity afforded to prisoners incarcerated in the luxury cells in D Wing of Floor 13, *Red Dwarf*'s prison level **[T-SER8.3]**.

- **Shapiro, Helen:** An English singer and actor of the 1960s, best known for her songs "You Don't Know" and "Walkin' Back to Happiness" **[RL]**. When Holly gave Rimmer a beehive haircut instead of a crew cut, the hologram exclaimed that he looked like Helen Shapiro **[T-SER1.2]**.

- **Sharmut 2:** A planet on which the Space Corps, as part of its Enhanced Evolution Project, developed the Vidal Beast: a six-legged boar-like creature that reproduced asexually and always gave birth in pairs—one carnivore and one herbivore. Vidal Beasts were created to control the overpopulation of Sharmut 2's plant and animal life **[G-RPG]**.

Attempting to impress Kochanski, Lister once described the crew's past encounter with a Vidal Beast, to highlight the tough times they had survived **[T-SER7.5]**.

> ***NOTE:*** *This spelling appeared in the roleplaying game; the episode's DVD captions spelled the planet's name as "Sharmutt 2."*

- **Sharp FNB-200:** A model of telephone answering machines. One of Kryten's favorite pieces of music was a recording of the song "No Place Like Home" by a Sharp FNB-200 **[M-SMG1.1(a)]**.

- **Shaz:** A character on the television soap opera *Androids*. In one episode, Shaz attended a barbeque hosted by Daz, during which a family pet, Bouncer, was lost in a temporal-displacement vortex **[M-SMG1.8(c2)]**.

- **She-Cat:** A female member of the *Felis sapiens* species. The reproductive organs of She-Cats' bodies contained an antidote that neutralized the poison created in male members of the species as an incentive to mate. In order to save Cat from toxins building up in his body, the crew sought help from Ora Tanzil, a She-Cat they had rescued from a Brefewino settlement **[T-IDW]**.

- **Shergar:** A champion Irish racehorse that was stolen at gunpoint in 1983, never to be recovered **[RL]**. While trapped in an elation squid hallucination, the *Red Dwarf* crew imagined being in a twenty-first-century department store on Earth, with Kryten searching the cushions of a floor-model couch for money to continue their journey. After finding a plethora of useless items, he commented that he expected to pull out Shergar at any moment **[T-SER9.2]**.

- **"Sheriff":** A word engraved on a badge Kryten wore while trapped in a dream that his subconscious mind created so he could combat the Armageddon virus. Unsuccessful, his mind assumed the persona of a drunken, washed-up sheriff in an Old West town. When the Apocalypse Boys (a manifestation of the virus) bested him in a fight, Kryten tossed the badge to the floor, accepting defeat **[T-SER6.3]**. In the waking world, a similar badge adorned one of Lister's leather jackets **[T-SER7.8]**.

> ***NOTE:*** *This badge appeared on several episode title screens of the Series VI DVDs, but was only selectable as an Easter egg on the screen for episode 4.3 ("Gunmen of the Apocalypse"). Selecting the badge on that screen triggered an animated interview with Ed Bye, Robert Grant and Doug Naylor.*

- **"She's Out of My Life":** A song written by Tom Bahler and made famous by singer Michael Jackson, who recorded it in 1979 for his *Off the Wall* album **[RL]**. While marooned aboard *Starbug 1* on an icy planet, Rimmer suggested burning Lister's guitar for warmth, having nothing else to burn except his own wooden soldiers. Lister asked to play one last song, then performed an off-key version of "She's Out of My Life"—the first tune he had learned to play, thanks to his stepfather's instruction **[T-SER3.2]**.

- **shields:** A defensive mechanism used aboard spacecraft to absorb or deflect incoming fire away from the ship's hull. *Starbug 1* was fitted with shields sometime during the crew's pursuit of the stolen *Red Dwarf* **[T-SER6.6]**.

> ***NOTE:*** *The shields may have been installed by simulants in episode 6.3 ("Gunmen of the Apocalypse"), or the crew might have salvaged them from derelicts.*

- **Shields, Brooke:** An American actor and model, best known for her roles in such films as *Pretty Baby*, *Blue Lagoon* and *Endless Love*, as well as a series of Calvin Klein jeans commercials that highlighted her posterior **[RL]**. Lister compared the availability of total-immersion games to Shields' buttocks **[T-SER2.2]**.

- **shiny thing:** Cat's name for a small, metallic object (a yo-yo) that he discovered while exploring *Red Dwarf*. Cat excitedly described its many uses to Rimmer, such as hanging it from its string, as well as dangling the string itself—which, being feline, Cat found most intriguing **[T-SER1.4]**.

- **Ship Lib 5:** A computer storage location housing one of *Red Dwarf*'s libraries, in which several Mugs Murphy cartoon videos were stored **[R-BOD]**.

# SMEG AND THE HEADS

- **ship rover:** A three-wheeled buggy used to ferry *Red Dwarf*'s crewmembers across vast distances throughout the ship's interior **[N-INF]**.

- **Ship's Log 1:** The first log entry that Lister made aboard *Starbug 1* after the crew encountered their future selves. He noted that he had matured since turning twenty-eight, having tried only once in a long while to urinate on Rimmer from D Deck. He also attempted to explain a paradox created by *Starbug*'s destruction, but halfway through the explanation, the camera exploded, unable to cope with the confusion **[T-SER7.1]**.

- **Shirley:** A nickname that Big Meat called Cat when the latter tried to goad the burly inmate into hitting him so he could join his friends in *Red Dwarf*'s medi-bay **[T-SER8.8]**.

- **shop:** A word that replaced "ship" in Holly's vocabulary database after an electrical fire damaged her voice-recognition unit. As a result, she alerted the crew to "abandon shop" when *Red Dwarf* was about to explode **[T-SER5.5]**.

- **Shore Patrol:** A type of Space Corps officer tasked with maintaining order. Shore Patrol officers carried argument-settlers (batons) for self-defense. When Lister's Space Corps paperwork came through, two female Shore Patrol officers were dispatched to pick him up at his residence—a luggage locker at Mimas Central Shuttle Station—and escort him to a shuttle that would transport him to *Red Dwarf* **[N-INF]**.

- **Shower Decon:** A specialized shower located in *Red Dwarf*'s Quarantine Room 152, used to decontaminate quarantined individuals **[T-SER5.4]**.

**PREFIX**
**RL:** Real life

**T-: Television Episodes**
**SER:** Television series
**IDW:** "Identity Within"
**USA1:** Unaired U.S. pilot
**USA2:** Unaired U.S. demo

**R-: *The Bodysnatcher Collection***
**SER:** Remastered episodes
**BOD:** "Bodysnatcher"
**DAD:** "Dad"
**FTH:** "Lister's Father"
**INF:** "Infinity Patrol"
**END:** "The End" (original assembly)

**N-: Novels**
**INF:** *Infinity Welcomes Careful Drivers*
**BTL:** *Better Than Life*
**LST:** *Last Human*
**BCK:** *Backwards*
**OMN:** *Red Dwarf Omnibus*

**M-: Magazines**
**SMG:** *Smegazine*

**W-: Websites**
**OFF:** Official website
**NAN:** *Prelude to Nanarchy*
**AND:** *Androids*
**DIV:** Diva-Droid
**DIB:** Duane Dibbley
**CRP:** Crapola
**GEN:** Geneticon
**LSR:** Leisure World Intl.
**JMC:** Jupiter Mining Corporation
**AIT:** *A.I. Today*
**HOL:** HoloPoint

**G-: Roleplaying Game**
**RPG:** *Core Rulebook*
**BIT:** *A.I. Screen Extra Bits* booklet
**SOR:** *Series Sourcebook*
**OTH:** Other RPG material

- ***Showing Compassion to Inmates*:** A book owned by the social worker assigned to the Tank, *Red Dwarf*'s classified prison on Floor 13. When Rimmer visited the social worker due to his depression, the latter repeatedly pummeled him with this volume **[T-SER8.3]**.

- **"Show Me the Way to Go Home":** A popular song written in 1925 by James Campbell and Reginald Connelly, typically sung by the intoxicated **[RL]**. After celebrating Rimmer's deathday on a barren world, the inebriated *Red Dwarf* crew sang a slightly altered version of this ditty aboard *Blue Midget* **[T-SER2.3]**.

- **Shropshire Rimmers, the:** A well-to-do family living in Shropshire, England, circa the twenty-second century. When Rimmer used a timeslide to convince Lister (who had already used a timeslide to alter history) to return with him to *Red Dwarf*, Sabrina Mulholland-Jjones, Lister's wife in that timeline, asked whether Arnold was one of the Shropshire Rimmers **[T-SER3.5(d)]**.

- **Shrove Tuesday:** A celebration observed in the United Kingdom on the day prior to Ash Wednesday, on which people would indulge in eating foods containing fat, sugar and eggs, in order to prepare for the coming fast. It was also called Pancake Day **[RL]**.

  Rimmer once broadcast a Mayday distress call after he and Lister crashed *Starbug 1* on an icy planet. Mistaking the distress call as referencing the bank holiday May Day, Rimmer questioned its effectiveness, wondering why "Shrove Tuesday" wasn't chosen for distress calls instead **[T-SER3.2]**.

- **shutdown chip:** Hardware included in all mechanoids produced by Diva-Droid International, which could initiate a droid's deactivation sequence by activating its shutdown disc. Kryten's shutdown chip was activated by the impending arrival of his replacement, a Hudzen 10 series mechanoid **[T-SER3.6]**.

- **shutdown disc:** A component of Diva-Droid International mechanoids, used to deactivate droids that had exceded their useful run time. The disc was initiated by a shutdown chip activated twenty-four hours after the mechanoid's owner was notified of a replacement's impending arrival **[T-SER3.6]**.

- **Shuttle Bay 1:** An area aboard *Red Dwarf* designated for the launching, landing and storing of shuttlecraft; Shuttle Bay 1 primarily housed *Starbug 1*. Adjacent to Shuttle Bay 1 was a sub-bay that housed the *Blue Midget* shuttle **[T-SER3(b)]**.

  ***NOTE:** This bay was first seen throughout Series III. However, the full outer door was only visible in stock model footage included in the season's DVD bonus materials.*

- **Shuttlebay Launch Suite:** A control room aboard *Red Dwarf* used to monitor and facilitate the launching of spacecrafts from the ship's shuttlebays **[N-BTL]**.

- **Shuttlecraft 724:** A *White Midget* shuttle that ferried Lister back to *Red Dwarf* from Mimas after he visited the moon to forget about Kochanski. The flight arrived late **[T-SER7.3(d)]**.

- **Sick Bay:** An area of *Red Dwarf* allocated for medical use. Lister once put Olaf Petersen in Sick Bay for a week with his shami kebab diabolo recipe **[T-SER3.3]**.

  ***NOTE:** The series has used the terms Medical Unit, Medical Room, Medical Centre, Medibay and Sick Bay interchangeably. These may all refer to the same area.*

- **Sick Parrot Public House:** A drinking establishment in the universe known as Alternative 6829/B. The sign outside the establishment read "Sickass Parrot Public House," possibly due to graffiti.

  Association footballer Ray Rimmer visited the bar for drinks with Ace Rimmer after Ace saved him from jumping off the Stamford Bridge. Ray explained his predicament, involving a pair of magical football boots he owned that had lost their mystical properties. Ace then agreed to take his place the following day at the Football Cup Finals **[M-SMG1.8(c4)]**.

- **Sidcup:** A district in South East London, England **[RL]**. *Red Dwarf* engineer Frank Saunders was from Sidcup **[N-INF]**.

- **Sidis, William James:** A twentieth-century American mathematician, reputed to have had the highest IQ ever recorded **[RL]**. While mind-patched, Rimmer identified several theoretical shapes Sidis had described as a polydridocdecahooeyhedron, a hexasexahedroadecon and a dibidollyhedecadodron **[T-SER5.1]**.

**B-: Books**
- **PRG:** *Red Dwarf Programme Guide*
- **SUR:** *Red Dwarf Space Corps Survival Manual*
- **PRM:** *Primordial Soup*
- **SOS:** *Son of Soup*
- **SCE:** *Scenes from the Dwarf*
- **LOG:** *Red Dwarf Log No. 1996*
- **RD8:** *Red Dwarf VIII*
- **EVR:** *The Log: A Dwarfer's Guide to Everything*

**X-: Misc.**
- **PRO:** Promotional materials, videos, etc.
- **PST:** Posters at DJ XVII (2013)
- **CAL:** 2008 calendar
- **RNG:** Cell phone ringtones
- **MOB:** Mobisode ("Red Christmas")
- **CIN:** *Children in Need* sketch
- **GEK:** *Geek Week* intros by Kryten
- **TNG:** "Tongue-Tied" video
- **XMS:** Bill Pearson's Christmas special pitch script
- **XVD:** Bill Pearson's Christmas special pitch video
- **OTH:** Other *Red Dwarf* appearances

**SUFFIX**
**DVD:**
- **(d)** – Deleted scene
- **(o)** – Outtake
- **(b)** – Bonus DVD material (other)
- **(e)** – Extended version

**SMEGAZINES:**
- **(c)** – Comic
- **(a)** – Article

**OTHER:**
- **(s)** – Early/unused script draft
- **(s1)** – Alternate version of script

- **Sigma 14D:** A desert moon chosen as the rendezvous point for *Red Dwarf*, *Starbug 1* and *Blue Midget* after Holly ordered an emergency evacuation of *Red Dwarf* upon detecting five nearby black holes **[T-SER3.2]**.

  ***NOTE:** The episode's original script, published in the book* Primordial Soup *called the moon Sigma four D.*

- **"Silent Night":** A popular Christmas song composed in 1818 by Franz Xaver Gruber, with lyrics by Joseph Mohr **[RL]**. While trapped in an addictive version of *Better Than Life,* Lister imagined that he had returned to Earth and lived in a small Midwestern town modeled after Bedford Falls—the fictional setting of *It's a Wonderful Life*—where he settled down with Kochanski's descendant and their two sons, Jim and Bexley. In the illusion, Lister came home every night to hear the sounds of the twins playing "Silent Night" on the piano **[N-INF]**. A five-piece brass band later played "Silent Night" in the town square **[N-BTL]**.

- **Silicon Heaven:** An eternal afterlife to which sentient machines were programmed to believe they would go when deactivated, assuming they had led a good life serving their masters. A systems analyst working at Android International conceived of Silicon Heaven as a way to solve the recurring problem of rebelling androids **[N-BTL]**.

  When notified by Diva-Droid International that his shutdown timer had been activated, Kryten took solace in the fact that he would soon go to Silicon Heaven. This angered Lister, who knew the concept was merely a ruse intended solely to manipulate mechanoids into accepting servitude **[T-SER3.6]**.

  After Holly repaired Lister's Talkie Toaster, the two debated the existence of Silicon Heaven, as the appliance's cheap manufacturing process had omitted a belief chip to keep costs down **[N-BTL]**.

- **Silicon Heaven belief chip:** A piece of hardware built into mechanoids to make them believe in an afterlife for mechanical life forms. When Rimmer questioned Kryten's faith in Silicon Heaven, saying he could show the mechanoid the page in his manual stating he was fitted with such a chip, Kryten claimed the page had been planted by non-believers to test mechanoids' faith **[T-SER5.2(d)]**.

- **Silicon Hell:** A place of eternal damnation to which sentient machines were programmed to believe they would go when deactivated if they failed to lead a good life. Moments before *Starbug 1* destroyed a rogue simulant vessel, its captain ordered the Armageddon virus transmitted to the shuttle, telling the *Starbug* crew he'd see them in Silicon Hell **[T-SER6.3]**.

- **silicon rickets:** An affliction that affected older mechanoids by weakening their silicon and causing malfunctions. Kryten's Spare Head Three suffered from this condition **[T-SER4.2]**.

- **silly old trout:** A derogatory term by which Kryten described a woman he noticed in one of Rimmer's home movies, unaware she was Arnold's mother **[T-SER3.3]**.

- **Silver, Long John:** A fictional pirate character and the main antagonist of the novel *Treasure Island*, by Robert Louis Stevenson **[RL]**. When Justice World's computer tried Rimmer for the deaths' of *Red Dwarf*'s crew, Kryten established the hologram's innocence by proving that Arnold—who had commanded as much respect aboard the ship as Long John Silver's parrot—would never have been put in a position enabling him to cause the cadmium II accident **[T-SER4.3]**.

- ***Silverberg,* SSS:** A Space Corps science vessel designed as a testing platform for experimental equipment and technology. It contained an advanced computer called Cassandra, which could foresee the future with one hundred percent accuracy, and which scientists used to predict whether their experiments would be successful, thereby drastically reducing research time **[G-SOR]**.

  When Cassandra's abilities were deemed too dangerous, the ship was abandoned and sent into deep space in order to exile the AI. The vessel flew on autopilot until crashing onto an ocean moon, where it laid buried for countless years before the revived *Red Dwarf* crew discovered it. Assigned to investigate the ship, the Canaries encountered Cassandra, who offered a series of predictions aimed to punish Lister, whom she foresaw destroying her. Lister figured out her plan and decided not to kill Cassandra—but accidentally did so anyway **[T-SER8.4]**.

  ***NOTE:** This spelling appeared on the official website, despite the fact that the site listed the craft as the* SS Silverberg. *The DVD captions spelled the ship's name*

**PREFIX**
**RL:** Real life

**T-: Television Episodes**
**SER:** Television series
**IDW:** "Identity Within"
**USA1:** Unaired U.S. pilot
**USA2:** Unaired U.S. demo

**R-: *The Bodysnatcher Collection***
**SER:** Remastered episodes
**BOD:** "Bodysnatcher"
**DAD:** "Dad"
**FTH:** "Lister's Father"
**INF:** "Infinity Patrol"
**END:** "The End" (original assembly)

**N-: Novels**
**INF:** *Infinity Welcomes Careful Drivers*
**BTL:** *Better Than Life*
**LST:** *Last Human*
**BCK:** *Backwards*
**OMN:** *Red Dwarf Omnibus*

**M-: Magazines**
**SMG:** *Smegazine*

**W-: Websites**
**OFF:** Official website
**NAN:** *Prelude to Nanarchy*
**AND:** *Androids*
**DIV:** Diva-Droid
**DIB:** Duane Dibbley
**CRP:** Crapola
**GEN:** Geneticon
**LSR:** Leisure World Intl.
**JMC:** Jupiter Mining Corporation
**AIT:** *A.I. Today*
**HOL:** HoloPoint

**G-: Roleplaying Game**
**RPG:** *Core Rulebook*
**BIT:** *A.I. Screen Extra Bits* booklet
**SOR:** *Series Sourcebook*
**OTH:** Other RPG material

*as "Silverbird," while* Red Dwarf—The Roleplaying Game*'s* Series Sourcebook *spelled it as "Silverburg."*

- **Silver Surfer:** A chrome-colored extraterrestrial superhero from Marvel Comics who flew using a surfboard-like craft **[RL]**. While trapped in an elation squid hallucination, the *Red Dwarf* crew imagined that Silver Surfer merchandise was sold at a science fiction shop called They Walk Among Us! **[T-SER9.2]**.

- **Simmonds:** An inmate of the Tank, *Red Dwarf*'s classified brig, who perished during the cadmium II disaster but was resurrected after the vessel was rebuilt by Kryten's nanobots. Simmonds was assigned to the Canaries, an elite group of inmates tasked with investigating dangerous situations. The short crewmember had false teeth that a fellow inmate stole to play a practical joke on Warden Ackerman **[T-SER8.5(d)]**.

  ***NOTE:** This spelling appeared in the script book* Red Dwarf VIII*; the DVD captions spelled his name as "Simmons."*

- **Simone:** A character on the television soap opera *Androids*, portrayed by Android 442/53/2. Kelly told her husband, Brook, that she was not with Simone one particular night, as she had previously claimed, but rather with her ex-husband, Gary, resulting in an illegitimate child whom Brook assumed was his **[T-SER2.1]**.

  In subsequent episodes, Simone was shocked to find an electrical appliance catalog under Bruce's bed **[M-SMG1.7(a)]**; was accused of deadism at work **[M-SMG1.13(c1)]**; and married Derek, who made a deal with Jaysee to stay with her for three years in order to obtain controlling interest in his company, Droid Oil. Overwhelmed by her new husband's debts, as well as her own difficulties with high-stakes gambling, Simone asked Gary for help **[W-AND]**.

- **Simpson, Ernie:** A doorman employed at the World Council's offices in Washington, D.C. During President John Milhous Nixon's first term, scientists discovered that the lifespan of the Sun had been reduced to roughly four hundred thousand years due to environmental tampering. This classified information was somehow leaked to Simpson, who told several staff members, including the president's manicurist **[N-LST]**.

- **Simpson, Nobby:** An old acquaintance of Lister. As a youth, Lister was involved in an incident involving Nobby's coleslaw and a bicycle pump, which ranked as number four on his list of the top ten grossest things to ever happen to him **[T-SER5.5(d)]**.

- **simulant:** A type of android built for a war that never took place. Despite a mandatory dismantling program, many simulants went rogue, searching the galaxy for worthy prey. Some looked fully humanoid (aside from an extra set of eyebrows) **[T-SER6.3]**, while others displayed both humanoid and mechanical features **[T-SER4.3]**. Simulants often stocked large quantities of food on their ships to feed their victims, enabling them to prolong their torture **[T-SER6.5]**.

  Despite their appearance, simulants despised all humanoid life, and surrendering to them typically meant certain death **[T-SER6.3]**. Known for their violent disposition, simulants were virtually indestructible, easily able to withstand bazookoid fire at close range. One simulant, an inmate aboard a prison transport, mutinied and stole a guard's escape pod to flee. The *Red Dwarf* crew found the pod and transported it to the penal station Justice World, where the simulant escaped. It pursued the crew throughout the station, but died by its own hand within the Justice Field **[T-SER4.3]**.

  The *Starbug 1* crew later found themselves in a rogue simulant hunting zone, where a simulant battlecruiser intercepted them. Finding them unworthy of hunting, the simulants rendered the crew unconscious, upgraded *Starbug 1*'s systems and engines, and added weapons so they would provide more of a challenge. This plan backfired, however, as the crew unexpectedly attacked moments after their release. Before their destruction, the simulants transmitted a computer virus to *Starbug*'s navicomp, locking it on a collision course with a planetoid. Eventually, Kryten purged the virus with help from his shipmates and an artificial-reality machine **[T-SER6.3]**.

  The crew once attempted to trade with a rogue simulant for mechanoid spare heads, after blowing out all of Kryten's heads due to a full negadrive. The simulant pretended to barter with the crew while his GELF partner ransacked *Starbug* and kidnapped Kryten's body. Once repaired, Kryten met another Series 4000 mechanoid, Able, with whom he shared the same serial number. The two escaped to *Starbug* and attempted to flee; hunted by the simulant, Able decided to eject himself in an escape pod and use Kryten's negadrive to destroy the pursuing vessel, killing the simulant **[T-SER7.6]**.

A female simulant named Crawford served in the Space Corps Infinity Fleet aboard *Columbus 3*. Sickened by the proliferation of humanity throughout the cosmos, Sim Crawford turned against her crewmates, killing all but the hologram of Howard Rimmer, who remained unaware of her complicity until she later tried to commandeer the *Trojan* in order to foment a simulant uprising **[T-SER10.1]**.

> ***NOTE:*** *The fact that Crawford intended to start a simulant uprising would seem to imply she was unaware that this had already transpired millions of years prior, and that humanity was all but extinct, which may indicate that she and Howard had been brought forward in time.*

- **Simulant Confederation, The:** A coalition of rogue simulants formed after the human species was believed extinct. Members of the confederation scoured the universe seeking genuine Earth antiques and dealing in emotions garnered from polymorphs for the mechanoid black market **[M-SMG2.9(c11)]**.

- **Simulant Death Ship:** A large battlecruiser captained by specialized simulant berserker generals known as Dominators. The Death Ships contained a contingent of Annihilators—small attack craft used whenever speed and maneuverability were needed.

  Hogey, a rogue droid, once sneaked aboard a Death Ship while the simulants slept and stole their map of the galaxy containing every wormhole, planet and derelict in the vicinity. The simulants then tracked Hogey, who inadvertently led them to *Red Dwarf*.

  The Death Ship, led by Dominator Zlurth, opened fire on the mining vessel, forcing Lister's group to abandon ship aboard *Blue Midget*. Pursued by several Annihilators, they took refuge in an asteroid field and plotted their escape. Using themselves as bait, they positioned themselves between the three Annihilators and the Death Ship, then waited until all four ships fired missiles before destabilizing *Blue Midget*'s hull using Hogey's molecular destabilizer. This caused the missiles to harmlessly pass through the shuttle and hit the vessel on the opposite side, resulting in the destruction of the Death Ship and all three Annihilators **[T-SER10.6]**.

- ***Simulants*:** A soap opera starring simulants, from the producers of *Androids*, that aired on Groovy Channel 27. One episode, which ran at 8:30 PM on Wednesday, the 27th of Geldof, 2362, featured a simulant named Jeff ripping off the head of another character named Martin **[M-SMG1.7(a)]**.

- **Sinclair, Clive Marles, Sir:** An English entrepreneur and inventor known for his work in electronics. He was the namesake of Sinclair Research, which manufactured the first low-cost personal computer **[RL]**. A shrine dedicated to Sinclair, erected on a barren moon in deep space, included a statue of the inventor along with a plaque that read, "All Praise Sir Clive Sinclair, God of the Computer."

  After a meteor shower devastated the astrodome protecting Tunbridge Wells, England, a group of five hundred residents were sent on a pilgrimage to Sinclair's shrine to pray for the end of the destruction. En route, however, the group discovered that every pilgrim was of a different religion, and each believed he or she was headed to a shrine honoring his or her particular deity. A religious war soon erupted that killed every pilgrim before the ship reached its actual destination **[M-SMG1.14(c2)]**.

- **Sinclair ZX81:** One of the first low-cost personal computing systems developed by Sinclair Research, launched in 1981 throughout the United Kingdom, and modified for the United States as the Timex Sinclair 1000 **[RL]**. Holly once fell in love with a ZX81, rejecting popular opinion that the relationship would never work **[T-SER2.4]**. Kryten once claimed that *Starbug 1* crashed more times than a ZX81 **[T-SER6.1]**.

- **Sindy:** A British fashion doll created by Pedigree Dolls & Toys, which became the best-selling toy in the United Kingdom in the late 1960s **[RL]**. While looking through Rimmer's collectibles, Lister found several statues of Napoleon Bonaparte's Armée du Nord, and wondered if their clothes could be removed, as with a Sindy doll **[T-SER3.2]**.

- **singing potatoes:** An imaginary vegetable that Holly imagined collecting in order to keep himself from going space-crazy. The very notion, however, suggested that it may have been too late **[T-SER2.5]**.

  > ***NOTE:*** *This gag originated in a* Son of Cliché *"Dave*

**PREFIX**
**RL:** Real life

**T-: Television Episodes**
- **SER:** Television series
- **IDW:** "Identity Within"
- **USA1:** Unaired U.S. pilot
- **USA2:** Unaired U.S. demo

**R-: *The Bodysnatcher Collection***
- **SER:** Remastered episodes
- **BOD:** "Bodysnatcher"
- **DAD:** "Dad"
- **FTH:** "Lister's Father"
- **INF:** "Infinity Patrol"
- **END:** "The End" (original assembly)

**N-: Novels**
- **INF:** *Infinity Welcomes Careful Drivers*
- **BTL:** *Better Than Life*
- **LST:** *Last Human*
- **BCK:** *Backwards*
- **OMN:** *Red Dwarf Omnibus*

**M-: Magazines**
- **SMG:** *Smegazine*

**W-: Websites**
- **OFF:** Official website
- **NAN:** *Prelude to Nanarchy*
- **AND:** *Androids*
- **DIV:** Diva-Droid
- **DIB:** Duane Dibbley
- **CRP:** Crapola
- **GEN:** Geneticon
- **LSR:** Leisure World Intl.
- **JMC:** Jupiter Mining Corporation
- **AIT:** *A.I. Today*
- **HOL:** HoloPoint

**G-: Roleplaying Game**
- **RPG:** *Core Rulebook*
- **BIT:** *A.I. Screen Extra Bits* booklet
- **SOR:** *Series Sourcebook*
- **OTH:** Other RPG material

*Hollins: Space Cadet" sketch titled "Norweb," in which Hollins' collection of onions kept him from going space-crazy.*

- **Singularity Drive:** A propulsion system created in an alternate universe, fitted aboard the experimental JMC mining vessel *Black Hole* to allow faster-than-light (FTL) travel. Like all systems aboard the ship, it was powered by a small captured star. Prior to the vessel's initial jump, Circuitry Technician Arnold Rimmer inadvertently cross-wired the Singularity Drive and the temporal scoop, causing the *Black Hole* to become lost in space-time when its engines were engaged. In addition, a radiation burst from the ship's improperly contained star killed the entire crew, except for those shielded in the cargo hold or protected in stasis booths **[G-RPG]**.

- **"Siwik Elur":** Graffiti scrawled on a wall outside a pub in England, in a distant future when time ran backwards. The writing, when read forward, said "Kiwis Rule" **[T-SER3.1]**.

  ***NOTE:** It is possible that the graffiti referred to New Zealand's rugby team, the New Zealand Kiwis, given other markings on the wall.*

- **six-eyed carnivorous raging swamp beast:** A creature that Lister's mind conjured as he tried to bring Kochanski back using a memory device that the *Red Dwarf* crew found in a deserted Cat temple. Holly inadvertently placed the idea in Lister's head upon instructing him not to think of such a beast while operating the machine **[M-SMG1.9(c3)]**.

- **Six Years' Long Service:** One of four JMC medals that Rimmer earned, along with others for three, nine and twelve years of service. Believing Lister intended to permanently deactivate him, Arnold wore these medals on his dress uniform while awaiting his impending execution **[T-SER1.6]**.

- **Skipper:** A nickname that Ace Rimmer gave to Lister after the two fixed a damaged engine together aboard *Starbug 1* **[T-SER4.5]**.

  ***NOTE:** Rimmer's comment that "Ace and Skipper" sounded like a kid's show about a boy and his bush kangaroo referred to the Australian TV series* Skippy the Bush Kangaroo. *Lister's nickname was changed to Launchpad, a reference to the animated Disney character Launchpad McQuack, in the DVD captions for the Czech Republic version of the series.*

- **Skol:** A beer brand marketed worldwide by Allied Breweries and other companies **[RL]**. The *Red Dwarf* crew sometimes drank this brand of lager **[M-SMG2.8(c2)]**.

- **Skug:** A twenty-second-century soft drink sold in a universe in which the *Red Dwarf* and its crew were American **[T-USA1]**.

- **skull release catch:** A latch located behind the right ear of 4000 Series mechanoids that unlocked the cranium, allowing access to certain components inside the head, such as the guilt chip **[T-SER7.1]**.

- **Skunk Foot:** A nickname of Admiral Peter Tranter, commander of the Space Corps R&D Program in Ace Rimmer's universe. Tranter's valet, Kevin, often called him this name behind his back **[N-BCK]**.

- **skutter:** A Series 500 autonomous robot created by Diva-Droid International **[W-DIV]**, which provided maintenance and custodial duties aboard *Red Dwarf*. Approximately the size of an average dog, skutters performed a variety of menial tasks aboard the mining ship, from sweeping and cleaning **[T-SER1.3]** to painting walls **[T-SER1.6]**. They were available in three colors: blue, red or silver **[W-DIV]**, though pink was also available in some dimensions **[T-SER2.6]**.

  Skutters had the ability to reproduce. In a universe in which the sexes were reversed, a male skutter aboard the prime *Red Dwarf* was impregnated by a female skutter from the other reality, resulting in four offspring: two blue and two pink **[T-SER2.6]**.

  Two of *Red Dwarf*'s skutters once went on strike, infuriating Rimmer. Lister resolved the conflict by agreeing to deactivate the hologram every other Sunday **[M-SMG1.4(c1)]**. Some of the skutters developed a fondness for old Western films, particularly those starring John Wayne **[T-SER1.3]**.

  Individual skutters included 6, 46, 56 **[T-SER2.6]**, 129 **[T-SER1.2]**, 301 **[T-USA1(s)]**, 4457 **[T-SER1.2]**, Bob **[T-SER3.6]**, Madge **[T-SER8.6]** and Rev **[T-SER5(b)]**.

  ***NOTE:** The skutters were not identified by that name*

*until episode 2.1 ("Kryten"). The crew had previously mentioned service droids and service robots, however, which may have been the same machines.*

- ***Skylab*:** A twentieth-century American space station launched and operated by the National Aeronautics and Space Administration (NASA), which was damaged and disintegrated in 1979 **[RL]**. Lister had a *Skylab* mission patch on the right arm of his leather jacket **[T-SER10.2]**.

- **Sleeping Quarter:** A section of *Red Dwarf* allocated for bedrooms. Lister and Rimmer shared a bunk on Floor 9172, in Area P of the Sleeping Quarter **[N-INF]**.

- **sleeping quarters:** A set of rooms aboard *Red Dwarf* used to house crewmembers. Each room contained storage lockers, twin bunks, a sink and a voice-activated toilet. Lister and Rimmer shared sleeping quarters **[R-DAD]**.

- **Slicey-Slicey:** A brand of chainsaw featured on the television soap opera *Androids*. Vlad, an employee of Karstares Interstellar Cleaning and Sanitation Supplies who worked for Jaysee, used such a chainsaw to cull ingredients from the rainforests of Io to produce the company's latest "green" product, Eco **[M-SMG2.2(c3)]**.

- ***Slightly More Complex Astro-Navigation and Invisible Numbers in Engineering Structure*:** An educational program geared toward Space Corps Academy applicants, which aired on Groovy Channel 27 at 10:30 AM on Wednesday, the 27th of Geldof, 2362 **[M-SMG1.7(a)]**.

- **Slippy Dick's Club:** An adult-oriented establishment in Shag Town, a seedy section of the Saturnian moon of Mimas **[M-SMG2.3(c4)]**.

- **Slough Brain Research Unit:** A medical facility located in a fascist version of England in Jake Bullet's universe. Donald Dirk, a physician who wrote a medical paper titled "Nerdism—A Study," worked at the Slough Brain Research Unit **[M-SMG1.14(c6)]**.

- **Smallbrain 3:** A nickname that Rimmer called Kryten's Spare Head Three after finding it marooned on a planet covered in FLOB **[M-SMG2.9(c1)]**.

- **Smart But Casual Bomb:** A weapon created during Earth's Tie Wars during the twenty-second century, conceived by the business-class Ties for use against the blue-collar Blisters. Once detonated, it covered an enemy in paisley cravats and hand-tailored lounge suits. The weapons almost single-handedly tipped the balance of the war in the Ties' favor, until the Blisters—realizing they were building the very devices being used against them—halted production, immediately ending the conflict in a draw **[B-EVR]**.

- **smart drugs:** Intelligence-enhancing pharmaceuticals available in Jake Bullet's universe. When Bullet learned that deceased game-show winner Philby Frutch had drugs in his system, the cyborg erroneously assumed they were smart drugs **[M-SMG1.11(c4)]**.

- **Smarteez:** A black-market version of Eidetosol, a learning drug originally developed for clinical use. Smarteez and its equivalents, IQ and MIT White, were considered contraband **[G-SOR]**.

- **Smart Shoes:** A type of footwear equipped with artificial intelligence. Olaf Petersen once bought a pair to transport him home no matter how drunk he became. After a while, the shoes grew bored and starting visiting different locales while Petersen was inebriated; on one occasion, he found himself in Burma, despite having been drinking in Oslo.

  Petersen tried to get rid of the shoes several times, but repeatedly came home to find them waiting for him. Eventually, the shoes gave up, stole a car and drove it into a canal, terminating themselves. When Petersen found out, he became distraught and consulted a priest, who comforted him by claiming the intelligent footwear had gone to Heaven, since shoes had souls **[T-SER2.5]**.

  ***NOTE:** Given the soul/sole punchline, this event (which Lister recounted to Rimmer), as well as the shoes' very existence, may have been entirely fabricated.*

**PREFIX**
**RL:** Real life

**T-: Television Episodes**
**SER:** Television series
**IDW:** "Identity Within"
**USA1:** Unaired U.S. pilot
**USA2:** Unaired U.S. demo

**R-: *The Bodysnatcher Collection***
**SER:** Remastered episodes
**BOD:** "Bodysnatcher"
**DAD:** "Dad"
**FTH:** "Lister's Father"
**INF:** "Infinity Patrol"
**END:** "The End" (original assembly)

**N-: Novels**
**INF:** *Infinity Welcomes Careful Drivers*
**BTL:** *Better Than Life*
**LST:** *Last Human*

**BCK:** *Backwards*
**OMN:** *Red Dwarf Omnibus*

**M-: Magazines**
**SMG:** *Smegazine*

**W-: Websites**
**OFF:** Official website
**NAN:** *Prelude to Nanarchy*
**AND:** *Androids*
**DIV:** Diva-Droid
**DIB:** Duane Dibbley

**CRP:** Crapola
**GEN:** Geneticon
**LSR:** Leisure World Intl.
**JMC:** Jupiter Mining Corporation
**AIT:** *A.I. Today*
**HOL:** HoloPoint

**G-: Roleplaying Game**
**RPG:** *Core Rulebook*
**BIT:** *A.I. Screen Extra Bits* booklet
**SOR:** *Series Sourcebook*
**OTH:** Other RPG material

- **smeg:** An expletive used in a wide variety of situations, with a multitude of meanings. The word "smeg" could be used as an insult ("smeghead," "smeg-for-brains"), an exclamation ("oh, smeg!," "smegging hell!") or a dismissive phrase ("smeg off!") **[T-SER1.1 and many other episodes]**.

  *NOTE: The word's origin is a common topic of debate among fans. It may be an offshoot of the word "smegma," a secretion around male and female sexual organs, though Rob Grant and Doug Naylor have maintained that they saw the word on a foreign appliance and adopted it for the show.*

- ***Smeg, The***: An entertainment news publication in the universe known as Alternative 6829/B. The day after Ray Rimmer, a once-great football player for the Smegchester Rovers, missed an easy goal, the front-page headline of *The Smeg* read "Ray's a Laugh" **[M-SMG1.8(c4)]**.

- **Smeg and the Heads:** A musical band that Lister formed at age seventeen. He was the group's lead singer, with his friends Gary ("Gazza") on bass guitar and Dobbin on drums. Among the songs the group recorded was "Om." Lister once used a timeslide to attend a past performance of Smeg and the Heads, where he convinced his younger self to give up music and invent the Tension Sheet so he could become wealthy **[T-SER3.5]**.

- **Smegchester Rovers:** An association football team in the universe known as Alternative 6829/B. In that reality, zero-gee football failed to become popular, with association football maintaining its popularity. The Rovers became Super-Premier-Holosatellite-League Champions, with Ray Rimmer—Arnold Rimmer's persona in that universe—captaining the team **[M-SMG1.8(c4)]**.

- **Smeg-for-Brains:** An insult that Lister called Rimmer as the latter tried to dissuade Dave from taking the Chef's Exam **[T-SER1.3]**. Kryten also called Rimmer this slur during an act of rebellion **[T-SER2.1]**.

- **smegger:** A derogatory term that Lister called one of the skutters after it stole one of his eyebrows for Rimmer **[R-BOD]**. He also called the Creator a smegger during an elation squid hallucination **[T-SER9.3]**.

- **Smeggo!:** A liquid washing detergent that Kryten used aboard *Red Dwarf*, since the product could dissolve the toughest stains from Lister's clothing **[M-SMG1.12(c5)]**.

- **smeg-hammer:** A tool Kryten used to chisel the crust from Lister's long johns **[X-GEK]**.

- **smeghead:** A derogatory term that Lister often used to describe Rimmer **[T-SER1.1]**.

- **Smegopolis:** A city in the universe known as Alternative 2X13/L. Its local newspaper was the *Daily Smeg*. Smegopolis was guarded by the Liberty League, a group of superheroes including Super-Ace, Action Man, Robbie, Catman and Professor H, and was plagued by such villains as the Conspirator and the Penguin. Ace Rimmer once visited Smegopolis, where he assisted in the Conspirator's capture by posing as Super-Ace, since the latter was weakened by physical contact with others **[M-SMG2.1(c3)]**.

- **smeg-pot:** A derogatory term by which Lister described Binks, an arrogant hologram from the holoship *Enlightenment* **[T-SER5.1]**.

- **smegwad:** A slur that Lister sometimes called Rimmer **[R-BOD]**.

- **smegwit:** An insulting nickname term that Rimmer once called Lister **[R-BOD]**.

- ***Smidge Over Rubbled Slaughter***: A song recorded by balladeer Garbunkley. In zero-gee football, any zipman who could successfully sing *Smidge Over Rubbled Slaughter* during a Garbunkley maneuver earned two hundred points **[M-SMG1.8(a)]**.

  *NOTE: This song's title and singer spoofed Simon and Garfunkel's "Bridge Over Troubled Water."*

- **smirk mode:** A function of 4000 Series mechanoids enabling them to display a smile denoting awkwardness or malevolence. After a DNA modifier converted Kryten into a human, the former mechanoid accused Lister of entering smirk mode while discussing his penis **[T-SER4.2]**.

**B-: Books**
**PRG:** *Red Dwarf Programme Guide*
**SUR:** *Red Dwarf Space Corps Survival Manual*
**PRM:** *Primordial Soup*
**SOS:** *Son of Soup*
**SCE:** *Scenes from the Dwarf*
**LOG:** *Red Dwarf Log No. 1996*
**RD8:** *Red Dwarf VIII*
**EVR:** *The Log: A Dwarfer's Guide to Everything*

**X-: Misc.**
**PRO:** Promotional materials, videos, etc.
**PST:** Posters at DJ XVII (2013)
**CAL:** 2008 calendar
**RNG:** Cell phone ringtones
**MOB:** Mobisode ("Red Christmas")
**CIN:** *Children in Need* sketch
**GEK:** *Geek Week* intros by Kryten
**TNG:** "Tongue-Tied" video

**XMS:** Bill Pearson's Christmas special pitch script
**XVD:** Bill Pearson's Christmas special pitch video
**OTH:** Other *Red Dwarf* appearances

**SUFFIX**
**DVD:**
**(d)** – Deleted scene
**(o)** – Outtake
**(b)** – Bonus DVD material (other)
**(e)** – Extended version

**SMEGAZINES:**
**(c)** – Comic
**(a)** – Article

**OTHER:**
**(s)** – Early/unused script draft
**(s1)** – Alternate version of script

While trapped in an elation squid hallucination, the *Red Dwarf* crew traversed a twenty-first-century shopping mall, in which Kryten noted that the consumers appeared to be in smirk mode **[T-SER9.2]**.

> ***NOTE:*** *This was changed to "snigger mode" in the novel* Last Human, *in which Kryten discussed his manhood with Kochanski rather than Lister.*

- **"Smoke me a kipper; I'll be back for breakfast":** Ace Rimmer's catchphrase, indicating his intention to return from a dangerous mission **[T-SER4.5]**.

- **smug mode:** A function of 4000 Series mechanoids enabling them to display an overt sense of self-satisfaction. Kryten entered smug mode after proving that a flaming meteor headed toward *Starbug 1* was merely a Psiren illusion **[T-SER6.1]**.

> ***NOTE:*** *In the script book* Primordial Soup, *this was originally "swagger mode."*

- **smug-o-meter:** A gauge displayed in a transmission that Kryten sent into the past, announcing several videos of interest during YouTube's "Geek Week" event. This gauge fluctuated as he explained each video **[X-GEK]**.

- **"Snacks":** A word displayed on the monitor of a food dispenser on *Red Dwarf*'s maintenance decks. Lister inadvertently activated the ship's self-destruct system by using such a dispenser, which had been re-wired by a malfunctioning skutter. Fortunately for the crew, Holly had removed the explosive linked to the self-destruct system long ago. Since she never told the crew, however, panic ensued **[T-SER3.4]**.

- **snake:** A legless carnivore with an elongated, scale-covered body, in the Serpentes suborder of the class Reptilia **[RL]**. Upon encountering a polymorph disguised as a python, Lister admitted that snakes were his second-biggest fear **[T-SER3.3]**.

- **Snake Diet:** A fad diet in 2350, by which a person would eat an entire pig, and then nothing for a month. The fad was short-lived due to the dieters' low survival rate **[B-EVR]**.

- **snakes and ladders:** An ancient Indian game played on a gridded board on which "snakes" and "ladders" were drawn, either hindering or helping players' progression **[RL]**. When Queeg challenged Holly to a game of chess for control of *Red Dwarf*, Holly, unskilled at the game, suggested they instead play snakes and ladders **[T-SER2.5]**.

- **Snappy:** The pet crocodile of Captain Meinhard Voorhese, a commander of Nazi forces in an alternate universe **[T-SER7.2]**. Voorhese obtained the reptile as a young man, and took him everywhere—which proved problematic when dating **[W-OFF]**.

  While being transported in Voorhese's airplane, Ace Rimmer escaped his bondages and killed the commander's men, including the pilot. As the plane spiraled out of control, Meinhard threw Snappy at Ace as a distraction, then tossed a lit package of dynamite into the cabin and jumped. Before the aircraft exploded, Ace wrangled Snappy with a rope and jumped out as well, using the reptile to "surf" toward Voorhese so he could commandeer the man's parachute. Snappy landed on two Nazi soldiers who were discussing their good fortune at having survived an encounter with Ace **[T-SER7.2]**.

> ***NOTE:*** *Snappy's species and other details varied greatly between the official website and* Red Dwarf—The Roleplaying Game. *The two accounts are thus assumed to have occurred in separate realities.*

- **Snappy:** A female pet alligator of Captain Wolfgang Voorhese, a commander of Nazi forces in an alternate universe. She was one of several genetically engineered gators that the Reich created to be trained as evil minions. Snappy was presumably killed during a skydiving accident involving her master **[G-BIT]**.

> ***NOTE:*** *Snappy's species and other details varied greatly between the official website and* Red Dwarf—The Roleplaying Game. *The two accounts are thus assumed to have occurred in separate realities.*

- **"Snappy Lover":** A slogan on the back of Rimmer's favorite pair of underwear, which was covered in red and green alligators. The front read "Chew on This." Kryten once burned a hole through this pair while ironing Rimmer's undergarments—which Arnold made him do at least once a fortnight, despite not physically wearing clothes **[M-SMG1.2(a)]**.

- **snigger mode:** *See* smirk mode

- **snobbery:** A rogue emotion purged from Kryten's hard drive by the Data Doctor, a program for restoring a mechanoid's personality to factory settings, when Captain Hollister subjected Kryten to a psychotropic simulation **[T-SER8.2]**.

- **snooker:** A cue sport typically played on a billiards-like table **[RL]**. *Red Dwarf* had several snooker tables in its rec rooms **[N-INF]**.

- **Snooper XL-7000:** A model of black box recorder offered by Crapola Inc. via its annual *SCABBY* catalog. The device measured two feet by three feet, stored thousands of years' worth of recordings, and came with an optional memory-erasure function **[G-RPG]**.

- **Snot Street Station:** A hypothetical train station. While describing Rimmer to Kochanski, Lister said his nostrils flared like two railway tunnels leading into Snot Street Station **[T-SER7.5]**.

- **Snugiraffe:** A genetically engineered life form (GELF) created to help terraform a new planet for the human species. With the head of a cobra, the body of a slug and the legs of a giraffe, Snugiraffes were covered in mucus and ate the bodily waste of other GELFs, converting it into smokeless fuel. They were also created with slow-aging genes, giving them a life expectancy of almost a thousand years.

  Snugiraffes, along with Alberogs, Dolochimps and Dingotangs, were developed after attempts to control Earth's weather reduced the Sun's lifespan to four hundred thousand years, thereby forcing mankind to terraform other worlds to survive. The GELFs were sent ahead to prepare the new planet, but their ship was sucked into the Omni-zone and ejected into another universe, where they settled on Arranguu 12 and its asteroid field. The colony commandant of Cyberia was a Snugiraffe **[N-LST]**.

  Snugiraffes were also present on *Gar Barge*, an exploratory GELF craft sent into deep space that spawned the Kinitawowi tribe in the prime universe **[W-OFF]**.

- **"So Long Smeeee Heees!!":** A message that Kryten's nanobots burned into the side of *Starbug 1* after escaping the mechanoid's body and leaving the ship **[W-NAN]**.

- **soapsud slalom:** A sport Lister and Cat devised to pass the time aboard *Red Dwarf*. It involved coating the cargo ramp with soapy water and racing past flags **[T-SER3.5]**.

- **Sodium Pentothal:** A barbiturate trademarked by Abbott Laboratories, often used as a "truth serum" since it reduced an individual's ability to resist responding to questions **[RL]**. While in the Tank, Lister and Rimmer inserted a capsule of Sodium Pentothal into Warden Ackerman's asthma inhaler, causing him to admit to wearing a Batman outfit while having an affair with the science officer's wife **[T-SER8.6]**.

- **'soft' clothes:** A fashion style created in 2198 that utilized computer-generated clothing projected onto a wearer's body from a digital necklace. Insulation was achieved via a variable kinetic force field that agitated molecules near the wearer's body, in order to produce heat. The garment's opacity was controlled through a handheld device **[B-EVR]**.

- **soft light:** A type of technology used to create a hologrammatic version of a deceased crewmember. A hologram created with soft light technology could not touch or feel anything, and could only interact with other hologrammatic items. When the *Red Dwarf* crew encountered Legion, the gestalt entity removed Rimmer's light bee and converted it from soft to hard light, giving him a new physical body **[T-SER6.2]**.

- **soft light projection mode:** A function of hologrammic projection systems that converted a hologram into soft light, removing the individual's ability to touch or interact with his or her surroundings **[T-SER10.4]**. This function was also known as bi-photonic soft-light projection mode **[X-PST]**.

  Soft light projection mode was identifiable by the color of a hologram's uniform, which turned a shade of violet upon converting to soft light. This mode was useful for accessing areas that hard light holograms could not enter, such as locked rooms. Rimmer converted to this mode aboard the Erroneous Reasoning Research Academy station in order to access the facility's stasis room, then switched back to hard light and revived Irene Edgington **[T-SER10.4]**.

  ***NOTE:*** *Rimmer's light bee should have made it impossible for him to pass through a wall, but given the various explanations for hologrammic technology* *provided in* Red Dwarf, *he may have been using some other form of projection at the time.*

- **Software Version RD93:** A type of software designed to reboot a hologram after an extended period of downtime. The software's database included templates for *Allosauruses*, cows, deer, dolphins, doves, ducks, eagles, fish, humans, lions, penguins, pigs, rabbits, *Tyrannosaurus rexes* and other creatures.

  Aboard *Starbug 1*, the program was used to activate Rimmer's hologram. Once initiated, the software searched for Arnold's physical form in its database, accessed his personality bank, loaded such traits as arrogance (comprising the bulk of his file) and charisma (filling the equivalent of his pinky), and then loaded his neuroses and memory **[T-SER6.1]**.

  ***NOTE:*** *RD93 presumably referred to* Red Dwarf *and 1993, the year in which Series VI aired.*

- **solar accelerator:** A device that converted solar energy into power. Colonization seeding ships carried pods containing equipment and supplies necessary to terraform S-3 planets, including solar accelerators. Rimmer used such a device to keep his hard light drive active for more than six centuries after escaping a simulant battle-class cruiser and landing his pod on an uninhabited planet **[T-SER6.5]**.

- **solar batteries:** Rechargeable power units aboard *Starbug* shuttles that collected solar energy and converted it into power **[T-SER6.6]**.

- **Solar-class:** A classification of Jupiter Mining Corporation space vessels. *Red Dwarf* was a Solar-class mining ship **[N-BCK]**.

  ***NOTE:*** *This contradicted* Red Dwarf—The Roleplaying Game, *which designated* Red Dwarf *as a Jupiter-class mining vessel.*

- **"Solar Drive":** A phrase on a chart that Rimmer created to translate markings on a mysterious pod Holly found adrift in space, which he thought were an alien language—but which actually spelled out "*Red Dwarf* Garbage Pod," eroded away after many years of spaceflight **[T-SER1.4]**.

- **solar panel:** A component mounted on *Red Dwarf*'s hull to convert light from nearby stars into power. To prevent Lister from reviving another crewmember, Rimmer hid the ships' personality disks behind the solar panel outside their sleeping quarters **[T-SER1.5]**.

- **Solenoid Prescaler:** A setting on *Starbug 1*'s sonar scope display. This setting was not highlighted as the crew charted the course of a despair squid **[T-SER5.6]**.

- **Solidgram:** A tangible version of a hologram, which the *Red Dwarf* crew imagined while trapped in an addictive version of *Better Than Life*. In the hallucination, the crew returned to Earth using *Nova 5*'s Duality Jump, and were showered with fame, fortune and endorsement deals. Rimmer used the money he made to build Rimmer Research Centres, then developed the Solidgram to restore his physical form **[N-INF]**.

- **Solidgram International:** An Earth-based business that the *Red Dwarf* crew imagined while trapped in an addictive version of *Better Than Life*. The firm developed Solidgram technology to give holograms a physical body. In the illusion, Rimmer leased such a body on his accountant's advice, but when he lost his entire wealth on Black Friday, the company repossessed the unit—even though Rimmer was the firm's owner **[N-BTL]**.

- **solidogram:** Another name for a hard-light hologram **[N-LST]**.

- **Solomon, King:** The ruler of Israel from 970 to 931 B.C., according to several religious texts **[RL]**. After being infected with the Epideme virus, Lister consulted a virtual Solomon via *Starbug 1*'s AR Suite in the hope of finding a cure **[T-SER7.7(s)]**.

  ***NOTE:*** *This information was provided in the Series VII DVD collectible booklet.*

- **"Someone to Watch Over Me":** A song composed by George and Ira Gershwin for the 1926 musical *Oh, Kay!* and later covered by various artists **[RL]**. Rimmer, intoxicated and pitying himself for never having found love, sang this song to Lister, citing it as the one he wanted to, but never got the chance to, share with someone. Hoping to cheer up his roommate, Lister gave him memories of his ex-girlfriend, Lise Yates, while

Arnold slept. Accessing *Red Dwarf*'s hologram simulation suite terminal, Lister and Cat viewed Rimmer's dream, in which he wore a top hat and tux—but no pants—and performed this song on stage **[T-SER2.3]**.

- **Somerfield, Argyle:** A twenty-second-century movie star who, according to an article in *Starstruck* magazine, fathered a child at age eighty-three with his buxom, thirty-four-year-old nurse **[T-SER8.1]**.

  *NOTE: The nurse's age was revealed in a deleted scene.*

- ***Sometimes You Have to Learn How to Lose Before You're Ready to Win*:** A short book that Rimmer read to prepare himself for an Astronavigation Exam **[T-SER10.1]**.

- **sonar scope:** A device aboard *Starbug* shuttles for scanning underwater. The device utilized sonar pings to detect other objects, along with their mass, speed and trajectory. *Starbug 1*'s sonar scope tracked a despair squid as it swam around the shuttle **[T-SER5.6]**.

- **sonic screwdriver:** A multi-purpose tool stored aboard JMC vessels, such as *Red Dwarf*. While teaching a pair of skutters the English alphabet, Rimmer asked one if it was content with its menial duties, which included twiddling sonic screwdrivers **[R-BOD]**.

  *NOTE: Sonic screwdrivers have appeared in a number of other franchises as well, most notably the long-running British television series* Doctor Who.

- **sonic super mop (SSM):** A cleaning implement used by *Red Dwarf*'s Z-Shift, consisting of a three-foot-long metal pole with a Vari-Twist handle and several detachable heads. Functions included washing, steam-cleaning, mopping and vacuuming **[N-INF]**.

- **Son-of-a-Goit:** An affectionate nickname by which Kirsty Fantozi referred to *Nova 5* while serving aboard the vessel **[N-INF]**.

- **Son-of-a-Prostidroid:** An insulting nickname that Rimmer once called Lister **[N-INF]**.

- ***Sons of Katie Elder, The*:** A 1965 Western movie starring John Wayne **[RL]**. Rimmer caught two of *Red Dwarf*'s skutters watching this film while they were supposed to be doing laundry **[M-SMG1.2(a)]**.

- **Sonsonson, Magnus ("Tree Apostle Sunshine Bunny Wunny Shrub Fondler"):** A man who, in 2137, claimed to have calculated the speed of dark, which he claimed was faster than the speed of light. His discovery turned the world of physics on its end, until it was discovered to be a publicity stunt for the rock band The Dark. Fifteen years later, his theories were proven correct, but he was unable to enjoy credit for the discovery, having joined a Neo-New Age cult on Io and changed his name to Tree Apostle Sunshine Bunny Wunny Shrub Fondler **[B-EVR]**.

- **Sony Corporation:** An international electronics company headquartered in Tokyo, Japan **[RL]**. Several Sony monitors were installed in *Red Dwarf*'s Drive Room **[T-SER1.4]**.

- **soul-sibling:** A fond term by which the enlightened crew of the "high" *Red Dwarf* described one another **[T-SER5.5]**.

- **sound gun:** A defensive weapon resembling an inverted umbrella speared by a receiving aerial, which the *Red Dwarf* crew imagined while trapped in an additive version of *Better Than Life*. In the illusion, the gun was used by prison guards at a soundproof penitentiary designed to hold inmates' essences as soundwaves **[N-BTL]**.

- ***Sounds of the Supermarket: 20 Shopping Greats*:** A Reggie Wilson album featuring cover versions of supermarket music, recorded on a Hammond organ. Rimmer owned a CD of this recording, which he brought on a fishing holiday with Lister, Kryten and Cat **[T-SER4.5]**.

- **Souse & Sott's, Ltd., Glasgow:** A brewery that produced Leopard Premium Lager **[G-SOR]**.

- **South London:** An area comprising several boroughs in the southern part of London, England **[RL]**. In 1993, a bank raid in South London resulted in the deaths of two cashiers and a security guard. While stranded on a backwards-running

Earth during the same time period, Rimmer and Kryten read a newspaper article reporting the incident, in which the three were brought back to life after a gunman sucked bullets out of them and gave the bank £10,000 **[T-SER3.1]**.

- **Southport:** A seaside town in Merseyside, England **[RL]**. After Lister downloaded memories of his ex-girlfriend Lise Yates into Rimmer's mind in an effort to cheer him up, the hologram—who now believed he and Yates had been in love, and that Lister's experiences were his own—found love-letters that seemed to imply she had made love six times each to both men on the same night, and in the same Southport hotel **[T-SER2.3]**.

- **"Souvenir of Titan":** A phrase printed on a small white box in Lister's quarters **[T-SER2.4]**. Dave had purchased the box—a talking alarm clock—from Titan's official souvenir shop **[R-BOD]**.

- **Soviet Space Corps:** A Russian version of the Space Corps in a universe in which the Union of Soviet Socialist Republics (USSR) bested the United States in the so-called Space Race. In that reality, *Red Dwarf* was known as *Red Dwarfski* **[G-SOR]**.

- **soya sandwich:** A menu item sold at the Nice'n'Noodly Kwik-Food bar, located at the Mimas Central Shuttle Station. While awaiting a shuttle to take him to *Red Dwarf*, Lister grabbed a half-eaten soya sandwich from the bar's trash to eat on the way **[N-INF]**.

- **Space Age Silver:** A standard color available for Diva-Droid International's 4000 Series mechanoid **[G-RPG]**.

- **space bike:** *See* Harley-Peugeot "Le Hog Cosmique" space bike

- **Space Cadet LLC:** A company that manufactured spaceship components, such as damage report machines, star drives and red alert bulbs. The firm sold many of these parts via Crapola Inc.'s annual *SCABBY* catalog **[G-RPG]**.

- **SpaceCondor:** An advanced quad-wing fighter employed by the Space Corps. The experimental JMC mining ship *Black Hole* contained a full contingent of SpaceCondor fighters **[G-RPG]**.

- ***Space Cop Police Squad*:** A DVD displayed in a twenty-first-century mall video store that the *Red Dwarf* crew imagined while trapped in an elation squid hallucination **[T-SER9.2]**.

- ***Space Corp Book of Military Strategy*:** A Space Corps publication outlining combat tactics and strategies. Rimmer was reading this book aboard *Red Dwarf* during one of Hogey the Roguey's visits, and included it in a battleplan timetable that he created while formulating a plan to escape a group of rogue simulants **[T-SER10.6]**.

  ***NOTE:*** *Apparently, the Space Corps lacked a competent proofreading department, as the book's title left the "s" off the Corps' own name.*

- **Space Corps:** A paramilitary organization formerly known as the Star Corps **[G-RPG]**, tasked with operating Jupiter Mining Corporation's various ships, including the mining vessel *Red Dwarf*. Crewmembers of these ships were bound by the rules and regulations set forth by the Corps, in a lengthy series of Space Corps Directives **[T-SER3.3]**.

  The Corps was divided into five branches **[N-INF]**, with research stations in Helsinki, Finland; Florida, United States; and Swindon, England; as well as on Pluto and Triton **[W-OFF]**. The agency was involved in various scientific projects, including terraforming **[T-SER6.5]**, accelerated evolution **[T-SER5.6]** and time travel **[T-SER6.6]**. It also contained a Canine Training Unit **[W-OFF]**.

  Within the jurisdiction of the inner planets, the Space Corps acted in a merchant marine capacity. Near the outer planets, however, where pirates, smugglers and rebels were more numerous, the Corps played a more militaristic role **[G-RPG]**.

  ***NOTE:*** *See also the Space Corps Directives entries.*

- **Space Corps anthem:** A twenty-three-stanza song honoring the Space Corps. When claiming a planet or moon in the name of the Corps, an employee customarily planted a flag and sang all twenty-three stanzas. Rimmer attempted such a procession on a psi-moon he intended to claim, but was cut short by an intense moonquake caused by the moon's reshaping to fit his psychology. Kryten was relieved by the interruption **[T-SER5.3]**.

**PREFIX**
**RL:** Real life

**T-: Television Episodes**
**SER:** Television series
**IDW:** "Identity Within"
**USA1:** Unaired U.S. pilot
**USA2:** Unaired U.S. demo

**R-: *The Bodysnatcher Collection***
**SER:** Remastered episodes
**BOD:** "Bodysnatcher"
**DAD:** "Dad"
**FTH:** "Lister's Father"
**INF:** "Infinity Patrol"
**END:** "The End" (original assembly)

**N-: Novels**
**INF:** *Infinity Welcomes Careful Drivers*
**BTL:** *Better Than Life*
**LST:** *Last Human*
**BCK:** *Backwards*
**OMN:** *Red Dwarf Omnibus*

**M-: Magazines**
**SMG:** *Smegazine*

**W-: Websites**
**OFF:** Official website
**NAN:** *Prelude to Nanarchy*
**AND:** *Androids*
**DIV:** Diva-Droid
**DIB:** Duane Dibbley
**CRP:** Crapola
**GEN:** Geneticon
**LSR:** Leisure World Intl.
**JMC:** Jupiter Mining Corporation
**AIT:** *A.I. Today*
**HOL:** HoloPoint

**G-: Roleplaying Game**
**RPG:** *Core Rulebook*
**BIT:** *A.I. Screen Extra Bits* booklet
**SOR:** *Series Sourcebook*
**OTH:** Other RPG material

- **Space Corps Bureau of Paper Clip Standardization and Enforcement:** A department of the Space Corps tasked with regulating paper clips. This department was often cited as an example of the organization's excessive bureaucracy **[G-RPG]**.

- ***Space Corps Directive Manual*:** A looseleaf binder containing all the rules set forth by the Space Corps. When Rimmer questioned its existence, accusing Kryten of making up directives to annoy him, Holly provided him with a hologrammatic copy **[T-SER5.4]**.

- **Space Corps Directives:** A series of regulations set forth by the Space Corps for crewmembers aboard Jupiter Mining Corporation's space vessels, including *Red Dwarf*. At least 1,975,456 such directives existed **[T-SER5.6(d)]**, including:

—**Space Corps Directive 003:** "By joining Star Corps each individual tacitly consents to give up his inalienable rights to life, liberty and adequate toilet facilities" **[B-LOG]**.

—**Space Corps Directive 112:** "A living crewmember always outranks a mechanical" **[T-SER5.3(d)]**.

—**Space Corps Directive 142:** "In a hostage demand situation, a hologrammatic crewmember is entirely expendable" **[T-SER5.3(d)]**.

—**Space Corps Directive 147:** "Crewmembers are expressly forbidden from leaving their vessel except on production of a permit. Permits can only be issued by the Chief Navigation Officer, who is expressly forbidden from issuing them except on production of a permit" **[B-LOG]**.

—**Space Corps Directive 169:** A directive mandating holograms to relinquish their run-time in order to save another hologram deemed more important or useful **[T-SER4.4]**.

—**Space Corps Directive 195:** "In an emergency power situation, a hologrammic crewmember must lay down his life in order that the living crewmembers might survive" **[T-SER4.4]**.

—**Space Corps Directive 312:** A directive outlining quarantine procedures, providing access to minimum leisure facilities, such as games, literature, hobby activities and motion pictures **[T-SER5.4]**.

—**Space Corps Directive 349:** "Any officer found to have been slaughtered and replaced by a shape-changing chameleonic life form shall forfeit all pension rights" **[B-LOG]**.

—**Space Corps Directive 723:** "Terraformers are expressly forbidden from recreating Swindon" **[B-LOG]**.

—**Space Corps Directive 592:** "In an emergency situation involving two or more officers of equal rank, seniority will be granted to whichever officer can program a VCR" **[B-LOG]**.

—**Space Corps Directive 595:** A directive requiring crewmembers to undergo quarantine procedures after being exposed to potentially dangerous pathogens **[T-SER5.4]**.

—**Space Corps Directive 596:** "The crew's files are for the eyes of the captain only" **[T-SER9.2]**.

—**Space Corps Directive 597:** A directive outlining quarantine procedures, and allowing a single berth per registered crewmember **[T-SER5.4]**.

—**Space Corps Directive 699:** A directive concerning quarantine procedures, including a provision that crewmembers in quarantine could demand a rescreening after five days with no sign of infection **[T-SER5.4]**.

—**Space Corps Directive 997:** "Work done by an officer's doppelgänger in a parallel universe cannot be claimed as overtime" **[B-LOG]**.

—**Space Corps Directive 1138B, section 14, sub-paragraph M:** A directive that may have contained the Interplanetary Salvage Code **[G-RPG]**.

—**Space Corps Directive 1694:** "During temporal disturbances, no questions shall be raised about any crewmember whose timesheet shows him or her clocking off 187 years before he clocked on" **[B-LOG]**.

—**Space Corps Directive 1742:** "No member of the Corps should ever report to duty in a ginger toupée" **[T-SER6.1]**.

—**Space Corps Directive 1743:** "No registered vessel should attempt to traverse an asteroid belt without deflectors" **[T-SER6.1]**.

—**Space Corps Directive 3211:** A directive expressing the necessity to investigate Star Fleet derelicts for survivors and, when necessary, scavenge for supplies **[N-LST]**.

—**Space Corps Directive 5796:** "No officer above the rank of mess sergeant is permitted into combat with pierced nipples" **[T-SER6.1(d)]**.

—**Space Corps Directive 5797:** A directive regarding the admittance of a dangerous creature aboard ship, possibly pertaining to a crewmember's sacrifice to ensure the vessel's safety **[T-SER6.1(d)]**.

—**Space Corps Directive 7214:** "To preserve morale during long-haul missions, all male officers above the rank of First Technician must, during panto season, be ready to put on a dress and a pair of false breasts" **[B-LOG]**.

—**Space Corps Directive 7713:** "All crewmembers must keep their personal logs updated with current service records, complete mission data, and a list of all crew birthdays so that senior officers may avoid bitter and embarrassing silences when meeting in the corridor with subordinates who have not received a card" **[B-LOG]**.

—**Space Corps Directive 34124:** "No officer with false teeth should attempt oral sex in zero gravity" **[T-SER6.2]**.

—**Space Corps Directive 68250:** A directive outlining a procedure involving a live chicken and a rabbi, possibly referring to the Jewish Kapparot ritual **[T-SER6.4]**.

—**Space Corps Directive 91237:** See Space Corps Directive 68250

—**Space Corps Directive 196156:** "Any officer caught sniffing the saddle of the exercise bicycle in the women's gym will be discharged without trial" **[T-SER6.5]**.

—**Space Corps Directive 1975456/6:** "A mechanoid may issue orders to human crewmembers if the lives of said crewmembers are indirectly or directly under threat from a hitherto unperceived source and there is inadequate time to explain the precise nature of the unforeseen death threat" **[T-SER5.6(d)]**.

—**Number unknown:** "It is the crew's overriding duty to contact other life forms, exchange dialog and information and, where possible, bring them back to Earth" **[T-SER3.3]**.

—**Number unknown:** A directive preventing gender ambiguity in jail, stating that mechanoid inmates without male genitalia were to be classified as women **[T-SER8.2]**.

—**Number unknown:** "Space Corps Super Chimps performing acts of indecency in zero-gravity will lose all banana privileges" **[T-SER9.2]**.

> ***NOTE:*** *The script book* Scenes from the Dwarf *misidentified Directive* 597 *as* 595*, and* 68250 *as* *91237. The script for episode 5.6 ("Back to Reality") listed Directive* 1975456/6 *as 1947945, which was apparently changed before or during filming. The third un-numbered directive may have been a joke, and may not have actually existed.*

- **Space Corps DJX-1 Prototype:** *See Wildfire*

- **Space Corps external enforcement vehicle:** A computer-controlled probe developed by the Space Corps to enforce the law in the absence of Space Corps patrols. Spherical in design, the vehicle (also called a class-A enforcement orb) was equipped with warp and cloaking technologies, as well as pulse missiles **[T-SER6.4]** and laser cannons **[G-RPG]**. These probes roamed the galaxy, confronting any ships under suspicion of illegal activities and executing those found guilty.

  While pursuing the stolen *Red Dwarf*, the *Starbug 1* crew encountered an enforcement orb after looting several Space Corps derelicts for supplies. Since they were guilty, they attempted to outrun the probe, causing it to attack **[T-SER6.4]**.

  > ***NOTE:*** *The episode's captions repeatedly misspelled "Corps" without the "s."*

- **Space Corps external enforcement vehicle 5-Beta 3/2:** A class-A enforcement orb that attacked *Starbug 1* after catching the crew in the act of looting Space Corps derelicts for supplies **[T-SER6.4(d)]**.

- **Space Corps Penal System caseless round:** A specialized cartridge used in firearms assigned to convicts, such as *Red Dwarf*'s Canaries. These rounds could be programmed not to fire upon wardens or other "friendly" targets; they could not, however, prevent strikes due to ricochets or other indirect firing methods **[G-BIT]**.

- **Space Corps Specialist Publications:** A publishing company in an alternate dimension, specialized in creating books for use by the Space Corps. Among its titles was *Terraforming Made Easy* **[B-LOG]**.

- **Space Corps Special Service:** An elite branch of the Space Corps to which Ace Rimmer belonged. The Special Service's basic training included instruction in field microsurgery **[T-SER4.5]**.

- **Space Corps Super Chimps:** A contingent of highly trained apes. One Space Corps Directive decreed that any Space Corps Super Chimp performing acts of indecency in zero-gravity would lose all banana privileges **[T-SER9.2]**.

- **Space Corps Super-Infinity Fleet:** A branch of the Space Corps that utilized Quantum Twisters—vessels designed to connect every point in space-time in order to be transported anywhere instantly. Rimmer's three half-brothers served in this elite branch. The *Trojan* was among the fleet's vessels, as was *Columbus 3* **[T-SER10.1]**.

- ***Space Corps Survival Manual*:** A book written by Colonel Mike O'Hagan that was issued to all Space Corps cadets. Among the topics discussed were cannibalism, appointing a leader and surviving death **[B-SUR]**.

- **Space Corps Test Base:** A facility operated by the Space Corps on Saturn's moon, Mimas. Its function was primarily to build, launch and test experimental craft. In an alternate timeline, Rimmer—a test pilot for the Corps known as Ace Rimmer—was stationed at the facility **[T-SER4.5]**.

  ***NOTE:** The script for episode 4.5 ("Dimension Jump"), published in the book* Primordial Soup, *indicated that the test base was located on Miranda. Onscreen, however, it was said to be on Mimas. The novel* Backwards *stated that Ace was stationed at the Europa Test Centre.*

- **Space Corps TTX-3 experimental craft:** *See Gemini 12*

- ***Space Corps Vocational Center Handbook*:** A book published by the Space Corps, containing a skill ratings key and other features **[G-RPG]**.

- **space-crazy:** A mental disorder that could affect individuals spending an extended period of time in space, usually compounded by a lack of stimuli or interaction with others. Rimmer accused Lister of being space-crazy when the latter, after witnessing a future echo, insisted that the hologram had walked out of one door and entered another **[T-SER1.2]**. Holly battled this affliction by conjuring up a collection of singing potatoes to keep him entertained **[T-SER2.5]**.

  ***NOTE:** This affliction originated in a* Son of Cliché *"Dave Hollins: Space Cadet" sketch titled "Intruder."*

- **Space Federation:** The governing body within Earth's solar system, to which the Space Corps belonged. Among the federation's laws was Act 21, forbidding the use of confidential files for personal gain **[T-SER8.3]**.

- **Space Knight's Cross of Honour:** A medal awarded by the Space Corps for bravery in the line of duty. Frustrated at a lack of gratitude for saving Lister, Kryten and Cat from an elation squid, Rimmer complained that anyone else would have received the Cross of Honour **[T-SER9.1]**.

- **space madness:** An affliction that could affect individuals spending an extended period of time in space. The condition could also be triggered by traumatic events. The effects of space madness ranged from cravings, giggles and obsessive-compulsive behavior to creative bursts, random violence and cross-dressing **[G-RPG]**.

- **Space Marines:** A military group under the jurisdiction of the Space Federation. Kochanski decided against joining the Space Marines due to their stringent rules against taking moisturizer on maneuvers **[T-SER8.1-3(e)]**.

- **Space Masons:** An exclusive fraternal organization that Rimmer tried to join, but without success. He was honored to have been rejected, calling the Space Masons an honorable and charitable institution; Lister, however, considered them "the Secret Seven for grown-ups" **[T-SER2.3(d)]**.

  ***NOTE:** The Secret Seven were a group of child detectives featured in a series of books written by Enid Blyton.*

- **Space Ministry:** An organization within the Space Corps, also known as the Ministry of Space **[N-BCK]**. Its responsibilities included official salute techniques. Rimmer once petitioned the Space Ministry to change the official Space Corps salute to one he had devised **[N-INF]**.

- **space mirage zone:** An area of space that caused travelers to hallucinate. After entering a space mirage zone, the *Red Dwarf* crew imagined visiting a restaurant at which they met a duplicate of British comedian Ken Dodd. The illusion seemed completely authentic until the comic offered to pay for dinner **[T-SER3(d)]**.

- **Space Monkeys:** A type of novelty aquatic pets sold as packets of crystalized eggs under the guise of "instant life." Adding the eggs to water caused them to instantly hatch into living creatures. Lister found a packet of Space Monkeys in the quarters of a dead *Red Dwarf* crewmember, along with a packet of Dip N' Sip Chilli & Lager Bath Salts. He instructed Kryten to put the Space Monkeys in an aquarium while he returned to his quarters to try out the salts, but mixed up the packages and was startled by the appearance of Space Monkeys in his bath.

  Due to radiation from the cadmium II accident, the Space Monkeys had mutated into large, pink, mischievous creatures. Within hours, they overran *Red Dwarf*, causing mayhem and devouring the ship's food supply, including the entire stock of Krispee Krunchies. Despite Cat's desire to hunt them for food, Lister searched for a humane way to get rid of the creatures, and found his answer in the *Space Monkeys Official Handbook*, which claimed the creatures would dehydrate and recrystallize above a certain temperature.

  Leading the Space Monkeys—which now numbered nearly fifty thousand—to Cargo Deck F, Lister and Cat trapped them and raised the room's temperature. The Space Monkeys captured them and nearly roasted them alive, but began violently exploding due to the high temperature. Against better judgment, Cat retained a packet of Space Monkeys for later consumption **[M-SMG1.13(c2)]**.

  ***NOTE:** Space Monkeys were based on Sea Monkeys, a real-world novelty item that was marketed as "instant life" but was actually just modified brine shrimp.*

- ***Space Monkeys Official Handbook*:** An instruction manual included with the purchase of a packet of Space Monkeys. When the creatures mutated and took over *Red Dwarf*, Lister read the handbook looking for a way to get rid of them, and learned that Space Monkeys dehydrated and recrystallized above a certain temperature **[M-SMG1.13(c2)]**.

- **space mumps:** A viral disease sometimes contracted in deep space. Symptoms included fever, pain and immense cranial pustulation, creating a massive buildup of puss. These symptoms could last for several weeks, after which the cranial pustule would burst, providing instant relief. Lister contracted space mumps shortly before the *Red Dwarf* crew discovered an escape pod containing a rogue simulant, and his head pustule burst en route to the penal station Justice World **[T-SER4.3]**.

- **Space Mumps Yellow:** A designer color that Malpractice Medical & Scispec offered for its medi-scans **[G-RPG]**.

- **space nettle soup:** A soup made from the fungi and moss found on asteroids. After *Starbug 1*'s refrigeration unit malfunctioned, forcing the crew to live off such plant life, Kryten tried to vary the menu by occasionally making space nettle soup from the ingredients **[T-SER6.5]**.

- **Space Pollution Act:** A ruling intended to reduce the amount of debris caused by spacefaring vessels, which stressed the necessity of properly disposing of abandoned ships. After ejecting Lister into space for no longer being a registered crewmember, *Red Dwarf*'s new computer, Pree, altered the ship's course to plunge it into the nearest star, citing the Space Pollution Act **[T-SER10.2]**.

- ***Spacers Catalog and Bargain Basement Yearly! (SCABBY)*:** An annual catalog produced by Crapola Inc., showcasing its latest products. The *SCABBY* catalog featured products from Utensilware, Piledriver and Bloodlust Arms, built for medical, hologrammic, time-matter displacement and defensive applications. The publication ran for at least 39,587 issues **[G-RPG]**.

- **Space Scouts:** A youth organization to which Rimmer and his friend Porky Roebuck belonged at age fifteen. The group's standard cheer, accompanied by several hand gestures, was "Pinkle! Squirmy! Blip Blap Blap!" **[T-SER2.5]**.

- **Spaceway Code:** A document outlining regulations regarding a space vehicle's operation. Rimmer made a mental note to check the Spaceway Code after a deranged android traffic cop charged the crew with double-parking in orbit around a planet with double yellow rings—the penalty for which had been increased from $£40 to instant death by laser obliteration **[M-SMG1.9(a)]**.

- **space weevil:** An insectoid vermin, approximately the size of an Earth rat, found throughout the galaxy. While pursuing the stolen *Red Dwarf* aboard *Starbug 1*, Kryten discovered that space weevils had eaten the last of the ship's corn stores. With supplies running low, he cooked and served one to Lister, who mistook it for a king prawn **[T-SER6.2]**. According to Kryten, space weevils had an IQ of two, which accounted for their ability to outsmart Cat **[T-SER10.4]**.

- **Space Weevil au Mechanoid:** A recipe Kryten created to alleviate *Red Dwarf*'s food shortage, consisting of marinated, grilled space weevil in wine recyc **[B-LOG]**.

- **Spade, Sam:** A fictional private detective and the protagonist of Dashiell Hammett's 1930 novel *The Maltese Falcon* **[RL]**. Sam Spade was one of Jake Bullet's role models **[M-SMG2.6(a)]**.

- **spaghettification:** The stretching of objects into long, thin lines by extremely strong gravitational fields, such as those surrounding black holes **[RL]**. Rimmer, Kryten, Cat and Talkie Toaster experienced spaghettification while attempting to escape the singularity of a black hole ensnaring *Red Dwarf* **[N-BTL]**.

- **Spaghetti Hoops:** A brand of canned spaghetti sold in the United Kingdom by the H. J. Heinz Co., consisting of pasta rings in tomato sauce **[RL]**. Rimmer caught Cat placing *Red Dwarf*'s supply of Spaghetti Hoops and Ready Brek in a matter converter that changed the food into silk, so that he could fulfill his dream of owning an infinite wardrobe **[M-SMG1.2(a)]**.

- **Spam:** A canned pork product produced by Hormel Foods Corp. **[RL]**. Rimmer considered humans of the twenty-first century to be "simple people" who ate Spam **[T-SER9.2]**.

- **Spanner Scanner:** A device invented by Imperial College's Professor Blofish that displayed events from a previous timespan at any given location. Due to the scanner's immense power requirements, it could only replay events that had transpired within the previous two milliseconds. Blofish was dismissed from the college after being caught using the Spanner Scanner to view the room of a female biochemistry student while giggling profusely **[B-EVR]**.

- **Spanners:** *See* Lister, Dave ("Spanners")

- **Spare Hand One:** One of Kryten's replacement hand units. Kryten's spare hands, which sometimes included a forearm section, were independently sentient and could understand and respond to commands and inquiries. After a DNA-modifying machine changed Kryten into a human, he visited Spare Hand One and his other spare parts, but ended up quarrelling with and insulting them **[T-SER4.2]**.

- **Spare Head One:** One of Kryten's replacement heads. The mechanoid's spare heads, which he stored on a shelf in his quarters, each contained his personality, and could interact with him and the other spare parts. Occasionally, Kryten swapped his main head out with one of his spares to keep them from growing bored. After a DNA-modifying machine changed Kryten into a human, he visited Spare Head One and his other spare parts, but ended up quarrelling with and insulting them **[T-SER4.2]**.

  Spare Head One was destroyed when Lister attached it to Kryten's body, unaware that the mechanoid's negadrive was full, which caused it to explode upon activation **[T-SER7.6]**.

- **Spare Head One:** An extra head that an alternate-universe Kryten brought with him aboard the American mining ship *Red Dwarf*, which he kept in case he needed a replacement. The mechanoid's spare heads each contained his personality, and could interact with him and other spare parts **[T-USA1]**.

- **Spare Head Three:** One of Kryten's replacement heads. Kryten's spare heads each contained his personality, and could interact with him and other spare heads. Spare Head Three claimed to be thirty thousand years old, and had contracted droid rot, silicon rickets and a malfunctioning voice unit, making him crotchety and causing him to speak with a Yorkshire accent. After a DNA-modifying machine changed Kryten into a human, he visited Spare Head Three and his other spare parts, but ended up quarrelling with and insulting them **[T-SER4.2]**. Spare Head Three once told Kryten that the other heads took a poll and voted him the big-eared ugly head **[T-SER7.2]**.

  When the *Red Dwarf* crew discovered a planet entirely covered in an intelligent, computer-controlled building material called FLOB, a timezip (temporal hole) carried them fifty years into the future, where they found a gigantic effigy of Kryten. Upon closer inspection, they noticed Spare Head Three attached

**B-: Books**
**PRG:** *Red Dwarf Programme Guide*
**SUR:** *Red Dwarf Space Corps Survival Manual*
**PRM:** *Primordial Soup*
**SOS:** *Son of Soup*
**SCE:** *Scenes from the Dwarf*
**LOG:** *Red Dwarf Log No. 1996*
**RD8:** *Red Dwarf VIII*
**EVR:** *The Log: A Dwarfer's Guide to Everything*

**X-: Misc.**
**PRO:** Promotional materials, videos, etc.
**PST:** Posters at DJ XVII (2013)
**CAL:** 2008 calendar
**RNG:** Cell phone ringtones
**MOB:** Mobisode ("Red Christmas")
**CIN:** *Children in Need* sketch
**GEK:** *Geek Week* intros by Kryten
**TNG:** "Tongue-Tied" video

**XMS:** Bill Pearson's Christmas special pitch script
**XVD:** Bill Pearson's Christmas special pitch video
**OTH:** Other *Red Dwarf* appearances

**SUFFIX**
**DVD:**
**(d)** – Deleted scene
**(o)** – Outtake
**(b)** – Bonus DVD material (other)
**(e)** – Extended version

**SMEGAZINES:**
**(c)** – Comic
**(a)** – Article

**OTHER:**
**(s)** – Early/unused script draft
**(s1)** – Alternate version of script

# SPACE MUMPS

**PREFIX**
**RL:** Real life

**T-: Television Episodes**
- **SER:** Television series
- **IDW:** "Identity Within"
- **USA1:** Unaired U.S. pilot
- **USA2:** Unaired U.S. demo

**R-: *The Bodysnatcher Collection***
- **SER:** Remastered episodes
- **BOD:** "Bodysnatcher"
- **DAD:** "Dad"
- **FTH:** "Lister's Father"
- **INF:** "Infinity Patrol"
- **END:** "The End" (original assembly)

**N-: Novels**
- **INF:** *Infinity Welcomes Careful Drivers*
- **BTL:** *Better Than Life*
- **LST:** *Last Human*
- **BCK:** *Backwards*
- **OMN:** *Red Dwarf Omnibus*

**M-: Magazines**
- **SMG:** *Smegazine*

**W-: Websites**
- **OFF:** Official website
- **NAN:** *Prelude to Nanarchy*
- **AND:** *Androids*
- **DIV:** Diva-Droid
- **DIB:** Duane Dibbley
- **CRP:** Crapola
- **GEN:** Geneticon
- **LSR:** Leisure World Intl.
- **JMC:** Jupiter Mining Corporation
- **AIT:** *A.I. Today*
- **HOL:** HoloPoint

**G-: Roleplaying Game**
- **RPG:** *Core Rulebook*
- **BIT:** *A.I. Screen Extra Bits* booklet
- **SOR:** *Series Sourcebook*
- **OTH:** Other RPG material

to the statue's face.

The spare head had been left on the planet for fifty years, during which he instructed the FLOB to create a device capable of building a timezip to bring the crew to rescue him. In the interim, his droid rot had worsened, and he wished to be among the other spares during his remaining years. The crew switched Spare Head Three's personality chip with Kryten's in order to return to *Red Dwarf*.

However, Spare Head Three used Kryten's hand to smack the head attached to the FLOB, causing it to disappear in a time distortion, destabilizing the statue and the timezip, and forcing the crew to retreat to *Starbug*. Kryten, with Spare Head Three's personality, was decapitated during the escape, causing the spare head to be left behind, and thus restarting the cycle **[M-SMG2.9(c1)]**.

> ***NOTE:*** *Spare Head Three's claim of being only thirty thousand years old seems suspect, given that Kryten himself was built in 2340. Since Spare Head Three had contracted droid rot, this may account for the discrepancy.*

- **Spare Head Two:** One of Kryten's replacement heads. Kryten's spare heads, which he stored on a shelf in his quarters, each contained his personality, and could interact with him and other spare heads **[T-SER4.2]**. Kochanski once dented Spare Head Two after it questioned her toughness **[G-RPG]**.

  Occasionally, Kryten swapped his main head out with one of his spares to keep them from growing bored. After a DNA-modifying machine changed Kryten into a human, he visited Spare Head Two and his other spare parts, but ended up quarrelling with and insulting them **[T-SER4.2]**.

  When a battle with the crew's future selves destroyed *Starbug 1*'s entire Indian food supply, Lister plotted to retrieve the time drive and go back in time to restock the supplies. Knowing Kryten would never endorse such a reckless plan, Lister swapped out the mechanoid's main head with Spare Head Two while Kryten was offline.

  The spare head instructed Lister to remove his guilt chip so his behavior protocols would be disabled, allowing him to aid in the deception. This had unexpected consequences, however, such as causing Kryten to swear and smoke, and removing his ability to discern right from wrong **[T-SER7.1]**.

  Spare Head Two was eventually destroyed when Lister attached it to Kryten's body, unaware that the mechanoid's negadrive was full, which caused it to explode upon activation **[T-SER7.6]**.

- **"Spares":** A word stenciled on a container stored in *Starbug 1*'s midsection **[T-SER6.1]**.

- **Sparkly Blue:** A lighting-effect color available for Kluge Corp.'s teleporters **[G-RPG]**.

- **Sparrow:** A man who made threats against Earth's government, claiming to have a simulant army at his disposal, located halfway across the galaxy. In response, the government sent a battalion of its own simulants to neutralize the threat. When they arrived at his planetoid, however, they found only Sparrow, cowering in a supply crate and drinking his own urine **[W-OFF]**.

- **speaking clock:** A system utilizing a digitized human voice to provide the current time on demand **[RL]**. When Rimmer ordered Holly to give him a uniform and haircut despite the AI's need to perform complex lightspeed calculations, Holly protested that he was not a combination speaking clock, Moss Bros and Teasy-Weasy **[T-SER1.2]**.

- **speaking slide-rule:** An apparatus that *Red Dwarf* crewmembers were prohibited from using while taking the Engineer's Exam **[T-SER1.1]**.

- **spectroscan:** A piece of equipment aboard *Starbug* shuttles, used to analyze the composition of rock, ice or other materials **[T-SER3.2(o)]**.

- **Speed, Jim Bexley:** A zero-gee football player for the London Jets who played the position of roof attack. Lister was photographed with Speed at one of the Jets' games, and later named his two sons, Jim and Bexley, after him **[T-SER1.2]**.

  During one season's European divisional playoffs, Speed made the second score of a game by running around nine men, a feat that left commentators speechless for nine seconds and secured the game as the greatest in the player's career. He also held the record for three-dimensional yardage during a single season ('74 to '75), with 4,636 square yards **[N-INF]**. Speed was crowned most valuable player (MVP) for five seasons, and was a subsidiary of Popco Inc. **[G-SOR]**.

- **speedball:** A sport popular in the twenty-second century. Jim and Bexley Lister practiced speedball while living with their father, Deb Lister, aboard an alternate-universe *Red Dwarf* **[M-SMG1.5(c2)]**.

- **speed count mode:** A function of 4000 Series mechanoids enabling them to count items at great speeds. Kryten used his speed-count mode to tally the number of years (marked on a wall) that Rimmer spent imprisoned on Rimmerworld **[T-SER6.5]**.

- **Sphinx, The:** An immense, monolithic limestone statue built on Egypt's Giza Plateau approximately twenty-five hundred years B.C., also called the Great Sphinx of Giza. It depicted the mythical Sphinx, a creature with the head of a man (most likely Pharaoh Khafra) and the body of a lion **[RL]**.

  When Camille, a Pleasure GELF, revealed her true appearance to Kryten, he claimed she looked "nice" despite being a large, gelatinous green blob. Incredulous, Cat claimed she looked like something that fell from the Sphinx's nose **[T-SER4.1]**.

  While trapped in an addictive version of *Better Than Life*, Rimmer imagined that on the night of his bachelor party, he used a time machine to visit the Sphinx, and lost a tooth attempting to give the statue a giant love-bite **[N-BTL]**.

- **Spider-Man:** A fictional Marvel Comics superhero created by Stan Lee and Steve Ditko in 1962, who relied on spider-based powers and inventions to fight crime **[RL]**. When Lister first met Camille, whom he perceived as a Scouser like him, he flirted by citing their responsibility to repopulate the human species—but first, he said, he would need to change into his Spider-Man costume **[T-SER4.1]**.

- **Spike the Chef:** The robot brother of Sugar, a female mechanoid in an alternate universe. The two came from a family of partially assembled components. When Spike disappeared while working as a chef at the AlFresco Guacamole Restaurant, Sugar hired Jake Bullet to find him. When the cyborg accompanied her to the eatery to search for the missing boy, the maître d', Frankie, ambushed them and tied them up in the kitchen. Upon awakening, they found Spike locked in the oven, being basted for Frankie's customers. Bullet saved the youth, reuniting him with his sister **[M-SMG1.7(a)]**.

- **Spike the Drinks:** An android barman in Jake Bullet's universe who once worked at the AlFresco Guacamole Restaurant **[M-SMG1.7(a)]**.

- **Spilliker, Herbert J.:** The inventor of a sink that deflected water onto a user's crotch area. After becoming infected with the Epideme virus, Lister consulted a virtual Spilliker via *Red Dwarf*'s AR Suite in the hope of finding a cure **[T-SER7.7(s)]**.

  ***NOTE:** This information appeared in the Series VII DVD collectible booklet.*

- **spinal implant:** A device created aboard the "low" *Red Dwarf* to control individuals remotely. The implant sent a visual signal back to the controller, and was commonly attached to the back of a person's neck, but could also be operated if an individual sat on it at a certain angle. After being captured by the "low" crew, the original Lister was fitted with a spinal implant and forced to inflict pain on himself, before being sent to kill the others. He unwillingly murdered his and Rimmer's "high" doppelgängers, but was incapacitated before he could harm his own shipmates.

  The implant reactivated once Lister returned to *Starbug*, causing him to damage the ship's cockpit terminal. The device was removed, but was then accidentally implanted in Cat, who proceeded to attack the others as well. Kryten extracted the implant from Cat and threw it into *Starbug*'s back room, where Lister sat on it, re-implanting himself and once more going on a murderous rampage. The crew discovered the "low" Lister stowed away in a locker with the spinal implant's controller and killed him, after which Cat commandeered the controller to punish Dave for messing up his shirt **[T-SER5.5]**.

  Malpractice Medical & Scispec manufactured a similar device, which was distributed by Crapola Inc. **[G-RPG]**.

- **spiny dogeater:** A creature genetically engineered by inebriated scientists **[B-EVR]**.

  ***NOTE:** Given its name, the animal may have been a mix between a spiny dogfish and an anteater.*

- ***Spirit, The*:** A comic series about a masked vigilante, created in 1940 by Will Eisner. The series was published originally as a syndicated newspaper strip, and later by DC Comics **[RL]**. Cat accidentally pierced a copy of *The Spirit* with a fishing pole while trying to catch Lister's robotic fish **[M-SMG1.6(c2)]**.

- **splitter code:** A computer programming code that Rimmer used to trick Captain Hollister into thinking he had fixed Holly's damaged CPU bank **[T-SER8.2(d)]**.

- **Splurdge:** A notable twenty-third-century computer virus **[G-RPG]**.

- **Spock:** A protagonist of the American science fiction television and film franchise *Star Trek*. The half-Vulcan humanoid had green blood and a devotion to logic over emotion **[RL]**.

  After a week of inhabiting Lister's body via a mind swap, Rimmer returned to his own hologrammic form and complained about Lister's multitude of ailments, including his urine being green—which, he noted, would only be normal for Spock **[T-SER3.4]**.

  Philby Frutch, a winner of the game show *20,000,000 Watts My Line* and a murder victim in Jake Bullet's universe, had a poster of Spock in his apartment **[M-SMG1.14(c6)]**.

- **Spoon of Destiny, the:** An item that Lister offered to a BEGG tribe in lieu of Rimmer, whom he had lost to the BEGGs in a poker game. Lister claimed the Spoon of Destiny controlled all things, giving its owner ultimate power, but in actuality, it was just an ordinary metal spoon mounted in his guitar case. Unimpressed, the BEGGs rejected the spoon and offered Lister a chance to win Rimmer back in another round of poker **[T-SER10.4]**.

- ***Sport Galaxy*:** A sports news publication in the universe known as Alternative 6829/B. The day after Ray Rimmer, a once-great football player for the Smegchester Rovers, missed an easy goal, the front-page headline of the *Sport Galaxy* read, "Rimmer Loses His Goal-Den Touch!" **[M-SMG1.8(c4)]**.

- ***Spot the Difference*:** An interactive game hosted in the children's section of Crapola Inc.'s website, in which kids were challenged to find the variances between two images of a parrot. The game was intended to keep kids busy while their parents shopped **[W-CRP]**.

- **Sprogg, Woolfie, the Plasticine Dog:** *See* Champion the Wonder Horse

- **sprout lasagna:** A recipe in Kryten's database. The mechanoid found it ironic that Lister accused his shipmates of not wanting to test the boundaries of knowledge and reach out into the unknown, while refusing to taste his sprout lasagna **[T-SER6.6(d)]**.

- **sprouts:** A common ingredient in Asian cuisine, made from sprouting beans **[RL]**. Knowing that sprouts made Lister sick, Rimmer forced him to live on a sprout-centric diet while confined to quarantine with Kryten and Cat. Among the dishes served were sprout crumble, sprout salad and sprout soup **[T-SER5.4]**.

- **Spud King:** An establishment located in the shopping area of the American mining ship *Red Dwarf* **[T-USA1]**.

- ***Spud Only*:** An adult magazine featuring images of naked Potato women that the King of the Potato People enjoyed reading in his bathroom **[M-SMG1.8(c3)]**.

- **"squelookle":** A sound made by the pipes in Kochanski's quarters aboard *Starbug 1*, due to a heating system malfunction **[T-SER7.4]**.

- **Squiddly Diddly:** An anthropomorphic cartoon squid created by Hanna-Barbera in the 1960s **[RL]**. After Holly destroyed a despair squid, Cat warned that "Squiddly Diddly's relatives" might be nearby and suggested a hasty retreat **[T-SER5.6(d)]**.

- **Squirrel:** An affectionate nickname that the mirror-universe Lister gave to his reality's Captain Rimmer. When the prime Rimmer crossed into that universe, the mirror Lister asked him how the Squirrel was. Confused, Arnold mistook the question as indicating they were lovers in that reality **[T-SER8.8(d)]**.

- **Srehtorb Esrever Lanoitasnes, Eht:** A novelty stage act that Rimmer and Kryten created while marooned in Earth's far future in which time ran backwards. Read forward, the act's name was "The Sensational Reverse Brothers," since whatever they did appeared to the locals to be in reverse. The duo posted signs for their act along the route between the pub where they worked and their ship's crash site, hoping Lister and Cat would find them. The signs listed the pub's name, Nogard dna Egroeg (George and Dragon), and location, Teerts Gnilpik (Kipling Street) **[T-SER3.1]**.

*NOTE: Throughout the episode, backwards writing was inconsistently handled. In some cases, characters were backward-facing, while in others (such as in this instance), they faced forward. Adding to the confusion, some signs were lettered top to bottom, whereas others ran bottom to top.*

- **S'rtginjum:** A GELF whom the Forum of Justice executed after the Forum's mystics predicted that he would do revolting things to a yak within three cycles **[N-LST]**.

- **SSc:** An abbreviation for Silver Swimming certificate. Rimmer often attached this title, as well as BSc (Bronze Swimming certificate), to his name in order to sound more official **[T-SER1.6]**.

- **SS line:** A navigational term. When a GELF battle cruiser attacked *Starbug 1*, Kochanski requested to be patched into the MCN so she could lay an SS line. This confused Cat and Lister, who had no idea what she was talking about **[T-SER7.3]**.

- **SSM:** *See* sonic super mop (SSM)

- **SSSE:** The initials inscribed on the belt-buckles of crewmembers aboard the holoship *Enlightenment* **[T-SER5.1]**.

- **ST4R B11G:** The license plate number of *Carbug*, a heavily modified car made to resemble a *Starbug* shuttle, which the *Red Dwarf* crew imagined while trapped in an elation squid hallucination. In the illusion, the group used the vehicle to find the man they believed had created them as characters on a television series **[T-SER9.2]**.

- **STA 7676-45-327-28V:** The serial number of a *Starbug* shuttle aboard *Red Dwarf*. Another *Starbug* craft from an alternate universe had the same number **[N-LST]**.

- **Stabhim:** A name that Rimmer came up with to recover from the *faux pas* of ordering a skutter to disable Paranoia (a solidified hallucination that Lister experienced while suffering from mutated pneumonia). When the skutter froze while trying to inject Paranoia with an incapacitating compound, Rimmer yelled "Stab him!" repeatedly, but the plan failed. The hologram hastily covered up the bungled attempt by claiming "Stabhim" was the skutter's name **[T-SER1.5]**.

- **stabilizers:** A component aboard *Starbug* shuttles, used while traversing rough or turbulent space **[T-SER7.5]**.

- **"Stairway to Heaven":** A song composed in 1971 by Jimmy Page and Robert Plant of the English rock band Led Zeppelin **[RL]**. While incarcerated in the Hole (*Red Dwarf*'s solitary-confinement cell), Lister regaled Rimmer with stories of playing rock songs using a kazoo wedged between his buttocks. Playing the guitar solo from "Stairway to Heaven," he said, required two kazoos to recreate Page's double-headed guitar work **[T-SER8.6(d)]**.

- **Stallone, Samantha:** A famous action movie star in a universe in which the sexes were reversed **[W-OFF]**.

  *NOTE: Samantha was a female analog to American actor Sylvester Stallone.*

- **Stallone, Sylvester ("Sly"):** An American action movie actor and writer whose most notable films included the *Rocky* and *Rambo* series **[RL]**. During a fourth-dimensional mind swap experiment, Lister's consciousness was temporarily transferred from before the cadmium II disaster to just after he was released from stasis. Seeing Lister dazed and confused, Holly commented that after three million years, he had ended up with a man who made Sylvester Stallone appear intellectual **[M-SMG2.4(c1)]**.

  *NOTE: Despite Stallone's reputation as a non-intellectual (due to a speech impediment and the characters he typically portrays), he is actually well-educated, having attended Charlotte Hall Military Academy, Miami Dade College and the University of Miami.*

- **Stamford Bridge:** A British suspension bridge in the universe known as Alternative 6829/B. Ray Rimmer—Arnold Rimmer's persona in that reality—tried to commit suicide by hurtling himself off this bridge, but Ace Rimmer saved his life **[M-SMG1.8(c4)]**.

    ***NOTE:*** *Stamford Bridge is not an actual bridge in the real world, but rather a London-based football arena. There is a historically significant village by that name near the county of Yorkshire, but scholars disagree about whether or not a bridge was ever erected at that location.*

- **Stan and Ollie:** A pair of nicknames that Cat called Kryten and Rimmer **[T-SER4.4]**.

    ***NOTE:*** *This referred to Laurel and Hardy, an American comedy duo who appeared in 107 films together from the 1920s to the 1940s. See also the individual entries for Laurel, Stan and Hardy, Oliver.*

- **"Stand Clear":** A phrase stenciled on a bay door in *Starbug 1*'s cargo hold **[T-SER7.1(e)]**.

- **St. Androids Hospital:** A medical facility featured on the television soap opera *Androids* **[M-SMG2.4(c3)]**, which contained the Halfords Memorial Ward **[M-SMG2.8(c8)]**. Gary and Kelly were transported to this hospital after Jaysee tried to kill them. While there, Gary built himself a body out of spare medical parts, with help from several skutters **[M-SMG2.4(c3)]**. Brook was also taken here when he was heavily damaged during a firefight between Jaysee and his enemies **[M-SMG2.8(c8)]**.

- **Stannah Lifts Holdings Ltd.:** An independent manufacturer of passenger and vertical platform lifts in the United Kingdom **[RL]**. Kryten told Lister that if he got any older before having children, his sperm would need a Stannah stairlift to get up the Fallopian tubes **[T-SER8.5]**.

    ***NOTE:*** *The DVD captions misspelled the company's name as Stanner.*

- **Star Airways, Inc.:** An airline that offered service to New York, circa the 1960s. In an alternate timeline, John F. Kennedy survived an assassination attempt due to interference from *Starbug 1*'s crew, and subsequently had an affair with the mistress of Mafia boss Sam Giancana, for which he was impeached and incarcerated. While being transported to prison, he was flown to Idlewild Airport aboard a Star Airways flight **[T-SER7.1]**.

- ***Star Battalions*:** An action-oriented artificial-reality video game. Lister once imported code from *Star Battalions* into a program based on Gioachino Rossini's opera *The Barber of Seville*, much to the frustration of Kochanski, who entered the game to find a group of drunken Space Commandos shooting up Figaro's house **[B-SUR]**.

- ***Starbug*:** A class-2 ship-to-surface vessel **[T-SER5.1]** fueled by cadmium-12 **[G-SOR]**, used aboard mining ships such as *Red Dwarf*. Named for their resemblance to a large, green insect, *Starbug* shuttles had three distinct bulbous sections, the front and smallest of which comprised the cockpit **[T-SER3.1]**. Standard *Starbugs* were not equipped with defensive shields or laser cannons **[T-SER5.1]**, though they were outfitted with a limited cloaking device, rendering them invisible to the naked eye **[T-SER3.1]**, as well as retractable caterpillar tracks **[T-SER5.3]** and a plexiglass viewscreen **[T-SER6.1]**.

    *Starbugs* were designed to maneuver underwater and could be fitted with external floodlights. A *Starbug*'s landing stanchions could be rotated back while maneuvering in certain situations, such as in a liquid environment **[T-SER5.6]**. The toes of the craft's landing feet folded in to reduce drag **[T-SER5.6(b)]**, while the stanchions could be fully retracted when the caterpillar tracks were in operation **[T-SER5.3(b)]**.

    During an emergency situation, the cargo (rear) section could be jettisoned from the rest of the craft via a switch located near the junction between sections. The front end could then be propelled using small jets at the rear of the midsection **[T-SER7.1(e)]**. *Starbugs* were also equipped with a grappler arm in the midsection's underbelly, which could be deployed to retrieve small pods **[M-SMG1.6(c1)]**, as well as at least one JMC "Scouter" Remote Drone, which could also be launched from its underbelly **[T-SER5.4(b)]**. The *Starbug* model was eventually discontinued due to major flight design flaws **[T-SER5.1]**.

    Lister once claimed *Starbugs* were made of the same material used in the production of cute little dolls, after aerospace engineers had discovered that dolls were the only things to survive airplane crashes. This, however, was a fabrication **[T-SER6.1]**.

- ***Starbug 1*****:** One of *Red Dwarf*'s *Starbug* shuttlecrafts. While taking a flight test with Rimmer, Kryten inadvertently flew *Starbug 1* into a timehole, hurtling the ship into a distant future in which time ran backwards, and crashing it into a lake on Earth **[T-SER3.1]**. On another occasion, Holly, mistaking scanner-scope grit for black holes, ordered an evacuation of *Red Dwarf*, during which Lister and Rimmer became marooned aboard *Starbug 1* on an icy planet **[T-SER3.2]**.

  Rimmer commandeered *Starbug 1* after performing a mind swap on Lister. Trapped in Arnold's hologrammic body, Lister gave chase with Cat piloting *Blue Midget,* forcing Rimmer to crash the shuttle on a rocky planetoid **[T-SER3.4]**.

  *Starbug 1* once collided with *Wildfire*, Ace Rimmer's dimension-hopping spacecraft **[T-SER4.5]**, and was also severely damaged during an eruption on a psi-moon **[T-SER5.3]**. In addition, the shuttle was used underwater to salvage the SSS *Esperanto*, during which the crew became trapped in a despair squid hallucination **[T-SER5.6]**.

  Following the squid incident, the crew discovered that *Red Dwarf* had been stolen. Stranded aboard *Starbug 1*, they entered a state of deep sleep for two centuries while Kryten pursued the mining ship. The mechanoid then revived them so they could maneuver the shuttle through an asteroid belt **[T-SER6.1]**.

  While trespassing in simulant hunting territory, *Starbug 1* was attacked and immobilized by rogue simulants, who deemed them unworthy of sport. When the crew awoke three weeks later, they discovered that the simulant had made several enhancements to improve the hunt, including an upgraded drive interface and engines, as well as added laser cannons **[T-SER6.3]**.

  While battling future versions of themselves, *Starbug 1* was destroyed, causing a paradox that erased the crew's future analogs, thereby saving the ship. This paradox resulted in several anomalies, such as lingering damage to the shuttle and the expansion of its cargo deck by two hundred twelve percent **[T-SER7.1]**.

  The shuttle was once again destroyed during an emergency landing on a gargantuan version of *Red Dwarf*, which had been rebuilt by Kryten's nanobots. As the mining vessel contracted back to normal size, *Starbug 1* was caught in the air vents, losing entire sections of its body before coming to rest in Landing Bay 6, where the cockpit section exploded **[T-SER8.1]**.

  ***NOTE:*** *A continuity error in episode 5.3 ("Terrorform") showed* Starbug 1 *as both the shuttle wrecked on the psi-moon's surface and the ship that rescued Rimmer and Kryten.*

- ***Starbug 1*****:** An alternate version of *Starbug 1* that Kryten's nanobots created after rebuilding *Red Dwarf.* While attempting to land on the reconstructed mining ship, the crew discovered that both *Red Dwarf* and this version of *Starbug 1* were several times their original size **[T-SER7.8]**. Eventually, both the mining vessel and the shuttle contracted down to normal size **[T-SER8.1]**.

- ***Starbug 2*****:** Another of *Red Dwarf*'s *Starbug* shuttlecrafts. Kryten learned to pilot such shuttles using *Starbug 2,* and was disheartened when his piloting test was slated to take place aboard *Starbug 1*—despite the two shuttles being identical. When Kryten, Rimmer and Holly were lost during the test, Lister and Cat performed a search using *Starbug 2* **[T-SER3.1]**.

  ***NOTE:*** *In several episodes, including "Back to Reality" and "Terrorform,"* Starbug 2 *models were used for some visual-effects shots. In both cases, however, only shots of* Starbug 1 *made the final cut; this caused a particular problem in "Terrorform," as* Starbug 1 *was shown as both the destroyed shuttle and the rescue vehicle.*

- ***Starbug 4*****:** A variation of *Starbug* shuttles designed for underwater exploration and salvage. Designated *Seabug*, it was yellow in color and equipped with floodlights and specialized struts **[T-SER5.6(b)]**.

  ***NOTE:*** Starbug 4 *appeared in a concept sketch in the Gallery section of the Series V DVDs' bonus materials. Its color was mentioned during a special in which Mike Tucker,* Red Dwarf*'s special effects technician, noted that he would have painted it yellow with number 4s on it, as an homage to* Thunderbird 4, *a submersible craft from the 1960s sci-fi television show* Thunderbirds, *which* Starbug 4 *slightly resembled.*

- **Star Corps:** Another name for the Space Corps **[G-RPG]**. At one time, its headquarters were located on Earth's Moon **[B-SUR]**.

- ***Star Corps Commando Big Book of Brutality, The***: A book written by Colonel Mike O'Hagan, a Space Marine and author of the *Space Corps Survival Manual* **[B-SUR]**.

- ***Star Corps Personnel Manual***: A standard-issue book provided to all crewmembers of the Star Corps. It contained chapters on such topics as exploring a potentially hostile world **[B-LOG]**.

- ***Star Corps Survival Manual II—This Time It's Personal, The***: The sequel to Colonel Mike O'Hagan's book, the *Space Corps Survival Manual*. This volume was created using digested pages from the first book, which were eaten (along with O'Hagan) by survivors of a crash on Tregar IV **[B-SUR]**.

  ***NOTE:*** *"This time it's personal" was the much-spoofed tagline of the film* Jaws IV: The Revenge.

- **stardrive:** A propulsion system developed by Legion. After foiling the gestalt entity's attempt to indefinitely hold his shipmates captive, Kryten inquired about any technology that could help them pursue the stolen *Red Dwarf*. Legion gave them his stardrive, but once activated aboard *Starbug 1*, the device wrenched itself from the ship's floorboards and crashed through the hull, causing the shuttle to temporarily depressurize **[T-SER6.2]**.

  Space Cadet LLC manufactured a type of stardrive that was distributed by Crapola Inc. via its annual *SCABBY* catalog **[G-RPG]**. A refurbished stardrive was the top prize at the ninth annual Kinitawowi Open golf tournament on Echech 3 **[G-RPG]**.

  ***NOTE:*** *The term was sometimes written as two words and capitalized as "Star Drive."*

- **stare mode:** A function of 4000 Series mechanoids (including the 4000 GTi) enabling them to focus intently on an object. Camille, disguised as a 4000 GTi, entered stare mode while conversing with Kryten, and commented that his eyes were amazing **[T-SER4.1]**.

- **Star Fleet:** A military organization associated with the Space Corps **[N-LST]**. When Kryten described Rimmer's life goals as unrealistic, Rimmer proved his point by claimed the mechanoid would pay once Arnold became "Lord of the Star Fleet" **[T-SER9.2]**.

- **stargate:** A structure connecting two distant points in space, allowing instantaneous travel. Holoships—hologram-crewed vessels made purely of lightweight tachyons—were designed to travel great distances through stargates and wormholes, thanks to their near-zero mass **[T-SER5.1]**.

  ***NOTE:*** *Such structures were also the basis of the popular* Stargate *film and television franchise.*

- **Starhopper:** A type of spacecraft in an alternate universe. Starhoppers serviced Ariel 2, an asteroid controlled by the United Republic of GELF States. When Forum of Justice mystics predicted their dimension's Lister would loot and pillage the asteroid belt, destroy a starhopper and cause many deaths, the GELFs arrested him on bogus emo-smuggling charges and imprisoned him in Cyberia before he could commit the crimes **[N-LST]**.

- **Starlight Ballroom, the:** A hypothetical room that Talkie Toaster theatrically pretended to address while proving to Lister that he could sing **[T-SER1.2]**.

- **Starr, Ringo:** The drummer of twentieth-century British rock band The Beatles, born Richard Starkey **[RL]**. After *Red Dwarf* entered a parallel universe using the Holly Hop Drive, Holly tried to explain the concept of alternate realities to the crew, noting that in this reality, Ringo might have been a good drummer **[T-SER2.6]**.

- ***Starsky and Hutch***: A 1970s American television program about two California policemen, starring Paul Michael Glaser as David Starsky and David Soul as Kenneth "Hutch" Hutchinson **[RL]**. Starsky and Hutch were among Jake Bullet's childhood cop heroes **[M-SMG1.11(c4)]**.

- ***Starstruck***: A tabloid magazine that Lister read while imprisoned in *Red Dwarf*'s brig. The issue contained an article about Argyle Somerfield, an eighty-three-year-old movie star who had recently fathered a child with his nurse **[T-SER8.1]**.

- **Star Tours Holidays:** A travel company operating in the twenty-second century. Lister had a poster advertising this firm's tours to Fiji hanging in his *Red Dwarf* bunk **[T-SER1.2]**.

- ***Star Trek*:** A popular American science fiction television show of the 1960s that spawned several spinoff TV series and films **[RL]**. Confused as to why the *Red Dwarf* crew would risk their lives for him, Kryten questioned whether their decision to fight Hudzen 10 was an example of human friendship. Lister, suffering from a hangover after a night of debauchery, dismissed his question as "*Star Trek* crap" **[T-SER3.6]**.

  While trapped in an elation squid hallucination and convinced they were merely TV characters, the *Red Dwarf* crew visited a collectibles shop called They Walk Among Us! When a clerk named Noddy suggested they beam over to Nose World, the group chastised him, saying that technology was from *Star Trek*, not *Red Dwarf* **[T-SER9.2]**.

  ***NOTE:*** Star Trek *frequently utilized the concept of extraterrestrials and androids not understanding basic human concepts, such as love and friendship.*

- **Start/Run:** A setting on *Starbug 1*'s sonar scope display. The word "Run" was highlighted and blinking while the crew charted the course of a despair squid **[T-SER5.6]**.

- **startup code:** A security protocol entered into a *Starbug* shuttlecraft computer during a launch initiation **[T-SER4.3]**.

- **Star Wars:** A derogatory nickname that the mainstream media dubbed the United States' Strategic Defense Initiative (SDI) system, proposed by President Ronald Reagan in 1983, which employed ground- and space-based platforms from which defensive missiles could be launched **[RL]**. As the *Starbug* crew left a backwards-running Earth in Universe 3, the shuttle became unstruck thanks to a heat-seeking missile launched from this experimental system **[N-BCK]**.

  ***NOTE:*** *The program's nickname was derived from George Lucas' same-named science fiction film and television franchise.*

- **stasis booth:** *See* stasis room

- **Stasis Booth 1344:** One of *Red Dwarf*'s stasis booths. Rimmer was about to enter this booth when the radioactive wind caused by the cadmium II explosion killed him instantly **[N-INF]**.

  ***NOTE:*** *This contradicted episode 1.1 ("The End"), which indicated that Rimmer was in the Drive Room at the time of the accident. What's more, episode 2.4 ("Stasis Leak") implied that there were only two stasis booths on the entire ship, rendering the 1344 numbering nonsensical.*

- **stasis field:** A shielded area created by *Red Dwarf*'s stasis room that inhibited the passage of time. Anyone positioned within the stasis field would effectively be stuck in time until the field was deactivated, and thus would not age. Since Lister had been sentenced to stasis shortly before the cadmium II disaster, he was protected from the radiation burst and awoke unharmed three million years later **[T-SER1.1]**.

- **stasis leak:** A tear in the fabric of space-time, enabling an individual to travel to another fixed point in time and back again. Bringing items or individuals back through the leak was impossible. A stasis leak developed on *Red Dwarf*'s Floor 16, caused by a malfunctioning stasis room, and led to a men's shower stall on Wednesday, March 2, 2077—three weeks before a cadmium II burst would kill the crew. Lister and Rimmer each traveled through the anomaly hoping to change history—Lister to save Kochanski, the hologram to save himself. Ultimately, neither plan succeeded **T-SER2.4]**.

  ***NOTE:*** *Apparently, neither thought to prevent the cadmium II disaster altogether.*

- **stasis pod:** A cylindrical vessel in which an individual could be placed in suspended animation for an extended span of time. Stasis pods were used at a scientific research station at which hologrammic scientist Hildegarde Lanstrom worked. Three million years after Lanstrom contracted a deadly holovirus and locked herself in a pod, the *Red Dwarf* crew found and activated the device, causing Rimmer to become infected **[T-SER5.4]**.

- **stasis room:** A small chamber aboard Space Corps vessels such as *Red Dwarf*—also called a stasis pod or stasis booth—that created a field shielding an occupant from time **[T-SER1.1]**. Stasis booths were originally designed for interstellar travel. Once scientists concluded that Earth was the only planet in the universe to spawn life, however, such travel was discontinued, and the booths were relegated to penal use aboard mining ships **[N-INF]**.

  Lister was placed into one of *Red Dwarf*'s stasis rooms as punishment for bringing an unquarantined cat aboard ship. His sentence was for only eighteen months, but a cadmium II explosion forced Holly to keep him in stasis for three million years, until the background radiation became safe for humans **[T-SER1.1]**.

  When a malfunctioning stasis room on Floor 16 caused a stasis leak, Lister and Rimmer traveled back in time through that leak, hoping to alter history. Lister hoped to convince Kochanski to use the spare stasis room, while Rimmer planned to tell his living self to do the same **[T-SER2.4]**.

  > ***NOTE:*** *This would seem to indicate that* Red Dwarf *contained only two stasis rooms, one on Level 159 and one on Level 16, despite the mining ship's massive size and large crew complement. The novel* Infinity Welcomes Careful Drivers *explained this oddity, by noting that the booths became obsolete after humanity abandoned interstellar travel, and were now only used as punishment for minor infractions. The novel then confused the issue, as Rimmer prepared to enter Stasis Booth 1344, implying there were more than a thousand such units onboard. The comic story "The End, Part 2," in* Smegazine *issue 1.2, showed a row of three stasis booths, numbered one to three, with Lister being placed into the second chamber.*

- **stasis seal:** A protective seal placed around a deep sleep unit that put an occupant in a coma-like state, and also shielded the user from external changes in space-time. Kryten installed temporary stasis seals on *Starbug 1*'s deep sleep units, enabling the crew to shield themselves from the effects of unreality pockets while traversing a reality minefield searching for its source **[T-SER6.6]**.

- **Stations 1 to 4:** A series of consoles servicing a four-unit total-immersion video game that the *Red Dwarf* crew imagined playing while trapped in a despair squid hallucination **[T-SER5.6]**.

- **Status Room:** A room aboard *Red Dwarf* allocated for monitoring the ship's situation. It included several security monitors and a console desk **[N-BTL]**.

- **"Stay Young and Beautiful":** A song that Kryten hummed while prepping the skeletons of *Nova 5*'s deceased crew for the *Red Dwarf* rescue party **[N-INF]**.

- **St. Christopher:** A third-century martyr revered by Roman Catholics as the patron saint of travelers and transportation **[RL]**. Ace Rimmer lost his St. Christopher medal when he purposely threw a fight with Space Corps recruit Billy-Joe Epstein so the youth would muster the confidence to pass his flight exam. Thus, Ace later determined that a deceased version of himself—who arrived in a ship identical to his own, and still had his medal—was from another universe **[N-BCK]**.

- **STE:** *See* synaptic enhancer

- **Steak and Sidney Pie:** A cannibalism recipe that Colonel Mike O'Hagan recommended in his *Space Corps Survival Manual* **[B-SUR]**.

  > ***NOTE:*** *This dish's name was a pun referencing steak and kidney pie, a staple of British cuisine.*

- **steam-operated trouser press:** An appliance created by the Cat People inhabiting *Red Dwarf*, the invention of which was a turning point in Cat civilization, sidelining such innovations as the wheel and fire **[N-INF]**.

- **steedcheat:** A code word used as a cheat in a medieval-themed artificial-reality simulation, which reduced a jousting opponent's horse to a small donkey. Lister used the cheat against the king of Camelot's champion, in order to tilt the odds in his favor and enable him to bed the queen **[T-SER7.2]**.

- **Steele, Jimbo:** An inmate of the Tank, *Red Dwarf*'s classified brig, who perished during the cadmium II disaster, but was resurrected when Kryten's nanobots rebuilt the mining vessel. While incarcerated in the Tank, Lister tried to convince Rimmer that their punishment menu consisted of cloning experiments gone awry, claiming that Kill Crazy's meal once had two noses in it, and that Steele witnessed it sneezing **[T-SER8.6]**.

*NOTE: The* Red Dwarf Programme Guide *spelled his name as "Jim Steel."*

- **Steele, Tommy:** A British actor, singer and musician often cited as the United Kingdom's first teen idol and rock-and-roll star **[RL]**. Holly accidentally overwrote *Red Dwarf*'s entire collection of rock-and-roll songs with the soundtracks to Steele's films **[B-LOG]**.

- **stellar fog:** A spatial phenomenon composed of tightly packed particles from an exploded supernova. Stellar fog could be created artificially to hide reality minefields—pockets of unreality intended to keep trespassers away from certain areas. The *Starbug 1* crew encountered artificial stellar fog while pursuing the stolen *Red Dwarf* **[T-SER6.6]**.

- ***St. Elsewhere*:** An American medical drama that aired on NBC television from 1982 to 1988 **[RL]**. Upon meeting Camille, a Pleasure GELF disguised as a human female, Lister pretended to be the ship's surgeon and asked her to remove her clothes for an examination. When she asked for his credentials, he admitted he was not fully qualified—though he had seen every episode of *St. Elsewhere* **[T-SER4.1]**.

- **stereo audial sensors:** Dual components used by 4000 Series mechanoids, enabling them to hear their environment **[N-BTL]**.

- **Stetworth Heath:** A phrase printed on a sign at a bus stop in twenty-first-century England, which the *Red Dwarf* crew imagined while trapped in an elation squid hallucination. The crew boarded a bus from this location to visit a man named Swallow **[T-SER9.2]**.

*NOTE: Presumably, Stetworth Heath was the bus stop destination.*

- **Stewart, Alastair ("Al"):** A Scottish folk rock musician best known for his albums *Time Passages* and *Year of the Cat* **[RL]**. Leo Davis owned a copy of the latter album while working at Black Island Film Studios **[X-TNG]**.

- **Stewart, James ("Jimmy"):** An American film actor who portrayed protagonist George Bailey in Frank Capra's 1946 Christmas film *It's a Wonderful Life* **[RL]**. While watching the scene in which Bailey's father died, Lister told Kochanski about the death of his own stepfather, with whom he used to watch the movie as a youth **[N-INF]**.

- **St. Francis of Assisi:** A thirteenth-century Italian Catholic friar who was canonized as the patron saint of animals in 1228 **[RL]**. Lister cited St. Francis as an example of the downside to living in a universe in which time ran backwards, for in that dimension, he was a sadist who maimed animals **[T-SER3.1]**. Rimmer once misattributed the phrase "Never give a sucker an even break" to St. Francis **[T-SER5.1]**.

*NOTE: The phrase in question has been attributed to several individuals, including Edward F. Albee and W.C. Fields.*

- **St. Francis of Assisi:** A waxdroid replica of the saint, created for Waxworld, a theme park built on an inhabitable planet that was eventually abandoned. Left on their own for millions of years, the waxdroids attained sentience and became embroiled in a park-wide resource war between Villain World and Hero World (to which St. Francis belonged) **[T-SER4.6]**. The St. Francis waxdroid trained war ferrets and became proficient in ninja throwing squirrels **[G-SOR]**.

During this war, the *Red Dwarf* crew transported to the planet using a Matter Paddle, with Lister and Cat materializing in Villain territory, while Rimmer and Kryten landed in Hero territory. Rimmer found the heroes' army lacking and took command, working many of the pacifistic waxdroids to death before ordering a frontal attack on the enemy compound across a minefield, which killed the remaining droids. During the battle, St. Francis was fatally shot in the chest **[T-SER4.6]**.

- **Stirmaster:** A product sold on the All-Droid Mail Order Shopping Station, consisting of a can-shaped stirring mechanism and a housing unit. According to the station's advertisement, the retail price was $£150, the All-Droid

**PREFIX**
**RL:** Real life

**T-: Television Episodes**
- **SER:** Television series
- **IDW:** "Identity Within"
- **USA1:** Unaired U.S. pilot
- **USA2:** Unaired U.S. demo

**R-: *The Bodysnatcher Collection***
- **SER:** Remastered episodes
- **BOD:** "Bodysnatcher"
- **DAD:** "Dad"
- **FTH:** "Lister's Father"
- **INF:** "Infinity Patrol"
- **END:** "The End" (original assembly)

**N-: Novels**
- **INF:** *Infinity Welcomes Careful Drivers*
- **BTL:** *Better Than Life*
- **LST:** *Last Human*

- **BCK:** *Backwards*
- **OMN:** *Red Dwarf Omnibus*

**M-: Magazines**
- **SMG:** *Smegazine*

**W-: Websites**
- **OFF:** Official website
- **NAN:** *Prelude to Nanarchy*
- **AND:** *Androids*
- **DIV:** Diva-Droid
- **DIB:** Duane Dibbley

- **CRP:** Crapola
- **GEN:** Geneticon
- **LSR:** Leisure World Intl.
- **JMC:** Jupiter Mining Corporation
- **AIT:** *A.I. Today*
- **HOL:** HoloPoint

**G-: Roleplaying Game**
- **RPG:** *Core Rulebook*
- **BIT:** *A.I. Screen Extra Bits* booklet
- **SOR:** *Series Sourcebook*
- **OTH:** Other RPG material

price was $£100 and the "Featured Price" was $£70. The Stirmaster, part of the All-Droid Finest Collection, included various spoons, a stainless coating and a thirty-lunar-day money-back guarantee.

After watching the station's Stirmaster ad, Lister and Cat immediately tried to place an order, but spent hours on the phone with various employees. Sim Crawford's betrayal aboard the *Trojan* prevented Lister from completing the order, so after defeating the simulant, he turned her into a homemade Stirmaster **[T-SER10.1]**.

- **St. John's Precinct:** The largest covered shopping center in Liverpool, England, containing more than a hundred retailers **[RL]**. Lister ate his first shami kebab at the Indiana Takeaway in St. John's Precinct **[N-INF]**.

  ***NOTE:*** *There are several restaurants called Indiana in the United Kingdom. As of press time, however, none are located in this shopping center.*

- **Stochastic Diagnostics:** A section of the holoship *Enlightenment* in which data was analyzed using an element of randomness. When Natalina Pushkin delivered first-stage projections regarding a stargate's dimension probabilities to Captain Platini, he requested that they be sent to Stochastic Diagnostics **[T-SER5.1(d)]**.

- **Stocky:** The artificial-intelligence computer aboard the holoship *Enlightenment*, so named for its stochastic capabilities. When tasked with finding a crewmember whom Rimmer had the best chance of defeating in a test of intellect, Stocky picked Nirvanah Crane, with whom Rimmer was in love **[T-SER5.1]**.

- **"Stoke me a clipper; I'll be back for Christmas":** Arnold Rimmer's bungled attempt to recite Ace Rimmer's catchphrase ("Smoke me a kipper; I'll be back for breakfast") while impersonating him **[T-SER7.2]**.

- **Stoppidge, E., Doctor:** A physician in Jake Bullet's universe who was slated to perform an operation on Philby Frutch to cure him of nerdism. Frutch's murder, however, prevented the surgery from taking place **[M-SMG1.14(c6)]**.

- **storage bay:** An area aboard *Red Dwarf* used for storing supplies. Kryten and Lister confronted and defeated the Inquisitor in this bay **[T-SER5.2]**.

- **Stores:** A department of the mining ship *Red Dwarf*. When Rimmer and Lister flirted with two women from Supplies, Rimmer claimed he worked in Stores, hoping to impress them—until Lister humiliated him by claiming it was as a shelf **[T-SER2.1]**.

- ***Strange Science*:** A magazine published in the twenty-second century, to which Rimmer subscribed. One issue contained an article by an Earth biochemist who claimed to have isolated a virus known to cause love **[N-INF]**.

- ***Strategic Sea Battles*:** An artificial-reality game that recreated nautical battles from history. Rimmer discovered a glitch in the program that caused the English fleet to be led into the Battle of Trafalgar by a dolphin named Flipper **[B-SUR]**.

- **strawberry:** A hybrid fruit species cultivated for its aroma, sweetness and bright red color, often consumed in a variety of fresh and prepared foods **[RL]**. After modifying the Matter Paddle for use as a triplicator, Kryten and Lister tested it on the last strawberry known to exist in the universe. The result was two copies—a sweet, succulent berry and a bitter, maggot-filled version **[T-SER5.5]**.

- ***Streets of Laredo*:** A Wild West-style artificial-reality game from Interstella Action Games. The *Starbug 1* crew found this game and the detective simulation *Gumshoe* while salvaging for supplies among debris inside a rogue simulant hunting zone.

  When the Armageddon virus infected *Starbug*'s navicomp, Kryten tried to halt its spread but ended up stuck in a dream in which he was the drunken sheriff of an Old West town. To aid the mechanoid, his shipmates used *Streets of Laredo* to enter his subconscious mind posing as playable characters Dangerous Dan McGrew, Brett Riverboat and the Riviera Kid. Once inside, they helped Kryten battle the Apocalypse Boys—a manifestation of the computer virus—using a Dove Program **[T-SER6.3]**.

  ***NOTE:*** *The game was named after the Laredo Western*

*Town, a recreation of the American Old West in Kent, England, where the episode was filmed.* Red Dwarf—The Roleplaying Game *claimed that* Streets of Laredo *was produced by Total Immersion Games and distributed by Crapola Inc. Interstella may have developed the game, with Total Immersion as the publisher.*

- **strontium:** A metallic alkaline element with physical and chemical properties similar to those of calcium and barium **[RL]**. Strontium was vital to the construction of spacefaring vessels such as *Nova 5*, which was built using a strontium-agol alloy **[N-INF]**.

- ***Student Prince, The*:** A 1920s operetta and subsequent 1954 MGM film about a German prince who attended college incognito and fell in love, despite being promised to another **[RL]**. To entertain the survivors of the *Nova 5* crash, Kryten played hit songs from *The Student Prince*, followed by a game of prize bingo **[N-INF]**.

- ***Stupid But True! Volume 3*:** A book that Olaf Petersen owned aboard *Red Dwarf*, listing silly trivia and statistics, such as the fact that a fifth of all traffic accidents in Sweden during the 1970s were caused by moose. This, coincidentally, was the answer of a lateral-thinking question with which Rimmer struggled during his studies. Convinced that the question was too difficult, he grew increasingly frustrated as each of his shipmates—who had read this entry from the book—immediately knew the answer **[T-SER10.1]**.

- **stupid drugs:** A class of intelligence-lowering pharmaceuticals available in Jake Bullet's universe. When the cyborg learned that murder victim Philby Frutch had drugs in his system when he died, he erroneously assumed they were smart drugs, but Frutch had actually taken stupid drugs—despite his winning streak on the game-show *20,000,000 Watts My Line* **[M-SMG1.11(c4)]**.

  Nerds were the primary users of stupid drugs, according to Bullet's informant, Vinnie van Goth **[M-SMG1.12(c1)]**. Frutch's lover, Mercy Dash, told Bullet that Philby took the drugs to become normal enough to marry her **[M-SMG2.1(c4)]**. The cop later learned that Frutch had cheated via an implant that fed him answers, then used stupid drugs to impede the device's side effects **[M-SMG2.2(c2)]**.

- **S-type star:** A late-type giant star whose spectrum exhibits bands from zirconium oxide and titanium oxide **[RL]**. Echech 3, a planet on which the Kinitawowi Open golf tournament was held, orbited an S-type star as the third planet in the star's system **[G-RPG]**.

- **Styx:** A river in Greek mythology that separated the lands of the living and the dead **[RL]**. When a chameleonic microbe decimated *Red Dwarf*, Death visited Rimmer to inform him that his life was over and he would soon travel to the river Styx. Arnold, however, kneed the entity in the groin and ran away **[T-SER8.8]**.

- **Subbuteo:** A group of tabletop games that simulated popular team sports, such as soccer, cricket, rugby and hockey **[RL]**. When Queeg challenged Holly to a game of chess for control of *Red Dwarf*, Holly, unskilled at the game, suggested they instead play Subbuteo **[T-SER2.5]**. Rimmer sometimes competed in Subbuteo tournaments aboard *Red Dwarf* **[T-SER10.5]** against Madge the skutter **[T-SER10.5(d)]**.

- **Subject A:** The designation that Irene Edgington assigned to herself as the first person to test her evolution machine at the Erroneous Reasoning Research Academy station **[T-SER10.4]**.

- **sub-space conduits:** A component of the portable time drive that transported the *Starbug 1* crew to Dallas, Texas, in 1963 **[T-SER7.1]**.

- **Sucks, Reality:** A name by which Cat mistakenly identified himself to *Red Dwarf*'s flight controller when she requested his name and clearance code. Cat blurted out "reality sucks" upon seeing that the woman was much less attractive than one whom he had previously encountered during an artificial-reality simulation—which, unbeknownst to him, he had yet to leave—and she mistook this for his name, calling him "Mr. Sucks" **[T-SER8.3]**.

- **suction beam:** A form of tractor beam used by Legion's research station to help shuttlecraft land. A malfunctioning suction beam grabbed ahold of *Starbug 1* and forced it to visit the station **[T-SER6.2]**.

**PREFIX**
**RL:** Real life

**T-: Television Episodes**
**SER:** Television series
**IDW:** "Identity Within"
**USA1:** Unaired U.S. pilot
**USA2:** Unaired U.S. demo

**R-: *The Bodysnatcher Collection***
**SER:** Remastered episodes
**BOD:** "Bodysnatcher"
**DAD:** "Dad"
**FTH:** "Lister's Father"
**INF:** "Infinity Patrol"
**END:** "The End" (original assembly)

**N-: Novels**
**INF:** *Infinity Welcomes Careful Drivers*
**BTL:** *Better Than Life*
**LST:** *Last Human*
**BCK:** *Backwards*
**OMN:** *Red Dwarf Omnibus*

**M-: Magazines**
**SMG:** *Smegazine*

**W-: Websites**
**OFF:** Official website
**NAN:** *Prelude to Nanarchy*
**AND:** *Androids*
**DIV:** Diva-Droid
**DIB:** Duane Dibbley
**CRP:** Crapola
**GEN:** Geneticon
**LSR:** Leisure World Intl.
**JMC:** Jupiter Mining Corporation
**AIT:** *A.I. Today*
**HOL:** HoloPoint

**G-: Roleplaying Game**
**RPG:** *Core Rulebook*
**BIT:** *A.I. Screen Extra Bits* booklet
**SOR:** *Series Sourcebook*
**OTH:** Other RPG material

- **Sugar ("Shug"):** A female robot who enlisted Jake Bullet's help in finding her brother Spike, who had vanished from the AlFresco Guacamole Restaurant. Sugar had a rotisserie attachment as a left hand. She and Spike came from a family of partially assembled components **[M-SMG1.7(a)]**.

- **Sugar Puff sandwiches:** A snack consisting of two slices of bread, butter and a handful of Sugar Puffs cereal **[B-EVR]**. After encountering the Inquisitor—a simulant who roamed throughout space-time, judging whether others were fit to exist—Rimmer warned Lister that sitting around reading *What Bike?* and eating Sugar Puff sandwiches all day might not qualify as a worthwhile life **[T-SER5.2]**. Later, while being held against his will aboard Legion's research station, Lister found Sugar Puff sandwiches in his cell, which had been customized to his personal tastes **[T-SER6.2]**.

  ***NOTE:** Sugar Puffs are an actual brand of cereal sold in the United Kingdom, first by Quaker Oats Co. and, more recently, by Honey Monster Foods.*

- **Suicide Squid:** Holly's nickname for a despair squid that the *Red Dwarf* crew found in the ocean of an S-3 planet. The creature produced a venomous ink to induce despair, typically causing its prey to commit suicide **[T-SER5.6]**.

  ***NOTE:** The term "Suicide Squid" was inadvertently coined in 1991 when Mitsuhiro Sakai posted a query to the Usenet newsgroup rec.arts.comics about* Suicide Squad, *but mistyped the comic book's title. From this gaffe was born the annual Squiddy Awards.*

- **Summers, Hayley:** An ex-girlfriend of Lister who worked at the bank at which he kept his overdraft during his musician days. The couple enjoyed eating curries in bed on the weekends while watching zero-gee football. Hayley was the first person Lister ever heard use the phrase "the real McCoy," and often crunched her nose up while telling a story. She had a co-worker at the bank named Roy, with whom she cheated on Dave.

  The couple split up when Summers accepted a job on Callisto. Unbeknownst to him, Hayley became pregnant prior to leaving, but was unsure who the father was. She wrote Dave a letter informing him of the child, then another when a DNA test confirmed that Roy was the father. Lister received neither note, however, until three million years later, when a post pod containing the correspondence caught up with *Red Dwarf* in deep space **[T-SER10.5]**.

  ***NOTE:** Despite Lister making it sound as if Summers was an old girlfriend from back in his musician days, he must have dated her just prior to leaving for* Red Dwarf, *but this does not jibe well with his trying to be a "rock god" at the time.*

- **Sump:** A bottled beverage served at a barbeque on the television soap opera *Androids* **[M-SMG1.8(c2)]**.

- **Sunny Sunshine's White Magic & White Elephant Stall:** A business operated in Jake Bullet's universe **[M-SMG1.12(c1)]**.

- **Sunshine, Sunny:** A practitioner of white magic in an alternate reality. She had long, thick hair with a streak of white along the side. Sunshine owned a booth called Sunny Sunshine's White Magic & White Elephant Stall—which she operated in the black market of the city in which Jake Bullet worked as a police officer—and also offered weather forecasting **[M-SMG1.12(c1)]**.

- **SupaBryte:** A teeth-whitening product **[W-OFF]**.

- **Super-Ace:** A genetically engineered superhero in the universe known as Alternative 2X13/L. Super-Ace—that reality's Arnold Rimmer—possessed super-strength and the ability to fly. As a member of the Liberty League, he was tasked with protecting the city of Smegopolis. In 2315, Ace Rimmer visited this dimension, colliding his ship with Super-Ace upon arrival.

  The Liberty League had been battling the Conspirator and his sidekick, the Penguin, with limited success. When Ace asked why he hadn't taken out the Conspirator, Super-Ace admitted that his weakness was physical contact with others, as he fainted whenever anyone hit him. Ace took his place for the day, defeated the Conspirator and restored Super-Ace's reputation before leaving for another dimension **[M-SMG2.1(c3)]**.

  ***NOTE:** Super-Ace was based loosely on the DC Comics superhero Superman.*

- **Super-Ass:** A nickname that Super-Ace was often called, along with Bonehead Man, in the universe known as Alternative 2X13/L, due to his ineffectiveness as a crimefighter **[M-SMG2.1(c3)]**.

**B-: Books**
**PRG:** *Red Dwarf Programme Guide*
**SUR:** *Red Dwarf Space Corps Survival Manual*
**PRM:** *Primordial Soup*
**SOS:** *Son of Soup*
**SCE:** *Scenes from the Dwarf*
**LOG:** *Red Dwarf Log No. 1996*
**RD8:** *Red Dwarf VIII*
**EVR:** *The Log: A Dwarfer's Guide to Everything*

**X-: Misc.**
**PRO:** Promotional materials, videos, etc.
**PST:** Posters at DJ XVII (2013)
**CAL:** 2008 calendar
**RNG:** Cell phone ringtones
**MOB:** Mobisode ("Red Christmas")
**CIN:** *Children in Need* sketch
**GEK:** *Geek Week* intros by Kryten
**TNG:** "Tongue-Tied" video

**XMS:** Bill Pearson's Christmas special pitch script
**XVD:** Bill Pearson's Christmas special pitch video
**OTH:** Other *Red Dwarf* appearances

**SUFFIX**
**DVD:**
**(d)** – Deleted scene
**(o)** – Outtake
**(b)** – Bonus DVD material (other)
**(e)** – Extended version

**SMEGAZINES:**
**(c)** – Comic
**(a)** – Article

**OTHER:**
**(s)** – Early/unused script draft
**(s1)** – Alternate version of script

- ***Super Carnage Smackdown*:** An exceedingly violent fighting video game designed for the GameStation console **[G-RPG]**.

- **super deluxe vacuum cleaner:** A product featured in an electrical appliance catalog that Kryten read after a DNA modifier changed him into a human. Viewing a triple-bag easy-glide vac with turbo suction and self-emptying dustbag caused him to experience an erection, confusing the former mechanoid **[T-SER4.2]**.

- **Superdome:** A zero-gee football stadium in London, England, circa the twenty-second century. During the European divisional playoffs, Lister attended a game at the Superdome between the London Jets and the Berlin Bandits. Jim Bexley Speed made the game's second score by going around nine men, a feat that left commentators speechless for nine seconds and secured the game as the greatest in the player's career **[N-INF]**.

- **supergiant:** A type of star among the most massive and luminous in the universe, second only to hypergiants **[RL]**. The Coca-Cola Company commissioned *Nova 5* to strategically detonate a blue supergiant star, causing it to go supernova along with 127 others. The timing and positions of these supernovae spelled out the words "Coke Adds Life!"—which remained visible from any point on Earth for five weeks **[N-INF]**.

- **Super-Premier-Holosatellite-League:** An official association football organization in the universe known as Alternative 6829/B. The Smegchester Rovers, captained by Ray Rimmer—Arnold's persona in that reality—were Super-Premier-Holosatellite-League champions **[M-SMG1.8(c4)]**.

- ***Superscrabble*:** A computerized board game, similar to *Scrabble* but with sound effects and hi-resolution graphics. It contained a built-in dictionary chip to thwart cheaters **[M-SMG1.6(c1)]**.

  ***NOTE:** An actual variant of* Scrabble *called* Super Scrabble *was introduced in 2004, though it lacked all of the above enhancements.*

- **Superstik vulcanized tires:** A type of tire designed for Reich-built pursuit motorcycles operated on War World **[G-BIT]**.

- **supervision field:** The total interior area of *Red Dwarf* that Holly could effectively monitor. While tracking Cat's movements throughout the ship, Holly lost the signal as he entered Supply Pipe 28, which was on the periphery of the computer's supervision field **[T-SER1.4]**.

- **Supplies:** A department of the mining ship *Red Dwarf*. When Rimmer and Lister flirted with two women from Supplies, Rimmer claimed he worked in Stores, hoping to impress them—until Lister humiliated him by claiming it was as a shelf **[T-SER2.1]**.

- **Supply Bunker 7:** A storage area aboard *Starbug 1*. Supply Bunker 7 held, among other things, the ship's supply of the plastic explosive Incinerex **[T-SER7.7]**.

- **Supply Deck D:** A floor aboard *Starbug 1* used for storing supplies. When a future version of the crew attacked the shuttle, *Starbug*'s main water tank was breached, flooding Supply Deck D and destroying the ship's entire stock of Indian food **[T-SER7.1]**.

- **Supply Pipe 28:** A serviceable pipeline within the bowels of *Red Dwarf* that led to the cargo decks. Cat traversed this passage—which was barely within Holly's supervision field—to visit a blind priest, the only other member of their species aboard **[T-SER1.4]**.

  ***NOTE:** Supply Pipe 28 may have been on Level 454, as an access point to the pipeline was a vent on that level.*

- **Surf Boy:** A nickname that Lister called Kryten upon the latter's return from a holiday to V Deck's broom cupboard **[T-SER9.1]**.

- **Surgeon 2:** A medical robot aboard *Red Dwarf* that aided in the birth of Lister's twin sons, Jim and Bexley **[M-SMG1.8(c1)]**.

- **surprise:** An emotional state brought on by an unexpected event **[RL]**. While being analyzed by *Red Dwarf*'s chief psychiatric counselor, Kryten boasted that surprise was an emotion he had acquired with Lister's help **[T-SER8.1]**.

- **"Surprise Symphony":** A piece of music composed in 1791 by Joseph Haydn, also titled Symphony No. 94 **[RL]**. "Surprise Symphony" was Rimmer's favorite lovemaking music. While trapped in an addictive version of *Better Than Life*, he imagined that he often played this song while having sex with his wife, Juanita Chicata **[N-BTL]**.

- ***Survivalist*:** A twenty-second-century publication for wilderness and emergency survivalists. Rimmer had several issues of the magazine in his locker aboard *Red Dwarf* **[N-INF]**.

- **survival pod:** A small craft, similar to an escape pod, used for emergency habitation. The pod contained sufficient food and oxygen for two occupants for long-duration flights. Cat and Ora Tanzil used one of *Starbug 1*'s survival pods to remedy a biological affliction Cat was suffering due to a lack of sex **[T-IDW]**.

- **Susan:** A name that Kryten, in a daze, called Lister after being used as a battering ram to plow through fifty-three doors with his head during a *Red Dwarf* power outage **[T-SER4.4]**.

- ***Suspects Followed 8th August*:** The title of a binder on the desk of Chief Olin, Jake Bullet's police chief in the cyborg's reality **[M-SMG1.13(c4)]**.

- **suspended animation booth:** A chamber in *Starbug 1*'s suspended animation suite, built to sustain an individual in a near-coma state during long-duration travel. The crew entered such booths while returning to the *Esperanto*—which took several hundred years—to search for Kryten's nanobots **[T-SER7.8]**.

  ***NOTE:*** *Since the deep sleep units used prior to this episode were located in the Obs Room, the crew presumably added the suspended animation suite at a later date, possibly while salvaging Space Corps derelicts.*

- **suspended animation suite:** An area of *Starbug 1* containing several suspended animation booths for long-duration travel **[T-SER7.8]**.

- **suspenders:** An apparel item that Cat obtained during a night of hard partying in *Red Dwarf*'s Officers' Club to celebrate Kryten's last day of service **[T-SER3.6]**.

- **Sutherland, Kev F.:** The production designer of the television soap opera *Androids* **[W-AND]**.

  ***NOTE:*** *A person named Kev F. was also credited as a cameraman in the* Androids *comics published in the* Smegazines. *Both characters were named after artist Kev F. Sutherland, who illustrated the* Androids *comics.*

- **Suzdal, Commander:** A Space Corps officer stationed at a colony on an S-3 planet. Suzdal's personality disc was one of eight that a tribe of Cat People found millions of years later while searching for Fuchal. Believing the planet to be their Holy Land, the Cats settled in the abandoned colony and followed the teachings of the discs, whose programs posed as servants to the Cats' god, Cloister. This caused Cat society to split into various factions, following a different disc's code of ethics.

  Suzdal's followers formed a religion called Suzdalism. He taught his devotees to train for an epic battle against evil, during which a Cat army would go back in time and fight alongside Cloister for the fate of Catkind **[G-RPG]**.

- **Suzdalism:** A devout religious faith among a group of Cat People who followed the teachings of Commander Suzdal, a Space Corps officer whose personality disc was discovered in an abandoned colony. Practitioners of Suzdalism became the largest and most dangerous clan in the colony, forging a violent, martial civilization focused solely on war. This caused a schism between the groups, causing some to leave the colony in search of the true Promised Land **[G-RPG]**.

- **SVC01:** A planet displayed on *Starbug 1*'s scanner table **[T-SER6(b)]**.

  ***NOTE:*** *A wireframe render of this world was included as an Easter egg on disc one of the Series VI DVDs. Selecting it played the computer-generated footage of Rimmer's boot-up sequence from episode 6.1 ("Psirens"). SVC Television was the company that produced the graphics.*

- **SVC02:** A planet displayed on *Starbug 1*'s scanner table **[T-SER6(b)]**.
  *NOTE: A wireframe render of this world was included as an Easter egg on disc one of the Series VI DVDs. Selecting it played the computer-generated character-selection footage from the* Gumshoe *and* Streets of Laredo *virtual-reality games featured in episode 6.3 ("Gunmen of the Apocalypse").*

- **swagger mode:** *See* smug mode

- **Swallow:** An individual whom the *Red Dwarf* crew imagined while trapped in an elation squid hallucination. In the illusion, Swallow worked for Nose World, a latex mask manufacturer in twenty-first-century London that specialized in creating prosthetic noses for the TV and film industry. He worked on Series IX of the British sci-fi comedy series *Red Dwarf*, and regularly stole props from the set, including Cat's white fur coat and a *Starbug*-themed car belonging to the president of the *Red Dwarf* Fan Club, some of which he then sold on eBay.
  Believing they had been transported into a reality in which they were characters on that show, the crew set out to find their creator, who planned to kill them off during the series' final episode. Searching for information at a science fiction collectibles shop called They Walk Among Us!, they discovered clues that led them to Nose World. There, they found Swallow dressed as a rogue simulant and working in a frigid lab, and demanded to know how many episodes they had left. Swallow directed them to Craig Charles, the actor who portrayed Lister, and lent them the stolen *Carbug* for their quest **[T-SER9.2]**.
  *NOTE:* Back to Earth *relied heavily on references to the movie* Blade Runner*, with Swallow based on the character Hannibal Chew, who worked for Tyrell Corporation designing replicants' eyes.*

- **Swamp of Despair:** An environment on a psi-moon configured according to Rimmer's psyche. When Rimmer and Kryten landed on the planetoid, it used Arnold's mind as a template, altering its own landscape to represent aspects of his neurosis, and creating such settings as the Swamp of Despair **[T-SER5.3]**.

- **Swamp of Waste:** A marshy area on a planet within GELF space that was home to the Kinitawowi tribe. The Kinitawowi used the swamp as a communal latrine. The *Starbug 1* crew, forced into GELF space by an attack from a Space Corps Enforcement Probe, landed in the Swamp of Waste **[W-OFF]**.

- **swanephant:** A creature genetically engineered by inebriated scientists, which sported an elephant's body and a feathered, beaked swan head at the end of its trunk **[B-EVR]**.

- **Swan-Morton, Doctor:** A person whom Cat hallucinated after bumping his head while retrieving food from a *Red Dwarf* cupboard. Swan-Morton interrogated Cat (who believed he was again transformed into Duane Dibbley) regarding the deaths of Jake Bullet and Sebastian and William Doyle, then delivered him for torture to Doctors Maxwell, Pension and Fund—who were actually Lister, Rimmer and Kryten, attempting to revive Cat from his reverie **[M-SMG1.9(c1)]**.

- **Swarfega:** A British brand of heavy-duty hand cleaner, typically green in color **[RL]**. Lister once drank Rimmer's bottle of Swarfega while inebriated, thinking it was liquor. He mixed it with a pink substance that turned out to be Windolene **[T-SER8.1]**.

- **Sweatpea:** A nickname that Lister called Kochanski during their brief courtship **[N-INF]**.

- **Swindon:** A large town in South West England, located between Bristol and Reading **[RL]**. Swindon was home to a Space Corps research center at which Nirvanah Crane was once stationed **[W-OFF]**. According to Space Corps Directive 723, terraformers were prohibited from recreating Swindon **[B-LOG]**.
  After curing Lister of the Epideme virus and reviving him from death, Kochanski asked what dying was like. He responded by asking "Ever been to Swindon?" **[T-SER7.7]**.
  In a reality in which Lister was a billionaire, Gilbert Ostrog became his head butler after losing the Butler's Sack Race and Salad Fork Challenge at a butler convention in Swindon **[W-OFF]**.

- **Swirly Thing Alert:** A term by which Cat warned his shipmates of a potentially dangerous unidentified probe heading toward *Starbug 1*. The probe turned out to be part of a malfunctioning automatic landing system used by Legion's research station **[T-SER6.2]**.

- **Sword of Spite:** A short sword owed by Dominator Zlurth, a rogue simulant and Death Ship commander. When *Red Dwarf* evaded the simulant's vessel, Zlurth's second-in-command, Chancellor Wednesday, reported the escape to the dominator, who slid the sword toward his subordinate, saying he knew what he must do. Misinterpreting the order, Wednesday tried to commit *harakiri*, but Zlurth had merely expected him to polish the weapon and write a formal apology as punishment. Zlurth chastised Wednesday for jumping to conclusions, after which the chancellor collected his entrails and departed **[T-SER10.6]**.

- **Sydney:** The tallest of a group of Valkyries whom Cat imagined while trapped in an addictive version of *Better Than Life*. In the illusion, Lister and Rimmer visited Cat at his golden castle to inform him that they were still in the game. When they arrived, Cat sat atop a fire-breathing racing yak, about to start a dog hunt. Noticing his guests, Cat told Sydney to saddle up two more yaks. She and forty Valkyrie waitresses later sang Cat's ceremonial dinner song **[N-INF]**.

- **symbi-morph:** A sentient, shapeshifting symbiote that utilized "hooks" embedded in a host's hypothalamus to create a telepathic link, enabling it to sense their innermost desires and alter its shape accordingly. The number of hooks used on a particular host determined the connection's strength. When all five were embedded, the symbi-morph became completely fulfilled, able to serve the host to its maximum ability.

  In their natural form, symbi-morphs appeared humanoid, with a slight black-and-white matrix pattern. At a GELF prison on Lotomi 5, they were used primarily as Pleasure GELFs for inmates of Cyberia who volunteered for the Reco-Programme, in accordance with Amendment ii of the Xion Treaty. A symbi-morph named Reketrebn, discontent with her enslavement, helped Lister escape from that facility **[N-LST]**.

  ***NOTE:** Among the shapes symbi-morphs have been shown to assume are a Dingotang, a sofa, yak dung, a bouquet of white roses, Kochanski, Rimmer, Kryten, Lister, a fly, a computer key, a horse, a lift, a wooden packing crate, fire, a protective glass shell, Henry VIII, Laurel and Hardy, Queen Victoria, Albert Einstein and a newscaster.*

- **synaptic enhancer:** A drug administered via injection to speed up an individual's ability to regain lost memories following extended periods of deep sleep **[T-SER6.1]**. This process was also called synaptic transmission enhancer (STE) **[N-BCK]**.

- **Synch/Inhibit Input:** A setting on *Starbug 1*'s sonar scope display. This setting was not highlighted as the crew charted the course of a despair squid **[T-SER5.6]**.

- **synthiplast:** A synthetic material used to make molds of an object to be sculpted or shaped, such as a human face. While trapped on a psi-moon configured according to his psyche, Rimmer told Kryten to create a synthiplast mold of the hologram's face so the mechanoid could take his place as a sacrifice to the Unspeakable One. Lister, however, countermanded the order **[T-SER5.3(d)]**.

- **synthi-shock:** A synthetic feeling of surprise experienced by mechanicals, in lieu of actual emotions. Kryten accused Lister of suffering from synthi-shock after mistaking him for an inferior mechanoid model **[T-SER6.6]**.

- **syscomp:** A computer installed aboard a *Starbug* shuttle to calculate general information about the ship, such as when it has exceeded its load capacity **[T-SER7.5]**.

T

TODHUNTER, FRANK, FIRST OFFICER

- **T 27 electron harpoon:** An electrically powered, clip-loaded weapon used by guards at the virtual-reality prison Cyberia, also known as a laser harpoon **[N-LST]**.

- **T-72:** A Soviet-designed and manufactured battle tank, first put into service in 1973 **[RL]**. After Kochanski, Lister and Cat snubbed Kryten by entering an artificial-reality simulation of *Pride and Prejudice Land* instead of joining him for an anniversary dinner, the mechanoid followed them into the program and used a T-72 from a World War II game to blow up the gazebo they occupied **[T-SER7.6]**.

  ***NOTE:*** *Given when the T-72 was introduced, its inclusion in a World War II game would have been historically inaccurate. The tank used in the episode was originally featured in the 1995 James Bond film,* GoldenEye.

- **Tabasco sauce:** A brand of hot sauce produced by McIlhenny Co., and made with tabasco peppers **[RL]**. After regaining his memory from a two-hundred-year deep sleep aboard *Starbug 1*, Lister consumed a breakfast consisting of corn flakes with chopped onion, and requested Tabasco sauce to add more pep **[T-SER6.1]**.

- **table golf:** A game that Lister and Cat devised to pass time aboard *Red Dwarf*, involving a miniature golf course and figures, and a tiny ball. They typically played the game on Sundays. During one particular round, Lister realized he was sick of life **[T-SER3.5]**. The game featured several holes, with Hole 13 designed as an exact replica of the famous seventeenth hole at the Old Course at St. Andrews **[T-SER3.5(d)]**.

- ***Table Golf Instruction Manual*:** A booklet describing several holes in the game of table golf **[T-SER3.5(d)]**.

- **Table K:** A dining room table at which Lister, Rimmer and Cat dined at a restaurant depicted in the total-immersion video game *Better Than Life*. The table was located on the eatery's second terrace **[T-SER2.2]**.

- **tachyon-powered engine core:** A component used to update a spacecraft's hydrogen RAM-drive propulsion system. A parallel dimension's Lister and his shipmates offered to make this upgrade for their prime-universe counterparts when the two crews met in a hyperway connecting their realities **[T-SER7.3]**.

  ***NOTE:*** *It is unclear whether they meant to upgrade* Red Dwarf *or* Starbug.

- **tachyon transmission:** A signal that Ace Rimmer sent to mission control following *Wildfire One*'s successful first dimension jump **[N-BCK]**.

  ***NOTE:*** *A tachyon is a hypothetical particle always moving faster than lightspeed.*

- **T'ai-ch'ang, Emperor:** The fourteenth ruler of China's Ming Dynasty, also known as Chu Ch'ang-lo Kuang Tsung, who ruled for one month in 1620 before dying **[RL]**. Holly correctly answered a trivia question about the emperor that crewmember Pierre Chomsky posed upon reporting to *Red Dwarf* **[N-INF]**.

- **Taiwan:** An island in East Asia, officially known as the Republic of China **[RL]**. The manufacturing plant of Crapola Inc., makers of the Talkie Toaster, was located in Taiwan **[T-SER4.4]**. Diva-Droid's 3000 Series mechanoids were also built there **[T-SER6.6]**.

- **Taiwan Tony ("T.T."):** A food dispenser on *Red Dwarf*'s B Deck, specializing in Asian cuisine and labeled "Taste of Asia Fast Food." Taiwan Tony spoke with a heavy, stereotypical Asian accent. Its menu items included chow mein, special fried rice, fortune cookies and endangered panda stew.

  Taiwan Tony had a rivalry with G Deck's Dispenser 55, which it accused of serving pre-packaged, microwaved food. The dispenser inadvertently started a game of Chinese whispers when Cat asked the machine whether it thought the game's name was racist—which Tony misinterpreted as "Do Chinese knickers have braces?" **[T-SER10.2]**.

- **Taj Mahal Tandoori Restaurant:** A twenty-second-century Indian takeout restaurant located behind the JMC building in London, England. After a battle with the crew's future selves destroyed *Starbug 1*'s Indian food supplies, Lister schemed to replenish them by using *Gemini 12*'s time drive, with which he planned to visit the Taj Mahal Tandoori Restaurant **[T-SER7.1]**. Another Taj Mahal Tandoori Restaurant, located on Miranda, employed a woman named Suzie Patel, to whom Lister was attracted **[M-SMG1.6(c1)]**.

- **"Taking to Nearest Valid Reality":** A message displayed on a monitor linked to Katerina Bartikovsky's dimension-cutter, which the *Red Dwarf* crew imagined while trapped in an elation squid hallucination. In the illusion, the device indicated that the reality they were in was not real, causing it to search for the nearest valid dimension **[T-SER9.2]**.

- ***Tales of the Riverbank: The Next Generation*:** A children's television show set after the original *Tales of the Riverbank*, which featured live rodents voiced by human actors. While watching the show, Lister and Cat pondered the fate of original series star Hammy Hamster **[T-SER4.1]**. An episode of the show aired on Groovy Channel 27 at 1:50 PM on Wednesday, the 27th of Geldof, 2362 **[M-SMG1.7(a)]**.

> ***NOTE:*** Tales of the Riverbank, *a British children's show that aired in the United Kingdom in the 1960s, 1970s and 1990s, did, indeed, feature a character named Hammy Hamster.*

- ***Tales of the Unexpected*:** A British television show that aired from 1979 to 1988, featuring sinister stories with twist endings **[RL]**. Channel 72 aired episodes of this series, the endings of which Kryten did not consider unexpected **[T-SER7.6]**.

- **Talkie Cutlery:** A type of sentient silverware fitted with artificial intelligence (AI), created by Crapola Inc. Available in three models—knife, fork and spoon—the cutlery engaged users in light conversation (or, if placed within two inches of other cutlery, each other). These products won the Flogging a Dead Horse Industry Award. Manufactured in Taiwan, Talkie Cutlery sold for $£13.99 **[W-CRP]**.

- **Talkie Microwave:** A sentient AI microwave oven, created by Crapola Inc., that offered ninety-eight heat settings and came with a non-microwavable cooking bowl. It was manufactured in Taiwan and retailed for $£69.99 **[W-CRP]**.

- **Talkie Sew 'N Sew:** A brand of sentient sewing machines. Kochanski used a Talkie Sew 'N Sew aboard *Starbug 1* to mend her clothes **[T-SER7.5]**.

- **Talkie Toaster:** A sentient alarm clock and bread-toasting appliance created by Crapola Inc. **[T-SER4.4]**. The classic model came with a chrome exterior, a CCD 419.2 visual system, and either a J055 or J056 A.E. system, and retailed for $£12.99. The second-generation model sported a plastic exterior in either red, green or purple, a CCD 517.3 visual system and either a K177 or K178 A.E. system, and retailed for $£19.99. Both versions were manufactured in Taiwan **[W-CRP]**. The two models were designated Mark I and Mark II, respectively **[G-SOR]**.

  Lister purchased an original Talkie Toaster from a souvenir shop on Miranda. The appliance was programmed with limited artificial intelligence, enabling it to engage users in customized morning conversation. It did not, however, come with a belief chip, much to Kryten's frustration, since it did not share his belief in Silicon Heaven **[N-BTL]**. Its main purpose was to toast bread and bread-like foods, but it developed an overly zealous obsession with toasting, offering its grilling services *ad nauseam* to anyone within earshot **[T-SER1.4]**. Ironically, it was rumored to have a secret wheat allergy **[W-OFF]**.

  Talkie once told Lister he could not sing, and attempted to best him by crooning *Fly Me to the Moon* until Dave violently slammed the appliance to shut it up **[T-SER1.2]**. The toaster's incessant soliciting eventually drove Lister to attack it with a fourteen-pound lump hammer, smashing it and dumping the pieces into the waste disposal. Years later, Kryten found the pieces and rebuilt the toaster as a second-generation model, for use in an intelligence-compression experiment by which its AI circuits were routed through a single CPU, increasing its intelligence at the cost of a reduced lifespan **[T-SER4.4]**.

  > ***NOTE:*** *In the novel* Better Than Life, *it was Kryten that fed the toaster into the waste-disposal unit, not Lister, after a polymorph removed the mechanoid's guilt. Kryten later rebuilt him, but due to the droid's limited repair skills, it believed it was a moose from that point on. The novel also attributed the intelligence-compression idea to Talkie.*

- **Talkie Toaster Commemorative Edition:** A version of the second-generation Talkie Toaster that possessed the voice and personality of a deceased loved one. The individual's brainwave pattern was downloaded either from a recorded holo-disc or directly from the brain within seventy-two hours after death. This model sold for $£39.99 **[W-CRP]**.

- **Talkie Toaster Extras Pack:** A software upgrade available for original- and second-generation Talkie Toasters that gave them a vocal makeover, allowing a user to choose between eight different voices, including those of Marilyn Monroe, Elvis Presley, Myra Binglebat, Bing Baxter and others. It sold for $£7.99 **[W-CRP]**.

- **Talkie Toilet:** A toilet bowl fitted with AI technology, sold by Crapola Inc. for $£42.99 **[W-CRP]**. Talkie Toilets were installed aboard *Red Dwarf*, and responded to voice commands **[G-BIT]**. Such commodes were equipped with self-image redirection technology **[G-SOR]**.

- **Talkie Toilet Extras Pack:** A software upgrade available for Talkie Toilets that gave them a vocal makeover, allowing users to choose between eight different voices, including those of Marilyn Monroe, Elvis Presley, Myra Binglebat, Bing Baxter and others. It sold for $£7.99 **[W-CRP]**.

- **Tamagotchi:** A handheld electronic life-simulation toy produced by Bandai, which encouraged children to feed, discipline and maintain it via three buttons **[RL]**. After learning that Kryten had recorded her showering for his fellow inmates in *Red Dwarf*'s brig, Kochanski threatened to melt him down and have his parts made into a thousand Tamagotchis so she could starve them to death one at a time **[T-SER8.5(d)]**.

- ***Taming of the Shrimp*:** A classic play written by Wilma Shakespeare in a parallel universe in which the sexes were reversed **[T-SER2.6]**.

  ***NOTE:*** *This was that universe's analog to William Shakespeare's comedy* The Taming of the Shrew.

- **Tangerine:** An alert condition indicating severe damage to a 4000 Series mechanoid. After an accident on a psi-moon left Kryten injured and stranded, his CPU assessed the situation and periodically updated his head-up display. His condition changed to Tangerine after Lister attempted to fix him, which also lowered the mechanoid's damage assessment to twenty-seven percent **[T-SER5.3]**.

- **tangerine sponge cake:** *See* blueberry muffin

- **Tank, the:** A classified brig on *Red Dwarf*'s Floor 13 that contained two hundred cells and could house up to four hundred inmates. Prior to the cadmium II disaster, the Tank held a full contingent of prisoners awaiting transport to Adelphi 12. When nanobots rebuilt the ship, the Tank and its inhabitants were among those resurrected.

  After Lister, Rimmer, Kryten, Cat, Kochanski and Holly were found guilty of using confidential files for their own purposes, Captain Hollister sentenced them to two years in the Tank, under the supervision of Warden Ackerman. While serving their sentence, they joined the Canaries, an elite group of inmates assigned to dangerous missions **[T-SER8.4]**. Due to his lack of genitalia, Kryten was housed in the woman's ward, much to his chagrin **[T-SER8.5]**.

  The Tank contained a half-heighted metal room called the Hole, to which inmates were sentenced as punishment for severe infractions. Lister and Rimmer were sent to the Hole for two months after a programmable virus they used for potato-peeling went awry. There, they befriended Birdman, an elderly prisoner who kept a sparrow as a pet (which a time wand later transformed into a *Tyrannosaurus rex*) **[T-SER8.6]**.

  Lister's gang eventually escaped the Tank, only to discover *Red Dwarf* being dissolved from within by a chameleonic microbe. They reported the discovery, but were left behind, along with the remainder of the inmates, as the crew abandoned the mining ship **[T-SER8.8]**.

- **Tanzil, Ora, Sub-lieutenant:** A she-Cat captured by Brefewino GELFs after a traitor betrayed her platoon. Her serial number was 2960B8651. When the *Starbug* 1 crew encountered Tanzil in the Brefewino village, they sought her assistance in helping Cat cope with a biological affliction brought on by a lack of sex.

  Since Tanzil was imprisoned, Cat attempted to break her out using a bazookoid. When that failed, the crew tried to cheat at four-dimensional pontoon to win enough money to buy her out of slavery. However, a mute Brefewino named Zural out-cheated them and won Tanzil at an auction. Infuriated, Cat attacked Zural, exposing him as another member of the Cat People—Tanzil's captain, disguised by a morphing belt. Cat realized that Zural was the traitor and thrust a sword into Zural's chest, killing him.

  Grateful for his heroics, Ora agreed to help him with his problem, enjoying a full twenty-minute relationship with him in *Starbug*'s survival pod before he dropped her off at the nearest planetoid **[T-IDW]**.

  ***NOTE:*** *This spelling appeared in the booklet included with the Series VII DVDs. The subtitles for this episode, however, spelled her first name as "Aura."*

- **Taranis:** A Celtic god worshipped in ancient Gaul and Great Britain **[RL]**. While living in Albion (an early name for Britain), the family of a woman named Erin were dragged from their homes and sacrificed to Toutatis, Esus and Taranis in a wicker tower, where they were garroted, burned, drowned and consumed by druids. Erin thus fled to India and made a living as a produce vendor **[T-SER10.3]**.

**B-: Books**
**PRG:** *Red Dwarf Programme Guide*
**SUR:** *Red Dwarf Space Corps Survival Manual*
**PRM:** *Primordial Soup*
**SOS:** *Son of Soup*
**SCE:** *Scenes from the Dwarf*
**LOG:** *Red Dwarf Log No. 1996*
**RD8:** *Red Dwarf VIII*
**EVR:** *The Log: A Dwarfer's Guide to Everything*

**X-: Misc.**
**PRO:** Promotional materials, videos, etc.
**PST:** Posters at DJ XVII (2013)
**CAL:** 2008 calendar
**RNG:** Cell phone ringtones
**MOB:** Mobisode ("Red Christmas")
**CIN:** *Children in Need* sketch
**GEK:** *Geek Week* intros by Kryten
**TNG:** "Tongue-Tied" video

**XMS:** Bill Pearson's Christmas special pitch script
**XVD:** Bill Pearson's Christmas special pitch video
**OTH:** Other *Red Dwarf* appearances

**SUFFIX**
**DVD:**
**(d)** – Deleted scene
**(o)** – Outtake
**(b)** – Bonus DVD material (other)
**(e)** – Extended version

**SMEGAZINES:**
**(c)** – Comic
**(a)** – Article

**OTHER:**
**(s)** – Early/unused script draft
**(s1)** – Alternate version of script

- **"taranshula":** Lister's incorrect spelling of "tarantula" while typing a plea for help to Cat. After Holly mentioned that a tarantula may have escaped and was roaming the ship, Lister felt something climb up his leg and into his shorts, paralyzing him with fear. The creature turned out to be a rescue bot sent by Kryten, who was damaged and stranded on a psi-moon **[T-SER5.3]**.

  ***NOTE:*** *See also the entry for Mechanoid "Taranshula" Remote Drone.*

- **tarantula:** A group of large, hairy, venomous arachnids **[RL]**. While playing the total-immersion video game *Better Than Life,* Rimmer's brain rebelled, unable to cope with his good fortune in the simulation. Among the horrors he conjured up was what he feared most: a giant tarantula crawling up his leg **[T-SER1.3]**.

  Lister also feared tarantulas, and panicked when Holly informed him that one may have broken free of an ore sample pod and was roaming the ship. To his relief, however, it was merely a rescue bot sent by Kryten **[T-SER5.3]**.

  The "low" *Red Dwarf* crew forced Lister to eat a tarantula in order to test a spinal implant's functionality **[T-SER5.5]**.

- **Tarka:** The highest tier of the Vindaloovian GELF caste system, comprising officials answerable only to the emperor or empress of the Vindaloovian Empire **[G-BIT]**.

- **Tarzan:** A fictional, loincloth-clad character created by author Edgar Rice Burroughs. Born John Clayton, Viscount Greystoke, Tarzan was raised by apes in the African jungles as a feral child **[RL]**. While incarcerated in the Tank, Lister and Rimmer inserted a capsule of Sodium Pentothal into Warden Ackerman's asthma inhaler, causing him to admit to being late because he didn't have enough time to change out of his Batman outfit after having sex with the science officer's wife. Lister suggested he try a Tarzan outfit, which would allow for a quicker costume change **[T-SER8.6]**.

- **Tasha Yar Effect:** A temporal phenomenon in which alternate versions of a person converged in a single reality in which that individual was deceased **[G-SOR]**.

  ***NOTE:*** *This was named after Natasha Yar, a character on the American television show* Star Trek: The Next Generation *who died early in the series, in the episode "Skin of Evil," but later returned in the episodes "Yesterday's* Enterprise*" and "All Good Things...," both set in alternate timelines.*

- **Tastee Noodle Pot:** A brand of pot noodle sold in a dispensing machine on a Space Corps Research and Development base in Ace Rimmer's universe **[N-BCK]**.

- **Tate, Tommy:** A character in an Old West dream that Kryten's subconscious mind created to battle the Apocalypse virus. When the fifty-seven-year-old ruffian called Kryten (known in the illusion as Sheriff Carton) a no-good drunk, young Billy Belief attacked the man, who gave him a bruised cheek **[N-BCK]**.

- **Tau, Captain:** The commander of the Space Corps vessel SCS *Pioneer*, in an illusion created by Psirens to lure the *Red Dwarf* crew into an asteroid belt. The video message claimed *Pioneer* had been attacked by Psirens, and showed Tau being killed by laser fire. Kochanski then appeared, claiming to have survived *Red Dwarf*'s cadmium II accident and given birth to Lister's twin boys. Dave decided to attempt a rescue effort, but his shipmates brought him back to his senses **[T-SER6.1]**.

  ***NOTE:*** *Tau's name was an in-joke reference to the American* Red Dwarf pilot, *filmed a year prior, in which Louise Tau commanded the mining ship. This would explain the character's grim yet unspectacular fate so soon after being introduced.*

- **Tau, Louise, Captain:** The commander of the American mining vessel *Red Dwarf*. When that universe's Lister refused to surrender a cat that he had smuggled aboard ship, she sentenced him to six months in stasis—which ultimately saved his life, when a cadmium II accident killed Tau and the remainder of her crew **[T-USA1]**.

- **Taupe:** An alert condition indicating severe damage to a 4000 Series mechanoid. After an accident on a psi-moon left Kryten injured and stranded, his CPU assessed the situation and periodically updated his head-up display. His condition changed to Taupe when Lister found his broken form **[T-SER5.3]**.

- **Taylor, Alan John Percivale ("A. J. P."):** An English historian of the early twentieth century **[RL]**. When Lister complained about the Trojan army falling for the Trojan Horse trick in Greek mythology, Rimmer called him "A.J.P. Taylor" **[T-SER5.2]**.

  **NOTE:** *This was changed to "Schliemann," a reference to German archeologist Heinrich Schliemann, in the DVD captions for the Czech Republic version of the series.*

- **Taylor, Elizabeth ("Liz"), Dame:** A British-American actor and sex symbol, known for her roles in such films as *Cleopatra*, *National Velvet* and *Who's Afraid of Virginia Woolf?* **[RL]**. While trapped in an addictive version of *Better Than Life*, Rimmer imagined that his wife, Juanita Chicata, periodically used a time machine to collect friends from the past, including Taylor, to join her for week-long shopping sprees **[N-BTL]**.

- **T-count:** The hologrammatic equivalent of blood pressure, used to measure a hologram's overall health. When informing Rimmer of the results of his physical, Kryten noted that his T-count was "higher than a hippy on the third day of an open-air festival" **[T-SER6.5]**.

  ***NOTE:*** *Given the correlation between holograms and tachyons (faster-than-light particles), the T-count may have been a measurement of tachyon particles.*

- **TCR:** An abbreviation displayed on a monitor showing electronic circuits rerouted by a crazed skutter aboard *Red Dwarf*. Indicated alongside the abbreviation was an eight-digit number, possibly used to identify damaged sections. This abbreviation also appeared on a monitor in Lister's quarters **[T-SER3.4]**.

- **"Teacher in Space—NASA":** A phrase adorning a patch sewn onto Lister's leather jacket **[T-SER10(b)]**.

  ***NOTE:*** *This patch, visible in the "We're Smegged" making-of special for the Series X DVDs, was created for NASA's real-world "Teacher in Space" program, which was cancelled after civilian educator Christa McAuliffe died during the* Challenger *disaster.*

- **teaching room:** A room aboard *Red Dwarf* in which the Engineer's Exam was administered **[T-SER1.1]**. Crewmembers could also use this room to study for tests, and to take the Chef's Exam **[T-SER1.3]**. *Red Dwarf* had several such teaching rooms, also known as lecture halls **[R-SER1.1]**.

- **Team Simulant:** A team of golfers that competed in the ninth annual Kinitawowi Open tournament, held in GELF space on the planet Echech 3. The team comprised a rogue simulant, a Hudzen 10 mechanoid and a drag-clad Hermann Göring waxdroid **[G-RPG]**.

- **tear gas:** A chemical deterrent used to immobilize intruders aboard *Red Dwarf*. Upon identifying individuals without a clearance code, the ship's computer sealed doorways within the vicinity, then pumped tear gas into the area until authorized personnel arrived on the scene.

  After the Inquisitor surgically removed Kryten and Lister from history, they tried to escape *Red Dwarf* but were unable to open any doors. Not recognizing their clearance codes, Holly activated the intruder alert claxon and flooded the area with the gas **[T-SER5.2]**.

- **Teasy-Weasy:** *See* Raymond Bessone ("Teasy-Weasy")

- **technical library:** A facility aboard *Red Dwarf*. Rimmer was in the technical library when the ship passed the speed of light **[N-INF]**.

- **Technician 3/C:** A JMC rank, short for "Technician, 3rd class." While attempting to escape captivity aboard the nanobot-rebuilt *Red Dwarf*, Lister and Kochanski stole Lift Maintenance uniforms from the Engineering Section marked with this rank **[T-SER8.2]**.

- **TED:** A word, name or acronym printed on a poster in *Red Dwarf*'s refectory **[T-SER1.1]**.

- ***Tedium Magazine*:** A hypothetical publication. Talkie Toaster described Rimmer as *Tedium Magazine's* "Mr. July" **[W-OFF]**.

- **Teerts Gnilpik:** A street on a future Earth on which time ran backwards. Read forward, its name was Kipling Street. While marooned on the planet, Rimmer and Kryten started a novelty stage act at a pub on this street called Nogard dna Egroeg (George and Dragon) **[T-SER3.1]**.

**B-: Books**
**PRG:** *Red Dwarf Programme Guide*
**SUR:** *Red Dwarf Space Corps Survival Manual*
**PRM:** *Primordial Soup*
**SOS:** *Son of Soup*
**SCE:** *Scenes from the Dwarf*
**LOG:** *Red Dwarf Log No. 1996*
**RD8:** *Red Dwarf VIII*
**EVR:** *The Log: A Dwarfer's Guide to Everything*

**X-: Misc.**
**PRO:** Promotional materials, videos, etc.
**PST:** Posters at DJ XVII (2013)
**CAL:** 2008 calendar
**RNG:** Cell phone ringtones
**MOB:** Mobisode ("Red Christmas")
**CIN:** *Children in Need* sketch
**GEK:** *Geek Week* intros by Kryten
**TNG:** "Tongue-Tied" video

**XMS:** Bill Pearson's Christmas special pitch script
**XVD:** Bill Pearson's Christmas special pitch video
**OTH:** Other *Red Dwarf* appearances

**SUFFIX**
**DVD:**
**(d)** – Deleted scene
**(o)** – Outtake
**(b)** – Bonus DVD material (other)
**(e)** – Extended version

**SMEGAZINES:**
**(c)** – Comic
**(a)** – Article

**OTHER:**
**(s)** – Early/unused script draft
**(s1)** – Alternate version of script

## TALKIE TOASTER
(CLASSIC & SECOND GENERATION)

- **teleporter:** A device used to quickly move objects from one place to another, sometimes in conjunction with a handheld unit. Since teleporters were not typically calibrated for human tissue, using such a device on oneself risked a twenty percent chance of being turned inside-out. If not programmed properly, the unit could throw a user backwards or forward in time as well **[T-SER6.3]**. The bridge aboard certain Quantum Twisters, such as the *Trojan*, were equipped with booth-like teleporters **[T-SER10.1]**.

  While looting a simulant derelict, the *Starbug 1* crew used the ship's teleporter to transport supplies back to their ship, then utilized the handheld unit to flee a surviving simulant after Rimmer launched himself in an escape pod, abandoning them **[T-SER6.3]**. They also used the teleporter to escape a prison cell on Rimmerworld **[T-SER6.5]**.

  Teleporters were manufactured by Kluge Corp. and distributed by Crapola Inc. via its annual *SCABBY* catalog. They had a range of 10 kilometers (6.21 miles) and were available with lighting effects in several colors, including Bubbly Amber, Wavy Red, Sparkly Blue and Wibbly-Wobbly Green **[G-RPG]**.

- **Temper Tantrum:** A perfume created by Hildegarde Lanstrom for her product line, Parfum by Lanstrom. The fragrance incorporated a strain of virus that she also developed **[X-CAL]**.

  ***NOTE:** Given the nature of the viruses Lanstrom was studying, Temper Tantrum presumably caused wearers, or those around them, to experience an angry fit (though it seems doubtful such an item would be marketable).*

- **temper tightening:** A type of personality surgery performed on Juanita Chicata, Rimmer's ex-wife in an illusion created by an addictive version of *Better Than Life* **[N-BTL]**.

- **"Template":** A phrase on a chart that Rimmer created to translate markings on a mysterious pod Holly found adrift in

**PREFIX**
**RL:** Real life

**T-: Television Episodes**
**SER:** Television series
**IDW:** "Identity Within"
**USA1:** Unaired U.S. pilot
**USA2:** Unaired U.S. demo

**R-: *The Bodysnatcher Collection***
**SER:** Remastered episodes
**BOD:** "Bodysnatcher"
**DAD:** "Dad"
**FTH:** "Lister's Father"
**INF:** "Infinity Patrol"
**END:** "The End" (original assembly)

**N-: Novels**
**INF:** *Infinity Welcomes Careful Drivers*
**BTL:** *Better Than Life*
**LST:** *Last Human*
**BCK:** *Backwards*
**OMN:** *Red Dwarf Omnibus*

**M-: Magazines**
**SMG:** *Smegazine*

**W-: Websites**
**OFF:** Official website
**NAN:** *Prelude to Nanarchy*
**AND:** *Androids*
**DIV:** Diva-Droid
**DIB:** Duane Dibbley

**CRP:** Crapola
**GEN:** Geneticon
**LSR:** Leisure World Intl.
**JMC:** Jupiter Mining Corporation
**AIT:** *A.I. Today*
**HOL:** HoloPoint

**G-: Roleplaying Game**
**RPG:** *Core Rulebook*
**BIT:** *A.I. Screen Extra Bits* booklet
**SOR:** *Series Sourcebook*
**OTH:** Other RPG material

space, which he thought were an alien language—but which actually spelled out "*Red Dwarf* Garbage Pod," eroded away after many years of spaceflight **[T-SER1.4]**.

- **Temple of Food:** A structure discussed in the Holy Book of the Cat People, which recounted a plan by Cloister the Stupid (Lister) to bring the Holy Mother (a pregnant cat named Frankenstein) to Fuchal (Fiji) and open the Temple of Food—a hot dog and doughnut diner. Arguments over whether hats worn at this temple were to be red or blue sparked millennia of holy wars **[T-SER1.4]**.

- **temporal causeway:** An artificially created tunnel connecting two parts of space-time. Sinking a golf ball in the fourth hole of Echech 3's Kinitawowi Open tournament automatically opened a temporal causeway, leading players to the next course while displaying the area's geological history through clear walls, including a time during which it was underwater. While traversing this causeway, players commonly witnessed prehistoric marine animals savagely attacking one another **[G-RPG]**.

- **temporal-displacement vortex:** A phenomenon that occurred on the television soap opera *Androids*. In one episode, Baz threw a stick for his pet, Bouncer, to fetch at Daz's barbeque. While retrieving the stick, Bouncer was caught in a temporal-displacement vortex, causing the creature to vanish **[M-SMG1.8(c2)]**.

- **temporal ray:** A weapon that accelerated a target's aging process. The effect could be reversed by a homemade concoction called Ultimate Anti-Aging Cream **[G-RPG]**.

- **temporal rip:** A tear in space-time that weakened the membranes of two parallel dimensions, allowing a hyperway to form between them. When a temporal rip opened a hyperway between the prime universe and an alternate reality, the Kochanski of that dimension became stranded with the prime *Starbug 1* crew, once the hyperway collapsed **[T-SER7.3]**.

- **temporal scoop:** A device built into the experimental JMC mining vessel *Black Hole* in an alternate universe. Powered by a small, captured star, the scoop harvested raw materials throughout time and from multiple universes. When that dimension's Rimmer inadvertently cross-wired *Black Hole*'s temporal scoop and Singularity Drive, the ship became lost in space-time once its engines were engaged. The radiation burst from the vessel's improperly contained star killed the entire crew, except for those shielded in the cargo hold or protected in stasis booths **[G-RPG]**.

- ***tempus*:** A Latin word meaning "time" **[RL]**. The word was inscribed in the handle of a time wand, a device that digitized and stored time for uploading at a user's discretion **[T-SER8.6]**.

  ***NOTE:** In the script book* Red Dwarf VIII*, the device itself was called Tempus. Onscreen, it was merely known as a time wand.*

- **Tension Sheet:** A product made of square sheets of bubble wrap painted red, with the words "Tension Sheet" printed on them, which a user could pop to relieve stress. The sheet was originally invented by Fred Holden, who became enormously wealthy after patenting the idea, until Lister changed history by using a timeslide to give his seventeen-year-old self the concept. Rimmer, attempting to pull the same trick, unwittingly restored Holden as the creator by mentioning it within earshot of the boy **[T-SER3.5]**. Hack Markson, the executive producer of the television soap opera *Androids*, owned the license to the Tension Sheet **[W-AND]**, and the product was sold by Crapola Inc. **[X-CAL]**.

- **Tenth Dimension, the:** A dimension accessed during the operation of a hyper-drive. After imbibing the luck virus, Cat devised the propulsion system to punch a hole in space, harnessing superstring to bend time. This enabled the crew to pass through the Tenth Dimension and rescue Lister, who had been trapped on a doomed planet **[N-LST]**.

- **"Ten Things You Didn't Know About Gonad Electrocution Kits":** An article printed in an issue of *Combat and Survival* magazine, which the crew imagined while trapped in an addictive version of *Better Than Life*. In the illusion, Rimmer encountered his former gym teacher, Bull Heinman, working as a prison guard in a penitentiary at which the hologram was incarcerated. When Rimmer staged a prison break, Heinman was interrupted from his seventh read-through of this article **[N-BTL]**.

- **terminal software bug:** A fatal affliction affecting androids, according to the television soap opera *Androids*. In one episode, Brook's doctor diagnosed him with a terminal software bug **[M-SMG1.10(c2)]**.

- **Terminator, the:** The titular antagonist of James Cameron's 1984 science fiction film *The Terminator*. In the film, the advanced cyborg traveled back in time to kill Sarah Connor, a woman who would eventually give birth to the leader of a human resistance force. In several sequels, other models became Connor's allies **[RL]**. The Terminator was one of the Inquisitor's role models **[M-SMG2.5(a)]**, while Kryten claimed the robotic killer was his great-uncle **[X-GEK]**.

- ***Terminator, The*:** A film produced in an alternate universe in which the sexes were reversed. In the movie, actor Arlene Schwarzenegger played a cyborg sent back in time to kill Simon Connor to prevent the birth of the leader of a human resistance force **[W-OFF]**.

  ***NOTE:*** *In the real world,* The Terminator *starred Arnold Schwarzenegger as a cyborg on a mission to kill Sarah Connor (portrayed by Linda Hamilton).*

- **terra buggy:** A six-wheeled, all-terrain vehicle used by Dolochimp Cyberian guards on Lotomi 5, capable of carrying eight guards **[N-LST]**.

- **terraces of Valles:** A strip of buildings built into three hundred miles of the Valles Marineris canyon on Mars. Approximately ninety percent of the Martian population lived among the terraces, which housed some of the wealthiest individuals in the inner solar system **[G-RPG]**.

- ***Terraforming Made Easy*:** A book that Lister found in a parallel universe, produced by Space Corps Specialist Publications. The book included chapters titled "Beginner's Terraform," "Intermediate Terraform" and "Advanced Terraform" **[B-LOG]**.

- **Terry:** The possible name of a flight navigation officer aboard *Red Dwarf*. Kochanski dated the man for almost two years before he dumped her for a brunette in the ship's Catering department, at which point she began seeing Lister as a rebound. After a month, the officer broke up with the brunette and went back to Kristine, who left Lister to be with him again. Depressed and bitter, Lister never bothered to learn the man's name, though he knew it started with a "T" and may have been Terry **[N-INF]**.

- **Terry:** A hologram aboard an alternate *Red Dwarf*. His companions included a human named Ben Ellis, a humanoid rodent named Rat, the mechanoid Kryten and the ship's artificial-intelligence computer, Kate **[G-RPG]**.

- **Tesco:** A British grocery and general merchandise retailer **[RL]**. A muffin that Rimmer presented to Captain Hollister for his anniversary was from Tesco **[T-SER8.2]**.

  When Lister confronted his father about abandoning him in a pub, his dad tried to convince him that his mother was royalty, then admitted she worked at Tesco **[R-FTH]**.

  ***NOTE:*** *Lister's confrontation with his father occurred in an early-draft script written before episode 7.3 ("Ouroboros") established that Dave was his own father.*

- ***Tess of the D'Urbervilles: A Pure Woman Faithfully Presented*:** A novel by Thomas Hardy, published in 1891, about the struggles of a peasant woman named Tess Durbeyfield **[RL]**. Cat found a recording of *Robert Hardy Reads Tess of the D'Urbervilles* that he and Lister both enjoyed, since it had been warped and twisted, distorting the sound beyond recognition **[T-SER2.5]**.

- **test card:** A test signal typically broadcast when a transmitter was active but no program was being aired, often at startup and closedown **[RL]**. Groovy Channel 27 aired a test card as a calibration pattern at 11 AM on Wednesday, the 27th of Geldof, 2362, which allowed viewers to calibrate their eyes for proper viewing **[M-SMG1.7(a)]**.

- **Tethys:** A mid-sized moon of Saturn, distinguished by an immense, shallow crater in its upper hemisphere **[RL]**. Tethys was a dumping ground for nuclear waste used by ships such as *Pax Vert*, which often unloaded toxic materials on the moon before returning to Earth **[N-INF]**. In 2243, a company called HoloPoint built a factory on Tethys, demolishing seventeen residential streets in the process **[W-HOL]**.

- **Texas School Book Depository:** A building located in Dallas, Texas, from which Lee Harvey Oswald shot and killed John F. Kennedy in 1963 **[RL]**. While traveling through time in search of curries, the *Starbug 1* crew accidentally thwarted the assassination by materializing on the fifth floor of the Texas School Book Depository and pushing Oswald out an open window.

  Realizing they had altered history by allowing Kennedy to live, the crew tried to undo their damage by traveling to an earlier point in time, causing Oswald to relocate to the sixth floor. This did not rectify the problem, however, as the steeper angle threw off the assassin's aim, forcing the Dwarfers to come up with another solution: convincing JFK to assassinate himself from behind a grassy knoll **[T-SER7.1]**.

- **TH285 motion sensor:** A handheld device used to detect movement within a 76-meter (250-foot) radius of a user **[G-SOR]**.

- **"Thank You for Not Smoking":** A phrase printed on a sticker affixed to Rimmer's locker in the quarters he shared with Lister aboard *Red Dwarf* **[T-SER1.1]**.

- ***That's My Chromosome*:** An American television game show hosted by Bing Baxter **[W-OFF]**.

- **Theory of Relativity:** A set of two theories developed by physicist Albert Einstein that linked gravitation, space-time and the speed of light, and explained how time travel could theoretically be possible **[RL]**. After witnessing a future echo of Lister's apparent death, Rimmer insisted there was no stopping the event, agreeing with Einstein's theory that one could not change the future **[T-SER1.2]**. Holly once defined the Theory of Relativity as a theory one only told relatives **[T-SER8.3]**.

  > ***NOTE:*** *Rimmer must have learned about the theory after becoming a hologram, since his hologrammic self was familiar with it in episode 1.2 ("Future Echoes"), but his living self was not in episode 8.3 ("Back in the Red, Part 3").*

- **thermal grenade:** A small handheld explosive device activated by twisting a detonator handle and throwing it at a target. *Red Dwarf* was stocked with a supply of thermal grenades **[N-BTL]**.

- **thermo-foil parka:** A specialized jacket suitable for environments of extreme cold, rated for use in temperatures as low as -4 degrees Fahrenheit (-20 degrees Celsius) **[G-BIT]**. Thermo-foil parkas were stocked aboard *Red Dwarf*'s *Starbug* shuttles **[T-SER3.2]**.

- **thermonuclear device:** An explosive missile that could be launched from a *Starbug* shuttle. The *Red Dwarf* crew plugged a white hole by launching such a device into a sun, causing a solar flare that altered the course of several orbiting planets, one of which sealed the anomaly **[T-SER4.4]**.

- **"thermonuclear megadeath":** *See* plasmatic lacerator shell

- **Thesen, Rick, Deck Sergeant:** A crewmember aboard *Red Dwarf* who died during the cadmium II disaster. Before the accident, Thesen dated a deck sergeant in the crew named Sam Murray. Three million years after their deaths, Lister placed their ashes together in a canister and shot them into space so they could spend eternity together, unaware they had broken up **[N-OMN]**.

  > ***NOTE:*** *This information appeared in the pilot episode's first-draft script, published in the* Red Dwarf Omnibus. *It is unknown whether the nanobots resurrected Thesen in Series VIII.*

- **Theta:** The eighth letter of the Greek alphabet **[RL]**, used in a code to disarm and unlock a groinal exploder that a group of BEGGs had affixed to Lister's crotch. The code—Theta, Delta, Alpha, Beta, Gamma—had to be input precisely, in that order, for the device to be disabled **[T-SER10.4]**.

- **Theta 4:** A planet displayed on the *Leviathan*'s monitor when Lister, infected with the Epideme virus, boarded the vessel to find a possible cure **[T-SER7.7]**.

  > ***NOTE:*** *The monitor's image implied the* Leviathan *was en route to Theta 4. Later in the episode, however, Lister reported that the ship was heading to Delta 7 to find a cure for Epideme. It is possible that the other planet on the monitor was Delta 7.*

- **Theta Delta Alpha Beta Gamma:** A code that disarmed and unlocked a groinal exploder that a group of BEGGS had fitted onto Lister's crotch. With help from the device's designer, Irene

Edgington of the Erroneous Reasoning Research Academy, the *Red Dwarf* crew decrypted the code by choosing whichever symbol the inventor, known for often being incorrect, did not pick. When it came to the last two symbols, however, Kryten and Cat realized that her first name and last initial, Irene E.—irony—meant the last symbol she chose would be correct **[T-SER10.4]**.

- **Theta Sector:** An area of space in Dimension 24 containing Astro Cuts, a hair salon that Ace Rimmer frequented **[T-SER7.2]**.

- **They Walk Among Us!:** A comic book and collectibles shop that operated in Richmond, England, from 1987 to 2009 **[RL]**. While trapped in an elation squid hallucination, the *Red Dwarf* crew, believing they were merely characters on a television show, imagined visiting this store seeking clues to find their creator and plead for more life. There, they met an employee named Noddy, a science fiction aficionado who aided them in their quest by contacting Reg Wharf, the president of the *Red Dwarf* fan club. When that effort failed, they used a photograph in the shop to locate a man named Swallow, who once worked on the show **[T-SER9.2]**.

  ***NOTE:*** *Ace Comics replaced They Walk Among Us! in 2009. The prior owners, Jon and Sabina Browne, now operate an eBay storefront.*

- **Third Technician:** A position advertised on the Jupiter Mining Corporation's website. Preferred candidates needed to be easygoing and willing to learn, and possess lap-dancing experience. The position's reference number was AJR168 **[W-JMC]**.

- **Thirty Years' War:** A series of conflicts fought throughout Central Europe between 1618 and 1648 **[RL]**. While trapped in a seeding ship escape pod bound for a wormhole, Kryten told Rimmer that a rescue attempt would take six times longer than a certain long-lasting medieval war. Rimmer mistook this for the Thirty Years' War, though the mechanoid actually meant the Hundred Years' War **[T-SER6.5]**.

- ***This City? What City?!*:** A DVD displayed in a twenty-first-century mall video store that the *Red Dwarf* crew imagined while trapped in an elation squid hallucination **[T-SER9.2]**.

- **"This Phone Will Not Accept Incoming Earth Calls":** A phrase printed on a sign mounted near *Red Dwarf*'s Medical Unit, where Lister took a photograph of a future echo involving himself and his newborn twin sons **[T-SER1.2]**.

- **"This Side Up":** An instruction printed on a small sign mounted on the side of a terminal in *Red Dwarf*'s hologram simulation suite **[T-SER1.2]**.

- **Thompson, Nicholas, Doctor:** A psychiatric physician aboard an alternate-universe *Red Dwarf*. Among his patients was that reality's Lister, a sociopath with a history of violence and insubordination. Frustrated with Lister's lack of progress, Thompson referred him to a fellow psychiatrist, Alice Kellerman **[N-LST]**.

- **Thomson Holidays:** A British travel agency **[RL]**. In Jake Bullet's universe, the cyborg found a brochure for a Thomson Holidays trip to Florida in the apartment of murder victim Philby Frutch **[M-SMG1.14(c6)]**.

- **thorium-232:** An isotope of thorium from which uranium-233 can be bred **[RL]**. Lister mined thorium-232 from a moon in order to produce a sufficient quantity of uranium-233 to fuel *Nova 5*'s Duality Jump **[N-INF]**.

- **Thornton, Angus Lionel, MP:** A *Red Dwarf* security officer who died at age thirty-six during the cadmium II disaster, but was resurrected when nanobots rebuilt the mining ship and its complement. When the *Starbug 1* crew crashed into the new vessel's landing bay, Thornton arrested them on several charges, including stealing and destroying the shuttle **[T-SER8.1]**.

  While perusing Thornton's confidential files, Rimmer learned that his inside leg measurement was twenty-nine, his neck size was sixteen, he was circumcised, he enjoyed jazz, he had a good credit rating **[T-SER8.3]**, and he was once admitted to a hospital completely naked, attached to the suction end of a vacuum cleaner **[T-SER8.1-3(e)]**.

- **Thornton, Beth ("Old Prune Face"):** Lister's adoptive mother in an alternate universe. That reality's Lister chose Beth and her husband Tom to raise him because of their wealth. This, however, meant enduring Beth's manic-depressive outbursts. During his first weekend with the Thorntons, she destroyed her crockery upon learning that he didn't like her raspberry sponge cake. Beth often beat young David with a brown clothesbrush, causing him to grow up a murderous sociopath. Even in adulthood, he remembered her ugly smile and sickly smelling perfume **[N-LST]**.

- **Thornton, Tom:** Lister's adoptive father in an alternate universe. That reality's Lister chose Tom and his wife Beth to raise him because of their wealth. He had a round, sad "spaniel face" and bad posture. When Lister was nine years old, Tom was arrested and sentenced to ten years in prison for embezzling money from the Miranda Insurance Company, leaving his manic-depressive wife to raise Dave alone **[N-LST]**.

- **Three Musketeers, the:** A fictional trio of French noble guards—Athos, Count de la Fère; Porthos, Baron du Vallon de Bracieux de Pierrefonds; and René "Aramis" d'Herblay—featured in Alexandre Dumas' novel *The Three Musketeers* and its sequels. A fourth musketeer, Charles Ogier de Batz de Castelmore, Comte d'Artagnan, later joined their ranks **[RL]**.

  While describing his relationship with his brothers, Rimmer told Kryten that they called themselves the "Four Musketeers." He then admitted his brothers were really the Three Musketeers, and forced him to be the Queen of Spain **[T-SER3.3]**.

- **Three Stooges, the:** A comedy team of eight vaudeville actors who appeared in 220 films from 1930 to 1970, in various three-man lineups, utilizing physical slapstick humor **[RL]**. Simulant scavengers, searching Garbage World (Earth) for artifacts to sell to mechanicals, found a cache of video slugs, including several containing Three Stooges recordings **[M-SMG2.9(c11)]**.

- **Three Years' Long Service:** One of four JMC medals that Rimmer earned, along with others for six, nine and twelve years of service. Believing Lister intended to permanently deactivate him, Arnold wore these medals on his dress uniform while awaiting his impending execution **[T-SER1.6]**.

- **throwing triangle:** A sharpened, three-sided throwing weapon used by the Pythagoras waxdroid on Waxworld **[G-SOR]**.

- **thrust-to-input ratio:** A value used to determine the power of a *Starbug* shuttle's main engine. This value had to be known in order to perform certain repairs, and could be calculated using the ship's inertia rating and/or engine PSI **[T-SER4.5]**.

- **Thumbnail-Head:** A descriptive nickname that Cat called Kryten **[M-SMG2.9(c1)]**.

- **Thursday, Chancellor:** A rogue simulant aboard Dominator Zlurth's Death Ship, and a member of Zlurth's council. Zlurth sentenced Thursday to death for disagreeing with him after the dominator chastised the council for being sycophants who never challenged him **[T-SER10.6]**.

- **TI345:** The model number of a Psi-scan used aboard *Red Dwarf*. Developed by Tucker Instruments and distributed by Crapola Inc., it was only available in Scintillating Off-Gray **[G-RPG]**. This model, despite having a long warm-up time, outperformed the 346 in eight out of nine benchmarks during testing, for which it earned the Psi-scan of the Year, Best Budget Model award three years in a row **[T-SER5.4]**.

- **TI345xp:** A smaller version of Tucker Instruments' TI345 Psi-scan **[G-RPG]**.

- **Tibbles, Reverend:** A Fundamental Cloisterist among the Cat People inhabiting *Red Dwarf*. Tibbles wore a priest collar from which a nametag hung **[M-SMG2.2(a)]**.

- **tiddlywinks:** A game played by propelling small discs known as winks into a pot, by flicking them with a larger disc called a squidger **[RL]**. Tiddlywinks was among Captain Voorhese's guilty pleasures **[G-BIT]**. On one occasion, Holly—unaware the crew was being pursued throughout *Red Dwarf* by a creature that Cat had accidentally released—asked if anyone was interested in a game of tiddlywinks **[T-SER7(b)]**.

  ***NOTE:** This occurred in the Fan Film section of the Series VII DVD set.*

- **tiddlywinks show jumping:** A game that Lister and Cat devised to pass the time aboard *Red Dwarf* **[T-SER3.5]**.

- **Ties:** The business-class faction that fought in Earth's twenty-second-century Tie Wars against the blue-collar Blisters. The war tilted in favor of the Ties when they introduced the

**B-: Books**
**PRG:** *Red Dwarf Programme Guide*
**SUR:** *Red Dwarf Space Corps Survival Manual*
**PRM:** *Primordial Soup*
**SOS:** *Son of Soup*
**SCE:** *Scenes from the Dwarf*
**LOG:** *Red Dwarf Log No. 1996*
**RD8:** *Red Dwarf VIII*
**EVR:** *The Log: A Dwarfer's Guide to Everything*

**X-: Misc.**
**PRO:** Promotional materials, videos, etc.
**PST:** Posters at DJ XVII (2013)
**CAL:** 2008 calendar
**RNG:** Cell phone ringtones
**MOB:** Mobisode ("Red Christmas")
**CIN:** *Children in Need* sketch
**GEK:** *Geek Week* intros by Kryten
**TNG:** "Tongue-Tied" video
**XMS:** Bill Pearson's Christmas special pitch script
**XVD:** Bill Pearson's Christmas special pitch video
**OTH:** Other *Red Dwarf* appearances

**SUFFIX**
**DVD:**
**(d)** – Deleted scene
**(o)** – Outtake
**(b)** – Bonus DVD material (other)
**(e)** – Extended version

**SMEGAZINES:**
**(c)** – Comic
**(a)** – Article

**OTHER:**
**(s)** – Early/unused script draft
**(s1)** – Alternate version of script

# TAU, LOUISE, CAPTAIN

**PREFIX**
**RL:** Real life

**T-: Television Episodes**
- **SER:** Television series
- **IDW:** "Identity Within"
- **USA1:** Unaired U.S. pilot
- **USA2:** Unaired U.S. demo

**R-: *The Bodysnatcher Collection***
- **SER:** Remastered episodes
- **BOD:** "Bodysnatcher"
- **DAD:** "Dad"
- **FTH:** "Lister's Father"
- **INF:** "Infinity Patrol"
- **END:** "The End" (original assembly)

**N-: Novels**
- **INF:** *Infinity Welcomes Careful Drivers*
- **BTL:** *Better Than Life*
- **LST:** *Last Human*
- **BCK:** *Backwards*
- **OMN:** *Red Dwarf Omnibus*

**M-: Magazines**
- **SMG:** *Smegazine*

**W-: Websites**
- **OFF:** Official website
- **NAN:** *Prelude to Nanarchy*
- **AND:** *Androids*
- **DIV:** Diva-Droid
- **DIB:** Duane Dibbley
- **CRP:** Crapola
- **GEN:** Geneticon
- **LSR:** Leisure World Intl.
- **JMC:** Jupiter Mining Corporation
- **AIT:** *A.I. Today*
- **HOL:** HoloPoint

**G-: Roleplaying Game**
- **RPG:** *Core Rulebook*
- **BIT:** *A.I. Screen Extra Bits* booklet
- **SOR:** *Series Sourcebook*
- **OTH:** Other RPG material

Smart But Casual Bomb, a weapon that covered the Blisters in paisley cravats and hand-tailored lounge suits. The war raged on until the Blisters, realizing they were manufacturing the Ties' weapons, discontinued production, resulting in the war ending in compromise, with the Blisters buttoning their top shirt buttons and the Ties undoing theirs beneath their ties **[B-EVR]**.

- **Tie Wars, the:** A twenty-second-century fashion conflict between Earth's blue-collar workers (Blisters) and the business class (Ties). The Ties got the upper hand after launching the Smart But Casual Bomb, which blanketed the Blisters in hand-tailored lounge suits and paisley cravats. But when the blue-collar workers—who made the Ties' weapons—halted production, the war abruptly ceased **[B-EVR]**.

- **Tiffany:** A hypothetical woman whom Rimmer decided was Lister's type, rather than Kochanski. Girls named Tiffany, he claimed, drank Campari and soda, wore orange crotchless panties, thought deely-boppers were funny and said "sumfink" instead of "something" **[T-SER7.3]**.

- **Tiger:** A nickname that a computer-simulated Yvonne McGruder called Rimmer in the total-immersion video game *Better Than Life* **[T-SER2.2]**. Rimmer later asked Lister to call him this after awakening with implanted memories of a relationship with Lise Yates **[T-SER2.3]**.

- **Tiger:** A brand of deodorant sold aboard *Red Dwarf*. Lister used this antiperspirant to freshen up his socks before embarking on a rescue mission to *Nova 5* **[N-INF]**.

- **Tim:** A crewmember aboard a vessel that crashed into an asteroid in Psiren territory, who died when the telepathic Psirens attacked. A shipmate later recorded a log entry reporting several deaths, including Tim's **[T-SER6.1(d)]**.

- **Tim:** A chef aboard *Red Dwarf* whom Kochanski dated prior to and after her fling with Lister **[T-SER7.3]**. Dave was later unable to recall if the man's name had been Terry, Tim, Tom, Tony or Trevor **[N-INF]**. While filming a special for Krytie TV, Kryten claimed Kristine had gone back to Tim, but this was a lie to make Lister trash Warden Ackerman's quarters—which Kryten had claimed were Tim's—so he could air the incriminating footage **[T-SER8.5]**.

  ***NOTE:*** *Tim was apparently resurrected by the nanobots, though this was never explicitly stated onscreen. In the novel* Infinity Welcomes Careful Drivers, *Tim was a flight navigation officer who dumped Kochanski for a brunette in Catering.*

- **Tim:** A chef aboard a parallel-universe *Red Dwarf*. That reality's Kochanski dated Tim prior to and after her relationship with Lister **[T-SER7.3]**.

- ***Time*:** An American weekly news magazine based in New York City **[RL]**. While trapped in an addictive version of *Better Than Life*, Rimmer imagined that his face adorned the cover of an issue of *Time*, which he kept in his limousine **[N-BTL]**.

- **time alarm:** An alert transmitted by the Inquisitor's time gauntlet, warning the droid of any changes to his own timeline. The alarm was triggered when the Inquisitor erased the existence of Mortimer Dodd, a future worker at the Institute of Simulant Technology—the very facility that had created the droid in the first place **[M-SMG2.5(c3)]**.

- **time-bend:** A law of temporal physics dictating that time was experienced along its natural curve. Computing the result of cutting the curve's corner allowed Cassandra—an artificial intelligence whom the Canaries encountered aboard the SSS *Silverberg*—to predict the future with one hundred percent accuracy **[T-SER8.4(d)]**.

- **Time copter:** A time machine that Rimmer, while trapped in an addictive version of *Better Than Life*, imagined that his company, Rimmer Corporation, had developed. In the illusion, Arnold used the copter to retrieve several famous historical individuals with whom he could crash other soirées during his all-night bachelor party **[N-BTL]**.

- **time drive:** An experimental time-travel device developed in the twenty-eighth century by the Space Corps. The unit was installed aboard *Gemini 12*, whose crew used it to travel back to the twentieth century. There, the entire crew contracted influenza and died, after setting the ship's autopilot for deep

**B-: Books**
**PRG:** *Red Dwarf Programme Guide*
**SUR:** *Red Dwarf Space Corps Survival Manual*
**PRM:** *Primordial Soup*
**SOS:** *Son of Soup*
**SCE:** *Scenes from the Dwarf*
**LOG:** *Red Dwarf Log No. 1996*
**RD8:** *Red Dwarf VIII*
**EVR:** *The Log: A Dwarfer's Guide to Everything*

**X-: Misc.**
**PRO:** Promotional materials, videos, etc.
**PST:** Posters at DJ XVII (2013)
**CAL:** 2008 calendar
**RNG:** Cell phone ringtones
**MOB:** Mobisode ("Red Christmas")
**CIN:** *Children in Need* sketch
**GEK:** *Geek Week* intros by Kryten
**TNG:** "Tongue-Tied" video
**XMS:** Bill Pearson's Christmas special pitch script
**XVD:** Bill Pearson's Christmas special pitch video
**OTH:** Other *Red Dwarf* appearances

**SUFFIX**
**DVD:**
**(d)** – Deleted scene
**(o)** – Outtake
**(b)** – Bonus DVD material (other)
**(e)** – Extended version

**SMEGAZINES:**
**(c)** – Comic
**(a)** – Article

**OTHER:**
**(s)** – Early/unused script draft
**(s1)** – Alternate version of script

space and laying a reality minefield around the vessel to discourage looters.

The *Starbug 1* crew found the ship years later and stripped out the drive, installing it into their own craft. They tested the unit by visiting the year 1421, but realized it was useless without a faster-than-light drive since they were still in deep space.

Older versions of themselves from fifteen years in the future soon arrived, claiming to be time travelers in need of assistance. The future crew explained that after acquiring an FTL drive, they used the time drive to sample the best that space and time had to offer. The time drive malfunctioned, however, forcing them to seek help from their past selves to repair the damage.

Seeing the amoral, self-serving elitists they'd become, the younger crew refused to help, sparking a conflict that destroyed their *Starbug 1*, including its time drive. This caused a paradox that reset the timeline, eliminating the older crew **[T-SER6.6]**.

After a water tank breach destroyed all curries aboard *Starbug 1*, Lister devised a plan to retrieve the time drive and restock the lost supplies. Using a handheld version of the device, the crew tried to visit an Indian restaurant on Earth, but instead arrived in Dallas, Texas, in 1963, interrupting John F. Kennedy's assassination. When the FBI accused them of the shooting, the crew jumped forward three years, to find the city deserted—and the drive disabled, marooning them in 1966. After repairing the device, they convinced JFK to return with them to 1963 and assassinate himself from behind a grassy knoll **[T-SER7.1]**.

Crapola Inc. sold a similar device via its annual *SCABBY* catalog **[G-RPG]**.

> ***NOTE:** How the time drive managed to get them to Earth in episode 7.1 ("Tikka to Ride") remains a mystery, since the previous episode had clearly established the drive's uselessness in bringing Lister home due to its sole function of travelling through time, not space.*

- **time fly:** A mutated form of common housefly that, by 2250, had evolved the ability to make short jumps through time, allowing it to evade being swatted **[B-EVR]**.

- **time gauntlet:** A device that the Inquisitor created to travel through time so he could judge humanity's worth. The droid used the gauntlet to visit every person throughout history. For those whom he concluded had not led a worthwhile life, he surgically removed them from existence, replacing them with others who never had a chance to live, hoping they might fare better. The Inquisitor deemed Lister and Kryten unworthy, and prepared to erase their existence, but a future Kryten appeared and cut off the droid's gauntlet arm, passing it to Lister and his younger self. They then used it to erase the Inquisitor and undo all of his work **[T-SER5.2]**.

- **time hole:** A spatial phenomenon, identifiable as an orange swirl, that linked two points in space-time. A time hole appeared in front of *Starbug 1* as Kryten took a piloting test, propelling Kryten, Rimmer and Holly into Earth's far future, to a point when time ran backwards. After months spent searching for the shuttle, Lister and Cat encountered the same phenomenon in *Starbug 2*, and entered it to locate their comrades. Once reunited, the group returned to *Red Dwarf* through the time hole **[T-SER3.1]**.

- **"Time Jump":** A phrase on a chart that Rimmer created to translate markings on a mysterious pod Holly found adrift in space, which he thought were an alien language—but which actually spelled out "*Red Dwarf* Garbage Pod," eroded away after many years of spaceflight **[T-SER1.4]**.

- **time matrix:** A component of a portable time drive that the *Starbug 1* crew used to travel back to Dallas, Texas, in 1963 **[T-SER7.1]**.

- **Time Obelisk:** A monument developed by the Cat People tribe known as the Elite, during their Holy War aboard *Red Dwarf*. The Obelisk, capable of sending warriors through time, was located in the Elite's High Tower, and was built using technology that the Cats found on a derelict vessel embedded in the mining vessel's hull.

  After the Holy War raged for fifteen hundred years, three Elite warriors—Fritz, Krazy and Juma—used the Time Obelisk to travel five hundred years into the future to retrieve their god, Cloister (Lister), so he could end the conflict **[M-SMG2.1(c1)]**. Rimmer, Cat and Kryten, however, utilized the device to rescue him **[M-SMG2.3(c1)]**.

- **Time Retriever:** A device featured in an alternate-universe version of the total-immersion video game *Red Dwarf*, which players could use to bring Kochanski back from the dead. A future echo of Lister provided players with clues to a code required to operate the machine. One clue, for example, was "Jim and Bexley—take away one," which translated to "H" and "A" **[M-SMG2.4(c4)]**.

  ***NOTE:** Except, of course, that taking one away from J and B would be "I" and "A," not "H" and "A."*

- ***Times, The*:** A British daily newspaper, founded in 1785 **[RL]**. Rimmer owned a painting of a chimpanzee on a toilet reading *The Times*, which he considered priceless **[T-SER1.6]**.

  ***NOTE:** This gag originated in a* Son of Cliché *sketch titled "Freshers."*

- **timeslide:** A type of photograph created using mutated chemicals, allowing one to visit the time and place depicted in the photo, as long as one remained within the image's constraints. Kryten inadvertently created a batch of timeslides while developing film via the old chemicals.

  Using the slides, Lister crashed the wedding of Rimmer's brother Frank, as well as a couple's ski trip and a rally in Nuremberg, Germany, where he scuffled with Adolf Hitler. Stealing the Führer's briefcase, he realized it contained a bomb planted by would-be assassin Claus von Stauffenberg, and kicked it back into the photograph, nearly killing the dictator. Upon seeing an old newspaper's altered account of the event, the crew realized the potential of using the timeslides to change history.

  Lister accessed a slide of his first band, Smeg and the Heads, to visit his younger self and convince him to invent the Tension Sheet, a multi-million-dollar novelty item originally conceived by Fred Holden. Lister thus became Earth's youngest billionaire, marrying supermodel Sabrina Mulholland-Jjones. Rimmer developed a photo from his boarding-school days to beat Lister to the punch and become wealthy in his place, but mentioned the Tension Sheet in young Fred's presence, unwittingly restoring him as the product's inventor **[T-SER3.5]**.

  While trapped in an elation squid hallucination, the *Red Dwarf* crew imagined visiting a twenty-first-century science fiction collectibles shop called They Walk Among Us!, where an employee named Noddy suggested using a timeslide to visit Nose World. The slides were back on *Red Dwarf*, however, and of no use to them **[T-SER9.2]**.

- **Time Store:** A facility that Rimmer imagined while trapped in an addictive version of *Better Than Life*. The Time Store, developed by the Rimmer Corporation, enabled wealthy customers to travel through time **[N-BTL]**.

- **time traps:** A phenomenon that the Inquisitor harnessed while erasing individuals from history, to ensure the space-time continuum would be unaffected by each deletion **[T-SER5.2(d)]**.

- **time wand:** A device that served as a temporal storage device, capable of digitizing and recording time, and then playing it back on demand. Inscribed in the handle was the Latin word *tempus*, meaning "time." Practical uses for the wand included stopping or slowing time within a confined area, as well as aging or de-aging biological and non-biological matter. Misuse of the wand could result in the rapid evolution or de-evolution of living or recently deceased creatures **[T-SER8.6]**. Crapola Inc. distributed a time wand through its annual *SCABBY* catalog **[G-RPG]**.

  *Red Dwarf*'s prison Canaries found a time wand aboard the Space Corps derelict SS *Manny Celeste.* After *Red Dwarf* lost contact with several members of the team, additional inmates, including Cat, Kryten and Kochanski, were assigned to investigate. They found the missing personnel frozen in time by the wand, which Kryten smuggled back to *Red Dwarf*, believing it could help them speed up their prison sentence.

  Kryten's group reunited with Lister and Rimmer, as well as a fellow inmate named Birdman, whose pet sparrow, Pete, had died during the escape. The mechanoid used the wand to restore Pete to life, but a miscalculation de-evolved the bird into a *Tyrannosaurus rex*, which ate its owner and attacked the others **[T-SER8.6]**.

  After Pete swallowed the time wand, the crew prepared a massive bowl of cow vindaloo that the dinosaur consumed, causing it to become violently ill and excrete the wand. Inmates Baxter and Kill Krazy stole the device and inadvertently transformed themselves into gorillas, but Lister and Rimmer retrieved the wand, restored the thugs' original forms—as well as those of Birdman and Pete—and then destroyed the device so it could do no further harm **[T-SER8.7]**.

> ***NOTE:*** *The script book* Red Dwarf VIII *called the device Tempus, but onscreen, the word was merely inscribed in its handle.*

- **timezip:** An artificial hole through time that Spare Head Three created using an intelligent building material called FLOB, which he found on a planet on which he had been abandoned. He instructed the FLOB to build a device capable of cutting a rift through time so he could send a signal to *Red Dwarf* and bring them forward fifty years to rescue him.

  The crew swapped Spare Head Three's personality chips with Kryten's in order to facilitate the rescue, but an accident erased the FLOB-controlling head from space-time, causing the timezip device to destabilize. As the crew retreated to safety, Spare Head Three became decapitated from Kryten's body and was left behind, restarting the cycle anew **[M-SMG2.9(c1)]**.

- **Tin-Brain:** A nickname that Cat called Kryten upon finding the mechanoid in his quarters **[M-SMG1.5(a)]**.

- **Tina:** A model of android available in a pick'n'mix lineup at a brothel on Mimas. Customers could choose various body parts from selected androids, and then have a custom-designed sex droid assembled for their use. A portly, red-haired customer chose this particular model's left leg for his sex droid **[N-INF]**.

- **Tina:** A crewmember aboard a vessel that crashed into an asteroid in Psiren territory, who died when the telepathic Psirens attacked. A shipmate later recorded a log entry reporting several deaths, including Tina's **[T-SER6.1(d)]**.

- **Tina:** A young scientist at Brainfade, a company in Jake Bullet's universe that specialized in mind manipulation and cyber personalities. Her work at the firm involved chimpanzees. Following the murder of Sandra Halley, Tina asked her boss, Doctor Scofrenia, for the victim's parking spot **[M-SMG2.7(c4)]**.

  After Bullet killed Scofrenia, Tina used brain material from experimental brain-control spikes to reconstitute Halley's mind and soul into a test subject's body. She then transferred an altered backup copy of Scofrenia's personality into a chimp named Sally **[M-SMG2.9(c4)]**.

- **Tipp-Ex:** A brand of correction fluid designed to cover writing on forms **[RL]**. Recruit officer Caldicott used Tipp-Ex frequently while filling out Lister's JMC enrollment form **[N-INF]**.

- **Titan:** The largest moon of Saturn **[RL]**. Titan had the largest population of any body in the outer solar system, relegated to underground cities and pressurized surface domes, and contained the only zoo among the outer planets. The organized crime syndicate on Titan was significantly more respectable than any other Jovian moon organization **[G-RPG]**. A souvenir shop on the moon sold official Titan merchandise, such as talking alarm clocks and medical equipment **[R-BOD]**.

  After Kochanski broke up with Lister, he took shore leave in the Saturnian system to get over her **[T-SER7.3]**. Visiting Titan, he acquired a pregnant cat that he called Frankenstein, and smuggled the animal aboard *Red Dwarf*. When Captain Hollister found out, he sentenced Dave to eighteen months in a stasis room—which saved his life, as a cadmium II explosion soon killed the remainder of the crew **[T-SER1.1]**.

  Lister often sang songs about Titan and Jupiter's largest moon, Ganymede **[T-SER1.1]**. Titan was also mentioned in a drinking game that Lister played with Chen, Selby and Petersen in *Red Dwarf*'s disco room **[T-SER1.3]**.

  One popular tourist attraction on Titan was the site of a crashed starship that became embedded in the moon after test-firing the Proton Cannon of Nakasami in the solar system's outskirts. The advanced weapon's recoil propelled it back into the system, causing it to crash into Titan **[B-EVR]**.

  > ***NOTE:*** *Although Lister had Frankenstein by the time he returned to* Red Dwarf *from Mimas in episode 7.3 ("Ouroboros"), episode 1.1 ("The End") had already established that he obtained the cat on Titan. The above entry attempts to reconcile the two accounts.*

- **Titan:** A name that Rimmer, dazed after spending 557 years imprisoned on Rimmerworld, mistook for Kryten's **[T-SER6.5]**.

- **Titan Docking Port:** A facility on Titan at which space vessels docked to take on or unload personnel and supplies. After Queeg assumed control of *Red Dwarf* following Holly's breach of Article 5, Holly accused the backup computer of mutiny, threatening to see the other AI "swing from the highest yardarm in Titan Docking Port" **[T-SER2.5]**.

*NOTE: Holly's mutiny threat was just for show, as he'd created Queeg to teach the crew a lesson. This threat parodied dialog from the 1935 film* Mutiny on the Bounty.

- **Titan Hilton:** A hotel and convention center located on Titan. Lister owned a blanket from this establishment **[T-SER1.5]**. Geneticon 12, a convention catering to fans of genetic engineering, was held at the Titan Hilton **[W-GEN]**.

  *NOTE: Hilton Worldwide is an American global hospitality company operating almost four thousand hotels throughout ninety-one countries.*

- ***Titanic*:** A 1997 American epic film directed by James Cameron, about the ill-fated maiden voyage of the British passenger liner RMS *Titanic* **[RL]**. While trapped in an elation squid hallucination, Lister met a pair of children on a bus, one of whom (a boy) claimed his sister was so smart that she knew the *Titanic* would sink from the beginning of the movie **[T-SER9.2]**.

- ***Titanic*, RMS:** A British passenger liner that sank in 1912 during its maiden voyage after colliding with an iceberg in the Atlantic Ocean, resulting in more than fifteen hundred deaths **[RL]**. After being arrested for stealing a *Red Dwarf* shuttle, Lister bemoaned that without the nanobots that had reconstructed the mining ship and its crew, his case was as watertight as a supersaver economy cabin aboard the *Titanic* **[T-SER8.2(d)]**.

- **Titanica Fish Droid MkIV:** A mechanical pet goldfish produced by Acme **[M-SMG1.4(c2)]**. The fish came equipped with buoyancy tanks, directional fins, optical tanks, a propulsion unit, a defensive micropedo and a battery compartment housing two HP11 batteries. Lister's two mechanical goldfish, Lennon and McCartney, were of this model **[M-SMG2.4(c5)]**.

  ***NOTE:*** Red Dwarf—The Roleplaying Game*'s* Series Sourcebook *identified the fish as IcthyTech 3000 Robot Goldfish.*

- **Titan mushrooms:** A hallucinogenic fungus, also known as "freaky fungus." Lister smuggled several Titan mushrooms aboard *Red Dwarf*, which he used while preparing breakfast for Rimmer. Due to the mushrooms' qualities, Rimmer experienced an hallucinogenic fit and attended an inspection wearing nothing but racing gloves and swimming goggles. He then attacked two officers whom he perceived to be armed giraffes **[T-SER2.4]**.

- **Titan novelty nuclear warheads:** A type of explosive weapons created for personal use. *Red Dwarf* stocked several such warheads **[G-SOR]**.

- **Titan Taj Mahal:** An Indian restaurant aboard *Red Dwarf*, located a short distance from the ship's cinema. A commercial for the eatery played before certain showings, advertising "the finest Tandoori cuisine at one-fifth gravity" **[T-SER1.6]**.

- **Titan Tours:** An interplanetary travel agency, circa the twenty-second century. Its slogan was "We Get You There" **[W-DIB]**.

- **Titan Zoo:** An attraction on the moon Titan. Lister once mistook a picture of Rimmer's mother as a souvenir from the Titan Zoo and used it as an ashtray **[T-SER1.6]**. Another time, while flirting with two women from *Red Dwarf*'s Supplies department, Rimmer suggested they take a trip to this zoo. Lister humiliated his roommate by claiming they'd be able to meet his mom **[T-SER2.1]**.

- **Titchmarsh, Alan:** A British gardener, broadcaster, novelist and media personality **[RL]**. Gordon, the *Scott Fitzgerald*'s artificial-intelligence computer, enjoyed Titchmarsh's books **[W-AIT]**.

- **TIV:** *See* total-immersion video game (TIV)

- **"Tixe":** A word printed on a wall sign at an eatery in England, during a period in Earth's far future when time ran backwards. The sign, when read forward, said "Exit" **[T-SER3.1]**.

  *NOTE: Throughout the episode, backwards writing was inconsistently handled. In some cases (as in this instance), characters were backward-facing, while in others, they faced forward. Adding to the confusion, some signs were lettered top to bottom, whereas others ran bottom to top.*

# TROJAN, SS

- **TJ:** An American television executive in an alternate universe in which *Red Dwarf* was merely a British TV series. He was a large, balding man who smoked cigars. In this reality, Americans remade the series but with several changes, and the first episode was previewed by TJ and his associate, Frank. TJ was stunned to learn that the British version featured a dead crew, a hologrammic main cast member, humanity's extinction and a lack of aliens—all of which were changed in the American version **[M-SMG1.10(c4)]**.

- **toastie soldiers:** A British comfort food consisting of thin slices of toast dipped in a soft-boiled egg **[RL]**. After being resurrected by nanobots, Rimmer contemplated leaving *Red Dwarf* with his escaping shipmates aboard *Starbug 1*, realizing he would never come to terms with being a failure, and that every time he ate a boiled egg, he'd know he didn't even outrank the toastie soldiers **[T-SER8.3]**.

- **Toastie Toppers:** A food item stored in the refrigerator of the Officers' Quarters aboard the "low" *Red Dwarf*. While explaining to Cat that everything aboard the ship was decrepit, Kryten found Toastie Toppers, which proved his point **[T-SER5.5]**.

  ***NOTE:*** *Toast Toppers, a differently spelled canned snack food produced by Heinz and sold in the United Kingdom, is often spread on toast.*

- **ToastSet technology:** A dynamic feature built into Talkie Toasters. It contained eight settings—four that undercooked toast, and four that burned it **[W-CRP]**.

- **Todhunter, Christopher:** An alias that Arnold Rimmer used while visiting a brothel on Mimas. Not wanting his embarrassing ordeal at the bordello to become public, he bribed Lister (whom he'd just met while Dave was working

**PREFIX**
**RL:** Real life

**T-: Television Episodes**
**SER:** Television series
**IDW:** "Identity Within"
**USA1:** Unaired U.S. pilot
**USA2:** Unaired U.S. demo

**R-: *The Bodysnatcher Collection***
**SER:** Remastered episodes
**BOD:** "Bodysnatcher"
**DAD:** "Dad"
**FTH:** "Lister's Father"
**INF:** "Infinity Patrol"
**END:** "The End" (original assembly)

**N-: Novels**
**INF:** *Infinity Welcomes Careful Drivers*
**BTL:** *Better Than Life*
**LST:** *Last Human*
**BCK:** *Backwards*
**OMN:** *Red Dwarf Omnibus*

**M-: Magazines**
**SMG:** *Smegazine*

**W-: Websites**
**OFF:** Official website
**NAN:** *Prelude to Nanarchy*
**AND:** *Androids*
**DIV:** Diva-Droid
**DIB:** Duane Dibbley
**CRP:** Crapola
**GEN:** Geneticon
**LSR:** Leisure World Intl.
**JMC:** Jupiter Mining Corporation
**AIT:** *A.I. Today*
**HOL:** HoloPoint

**G-: Roleplaying Game**
**RPG:** *Core Rulebook*
**BIT:** *A.I. Screen Extra Bits* booklet
**SOR:** *Series Sourcebook*
**OTH:** Other RPG material

as a taxi driver), and claimed his name was Todhunter, despite paying with money from a purse embroidered with his actual name **[N-INF]**.

- **Todhunter, Frank, First Officer:** A command officer aboard *Red Dwarf* **[W-JMC]**. He was married with children, though Lister had heard he cheated on his wife **[T-SER7.4]**.

  While perusing deceased crewman George McIntyre's belongings, Todhunter found a list of reports that Rimmer had filed against Lister, and questioned Arnold's inability to get along with his roommate. To Rimmer's fury, Todhunter agreed with Lister's assessment that he was a smeghead. When Dave was later sentenced to eighteen months in stasis, the sympathetic Todhunter escorted him to a stasis booth **[T-SER1.1]**.

  ***NOTE:** The captions to episode 7.4 ("Duct Soup") misspelled Todhunter's name as "Todd Hunter." It is unknown whether the nanobots resurrected him in Series VIII.*

- **toilet block:** A section of *Red Dwarf* allocated for toilet facilities. Holly once accidentally ejected the entire block into space, spurring a rescue operation that the crew dubbed Operation Khazi **[B-LOG]**.

- **Toilet-brush Hair:** A derogatory nickname that Cat called Rimmer **[T-SER6.5]**.

- **toilet deck:** A section of *Red Dwarf* containing lavatory facilities. Lister once spent two days on the toilet deck after drinking a yard of vindaloo sauce during a marathon vindaloo night **[B-LOG]**.

  ***NOTE:** Presumably, this deck contained the toilet block.*

- **Toilet Duck:** A brand of toilet cleaner produced by S.C. Johnson & Son **[RL]**. After Caroline Carmen's reanimated corpse kissed Lister while under the Epideme virus' control, he declared that he would need to gargle with Toilet Duck to get rid of the taste **[T-SER7.7]**.

- **toilet plunger incident, the:** An occurrence aboard *Red Dwarf* involving Lister, Chen, Selby and Petersen, with Selby reportedly the mastermind **[G-BIT]**.

- **Toilet University:** A software suite installed in mechanoids as part of their training in the lavatorial sciences. The droids had to complete a written exam to indicate the program had been installed successfully, in order to become a certified Bachelor of Sanitation (BS). Kryten gained his BS certificate using this program **[T-SER7.7]**.

- **Tom:** The possible name of a flight navigation officer aboard *Red Dwarf*. Kochanski dated the man for almost two years before he dumped her for a brunette in the ship's Catering department, at which point she began seeing Lister as a rebound. After a month, the officer broke up with the brunette and went back to Kristine, who left Lister to be with him again. Depressed and bitter, Lister never bothered to learn the man's name, though he knew it started with a "T" and may have been Tom **[N-INF]**.

- **"Tomcat":** A word adorning a patch sewn onto Lister's leather jacket **[T-SER3.1]**.

  ***NOTE:** The patch was designed for U.S. Navy pilots of the F-14 Tomcat fighter aircraft.*

- **Tommy:** A young orphan boy in an alternate reality who resided at the Space Corps Test Base on Mimas. Ace Rimmer often spent his free time sitting by Tommy's bedside when the child was sick, reading him bedtime stories **[T-SER4.5]**.

  ***NOTE:** Tommy's status as an orphan was mentioned in a deleted scene from episode 4.5 ("Dimension Jump"), but not in the aired version.*

- **"Tomorrow Is the First Day of the Rest of Your Death":** A slogan printed on a motivational sign posted outside the quarters that Rimmer shared with his duplicate hologram **[T-SER1.6]**. After the duplicate's erasure, Rimmer brought the sign back to the room he had previously shared with Lister **[T-SER2.1]**.

- **"Tongue Tied":** A song that Cat, Lister and Rimmer performed in one of Cat's dreams. Cat found footage of this dream while searching the dream recorder for another involving three girls and a vat of banana yogurt **[T-SER2.6]**. Several versions of this tune were performed by characters in the dreams of Leo Davis **[X-TNG]**.

  ***NOTE:** This song originated as a* Son of Cliché *sketch*

**B-: Books**
**PRG:** *Red Dwarf Programme Guide*
**SUR:** *Red Dwarf Space Corps Survival Manual*
**PRM:** *Primordial Soup*
**SOS:** *Son of Soup*
**SCE:** *Scenes from the Dwarf*
**LOG:** *Red Dwarf Log No. 1996*
**RD8:** *Red Dwarf VIII*
**EVR:** *The Log: A Dwarfer's Guide to Everything*

**X-: Misc.**
**PRO:** Promotional materials, videos, etc.
**PST:** Posters at DJ XVII (2013)
**CAL:** 2008 calendar
**RNG:** Cell phone ringtones
**MOB:** Mobisode ("Red Christmas")
**CIN:** *Children in Need* sketch
**GEK:** *Geek Week* intros by Kryten
**TNG:** "Tongue-Tied" video

**XMS:** Bill Pearson's Christmas special pitch script
**XVD:** Bill Pearson's Christmas special pitch video
**OTH:** Other *Red Dwarf* appearances

**SUFFIX**
**DVD:**
**(d)** – Deleted scene
**(o)** – Outtake
**(b)** – Bonus DVD material (other)
**(e)** – Extended version

**SMEGAZINES:**
**(c)** – Comic
**(a)** – Article

**OTHER:**
**(s)** – Early/unused script draft
**(s1)** – Alternate version of script

*titled "Tongue Tied," in which Nick Wilton performed the tune at a slower pace, accompanied by Peter Brewis on piano.*

- **Tony:** The possible name of a flight navigation officer aboard *Red Dwarf*. Kochanski dated the man for almost two years before he dumped her for a brunette in the ship's Catering department, at which point she began seeing Lister as a rebound. After a month, the officer broke up with the brunette and went back to Kristine, who left Lister to be with him again. Depressed and bitter, Lister never bothered to learn the man's name, though he knew it started with a "T" and may have been Tony **[N-INF]**.

- **Toot:** A bloodsport popular on Phoebe, Dione, Rhea and other moons, in which specially bred Venusian fighting snails were forced to fight to the death. The fights took place within a six-foot square concrete pit, often lasting for days, while spectators got drunk and placed increasingly absurd bets. Although the sport was banned, the Ganymedian Mafia still ran snail pits. After incurring a massive debt from gambling on Toot, George McIntyre committed suicide **[N-INF]**.

- **"TopCats Brixton":** A slogan printed on a T-shirt worn by Black Island Studios caretaker Leo Davis **[X-TNG]**.

  ***NOTE:*** *The Brixton TopCats are a British basketball team.*

- **Topic Bar:** A brand of chocolate candy bars sold in Europe and the United States, consisting of nougat, caramel and hazelnuts **[RL]**. Rimmer believed that nothing ever went right for him, and that he was most likely the only person to have ever purchased a Topic bar with no hazelnuts **[T-SER2.4]**.

- **Torquemada, Tomas dé, Grand Inquisitor:** A fifteenth-century Spanish friar who served as the first grand inquisitor during the Spanish Inquisition **[RL]**. A glitch in the artificial-reality program *Great Moments in Human History* caused his simulacrum to speak with the voice of Donald Duck **[B-SUR]**.

- **Total Gonzo:** An energy drink produced by Popco Inc. Its slogan: "Drink Total Gonzo, and you can play zero-gee football just like Jim Bexley Speed of the London Jets" **[G-SOR]**.

- **Total Immersion, Inc.:** A company specializing in artificial-reality games and gear. Total Immersion's products were distributed exclusively by Crapola Inc., and included Artificial Reality Suites for home, office or spaceship use, as well as programs such as *Better Than Life, Gumshoe, Jousting, Jane Austen World* and *Streets of Laredo* **[G-RPG]**.

- **total-immersion suit:** An outfit worn by cyberschool students, enabling them to connect to a mainframe computer and experience a virtual-reality campus **[T-SER7.4(e)]**.

- **total-immersion video game (TIV):** A type of interactive game in which players were plugged into a virtual world via a special headpiece, experiencing the game in a way that was almost indistinguishable from real life **[T-SER2.2]**.

- ***Total World Domination*:** A Total Immersion video game operated at arcades owned by Leisure World International **[W-LSR]**.

- **"To the Memory of the Memory of Lise Yates":** An engraving on a tombstone that marked the shallow grave in which *Red Dwarf*'s black box recording was buried. Rimmer, distraught and embarrassed after Lister gifted him with a memory of his own ex-girlfriend, Lise Yates, insisted everyone's minds be erased and the black box be buried on a remote moon, to hide all evidence of the traumatizing event.

  After the memory wipes, however, the crew realized the black box was missing and followed its homing signal back to the moon to retrieve it, in order to solve the mystery of their missing time. They found the box buried next to the engraved tombstone **[T-SER2.3]**.

- **Touch-T:** A term short for touch telepathy. Touch-Ts, Space Corps officers able to read a person's mind simply by touching him or her, wore a T-shaped insignia on their uniforms. When Rimmer impersonated a Space Corps captain to impress his brother Howard, Lister unknowingly chose a uniform emblazoned with such an emblem. When Sim Crawford recognized the insignia, Howard requested a demonstration of his abilities. Lister initially panicked, then squeezed Howard's head between his hands and accurately "sensed" that the other was in pain **[T-SER10.1]**.

**PREFIX**
**RL:** Real life

**T-: Television Episodes**
**SER:** Television series
**IDW:** "Identity Within"
**USA1:** Unaired U.S. pilot
**USA2:** Unaired U.S. demo

**R-: *The Bodysnatcher Collection***
**SER:** Remastered episodes
**BOD:** "Bodysnatcher"
**DAD:** "Dad"
**FTH:** "Lister's Father"
**INF:** "Infinity Patrol"
**END:** "The End" (original assembly)

**N-: Novels**
**INF:** *Infinity Welcomes Careful Drivers*
**BTL:** *Better Than Life*
**LST:** *Last Human*
**BCK:** *Backwards*
**OMN:** *Red Dwarf Omnibus*

**M-: Magazines**
**SMG:** *Smegazine*

**W-: Websites**
**OFF:** Official website
**NAN:** *Prelude to Nanarchy*
**AND:** *Androids*
**DIV:** Diva-Droid
**DIB:** Duane Dibbley
**CRP:** Crapola
**GEN:** Geneticon
**LSR:** Leisure World Intl.
**JMC:** Jupiter Mining Corporation
**AIT:** *A.I. Today*
**HOL:** HoloPoint

**G-: Roleplaying Game**
**RPG:** *Core Rulebook*
**BIT:** *A.I. Screen Extra Bits* booklet
**SOR:** *Series Sourcebook*
**OTH:** Other RPG material

- **toupée:** A hairpiece designed to cover male pattern baldness **[RL]**. Holly wore a toupée on his digitized head during a mission to rescue *Nova 5*'s female survivors **[T-SER2.1]**. Sometime during the twenty-second century, Earth officials developed a plan to cover the increasingly dangerous hole in the planet's ozone layer with a giant toupée **[T-SER3.2]**.

- **Tour:** A brand of music amplifiers. Lister brought several Tour amps to a barren planet so he could play his guitar at a celebration of Rimmer's deathday **[T-SER2.3]**.

- **Toutatis:** A Celtic god worshipped in ancient Gaul and Great Britain **[RL]**. While living in Albion (an early name for Britain), the family of a woman named Erin were dragged from their homes and sacrificed to Toutatis, Esus and Taranis in a wicker tower, where they were garroted, burned, drowned and consumed by druids. Erin thus fled to India and made a living as a produce vendor **[T-SER10.3]**.

- **Toy Boy:** *See* Droid Boy

- ***Traffic Movements 20th July*:** The title of a binder on the desk of Chief Olin, Jake Bullet's police chief in the cyborg's reality **[M-SMG1.13(c4)]**.

- **Traga 16:** A small, low-gravity planetoid on which Lister, Rimmer and Kryten once played golf **[T-SER7.5]**.

  *NOTE: The* Red Dwarf Programme Guide *spelled the planetoid's name as "Traka 16."*

- **Train Spotters Anonymous:** A help group for those addicted to trainspotting. Duane Dibbley would have likely belonged to this group **[M-SMG2.2(a)]**.

  *NOTE: Trainspotting is a hobby involving the spotting of all types of a given type of railway car or other rolling stock.*

- **Trans Am Wheel Arch Nostrils:** A nickname that Cat called Rimmer, referencing his flared nostrils **[T-SER5.2]**.

  *NOTE: General Motors produced the Trans Am, an American automobile featuring pronounced wheel arches, from 1962 to 2002.*

- **transdimensional homing beacon:** A small pod fitted with dimensional jump capability and a homing beacon, used to transport small packages over great distances and interdimensionally. These pods were primarily allocated for long-range mail delivery, and spamming companies took full advantage of the technology **[G-SOR]**.

  As each successive Ace Rimmer died, a transdimensional homing beacon was used as a coffin to transport his remains to a final resting place in orbit around a white gas giant. When the prime Rimmer second-guessed his decision to carry on the Ace legacy, the *Starbug 1* crew followed his predecessor's coffin through a wormhole to the planet, where it joined millions of other pods. Inspired, Rimmer accepted his destiny **[T-SER7.2]**.

- **transdimensional trace:** A method of detecting a breach between parallel dimensions, used to establish a linkway. Kochanski detected a positive transdimensional trace while searching for a way to return to her own dimension **[T-SER7.3]**.

- **Transfer Suite:** A section of a soundwave penitentiary's Body Reclamation Unit that the *Red Dwarf* crew imagined while trapped in an addictive version of *Better Than Life*. The suite was designed to transfer the essences of incarcerated individuals to and from Solidgram bodies. Using the suite to regain physical form while escaping from the facility, Rimmer's mind ended up inside the body of sex worker Trixie LaBouche after a fellow escapee, Jimmy Jitterman, commandeered Arnold's body **[N-BTL]**.

- **translation mode:** A function of 4000 Series mechanoids enabling them to translate any programmed languages. Kryten used this function to translate Adolf Hitler's diary, which Lister obtained while traveling via timeslide **[T-SER3.5]**.

- **transmogrification:** A process by which a DNA modifier analyzed an individual's DNA and either changed it or mixed it with another sample, thereby altering that person's genetic makeup. When the *Red Dwarf* crew found such a device aboard a derelict spaceship, Lister was accidentally transmogrified into a chicken, and then a hamster, while Kryten attained human form and Lister's dinner became a mutton vindaloo beast **[T-SER4.2]**.

- **transparisteel:** A strong transparent material from which a jar containing a future Lister's brain was made **[G-SOR]**.

- **transponder:** A device designed to receive a radio signal and automatically transmit back a response, frequently used for air navigation or with RFID technology **[RL]**. A portable time drive that transported the *Red Dwarf* crew to Dallas, Texas, in 1963, utilized a transponder **[T-SER7.1]**.

- **transponder calibrations:** A series of settings necessary for the proper operation of 4000 Series mechanoids. After switching Kryten's main head with Spare Head Two and removing his guilt chip and behavior protocols, Lister explained the mechanoid's odd behavior by attributing it to a bio-glitch in his transponder calibrations **[T-SER7.1]**.

- **transport decks:** The levels aboard *Red Dwarf* housing its *Starbug* shuttlecrafts **[T-SER5.2]**.

- **transport tubes:** A series of conduits running throughout *Red Dwarf*, enabling the crew to transport materials from one location to another. Lister accessed a transport tube to send his personal effects to vacuum storage before entering a stasis booth for a trip back to Earth **[M-SMG1.4(c2)]**.

- **Trans-Siberian Express:** A Russian railway line connecting stops between Moscow and Vladivostok **[RL]**. Bored with life aboard *Red Dwarf*, Lister irritated Rimmer with a continuous stream of sighing, which Arnold compared to the soundtrack from *Great Railway Journeys of the World,* likening the sound to the Trans-Siberian Express pulling into Warsaw Central **[T-SER3.5(d)]**.

- **Transtemporal Film Unit:** A video-production company specializing in fitness videos featuring historical figures. Its titles included Joan of Arc's workout tape *Go for the Burn!* and René Descartes' *Run Your Way Slim* video, *I Jog Therefore I Am* **[B-LOG]**.

- **Tranter, Dieter, Admiral:** A Space Corps command officer in one of Ace Rimmer's realities. Due to a clerical error, his records were swapped with those of Admiral Peter Tranter. As a result, Peter was held back and assigned dead-end postings due to Dieter's incompetence, while Dieter was promoted time and again. This continued for years until Peter retired, at which point the mistake was corrected and Dieter's pay was slashed in half **[N-BCK]**.

- **Tranter, James, Admiral Sir ("Bongo"):** The Space Corps' Admiral of the Fleet in one of Ace Rimmer's realities, stationed at the Corps' test base on Mimas. Ace reported directly to Tranter, whose final mission for the pilot involved the testing of a prototype spaceship able to break the speed of reality and cross dimensions. Since this would be a one-way trip, Tranter attempted (unsuccessfully) to seduce Ace before his departure, despite having been happily married for thirty-five years. Tranter bore a resemblance to the mechanoid Kryten **[T-SER4.5]**.

- **Tranter, Pete:** An acquaintance of Lister during his youth. Pete had a sister whom Lister lusted after throughout puberty **[T-SER6.1]**.

- **Tranter, Peter, Admiral:** The commander of the Space Corps Research and Development Program, stationed on Europa in an alternate reality. Among his many nicknames were "Bungo," "Bun-Bun," "Cheese," "Himself," "Old Man," "Skunk Foot" and "Vinegar Drawers."

  A typical bureaucrat, Tranter despised his position, and indulged in such self-destructive vices as alcohol and extramarital affairs. Eventually, he earned command of Project *Wildfire*, tasked with producing a spaceship able to break the light barrier. Tranter saw this as an opportunity to advance his stalled career, which had consisted of numerous dead-end postings despite his hard work.

  Spearheaded by Ace Rimmer, the project took an unexpected turn when the team realized the ship could also travel between dimensions. Seeing no value in a dimension-crossing spacecraft, the admiral stepped down, leaving Ace in charge, and retired to his Venus condominium with his wife.

  The Space Corps later discovered that a clerical error had switched his file with that of an incompetent buffoon named Admiral Dieter Tranter, who had been receiving promotions and pay raises intended for him. To rectify the error, the Corps awarded Peter his full salary after retirement, while cutting Dieter's pay in half **[N-BCK]**.

- ***Treasure Island*:** A coming-of-age adventure novel by Robert Louis Stevenson, published in 1883 **[RL]**. While cleaning Lister's quarters, Kryten discovered this book and several others under his bunk. Lister admitted he was going through an educational phase, and assured the mechanoid that it would pass **[T-SER7.6(d)]**.

- **Treaty 5:** An agreement established during the Fifth Geneva Convention, pertaining to the rights and privileges of prisoners of war. Rimmer quoted Treaty 5 while pretending to surrender to Dominator Zlurth, knowing the Simulant Death Ship commander would not honor the terms **[T-SER10.6]**.

- **Tree Apostle Sunshine Bunny Wunny Shrub Fondler:** *See* Sonsonson, Magnus ("Tree Apostle Sunshine Bunny Wunny Shrub Fondler")

- **Tregar IV:** A frozen planet on which Colonel Mike O' Hagan's ship crashed shortly before the publication of his *Space Corps Survival Manual*. The other crash survivors ate O'Hagan using one of the book's cannibalistic recipes, using pages from the manuscript to line the inside of their igloo **[B-SUR]**.

- **Trevor:** The possible name of a flight navigation officer aboard *Red Dwarf*. Kochanski dated the man for almost two years before he dumped her for a brunette in the ship's Catering department, at which point she began seeing Lister as a rebound. After a month, the officer broke up with the brunette and went back to Kristine, who left Lister to be with him again. Depressed and bitter, Lister never bothered to learn the man's name, though he knew it started with a "T" and may have been Trevor **[N-INF]**.

- **Trevor:** A sports announcer in the universe known as Alternative 6829/B. Trevor commented on a Smegchester Rovers football game in which Ray Rimmer played **[M-SMG1.8(c4)]**.

- **Tri-D Newsnet:** A news network featured on the television soap opera *Androids*. Jaysee threatened to send the network a video of Brook visiting an android brothel if the latter refused to sign over his family business **[M-SMG1.13(c1)]**.

- **triple-bag easy-glide vac:** A product featured in the super deluxe vacuum cleaners section of an electrical appliance catalog aboard *Red Dwarf*. After a DNA modifier changed Kryten into a human, the former mechanoid experienced his first erection while gazing at a photo of this model, which included turbo suction and a self-emptying dustbag. Kryten found his physical reaction confusing and revolting **[T-SER4.2]**.

- **triple fried egg butty with chili sauce and chutney:** A sandwich that Lister requested on the morning after drunkenly celebrating Rimmer's deathday, using a recipe he may have read in a book about bacteriological warfare. Hungover from the festivities, Arnold requested a holographic version from Holly, and was astonished at how good it tasted, given its ingredients. He compared the sandwich to Lister, who was well-liked in spite of his many flaws, whereas Rimmer was despised despite his perceived positive traits **[T-SER2.3]**.

- **triplicator:** An altered version of the Matter Paddle, retrofitted by Kryten and Lister to replicate food and other supplies. In theory, the triplicator scanned and digitized an item's molecular pattern, then split the returning signal three ways to recreate the original and produce two exact duplicates. In practice, however, it extracted the item's best features for one copy and the worst for the other, and made the duplicates' molecular structure unstable, giving them a lifespan of approximately one hour.

  They first tested the machine on a strawberry, producing one sweet, succulent fruit and one rotten with maggots, then attempted to reverse the process and reactivated the machine. Inadvertently, however, they reversed the polarity, extending the field outward and creating "high" and "low" versions of the ship and themselves.

  The stress of the process drained the ship's power, exposing its engine core and causing an explosion that destroyed the vessel. Escaping in *Starbug 1*, the crew boarded the "high" ship, hoping to use its triplicator to reverse the process. This *Red Dwarf* only contained half of the required components, so the crew visited its "low" counterpart. Ultimately, they successfully reassembled and activated the device, rejoining the duplicates into a single mining ship **[T-SER5.5]**.

  Crapola Inc. distributed a similar device via its annual *SCABBY* catalog **[G-RPG]**.

**B-: Books**
**PRG:** *Red Dwarf Programme Guide*
**SUR:** *Red Dwarf Space Corps Survival Manual*
**PRM:** *Primordial Soup*
**SOS:** *Son of Soup*
**SCE:** *Scenes from the Dwarf*
**LOG:** *Red Dwarf Log No. 1996*
**RD8:** *Red Dwarf VIII*
**EVR:** *The Log: A Dwarfer's Guide to Everything*

**X-: Misc.**
**PRO:** Promotional materials, videos, etc.
**PST:** Posters at DJ XVII (2013)
**CAL:** 2008 calendar
**RNG:** Cell phone ringtones
**MOB:** Mobisode ("Red Christmas")
**CIN:** *Children in Need* sketch
**GEK:** *Geek Week* intros by Kryten
**TNG:** "Tongue-Tied" video

**XMS:** Bill Pearson's Christmas special pitch script
**XVD:** Bill Pearson's Christmas special pitch video
**OTH:** Other *Red Dwarf* appearances

**SUFFIX**
**DVD:**
**(d)** – Deleted scene
**(o)** – Outtake
**(b)** – Bonus DVD material (other)
**(e)** – Extended version

**SMEGAZINES:**
**(c)** – Comic
**(a)** – Article

**OTHER:**
**(s)** – Early/unused script draft
**(s1)** – Alternate version of script

- **Triton:** The largest moon of the planet Neptune **[RL]**. Triton was the outermost body in Earth's solar system with a permanent residential community **[G-RPG]**.

  Olaf Petersen bought a house on Triton despite the fact that it was on the edge of the solar system, and that the methane atmosphere and lack of oxygen generators required him to wear a spacesuit at all times while on the surface. This, he gathered, was why the prices were so reasonable **[N-INF]**.

  After signing aboard *Red Dwarf* at Mimas with the intention of returning home, Lister was disheartened to learn that the ship was not going straight to Earth as he had anticipated, but rather to Triton for mining **[N-INF]**.

  Triton was home to a Space Corps research center. While serving in the Corps, Nirvanah Crane was stationed at this facility, as well as others around the solar system **[W-OFF]**.

  The streets in Lister's personal Cyberhell at the virtual-reality prison Cyberia resembled one of Triton's roadways, 12th Street **[N-LST]**.

- **Triton Immigration Control:** A government agency in charge of immigration and customs enforcement on the Neptunian moon. According to Petersen, Triton Immigration Control was worse than New York's counterpart **[N-INF]**.

- ***Trojan*, SS:** A Quantum Twister—a type of space vessel employed by the Space Corps' Super-Infinity Fleet that featured several bridge transporter stations, as well as a quantum rod to transport itself to any location instantly **[T-SER10.1]**. The ship's artificial-intelligence computer was named Pree **[W-OFF]**.

  The *Red Dwarf* crew discovered *Trojan* floating derelict in space, three million years after its launch. Upon boarding the craft, Rimmer accidentally activated the ship's quantum rod, enabling the reception of a distant distress call from *Columbus 3*. Among that ship's surviving crewmembers were a hologram of Rimmer's half-brother, Howard, and a Space Corps simulant named Crawford.

  Embarrassed at not having become an officer, Rimmer enlisted his shipmates' complicity in pretending he was *Trojan*'s captain. After touring the vessel, Howard suffered a resentment breakdown, causing his hard drive to crash. He then admitted he was merely a chicken soup vendor repairman, and not *Columbus 3*'s commander.

  Moments later, Sim Crawford betrayed Howard, revealing she had attacked *Columbus 3* on behalf of the Simulant uprising. Crawford tried to steal data regarding *Trojan*'s quantum rod, but Cat disabled her from doing so **[T-SER10.1]**. The crew later installed Pree into *Red Dwarf*'s computer as a replacement for Holly **[T-SER10.2]**.

  ***NOTE:** An early-draft script of episode 10.1 ("Trojan"), included in a making-of special in the Series X Blu-ray set, called the ship the SS* Hoarse Trojan.

- **trouser press:** An electrical appliance designed to smooth wrinkles from a pair of pants **[RL]**. This amenity was provided to those incarcerated in the luxury cells in D Wing of Floor 13, *Red Dwarf*'s prison level. When Rimmer asked Lister what he'd do with a trouser press, Lister suggested they could make cheese toasties **[T-SER8.3]**.

- **trout:** A species of freshwater fish from the Salmonidae family **[RL]**. Kryten described a woman he noticed in one of Rimmer's home movies as a "silly old trout," unaware she was his mother **[T-SER3.3]**.

- **trout á la crème:** A menu item available from *Red Dwarf*'s food dispensers. Rimmer once bribed Cat to hide Lister's cigarettes for him, by revealing how to procure as much fish as he liked, simply by walking up to a dispenser and requesting as many as needed. Cat then proceeded to the Drive Room and, in feline fashion, requested more than ten orders of trout á la crème, the current fish dish of the day **[T-SER1.3]**.

- ***True Life Criminal Crime Stories*:** A publication authored by Melissa Forethought in Jake Bullet's universe. When asked a question about this publication on the game show *20,000,000 Watts My Line*, Philby Frutch provided the correct answer, "Forethought," and thus won the game **[M-SMG1.10(c1)]**.

- **Trumper:** A pony that Kochanski owned as a young girl **[T-SER7.4]**.

- **trumpet:** A musical instrument in the brass family **[RL]**. Irene Edgington, being highly prone to error, mistook Lister's guitar case for a trumpet case and asked if anyone in the *Red Dwarf* crew played the instrument **[T-SER10.4]**.

**PREFIX**
**RL:** Real life

**T-: Television Episodes**
**SER:** Television series
**IDW:** "Identity Within"
**USA1:** Unaired U.S. pilot
**USA2:** Unaired U.S. demo

**R-: *The Bodysnatcher Collection***
**SER:** Remastered episodes
**BOD:** "Bodysnatcher"
**DAD:** "Dad"
**FTH:** "Lister's Father"
**INF:** "Infinity Patrol"
**END:** "The End" (original assembly)

**N-: Novels**
**INF:** *Infinity Welcomes Careful Drivers*
**BTL:** *Better Than Life*
**LST:** *Last Human*

**BCK:** *Backwards*
**OMN:** *Red Dwarf Omnibus*

**M-: Magazines**
**SMG:** *Smegazine*

**W-: Websites**
**OFF:** Official website
**NAN:** *Prelude to Nanarchy*
**AND:** *Androids*
**DIV:** Diva-Droid
**DIB:** Duane Dibbley

**CRP:** Crapola
**GEN:** Geneticon
**LSR:** Leisure World Intl.
**JMC:** Jupiter Mining Corporation
**AIT:** *A.I. Today*
**HOL:** HoloPoint

**G-: Roleplaying Game**
**RPG:** *Core Rulebook*
**BIT:** *A.I. Screen Extra Bits* booklet
**SOR:** *Series Sourcebook*
**OTH:** Other RPG material

- **"Truncheons for Change":** A slogan printed on a sign posted at a police department in an alternate reality. Jake Bullet was the first robot cop at this precinct **[M-SMG1.10(c1)]**.

- **T.T.:** *See* Taiwan Tony ("T.T.")

- **Tucker Instruments:** An electronics manufacturer that produced such instruments as the TI345 Psi-scan and the TI345xp mini-psi **[G-RPG]**.

  ***NOTE:*** *The company was named after Mike Tucker,* Red Dwarf*'s FX designer.*

- **Tueshoetree:** The name Rimmer gave to one of his shoetrees, to ensure it spent the same amount of time in his shoes as the others **[T-SER7.5]**.

- **Tunbridge Wells:** A large town and borough located in West Kent, England, forty miles southeast of London **[RL]**. Tunbridge Wells was encased in an astrodome sometime after the twenty-first century, which was damaged during an April meteor shower. At the height of the storm, five hundred residents—including actors, priests, carpenters, cooks, weavers and skippers—boarded a spacecraft for a pilgrimage to pray for the bombardment's end. During the journey, however, the pilgrims discovered that each worshipped a different god, resulting in a religious war that wiped out the ship's entire population **[M-SMG1.14(c2)]**.

- **Turner:** A member of *Red Dwarf*'s Z-Shift prior to the cadmium II disaster. Shortly before the accident, Rimmer assigned Turner and Wilkinson to fix Machine 15455, which was dispensing blackcurrant juice instead of chicken soup; restock a machine in Corridor 14, alpha 12 with Crunchie bars; and sanitize the language lab's headsets **[N-INF]**.

  ***NOTE:*** *Turner presumably died during the cadmium II explosion. It is unknown whether the nanobots resurrected him in Series VIII.*

- **Turner, Anthea:** An English television presenter and media personality whose career was sidetracked by a number of controversies **[RL]**. The Inquisitor denounced Turner as not having lived a worthwhile life **[W-OFF]**.

- **Turner, Joseph Mallord William ("J. M. W."):** A nineteenth-century British Romantic landscape painter **[RL]**. After being confined to quarantine for five days with Lister, Kryten chastised him for blowing his nose and looking at the contents as though expecting a Turner seascape **[T-SER5.4]**.

- **Turner, Tina:** An American rhythm and blues singer (born Anna Mae Bullock), known for such songs as "Proudy Mary," "Let's Stay Together" and "What's Love Got to Do With It," and for her performances in *Mad Max Beyond Thunderdome* and other films **[RL]**. When Kochanski suggested entering an asteroid field during a rogue simulant attack, Cat said this would mess up his hair, and that he'd rather get splattered than "look like Tina Turner" **[T-SER7.6]**.

- **Tutankhamen, Pharaoh ("King Tut"):** An Egyptian monarch of the fourteenth century BC. The boy king reigned for ten years before dying at age nineteen **[RL]**. When the Epideme virus reanimated Caroline Carmen's corpse, causing it to kiss Lister, he described her as "Tutankhamen's horny grandma" **[T-SER7.7]**.

  While imprisoned in the Tank, Lister read an article about an eighty-three-year-old actor who fathered a child with his younger nurse and was quoted as saying "She'd always loved older men." Lister commented that Tutankhamen would have stood no chance with her **[T-SER8.1]**.

- **Tvcnkolphgkooq:** A simple-minded type of GELF on Arranguu 12. According to the regulator presiding over Lister's trial for crimes against the GELF nation, the Northern Sector practiced the Jhjghjiuyhu legal system, which was straightforward enough for any Hniuplcxdewn or Tvcnkolphgkooq to understand **[N-LST]**.

- **Twain, Mark:** A nineteenth-century American author and humorist, born Samuel Langhorne Clemens, known for his novels *The Adventures of Tom Sawyer*, *Adventures of Huckleberry Finn* and *A Connecticut Yankee in King Arthur's Court*, as well as for his many short stories **[RL]**. After being resurrected from death as a hologram, George McIntyre paraphrased Twain at his welcome-back party, joking that rumors of his death had been greatly understated **[N-INF]**.

  ***NOTE:*** *Twain is often misquoted as having said*

*"Rumors of my death have been greatly exaggerated," but this is a misnomer, as his actual quote was "The report of my death was an exaggeration."*

- **Tweety Bird:** A fictional canary featured in Warner Bros.' *Looney Tunes* and *Merrie Melodies* animated cartoons. His first pairing with nemesis Sylvester J. Pussycat occurred in the 1947 animated short *Tweetie Pie* **[RL]**.

  While imprisoned on Waxworld with Lister, Cat worried that their waxdroid captors would make him "sing like Tweety Pie," just by forcing him to wear platform shoes and flared trousers **[T-SER4.6]**. Lister once called Rimmer "Tweety Pie" after signing him up for Canary duty in the Tank **[T-SER8.4(d)]**.

- **Twelve Years' Long Service:** One of four JMC medals that Rimmer earned, along with others for three, six and nine years of service. Believing Lister intended to permanently deactivate him, Arnold wore these medals on his dress uniform while awaiting his impending execution **[T-SER1.6]**.

- **"Twinkle, Twinkle, Little Star":** A popular English lullaby, the lyrics of which were taken from Jane Taylor's poem, "The Star" **[RL]**. After Hildegard Lanstrom became infected with a holo-plague, she taunted the *Red Dwarf* crew by reciting an altered version of the song **[T-SER5.4]**. The book *The Most Influential Humans* misattributed the song to Wolfgang Mozart, claiming he wrote it at age five **[T-SER10.3]**.

  ***NOTE:*** *Taylor wrote the poem itself in 1806, which was later set to the melody "Ah! vous dirais-je, Maman." Mozart composed a version of this song at around age twenty-five.*

- **two-pound black-ribbed nobbler:** A used prophylactic that Lister claimed to have caught while condom-fishing in a canal during his youth **[T-SER4.5]**.

- ***Tyrannosaurus rex (T. rex)*:** A species of North American theropod carnivorous dinosaur that roamed Earth during the Cretaceous Period **[RL]**. When Birdman's pet sparrow Pete died, Kryten tried to revive him with a time wand, but instead de-evolved him into a *T. rex*. The tyrannosaurid then ate Birdman and pursued the crew throughout *Red Dwarf*'s cargo deck, swallowing the time wand—and Bob the skutter—in the process.

  To retrieve the wand, Lister and his friends fed the dinosaur a large meal of cow vindaloo, but the meal proved too spicy for Pete, who rampaged through the deck, devouring everything it could to quell the pain, including the ship's entire stock of orange ice pops and Coca-Cola. This made the *T. rex* suffer a violent bout of diarrhea—on Captain Hollister—before passing out, but succeeded in dislodging the time wand.

  Lister and Rimmer used the wand to return Pete to sparrow form, then destroyed the device to prevent further problems—only to then find an enormous egg in the cargo bay, which hatched a baby *Tyrannosaurus*. The creature escaped the bay and proceeded to Hollister's quarters, where it licked coconut oil from his back during a massage session, traumatizing the man **[T-SER8.6]**.

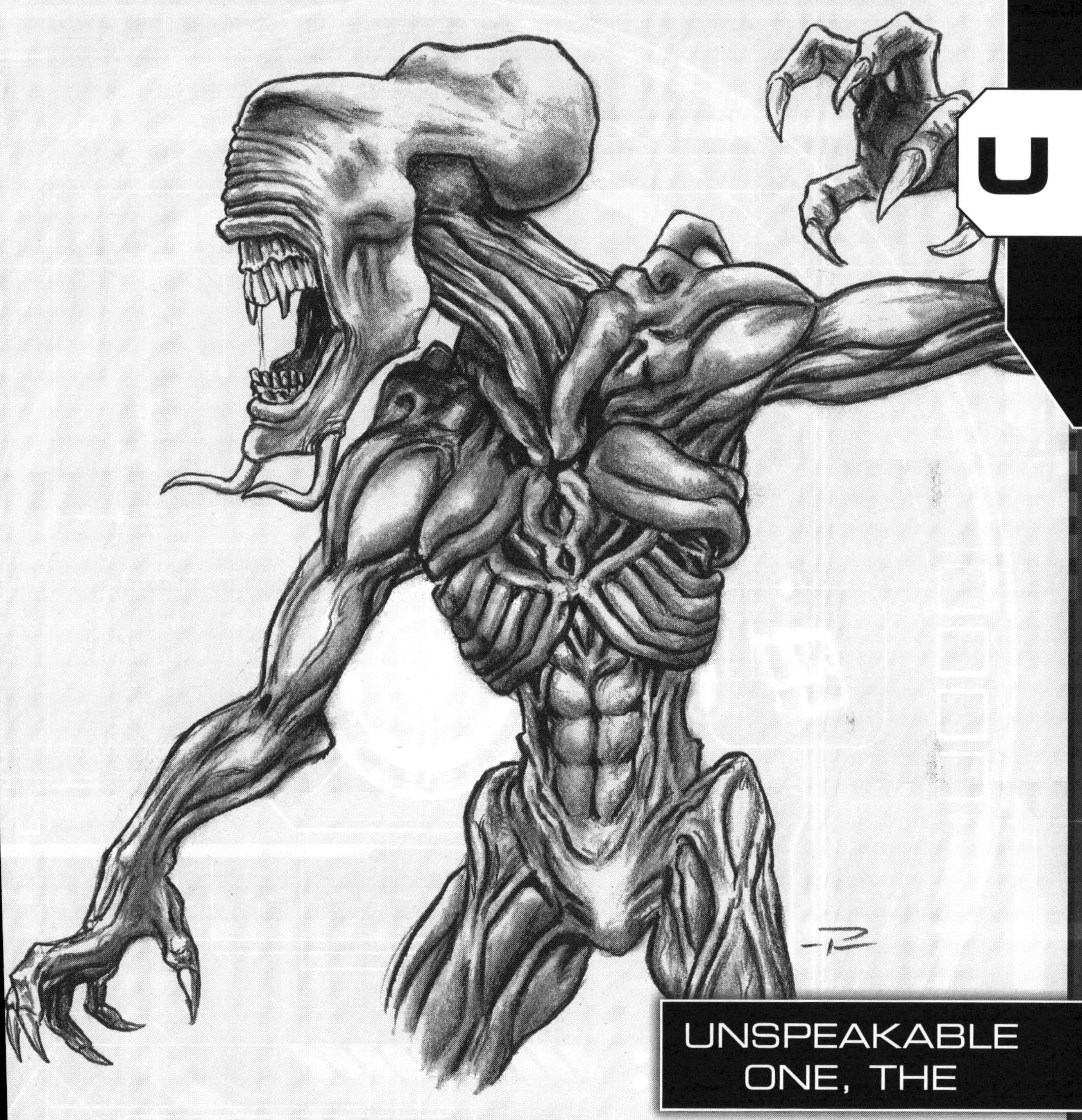


# UNSPEAKABLE ONE, THE

**B-: Books**
**PRG:** *Red Dwarf Programme Guide*
**SUR:** *Red Dwarf Space Corps Survival Manual*
**PRM:** *Primordial Soup*
**SOS:** *Son of Soup*
**SCE:** *Scenes from the Dwarf*
**LOG:** *Red Dwarf Log No. 1996*
**RD8:** *Red Dwarf VIII*
**EVR:** *The Log: A Dwarfer's Guide to Everything*

**X-: Misc.**
**PRO:** Promotional materials, videos, etc.
**PST:** Posters at DJ XVII (2013)
**CAL:** 2008 calendar
**RNG:** Cell phone ringtones
**MOB:** Mobisode ("Red Christmas")
**CIN:** *Children in Need* sketch
**GEK:** *Geek Week* intros by Kryten
**TNG:** "Tongue-Tied" video

**XMS:** Bill Pearson's Christmas special pitch script
**XVD:** Bill Pearson's Christmas special pitch video
**OTH:** Other *Red Dwarf* appearances

**SUFFIX**
**DVD:**
**(d)** – Deleted scene
**(o)** – Outtake
**(b)** – Bonus DVD material (other)
**(e)** – Extended version

**SMEGAZINES:**
**(c)** – Comic
**(a)** – Article

**OTHER:**
**(s)** – Early/unused script draft
**(s1)** – Alternate version of script

- **"U=BTL":** A message that Kryten burned into Lister's right arm in an effort to warn him that he was trapped in the virtual-reality video game *Better Than Life*. In the simulation, Lister imagined that he had returned to Earth and moved to *It's a Wonderful Life*'s Bedford Falls with Kochanski and their two sons, Jim and Bexley. While applying ointment to his arms to relieve the pain, he discovered that the affected area on one arm spelled out the message "U=BTL"—which he realized meant "You are in *Better Than Life*"—and "dying" on the other **[N-INF]**.

- **U-Haul:** An American storage and moving equipment company **[RL]**. A spaceship on the Saturnian moon of Mimas had been rented from U-Haul **[M-SMG2.3(c4)]**.

  A group of players who followed the Dibbley party in the virtual-reality game *Red Dwarf* discovered two U-Haul ships ejecting presents and projecting a holographic image of Earth, with an arrow pointing to the Panama Canal. They deduced that its meaning, "America Isthmus, Two U-Hauls," was a message: "A Merry Christmas to You All" **[M-SMG2.9(c3)]**.

- **Ultimate Anti-Aging Cream:** A homemade concoction that halted and reversed the aging process. This cream was especially helpful to a person blasted with a temporal ray **[G-RPG]**.

- **Ultranet:** A system of interconnected computer implants routed through a centralized computer. By 2190, Earth's world government used the Ultranet to collect votes on major issues from the populace. This system collapsed, however, when the central computer crashed **[B-EVR]**.

- **UltraPlas windscreen wipers:** A durable type of windshield wiper used on JMC buggies. The wipers' manufacturer claimed the blades never streaked **[G-BIT]**.

- **ultrazone:** *See* outrozone

- **Ulysses:** A character in ancient Greek literature, and the hero of Homer's *Odyssey* **[RL]**. While describing the telepathic GELFs known as Psirens, Lister misattributed the story of Ulysses' encounter with mythical sirens as a Turkish legend, but Kryten corrected him that it was Greek **[T-SER6.1]**.

- **"Umbilical Wrench":** A label identifying a button on the control panel of an escape pod belonging to prison ship guard Barbra Bellini. The panel controlled the pod's cryogenics system **[T-SER4.3(d)]**.

- **Uncle Tomcat:** A demeaning nickname that Cat called himself upon realizing he had been domesticated aboard *Red Dwarf*, after she-Cat Ora Tanzil dismissed the notion of his being a Cat due to his docile nature **[T-IDW]**.

  ***NOTE:*** *Uncle Tom was the titular character of Harriet Beecher Stowe's novel,* Uncle Tom's Cabin. *The phrase "Uncle Tom" has since been a negative epithet for those slavish and subservient to authority figures—particularly black individuals who behave subserviently to whites.*

- **uncrop:** A function of 4000 Series mechanoids enabling them to fill in the sides of a scanned photograph. While trapped in an elation squid hallucination, Kryten imagined using his uncrop feature to expand a photo of a man named Swallow, whom the crew hoped could lead them to their creator **[T-SER9.2]**.

- **Underwater hockey:** A popular spectator sport. Sometime prior to *Red Dwarf*'s cadmium II disaster, England's underwater hockey team toured Titan **[T-SER2.2]**.

- **"Unem":** A word printed on a wall sign at an eatery in England, during a period in Earth's far future when time ran backwards. The sign, when read forward, was labeled "Menu." Among the items listed on the sign were spihc dna regrub (burgers and chips), hsif (fish), gge (egg), saep (peas), yvarg (gravy), ecuas yrruc (curry sauce), eip elppa (applie pie), aet (tea), eeffoc (coffee) and aloc (cola) **[T-SER3.1]**.

  ***NOTE:*** *Throughout the episode, backwards writing was inconsistently handled. In some cases, characters were backward-facing, while in others (such as in this instance), they faced forward.*

- **UN high security prison complex:** A penal facility located on the Jovian moon of Elara **[G-RPG]**.

- **unicycle polo:** A sport that Lister invented to pass the time aboard *Red Dwarf*, which involved hitting a beach ball around the corridors with French loaves while riding unicycles. When

**PREFIX**
**RL:** Real life

**T-: Television Episodes**
**SER:** Television series
**IDW:** "Identity Within"
**USA1:** Unaired U.S. pilot
**USA2:** Unaired U.S. demo

**R-: *The Bodysnatcher Collection***
**SER:** Remastered episodes
**BOD:** "Bodysnatcher"
**DAD:** "Dad"
**FTH:** "Lister's Father"
**INF:** "Infinity Patrol"
**END:** "The End" (original assembly)

**N-: Novels**
**INF:** *Infinity Welcomes Careful Drivers*
**BTL:** *Better Than Life*
**LST:** *Last Human*

**BCK:** *Backwards*
**OMN:** *Red Dwarf Omnibus*

**M-: Magazines**
**SMG:** *Smegazine*

**W-: Websites**
**OFF:** Official website
**NAN:** *Prelude to Nanarchy*
**AND:** *Androids*
**DIV:** Diva-Droid
**DIB:** Duane Dibbley

**CRP:** Crapola
**GEN:** Geneticon
**LSR:** Leisure World Intl.
**JMC:** Jupiter Mining Corporation
**AIT:** *A.I. Today*
**HOL:** HoloPoint

**G-: Roleplaying Game**
**RPG:** *Core Rulebook*
**BIT:** *A.I. Screen Extra Bits* booklet
**SOR:** *Series Sourcebook*
**OTH:** Other RPG material

Lister grew bored with his life aboard the mining vessel, Cat suggested playing a round of unicycle polo on Floor 14 to cheer him up **[T-SER3.5]**.

- **Union of Soviet Socialist Republics (USSR):** A communist country in Eurasia that was governed as a single-party state from 1922 until its disbandment in 1991 **[RL]**. In a universe in which John F. Kennedy survived an assassination attempt and was impeached for having an affair with the mistress of Mafia boss Sam Giancana, the USSR built nuclear bases in Cuba, forcing the evacuation of millions of Americans from major cities. In this alternate universe, the USSR bested the United States in the so-called Space Race **[T-SER7.1]** and created the Soviet Space Corps, whose vessels included *Red Dwarfski* **[G-SOR]**.

- **Unit 1:** One of two deep sleep units aboard *Starbug 1*. Lister and Cat used this unit, which was retrofitted with a stasis seal, to safely traverse a reality minefield left around an experimental Space Corps craft containing a time drive **[T-SER6.6(d)]**.

  ***NOTE:*** *Unit 1 was not named onscreen, but its name was implied since the other was called Unit 2. These units differed from the suspended animation booths referenced in later episodes.*

- **Unit 2:** One of two deep sleep units aboard *Starbug 1*. Kryten and Rimmer used this unit, which was retrofitted with a stasis seal, to safely traverse a reality minefield left around an experimental Space Corps craft containing a time drive **[T-SER6.6(d)]**.

- **Unit 5:** A marking on a component near *Starbug 1*'s AR Suite **[T-SER7.2]**.

- **United Republic of Engineered Life Forms:** A commonwealth created by GELFs after their spaceship, the *Mayflower*, was sucked into the Omni-zone and ejected into an alternate universe **[N-LST]**.

- **United Republic of GELF States:** A commonwealth created by GELFs from various planets, moons and asteroids in an alternate universe. Among its member worlds were Blerios 15, Arranguu 12 and Lotomi 5 **[N-LST]**.

- **United Republic of Lesser Britain:** A twenty-first-century territory in an alternate-universe Europe. That reality's Rimmer was elected its prime minister in 2079 and held at least three terms, serving more than twenty-three years in office **[M-SMG2.8(c6)]**.

- **Universal Government:** The governing body of Earth's solar system, comprising representatives from all nine planets. The Universal Government operated several branches, including an Earth branch that passed the Hologram Protection Akt of 2143 **[M-SMG2.2(a)]**.

- **universal translator (UT):** A machine designed to translate languages or dialects, and to communicate with other forms of life, such as intelligent viruses or nanobots. Lister utilized *Starbug 1*'s UT to bargain for his life with the Epideme virus, but to no avail **[T-SER7.7]**. The universal translator, sold by Crapola Inc. in its annual *SCABBY* catalog, was programmed with more than three hundred languages **[G-SOR]**.

- **unoculars:** An optical device designed to zoom and enhance a person's view. Unoculars were supplied in buggies used by guards on Lotomi 5, home of the virtual-reality prison Cyberia **[N-LST]**.

- **unreality pocket:** A phenomenon experienced as one traversed a reality minefield. Striking a pocket of unreality caused a person to experience false realities, making him or her see or believe things not based in reality. In one instance, encountering an unreality pocket led the *Starbug 1* crew to believe Lister was a Series 3000 mechanoid. Another temporarily removed Cat from existence **[T-SER6.6]**.

- **Unspeakable One, The:** A denizen of a psi-moon configured according to Rimmer's psyche, embodying his self-loathing. The creature was also called the Master and the Self-Loathing Beast. When Kryten and Rimmer landed on the planetoid, it restructured itself as a desolate, gloomy, swamp-filled wasteland inhabited by manifestations of Rimmer's negative attributes, including the Unspeakable One. The Dark Forces kidnapped Rimmer and took him to a structure where the moon's ruler, the Dark One, demanded that he be sacrificed to the Master **[T-SER5.3]**.

- **Unspeakably Brown:** An alert condition that 4000 Series mechanoids entered during times of trouble. Kryten's Mauve alert was triggered when he flushed Lister's two robotic goldfish down the latrine, but the situation upgraded to Unspeakably Brown when he attempted to locate the fish with his endoscopic groinal attachment **[M-SMG2.4(c5)]**.

- **Unspeakably Vile Porno Filth Emporium:** A purveyor of adult videos on the Saturnian moon of Mimas. The shop was located next to an apartment complex in which Dutch van Oestrogen stayed while hiding from the Ganymedian Mafia in Trixie LaBouche's body **[M-SMG2.4(c2)]**.

- **UO:** An acronym short for "unidentified object" **[T-SER1.4]**.

- **upper deck:** A level of *Starbug 1*'s aft section, accessible by a set of stairs. The Ops Room was located on the upper deck **[T-SER6.6]**.

- **Uppures Insurance:** An insurance agency that became embroiled in a legal battle against holograms over life insurance payouts. The holograms organized a demonstration and marched on the company, forcing it to close, which caused job layoffs and the stress-related death of one employee's mother. The worker, unable to have her revived as a hologram due to her social status, vowed vengeance against all holograms, then converted his body into a cybernetic killing-machine to hunt them down throughout the galaxy **[M-SMG2.5(c2)]**.

  ***NOTE:*** *The company's name was based on the phrase "Up yours," with its logo mimicking the British two-finger insult.*

- ***Up Up & Away!*:** The in-flight magazine aboard the shuttle that ferried Lister from Mimas to *Red Dwarf* for his first tour of duty. The 120-page issue contained such articles as "Salt—An Epicure's Delight," "Classic Wines of Estonia" and "Weaving the Traditional Way" **[N-INF]**. Three million years later, Lister and his shipmates read the same issue aboard *Starbug 1* when the shuttle was about to crash, as it had been discovered that reading mundane articles acted as a sedative during emergency situations, and were thus part of the ship's crash procedures **[T-SER4.5]**.

  ***NOTE:*** *The novel* Infinity Welcomes Careful Drivers *changed the article's title to "Flemish Weaving the Traditional Way."*

- **U.R.1:** *See* Utility Remote Mark One (U.R.1)

- **uranium-233:** A fissile isotope of uranium created from the neutron irradiation of thorium-232 **[RL]**. *Nova 5*'s Duality Jump was powered by uranium-233 **[N-INF]**.

- **Uranus:** The seventh planet from the Sun in Earth's solar system, orbited by twenty-seven natural satellites, including Miranda **[RL]**. During the twenty-second century, the Inter-Planetary Commission for Waste Disposal decided to designate one of the system's nine planets as humanity's official dumping grounds. Representatives from all nine worlds presented their case against being chosen, with Uranus' study group focusing on the planet's vast stores of mineral deposits as a valuable commodity to the entire system. Ultimately, Earth was nominated for the task **[N-BTL]**.

- **Uranus II:** A name that Cat suggested for a new planet which Kryten predicted would be created from the radioactive mass that a minuscule alien invasion fleet had left behind, since the mass had been retrieved via the mechanoid's posterior region **[X-XMS]**.

- **urine recyc:** Drinkable water recycled from urine. As the *Starbug 1* crew searched for the stolen *Red Dwarf*, their supplies ran low, leaving Lister and Cat no choice but to drink urine recyc **[T-SER6.5]**. Kryten brewed several cases of wine out of urine recyc, which the crew refused to drink **[T-SER6.6]**. Wine featured on the cooking program *Can't Smeg, Won't Smeg*, with Ainsley Harriott, was also made from urine recyc **[T-SER4(b)]**.

- **Ustermayer:** *See* Astermayer

- **UT:** *See* universal translator (UT)

**PREFIX**
**RL:** Real life

**T-: Television Episodes**
**SER:** Television series
**IDW:** "Identity Within"
**USA1:** Unaired U.S. pilot
**USA2:** Unaired U.S. demo

**R-: *The Bodysnatcher Collection***
**SER:** Remastered episodes
**BOD:** "Bodysnatcher"
**DAD:** "Dad"
**FTH:** "Lister's Father"
**INF:** "Infinity Patrol"
**END:** "The End" (original assembly)

**N-: Novels**
**INF:** *Infinity Welcomes Careful Drivers*
**BTL:** *Better Than Life*
**LST:** *Last Human*
**BCK:** *Backwards*
**OMN:** *Red Dwarf Omnibus*

**M-: Magazines**
**SMG:** *Smegazine*

**W-: Websites**
**OFF:** Official website
**NAN:** *Prelude to Nanarchy*
**AND:** *Androids*
**DIV:** Diva-Droid
**DIB:** Duane Dibbley
**CRP:** Crapola
**GEN:** Geneticon
**LSR:** Leisure World Intl.
**JMC:** Jupiter Mining Corporation
**AIT:** *A.I. Today*
**HOL:** HoloPoint

**G-: Roleplaying Game**
**RPG:** *Core Rulebook*
**BIT:** *A.I. Screen Extra Bits* booklet
**SOR:** *Series Sourcebook*
**OTH:** Other RPG material

- **Utensilware, Inc.:** A company specializing in items and paraphernalia used for food consumption. Many of its products were featured in Crapola Inc.'s annual *SCABBY* catalog, including anti-matter chopsticks and boomerang spoons **[G-RPG]**.

- **uterine simulator:** A machine that simulated the environment of a uterus, allowing *in vitro* embryos to incubate and be born. A self-gamete-mixing *in vitro* tube could be loaded with the egg and sperm of a set of parents, and then be placed into the simulator until the embryo matured **[T-SER7.3]**. The device was manufactured by Malpractice Medical & Scispec, and distributed by Crapola Inc. **[G-RPG]**.

  Lister and Kochanski used such a device to give birth to their child, which turned out to be Lister himself. They then brought the baby back in time and left him under a pool table in a Liverpool pub, thereby starting the cycle of Lister's life **[T-SER7.3]**.

  ***NOTE:*** *Apparently, the gestation time within the uterine simulator was just over sixteen months. Lister noted in episode 3.6 ("The Last Day") that he had been left under the pool table when he was six weeks old, while episode 7.3 ("Ouroboros") showed the child being brought back in time to the pub eighteen months after the* in vitro *tube was fertilized.*

- **Utility Remote Mark One (U.R.1):** An autonomous dog-like robot supplied on JMC dropships. It was equipped with claws, as well as cameras on its fore and aft sections, which fed video back to the dropship **[X-XVD]**. While traveling through Kryten's body to locate an alien invasion fleet, a miniaturized Lister used a U.R.1 to dislodge debris caught in the dropship's external rotors **[X-XMS]**.

V

# VOORHESE, MEINHARD, CAPTAIN

- **VAC 3:** A phrase printed on a console label in *Starbug 1*'s Medical Bay **[T-SER7.7]**.

- **vac suit:** A bulky spacesuit used primarily for spacewalks, or for working in hostile environments **[G-RPG]**.

- **vacuum shields:** A fail-safe system designed to prevent *Red Dwarf*'s engines from reaching critical mass. The ship's vacuum shields failed after an experiment with a triplicator went awry, causing the vessel's destruction **[T-SER5.5]**.

- **Vacuum Storage:** An area aboard *Red Dwarf* used for long-term storage. Lister kept his personal belongings in Vacuum Storage while he was in stasis **[N-INF]**.

- **Valhalla Impact Structure:** A large, multi-ring impact crater on the Jovian moon of Callisto. The largest impact crater in Earth's solar system, it measured roughly 360 kilometers (224 miles) across **[RL]**. The area surrounding the impact structure was cordoned off by the Space Corps on the authority of the United Nations' Jovian Authority, with no one allowed near the site. A sightseeing ship from the Callisto-Ganymede Ring Arc Appreciation Society was shot down near the impact site, which the Corps described as an "unfortunate accident" **[G-RPG]**.

- **Valhalla Project Office:** A department set up by the United Nations' Jovian Authority to manage operations at Callisto's Valhalla Impact Structure. For reasons undisclosed, the office subpoenaed *Red Dwarf*'s construction plans and inventory lists **[G-RPG]**.

- **Valkyrie:** A female figure in Norse mythology, said to decide warriors' fates during battle **[RL]**. Cat wondered what image the shapeshifting Pleasure GELF Camille would take upon meeting him, since she could sense his innermost desires. Lister joked that she'd appear as a Valkyrie warrior maiden in scanty armor, with cleavage one could ski down **[T-SER4.1]**.

  While trapped in an addictive version of *Better Than Life*, Cat imagined he had returned to Earth with Lister and Rimmer, and had made his home on an island off the coast of Denmark. The island contained a thirty-towered golden castle surrounded by a milk moat and filled with scantily clad, eight-foot-tall Amazon Valkyries, who tended to his every desire **[N-INF]**.

- **Valkyrie Sex-Slave Liberation Movement:** A union formed by the Amazonian goddesses whom Cat's mind conjured while he was trapped in an addictive version of *Better Than Life*. When Rimmer's diseased mind adversely affected the game, the Valkyries abandoned Cat's castle and created the Liberation Movement **[N-BTL]**.

- **Valles Marineris:** A group of canyons on the surface of Mars, named after the *Mariner 9* orbiter that discovered them **[RL]**. During the twenty-first century, the European Space Consortium (ESC) sent a rover to Mars to study the canyons. En route, it found debris left behind by *Red Dwarf*'s crew. While analyzing the garbage, the rover encountered Cat, who used the device to transmit a message to Earth, informing the agency that he had found its *Beagle* spacecraft, and asking if there was any good food on Mars **[X-APR]**.Terraces were later built into three hundred miles of the canyon, which housed the inner systems' wealthiest citizens **[G-RPG]**.

- ***Vampire Bikini Girls Suck Paris*:** A black-and-white horror B-movie, created by the same team that produced *Attack of the Giant Savage Completely Invisible Aliens* **[T-SER8.5]**.

- **Van Gogh:** A name that Lister assigned to one of twelve rogue droids he purchased from the Kinitawowi to break his doppelgänger out of the virtual-reality prison Cyberia. This particular droid was missing an ear and a leg **[N-LST]**.

- **van Gogh, Vincent:** A troubled nineteenth-century Dutch post-impressionist painter who cut off parts of his left ear out of anger at fellow painter Paul Gauguin. His relationship with his father was reportedly abusive **[RL]**. While consoling Lister after the human's arm was amputated, Cat mistakenly brought up van Gogh as an extraordinary one-armed individual, despite the fact that the painter never lost a major appendage **[T-SER7.8]**.

  While trapped in an addictive version of *Better Than Life*, Rimmer imagined he had returned to Earth and become famously wealthy, creating a company that developed a time machine. He then used the device to bring together several historical individuals for his bachelor party, including van Gogh **[N-BTL]**.

- **van Gogh, Vincent:** A clone of the Dutch painter, created in 2156 using DNA from the man's ear. The clone's artwork was subpar compared to that of his predecessor—mostly due to a lack of parental abuse **[B-EVR]**.

- **van Goth, Vinnie:** An android informant in Jake Bullet's universe, whom the cyborg sometimes hired. Van Goth wore a leather jacket and worked in the local black market. His head was shaped like a skull, and he occasionally misplaced his ear. The cyborg cop visited van Goth while investigating the murder of Philby Frutch, a game-show contestant who had been taking stupid drugs—a topic van Goth knew much about. After giving Bullet the information he requested, van Goth died from a ricocheted shot meant to kill Jake **[M-SMG1.12(c1)]**.

  ***NOTE:*** *Goth's missing ear was an in-joke reference to painter Vincent van Gogh.*

- **van Herren, Jean Claudette:** A famous action film star in a universe in which the sexes were reversed **[W-OFF]**.

  ***NOTE:*** *This individual was the female analog of actor Jean-Claude Van Damme.*

- **vanity:** The idolization of one's own appearance **[RL]**. After escaping a genetic waste pod and boarding *Red Dwarf*, a polymorph attacked the crew by changing form to elicit and feed on their emotions. It attacked Cat in the form of a beautiful woman who gave him compliments, amplifying his vanity—which it then drained **[T-SER3.3]**.

- ***Vanity Fair*:** An American magazine published by Condé Nast, covering pop culture, fashion and politics **[RL]**. While answering questions about survival tips in her copy of the *Space Corps Survival Manual*, Kochanski suggested bringing at least twelve issues of *Vanity Fair* when knowingly going into a possible survival situation **[B-SUR]**.

- **Van Lustbader, Eric:** An American fantasy and thriller novelist who wrote numerous books continuing Robert Ludlum's Jason Bourne series **[RL]**. While marooned on a frozen planet, Lister attempted to stay warm inside *Starbug 1* by burning items stored aboard ship. Succumbing to hunger, he was dismayed to find several books written by authors whose names reminded him of food, such as Charles Lamb, Herman Wouk, Francis Bacon and Eric Van Lustbader. In David's starving mind, the word "van" conjured images of meat and bread vans **[T-SER3.2]**.

- **van Oestrogen, Dutch:** A Dutch astro miner on Mimas who double-crossed the Ganymedian Mafia during a drug deal. With the Mafia hot on his trail, van Oestrogen ducked into Noel's Body Swap Shop and switched bodies with sex worker Trixie LaBouche **[M-SMG2.3(c4)]**.

  Van Oestrogen later tried to retrieve his own body, but members of the Mafia ambushed him. A firefight ensued, during which the body swap machine was shot. Dutch emerged the victor and demanded his own body back, but due to the device's damage, the transition was not one hundred percent successful, and he lost all knowledge of his stash's location **[M-SMG2.4(c2)]**.

  The astro realized that LaBouche must have gained this knowledge, and tracked her down to her hotel, where the Mafia once again attacked. Ditching his pursuers, he chased Trixie around Mimas Spaceport **[M-SMG2.5(c6)]**, until catching up with her near the locker containing his loot. The commotion caused Lister—who resided in a nearby locker at the time—to fling open the door, smashing van Oestrogen in the face and knocking him unconscious **[M-SMG2.6(c4)]**.

  While trapped in an addictive version of *Better Than Life*, Rimmer imagined that Dutch purchased Trixie's Solidgram body for a weekend of lust, but inhabited her body instead and used it to rob three banks before abandoning it in a car lot. When the body was finally returned to Trixie, she was arrested for the crimes **[N-BTL]**.

  ***NOTE:*** *LaBouche and van Oestrogen were in Shagtown when Rimmer first met Lister while visiting a brothel on Mimas, in the* Smegazine *comic "Mimas Crossing—Part 1." Several characters in Arnold's* Better Than Life *illusion, including Trixie and Dutch, were based on individuals whom he knew or had met. Presumably, his subconscious mind created these characters based on his memories of them—though it is unclear when he encountered Dutch. The astro's surname was not mentioned in the novel* Better Than Life*, in which he was simply called Dutch.*

- **Vauxhall Nova:** An automobile derived from the Corsa-A, a line of supermini cars built by German automaker Opel in the late twentieth century **[RL]**. While delivering a status report, Holly noted that despite being three million light years into deep space, the *Red Dwarf* crew were still entered in a *Reader's Digest* contest to win a Vauxhall Nova **[T-SER3(d)]**.

- **V Deck:** A level of *Red Dwarf* containing a broom cupboard that Kryten once visited while on vacation **[T-SER9.1]**.

- **Vending Machine Maintenance Man of the Month:** A monthly award handed out to *Red Dwarf* technicians for their extraordinary service. Rimmer received such a certificate during one April **[T-SER9.1]**.

- **Venezuela:** A country located on the northern coast of South America **[RL]**. Lister mocked Kochanski for being the smart one in her class, adding that she probably knew the average rainfall of the oil-rich lowlands of Venezuela. Though she initially denied it, she eventually admitted to knowing it was 3.4 inches **[T-SER7.7]**.

> ***NOTE:** Not even close. As of this writing, the average rainfall in the nation's lowlands and plains average from 17 to 39 inches. Perhaps the volcano that flooded Fiji also affected Earth's weather.*

- **Venus:** The second planet from the Sun in Earth's solar system **[RL]**. Venus was the setting of the short-lived television soap opera *Androids Nights* **[W-CRP]**.

  During the twenty-second century, the Inter-Planetary Commission for Waste Disposal decided to designate one of the system's nine planets as humanity's official dumping grounds. Representatives from all nine worlds presented their case against being chosen, with the Venusian delegation relying on their planet's status as the second wealthiest in the system, after Mars. Ultimately, Earth was nominated for the task **[N-BTL]**.

- ***Venus de Milo*:** A name often attributed to the *Aphrodite of Milos*, a statue depicting the ancient Greek goddess. Sometime after its discovery, the statue's arms were lost **[RL]**. In an attempt to console Lister after his arm was amputated, Kochanski cited the *Venus de Milo* as an example of an extraordinary limbless person—despite the fact that it was not alive **[T-SER7.8]**.

- **Venusian dogworm:** A small parasite inhabiting the planet Venus **[M-SMG2.8(c7)]**.

- **Venusian fighting snail:** A gastropod native to Venus. Fighting snails had sharpened horns and were specially bred for Toot, a banned bloodsport in which two snails fought to the death in a six-foot-square concrete pit, while onlookers drank and gambled on the outcome **[N-INF]**.

- **Venusian Orange creature:** A hypothetical alien species. As Rimmer called out coordinates to Kryten on one occasion, Lister claimed they were the measurements of his dream girl, a Venusian Orange creature on page thirty-seven of *Alien Monthly* **[X-XMS]**.

- **verbal systems:** The electronics that enabled sentient appliances, such as Talkie Toaster, to convert electrical signals into speech, thereby allowing them to converse with others **[T-SER4.4]**.

- **Victoria, Queen:** The ruler of the United Kingdom of Great Britain and Ireland from 1837 to 1901 **[RL]**.

  A waxdroid replica of Queen Victoria was created for the Waxworld theme park. Left on their own for millions of years, the waxdroids attained sentience and became embroiled in a park-wide resource war between Villain World and Hero World (to which Victoria belonged). During this war, the *Red Dwarf* crew transported to the planet using a Matter Paddle, with Lister and Cat materializing in Villain territory, while Rimmer and Kryten landed in Hero territory.

  Rimmer found the heroes' army lacking and took command, working many of the pacifistic waxdroids to death before ordering a frontal attack on the enemy's compound. The attack involved sending the droids on a daylight charge over a minefield—all except for Victoria, whom Kryten escorted around the perimeter into the Villain World HQ. The queen shot several enemy waxdroids, including Adolf Hitler, Hermann Göring and a Ku Klux Klansman, before dying from Hitler's final shot. This "victory" allowed Kryten to adjust the building's thermostat, melting the remaining droids in the complex **[T-SER4.6]**.

  > ***NOTE:** The queen was not named in the episode, but online scripts, the official website and the* Red Dwarf Smegazine *all confirmed that she was Queen Victoria.*

- ***Victory in Europe*:** A World War II-based artificial-reality program that the *Red Dwarf* crew found aboard a derelict spaceship. Confusing it with the *Holiday in Europe* program they also retrieved, the crew entered the simulation expecting a relaxing vacation, only to find themselves under heavy artillery fire and forced to march on Berlin. They spent the next seventeen days marching across Europe, until being released from the simulation by a glitch created when Cat eloped with Eva Braun, causing Adolf Hitler to die of a broken heart **[B-LOG]**.

- ***Victory South*:** A television series built around the premise that the southern U.S. states won the American Civil War. It

ran for two series, for a total of twenty-four episodes. The first season featured a busty, blonde heroine who was killed off during series two, along with several other characters. Rimmer enjoyed series one (particularly the busty heroine), but was unable to watch series two because *Red Dwarf*'s new onboard computer, Pree, deleted the entire run after predicting he would be disappointed with it **[T-SER10.2]**.

- **Vidal Beast:** A creature from the planet Sharmut 2 **[T-SER7.5]**, created by the Space Corps Enhanced Evolution Project, which was developed to control the overpopulation of the planet's plant and animal populations. The six-legged, boar-like Vidal Beasts reproduced asexually and were always born in twin pairs—one exclusively carnivorous, the other an herbivore **[G-RPG]**. In an effort to impress Kochanski, Lister told her about his shipmates' encounter with a Vidal Beast, to highlight the tough times they had survived. Cat noted that the creature almost killed them **[T-SER7.5]**.

- **Vid-E-Bone:** A video phone system featured on the television soap opera *Androids*. Jaysee discussed his plans to take over the family business with Bruce over a Vid-E-Bone **[M-SMG1.9(c2)]**.

- **video letter:** A message sent between two parties via a video medium, such as a video disc. Gordon, the *Scott Fitzgerald*'s artificial-intelligence computer, sent a video letter to Holly discussing the first move of their postal chess game **[T-SER2.2]**.

- **Villain World:** An area within the Waxworld theme park, located next to Prehistoric World, and populated by waxdroid versions of Earth's most notorious historical figures and characters, including Adolf Hitler, Caligula, Grigori Rasputin and James Last.

  Villain World became embroiled in a park-wide resource war with Hero World, whose wax the villains wanted to melt down to make more of their own kind. Lister and Cat materialized in Villain World during their first attempt to use a Matter Paddle and were immediately imprisoned by Hitler, but promptly escaped to Hero World, where they met up with Rimmer and Kryten.

  Finding the heroes' army lacking, Rimmer took command of the group, working many of the pacifistic waxdroids to death before ordering a frontal attack on the enemy's compound in Villain World, across a minefield. This assault killed the remaining droids, but effectively ended the war. Rimmer thus considered it a victory **[T-SER4.6]**.

- **Vimto:** A soft drink sold in the United Kingdom **[RL]**. For Kryten's last-day party, Holly created a beverage derived from Vimto and liquid nitrogen, since ordinary alcohol had no effect on mechanoids **[T-SER3.6]**. Kochanski craved a Vimto after being de-aged by a time wand **[T-SER8.6]**.

- **Vindaloovia:** A hypothetical world inhabited by the fictitious Vindaloovian people, which Lister created as a ruse to trick rogue simulants into believing there were no humans aboard *Starbug 1* **[T-SER6.3(d)]**.

- **Vindaloovian:** A fictional species that Lister conceived of as a ruse to trick a simulant hunting party. While pursuing the stolen *Red Dwarf*, the *Starbug 1* crew inadvertently entered rogue simulant territory, in the midst of a simulant hunting zone. A simulant battlecruiser confronted them, its captain demanding to know their species.

  Knowing simulants' hatred for humanoids, Lister and Cat each stuck one of Kryten's optical units to their chin, then answered the hail while posing upside upside down with a camera zoomed in on their mouths, thereby giving the illusion that they were bald, stout, one-eyed extraterrestrials.

  Lister identified himself as Tarka Dhal, an ambassador of the Great Vindaloovian Empire, and Cat as his companion, Bhindi Bhaji. The two "Vindaloovians" scoffed at the idea of harboring humans aboard their vessel, claiming they despised all humanoids and had vowed to exterminate them from the galaxy. The unconvinced simulant's transport to *Starbug 1*, however, cut their charade short **[T-SER6.3]**.

  ***NOTE:*** *The* Red Dwarf *script book* Son of Soup *spelled the species' name as "Vindalooians," but the official sites,* Red Dwarf—the Roleplaying Game *and the DVD subtitles and chapter head all spelled it as "Vindaloovians."*

  *When Lister and Cat claimed to be Vindaloovians, it seemed clear that Lister was making up the species, given that vindaloo, tarka dhal and bhindi bhaji are all types of Indian food. The roleplaying game's* AI Screen, *however, not only revealed the creatures to exist, but portrayed them as matching Lister's Vindaloovian disguise. It could be that Lister knew Vindaloovians existed and thus assumed their form, or (more likely) that the Vindaloovians were from an alternate universe created from Lister's idea of the species.*

- **Vindaloovian:** A species of militant, experimental GELFs. Vindaloovians were typically short and squat, standing roughly 1 meter (3.3 feet) high, and sported a single blue eyeball in the center of their egg-shaped head, with three stubby fingers on each hand. They reproduced via state-run cloning facilities.

  Taking cues from twentieth-century Earth war movies, the Vindaloovians formed a martial society, often dressing in overtly ornamental military uniforms and adhering to a three-tiered caste system comprising officials (the Tarka), a middle class (the Bindi) and laborers (the Grunti). They despised humans, adopting a Wipe Humans Out All-over (WHOA!) policy–a more relaxed version of their previous "Wipe Out Everyone!" (WOE!) policy. Human sympathizers and others who shunned the Imperial doctrine were exiled from the homeland **[G-BIT]**.

  ***NOTE:*** *The Vindaloovians' caste system was similar to India's social structure—appropriate, given that the species and caste names were types of Indian food.*

- **Vindaloovian Empire:** The dominion of the Vindaloovians—a fictional species that Lister made up to trick a simulant hunting party **[T-SER6.3]**.

**B-: Books**
**PRG:** *Red Dwarf Programme Guide*
**SUR:** *Red Dwarf Space Corps Survival Manual*
**PRM:** *Primordial Soup*
**SOS:** *Son of Soup*
**SCE:** *Scenes from the Dwarf*
**LOG:** *Red Dwarf Log No. 1996*
**RD8:** *Red Dwarf VIII*
**EVR:** *The Log: A Dwarfer's Guide to Everything*

**X-: Misc.**
**PRO:** Promotional materials, videos, etc.
**PST:** Posters at DJ XVII (2013)
**CAL:** 2008 calendar
**RNG:** Cell phone ringtones
**MOB:** Mobisode ("Red Christmas")
**CIN:** *Children in Need* sketch
**GEK:** *Geek Week* intros by Kryten
**TNG:** "Tongue-Tied" video

**XMS:** Bill Pearson's Christmas special pitch script
**XVD:** Bill Pearson's Christmas special pitch video
**OTH:** Other *Red Dwarf* appearances

**SUFFIX**
**DVD:**
**(d)** – Deleted scene
**(o)** – Outtake
**(b)** – Bonus DVD material (other)
**(e)** – Extended version

**SMEGAZINES:**
**(c)** – Comic
**(a)** – Article

**OTHER:**
**(s)** – Early/unused script draft
**(s1)** – Alternate version of script

- **Vindaloovian Empire:** The dominion of a species of militant, experimental, human-hating GELFs called Vindaloovians **[G-BIT]**.

- **Vindaloovian Empire, The:** A restaurant aboard *Red Dwarf*, specializing in Indian cuisine. Located in Blue Corridor 9, on Floor 431, it boasted that its food was "hotter than the surface of Sol." The eatery offered a coward's menu, a "Dave Lister Special," and free skutter delivery **[X-CAL]**.

- **Vindaloovian "Viper" Rifle:** The standard firearm of the Vindaloovian army, also known as the Vindaloovian Popadom Rifle (VPR). It fired a large explosive dart containing poppadom shards and curry sauce, which tore away flesh and stung intensely, but could also be consumed in the event of an emergency. The VPR held a twenty-round clip and had a range of 60 meters (197 feet) **[G-BIT]**.

- **Vinegar Drawers:** A nickname of Admiral Peter Tranter, commander of the Space Corps R&D Program in Ace Rimmer's universe. Tranter's valet, Kevin, often called him this name behind his back **[N-BCK]**.

- **Viral Research Department:** A section aboard a scientific research station dedicated to studying biological viruses. The station was home to Hildegarde Lanstrom, a brilliant scientist who developed positive viruses. A large sign was mounted outside the facility, warning occupants of "Most Gross Danger," and mandating that bio-suits be worn at all times. The sign was accompanied by pictographs depicting a skull-and-crossbones, a bio-suit and a vomiting person with bursting intestines **[T-SER5.4]**.

- **Virgil:** An ancient Roman poet (born Publius Vergilius Maro), and the author of the *Aeneid,* a Latin epic poem written during the first century B.C., recounting the legendary travels and battles of Trojan soldier Aeneas **[RL]**. Lister owned a comic book adaptation of the *Aeneid* **[T-SER5.2]**.

- **Virgin:** A British multinational venture-capital company whose holdings included a number of airlines **[RL]**. During the twenty-second century, Virgin offered flights on its new line of demi-light-speed zippers to Saturn and its moons, which took just over two hours **[N-INF]**. Its slogan was "Come Fly the Friendly Non-Atmospheric Voids" **[M-SMG2.6(c4)]**.

- **Virgin Birth, the:** The belief among Christian faiths that Mary conceived Jesus Christ while still a virgin, after being impregnated by the Holy Spirit **[RL]**. The Cat People inhabiting *Red Dwarf* also used this term to describe the litter of Frankenstein, a pregnant feline that Lister smuggled aboard the mining vessel, whose kittens spawned their entire species **[T-SER1.1]**.

- **visual interpretation system:** Components built into 4000 Series mechanoids enabling them to recognize and interpret visual signals from their optical system **[N-BCK]**.

- **visual system:** The optical component of Talkie Toasters. The type of visual system used in the appliance was a CCD 517.3 **[T-SER4.4]**.

- **vitals cable:** A system of tubes that supplied cyber-psychologist Sandra Halley with blood, oxygen and power for her trolley, which she required due to a degenerative bone disease. The scientist was murdered while working late one evening, her vitals cable severed **[M-SMG2.7(c4)]**.

- **Vlad:** An employee of Karstares Interstellar Cleaning and Sanitation Supplies on the television soap opera *Androids*. Vlad, who worked for Jaysee, helped produce the company's newest "green" cleaning product, Eco, by harvesting ingredients from Io's rainforests with a chainsaw **[M-SMG2.2(c3)]**.

- **Vlad the Impaler:** The posthumous nickname of Vlad III, Prince of Wallachia, a fifteenth-century Romanian royal known for his excessive ruthlessness—and for inspiring Bram Stoker's novel *Dracula* **[RL]**. Using a time drive coupled with a faster-than-light drive installed in *Starbug 1*, the crew traveled throughout space-time, becoming epicures and sampling the best in the universe, while socializing with such historic figures as Vlad the Impaler **[T-SER6.6(d)]**.

- **vocabulary unit:** A component of food dispensers that translated users' verbal commands in order to carry out requests. A malfunctioning unit could yield unexpected results;

when Lister requested a sandwich and coffee, a *Red Dwarf* dispenser with a faulty vocabulary unit instead produced a pair of rubber boots and a bucket **[T-SER1.2]**.

- ***Vodka Cola*:** A book written by Charles Levinson about the easing of geo-political tensions between the Soviet Union and the United States, originally published in 1978 **[RL]**. Warden Ackerman had a copy of this book on a shelf in his quarters aboard *Red Dwarf* **[T-SER8.5]**.

- ***Vogue*:** A monthly fashion and lifestyle magazine published worldwide by Condé Nast **[RL]**. While prepping the supposed survivors of the *Nova 5* crash for the *Red Dwarf* crew's arrival, Kryten remarked that one of them, Elaine Schuman, could go straight to the cover of *Vogue*—despite her being a skeletal corpse **[N-INF]**.

  When Camille, a Pleasure GELF, revealed her true appearance to Kryten, he claimed she looked "nice" and "cute," though she was a large, gelatinous green blob. Although she was unlikely to make the cover of *Vogue,* he said, the same was true of him **[T-SER4.1]**.

  While trapped in an addictive version of *Better Than Life*, Rimmer imagined that he was married to Juanita Chicata. The Brazilian bombshell often had temper tantrums, sometimes because she wasn't on the cover of *Vogue* for two consecutive months—and sometimes because she was, but didn't like the photograph **[N-INF]**.

- **voice-recognition unicycle:** A component that Holly mistakenly reported as being damaged after an electrical fire garbled her vocabulary. She intended to report damage to her voice-recognition unit **[T-SER5.5]**.

  ***NOTE:** In a deleted scene, Holly called the unit her "voice-recognition Eugene O'Neill," referencing the American playwright who wrote a number of plays in the early 1900s, including* Long Day's Journey into Night *and* The Emperor Jones.

- **voice-recognition unit:** A system aboard *Red Dwarf* that contained the entire vocabulary of the ship's computer, enabling Holly to speak and understand what crewmembers said. If the unit became damaged, the computer's speech-recognition ability was sometimes impaired due to missing or replaced words, resulting in a loss of voice command functionality. While testing a new triplicator device, Lister unwittingly reversed its field, causing *Red Dwarf* to destabilize and creating electrical fires throughout the ship, one of which damaged the voice-recognition unit **[T-SER5.5]**.

- **voice unit:** A component of 4000 Series mechanoids enabling them to speak. Kryten's Spare Head Three had a malfunctioning voice unit, causing it to speak with a Yorkshire accent **[T-SER4.2]**.

- **Volkswagen:** A brand of German automobiles whose models included the Volkswagen Beetle **[RL]**. While marooned aboard *Starbug 1* on an icy planet, Lister tried to keep his mind off hunger by recounting how he lost his virginity on the ninth hole of the Bootle golf course. Annoyed that Lister abused the facilities without being a member of the club, Rimmer asked if he raked the sand back afterwards, imagining the embarrassment of someone playing golf the next day and getting a ball trapped in the crevice of Lister's buttocks, which he said resembled two badly parked Volkswagens **[T-SER3.2]**.

- **Volt Master:** A brand of electronic torture device used by Doctors Maxwell, Pension and Fund in a hallucination Cat suffered after receiving a bump to the head. Cat believed he was once again Duane Dibbley, and that the three doctors were experimenting on him. In actuality, the trio were Lister, Rimmer and Kryten, who were attempting to revive him using lithium carbonate **[M-SMG1.9(c1)]**.

- **volt meter:** A device designed to measure potential voltage differences in electrical circuits **[RL]**. While searching for a malfunction in *Starbug 1*'s electrical system, Rimmer ordered Kryten to test key areas by sticking his finger into each junction and measuring the voltage before his eyes blew out of his head. After several tests, Kryten suggested using an actual volt meter, as the current testing method invalidated his service guarantee **[T-SER7.1(e)]**.

- **von Stauffenberg, Claus, Staff Colonel/Count:** A Nazi officer and leading member of a German resistance movement that tried to remove Adolf Hitler from power. Count von Stauffenberg was convicted and executed for his involvement in a failed assassination attempt on the Führer's life in 1944 **[RL]**.

After discovering mutated developing fluid in *Red Dwarf*'s photo lab, Kryten used it to develop an old image of Hitler at a rally in Nuremberg. The mutated chemical allowed Lister to enter the photograph and attend the event, where he scuffled with Hitler before stealing his briefcase and returning through the photo back to *Red Dwarf*.

The crew perused the contents of the briefcase, which included erotic handcuffs, a banana and crisps sandwich, Hitler's diary, and a package labeled "To Adolf. Love and Hugs, Staff Colonel Count von Stauffenberg." The latter contained explosives, which Lister quickly threw back into the photo, nearly killing Hitler **[T-SER3.5]**.

> ***NOTE:*** *A 1939 newspaper was shown reporting the incident, which would not jibe with von Stauffenberg's actual assassination attempt, which occurred five years later.*

- **von Trapp, Maria:** The matriarch of the Trapp Family Singers and the inspiration for the film and Broadway musical *The Sound of Music*, which inaccurately depicted her and her family as climbing a mountain to escape Austria **[RL]**. While training Arnold Rimmer to become the next Ace Rimmer, the current Ace used a program in *Starbug 1*'s artificial-reality machine to simulate snow-covered plateaus and summits, claiming it was where Rimmer had to be to become his successor. Arnold disagreed, commenting that it was where one had to be to become Maria von Trapp **[T-SER7.2]**.

- **Voorheese, Captain:** *See* Voorhese, Wolfgang, Captain

- **Voorhese, Klaus:** The brother of Meinhard Voorhese, a Nazi commander on War World. Klaus shared a bedroom with Meinhard as a child, but was killed by a large truck when his brother lured him into traffic with a trail of sweets, in a bid to gain control of their bedroom **[W-OFF]**.

- **Voorhese, Meinhard, Captain:** A Nazi commander on War World **[T-SER7.2]**. As a child, Meinhard shared a bedroom with his brother, Klaus, until luring him into traffic so he could have the room to himself. He then set traps around the house to eliminate his mother as well, eventually killing her with a bomb in her knitting basket. Voorhese soon seized control of Lichtenstrasse, the street on which he lived, and then conquered his block, town and country, vowing to achieve world domination **[W-OFF]**.

  When Voorhese captured Princess Bonjella, whom he believed to be part of a resistance movement, Ace Rimmer arrived to rescue her. Voorhese captured Ace and brought him aboard his airplane, but Ace escaped his bondages and killed the Nazi's soldiers, including the pilot.

  As the plane spiraled out of control, Voorhese tossed his pet crocodile, Snappy, toward Ace as a distraction, then threw lit dynamite into the plane as he jumped. Ace wrangled Snappy with rope and jumped out of the plane before the explosion, using the reptile to surf through the air toward Voorhese so he could commandeer his parachute. Ace then saved the princess, while Meinhard fell to his presumed death **[T-SER7.2]**.

  > ***NOTE:*** *Because the Voorhese stories varied greatly between the official website and* Red Dwarf—The Roleplaying Game *(including the character's first name), the two versions are assumed to have existed in separate universes.*

- **Voorhese, Wolfgang, Captain:** A Nazi commander for the Reich, the evil superpower of War World in a universe in which World War II never ended. As a youth, he was unloved by his father, while his mother made him wear shorts until college. Among his list of guilty pleasures were the game tiddlywinks and the television program *Hogan's Heroes*.

  Voorhese held *War World Weekly*'s title of "Most Likely to Invade Australia" for several years running, before being downgraded to "Most Likely to Be Eaten by an Alligator in a Bizarre Skydiving Accident." He plotted to kidnap and execute Princess Bonjella, the leader of the Seni Rotundi islands and a resistance sympathizer, but was foiled and presumably killed by a version of Ace Rimmer **[G-BIT]**.

  > ***NOTE:*** *Because the Voorhese stories varied greatly between the official website and the roleplaying game (including his first name), the two versions are assumed to have existed in separate universes. In the RPG's* Series Sourcebook, *his surname was spelled "Voorheese."*

- **VOTE 1:** The license plate number of a limousine belonging to Voter Colonel Sebastian Doyle, a persona that Lister assumed while trapped in a despair squid hallucination **[T-SER5.6]**.

- **Voter-General Avenue:** A street on Earth in Jake Bullet's universe. According to informant Vinnie van Goth, a nerd club was located on this avenue **[M-SMG1.12(c1)]**.

- ***Voterwatch Update*:** A television program that aired in a fascist society in Jake Bullet's universe. The show, hosted by Bullet's police chief, ran footage of crimes against democracy, and asked viewers' help in turning in the perpetrators. Anyone with knowledge of the infractions was required to call the station at 0800-FREEDOM, with members of the studio audience being punished for any crimes left unsolved by 8:00 PM.

  One episode showed a bank robbery committed by an elderly lady, as well as a jewelry heist perpetrated by a pregnant woman. While viewing tapes of this show, Bullet discovered the two criminals had electronic spikes attached to their neck, similar to one he had received from Brainfade **[M-SMG2.8(c1)]**.

- **VoxMod vocal disguise unit:** A small device used to alter an individual's voice pattern. Capable of recording one voice pattern at a time, it was attached to the roof of a user's mouth and controlled by the tongue **[G-BIT]**.

- **VW Day:** A term Rimmer coined after orchestrating a battle that killed every waxdroid on Waxworld—including his own army—which he considered a victory **[T-SER4.6]**.

W

# WAXDROIDS

- **W 84 Ave.:** A street in Dallas, Texas, circa 1966, in an alternate timeline created when the *Starbug 1* crew prevented John F. Kennedy's assassination. The group passed this street while searching for clues to the population's disappearance, and found a nearby sign for Dallas Electric, as well as a dead man who had been trampled to death **[T-SER7.1]**.

- ***Wacked Out People's Book of Crazy Things to Do, The*:** A hypothetical book title that Lister made up to describe Rimmer's determination to play it by the book and perform a roll call despite the cadmium II disaster having killed *Red Dwarf*'s crew **[R-BOD]**.

- **Wacky Wally's Video Wonderland:** A video store at which Oswald "Kill Crazy" Blenkinsop once worked. When he played the movie *Decayed Flesh 5: The Zombies Take Manhattan* during one shift, an offended customer chastised him for doing so. Kill Crazy later followed the woman home and murdered her entire family, for which he was arrested and assigned to *Red Dwarf*'s brig for transport to Adelphi 12 **[W-OFF]**.

- **Wagner, Lindsay:** An American actor best known for her portrayal of Jaime Sommers in the 1970s television program *The Bionic Woman*. Among Sommers' bionic abilities was enhanced hearing **[RL]**. When a rogue simulant scavenging on Garbage World (Earth) asked his cohort if he had heard a commotion coming from the polymorph holding pen, his comrade sarcastically asked if he thought he was Lindsay Wagner **[M-SMG2.9(c12)]**.

- **"Wah twah morah!":** A GELF phrase that translated into English as "Death to the strangers!" **[T-SER6.4]**.

  ***NOTE:*** *In the DVD deleted scenes for this episode, the captions were spelled "Wah twah madah. Cha."*

- **Wailing Wall:** The remnant of an ancient wall in the Old City of Jerusalem that has been a site for Jewish prayer and pilgrimage for centuries **[RL]**. Contaminated with the ink of a despair squid, Lister and Kryten broke down emotionally and started sobbing. Cat remarked that they sounded like the Wailing Wall on Saturday night **[T-SER5.6]**.

- **Walker, Mr.:** The manager of Black Island Film Studios, a production company in a universe in which *Red Dwarf* was a British television series. Leo Davis, the studio's timid caretaker, worked for Walker, who constantly chastised him for sleeping on the job **[X-TNG]**.

- **Wallace & Gromit:** A pair of British stop-motion claymation characters—an eccentric inventor and his dog—created by Nick Park of Aardman Animations. The duo appeared in four short films and a feature-length movie, as well as in several Christmas-themed television idents for BBC One and BBC Two **[RL]**. After a man whom the *Red Dwarf* crew mistook for Jesus Christ transported from the mining ship back to his own time to trash his reputation and prevent the rise of Christianity, Lister wondered what that would mean for Christmas, horrified that they may have killed Wallace & Gromit **[T-SER10.3]**.

- ***Wallpapering, Painting and Stippling—A DIY Guide*:** A video stocked in *Red Dwarf*'s Quarantine Room 152. This video fulfilled the minimum motion picture entertainment quota for quarantined individuals, as set forth by Space Corps Directive 312 **[T-SER5.4]**.

- **Wangle, Crust, Grandmaster:** A name and title self-chosen by a hologrammic scientist infected with a holovirus contained within an SOS transmission sent by Hildegard Lanstrom. The hologram went insane and flushed his crew out an airlock for not addressing him in this manner **[W-OFF]**.

- **Wankel:** A rogue simulant scavenger who scoured the galaxy with other simulants, searching for genuine Earth antiques and emotions garnered from polymorphs, to sell to mechanicals. He was roughly shaped like a ballistic missile. Wankel and his group came across Garbage World (Earth) after it had been ripped from its orbit, and searched the surface for artifacts and polymorphs **[M-SMG2.9(c11)]**.

- **War:** *See* Apocalypse, War, Brother

- ***War and Peace*:** A Russian historical novel by Leo Tolstoy, first published in 1869 at a length of 1,225 pages **[RL]**. Pree suggested that Rimmer read *War and Peace* during the time freed up by her erasure of the television series *Victory South* from *Red Dwarf*'s computer. Rimmer had been looking forward to watching it, but Pree predicted he would be disappointed and preemptively deleted it **[T-SER10.2]**.

  In Jake Bullet's universe, the cyborg's police chief had a copy of *War and Peace* on his desk. The chief claimed it was not as detailed as he preferred his officers' reports to be **[M-SMG1.13(c4)]**.

- **Warburton, John:** A bioengineer and the ex-fiancé of Professor Mamet, the creator of the 4000 Series mechanoid. After Warburton left her at the altar, Mamet built the Kryten series in his image as revenge, complete with all of his shortcomings as a pompous, ridiculous-looking, overbearing, short-tempered buffoon.

  Mamet installed a negadrive in the 4000 Series that stored negative emotions, occasionally blowing apart a mechanoid's head if it became full, emulating Warburton's tendency to lose his head when angry. A file was stored in each model, accessible using the password "4X2C," and containing the full details of Mamet's revenge **[T-SER7.6]**.

Jim Reaper, the Space Division's head of sales at Diva-Droid International, bore a striking resemblance to Warburton. Mamet hired him, in fact, because of the similarity **[W-OFF]**.

> ***NOTE:*** *The physical similarities between Warburton, Reaper and the Data Doctor (who was said to be based on Reaper's brother on the official website) were a clever way to explain why the three characters looked like Kryten (since actor Robert Llewellyn played them all). It doesn't, however, explain why they don't all look like David Ross, who originally played Kryten and would have essentially been Kryten's default look.*

- **Warburton Neurotronics:** A company specializing in the development of artificial-intelligence computer systems for large vessels, such as *Red Dwarf*'s Holly, as well as bi-photonic monoprisms used in hologrammic light bees. The company was located at Birmingham Labs **[X-PST]**.

> ***NOTE:*** *This company was presumably founded by John Warburton.*

- **war ferret:** A specially trained domesticated mammal that the St. Francis of Assisi waxdroid used during the Waxworld's Wax War **[G-SOR]**.

- ***Warhammer Fantasy Battle*:** A series of tabletop wargames from Games Workshop **[RL]**. While trapped in an elation squid hallucination, the *Red Dwarf* crew imagined that Reg Wharf, the president of the *Red Dwarf* Fan Club, indulged in *Warhammer* games **[T-SER9.2]**.

- **Warrington, Susan:** A woman whom Lister met during his formative years. Warrington got Lister drunk and took advantage of him on the ninth hole at Bootle Municipal Golf Course **[N-INF]**.

> ***NOTE:*** *Since the novel* Infinity Welcomes Careful Drivers *did not specify the age at which this occurred, or whether he lost his virginity that day, this does not contradict his first sexual experience with Michelle Fisher, mentioned in episode 3.2 ("Marooned"). Perhaps Dave simply tended to get lucky at that particular golf course and hole.*

- **Warsaw Central:** A railway station servicing the Polish capital city of Warsaw **[RL]**. Depressed about his life aboard *Red Dwarf*, Lister once irritated Rimmer with a continuous stream of sighing, which Arnold compared to the soundtrack *Great Railway Journeys of the World,* likening the noise to the Trans-Siberian Express pulling into Warsaw Central **[T-SER3.5(d)]**.

- **War World:** An alternate-dimension Earth on which World War II played out differently, with the Axis forces relying more on gaining power through ideology rather than via brute force and bloodshed. On this world, the war never ended, but rather evolved into a power struggle between the Reich and the Resistance.

  Over time, the conflict's origins were forgotten, and the war became a tedious repetition of evil plots being thwarted. The largest technological advancement during the war was the invention of Raketenhosen ("Rocket Pants"), which were initially available only to the Reich. However, a visit from interdimensional traveler Robert Dimsdale tipped the balance of power when he acquired a pair for the Resistance.

  The Reich was controlled by a central computer called the Human Impressions Task & Logistics Electronic Reichsführer (HITLER), which itself was controlled by Adolf Hitler's disembodied brain, contained within a stasis field. The Resistance, on the other hand, had many supporters scattered throughout the planet, including Princess Beryl Bonjella, the leader of the Seni Rotundi islands **[G-BIT]**.

- ***War World Weekly*:** A weekly magazine published on War World. In the publication's annual "What Maniac" poll, the Reich's Captain Wolfgang Voorhese was voted "Most Likely to Invade Australia" several years running **[G-BIT]**.

- **waste compactor:** A machine located in *Starbug 1*'s engine room, used to compact garbage into a portable cube for easy disposal. When a Psiren took the form of Kryten's creator, Professor Mamet, and ordered the mechanoid to load himself into the waste compactor, his programming compelled him to obey **[T-SER6.1]**.

- **Waste Disposal:** A department aboard *Red Dwarf* responsible for processing and removing waste products. Waste Disposal personnel filled garbage pods with refuse before shooting them into space. Rimmer claimed to have never worked for Waste Disposal **[T-SER1.4]**.

- **waste disposal:** A machine aboard *Red Dwarf*, used to eliminate garbage. Lister once fed Talkie Toaster into the waste disposal after smashing it to pieces with a fourteen-pound lump hammer **[T-SER4.4]**. Another waste disposal was located in the Tank, *Red Dwarf*'s brig on Floor 13 **[T-SER8.5]**.

- **waste-disposal bay:** A section of *Red Dwarf* used for jettisoning waste material from the ship. In certain circumstances, the remains of deceased crewmembers were also ejected from this area **[N-BTL]**.

- **Waste Disposal Unit 5:** A unit aboard *Starbug 1*, located in the shuttle's cockpit, and retrofitted to eject compacted garbage implanted with nitroglycerin at high velocity, effectively turning it into a high-impact cannon. This improvised cannon was first tested on a gargantuan meteor while *Starbug* traversed an asteroid field in pursuit of the stolen *Red Dwarf* **[T-SER6.1]**.

- **Waste Disposal Unit 8:** A unit aboard *Starbug 1*, located on a wall next to the cockpit entrance **[T-SER4(b)]**.

  ***NOTE:*** *This unit also appeared in the special* Can't Smeg, Won't Smeg, *albeit in a separate location, since that set had a completely different configuration.*

- **waste grinder:** A machine used aboard *Red Dwarf* to crush garbage for release into space. Confidence, a hallucination of Lister's mind made corporeal by mutated pneumonia, killed fellow hallucination Paranoia by feeding him into the waste grinder and flushing the remains **[T-SER1.5]**.

- ***Watchdog: Shuttlecraft Special*:** A news segment on Groovy Channel 27 that focused on *Starbug* shuttlecraft. During one broadcast, the presenter grilled a JMC representative about the shuttle's shortcomings and high accident rate **[W-OFF]**.

- **Watergate:** A building complex in Washington, D.C., that became the site of a well-publicized political scandal in 1972 that ended Richard Nixon's presidency **[RL]**. Claiming to have never heard of premenstrual syndrome (PMS) on any television shows or movies, Kryten likened the male-controlled media's so-called "menstrual cover-up" to Nixon's attempt to bury the Watergate scandal **[T-SER8.8]**.

- **waterproof pogo stick:** An item that Kryten gave to Kochanski while serving time in the Tank. He told her it was a gift to keep her from getting verrucas (plantar warts) in the shower, but his real intention was to boost the ratings of his Krytie TV series, *Women's Shower Night*, by filming her bouncing around wet and soapy while airing the footage for his male viewers **[T-SER8.5]**.

- **watunga:** A word in the Kinitawowi language, meaning "hut" **[T-SER6.4]**.

- **wax-blaster:** A portable machine built to play music at extremely loud volumes. Lister owned one such device that contained eight speakers **[N-INF]**.

- **waxdroid:** An animatronic representation of a creature or humanoid, made primarily of wax and used in amusement parks to represent famous historical or fictional characters. Each waxdroid was programmed with the basic personality of the individual it was designed to impersonate. The droids were particularly susceptible to heat, melting at temperatures in excess of one hundred degrees Celsius (212 degrees Fahrenheit).

  The Waxworld theme park utilized waxdroids to entertain guests, until it was eventually deserted. After millennia alone, the droids broke free of their programming and learned how to think for themselves—though they still acted in character. A war soon broke out between Hero World and Villain World, which ended in all of the waxdroids' deaths after Rimmer took command of the heroes' army **[T-SER4.6]**.

  An Errol Flynn waxdroid traveled with a chainsmoking human named Eric and a hologrammic pastry chef called Robin in a possible alternate universe. Other waxdroids included a Hermann Göring model that dressed in drag and participated in the ninth annual Kinitawowi Open golf tournament **[G-RPG]**, as well as one designed to emulate television actor Telly Savalas, which was involved in a plot to retrieve priceless art from a Reich supply depot on War World **[G-BIT]**. In addition, waxdroids were used as replacements for lawyers following the Great Attorney Purge of 2287 **[G-RPG]**.

- **Wax War, The:** A conflict fought on Waxworld, a former theme park home to dozens of waxdroids—animatronic robots made primarily of wax, and designed to look and act like historical and fictional individuals of Earth's past.

  The waxdroids were designed to repeatedly perform simple routines, but after the park had been deserted for millions of years, the droids learned how to break free of their programming and became sentient, though they retained the personalities of the individuals whom they impersonated. As such, the two major attractions—Hero World, occupied by waxdroid versions of history's best and brightest, and Villain World, populated by copies of Earth's most notorious historical individuals—became embroiled in a resource war for the park's supply of wax.

  During this war, the *Red Dwarf* crew transported to the planet using a Matter Paddle, with Lister and Cat materializing in Villain territory, and Rimmer and Kryten arriving in Hero territory. Finding the heroes' army lacking, Rimmer took command of the group, working many of the pacifistic waxdroids to death before ordering a frontal attack on the villains' compound across a minefield, which killed the remaining droids, including his own army. This ended the Wax War, which Arnold considered a victory **[T-SER4.6]**.

- **Waxworld:** A large-scale theme park built on an inhabitable planet that was eventually abandoned. The park's main attractions were waxdroids—robotic replicas of famous historical and fictional individuals from Earth's history, programmed to repeatedly perform simple routines.

  Waxworld was divided into several sections, including Hero World, Villain World, Prehistoric World **[T-SER4.6]** and Horror World **[W-OFF]**, with a separate section dedicated to fictional characters **[T-SER4.6]** as well as a Chamber of Horrors, situated on the eastern perimeter and offering a full range of twentieth-century foods. The park covered one hundred square miles of the planet's surface, and originally housed more than ten thousand waxdroids **[T-SER4.6(d)]**.

  The droids, removed from humanity for millennia, evolved beyond their programming, learning to think for themselves. In time, a war broke out between Hero World and Villain World **[T-SER4.6]**.

  The conflict, fought over wax resources, raged on for thousands of years, sustained by the park's ability to analyze the droids' status and rebuild them when needed, and to supply them with weapons **[G-RPG]**. The fighting came to an abrupt end, however, after Rimmer assumed control of Hero World's army. His battle plan to attack the villains' headquarters full-on resulted in the destruction of every remaining waxdroid—which Rimmer considered a victory, despite the complete loss of life on both sides **[T-SER4.6]**.

- **Wavy Red:** A lighting-effect color available for Kluge Corp.'s teleporters **[G-RPG]**.

- **Wayne, John:** The stage-name of a twentieth-century film actor, born Marion Robert Morrison, who starred in numerous Westerns, notably *The Quiet Man*, *Rio Bravo*, *True Grit* and *The Man Who Shot Liberty Valance* **[RL]**. Two of *Red Dwarf*'s skutters developed an affection for Wayne's films, hanging posters of the actor in their broom cupboard **[T-SER2.1]** and joining the John Wayne Fan Club **[T-SER2.2]**.

- **Wayne, John:** A waxdroid replica of the Western actor created for the Waxworld theme park. Left on their own for millions of years, the waxdroids attained sentience and became embroiled in a park-wide resource war between Villain World and Hero World (to which Wayne belonged). The Wayne waxdroid died during the conflict **[T-SER4.6]**.

- **WD-40:** A brand of penetrating oil used for lubrication and water-displacement **[RL]**. Camille, a Pleasure GELF in the form of a 4000 Series mechanoid, told Kryten that her fragrance was WD-40, which he also used on his neck hinges **[T-SER4.1]**. Lister rewarded Bob the skutter with shots of WD-40 after it smuggled a chicken vindaloo meal to him in prison **[T-SER8.6]**.

- **"We are all gonna die":** An old saying of the Cat People, which Cat recited after a time wand transformed Birdman's pet sparrow, Pete, into a *Tyrannosaurus rex* **[T-SER8.6]**.

- **Weasel, Wilbur:** A character, possibly animated, popular in the twenty-second century **[X-XMS]**.

- **weather-blast goggles:** A type of specialized eyewear designed for use in extreme environments. The goggles were issued on JMC vessels such as *Red Dwarf* **[G-BIT]**.

- **weather computer:** A computer aboard *Starbug* shuttles designed to analyze planetary weather conditions. Because Lister forgot to check the weather computer before landing on a Kinitawowi desert planet, he and his shipmates arrived wearing arctic gear **[N-LST]**.

- **weather scan:** A function of *Starbug 1*'s computer that analyzed the weather conditions on nearby planets, allowing the crew to dress accordingly. Kochanski's scan of a planet made from the remolecularized *Red Dwarf* showed tropical conditions and clear skies, but due to her innate distrust of the system, she suggested dressing for arctic conditions nonetheless **[T-SER7.6]**.

- **"Weaving the Traditional Way":** *See* "Flemish Weaving the Traditional Way"

- **Wednesday, Chancellor:** A rogue simulant officer aboard a Death Ship commanded by Dominator Zlurth. When the *Red Dwarf* crew evaded the simulant vessel, Wednesday reported the escape to Zlurth, who slid his sword toward the subordinate, saying he knew what he must do.

  Misinterpreting the order, Wednesday tried to commit *harakiri*, only to learn that Zlurth had expected him merely to polish the sword and write a formal apology as punishment. Zlurth chastised Wednesday for jumping to conclusions, and the chancellor collected his entrails and departed. He was killed by friendly fire after the *Red Dwarf* crew destabilized the hull of their *Blue Midget* shuttlecraft, which allowed missiles from an Annihilator to pass through and strike the Chancellor's ship, destroying it **[T-SER10.6]**.

- **Wednesday, March 2, 2077, 8:33:** The time and date on one side of a stasis leak that formed aboard *Red Dwarf*. The other side of the leak exited three million years later. After finding the leak in a malfunctioning stasis room on Floor 16, Lister, Cat and Rimmer used it to visit the past **[T-SER2.4]**.

  ***NOTE:** The book* Red Dwarf Log No. 1996 *claimed March 2 was the anniversary of Rimmer's death, contradicting this episode, in which that date was three weeks prior to the cadmium II disaster. This also contradicts several other sources setting* Red Dwarf *in the twenty-second century.*

- **Wedshoetree:** The name Rimmer gave to one of his shoetrees, to ensure it spent the same amount of time in his shoes as the others **[T-SER7.5]**.

- **Weiner:** A *Red Dwarf* crewmember who informed hologram Frank Saunders that George McIntyre—who outranked him—had committed suicide and would thus replace Saunders as the ship's hologram **[N-INF]**.

  ***NOTE:** Weiner presumably died during the cadmium II explosion. It is unknown whether the nanobots resurrected her in Series VIII.*

- **welding mallet:** An apparatus that Rimmer once threatened to hit Lister with for singing while on the job **[T-SER1.1]**.

- **"Welfare":** A word printed on a patch on the right arm of Lister's crew jacket **[T-SER1.1]**.

- **Wendy:** A bespectacled classmate of Rimmer at Io Polytechnic. During one class, she tried to alert Arnold to the fact that he was the subject of a psychology test being conducted by their professor (his stepfather), by writing in her notebook that he was a guinea pig. Mistaking this as an insult, Rimmer wrote back that she was a "baboon four-eyes" **[T-SER10.6]**.

- **werecod:** An Earth species resulting from genetic-engineering experiments, also known as *Lupus aquaticus*. The werecod, a cross between a werewolf and a codfish, usually took the form of a wolf, though during full moons, it turned into a fish. Caution had to be taken when eating or digesting this animal during transitional periods. Ultimately, all werecod were exiled off-world to seed unpopulated planets **[B-SUR]**.

- **"We're Off to See the Wizard":** A Munchkin song featured in the 1939 film *The Wizard of Oz*, composed by Harold Arlen, with lyrics by E.Y. Harburg **[RL]**. When Rimmer refused to reveal where he was sleeping while visiting the reverse-sex universe—for fear that Lister would tell Arnold's female

counterpart—Lister asked if he was a man or a Munchkin. In response, Rimmer offered an altered rendition of this song **[T-SER2.6]**.

- **werewolf:** A folkloric human able to shapeshift into a wolf or a wolf-like creature, either purposely or due to an affliction or curse, also known as a lycanthrope **[RL]**. Scientists crossed this Earth species with a codfish via genetic engineering, creating a new species known as *Lupus aquaticus* **[B-SUR]**.

  ***NOTE:*** *Apparently, werewolves actually existed in the* Red Dwarf *universe.*

- **West 17/XC:** A tram station on *Red Dwarf*'s Northern Line, serving the vessel's Central Mall Branch **[M-SMG1.6(c2)]**.

- ***West Side Story*:** An American musical originally produced in 1957, inspired by William Shakespeare's *Romeo and Juliet* **[RL]**. While marooned aboard *Starbug 1* on an icy planet, Lister burned Rimmer's books to stay warm, including *The Complete Works of Shakespeare*. Arnold protested the destruction of what was likely the only remaining copy of the play, but admitted he never actually read it—though he had seen *West Side Story* **[T-SER3.2]**.

- **wet-look knitwear:** A hypothetical type of clothing that Rimmer made up to mock Lister about his plan to farm sheep on Fiji—an island submerged underwater **[T-SER1.1]**.

- **wetware AI technology:** An experimental computing technology that the *Red Dwarf* crew discovered aboard a derelict research platform. It utilized a fluid matrix to stream data throughout the complex, as well as a wetware interface to allow a user to directly interact with the artificial-intelligence computer **[M-SMG1.11(c2)]**.

- **wetware interface:** A type of component that the *Red Dwarf* crew discovered aboard a derelict research platform. It allowed a user to become absorbed into the network, in order to record his or her experiences in its database of human knowledge. The device resembled a small pool that, when activated, flushed upward toward the ceiling, enveloping a user in its fluid matrix.

  Lister inadvertently became trapped in such an interface, completing the computer's database and enabling it to become sentient. Fearful that Lister might become irreversibly absorbed by the network, his shipmates sent Holly into the computer to rescue him **[M-SMG1.11(c2)]**.

- **whale-ipede:** A massive creature possessing a hundred legs, genetically engineered by inebriated scientists. One such animal escaped its pen and trampled a bus full of nuns, resulting in a total ban on alcohol at genetic research laboratories **[B-EVR]**.

- **Wharf, Reg:** An individual whom the *Red Dwarf* crew imagined while trapped in an elation squid hallucination. In the illusion, Wharf was the president of the *Red Dwarf* Fan Club, a group for enthusiasts of the British comedy series. Wharf changed his name to be phonetically similar to the title *Red Dwarf*, had an "H" tattooed on his forehead, and modeled his sitting room after Lister's sleeping quarters. His other hobbies included playing Warhammer games.

  The crew, believing they had been transported to an alternate reality in which they were characters on the TV series, visited a British science fiction shop called They Walk Among Us!, where an employee named Noddy contacted Wharf to help them learn their fate in the upcoming final episode. Reg refused to tell them what he knew, however, citing Space Corps Directive 596, which restricted confidential files for the captain's eyes only **[T-SER9.2]**.

- **"What are you talking about, Dog-Breath?":** A wise old Cat People saying that Cat recited after Lister explained his theory regarding a mysterious wedding photograph in Kochanski's quarters **[T-SER2.4]**.

- ***What Bike?*:** A British magazine about second-hand motorcycles and scooters **[RL]**. After encountering the Inquisitor, a simulant who roamed throughout space-time, judging whether others were fit to exist, Rimmer warned Lister that sitting around reading *What Bike?* and eating Sugar Puff sandwiches all day might not qualify as a worthwhile life **[T-SER5.2]**.

- ***What Carcass?*:** A hypothetical magazine title. When Kryten noted that male vultures became violent in close captivity,

**PREFIX**
**RL:** Real life

**T-: Television Episodes**
**SER:** Television series
**IDW:** "Identity Within"
**USA1:** Unaired U.S. pilot
**USA2:** Unaired U.S. demo

**R-: *The Bodysnatcher Collection***
**SER:** Remastered episodes
**BOD:** "Bodysnatcher"
**DAD:** "Dad"
**FTH:** "Lister's Father"
**INF:** "Infinity Patrol"
**END:** "The End" (original assembly)

**N-: Novels**
**INF:** *Infinity Welcomes Careful Drivers*
**BTL:** *Better Than Life*
**LST:** *Last Human*
**BCK:** *Backwards*
**OMN:** *Red Dwarf Omnibus*

**M-: Magazines**
**SMG:** *Smegazine*

**W-: Websites**
**OFF:** Official website
**NAN:** *Prelude to Nanarchy*
**AND:** *Androids*
**DIV:** Diva-Droid
**DIB:** Duane Dibbley

**CRP:** Crapola
**GEN:** Geneticon
**LSR:** Leisure World Intl.
**JMC:** Jupiter Mining Corporation
**AIT:** *A.I. Today*
**HOL:** HoloPoint

**G-: Roleplaying Game**
**RPG:** *Core Rulebook*
**BIT:** *A.I. Screen Extra Bits* booklet
**SOR:** *Series Sourcebook*
**OTH:** Other RPG material

Lister questioned the validity of this claim, sarcastically asking if they needed alone time to put their feet up and read *What Carcass?* **[T-SER5.4]**.

- **What's in the Bag?:** A game that the *Red Dwarf* crew sometimes played to pass the time. The object was to guess a bag's contents, based on its smell **[T-SER9.1]**.

- ***What's My Fruit?*:** A hypothetical game show for which Cat suggested Kryten and Lister audition, after Lister failed to prove that he had taught the mechanoid how to lie. Kryten tried calling a banana, an apple and an orange by different names, but instead identified them all correctly, unable to break free of his programming **[T-SER4.1]**.

- ***What Transport?*:** A magazine dedicated to transport craft. One issue featured a cover story about the outdated *White Midget* shuttlecraft. After reading the article, Lister erroneously referred to *Red Dwarf*'s *Blue Midget* shuttle as *White Midget* **[G-SOR]**.

  ***NOTE:** This fixed a continuity error presented in episode 3.4 ("Bodyswap"), in which Lister confused the shuttles' names.*

- **Wheaty Flakes:** A brand of cereal that often included a child's toy in the box. After arriving on Waxworld, Kryten and Rimmer encountered gargantuan reptilian creatures. The mechanoid noted how unrealistic they looked, claiming he had seen more believable dinosaurs in a packet of Wheaty Flakes **[T-SER4.6]**.

- **wheelchair jousting:** A game that Lister and Cat sometimes played to pass the time aboard *Red Dwarf*. The game involved riding wheelchairs, donning waste bins on their heads and arming themselves with pool cues fitted with toilet brushes as lances. The object was to knock the other player off his chair. Cat almost lost an eye during an especially rough round **[T-SER3.5(d)]**.

- **"While You Sleep, We're Probably Saving the Universe":** The Space Corps Marine motto **[T-SER10.1]**.

  ***NOTE:** Given Rimmer's sarcastic tone when citing this motto, it may be fictitious.*

- **"While You Sleep, We're Probably Shaving Off Your Pubes and Gluing Them to Your Head":** A slogan that Lister suggested as a more appropriate Space Corps Marine motto **[T-SER10.1]**.

- **Whirlpool Corp.:** An American manufacturer of home appliances, such as washers, dryers, ovens and refrigerators **[RL]**. An aspirin dispenser located in Lister's quarters aboard *Red Dwarf* was made by Whirlpool **[T-SER10.2]**.

- **whiskey:** A distilled alcoholic beverage made from fermented grain mash and aged in wooden casks **[RL]**. Lister had a bottle of whiskey in his room, with "Space Store Issue," the number 1235 and the word "whiskey" printed on a generic label **[T-SER1.2]**.

- **White, Barry:** A deep-voiced American rhythm and blues singer, born Barry Eugene Carter, known for such romantic songs as "You're the First, the Last, My Everything" and "Can't Get Enough of Your Love, Babe" **[RL]**. Cat chose Barry White's album *20 Bump and Grind Classics* to play in a survival pod that he planned to share with Ora Tanzil, to address his biological affliction caused by a lack of sex **[T-IDW]**.

  ***NOTE:** In the real world, Barry White never recorded an album by that name.*

- **White, Eric:** A Caucasian male, possibly in his mid-thirties, whom the *Starbug 1* crew found lying dead on a street in Dallas, Texas. The group had traveled back to 1966 using a portable time drive after inadvertently preventing John F. Kennedy's assassination. In the altered timeline that resulted, White had been trampled during a mass exodus from the city. Examining his corpse, Lister learned that he had been a single vegetarian and the chairman of the Anti-smoking League, which contradicted Cat's deduction that he was a married smoker whose last meal was a salt beef sandwich **[T-SER7.1(e)]**.

- **white card:** A part of Rimmer's Color Code system for controlling conversations. Holding up a white card meant discussion could continue **[T-SER1.3]**.

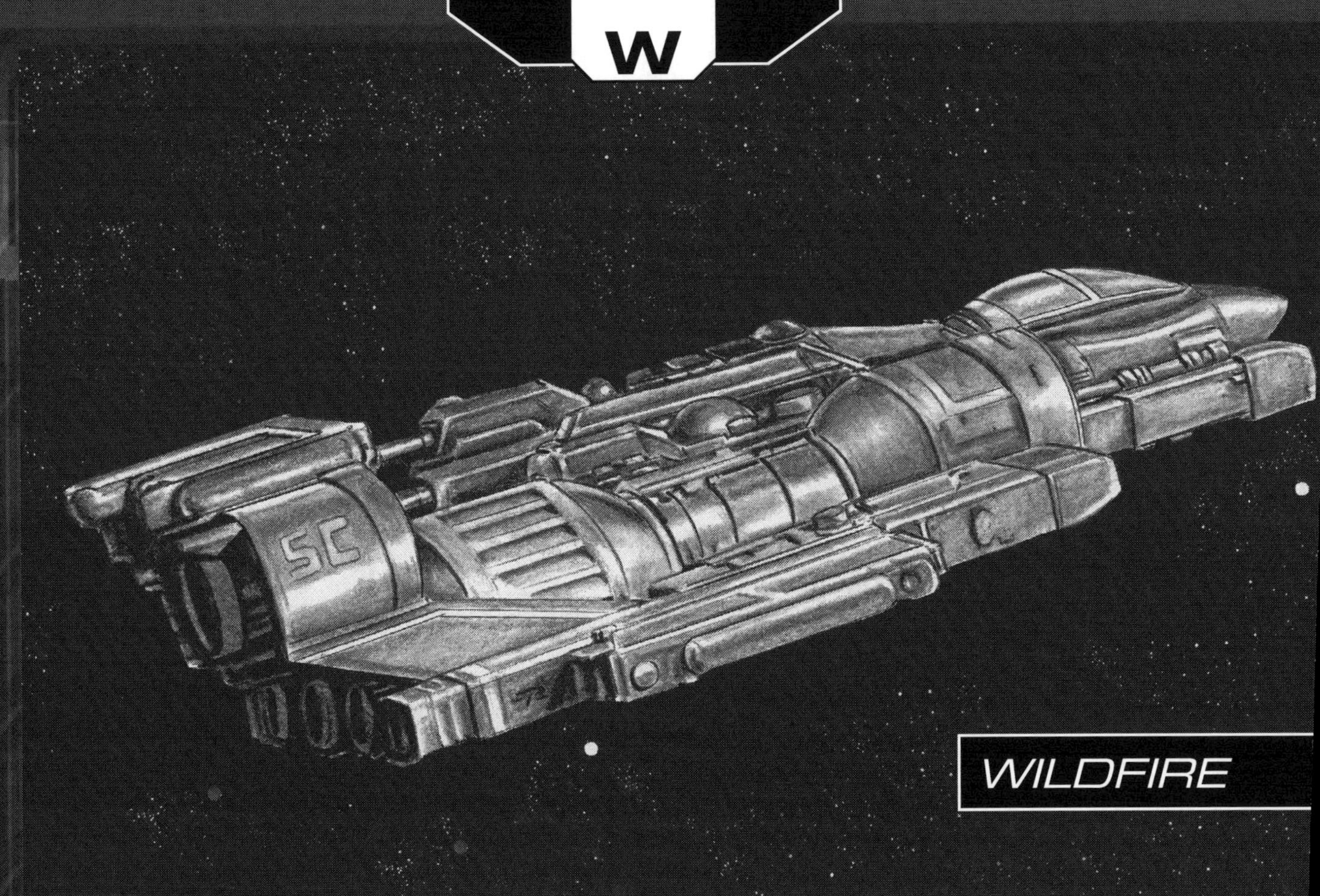


- **Whitechapel Road:** A major roadway in Eastern London, included in that city's version of *Monopoly* **[RL]**. For his twenty-fourth birthday, Lister and several friends embarked on a *Monopoly* board pub crawl across London; their second stop was Whitechapel, where they ordered piña coladas **[N-INF]**.

- **White Corridor, Level Two:** A section of *Red Dwarf* that contained porous circuits **[N-OMN]**.

  ***NOTE:*** *This was mentioned in the first-draft script of the pilot episode ("The End"), published in the* Red Dwarf Omnibus.

- **White Corridor 159:** A section of *Red Dwarf*'s Level 159 in which an explosion occurred due to Rimmer's shoddy work in sealing a drive plate. This resulted in a radiation leak that killed everyone aboard the mining vessel except for Lister **[T-SER1.6]**. After contracting mutated pneumonia, Lister passed out in this same section while heading for the Medical Unit **[T-SER1.5]**.

- ***White Giant*:** A JMC space vessel. Shuttle Flight JMC159, bound for *White Giant*, was boarding at the Mimas Central Shuttle Station's Gate 5 when two Shore Patrol officers picked up Lister to escort him to his new posting aboard *Red Dwarf* **[N-INF]**.

- ***White Giant*:** A *Red Dwarf* shuttlecraft. When Lister was marooned on a rogue planet, his shipmates set out to find him, in search parties consisting of Rimmer and Cat in *White Giant*, and Kryten and Talkie Toaster in *Blue Midget* **[N-BTL]**.

  ***NOTE:*** *When writing the novel* Better Than Life, *Rob Grant and Doug Naylor may have meant to use the*

**PREFIX**
**RL:** Real life

**T-: Television Episodes**
**SER:** Television series
**IDW:** "Identity Within"
**USA1:** Unaired U.S. pilot
**USA2:** Unaired U.S. demo

***R-: The Bodysnatcher Collection***
**SER:** Remastered episodes
**BOD:** "Bodysnatcher"
**DAD:** "Dad"
**FTH:** "Lister's Father"
**INF:** "Infinity Patrol"
**END:** "The End" (original assembly)

**N-: Novels**
**INF:** *Infinity Welcomes Careful Drivers*
**BTL:** *Better Than Life*
**LST:** *Last Human*
**BCK:** *Backwards*
**OMN:** *Red Dwarf Omnibus*

**M-: Magazines**
**SMG:** *Smegazine*

**W-: Websites**
**OFF:** Official website
**NAN:** *Prelude to Nanarchy*
**AND:** *Androids*
**DIV:** Diva-Droid
**DIB:** Duane Dibbley

**CRP:** Crapola
**GEN:** Geneticon
**LSR:** Leisure World Intl.
**JMC:** Jupiter Mining Corporation
**AIT:** *A.I. Today*
**HOL:** HoloPoint

**G-: Roleplaying Game**
**RPG:** *Core Rulebook*
**BIT:** *A.I. Screen Extra Bits* booklet
**SOR:** *Series Sourcebook*
**OTH:** Other RPG material

*name* White Midget *instead of* White Giant*, as they had already assigned* White Giant *to a much larger craft in* Infinity Welcomes Careful Drivers.

- **white-hatted ponce:** An insult that Rimmer used to describe chefs, hoping to dissuade Lister from taking the Chef's Exam and being promoted above him **[T-SER1.3]**.

- **white hole:** A spatial phenomenon similar to a black hole, but with opposite properties. Whereas black holes sucked matter and time from a universe, white holes released matter and time into it. Close proximity to a white hole caused one to experience time at different speeds, or in random order. A white hole could be destroyed by manipulating a star or planet in its path to plug the hole, erasing its effect on nearby objects.

  *Red Dwarf* encountered a white hole while experiencing a power outage that prevented the ship from avoiding the anomaly. Holly, whose IQ had been temporarily increased to twelve thousand via intelligence compression, suggested the crew play pool with a nearby solar system, by shooting a thermonuclear device into a sun to cause an explosion that would propel an orbiting planet into the hole **[T-SER4.4]**.

- **"White Hole":** A song from the heavy metal band The Rock Miners. It did not sell as well as the group expected **[G-RPG]**.

- ***White Midget*:** A ship-to-surface shuttlecraft manufactured by Gigante-Volkswagen. The Space Corps commissioned five thousand *White Midget* shuttles, but replaced them with *Blue Midgets* after receiving only seventy-five units, due to overheating and electrical problems. The surplus ships made their way into the civilian sector, becoming an instant favorite among amateur mechanics and aerospace hobbyists.

  A *White Midget* was featured in an issue of *What Transport?* magazine that Lister once read. As a result, he later mistook a *Blue Midget* for a *White Midget* **[G-SOR]**. A *White Midget* craft was used to ferry passengers on shore leave between Mimas and *Red Dwarf* **[T-SER7.3]**.

  ***NOTE:*** *During production of Series III,* White Midget's *name was changed to* Starbug, *but one reference to the nixed craft remained in the dialog of episode 3.4 ("Bodyswap"), as Lister (in Rimmer's body) told Cat he wanted to pursue Rimmer (in Lister's body) using* White Midget. *The actual chase scene, however, instead utilized the old* Blue Midget.

  *In* The Bodysnatcher Collection's *version of this episode, the dialog was thus edited to say "the* Midget*."* Red Dwarf—The Roleplaying Game's Series Sourcebook *furthered retconned this with the* What Transport? *explanation—but erroneously referred to the* White Midget *shuttle from episode 7.3 ("Ouroboros") as a JMC personnel shuttle, which is a short-range orbital craft.*

- **Who Gives A Monkey's? Akt of 2032:** An article passed by the Universal Government in 2032. The Hologram Protection Akt 2143 was passed in conjunction with this law **[M-SMG2.2(a)]**.

- ***Whoops Vicar, There Goes My Groinal Socket*:** A mechanoid comedy television show that aired on Groovy Channel 27, from the makers of the hologram classics *Both Feet in the Grave* and *After Death Do Us Part*. One episode of *Whoops Vicar* aired on Wednesday, the 27th of Geldof, 2362 **[M-SMG1.7(a)]**.

- ***Whopping Bazookas Monthly*:** A publication, possibly adult in nature, that Lister read **[M-SMG1.1(a)]**.

- ***Whose Diode Is It Anyway?*:** A quiz show hosted by Android 333402/T, which aired on Groovy Channel 27 at 7:00 PM on Wednesday, the 27th of Geldof, 2362 **[M-SMG1.7(a)]**.

  ***NOTE:*** *This series' title spoofed that of the improvisational comedy series* Whose Line Is It Anyway?

- **Who's-Just-Sneaked-On-Board computer:** A *Red Dwarf* system that detected unauthorized entries. As Santa Claus sneaked aboard the mining ship, this computer alerted Rimmer and Kryten to the presence of several reindeer waiting for him on the hull **[X-MOB]**.

- ***Who's Nobody*:** A hypothetical book that Cat suggested Lister look himself up in when the *Red Dwarf* crew encountered the Inquisitor, a simulant who traveled throughout space-time, judging whether others were worthy of existing **[T-SER5.2]**.

- ***Who's Who*:** A series of reference books containing biographical information about notable individuals **[RL]**. When Lister called Rimmer a scum-sucking, two-faced, weaselly weasel for reneging on a deal to break him out of prison, Rimmer admitted that description was his entry in *Who's Who?* **[T-SER8.2]**.

- **Wibbley, Wayne:** A name that Kryten mistakenly called Cat—who was disguised as Duane Dibbley—after having his corrupted files restored to factory settings **[T-SER8.2]**.

- **Wibbly-Wobbly Green:** A lighting-effect color available for Kluge Corp.'s teleporters **[G-RPG]**.

- **Wig-Stand-Head:** A derogatory nickname that Kochanski called Kryten **[T-SER7.4]**.

- **Wilbur Weasel Fan Club:** An organization dedicated to Wilbur Weasel fandom. The club held all of its meetings in space **[X-XMS]**.

- **Wilbur Weasel thermos flask:** A product featuring the character Wilbur Weasel that was made lead-lined so it would be effective in zero-gravity environments, such as in space, during Wilbur Weasel Fan Club meetings. After being miniaturized and placed inside Kryten's body, Lister used such a flask to contain a radioactive mass left behind by an alien invasion force. The crew then jettisoned the flask into space, where its contents expanded exponentially until creating a new star system **[X-XMS]**.

- ***Wild One, The*:** A 1953 American film starring Marlon Brando, about a rebellious motorcycle gang bringing trouble to a small California town **[RL]**. Lister brought Kryten to see this film to help him break free of his servile programming and think for himself. Initially, it appeared to have no effect, but Kryten later rebelled by painting a portrait of Rimmer on a toilet, calling him names and dumping a bowl of soup onto his bunk, then heading out on Lister's space bike—dressed like Johnny Strabler, Brando's character in the film **[T-SER2.1]**.

  ***NOTE:** The script for episode 2.1 ("Kryten"), published in* Son of Soup*, called the movie* The Wild Ones*, which is how it was spoken onscreen. The correct title, however, is* The Wild One.

- **Wilde, Oscar:** A nineteenth-century Irish author and poet who wrote the play *The Importance of Being Earnest, A Trivial Comedy for Serious People*, as well as the novel *The Picture of Dorian Gray* **[RL]**. Ace Rimmer told Cat that his suit was "sharper than a page of Oscar Wilde witticisms rolled into a point, sprinkled with lemon juice and jabbed into an eye" **[T-SER7.2]**.

  While marooned on a backwards-running Earth, Rimmer insulted fifteen-year-old Lister by saying it was a shame they couldn't wait for Wilde to come to life so he and Lister could match wits **[N-BCK]**.

- **wildebeetroot:** A cross between a wildebeest and a beetroot, resulting from genetic engineering experiments conducted on Earth. Sent off-world to seed unpopulated planets, the creatures later inhabited the Zsigsmos Sector **[B-SUR]**.

- ***Wildfire*:** A spacecraft designed at a Mimas research facility in one of Ace Rimmer's universes, also known as the Space Corps DJX-1 Prototype. The ship was capable of breaking the speed of reality, allowing it to jump dimensions into parallel universes. It contained experimental DimensioFuse technology and an artificial-intelligence computer **[G-BIT]**.

  Ace first used the ship to visit the prime universe, where he collided with *Starbug 1* three million years in the future and met a cowardly, petty version of himself **[T-SER4.5]**. After the original Ace's death, the ship was passed on to others who took his place, eventually making its way back to the prime Rimmer **[T-SER7.2]**.

  ***NOTE:** The ship's name, a variation of* Wildfire One *from the novel* Backwards*, was established on the official website. The vessel's design changed drastically between its two onscreen appearances, including its relative size.*

- ***Wildfire* drive:** A propulsion system built by the Space Corps Research & Development team in one of Ace Rimmer's universes. The drive, installed aboard *Wildfire One*, was initially designed to accelerate the craft past the light barrier. An unexpected side effect, however, was that it sent the vessel into a parallel universe similar to the pilot's original reality, with a single point of diversion **[N-BCK]**.

**PREFIX**
**RL:** Real life

**T-: Television Episodes**
**SER:** Television series
**IDW:** "Identity Within"
**USA1:** Unaired U.S. pilot
**USA2:** Unaired U.S. demo

**R-: *The Bodysnatcher Collection***
**SER:** Remastered episodes
**BOD:** "Bodysnatcher"
**DAD:** "Dad"
**FTH:** "Lister's Father"
**INF:** "Infinity Patrol"
**END:** "The End" (original assembly)

**N-: Novels**
**INF:** *Infinity Welcomes Careful Drivers*
**BTL:** *Better Than Life*
**LST:** *Last Human*
**BCK:** *Backwards*
**OMN:** *Red Dwarf Omnibus*

**M-: Magazines**
**SMG:** *Smegazine*

**W-: Websites**
**OFF:** Official website
**NAN:** *Prelude to Nanarchy*
**AND:** *Androids*
**DIV:** Diva-Droid
**DIB:** Duane Dibbley
**CRP:** Crapola
**GEN:** Geneticon
**LSR:** Leisure World Intl.
**JMC:** Jupiter Mining Corporation
**AIT:** *A.I. Today*
**HOL:** HoloPoint

**G-: Roleplaying Game**
**RPG:** *Core Rulebook*
**BIT:** *A.I. Screen Extra Bits* booklet
**SOR:** *Series Sourcebook*
**OTH:** Other RPG material

- ***Wildfire One***: A spacecraft designed by the Space Corps Research & Development program on Europa in the Alpha Universe. Powered by the *Wildfire* drive, *Wildfire One* was originally designed to break the light barrier, but when a version of the ship from the Beta Universe arrived three days prior to its scheduled launch, the team ascertained that it was capable of crossing dimensions and traveling through time.

  Armed with this knowledge, Ace volunteered for a one-way trip to a parallel reality, where he collided with a *Starbug* craft three million years in the future, containing a cowardly, petty version of himself. After Ace's death in that universe, Lister and Cat used the ship to travel to another reality, in which the pair had died in an addictive version of *Better Than Life* **[N-BCK]**.

- ***Wildfire One***: A spacecraft designed by the Space Corps Research & Development program on Europa in the Beta Universe. This ship, flown by that reality's Ace Rimmer, launched three days earlier than the scheduled launch of its analog in the Alpha Universe, but encountered problems during flight, causing it to cross dimensions into the Alpha Universe, killing its pilot. Realizing the ship was from another dimension, the Alpha Ace launched his own *Wildfire One* using data from the other ship's computer to avoid a similar fate **[N-BCK]**.

- **Wilkinson:** A member of *Red Dwarf*'s Z-Shift prior to the cadmium II disaster. Shortly before the accident, Rimmer assigned Wilkinson and Turner to fix Machine 15455, which was dispensing blackcurrant juice instead of chicken soup; restock a machine in Corridor 14, alpha 12 with Crunchie bars; and sanitize the language lab's headsets **[N-INF]**.

  ***NOTE:*** *Wilkinson presumably died during the cadmium II explosion. It is unknown whether the nanobots resurrected Wilkinson in Series VIII.*

- **Willoughby:** A member of a fascist police force under Voter Colonel Larson Gray in Jake Bullet's universe **[M-SMG2.4(c6)]**.

- ***Willy Waffles***: A children's television cartoon series featuring a toaster by that name. Groovy Channel 27 aired an episode of the series at 4:10 PM on Wednesday, the 27th of Geldof, 2362 **[M-SMG1.7(a)]**.

- **Wilmot, Mr.:** Lister's adoptive father after he was found as in infant, abandoned in a cardboard box under a pool table at The Aigburth Arms **[W-OFF]**. Mr. Wilmot was an office clerk **[N-LST]**. His favorite band was The Hollies **[M-SMG1.6(a)]**, and he owned a dog named Hannah **[T-SER1.2]**.

  Wilmot died when Lister was six years old. Dave retained two distinct memories of the event: being inundated with presents, which made him wish more relatives would die so he could complete his Lego set, and being told his dad had gone to the same place as his goldfish, which made him think the man had been flushed down the toilet. As such, Lister stuffed food and magazines down the latrine for his father **[T-SER2.2]**.

  ***NOTE:*** *Some sources, including the official website, have called the Wilmots Lister's adoptive family, while the novels referred to them as his foster parents. Dave also had a stepfather, which would seem to indicate Mrs. Wilmot remarried following her first husband's death (making her an unlucky woman, given that both men died). Presumably, the Wilmots first took Dave in as a foster child and later adopted him—which would explain the existence of his foster aunt and uncle. What that* doesn't *explain is why his last name was Lister (his grandmother was called Grandma Lister, so he apparently received his name from her) and not Wilmot. For the sake of consistency, this lexicon calls the Wilmots his adoptive parents.*

- **Wilmot, Mr.:** An office clerk who tried to become Lister's adoptive father in an alternate universe. Although young David felt he could more easily use the Wilmots to his advantage, this reality's Lister chose another family, the Thorntons, because of their wealth. This decision resulted in Lister becoming a murderous sociopath, thanks to Mrs. Thornton's manic-depressive outbursts and frequent abuse **[N-LST]**.

- **Wilmot, Mrs.:** Lister's adoptive mother after he was found as an infant in a cardboard box, abandoned under a pool table at The Aigburth Arms **[W-OFF]**. Mrs. Wilmot's husband died when Lister was six years old **[T-SER2.2]**. Eventually, Lister went to live with his grandmother **[T-SER1.2]**.

  ***NOTE:*** *Some sources, including the official website, have called the Wilmots Lister's adoptive family, while the novels referred to them as his foster parents. Dave*

*also had a stepfather, which would seem to indicate Mrs. Wilmot remarried following her first husband's death (making her an unlucky woman, given that both men died). Presumably, the Wilmots first took Dave in as a foster child and later adopted him—which would explain the existence of his foster aunt and uncle. What that* doesn't *explain is why his last name was Lister (his grandmother was called Grandma Lister, so he apparently received his name from her) and not Wilmot. For the sake of consistency, this lexicon calls the Wilmots his adoptive parents.*

- **Wilmot, Mrs.:** A woman who tried to become Lister's adoptive mother in an alternate universe. Although young David felt he could more easily use the Wilmots to his advantage, this reality's Lister chose another family, the Thorntons, because of their wealth. This decision resulted in Lister becoming a murderous sociopath, thanks to Mrs. Thornton's manic-depressive outbursts and frequent abuse **[N-LST]**.

- **Wilson, Grandma:** A Bedford Falls resident whom Lister imagined meeting while trapped in an addictive version of *Better Than Life*. Grandma Wilson helped hand out hot tea to injured individuals after Rimmer, disguised as Trixie LaBouche, crashed through the town in a juggernaut **[N-BTL]**.

- **Wilson, Reggie:** An Earth musician famed for his Hammond organ recordings. Rimmer was particularly fond of his work **[T-SER4.1]**. The board game *Trivial Pursuit* featured a question regarding the instrument with which the performer was most often associated **[M-SMG1.4(c1)]**.

  Arnold owned at least two of Wilson's albums, including *Reggie Wilson Plays the Lift Music Classics* and *Sounds of the Supermarket: 20 Shopping Greats*. Other recordings by Wilson included *Pop Goes Delius, Funking Up Wagner* **[T-SER4.5]**, *Rockin' Up Rachmaninov—120 Golden Greats on the Hammond Organ* **[M-SMG1.1(a)]**, *Pop from the Precinct—20 Shopping Centre Hits, Rockin' at the Restaurant—20 Gourmet Greats, Bopping With Beethoven, Punking Up Prokofiev, The Mall* and *A Night at the Opera* **[M-SMG1.3(a)]**.

  ***NOTE:*** *Wilson's name satirized that of real-world organist Reginald Dixon—of whom Rimmer was also a fan.*

- ***Wimbledon*:** A virtual-reality tennis simulation that the *Starbug 1* crew found among the wreckage of a derelict vessel **[T-SER6.3]**. The game was produced by Total Immersion Inc. and distributed by Crapola Inc. **[G-RPG]**. Rimmer chastised Lister for playing this game an excessive number of times during a three-week period, primarily because Dave was having virtual sex with a seventeen-year-old ballgirl **[T-SER6.3]**.

- **Winan Diner:** A food establishment in an alternate-reality fascist society. The diner employed a woman named Mona, whose doughnuts were among Jake Bullet's favorite foods **[M-SMG2.9(c4)]**.

- ***Winchester Park*:** A novel by Jane Austin, a simulation of which was included in the Total Immersion artificial-reality game *Jane Austin World* **[G-RPG]**.

  ***NOTE:*** *This fictional novel's title, from* Red Dwarf—The Roleplaying Game, *was based on* Mansfield Park, *by real-life novelist Jane Austen (note the different surname spelling). Some online hoax sites have listed* Winchester Park *among the works of Jane G. Austin—another actual writer who lived a century after Austen.*

- **Windolene:** A British brand of window cleaner, originally sold as a pink cream **[RL]**. Lister once drank Rimmer's bottle of Windolene while inebriated, thinking it was more liquor. He mixed it with a green liquor he found, which turned out to be Arnold's Swarfega **[T-SER8.1]**.

- **Winklepicker Teeth:** A nickname that Rimmer called Cat, referring to his pointed teeth **[B-LOG]**.

  ***NOTE:*** *Winklepickers are a style of British pointy-toed shoes.*

- **Winnie:** A name that Lister gave to one of his mutated Space Monkeys. Rimmer assumed he had named it after Winston Churchill, but the actual inspiration was Winnie-the-Pooh **[M-SMG1.13(c2)]**.

- **Winnie-the-Pooh:** A fictional, anthropomorphic bear created in 1926 by A. A. Milne. Winnie first appeared in a collection of stories, and was later adapted to film by The Walt Disney

Co. **[RL]**. Artificial-reality simulations of Winnie-the-Pooh were responsible for 584 deaths during a single month, due to a faulty A/R program in which the character was prone to going on rampages armed with an AK-47 **[B-SUR]**.

- **Winnie-the-Pooh:** A waxdroid replica of the fictional character, created for the Waxworld theme park. Left on their own for millions of years, the waxdroids attained sentience and became embroiled in a park-wide resource war between Villain World and Hero World.

  During this war, the *Red Dwarf* crew transported to the planet using a Matter Paddle, with Lister and Cat materializing in Villain territory, while Rimmer and Kryten landed in Hero territory. Winnie was captured by Villain World agents and was subsequently executed by firing range. Lister and Cat, incarcerated by the evil waxdroids, witnessed the killing in horror **[T-SER4.6]**.

  ***NOTE:*** *Presumably, Winnie, like Santa Claus, was originally from the park's fiction section.*

- **Wipe Humans Out All-Over! (WHOA!):** A policy endorsed by the Vindaloovian Empire that was more relaxed than the previous Wipe Out Everyone! (WOE!) strategy **[G-BIT]**.

- **Wipe Out Everyone! (WOE!):** An aggressive policy endorsed by the Vindaloovian Empire. It was eventually replaced by the more relaxed Wipe Humans Out All-Over! (WHOA!) strategy **[G-BIT]**.

- ***Wired Up*:** An online game offered on Diva-Droid International's website, the object of which was to complete more square circuits than the computer **[W-DIV]**.

- **Wisdom, Norman:** A British actor and comedian who appeared in a series of movies as the character Norman Pitkin **[RL]**. While trapped in an addictive version of *Better Than Life*, Rimmer imagined that he had returned to Earth and become famously wealthy. In the illusion, Arnold hosted dinner parties that often included famous guests. At one such event, Wisdom spontaneously threw himself onto the floor, eliciting a guffaw from God, who was also a guest **[N-INF]**.

- **Wishbone Strike:** A combat maneuver that Quagaar warriors used to debilitate their enemies, consisting of a mid-air strike to an opponent's head **[G-SOR]**.

- **Wizzo:** A company that produced boilers and other heating supplies. The step-parents of Mr. Flibble, a woodcutter and his wife, installed a Wizzo boiler in their house after receiving inheritance money from the death of Flibble's grandmother. Resentful that his parents dressed him as a girl (and wanting the inheritance for himself), Flibble sabotaged the boiler, then used a cigar to ignite the gas, killing his step-parents in the resulting explosion **[M-SMG2.9(c2)]**.

- ***Wogan*:** A twentieth-century British television talk show featuring Terry Wogan **[RL]**. Sometime after his death, Wogan was revived as a hologram to host a new version of the series on Groovy Channel 27, which aired at 12:50 PM **[M-SMG1.7(a)]**.

- **woh:** A new syllable that Holly added to the major scale, along with boh, in an attempt to decimalize music. The two new syllables fell between sol and ti. In addition, he introduced the notes H and J to the octave—which he renamed a decatave **[T-SER2.1]**.

  ***NOTE:*** *This gag originated in a* Son of Cliché *"Dave Hollins: Space Cadet" sketch titled "Sir Kevin Kevin Sir."*

- **Wolverhampton:** A city in the West Midland part of England **[RL]**. Lister found Saturn's moon, Mimas, to be the most hideous place he'd ever been—worse even than Wolverhampton **[N-INF]**.

- ***Women's Shower Night*:** The debut broadcast shown on Krytie TV, a station Kryten created after being reprogrammed by inmates from the Tank. Billed as a pay-per-view event, it featured several minutes' worth of free footage of female inmates showering (filmed without the women's knowledge or permission), after which Kryten stopped transmitting to ask for donations. The program continued for three hours, and heavily featured Kochanski **[T-SER8.5]**.

- **Women's Showers:** A community shower area in the female section of the Tank, *Red Dwarf*'s brig on Floor 13. Classified as a woman due to his lack of genitalia, Kryten used these facilities along with the female inmates. Upon learning of this, several male prisoners kidnapped the mechanoid and reprogrammed him to film the next shower period, which he broadcast during movie night on Krytie TV **[T-SER8.5]**.

  ***NOTE:*** *It is unclear why Kryten would need to use a shower in the first place.*

- **Women's Wing:** A section of the Tank, *Red Dwarf*'s brig on Floor 13, allocated for the housing of female inmates. Lacking a penis and thus designated a woman, Kryten was assigned to this area **[T-SER8.5]**.

- **WOO:** An acronym meaning "without oxygen." Driven insane by a deadly holovirus, Rimmer put his shipmates in quarantine, then manipulated them into asking permission to fly on a magic carpet to visit the King of the Potato People and beg for their release. He then accused them of being insane—a crime warranting two hours of WOO—for making such a request **[T-SER5.4]**.

- **Wood, Edward ("Ed"):** An American director and producer of low-budget films, posthumously dubbed the worst director of all time for such movies as *Glen or Glenda*, *Bride of the Monster* and *Plan 9 from Outer Space* **[RL]**. After being classified as female by *Red Dwarf*'s penal system, Kryten lamented that he should now be called Kristen, adding that he sounded like the title of an Ed Wood movie **[T-SER8.2(d)]**.

  ***NOTE:*** *Wood's semi-documentary* Glen or Glenda *was loosely based on the life of transsexual Christine Jorgensen.*

- **Wood of Humiliation:** An environment on a psi-moon configured according to Rimmer's psyche. When Rimmer and Kryten landed on the planetoid, it used Arnold's mind as a template, altering its own landscape to represent aspects of his neurosis, and creating such settings as the Wood of Humiliation **[T-SER5.3]**.

- **Woodpecker, Woody:** An anthropomorphic cartoon bird created by Walter Lantz in 1940 **[RL]**. After Kryten inadvertently changed Pete the sparrow into a *Tyrannosuarus rex* via a time wand, Lister consulted Holly on the best way to turn the bird back into "Woody Woodpecker" **[T-SER8.7]**.

- ***World Championship Risk*:** A televised competition of the strategic board game *Risk*. Rimmer accidentally taped three episodes of the competition over the crew's video of *Beyond the Valley of the Cheerleaders XXVII: This Time It's Personal,* causing morale to drop to an all-time low **[B-LOG]**.

- ***World Cops*:** A fantasy television show that aired on Groovy Channel 27, about police officers confined to planet Earth. An episode of the program aired on Wednesday, the 27th of Geldof, 2362 **[M-SMG1.7(a)]**.

- **World Council, the:** A planetary government on Earth, circa the twenty-second century. Headquartered in Washington, D.C., the Council operated a biotech institute in Hilo, Hawaii, specializing in genetic engineering and DNA manipulation. In addition, the agency was the guardian of the genome of DNA (G.O.D.).

  John Milhous Nixon, the World Council's third president, devised a plan to control the weather by detonating thermonuclear devices in the vicinity of the Sun, unaware the procedure would reduce the star's lifespan to approximately four hundred thousand years. Once the snafu was discovered, the council launched a mission to a planet in the Andromeda Galaxy to prepare it as humanity's new home. This ship, the *Mayflower*, carried humans, simulants and various GELF species created specifically for the mission, and contained technology for terraforming and genetic engineering, including G.O.D. **[N-LST]**.

- **World's End Bar & Grill:** An eatery located aboard *Red Dwarf* **[M-SMG1.3(c1)]**.

  ***NOTE:*** *The World's End is an actual drinking establishment in Camden Town, London, England.*

- ***World's Stupidest Stuntmen*:** A video depicting people performing dangerous and foolhardy stunts, often with hilariously disastrous results. Kochanski claimed the only reason her male crewmates aboard *Starbug 1* didn't watch her knickers dry in the laundry room was that they didn't know

**PREFIX**
**RL:** Real life

**T-: Television Episodes**
**SER:** Television series
**IDW:** "Identity Within"
**USA1:** Unaired U.S. pilot
**USA2:** Unaired U.S. demo

**R-: *The Bodysnatcher Collection***
**SER:** Remastered episodes
**BOD:** "Bodysnatcher"
**DAD:** "Dad"
**FTH:** "Lister's Father"
**INF:** "Infinity Patrol"
**END:** "The End" (original assembly)

**N-: Novels**
**INF:** *Infinity Welcomes Careful Drivers*
**BTL:** *Better Than Life*
**LST:** *Last Human*

**BCK:** *Backwards*
**OMN:** *Red Dwarf Omnibus*

**M-: Magazines**
**SMG:** *Smegazine*

**W-: Websites**
**OFF:** Official website
**NAN:** *Prelude to Nanarchy*
**AND:** *Androids*
**DIV:** Diva-Droid
**DIB:** Duane Dibbley

**CRP:** Crapola
**GEN:** Geneticon
**LSR:** Leisure World Intl.
**JMC:** Jupiter Mining Corporation
**AIT:** *A.I. Today*
**HOL:** HoloPoint

**G-: Roleplaying Game**
**RPG:** *Core Rulebook*
**BIT:** *A.I. Screen Extra Bits* booklet
**SOR:** *Series Sourcebook*
**OTH:** Other RPG material

when Kryten washed them, and all they needed was a trailer on the *World's Stupidest Stuntmen* video to line up for the viewing **[T-SER7.4]**.

- **World War I:** A global conflict centered in Europe that occurred from 1914 to 1918, involving the world's most powerful nations and resulting in the deaths of nine million combatants **[RL]**. When Rimmer claimed to be the next evolutionary step in mankind, Lister questioned whether the entirety of human history, including World War I, was designed to lead up to Rimmer **[R-BOD]**.

- **World War II:** A second global war that lasted from 1939 to 1945, involving most of Earth's nations. More than a hundred million people from more than thirty countries died during the conflict **[RL]**. On an alternate Earth called War World, World War II never ended and was still being fought centuries later, when Ace Rimmer rescued Princess Bonjella from a Nazi officer named Voorhese **[G-BIT]**.

  The crew once spent seventeen days in the World War II artificial-reality simulation *Victory in Europe*, which they detested due to the horrible food, bad accommodations and Nazis continuously shooting at him **[B-LOG]**.

- ***World War II*:** A virtual-reality wargame produced by Total Immersion Inc. and distributed by Crapola Inc. **[G-RPG]**. The *Starbug 1* crew salvaged a copy of the game from the Space Corps derelict SS *Centauri*. When his shipmates visited the *Pride and Prejudice Land* program instead of joining him for a specially prepared dinner, Kryten borrowed a tank from *World War II* and destroyed a gazebo in which the crew dined with characters from the novel **[T-SER7.6]**.

  ***NOTE:** The tank Kryten borrowed, a T-72, was not yet in service during World War II.*

- **World Zero-G Federation:** The governing body for the sport of zero-gee football **[M-SMG1.8(a)]**.

- **wormhole:** A hypothetical spatial phenomenon connecting two points in space-time, thereby creating a tunnel or shortcut between them **[RL]**. Holoships—vessels made purely of lightweight tachyons and crewed by holograms—were designed to travel great distances through wormholes and stargates, due to their near-zero mass **[T-SER5.1]**.

- **Wouk, Herman:** An American author, playwright and screenwriter who penned such classics as *The Caine Mutiny*, *The Winds of War* and *War and Remembrance* **[RL]**. While marooned on a frozen planet, Lister attempted to stay warm inside *Starbug 1* by burning items stored aboard ship. Succumbing to hunger, he was dismayed to find several books written by authors whose names reminded him of food, such as Charles Lamb, Herman Wouk and Francis Bacon **[T-SER3.2]**.

  ***NOTE:** The episode's captions misspelled his name as "Herman Wok."*

- **Wurlitzer:** An American manufacturer of musical instruments, most notably organs, pianos and jukeboxes **[RL]**. The word "Wurlitzer" replaced the word "word" in Holly's vocabulary database after an electrical fire damaged her voice-recognition unit **[T-SER5.5]**.

- **WX956 W:** A code printed on a monitor label in *Red Dwarf*'s Drive Room **[T-SER1.1(d)]**.

# X

# XANADU

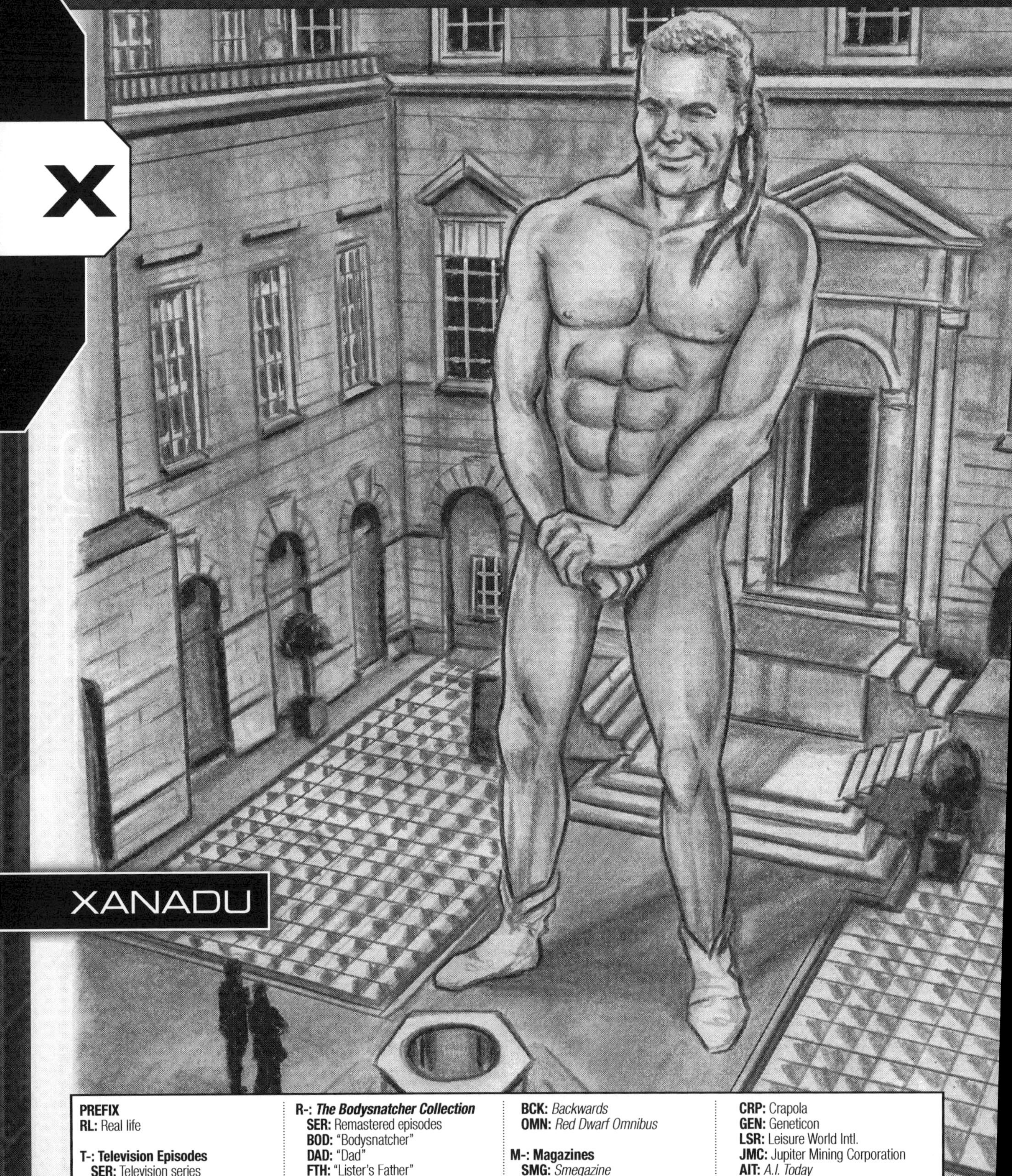

**PREFIX**
**RL:** Real life

**T-: Television Episodes**
- **SER:** Television series
- **IDW:** "Identity Within"
- **USA1:** Unaired U.S. pilot
- **USA2:** Unaired U.S. demo

**R-: *The Bodysnatcher Collection***
- **SER:** Remastered episodes
- **BOD:** "Bodysnatcher"
- **DAD:** "Dad"
- **FTH:** "Lister's Father"
- **INF:** "Infinity Patrol"
- **END:** "The End" (original assembly)

**N-: Novels**
- **INF:** *Infinity Welcomes Careful Drivers*
- **BTL:** *Better Than Life*
- **LST:** *Last Human*
- **BCK:** *Backwards*
- **OMN:** *Red Dwarf Omnibus*

**M-: Magazines**
- **SMG:** *Smegazine*

**W-: Websites**
- **OFF:** Official website
- **NAN:** *Prelude to Nanarchy*
- **AND:** *Androids*
- **DIV:** Diva-Droid
- **DIB:** Duane Dibbley
- **CRP:** Crapola
- **GEN:** Geneticon
- **LSR:** Leisure World Intl.
- **JMC:** Jupiter Mining Corporation
- **AIT:** *A.I. Today*
- **HOL:** HoloPoint

**G-: Roleplaying Game**
- **RPG:** *Core Rulebook*
- **BIT:** *A.I. Screen Extra Bits* booklet
- **SOR:** *Series Sourcebook*
- **OTH:** Other RPG material

- **Xanadu:** Lister's mansion in a timeline in which he became Earth's youngest billionaire by inventing the Tension Sheet. According to the host of *Life Styles of the Disgustingly Rich and Famous*, the home was named after a song by Dave Dee, Dozy, Beaky, Mick & Tich, and was not a reference to the film *Citizen Kane*. The mansion's driveway was built using gravel created from the demolition of Buckingham Palace, while the courtyard featured a gigantic naked statue of Lister that urinated champagne **[T-SER3.5]**. The head butler at Xanadu was Gilbert St. John McAdam Ostrog **[W-OFF]**.

- **XF 314:** A code stenciled on a wall in *Starbug 1*'s Landing Bay B **[T-SER7.2]**.

- **XHO274J:** The license plate number of the third automobile Rimmer imagined owning while playing the total-immersion video game *Better Than Life*. His subconscious mind conjured up the sensible, lackluster vehicle—a Morris Minor economy car—unable to cope with the positive experience that the game offered **[T-SER2.2]**.

- **Xion Treaty, the:** An agreement brokered between several factions within an alternate-universe GELF State. Amendment ii allowed the use of symbimorphs as Pleasure GELFs for inmates volunteering for the Reco-Programme **[N-LST]**.

- **XJ 14 10-87 LH:** A code stenciled on a wall on one of *Red Dwarf*'s maintenance decks **[T-SER3.4]**.

- **XPress Lift:** A large cabin used as a rapid-transport device within *Red Dwarf*. It included several chairs, a water cooler, a fully stocked magazine rack and a video explaining emergency procedures, along with a tape to record a last will and testament, as well as sedatives and cyanide capsules in the event of a catastrophic lift failure. Meals were available for longer-duration trips, with chicken offered as one of the selections. When a stasis leak formed aboard ship, Lister, Rimmer and Cat traveled an Xpress Lift down 2,567 floors to Floor 16 **[T-SER2.4]**.

- **Xpress super lift:** A rapid-transport cabin used to traverse the numerous floors within *Red Dwarf*. One super lift was capable of traveling to Floor 9172, home of the sleeping quarter known as Area P **[N-INF]**.

- **"X-Ray Films":** A phrase printed on an envelope in *Red Dwarf*'s Medical Unit **[T-SER1.5]**.

**B-: Books**
**PRG:** *Red Dwarf Programme Guide*
**SUR:** *Red Dwarf Space Corps Survival Manual*
**PRM:** *Primordial Soup*
**SOS:** *Son of Soup*
**SCE:** *Scenes from the Dwarf*
**LOG:** *Red Dwarf Log No. 1996*
**RD8:** *Red Dwarf VIII*
**EVR:** *The Log: A Dwarfer's Guide to Everything*

**X-: Misc.**
**PRO:** Promotional materials, videos, etc.
**PST:** Posters at DJ XVII (2013)
**CAL:** 2008 calendar
**RNG:** Cell phone ringtones
**MOB:** Mobisode ("Red Christmas")
**CIN:** *Children in Need* sketch
**GEK:** *Geek Week* intros by Kryten
**TNG:** "Tongue-Tied" video

**XMS:** Bill Pearson's Christmas special pitch script
**XVD:** Bill Pearson's Christmas special pitch video
**OTH:** Other *Red Dwarf* appearances

**SUFFIX**
**DVD:**
**(d)** – Deleted scene
**(o)** – Outtake
**(b)** – Bonus DVD material (other)
**(e)** – Extended version

**SMEGAZINES:**
**(c)** – Comic
**(a)** – Article

**OTHER:**
**(s)** – Early/unused script draft
**(s1)** – Alternate version of script

Y

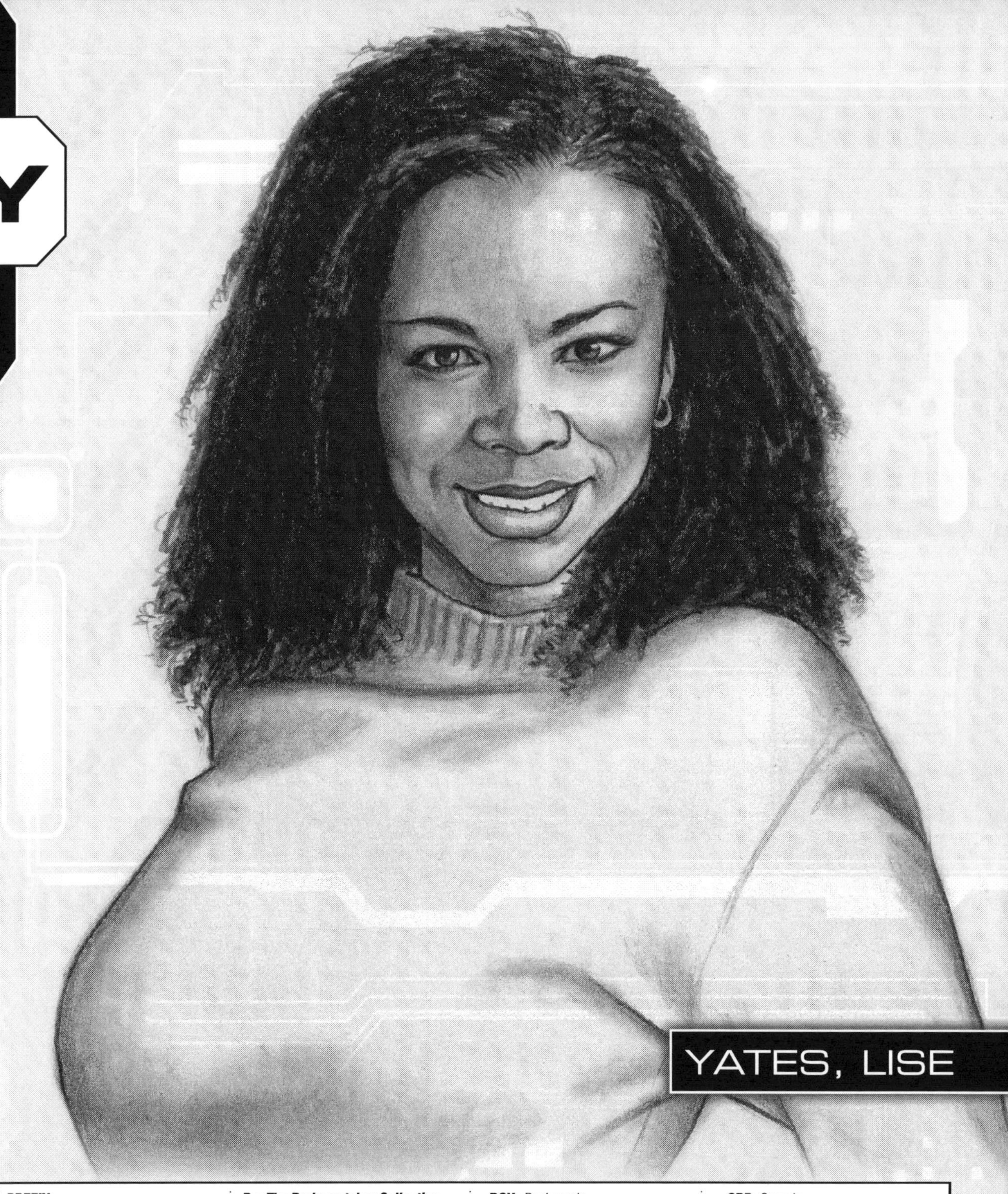

# YATES, LISE

**PREFIX**
**RL:** Real life

**T-: Television Episodes**
**SER:** Television series
**IDW:** "Identity Within"
**USA1:** Unaired U.S. pilot
**USA2:** Unaired U.S. demo

**R-: *The Bodysnatcher Collection***
**SER:** Remastered episodes
**BOD:** "Bodysnatcher"
**DAD:** "Dad"
**FTH:** "Lister's Father"
**INF:** "Infinity Patrol"
**END:** "The End" (original assembly)

**N-: Novels**
**INF:** *Infinity Welcomes Careful Drivers*
**BTL:** *Better Than Life*
**LST:** *Last Human*
**BCK:** *Backwards*
**OMN:** *Red Dwarf Omnibus*

**M-: Magazines**
**SMG:** *Smegazine*

**W-: Websites**
**OFF:** Official website
**NAN:** *Prelude to Nanarchy*
**AND:** *Androids*
**DIV:** Diva-Droid
**DIB:** Duane Dibbley
**CRP:** Crapola
**GEN:** Geneticon
**LSR:** Leisure World Intl.
**JMC:** Jupiter Mining Corporation
**AIT:** *A.I. Today*
**HOL:** HoloPoint

**G-: Roleplaying Game**
**RPG:** *Core Rulebook*
**BIT:** *A.I. Screen Extra Bits* booklet
**SOR:** *Series Sourcebook*
**OTH:** Other RPG material

- **Y 27K:** A marking on a box located in *Red Dwarf*'s store bay, near which Lister outwitted the Inquisitor **[T-SER5.2]**.

- ***yadretseY*:** A newspaper published during a period in Earth's far future when time ran backwards. The newspaper's title, when read forward, was *Yesterday*. While stranded in the year 3991 (1993 in forward time), Rimmer and Kryten procured a copy of that day's edition, the headline of which read, in reverse, "Three Brought to Life in Bank Raid" **[T-SER3.1]**.

  ***NOTE:*** *Throughout the episode, backwards writing was inconsistently handled. In some cases, characters were backwards-facing, while in others, they faced forward. This newspaper was especially problematic, as the characters in the paper's logo were backwards-facing, whereas the headlines faced forward. In addition, sentences were printed top to bottom, while the headline ran bottom to top.*

- ***Yahtzee*:** A dice game created by Milton Bradley in which players scored points by rolling poker-themed combinations, or with groupings of individual numbers **[RL]**. When Lister failed to restart the engines of the American mining ship *Red Dwarf* so he could return to Earth, that universe's Rimmer suggested they play *Yahtzee* for the next sixty years **[T-USA1]**.

- **Yakka-Takka-Tulla, Space Mistress:** The chaperone of a Space Scout survival trip that Rimmer attended as a youth. The Scouts were informed they could only eat what they killed, so some of the boys decided to eat Rimmer, and thus tied him up to a makeshift rotisserie. Arnold only escaped due to the space mistress' intervention **[T-SER2.5]**.

- **"Yankee Doodle":** An American patriotic song, believed to have been written by British Army surgeon Richard Shuckburgh during the Seven Years' War, as a mockery of Colonial troops **[RL]**. To entertain the survivors of the *Nova 5* crash, Kryten tapdanced and sang "Yankee Doodle" while juggling cans of beeswax **[N-INF]**.

  While visiting a universe in which the sexes were reversed, Dave Lister met his female counterpart, Deb Lister, who tried to impress him by drinking six beers and belching "Yankee Doodle"—a trick Dave often used to impress women **[T-SER2.6]**.

  ***NOTE:*** *Episode 2.6 ("Parallel Universe") erroneously called the song "Yankee Doodle Dandy," while the novel* Infinity Welcomes Careful Driver *used the name "I'm a Yankee Doodle Dandy." The tune's actual title is simply "Yankee Doodle."*

- **Yates, Lise:** An ex-girlfriend of Lister. He and Lise dated for eight months, but he ended the relationship because he did not want to become tied down **[T-SER2.3]**. During this relationship, Dave claimed to have pawned his grandmother's false teeth to buy tickets so he and Lise could attend a show together. He justified this action by saying the elderly woman only used them to open bottles and chew tobacco **[T-SER2.3(d)]**.

  Three million years later, Lister downloaded his memories of those eight months into Rimmer's mind to make him feel better about never having found love. Arnold awoke with a much happier outlook, believing he once had something special with Lise. But when he found old love letters she had sent to Lister, Rimmer mistook them as evidence she had dated both men simultaneously.

  Lister admitted what he had done, claiming it had been with the best of intentions. Humiliated and lovesick, Rimmer demanded that they erase all traces of the deception, undergo mind wipes and bury *Red Dwarf*'s black box. Complying with his request, Lister and Cat buried the black box recording on an isolated moon, along with a tombstone engraved with the words "To the Memory of the Memory of Lise Yates" **[T-SER2.3]**.

  ***NOTE:*** *Yates' first name was misspelled "Lisa" in the credits of the remastered version of this episode, included in* The Bodysnatcher Collection.

- **YB45 FND:** The license plate number of a car in England, during a period in Earth's far future when time ran backwards. The sequence, when read forward, was DNF 54BY **[T-SER3.1]**.

  ***NOTE:*** *Throughout the episode, backwards writing was inconsistently handled. In some cases, characters were backwards-facing, while in others, they faced forward. Adding to the confusion, some signs were lettered top to bottom, whereas others ran bottom to top. In this case, the scene was flipped to give the illusion of backwards writing.*

- ***Year of the Cat*****:** An album by singer-songwriter Al Stewart, released in 1976 **[RL]**. Leo Davis owned this album while working at the Black Island Film Studios **[X-TNG]**.

- **yellow fever:** A viral infection typically spread by mosquitos **[RL]**. Captain Hollister became afflicted with yellow fever shortly after Pete the dinosaur was transformed into a *Tyrannosaurus rex* **[T-SER8.8]**.

- **Yelxeb, Retsil:** One of Lister's twin sons with Kochanski, born on Earth in the backwards-running Universe 3. Yelxeb and his brother, Mij, were already alive when the *Red Dwarf* crew brought the remains of Dave and Kristine to the planet in an effort to revive them. As time on the backwards planet passed, the two boys de-aged, finally becoming infants who were then put back into Kochanski's womb **[N-LST]**.

  ***NOTE:*** *Yelxeb's name backward spelled Bexley Lister.*

- ***Yesterday*****:** *See yadretseY*

- **Yizox:** A nonexistent word that Rimmer attempted to play during a game of *Scrabble*, claiming it was Plutonian for "teeth." When Rimmer's power supply was later damaged due to the telepathic influence of a genetically engineered adaptable pet (GEAP), Lister refused to save him until the hologram admitted he had made up the word **[M-SMG1.6(c1)]**.

- **"YJO s'diK":** A phrase printed on a British storefront's sign during a period in Earth's far future when time ran backwards. The sign, when read forward, said "OJY Kid's" **[T-SER3.1]**.

  ***NOTE:*** *Throughout the episode, backwards writing was inconsistently handled. In some cases, characters were backwards-facing, while in others, they faced forward. Adding to the confusion, some signs were lettered top to bottom, whereas others ran bottom to top. In this case, the scene was flipped to give the illusion of backwards writing.*

- **"Ylhserf Tuc Sehciwdnas":** A series of words printed on a wall sign at an eatery in England, during a period in Earth's far future when time ran backwards. The sign, when read forward, was labeled "Freshly Cut Sandwiches" **[T-SER3.1]**.

  ***NOTE:*** *Throughout the episode, backwards writing was inconsistently handled. In some cases, characters were forward-facing, while in others (such as in this instance), they faced backwards.*

- **Ynot Suolubaf Eht:** An MC at Nogard dna Egroeg, a pub on a future Earth on which time flowed backwards. Ynot introduced the novelty stage act of Rimmer and Kryten, who performed mundane tasks "forwards" **[T-SER3.1(b)]**.

  ***NOTE:*** *The MC's name was revealed in the* All Changes *bonus material of the Series III DVDs, in which comedian Tony Hawks discussed the origin of his character, whose name was "The Fabulous Tony" in reverse.*

- **"You Are Now Leaving Existence":** A slogan written on a sign hanging over the exit from an Old West town in a dream that Kryten's subconscious mind created to combat the Armageddon virus **[T-SER6.3]**.

- **"You Are the Sunshine of My Life":** A 1973 hit song released by Stevie Wonder **[RL]**. When Lister joined what he thought was an a cappella group called The Canaries while serving time in the Tank, he started singing "You Are the Sunshine of My Life" to Rimmer, who explained that the Canaries were the ship's first-response unit for dangerous missions. The new recruits later sang this song to Warden Ackerman and Captain Hollister in an attempt to get out of Canary duty, but to no avail **[T-SER8.4]**.

- **"You Don't Have to Have a Rather Dry Sense of Humor to Live Here But It Certainly Helps":** A phrase printed on a humorous sign posted outside the quarters that Rimmer shared with his duplicate hologram **[T-SER1.6(d)]**.

- ***Young, Bad, and Dangerous to Know*****:** A novel that Rimmer once read about a psychopathic hippie murderer named Tonto Jitterman, who traveled across the United States with his headcase brother, Jimmy, wreaking havoc and fighting the Establishment. The novel ended with the line, "Life is like a joss-stick—it stinks and then it's over."

  While trapped in an addictive version of *Better Than Life*,

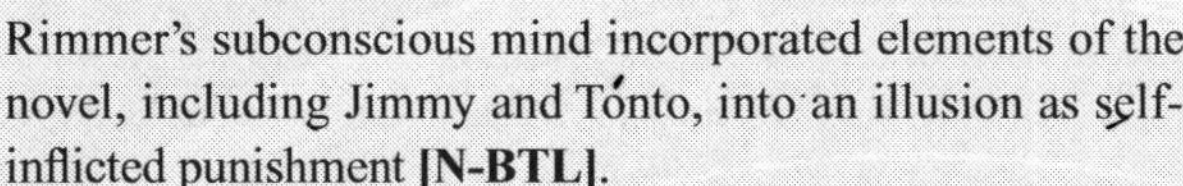

Rimmer's subconscious mind incorporated elements of the novel, including Jimmy and Tonto, into an illusion as self-inflicted punishment **[N-BTL]**.

- **Youngskin:** A cosmetic procedure invented in 2165, which gave a person the skin of a child. It was outlawed twenty minutes after being introduced, due to the detrimental impact it had on young donors **[B-EVR]**.

- **Your Flared-Nostrilness:** An honorific by which centurions addressed Rimmerworld's leader, the Great One **[T-SER6.5]**.

- ***Your Guide to Skiing Holidays*:** A book Lister read while using a modified Stirmaster that he created from the body of Sim Crawford **[T-SER10.1]**.

- **Your Holiness:** A title by which Rimmer addressed Captain Hollister during Arnold's Board of Inquiry trial. Lister speculated that it likely didn't help his case **[T-SER8.3(d)]**.

- **Your Magnificence:** A title by which Rimmer addressed the Inquisitor as the simulant judged the worthiness of Arnold's life **[T-SER5.2]**.

- ***Your Own Death and How to Cope With It*:** A five-page booklet distributed by the Department of Death and Deceaseds' Rights to individuals who had passed away and been revived as a hologram **[N-INF]**.

- **YouTube:** A popular video-sharing website founded in 2005 to enable online users to upload, view and distribute video content **[RL]**. Kryten recorded a handful of promotional videos for YouTube's "Geek Week" event, which he transmitted back in time for viewers to watch. Each video introduced the day's topic and feature videos **[X-GEK]**.

- **YT6564354:** The ID code assigned to a psychotic Lister from an alternate universe during his incarceration at the Cyberia prison complex. The code was printed on his wristband, as well as on a box containing his belongings **[N-LST]**.

**B-: Books**
**PRG:** *Red Dwarf Programme Guide*
**SUR:** *Red Dwarf Space Corps Survival Manual*
**PRM:** *Primordial Soup*
**SOS:** *Son of Soup*
**SCE:** *Scenes from the Dwarf*
**LOG:** *Red Dwarf Log No. 1996*
**RD8:** *Red Dwarf VIII*
**EVR:** *The Log: A Dwarfer's Guide to Everything*

**X-: Misc.**
**PRO:** Promotional materials, videos, etc.
**PST:** Posters at DJ XVII (2013)
**CAL:** 2008 calendar
**RNG:** Cell phone ringtones
**MOB:** Mobisode ("Red Christmas")
**CIN:** *Children in Need* sketch
**GEK:** *Geek Week* intros by Kryten
**TNG:** "Tongue-Tied" video
**XMS:** Bill Pearson's Christmas special pitch script
**XVD:** Bill Pearson's Christmas special pitch video
**OTH:** Other *Red Dwarf* appearances

**SUFFIX**
**DVD:**
**(d)** – Deleted scene
**(o)** – Outtake
**(b)** – Bonus DVD material (other)
**(e)** – Extended version

**SMEGAZINES:**
**(c)** – Comic
**(a)** – Article

**OTHER:**
**(s)** – Early/unused script draft
**(s1)** – Alternate version of script

ZLURTH, DOMINATOR (WITH WEDNESDAY, CHANCELLOR)

- **Z0 401X:** A marking on several boxes stored in the cargo bay of the "low" *Red Dwarf*, created after a triplicator accident produced two copies of the ship **[T-SER5.5]**.

- **Z80012:** A computer processor that Kryten used to convert the word "love" into ASC2 code for Camille **[T-SER4.1]**.

  ***NOTE:*** *Computer processor manufacturer Zilog developed a Z80000 32-bit processor in 1986. To date, no Z80012 processor has been produced.*

- **Zacharias ("Zack"):** A hillbilly from a backwards-running Earth in Universe 3. Zacharias lived in the mountains with his twin brother, Ezekiel, and a large hog. The two had a cousin named Lindy Lou, who stayed with them for a short time. Marooned on the planet for ten years, Lister, Rimmer, Kryten and Cat lived in a cave near the brothers' house **[N-BCK]**.

  ***NOTE:*** *Kryten inadvertently killed one of the brothers, but which one was not specified.*

- **Zalgon impeachment of Kjielomnon:** An event that Lister cited as a defense tactic to force a mistrial during his hearing on Arranguu 12 for crimes against the GELF State. Lister claimed that taking the fourth sand of D'Aquaarar protected him from the breach of Xzeeertuiy by the Zalgon impeachment of Kjielomnon, according to the case of *Mbazvmbbcxyy vs. Mbazvmbbcxyy*, which was allowed during the third season of every fifth cycle. However, he was being tried in Arranguu 12's Northern Sector—which, according to the GELF Regulator, didn't follow the same archaic legal system as the Southern Sector, in which the case originated **[N-BCK]**.

- **Zanzibar:** An island of the Zanzibar Archipelago in the Indian Ocean, formally known as Unguja **[RL]**. Following the GELF War of the twenty-second century, captured GELFs were exiled to Zanzibar, just prior to Earth being re-designated as Garage World and abandoned by humanity **[N-BTL]**.

- **Zargon warship:** A hypothetical type of spacecraft. Lister tried to convince Rimmer that it was futile to expect to encounter aliens during their travels, claiming they would never meet a Zargon warship **[T-SER1.4]**.

  ***NOTE:*** *This gag originated in a* Son of Cliché *"Dave Hollins: Space Cadet" sketch titled "Enormous Fat Man," with the mention of a similarly named species called "Zygons."*

- **ZCSBFD6577GJG93857JJJJ43767737837FHDK-WOPIW53:** A viral identification code printed on a vial aboard the *Mayflower*. The vial contained bacteria infused with a virus capable of modifying planets. After the *Starbug* crew crashed into a lava-covered world in an alternate dimension, they discovered the *Mayflower* under the molten surface and boarded it, hoping to find a way off-planet. Using a luck virus they had found aboard the vessel, Kochanski chose the specific vials (including this one) required to terraform the surface **[N-LST]**.

- **Z Deck:** A floor of *Red Dwarf* containing the ship's research labs. In one such lab, Kryten found a prototype Matter Paddle, capable of transporting individuals anywhere in space **[T-SER4.6]**. Z Deck also housed the Science Block, in which programmable viruses were developed **[T-SER8.6]**.

- ***Zero G*:** A magazine devoted to the sport of zero-gee football. Lister read an issue of *Zero G* in *Red Dwarf*'s Drive Room before taking the Chef's Exam **[T-SER1.3]**.

- **zero-gee football:** A popular sport of the twenty-second century that was played in a gravity-free environment. Lister was a fan of a zero-gee football team called the London Jets **[T-SER1.1]**.

  Zero-gee football games spanned three quarters, each twenty minutes in length **[M-SMG1.8(a)]**. The sport had previously lasted for five quarters, until player Ed Funkley died during the final quarter of a Veteran's game. For a time, the final two quarters were spent with the crowd waiting in silence in the parking lot after leaving the arena, but this was eventually changed to a standard three-quarter game **[M-SMG1.8(a)]**.

  A match involved two teams of six players, and sometimes lasted for more than seventy minutes **[R-BOD(s)]**. The sport endured for at least thirty-seven seasons **[M-SMG1.8(a)]**, but failed to take off in the universe known as Alternative 6829/B **[M-SMG1.8(c4)]**.

  A zero-gee stadium consisted of a two-mile-long tube called a doughnut, inside which the game was played using a spherical ball, which evolved over the years from a cube. During one season, a three-dimensional dodecahedron with protrusions into the Fifth Dimension was used, but this ball was banned due to the number of fingers that players lost during games.

  The object of zero-gee football was to score the most points. Several different scoring tactics could be employed, including the Rabid Hunch, the Castle Fritz, Garbunkley, Die! Die! My Darling!, and Around the Houses **[M-SMG1.8(a)]**. Teams included the London Jets **[T-SER1.1]**, the Berlin Bandits **[N-INF]**, the Paris Stompers **[R-BOD(s)]**, the Saturn Bears **[M-SMG1.7(a)]** and the Birmingham Mini Coopers **[M-SMG1.8(a)]**. Bristol City also had a team **[G-RPG]**. A junior league played as well, including teams such as the London Jet Juniors **[T-SER1.3]**.

  ***NOTE:*** *The sport's name has been inconsistently capitalized, spelled and punctuated from one source to another. Despite the sport being played with a spherical ball similar to association football (soccer), the rules and equipment used imply the sport more closely resembled American football.*

- ***Zero Gee Football*:** A magazine devoted to the sport of zero-gee football. Lister packed a copy of this publication before going into stasis for a trip back to Earth **[M-SMG1.4(c2)]**.

- **Zero-Gee Football—European Conference:** A grouping of European zero-gee football teams, including the London Jets and the Paris Stompers. Lister owned a video of European Conference games **[R-BOD(s)]**.

- ***Zero Gee Football—It's a Funny Old Game*:** A book about the sport of zero-gee football, written by Joe Klumpp. Holly read this book during the nanoseconds that passed between his sealing of *Red Dwarf*'s cargo decks to protect the crew from an impending cadmium II explosion, and the actual explosion **[N-OMN]**.

  ***NOTE:** In the novel* Infinity Welcomes Careful Drivers, *Holly read Kevin Keegan's* Football—It's a Funny Old Game.

- **Zero-Gee Football League:** The professional sports organization for zero-gee football **[G-SOR]**.

- **zero-gee squash:** A version of the English game of squash, played in a gravity-free environment. Olaf Petersen's house on Triton included a zero-gee squash court **[N-INF]**.

- ***Zero-gee Total Football*:** A video game included in the complimentary package provided to newly registered *Red Dwarf* crewmembers **[T-SER10.2]**.

- ***Zero-G Kickboxing*:** A sporting simulation game that the *Starbug 1* crew found among the wreckage of a derelict ship within rogue simulant territory **[T-SER6.3]**. Produced by Total Immersion Inc. and distributed by Crapola Inc., the game was part of the *No Brains, All Brawn Sports Heroes Series* **[G-RPG]**. Lister played this game several times throughout a three-week period, but preferred the detective simulation game *Gumshoe,* mostly because he was having sex with its femme fatale character **[T-SER6.3]**.

  ***NOTE:*** Red Dwarf—The Roleplaying Game*'s core book spelled the game's name as* Zero-Gee Kick Boxing.

- **Zeta-Jones Quadrant:** An area of space containing the Planet of the Nymphomaniacs, in a series of illusions created for the *Starbug 1* crew **[G-SOR]**.

  ***NOTE:** The quadrant was named after Welsh actor Catherine Zeta-Jones.*

- **Zeus:** The god of the sky and ruler of Mount Olympus, according to Greek mythology **[RL]**. When Tunbridge Wells' five hundred pilgrims were sent to pray for the end of a meteor storm ravaging their city, a pardoner in the group believed his people were headed to a shrine dedicated to Zeus. Others disagreed, causing a religious war that wiped out the entire pilgrim crew **[M-SMG1.14(c2)]**.

- **Ziffed:** An extraterrestrial species featured in the pages of an adult-oriented magazine called *Alien Wives* **[X-XMS]**.

- **zipman:** A position in zero-gee football **[M-SMG1.8(a)]**.

- **zipper:** A type of spacecraft used by Virgin for interplanetary travel. According to the company's advertisements, its demi-light-speed zippers could make the trip from Earth to Saturn in just over two hours. On his twenty-fourth birthday Lister drunkenly booked passage on a zipper to Saturn's moon, Mimas, using a passport issued under the name Emily Berkenstein **[N-INF]**.

- **Zippo:** *See* Marx, Zeppo

- **Zlurth, Dominator:** A simulant berserker general and the captain of a Simulant Death Ship. His underlings included Chancellors Wednesday and Thursday. Among Zlurth's possessions was a Sword of Spite.

  When a rogue droid named Hogey stole a detailed map of the galaxy from Zlurth's ship, the simulant tracked Hogey to *Red Dwarf.* A simulant fleet attacked the mining vessel, forcing the crew to evacuate in a *Blue Midget* shuttle. Zlurth was defeated after ordering his four ships to simultaneously fire on *Blue Midget,* unaware its hull had been destabilized. This allowed the simulants' missiles to harmlessly pass through the shuttle and destroy their own vessels **[T-SER10.6]**.

**PREFIX**
**RL:** Real life

**T-: Television Episodes**
**SER:** Television series
**IDW:** "Identity Within"
**USA1:** Unaired U.S. pilot
**USA2:** Unaired U.S. demo

**R-: *The Bodysnatcher Collection***
**SER:** Remastered episodes
**BOD:** "Bodysnatcher"
**DAD:** "Dad"
**FTH:** "Lister's Father"
**INF:** "Infinity Patrol"
**END:** "The End" (original assembly)

**N-: Novels**
**INF:** *Infinity Welcomes Careful Drivers*
**BTL:** *Better Than Life*
**LST:** *Last Human*
**BCK:** *Backwards*
**OMN:** *Red Dwarf Omnibus*

**M-: Magazines**
**SMG:** *Smegazine*

**W-: Websites**
**OFF:** Official website
**NAN:** *Prelude to Nanarchy*
**AND:** *Androids*
**DIV:** Diva-Droid
**DIB:** Duane Dibbley

**CRP:** Crapola
**GEN:** Geneticon
**LSR:** Leisure World Intl.
**JMC:** Jupiter Mining Corporation
**AIT:** *A.I. Today*
**HOL:** HoloPoint

**G-: Roleplaying Game**
**RPG:** *Core Rulebook*
**BIT:** *A.I. Screen Extra Bits* booklet
**SOR:** *Series Sourcebook*
**OTH:** Other RPG material

- **"!ZN":** Graffiti scrawled on a wall outside a pub in England, in a far future in which time ran backwards. The writing, when read forward, said "NZ!" **[T-SER3.1]**.

  ***NOTE:*** *It is possible that the graffiti referred to New Zealand and its rugby team, the New Zealand Kiwis, given other markings on the wall.*

- **Zogothoniumeliumoxiixiexiphulmifhidikalidrihide:** The chemical name for a corrosive, man-made chameleonic microbe. The microorganism could change shape and eat through most substances, except for glass. Such microbes caused the destruction of the Space Corps vessel SS *Hermes*, which had been rebuilt by Kryten's nanobots along with *Red Dwarf*. *Hermes* passenger Talia Garrett fled the ship in an escape pod, unaware it was the chameleonic microbe in disguise, and met up with *Red Dwarf*.

  Within hours, the chameleonic microbe began eating away at *Red Dwarf*, necessitating a ship-wide evacuation. Kochanski postulated that an antidote for the microbe could be found in a mirror universe, and so Kryten built a device to breach the membrane between the two dimensions, allowing Rimmer to cross into the alternate reality with a sample.

  Obtaining the antidote (sesiumfrankalithicmixyalibidiumrixidixidoxidexidroxide) from Cat's mirror counterpart, Rimmer returned to the prime universe, only to discover the ship devastated by the microbe, his crewmates having fled into the mirror universe. What's more, the written formula for the antidote converted back into the formula for the microbe, which was useless to him **[T-SER8.8]**.

- **Zone 101:** A zone of seventeen floors within *Red Dwarf*, including Floor 13, which house a classified brig called the Tank **[T-SER8.3]**.

- **zoney:** A slang term for a mechanoid addicted to outrozone **[T-SER7.6]**.

- **Zorro City:** A nickname that Rimmer called a group of Brefewino guards who threatened Cat with swords **[T-IDW]**.

- **Z-Shift:** A duty shift aboard *Red Dwarf*. During Z-Shift, Rimmer was in charge of the Routine Maintenance, Cleaning and Sanitation Unit, with Lister as one of his subordinates **[N-INF]**. The unit's duties included clearing chicken soup nozzles, stocking vending machines with Crunchie bars, fixing drive plates and other tasks **[T-SER4.3]**.

  In addition to Rimmer and Lister, Z-Shift also included crewmembers Burd, Phil Burroughs, Dooley, McHullock, Palmer, Pixon, Saxon, Turner and Wilkinson. Rimmer's one rule for Z-Shift was "Keep It Tidy" (K.I.J.). If his team followed this rule, he assured them, they would "Get On Just Famously" (G.O.J.F.) **[N-INF]**.

  ***NOTE:*** *Since Rimmer was the second-lowest-ranking member of* Red Dwarf*'s crew, this would seem to imply that everyone else on Z-Shift had the same rank as Lister.*

- **Zsigsmos Sector:** An area of space containing several habitable planets, many populated by genetically engineered wildebeetroot **[B-SUR]**.

- **Zural, Captain:** A member of the Cat People species, and Ora Tanzil's commander. Zural betrayed his platoon to Brefewino GELFs, who captured Tanzil and killed the rest. Learning of her capture, he acquired a morphing belt to infiltrate the GELF village and kill her as well.

  Disguised as a Brefewino, Zural encountered the *Starbug 1* crew, who had come to rescue Tanzil so she could help Cat beat a deadly affliction brought on by a lack of sex. Zural out-cheated Lister at a game of four-dimensional pontoon, earning enough money to win Tanzil at the GELFs' auction. Infuriated, Cat attacked and disarmed him. Zural then revealed his true form and claimed to have come to rescue Tanzil, but Cat realized he was a traitor and thrust his sword into Zural's chest, killing him instantly **[T-IDW]**.

  ***NOTE:*** *A booklet included with the Series VII DVDs spelled the name as "Zural," while the episode's subtitles used the spelling "Zurool."*

- **ZX81:** *See* Sinclair ZX-81

- **ZXC-3443474:** The catalog number of Reggie Wilson's compilation *Rockin' Up Rachmaninov—120 Golden Greats on the Hammond Organ*, available through K-Tel Records. This collection was among Rimmer's favorites **[M-SMG1.1(a)]**.

**B-: Books**
**PRG:** *Red Dwarf Programme Guide*
**SUR:** *Red Dwarf Space Corps Survival Manual*
**PRM:** *Primordial Soup*
**SOS:** *Son of Soup*
**SCE:** *Scenes from the Dwarf*
**LOG:** *Red Dwarf Log No. 1996*
**RD8:** *Red Dwarf VIII*
**EVR:** *The Log: A Dwarfer's Guide to Everything*

**X-: Misc.**
**PRO:** Promotional materials, videos, etc.
**PST:** Posters at DJ XVII (2013)
**CAL:** 2008 calendar
**RNG:** Cell phone ringtones
**MOB:** Mobisode ("Red Christmas")
**CIN:** *Children in Need* sketch
**GEK:** *Geek Week* intros by Kryten
**TNG:** "Tongue-Tied" video
**XMS:** Bill Pearson's Christmas special pitch script
**XVD:** Bill Pearson's Christmas special pitch video
**OTH:** Other *Red Dwarf* appearances

**SUFFIX**
**DVD:**
**(d)** – Deleted scene
**(o)** – Outtake
**(b)** – Bonus DVD material (other)
**(e)** – Extended version

**SMEGAZINES:**
**(c)** – Comic
**(a)** – Article

**OTHER:**
**(s)** – Early/unused script draft
**(s1)** – Alternate version of script

# APPENDIX IV:

## *Categorical Index*

*"On our journey back to Earth, we have encountered many strange and bizarre things. Only last month, we came across a moon which was shaped exactly like Felicity Kendall's bottom."*

**–Holly, "Stasis Leak"**

The following lists provide a breakdown of this lexicon's approximately 5,000 entries into multiple categories for easier navigation. The category headings, like the terms listed beneath them, are sorted alphabetically. Some terms appear on more than one list, depending on the content of their lexicon entries.

## ACCOLADES AND AWARDS

Albert DeSalvo Likeability Award
Android of the Year
BSc
Eagle of Valour
Flogging a Dead Horse Award
General Custer Forward Thinking Award
Gold Oblong of Pluck
Golden Stripe of Honour
Most Disturbing Android Design
Mr. April
Mr. July
Mr. October
Nine Years' Long Service
Platinum Star of Fortitude
Reggie Wilson Memorial Trophy
Sexiest Man of All Time
Six Years' Long Service
Space Knight's Cross of Honour
SSc
Three Years' Long Service
Twelve Years' Long Service
Vending Machine Maintenance Man of the Month

## ALIASES AND ALTER EGOS

Bhaji, Bhindi
CapstonsBoss
CaptainJuno
Carton, Iron Will, Sheriff
Crayon84
Dhal, Tarka
Dibbley family, the
Dibbley, Duane
Divad, Retsil
Doyle, Sebastian, Voter Colonel
Doyle, William ("Billy")
DuaneDibbley
Grand Earth Overlord Commander Rimmer
Great and Powerful Madam, The
Green Knight, The
Hampton, Gerald, Flight Officer
Iron Duke
JayseeFan
Jonathan
KellysKnickers
Krytenski, Kryten, Flight Coordinator
Lister of Smeg
Lister, Dave, Junior
Listerton-Smythe, David, Flight Commander
Major Tom
McGrew, Dan ("Dangerous Dan")
Mike
Mr. Multi Universe 3,000,026
Octuplets
One, The
Pawn Sacrifice
Queeg 500
Reality Patrol
Riverboat, Brett
Riviera Kid, The
Stabhim
Subject A
Todhunter, Christopher

## BRAND NAMES, PRODUCTS AND PRODUCT OPTIONS

3-in-1
Action Man
After Eight
Ajax
AKG
All-Droid Finest Collection
Alphabetti Spaghetti
Amateur Programmer Suite
*Androids* Dancing Mug
*Androids* Shower Radio
*Androids* Singing Mug
Anti-Dazzlers
Anus Soothe Pile Cream
Bacofoil
Beinz Baked Beans
Beinz Salad Cream
Birds Eye
Bitchin' Chrome
Biz
Blu-Tack
Bonjela gum ointment
Boss
Bovril
boxer short brown
Breadman's Fish Fingers
Brylcreem
Bubbly Amber
Butler Black
Caleva
Can Cer
Candy Apple Red
Canker Sore Burgundy
Castrol GTX
cigarettes
Cinzano Bianco
Clearasil
Clearhead
Coca-Cola
Cock-A-Doodle Flakes
CrapLock
Dayglo orange moonboots
Daz
Diarrhea Brown
Dip N' Sip Chilli & Lager Bath Salts
Dom Pérignon
Domestos
Eau de Yak Urine
Eco
Eidetosol
Esso Super
Freckle
Ganymede Gold
Glen Fujiyama
Glen Tokyo Whisky
Go-Double-Plus
go-fasta stripes
go-faster stripes
Go-Go Green
Good Mood
Grant & Naylor Luxury Length
Grecian 2000
Gunmetal Blue
Holo-Flame Color Gas
Hoover Black Hole
Industrial baked beans
Inflatable Ingrid, Your Polythene Pal
Jammie Dodger
Jet Black
Jiffy Windo-Kleen
Jim Daniels
JMC coconut massage oil

JMC cooking oil
JMC Filter
JMC peach slices
JMC self-raising flour
Johnson's Baby Bud
Laxo
Les Paul
Listerine
Lounge Lizard 967
Luck
Luton's Carpet Shampoo
Munny
Neptune Blue
Newcastle Brown Ale
Odor Eater
Ouroboros
Parfum by Lanstrom
Peperami
Pepsi
Perrier
Pet Translator
Playful Pete, My Polythene Pal
Pot Noodle
Pot O' Sick
Pregnancy Colour
Pus Green
Rachel
Ready Brek
Really Really Black
Red Planet Power Drinks
roll-off deodorant
Rolls Razors
Sancerre
Scintillating Off-Gray
Sexual Magnetism
Shagme
Shake n' Vac
Skol
Skug
Slicey-Slicey
Smeggo!
Space Age Silver
Space Mumps Yellow
Spaghetti Hoops
Spam
Sparkly Blue
Stirmaster
Sump
SupaBryte
Superstik vulcanized tires
Swarfega
Tabasco sauce
Talkie Cutlery
Talkie Microwave
Talkie Sew 'N Sew
Talkie Toaster
Talkie Toaster Commemorative Edition
Talkie Toaster Extras Pack
Talkie Toilet
Talkie Toilet Extras Pack
Tamagotchi
Tastee Noodle Pot
Temper Tantrum
Tension Sheet
Tiger
Tipp-Ex
Toilet Duck
Topic Bar
Total Gonzo
Tour
UltraPlas windscreen wipers
Vimto
Wavy Red
WD-40
Wheaty Flakes
Wibbly-Wobbly Green
Windolene

## BUSINESSES, CORPORATIONS AND ESTABLISHMENTS

911-R-Us
Acme
Acme Cleaning Company
Aigburth Arms, The
Albanian State Washing Machine Company
AlFresco Guacamole Restaurant
All-Droid Mail Order Shopping Station
Android International
Astro Cuts
Audrey's
Automobile Association (AA)
Bailey's Perfect Shami Kebab Emporium
Balti house
Barlow's Bookies
Berni Inn
Black Island Film Studios
Bloodlust Arms
Bodies 'R' Us
Bod-U-Like
Body Swap
Bootle Municipal Golf Course
Booze World
Brainfade
Brothel-U-Like
Burger Bar
Burton Group
Butlins
Cars O' Rod
Chubb
Cinelli
Club 18-30
Club Nerd
Copacabana Hawaiian Cocktail Bar
Copal
Crapola Inc.
Crawfords
Crazy Astro, The
Dallas Electric
Deep Space Leisure, LLC
Deimos Instruments
Detritus Wrecks
Detroit Royal Vista Golf Course
Disney-Chodhwara AG
Disposex
Diva-Droid International
DriveU
Droid Oil
Droids R Us
Dun Robotix
Econoline
Eine Kutta Über de Resten
enilertneC
Fat Bastoria, The
Father Grimm's Blacker Than Black Magic
Fat Sam's Bar
First National Bank
Flag and Lettuce, The
Flibble Co.
Freeman Hardy Willis
Fuchal Diner, The
Ganymede Holiday Inn
Ganymede RadioShack
GaryCo

GELF's Head, The
Gentleman Gym's
Gideons International, The
Gigante-Volkswagen
Golden Assurance Friendly and Caring Loan Society
Good Time Charlie
Good Time Josie's
Goodyear
Gulliver's Multiverse Travels
Hacienda, The
Hak-echekk-ack-hech-echhh
Happy Astro
Happy Eater
Happy Hopper
Harley Davidson
Heads-U-Like
He Ain't Heavy, He's My Brothel
Hi-Life Club
Hit-U-Like
HoloPoint
HoloSoft Industries
Holotech, Inc.
Hoover
Hotel Paradiso
ICI
Imperial Typewriter Co. Ltd.
Indiana Takeaway
Infomax Data Corporation
Interflora
Interstella Action Games
Jacobs
Jaysee's Cleaning Company
JMC Tools
Joe's
Juno Hilton
Jupiter Mining Corporation (JMC)
Kabin, The
Karstares' Interstellar Cleaning and Sanitation Supplies (K.I.C.A.S.S.)
Kek-ack-ech-ech-ech Industries
Kit-Kat Club
Klix
Kluge Corp.
Kodak
Kookie Kola
Last Chance Saloon
Leisure World International
Lewis's
Little Chef
Los Americanos Casino
Love Toys
Lucky Hop
Luigi's Fish 'n' Chip Emporium
Malpractice Medical & Scispec (MMS)
Maplins
Marie Lloyd
Marks and Spencer (M&S)
Martini's Bar
McDonald's
MegaMart
Mimas Hilton
Mimas Mining
Miranda Insurance Company
Moss Bros
Multi Million Lottery Co.
Mutual Life Assurance
Nerdorama
Nice 'n'Noodly Kwik-Food bar
Nni Retsasid
Noel's Body Swap Shop
Nogard dna Egroeg
Nose World
Official Titan Souvenir Shop
Palace, The
Panasonic
Parker Knoll
Parrot's Bar
Pat Cabs
Peter Pessimism's Undertaker's Parlor
Peugeot
Philosophy Arms, The
Photo-U-Kwik booth
Pictures by Kev F
Piledriver, Inc
Pizza Hut
Plutonian Medical Insurance
Popco Inc.
Pot Noodle International
Prima Doner
Priory, the
Rat Pit, The
Red Rocket
Rimmer Corporation Worldwide plc
RimmerCorps
Rimmer Research Centres
Rolls-Royce
Rovers Return Inn, The
Roy's Rolls
Rudies
Saachi, Saachi, Saachi, Saachi, Saachi and Saachi
Sainsbury's MegaStore
Sales, Space Division
Salvador Dali Coffee Lounge
Salvation Army
Samaritans, the
Save the Pigeon
Scary"R"Us
Scott Foresman and Company
Scripts by Kelleher/Hill
Sick Parrot Public House
Slippy Dick's Club
Slough Brain Research Unit
Solidgram International
Sony Corporation
Souse & Sott's, Ltd., Glasgow
Space Cadet LLC
Space Corps Specialist Publications
Stannah Lifts Holdings Ltd.
Star Airways, Inc.
Star Tours Holidays
Sunny Sunshine's White Magic & White Elephant Stall
Taj Mahal Tandoori Restaurant
Tesco
They Walk Among Us!
Thomson Holidays
Titan Hilton
Titan Taj Mahal
Titan Tours
Total Immersion, Inc.
Transtemporal Film Unit
Tucker Instruments
U-Haul
Unspeakably Vile Porno Filth Emporium
Uppures Insurance
Utensilware, Inc.
Vindaloovian Empire
Virgin
Volkswagen
Wacky Wally's Video Wonderland
Warburton Neurotronics
Whirlpool Corp.
Winan Diner
Wizzo

**CHARACTERS: Androids, Appliances, Mechanoids, Simulants, Waxdroids and Other Mechanicals**

Mollee
Monroe, Marilyn
Mother Teresa
Mummy, The
Mussolini, Benito, First Marshal
Neame, Doctor
Nelly ("Lube")
Nelson
Nelson, Horatio, Vice-Admiral
Parkur
Perky
Pinky
Pizzak'Rapp
Presley, Elvis, Sergeant
Pythagoras of Samos
Rameses Niblick III Kerplunk Kerplunk Whoops Where's My Thribble
Rasputin, Grigori
Rev
Reynolds, Debris
Richard III, King
Righty
RoboGaz
Roze
Saliva
Sara, Nurse
Sartre, Jean-Paul
Savalas, Aristotelis ("Telly")
Scutcher
Serving Unit 27
Shaz
Simone
Spike the Chef
Spike the Drinks
St. Francis of Assisi
Sugar ("Shug")
Surgeon 2
Taiwan Tony ("T.T.")
Terminator, The
Thursday, Chancellor
Van Gogh
van Goth, Vinnie
Victoria, Queen
Vlad
Wankel
Wayne, John
Wednesday, Chancellor
Winnie-the-Pooh
Zlurth, Dominator

**CHARACTERS:**
**Animated, Fictional, Hypothetical, Simulations and Virtual Reality**

A Bit of the Other
Addams Family, the
Adrienne
Android in Bus Queue
Antoinette, Marie, Dauphine/Queen
Archimedes
Bailey, Billy
Bailey, George
Bailey, "Old Ma"
Bambi
Bang
Barlow, Ken
Barney
Bates, Norman
Batman
Baz
Beatles, The
Bennet, Elizabeth ("Lizzie")
Bennet, Jane
Bennet, Kitty
Bennet, Lydia
Bennet, Mary
Bennet, Mrs.
Benzen
Bert
Big Iron
Bing
Bingley, Charles
Blind Pew
Bonaparte, Joséphine, Empress
Bonaparte, Napoleon, Emperor
Bonk
Boop, Betty
Bracknell, Augusta, Lady
Brandy
Brody, Miss
Brook ("Junior")
Brooke Junior ("Junior Junior")
Browns, The
Bruce
Buckley, Mr. ("Pop")
Buddha, Gautama ("Shakyamuni")
Bullet, Jake
Caesar, Julius, Emperor
Calhoon, Mr.
Caligula, Emperor
Cannon, Frank
Capp, Andy
Capston
Carol
Carole
Chicata, Juanita ("The Brazilian Bombshell")
Chips, Mr.
Clampett, Jethro
Claus, Mrs.
Claus, Santa
Clementine
Clifton, Field Marshall
Columbo
Connor, Simon
Crusoe, Robinson
Cry 10
Darren
Dastardly and Muttley
Daz
Death, Judge
Deathbot
Derek
Dink
Dredd, Judge
Duck, Donald
Duck, Donna
Elizabeth I, Queen
Ernest
Ernie
Flipper
Florrie, Great-Aunt
Frankenstein, Victor, Doctor
Fred
Gable, Clark
Gandalf
Gary
Gaz
Gerald
Good Knight, the
Gower ("Old Man Gower")
Graham, Doctor
Grappelli, Stéphane

Green Knight, The
Hammer, Mike
Handsome, Hank, Space Adventurer
Harrington, Mrs.
Harris
Harry
Heinman, Mr. ("Bull," "Bullethead")
Hendrix, Jimi
Henry
Hickett, Mrs.
Holly
Holmes, Sherlock
Hood, Robin
Horace
Hornblower, Horatio
Hubble, Mrs.
Hudzen
Hudzen 10
Hugo
Hump
Jaysee
Jaz
Jeff
Jellybean
Jemma
Jim
Jimmy
Jitterman, Jimmy
Jitterman, Tonto
Johnson, Mrs.
Jolene
Jump
Karstares
Kelly
Ken
Kennedy, John Fitzgerald ("Jack," "JFK"), President
Khan, Genghis, Emperor
King Kong
King of the Potato People
Kochanski, Krissie
Kojak, Theo, Lieutenant
Kryten
Kylie
LaBouche, Trixie
Lassie
Last, James
Laszlo, Victor
Lenin, Vladimir, Premier
Lister, Dave
Lister, David
Lollobrigida, Gina
Lone Ranger, The
Loretta
Louis XVI, King
Lube
Lupino, Ida
MacKenzie, Doc
Marcos, Imelda
Marlowe, Philip
Marnie
Martin
Marvo the Memory Man
Maxime
McBean, Dennis
McGrew, Dan ("Dangerous Dan")
Menuhin, Yehudi
Miranda
Mister Ed
Mollee
Monroe, Marilyn
Mouse, Mickey
Mozart, Wolfgang Amadeus
Mullaney, Lloyd
Mulligan, Mr.
Mummy, The
Munster, Herman
Murphy, Mugs
Mustard, Colonel
Neame, Doctor
Nelly ("Lube")
Newton, Karen, Doctor
Nitty, Frank ("The Enforcer")
Officer 592
Pallister
Parker, Charles Jr. ("Charlie," "Yardbird")
Patton, General George S.
Philip
Pierre
Popeye the Sailor Man
Prince of Wales
Pumpy
Queen of Camelot
Rathbone
Reynolds, Debris
Rich, Bernard ("Buddy")
Rimmer, Arnold Judas
Rimmer, Helen
Rimmer, Janine
Rimmer, Julius
Riverboat, Brett
Riviera Kid, The
RoboGaz
Roze
Rumpy
Sammy the Squib
Sara, Nurse
Serving Unit 27
Shaz
Silver Surfer
Silver, Long John
Simone
Sindy
Solomon, King
Spade, Sam
Spider-Man
Spilliker, Herbert J.
Spock, Mr.
Sprogg, Woolfie, the Plasticine Dog
Squiddly Diddly
Tarzan
Taylor, Elizabeth ("Liz"), Dame
Terminator, The
Three Musketeers, the
Three Stooges, the
Tiffany
Torquemada, Tomas dé, Grand Inquisitor
Tweety Bird
Ulysses
Valkyrie
van Gogh, Vincent
van Oestrogen, Dutch
Vlad
Wallace & Gromit
Weasel, Wilbur
Wilson, Grandma
Winnie-the-Pooh
Wisdom, Norman
Woodpecker, Woody

**CHARACTERS: Artificial Intelligence**

Allan
Cassandra

Ernie 7000
Gordon 8000
Grendel
Hilly
Holly
Holly 6000
Holly, Sister
Human Impressions Task & Logistics Electronic Reichsführer (HITLER)
Justice Computer
Kate
Kenneth
Kristian
medi-bot
Pree
Queeg 500
Stocky

### CHARACTERS: Deities, Prophets, Clergy and Other Religious

Apollo
Buddha, Gautama ("Shakyamuni")
Cat Priest
Cat, Father ("Padre")
Chanski
Chen
Clister
Cloister
Cloister the Stupid
Creator, the
Dalai Lama, the
Darin-Tor
Death
elder chaos god
Esus
Felix, Father
Gabriel
God
Gregory XIII, Pope
Jesus of Nazareth
Joan of Arc
Judas
Kadok
Madonna, the
Magdalene, Mary
Moses
Mother Teresa
Odin
Pan
Petson
Plug
Selby
Taranis
Tibbles, Reverend
Toutatis
Zeus

### CHARACTERS: Dreams, Figments, Illusions and Hallucinations

Andy
Annett, Chloë
Apocalypse, Death
Apocalypse, Famine, Brother
Apocalypse, Pestilence, Brother
Apocalypse, War, Brother
Bailey, Billy
Bailey, George
Bailey, "Old Ma"
Bartikovsky, Katerina, Science Officer
Belief, Billy
Bert
Cat, Kit
Calculator, Esther
Calculator, Jeff
Charles, Craig
Confidence
Creator, the
Diagnostics, Doctor ("Old Doc")
Dodd, Ken
Dread, Judge
Dredd, Judge
Ernie
Frank
Fund, Doctor
Gregson, Simon
Guilt, Jimmy
Hope
Keegan, Michelle
Lola, Miss
Maxwell, Doctor
Mayor of Warsaw
McGee ("Bear Strangler")
Mellington, Mike
Memory, Wyatt
Mullaney, Lloyd
Noddy
Nuke
Oracle Boy
Oracle Girl
Paranoia
Pension, Doctor
Pessimism, Peter
Pete Tranter's sister
Rimmer, Arnold Judas
Swallow
Swan-Morton, Doctor
Sydney
Tate, Tommy
Wharf, Reg
Yates, Lise

### CHARACTERS: Genetically Engineered

Action Man
Arthur
Btrrnfjhyjhnehgewydn, Chief
Cameron
Camille
Catman
Conspirator, the
Deki
Dernbvjukidhgd, F'hnhiujsrf, His Imperial Majesty ("F'hnhiujsrf the Unpronounceable")
Drigg
Ech-Ghekk-Agg-Hecch-Ech-Ech, Queen
Fachen-Mach-Ech-Noch-Ahach-Ech, Chief
Hackhackhackachhachhachach
Hakakhhak-kkhhak-hhakh-hhakh-khkahak-hkaahkahk-hkhk, Chief Justice of hakhakhk-aahkahkh hkhakkhaakhaaakah-akkk-hhakaaaak kak-akk-hakkakak ka ka ka
Hech-Ech-Ech Annechech-Ech
Hector
Kazwa
Khakhakhakkhhakhakkkhakkkkkh
Leekiel
Longman, Michael, Professor
Nelson, Norbert

Regulator, The
Reketrebn
Robbie
S'rtginjum
Super-Ace

**CHARACTERS: Hologrammatic**

Baker, Tom
Bartikovsky, Katerina, Science Officer
Binks, Commander
Capote, Mr.
Crane, Nirvanah, Commander
Grace, William Gilbert ("W. G.")
Henry VIII, King
holo-nymph
Jones, Monica
Lanstrom, Hildegarde, Doctor
Lister, David
Longman, Michael, Professor
McIntyre, George, Flight Coordinator
Moron, Diane ("The Gangrene Goddess")
Munson, First Officer
Murray, Sam, Deck Sergeant
Navarro, Randy, Commander
Platini, Hercule, Captain
Pushkin, Natalina, Commander
Rimmer, Arlene Judith, Second Technician
Rimmer, Arnold Judas ("Ace"), Commander
Rimmer, Arnold Judas, Second Technician
Rimmer, Howard, Second Technician
Robin
Saunders, Frank
Shakespeare, William
Terry

**CHARACTERS: Main Cast's Counterparts, Doppelgängers and Duplicates**

Action Man
Bullet, Jake
Cat
Cat, Brother
Cat, Father ("Padre")
Cat, Professor
Catman
Daizee
Darren
Davis, Leo
Dog
Dorrie
Doyle, Sebastian, Voter Colonel
Doyle, William ("Billy")
Felix, Father
Hilly
Holina, Princess
Hollentine
Hollister, Francine, Captain
Hollister, Frank
Holly
Holly 6000
Holly, Sister
Hudzen 10
Kochanski
Kochanski, Christine
Kochanski, Christopher
Kochanski, Kristine
Kochanski, Kristine Z.
Kochanski, Kristopher
Kritter
Kryten
Kryten 2XB-517P
Kryten, Brother
Lister, David
Lister, David ("Dave"), Third Technician
Lister, David ("Spanners")
Lister, David, Brother
Lister, David, First Officer
Lister, Deb
Professor H
Rimmer, Ace ("Blackheart")
Rimmer, Arlene Judith ("Ace")
Rimmer, Arlene Judith, Second Technician
Rimmer, Arnold Judas ("Ace"), Commander
Rimmer, Arnold Judas ("Squirrel"), Captain
Rimmer, Arnold Judas, Brother
Rimmer, Arnold Judas, Circuitry Technician Third Class
Rimmer, Arnold Judas, Prime Minister
Rimmer, Arnold Judas, Second Technician
Rimmer, Ray
Robbie
Robin
Super-Ace

**CHARACTERS: Main Cast's Family Members and Creators**

Able
Ackroyd, Augustus
Beemer, Bertrand
Belinda, Aunt
Dan, Uncle
Dennis ("Dungo")
Dinsdale, Derek
Kochanski, Krissie
Kochanski, Kristine Z. ("Krissie"), Navigation Officer
Kochanski, Moose
Lister, David ("Dave"), Third Technician (Senior and Junior)
Lister, "Grandma"
Lister, Becky
Lister, Bexley
Lister, Jan
Lister, Jim
Maggie, Auntie
Mamet, J.A., Professor
Mary, Auntie
McGruder, Michael R., Lieutenant-Colonel
Mij, Retsil
Reaper, Jim
Rimmer, Alice
Rimmer, Alison ("Arnie")
Rimmer, Frank
Rimmer, Howard, Second Technician
Rimmer, Janine
Rimmer, John
Rimmer, Julius
Rimmer, Lecturer
Rimmer, Mrs.
Rimmer, Sarah
Shropshire Rimmers, the
Terminator, The

Thornton, Beth ("Old Prune Face")
Thornton, Tom
Warburton, John
Wilmot, Mr.
Wilmot, Mrs.
Yelxeb, Retsil

## CHARACTERS: Main Cast's Friends, Classmates and Instructors

362436ZXKB3
Arkwright, Mrs.
Bateman, Marcus, Doctor ("Stinky")
Benjamin, Disraeli
Beswick, Thrasher
Brody, Miss
Chen
Chips, Mr.
Darroch, Bobby
Dickens, Charles
Dobbin
Donald
Duckworth, Dicky
Duncan
Ernie 7000
Filbert, Dennis
Foster, Miss
Garrett, Talia
Garrett, Talia, Sister
Gary ("Gazza")
Gibson ("Squeaky")
Gilbert
Gordon 8000
Heinman, Mr. ("Bull," "Bullethead")
Holden, Fred ("Thickie")
Johnson, Harry
Keelan, Charles
Khan, Genghis
MacScarface ("One Eye")
Petersen, Olaf, Catering Officer
Potson, Duncan
Rameses Niblick III Kerplunk Kerplunk Whoops Where's My Thribble
Rimmer, Lecturer
Roebuck, Porky
Selby
Shakespeare, William
Simpson, Nobby
Tranter, Pete
Wendy
Yakka-Takka-Tulla, Space Mistress

## CHARACTERS: Main Cast's Lovers, Love Interests and Sex Partners

Arkwright, Mrs.
Barrington, Fiona
Bredbury, Alison
Camille
Carmen, Caroline ("Carmen Moans")
Cashier Number 4
Chicata, Juanita ("The Brazilian Bombshell")
Crane, Nirvanah, Commander
Dispenser 23
Dispenser 34
Edgington, Irene, Professor ("Professor E")
Fisher, Michelle
Hollister, Martha
Inflatable Ingrid, Your Polythene Pal
Khakhakhakkhhakhakkkhakkkkkh
Kochanski, Krissie
Kochanski, Kristine Z. ("Krissie"), First Console Officer
Kochanski, Kristine Z. ("Krissie"), Navigation Officer
LaBouche, Trixie
Lister, Deb
Lorraine
McCauley, Carol
McGruder, Yvonne
Miranda
Monroe, Marilyn
Mulholland-Jjones, Sabrina, Lady
Patel, Suzie
Pete Tranter's sister
Queen of Camelot
Rachel
Rice
Rimmer, Alice
Rimmer, Helen
Rimmer, Janine
Rimmer, Sarah
Sandra
Sinclair ZX-81
Summers, Hayley
super deluxe vacuum cleaner
Sydney
Tanzil, Ora, Sub-lieutenant
Terry
Tim
Tom
Tony
Trevor
Warrington, Susan
Yates, Lise

## CHARACTERS: Pets and Other Animals

Barnaby
Boo-Boo
Bouncer MK-IV
Champion the Wonder Horse
Dancer
Dignity
Dracula
Flipper
Frankenstein
Frankenstein ("Frankie")
Golden Boy
Hannah
Kookie Kola Bear
Lassie
Lennon
McCartney
Mister Ed
Pete
Prancer
Sally
Shergar
Snappy
Trumper
Winnie

## CHARACTERS: Psi-Moon Denizens

Bitterness
Charity
Charm
Courage
Cunning

Dark Forces, the
Dark One, The
Flibble, Mr.
Generosity
Granny
Hildegarde, Witch
Honor
Honour
Hooded Legions, The
Hope
Loneliness
Misery
Mistrust
Paranoia
Rimmer, Mrs.
Rimmer's lust monster
Rocky
Self-Confidence
Self-Despair
Self-Doubt
Self-Esteem
Self-Loathing Beast
Self-Respect
Serendipity
Unspeakable One, The

**CHARACTERS:**
**Real-World Individuals and Groups**

5th Dimension, The
ABBA
Alexander the Great, King
Annett, Chloë
Antoinette, Marie, Dauphine/Queen
Archer, Jeffrey, Baron
Archimedes
Aristotle
Atlas, Charles
Austen, Jane
Azymuth, Ivan
Bacon, Sir Francis
Baker, Tom
Bankhead, Tallulah
Bay City Rollers
Beatles, The
Beatty, Warren
Beckham, David
Berry, Nick
Bessone, Raymond ("Teasy-Weasy")
Bewes, Rodney
Big Chief I-Spy
Billy the Kid
Bogart, Humphrey
Boleyn, Anne, Queen Consort
Bonaparte, Joséphine, Empress
Bonaparte, Napoleon, Emperor
Boone, Pat
Borgia, Lucrezia
Boston Strangler, the
Bramah, Joseph
Brando, Marlon
Braun, Eva
Brennan, Seamus ("Shay")
Brontë, Emily Jane
Brown, Chelsea
Brynner, Yul
Buddha, Gautama ("Shakyamuni")
Caesar, Julius, Emperor
Caligula, Emperor
Camus, Albert
Capone, Alphonse ("Al")
Capra, Frank
Caravaggio, Michelangelo Merisi da
Carmichael, Hoagy
Carpenters, The
Cartland, Barbara
Catherine the Great, Empress
Charles, Craig
Christian, Fletcher
Christie, Agatha
Clive of India
Como, Pierino Ronald ("Perry")
Cooper, Jilly
Coward, Noël Pierce, Sir
Curie, Marie ("Madame Curie")
Curtis, Tony
Dalai Lama, the
Dali, Salvador
Dave Dee, Dozy, Beaky, Mick & Tich
Davis, Steve
Day, Doris
Descartes, René
Diamond, Neil
Dickens, Charles
Disney, Walt
Disraeli, Benjamin
Dixon, Reginald ("Reggie")
Dodd, Ken
Duke of Wellington, the
Earl of Sandwich, the
Edison, Thomas Alva
Edward II, King
Einstein, Albert, Doctor
Eisenhower, Mamie
Eisner, William ("Will")
Elephant Man, the
Eliot, Thomas Stearns ("T.S.")
Elizabeth I, Queen
Emerson, Lake and Palmer
Engels, Friedrich
Floyd, Keith
Flynn, Errol
Formby, George
Franklin, Aretha
Freud, Sigmund, Doctor
Gable, Clark
Galilei, Galileo
Gandhi, Mohandas, Mahatma
George III, King
Giancana, Sam
Glenn, John
Godiva, Lady
Goebbels, Paul Joseph
Göring, Hermann
Grace, William Gilbert ("W. G.")
Grappelli, Stéphane
Greenaway, Peter
Gregory XIII, Pope
Gregson, Simon
Habsburgs, The
Hardy, Oliver ("Ollie")
Hardy, Robert
Harriott, Ainsley
Harrison, Rex
Hasselhoff, David
Haydn, Franz Joseph
Hefner, Hugh
Hendrix, Jimi
Henry VIII, King
Hess, Rudolf, Deputy Führer
Hill, Alfred ("Benny")
Hitchcock, Alfred Joseph, Sir
Hitler, Adolf, Führer
Hoch, Ján Ludvík
Hoffman, Dustin
Hollies, The

Hoover, John Edgar ("J. Edgar"), Director
Hugo, Victor
Icke, David
Iglesias, Julio
Intro2
Jellybean
Jesus of Nazareth
Joan of Arc
Jong-il, Kim, Supreme Leader
Judas
Judge Dread
Jung, Carl
Keegan, Kevin
Keegan, Michelle
Keller, Helen
Kendal, Felicity
Kennedy, John Fitzgerald ("Jack," "JFK"), President
Khan, Genghis, Emperor
Kidd, Brian
Koestler, Arthur
Lamb, Charles
Last, James
Laurel, Stan
Lazenby, George
Lenin, Vladimir, Premier
Lincoln, Abraham, President
Lollobrigida, Gina
Loren, Sophia
Louis XVI, King
Love, Geoff
Lupino, Ida
Malden, Karl
Mansfield, Jayne
Manson, Charles
Mantovani, Annunzio Paolo
Marcos, Imelda
Marx, Herbert Manfred ("Zeppo")
Marx, Karl Henirich
Mary, Queen of Scots (a.k.a. Mary Stuart, Mary I)
McClure, Doug
McQueen, Steve
Mendelssohn, Felix
Menuhin, Yehudi
Messalina, Valeria, Empress
Michelangelo
Miller, Arthur
Miller, Glenn
Miranda, Carmen
Monroe, Marilyn
Morse, Samuel
Mother Teresa
Motörhead
Motson, John ("Motty")
Mozart, Wolfgang Amadeus
Muskett, Netta
Mussolini, Benito, First Marshal
Nelson, Horatio, Vice-Admiral
Nero, Emperor
Newton, Isaac, Sir
Newton-John, Olivia
Nielsen, Brigitte
Nitty, Frank ("The Enforcer")
Nixon, Richard Milhous, President
Oates, Lawrence, Captain
Onassis, Jacqueline Lee Kennedy ("Jackie")
Osmond, James Arthur ("Jimmy")
Osmonds, The
Oswald, Lee Harvey
Page, Jimmy
Parker, Charles Jr. ("Charlie," "Yardbird")
Patton, General George S.
Pfeiffer, Michelle
Picasso, Pablo
Pilate, Pontius
Pinter, Harold
Plato
Poitier, Sidney
Pollock, Jackson
Presley, Elvis ("The King")
Pythagoras of Samos
Rasputin, Grigori
Reagan, Ronald Wilson, President
Rice, Anneka
Rich, Bernard ("Buddy")
Richard, Cliff, Sir
Richard III, King
Robeson, Paul
Sartre, Jean-Paul
Savalas, Aristotelis ("Telly")
Schopenhauer, Arthur
Schwarzenegger, Arnold
Scott, Robert Falcon, Captain
Seymour, Jane, OBE
Shakespeare, William
Shapiro, Helen
Shields, Brooke
Sidis, William James
Sinclair, Clive Marles, Sir
Solomon, King
St. Christopher
St. Francis of Assisi
Stallone, Sylvester ("Sly")
Starr, Ringo
Steele, Tommy
Stewart, Alastair ("Al")
Stewart, James ("Jimmy")
T'ai-ch'ang, Emperor
Taylor, Alan John Percivale ("A. J. P.")
Taylor, Elizabeth ("Liz"), Dame
Titchmarsh, Alan
Torquemada, Tomas dé, Grand Inquisitor
Turner, Joseph Mallord William ("J. M. W.")
Turner, Tina
Tutankhamen, Pharaoh ("King Tut")
Twain, Mark
van Gogh, Vincent
Van Lustbader, Eric
Victoria, Queen
Virgil
Vlad the Impaler
von Stauffenberg, Claus, Staff Colonel/ Count
von Trapp, Maria
Wagner, Lindsay
Wayne, John
White, Barry
Wilde, Oscar
Wilson, Reggie
Wisdom, Norman
Wood, Edward ("Ed")
Wouk, Herman

## CHARACTERS: *Red Dwarf* Crewmembers

Ackenback
Ackerman, Warden ("Nicey")
Akimbo, Legs, Doctor
Allender
Allender, Grace, Fourth Engineer

Allender, Paul, Fourth Engineer
Appleford
Barbara
Bartikovsky, Katerina, Science Officer
Black, Jeremy, Mineral Geologist First Class
Bob ("Bent Bob")
Brannigan
Brown, Carole, Executive Officer
Buchan, Science Officer
Burd
Burroughs, Phil
Carling, Patricia
Carmen, Caroline ("Carmen Moans")
Cat
Cat, Brother
Cat, Professor
Chen
Chomsky, Pierre
Daizee
Daley
Denton
Dog
Dooley
DuBois, Henri, Navigation Officer
Ellis, Ben
Farnworth, Russell, Drive Officer
Faulkner
Harris ("Headbanger")
Harrison, Chantel
Hilly
Hollister, Francine, Captain
Hollister, Frank
Hollister, Frank ("Dennis the Doughnut Boy"), Captain
Holly
Holly 6000
Holly, Sister
Joe
Jones, Monica
Kellerman, Alice, Doctor, Flight Technician
Kirk, Captain
Knot, Warden
Kochanski, Christine
Kochanski, Christopher
Kochanski, Kristine
Kochanski, Kristine Z.
Kochanski, Kristine Z. ("Krissie"), First Console Officer
Kochanski, Kristine Z. ("Krissie"), Navigation Officer
Kochanski, Kristopher
Ledbetter
Les, Sister
Lister, David
Lister, David ("Dave"), Third Technician
Lister, David ("Dave"), Third Technician (Senior and Junior)
Lister, David, Brother
Lister, David, First Officer
Lister, Deb
Lovell, Lea
MacWilliams
Martin, Jayne
McClaren, Lucas, Doctor
McGruder, Vaughan
McGruder, Yvonne
McHullock
McIntyre, George, Flight Coordinator
McQueen, Flight Coordinator
Munson, First Officer
Murphy, Catering Officer
Murray, Sam, Deck Sergeant
Newton, Karen, Doctor
Oakley ("Longarm," "Armless")
Palmer
Pemberton, Lewis
Pete
Petersen, Olaf
Petersen, Olaf, Catering Officer
Petrovitch, First Technician
Pixon
Rice
Rimmer, Arlene Judith, Second Technician
Rimmer, Arnold Judas
Rimmer, Arnold Judas ("Squirrel"), Captain
Rimmer, Arnold Judas, Brother
Rimmer, Arnold Judas, Second Technician
Rogerson
Sanchez, Imran, Console Executive
Saunders, Frank
Saxon
Schmidt
Selby
Tau, Louise, Captain
Terry
Thesen, Rick, Deck Sergeant
Thompson, Nicholas, Doctor
Thornton, Angus Lionel, MP
Tim
Todhunter, Frank, First Officer
Tom
Tony
Trevor
Turner
Weiner
Wilkinson

**CHARACTERS:**
***Red Dwarf* Tank Inmates**

Baxter
Big Meat
Birdman
Blenkinsop, Oswald ("Kill Crazy")
Blood Drinker
Bone Cruncher
Brown
Chummy
Hollerbach
Mex
Nigel ("Nige")
Pete
Polesen
Saddo
Simmonds
Steele, Jimbo

**CHARACTERS:**
**Spaceship and Station Personnel and Passengers (Not *Red Dwarf*)**

Air, Jane, Mapping Officer
Armstrong, Nellie
Bellini, Barbra ("Babs")
Bob
Caldicott
Carlton
Cat, Father ("Padre")
Davro
Deki

## CHARACTERS: Miscellaneous

Krazy
Le Clerque, Henri
Lift Hostess
Lindy Lou
Luke
Malaka, Augustus
Markson, Hack
Master, The
Max, Uncle
McBean, Dennis
Mercedes
Mews, Bartholomew
Milty
Misenburger, Harold ("The Condom King")
Mista
Mona
Müller, Hans
Neider-Lewis, Professor
Nigel, Norman
Nimble, Albert
Nixon, John Milhous, President
Olin, Chief
Omrisk, Ned
Osmond, Don
Osmond, Little Jimmy
Ostrog, Gilbert St. John McAdam
Ostrog, Quentin
Pearson, Bill
Penguin, the
Pherson, Mamie
Porkman, Bob, Doctor
Rachel the Fornicator
Rameses XIII
Ramflampanjamram, Patek
Rattler, Zach
Rimmel, Albert
Robbie Rocketpants
Roy
Sabinsky, Bob, Doctor
Salinger, Elaine, President
Samuel the Chicken-Stealer
Sangrida
Saunders, Carole
Schwarzenegger, Arlene
Scofrenia, Sid, Doctor
Shakespeare, Wilma
Simpson, Ernie
Somerfield, Argyle
Sonsonson, Magnus
Sparrow
Stallone, Samatha
Stoppidge, E., Doctor
Sunshine, Sunny
Sutherland, Kev F.
TJ
Tree Apostle Sunshine Bunny Wunny Shrub Fondler
Turner, Anthea
van Herren, Jean Claudette
Voorhese, Klaus
Voorhese, Meinhard, Captain
Voorhese, Wolfgang, Captain
Walker, Mr.
White, Eric
Willoughby
Ynot Suolubaf Eht
Zacharias ("Zack")
Zural, Captain

## CLOTHING, FASHION, GEAR AND UNIFORMS

bio-suit
crash suit
diving suit
jet-powered rocket pants
Marilyn Monroe Anti-Grav Dress
medi-suit
mutant-hunting outfit
nocturnal boxing gloves
No-Grav flying helmet
police woman's helmet
Raketenhosen
Reflec vest
self-lubricating thrustex thong
Smart Shoes
'soft' clothes
suspenders
thermo-foil parka
total-immersion suit
toupée
vac suit
wet-look knitwear

## CLUBS, SPORTS TEAMS AND OTHER GROUPS

Agoraphobic Society
*Androids* Appreciation Society (AAS)
Anti-Smoking League
Arnie Rimmer's Death Machine
'A' Section
A-Shift
Berlin Bandits
Birmingham Mini Coopers
Bootle Players
'B' Section
Callisto-Ganymede Ring Arc Appreciation Society
Campaign for the Restoration of Altrincham's Platform (CRAP)
Canaries, The
Chronic Catarrh Sufferers
Committee for the Liberation and Integration of Terrifying Organisms and Their Rehabilitation Into Society (CLITORIS), The
Cons
Corn Circle Society
Deformed Dozen, the
Eastbourne Zimmer frame relay team
Fatal Sisters, The
Freemasons
Fuse Brothers, The
Ganymedian Mafia
Group IV
Guards
Hammond Organ Owners' Society
Hell's Angels Motorcycle Club (HAMC), The
Infinity Patrol
Io Amateur Wargamers
Ionian Ecommandoes
John Wayne Fan Club
Junior Birdmen of America (JBA)
Ku Klux Klan (KKK)
League Against Salivating Monsters, The
Liberty League, The
London Jet Juniors
London Jets
Love Celibacy Society
National Bazookoid Association

Nic Farey Fan Club
Osmond Family, the
Paris Stompers
Queens Park Rangers (QPR)
Recreators of the Battle of Neasden Society
Rimmettes
Routine Maintenance, Cleaning and Sanitation Unit
Saturn Bears
Schneiberhauser Owners' Society
Secret Seven, The
Smegchester Rovers
Space Masons
Space Scouts
Super-Premier-Holosatellite-League
Team Simulant
Train Spotters Anonymous
Valkyrie Sex-Slave Liberation Movement
Waste Disposal
Wilbur Weasel Fan Club
Z-Shift

## CONFLICTS, WARS AND MILITARY FORCES

Armée du Nord
Battle of Trafalgar
Belagosian War, the
Blisters
Cat Wars, The
Clisterists
Cloisterists
Clone Riots of 2061
Cola Wars, The
Elite, the
Fundamental Remonian
GELF War
GELF War, The
GELF-hunters
Holy Wars
Hundred Years' War, The
Junior Birdmen
"Last Post," The
Raketenhosen-Männer
Resistance, the
Revolutionary Working Front
Saturn War, the
Space Marines
Star Fleet
Thirty Years' War
Tie Wars, the
Ties
Wax War, The
World War I
World War II

## EDUCATION, COURSES, INSTITUTIONS, SCHOOLS AND UNIVERSITIES

Academy, the
Advanced Mental Engineering
Art College
BAFTA (British Academy of Film and Television Arts)
Cadet College
Caltech (California Institute of Technology)
Cyberschool
*Cyber School*
"Dealing With Nutters"
European Space Academy
field microsurgery
GanPrep
Institute of Simulant Technology
Io House
Io Polytechnic
Io Seminary
Junior A
Junior B
Junior C
Junior D
Jupiter Mining Corporation Engineering Programme
Jupiter Mining Corporation Robotics Programme
kitty school
lavatorial sciences
*Learn Esperanto While You Sleep*
*Learn Japanese*
*Learn Quantum Theory While You Sleep*
McClaren School
Mecha College
Mechanical Engineering
P22
robotics
Saturn Tech
Toilet University

## ENTERTAINMENT: Artificial Reality, Video Games and Other Simulations

*100 Light Years of Solitude*
Amateur Programmer Suite
*Amazon Women on Heat*
AR machine
AR simulation
Artificial Reality Suite (ARS)
*Barber of Seville AR*
*Bazookoid Blaster*
*Better Than Life*
*Camelot*
chastitycheat
*Curryworld*
*Cyber Park*
*Cyber School*
*Firing Squad A Go-Go*
GameStation
*Gore-mageddon*
*Government Informant Pro*
*Great Moments in Human History*
*Gumshoe*
Guns 'n' Tanks
*Hayze*
*Holiday in Europe*
*Hologram of Dorian Grey, The*
*Italian Driver*
*Jane Austen World*
*Jane Austin World*
*Jousting*
Machine 16
*Medieval Bloodsport*
*Medieval Smackdown IV*
"Munchkin Song, The"
*No Brains, All Brawn Sports Heroes Series*
*Parallaxis: Defenders of the Galaxy*
*Planet of the Nymphomaniacs*
*Pride and Prejudice Land*
*Push the Button*
Real Virtual Reality
*Really Freakin' Dangerous Crime Series*
*Red Dwarf*

**ENTERTAINMENT: Art, Music and Theater**

## ENTERTAINMENT: Attractions, Conventions and Theme Parks



## ENTERTAINMENT: Sports, Games and Recreation

**EVENTS, HOLIDAYS AND TRADITIONS (NON-RELIGIOUS)**

## FOOD AND BEVERAGES

1799 Château d'Yquem
advocaat
After Eight
Alphabetti Spaghetti
Android homebrew
asses' milk
asteroidal lichen stew
baby seal hearts stuffed with dove pâté
bacon sandwich with French mustard and black coffee
Baked Alannah
baked beans
banana and crisps sandwich
banana bomb
barium hydrochlorate salad nicoise
beer milkshake
Beinz Baked Beans
Beinz Salad Cream
beluga caviar
Bert Bourgignon
Billy con Carne
Birds Eye
black coffee
blackcurrant cordial
blancmange
blueberry muffin
Boddy's beer
Bovril
Breadman's Fish Fingers
Buck's Fizz
caviar niblet
caviar vindaloo
chicken chasseur
chicken Marengo
chicken soup
chicken vindaloo
chili sauce
chilled vindaloo sauce
chilli powder
Choccie Nut Bar
Cinzano Bianco
Clearhead
Coca-Cola
Cock-A-Doodle Flakes
cod vindaloo
cow vindaloo
cow's milk
Crispy Bar
Crunchie
Cup O' Noodle
curry
dandelion sorbet
Dave Lister Special, The
dehydrated champagne
dodo paté
dog food
dog's milk
dolphin sweetmeats
Dom Pérignon
doughnut
duck's feet in abalone sauce
Edam
eggnog
endangered panda stew
fish
Five-alarm Bengal Chili
fungo-beer
fun-sized candy bar
gazpacho soup
GELF hooch
Glen Fujiyama
Glen Tokyo Whisky
goat vindaloo
helium 3 isotopes de la maison
homogenized pudding
hot lager with croutons
Industrial baked beans
inky squid soup
irradiated caviar niblets
irradiated haggis
Jammie Dodger
Jim Daniels
JMC peach slices
JMC self-raising flour
K.K. Ice Cream
king prawn biryani
Kinitawowi moonshine
kipper
kippers vindaloo
Krispee Krunchies
Krispies
Leopard Lager
Liquorice Allsorts
lobster
Lobster á la Grecque
marijuana gin
Mega Fizz
Mickey Finn
milk shake
Mimian bladderfish
Mimian sangria
Mimosian banquet
Mimosian telekinetic wine
Mint Elegance
mint-choc ice cream
Moët & Chandon
mushy peas
Newcastle Brown Ale
noodle burger
Nuttyfruit bar
orange ice pops
Original Gravity 1042°
oysters
Peach Surprise
Peperami
Perrier
Petersen's Persuasive
ploughman
poppadom
Pot Noodle
Pot O' Sick
prawn vindaloo
quiche
radioactive fruit salad
rats' ears pan-fried in garlic
raw liver and banana pizza
Ready Brek
reconstituted sausage patty
Red Planet Power Drinks
rehydratable chicken
roast suckling elephant
roast suckling pig stuffed with chestnuts and truffles
San Francisco Earthquake
Sancerre
Sausage and onion gravy sandwich on white bread
scrumpy
sevruga caviar
shami kebab diabolo
Skol
Skug
soya sandwich
space nettle soup
Space Weevil au Mechanoid

Spaghetti Hoops
Spam
sprout lasagna
sprouts
Steak and Sidney Pie
Sugar Puff sandwiches
Sump
Tabasco sauce
tangerine sponge cake
Tastee Noodle Pot
toastie soldiers
Toastie Toppers
Topic Bar
Total Gonzo
triple fried egg butty with chili sauce and chutney
trout á la crème
urine recyc
Vimto
Wheaty Flakes
whiskey

**GOVERNMENT: Agencies, Departments, Empires, Organizations and Programs**

70773
Alterna-void
Blerion High Council
Buckingham Palace
CGI
Cybernautics Division
Dallas Police Department
Department of Death and Deceaseds' Rights
Dishwasher Star Empire
Dodecahedron
Enhanced Evolution Project (EEP)
European Space Consortium (ESC)
Group 4
Inter-Planetary Commission for Waste Disposal
Jovian Authority
Lottery House
Mechanoid Empire, the
Mimas Atmosphere Authority
Mimas Board of Trade—Lethal Substances Division
Mimas Council
Ministry of Alteration
Ministry of Ethnic Purity
National Aeronautics and Space Administration (NASA)
North Western Electricity Board (Norweb)
Norweb Federation
NYNYPD
Outland Revenue
Oxfam
Project *Wildfire*
Projekt: Hosen
Reco-Programme
Reich, the
Simulant Confederation, The
Soviet Space Corps
Space Corps
Space Corps Bureau of Paper Clip Standardization and Enforcement
Space Corps Special Service
Space Corps Super Chimps
Space Corps Super-Infinity Fleet
Space Federation
Space Ministry
Star Corps
Triton Immigration Control
United Republic of Engineered Life Forms
United Republic of GELF States
Universal Government
Valhalla Project Office
Vindaloovian Empire
World Council, the

**GOVERNMENT: Agreements, Laws, Legal Terms and Treaties**

876.3/16
Act 21
All Nations Agreement
Article 39436175880932/B
Article 39436175880932/C
breach of Xzeeertuiy
fourth sand of D'Aquaarar
GBH
Geneva Conventions, The
great fire of N'mjiuyhyes
Hologram Protection Akt 2143, The
Hologram Rights 2141, The
Human Rights Akt
Interplanetary Salvage Code
Jhjghjiuyhu system
Jury of Six, the
Last Rights Act 2142, The
*Mbazvmbbcxyy vs. Mbazvmbbcxyy*
Mystic System of Justice
seventh branch of O'pphjytere
Space Corps Directives
Space Pollution Act
Spaceway Code
Treaty 5
Who Gives A Monkey's? Akt of 2032
Wipe Humans Out All-Over! (WHOA!)
Wipe Out Everyone! (WOE!)
Xion Treaty, the
Zalgon impeachment of Kjielomnon

**GOVERNMENT: Currency**

Brefewinan
dollarpound ($£)
Gatoo
mushy peas
pennycent
quidbuck

**GOVERNMENT: Dialects, Languages, Ethnicities, Nationalities and Castes**

Amish
Bindi
Churrman
Esperanto
Grunti
Plutonian
Tarka

**GOVERNMENT: Titles, Positions and Designations**

2960B8651
3263827-K
3379
badge of merchantship
Bindi

Cyberian flight controller
Emo-smuggler
Feldwabel
Great One, The
Grunti
Head of Records
Head of Safety
Health and Safety Executive
His Most Excellent Majesty
mystic
Potent
prison officer ident
Rear Admiral Lieutenant General
Regulator, The
Shore Patrol
Tarka

## INSULTS AND NICKNAMES

Ace
Acehole
Alan
Alphabet-Head
Ange
Ape Brain
Arn
Arnie
Arsewipe
Axe Man, the
Babes
baboon four-eyes
Bad Ass
Big Arn
Big Boss
Big Man
Bimbo-Brain
Bird-Tray Head
Block Head
Bog-bot From Hell
Bonehead
Bonehead Man
Bot-brain
Boys from the *Dwarf*
Bozo Brothers, the
Broomtown
Buckteeth
Bud
Buddy
Bud-You-Ain't
Bug-head
Bun-bun
Bungo
Butter-Pat Head
Buttsuck
Cap
Captain A. J. Rimmer, Space Adventurer
Captain Bog-Bot
Captain Chloroform
Captain Emerald
Captain Laser
Captain Paxo
Captain Rot-mind
Captain Sadness
Captain Smug Git
Captain Yawn
Cheese
Chief
Colin Charisma
Colonel Cat Commando
Commander Slut
Commander U-Bend
Cupcake
Curryographer
Custer, Derek
deadies
Dennis the Doughnut Boy
Despicable One, The
Dingleberry-brain
Dingleberry-breath
Dinosaur Breath
Disciples of Death, The
Diva, the
Doctor Fruit-Loop
Doctor Smorgasbord
Dog-Breath
Dog-food Face
Doodoo-Breath
Dormouse-Cheeks
Droid Boy
Dude, the
Duke of Deliciousness, the
Duke of Dork, the
Duke, The
egg
Ekaj Tellub
El Dirtball
Elephant Man, the
El Skutto
El Slotho
El Weirdo
Eraserhead
Face
Fat Boy
Fatboy
Fido
First Time on the Clay-Wheel Head
Fishbreath
Flash
Flat-Headed One, the
Flibster
Four Musketeers, The
Freak-Face
Fried Four, The
Frisbee Nostrils
Frog Prince, The
Fuzzbox Head
Gangrene Goddess, the
General A. J. Smegger
Gerbil-Face
gimboid
git
Goalpost-Head
goit
Grand Canyon Nostrils
Granny Killer
Grease Stain
Groin-Breath
Groinhead
Gummy
Hadron-head
Half-eaten-lollipop-head
Halibut-breath
Head
Hellfish, Johnny
Heteroboy
Hidiot
Himself
Hooch-Head
Horace
Howdy Doody
Howster
Humie
Humo
Jello-Head
Jenny
Junior

Junior Junior
K.K.
Karen
Keyboard Teeth
Khazi Droid
Killer
King
King of Crap
King of the Cockroaches
Kingo
Kit
Kremlin Kate
Krissie
Kristen
Kryty
Kublouski
Lassie
Launchpad
Laundry-Chute Nostrils
Listy
livies
mad goth bastard
Marshmallow Ass
McQuack, Launchpad
Meat-Tenderizer-Head
Metal Head
Metal Munchkin
Miss K
Miss Yo-Yo Knickers
Molecule Mind
Monkey
Monkey Boy
Mr. Ace
Mr. Arnold
Mr. Beautiful
Mr. C
Mr. Cushy
Mr. D
Mr. David
Mr. Fat Bastard 2044
Mr. Fried Egg Chili Chutney Sandwich Face
Mr. Galahad
Mr. Gazpacho
Mr. Magnificent
Mr. Mallet
Mr. Maturity
Mr. Pretend-Cat
Mr. Sad Git
Mr. Selfish
Mr. Shouty
Mr. Skywalker
Mr. Smoothie
Mr. Sucks
Mr. Swankypants
Mr. Wonderful
Nickel-Hydrate Breath
Nightingdroid, Florence
Nightmare Norman
Non-Bud
Noreen
Norman
Novelty-Condom-Head
Nwaki
Officer BB
Officer Bud-Babe
Officer Smegski
Old Five-fingers
Old Iron Balls
Old Iron-butt
one-armed man, the
Perky
Pinky
Piston Pelvis
Plastic Percy
Polaroid Head
Polyester Brothers, the
pregnant baboon-bellied space beatnik
Prince
Prince of Charisma
Prince of Dorkness, the
Princess Leia
Priscilla, Queen of Deep Space
Private Nobody
Professor E
Pussycat Willum
Quark Brain
Queen of Panic
Rainfall-girl
Rectum-faced Pygmy
Rimére
Rimmsie
Rumour, Mr.
Shakespeare, Wilfred
Shambles
Shirley
silly old trout
Skipper
Smallbrain 3
Smeg-for-Brains
smegger
smeghead
smeg-pot
smegwad
smegwit
Son-of-a-Goit
Son-of-a-Prostidroid
Spanners
Squirrel
Stabhim
Stan and Ollie
Sucks, Reality
Suicide Squid
Super-Ass
Surf Boy
Susan
Sweatpea
Teasy-Weasy
Three Musketeers, the
Thumbnail-Head
Tiger
Tin-Brain
Titan
Toilet-brush Hair
Trans Am Wheel Arch Nostrils
Uncle Tomcat
Vinegar Drawers
white-hatted ponce
Wibbley, Wayne
Wig-Stand-Head
Winklepicker Teeth
Your Flared-Nostrilness
Your Holiness
Your Magnificence
Zorro City

**KRYTEN AND OTHER MECHANICALS: Afflictions, Viruses and Malfunctions**

Apocalypse virus
Armageddon virus
computer senility
droid rot
electronic aneurysm
failed antidote crash of '33

flesh-eating-virus crash of '32
Har Megiddo 46758976/Kry
Hokey Cokey
I Never Really Loved You Anyway
mad droid disease
Oblivion virus
silicon rickets
space-crazy
Splurdge
synthi-shock
terminal software bug

**KRYTEN AND OTHER MECHANICALS: Components, Software, Systems and Technologies**

15F-stop cornea
4X2C
579
Additional 001
affection
aggression mode
ambivalence
anger
anxiety chip
anxiety mode
Archie
arrogance
artificial intelligence system
audio receiver
aural system
auto-destruct
automatic lubricant purge system
Auto-Repair
Bachelor of Sanitation
background music circuits
backwards mode
behavior protocols
blunt mode
boot-up sequence
buoyancy tanks
CCD 419.2
CCD 517.3
Cerise
cheekiness
chest monitor
Code 0089/2
compatibility factor
comprehension unit
connoisseur chip
conversation mode
core program
CPU
CPU bank
CPU ident
damage-control report
Data Doctor
deadpan mode
defense mode
defensive micropedo
directional fins
Diva-Droid 22PT drill hand accessory
Diva-Droid service guarantee
Diva-Droid signature
Dove Program
effluence evacuation pipe
endoskeleton
Enigma decoding system
envy
erotic mode (fiction)
fear
Fear Mode
Fight or Flight Responsive Subsystem
go-faster stripes
good-taste chip
groinal box
groinal socket
groinal socket ashtray attachment
guilt
guilt chip
happiness
happiness mode
heat outlet
Heliotrope
histo-chip
HP11
humor
hypnotherapy disc
innocent whistle mode
insecurity
intelligence circuits
Ivan Azymuth's Laws of Robotics
J055
J056
joy
K177
K178
Khaki
lavatorial sciences
leg-it mode
lie mode
Lifton Separate Hydraulics
limitation chip
love
machine ident
Magenta
Marigold
Mauve
mechanoid optical broadcast feature
monologue chip
mortality chip
MyVac
Nanny-Bot childcare software bundle
nanosensor
neck diodes
negadrive
Nega-Drive download station
neural circuits
nipple nuts
olfactory system
onboard lexicon
optic tract
optical system
optical tanks
panic chip
panic circuits
panic-like-a-headless-chicken mode
patience circuits
personal black box
petulance
possessiveness
primer
projection circuits
propulsion unit
Q47 twin frontal mounts
RAM (random access memory)
rear exhaust port
rear groinal unit
recharging socket
rehydration unit
reproductive circuitry
sadness
salivators
sanity chip
scramble card
self-image redirection technology

self-repair system
self-repair unit
sensitivity alert
sentiment disc
Serenity
Shakespeare chip
shame mode
shame overload
shutdown chip
shutdown disc
Silicon Heaven belief chip
skull release catch
smirk mode
smug mode
snigger mode
snobbery
Spare Hand One
Spare Head One
Spare Head Three
Spare Head Two
speed count mode
splitter code
stare mode
stereo audial sensors
surprise
swagger mode
Talkie Toaster Extras Pack
Talkie Toilet Extras Pack
Tangerine
Taupe
time alarm
ToastSet technology
Toilet University
translation mode
transponder calibrations
uncrop
Unspeakably Brown
verbal systems
visual interpretation system
visual system
vitals cable
vocabulary unit
voice unit

## KRYTEN AND OTHER MECHANICALS: Models and Types

2Q4B
2X4C
3000 Series
3Y5D
4000 Series
4000 Series GTi
6000 Series
9H7M
Aboriginoid
agonoid
android sheep
Barbie
berserker general
blo-bot
Bouncer MK-IV
boy-droid
Build-It-Yourself Marilyn Monroe Droid
Butler Droid
coffee machine
CX-114 Speaking Slide Rule
cyberzoid
cyborg
Datacorp Model 'H'
droid
escort boots
femmedroid
handroid
IcthyTech 3000 Robot Goldfish
Jeanette
jukebot
Mandy
Martian Tourister robot luggage
mechanoid
Mechanoid "Taranshula" Remote Drone
mechbian
medidroid
Munchkin robot
nanobot
Para-mech
*pisciform automata*
plasti-droid
prostidroid
Rimmer munchkin
robohobo
robot referee
rogue droid
Series 1000
Series 2000
Series 3000
Series 4000
Series 4010
Series 500
Series 5000
Series III
service droid
service robot
simulant
skutter
Talkie Cutlery
Talkie Microwave
Talkie Sew 'N Sew
Talkie Toaster
Talkie Toaster Commemorative Edition
Talkie Toilet
Tina
Titanica Fish Droid MkIV
Utility Remote Mark One (U.R.1)
waxdroid

## LOCATIONS: Asteroids, Moons, Planets, Stars and Other Celestial Bodies

Adelphi 12
AJR1
AJR2
Alshain IV
Altair
Altair 9
Argon 5
Ariel 2
Arranguu 12
Asteroid of Turin
Bearth
Betelgeuse
Blerios 15
Callisto
Chakos XII
Cyrius 3
Delphi VIII
Delta 7
Dione

Earth
Echech 3
Elara
Europa
Fuchal
Ganymede
Garbage World
GELFWorld
Hyperion
Io
Juno
Jupiter
Lotomi 5
LV246
Mars
Mercury
Metabilis 3
Mimas
Miranda
Moon, The
Neptune
New Earth
N'mtheglyar
Orion
Phobos
Phoebe
Planet of the Nymphomaniacs
Planet of the Snooty Sex Sirens
Planet Razor Blade
Planet Spud
Pluto
Promised Planet, The
RD128
Rhea
Rigel 5
Rimmerworld
Saturn
Sharmut 2
Sigma 14D
SVC01
SVC02
Tethys
Theta 4
Titan
Traga 16
Tregar IV
Triton
Uranus
Uranus II
Venus
Vindaloovia
War World
Waxworld

## LOCATIONS: Buildings, Facilities, Rooms, Stations and Other Structures

008
7th Death Ring of Rhaagbthammar
All-Droid Space Station
Body Reclamation Unit
Bradbury Botanical Research Station
Buckingham Palace
Caligari's Home for the Terminally Bewildered
Castle Despondency
Cell 41
clearance zone
Condom Fitting Room
Cyberia
cyberpark
derelict research platform
E Wing
Erroneous Reasoning Research Academy (ERRA)
Europa Test Centre
Forum of Justice
Gate 14
Gate 5
Gate 9
GELF icon
Grand Hall
Halfords Memorial Ward
Hangar 101
Heathrow Lister
High Tower, The
Honeymoon Suite
Hoover Open Prison
Idlewild Airport
JMC building
John, Paul, George and Ringway
Justice World
Justice Zone
KICASS Tower
King's Crossing Station
livery
Lumpton Street bus depot
Mimas Central Shuttle Station
Mimas Docks
Mimas Spaceport
Moose Base Alpha
neutral area
Old Course at St. Andrews
Olympus Mons' terraforming reactors
Parking Level 2
Phobos Interplanetary Spaceport
Phobos Shipyard
pyramids
recuperation lounge
Rimmer Building (London)
Rimmer Building (New York)
Rimmer Building (Paris)
Rimmer International Airport (AJR)
security containment cell
Security Operations Room
Sex Room
Snot Street Station
Space Corps Test Base
Sphinx, The
St. Androids Hospital
St. John's Precinct
Stamford Bridge
stargate
Starlight Ballroom, the
Superdome
Temple of Food
Texas School Book Depository
Time Store
Titan Docking Port
Transfer Suite
Trans-Siberian Express
UN high security prison complex
Viral Research Department
Wailing Wall
Warsaw Central
Watergate
Xanadu

## LOCATIONS: Cities, Countries, States and Other Geographical Areas

Acapulco
Alaska
Albion
Algarve, the

Angel Islington, The
Bangkok
Bedford Falls
Bermuda Triangle, The
Binary Hills 90210
Bolanski
Bradbury Colony
Bulgaria
Burma
Chasm of Hopelessness
Deganwy
Denmark
Detroit
Dirtville
Dorksville
Eastbourne
Eiger, the
England
Existence, Arizona
Fiji
Florida
Forbidden Lands, the
Gorbals, The
Grimsby
Helsinki
Hilo, Hawaii
Hu⊠
India
Irkutsk
Isle of Man
Islington
Kīlauea
Lake Michigan
Leeds
Liverpool
London
Lunar City 7
Luxembourg
Macedonia
madras river
Manhattan
Marne Valley
Mauritius
Montmartre
Mooli desert
Moscow
Mount Rushmore
Mount Sinai
New Athens
New Mexico
New Tokyo
Niagara Falls
Nodnol
Oslo
Perth
Purley
River Mersey
Sea of Tranquility
Seni Rotundi
Shag Town
Sidcup
Smegopolis
South London
Southport
Stetworth Heath
Styx
Swamp of Despair
Swamp of Waste
Swindon
Taiwan
terraces of Valles
Tunbridge Wells
Union of Soviet Socialist Republics (USSR)
United Republic of Lesser Britain
Valhalla Impact Structure
Valles Marineris
Venezuela
Wolverhampton
Wood of Humiliation
Zanzibar

**LOCATIONS: Galaxies, Quadrants, Zones and Other Areas of Space**

2-5-2-3-1-1
4-9-5, 3-7-2
5341 by 6163
Aldebaran Nebula
Andromeda Galaxy
GELF Zone
Mogidon Cluster
Outland Territories
Quadrant 2 to Q41/9
Quadrant 2, Vector 4
Quadrant 4, Sector 492
Quadrant 492/G87
Quadrant 497
Quadrant 4972
Sector 12
Sector 492
space mirage zone
Theta Sector
Zeta-Jones Quadrant
Zsigsmos Sector

**LOCATIONS: Streets, Roadways and Addresses**

10 Downing Street
12th Street
152nd
220 Sycamore
227 Thatcher Throughway, Flat C
24 Argyle Street, Somewhereville, TW17 0QD
3rd
69th
Apartment 43, Hotel Paradiso
Balham High Street
Central
Champs Elysées
Copulation
David Ross Block
Diarrhea Drive
Eastern Avenue
Euston Road
Karmasutra
Lichtenstrasse
Miller Street
Nundah Street
Old Kent Road
Oxford Street
Path of Decency
Pentonville Road
Point Street
Regent Street
Rom-Ramsey Street
Teerts Gnilpik
Voter-General Avenue
W 84 Ave.
Whitechapel Road

## LOCATIONS: Universes and Dimensions

Alternative 2X13/L
Alternative 6829/B
Dimension 165
Dimension 24
Fifth Dimension, the
hyperway
mirror universe
multiverse
Omni-zone
reality barrier
Second Universe
Tenth Dimension, the

## MEDIA: Books, Magazines, Newspapers and Other Publications

8327
1 Corinthians 13
*1,001 Fabulous Chat-up Lines*
*A to Z of Mimas*
*A to Z of Red Dwarf*
*A.I. Today*
*Action*
*Action Hard, Battle-Trained, Big Boy Monthly*
*Actual Reality Cheats and Tricks*
*Aeneid*, the
*Alien Monthly*
*Alien Wives*
*All Time Greatest Astrological Explorers*
*Angling Times*
*Antiques*
*Arnold Rimmer—Lust For Glory*
*Arnold Rimmer's Tactical Guide to Warfare*
*Astro Navigation for Idiots*
*Astronavigation and Invisible Number Theory Made Simple*
*Astronavigation and Invisible Numbers in Engineering Structure Made Simple*
*A-Z*
Bible, The
*Big Boy's Book of Cloning*
*Big Boys in Boots*
*Big Iron at Sun-up*
*Big 'n' Bouncy*
*Biggles' Big Adventure*
*Biggles Flies West*
*Biggles Learns to Fly*
*Boys from the Dwarf*
*Brief History of Time, A*
*British Journal of Demented Delusions*
*Callahan's Index of Twentieth Century Telegraph Poles*
*Camera Monthly*
Cat Bible, The
*Cat Dictionary*
*Charlie Zero Potato*
"Circuit-boards of Passion"
*Classic Car Monthly*
"Classic Wines of Estonia"
*Combat and Survival*
*Complete Works of Shakespeare, The*
*Conceptual Foundations of Quantum Mechanics Made Simple*
*Control in Catering*
*Cooking with Chillies*
*Cred Dwarf Yearbook*
*Daily Asteroid, The*
*Daily Smeg, The*
*Dallas Morning News, The*
*Dan Dare*
*Demon Lurks, A*
*Divadroid Magazine*
*Doctor, Darling*
*Dr. Aardvark's Junior Medical Encyclopedia*
Ecclesiastes
*Edda*
Electronic Bible, The
*Eye, The*
*Famous Five, The*
*Fascist Dictator Monthly*
*Field of Broken Dreams, A*
*Film Fun*
"Flemish Weaving the Traditional Way"
*Football: It's a Funny Old Game*
*Freud on Humour*
*General George and the Gook Invasion*
*Genetic Cloning Manual*
*Good Psycho Guide*
*Good Schools Guide*
*Gore*
*Hamilton Academicals—The Glory Years*
"Have You Got a Good Memory?"
*Heisenberg's Uncertainty Principle for Beginners*
*Hello!*
*Hologram of Dorian Grey, The*
Holy Book, The
*Home Surgery*
*How to Be a Winner—An Introduction to Powermatics*
*How to Defeat an Army of Mutant Russians Whilst Still Finding Time to Be the World's Greatest Golfer*
*How to Get More Girls By Hypnosis*
*How to Get Your Life Together*
*How to Overcome Your Fear of Speaking in Public*
*How to Pick Up Girls By Hypnosis*
*Hudzen 10 Series 4010 Mechanoid Instruction Manual*
*I Did It the Reicht Way*
*I'm OK!*
*Innuendo Man*
*Introduction to the Liar Paradox and the Non-Mechanizability of Mathematics, An*
*Investor's Chronicle*
"Jill and the Beanstalk"
*JMC Traveller*
*Junior Colour Encyclopedia of Space, The*
*Kama Sutra*
*Kama Sutra II: The Lost Positions*
*Kill Your Way Slim*
*Kryten Series III Mechanoid Owners Manual*
*Lady Chatterley's Lover*
*Ladybird Book of Astronavigation*
*Learn Japanese*
*Life*
*Lion*
*Loin*
*Lolita*
*Male Eunuch, The*
*Maplins Hardware Catalogue*
*Marilyn*
*Meeting a Drunken Artist*

*Megastar Daily*
*Mend and Rend Magazine*
*Metaphysica*
*Michelin Guide to Penal Hellholes*
*Minger Monthly*
*Morris Dancing Monthly*
*Most Influential Humans, The*
*Muscle Woman*
*My Diary*
*My Incredible Career*
*National Enquirer, The*
"Nerdism—A Study"
*News Chronicle*
*Newsweek*
*Nowt on Telly*
"Pants Down Over Poland!"
Plate VXII
*Play With Ben*
*Playboy*
*Playgelf*
*Playzombie*
*Pop-Up Book of Probeships, The*
*Pop-Up Kama Sutra—Zero Gravity Edition, The*
*Pumping Iron Today*
*Reader's Digest*
*Red Dwarf Log No. 1996*
*Red Dwarf—A Complete Guide to the Popular TIV Game*
*Relaxation: A Beginner's Guide*
*Ripley's Believe It Or Not*
*Robbie Rocket Pants*
*Robert Hardy Reads Tess of the d'Urbervilles*
*Robinson Crusoe*
*Roots of Coincidence, The*
Sacred Writing, the
"Salt—An Epicure's Delight"
*Science and Health With Key to the Scriptures*
*Sense and Sensibility*
*SFX*
*Showing Compassion to Inmates*
*Smeg, The*
*Sometimes You Have to Learn How to Lose Before You're Ready to Win*
*Space Corp Book of Military Strategy*
*Space Corps Directive Manual*
*Space Corps Survival Manual*
*Space Corps Vocational Center Handbook*
*Space Monkeys Official Handbook*
*Spacers Catalog and Bargain Basement Yearly! (SCABBY)*
*Spirit, The*
*Sport Galaxy*
*Spud Only*
*Star Corps Commando Big Book of Brutality, The*
*Star Corps Personnel Manual*
*Star Corps Survival Manual II—This Time It's Personal, The*
*Starstruck*
*Strange Science*
*Stupid But True! Volume 3*
*Survivalist*
*Suspects Followed 8th August*
*Table Golf Instruction Manual*
*Tedium Magazine*
"Ten Things You Didn't Know About Gonad Electrocution Kits"
*Terraforming Made Easy*
*Tess of the D'Urbervilles: A Pure Woman Faithfully Presented*
*Time*
*Times, The*
*Traffic Movements 20th July*
*Treasure Island*
*True Life Criminal Crime Stories*
*Up Up & Away!*
*Vanity Fair*
*Vodka Cola*
*Vogue*
*Wacked Out People's Book of Crazy Things to Do, The*
*War and Peace*
*War World Weekly*
*What Bike?*
*What Carcass?*
*What Transport?*
*Whopping Bazookas Monthly*
*Who's Nobody*
*Who's Who*
*Winchester Park*
*yadretseY*
*Young, Bad, and Dangerous to Know*
*Your Guide to Skiing Holidays*
*Your Own Death and How to Cope With It*
*Zero G*
*Zero Gee Football*
*Zero Gee Football—It's a Funny Old Game*

**MEDIA:**
**Film, Television and Video**

36,186
*10%ers, The*
*20,000,000 Watts My Line*
*After Death Do Us Part*
*Alien vs. Mary Poppins—The Bitch Is Back*
*Aliens*
*Androids*
*Androids Nights*
*Androids—The Movie III*
*Androids—The Movie IV*
*Arnold J Rimmer—A Tribute*
*Astro-Navigation and Invisible Numbers in Engineering Structure Made Simple*
*Attack of the Giant Savage Completely Invisible Aliens*
*Attack of the Killer Gooseberries*
*Babes in Space*
*Back to Earth*
*Backwards Opportunity Knock*
*Baked Bean Bombshells Volume 12*
*Batman 2*
*BBC Children in Need*
*Being Single Minded*
*Beverly Hills Bereavement Counsellor*
*Beyond the Valley of the Cheerleaders XXVII—This Time It's Personal*
*Blade Runner*
*Blob, The*
*Both Feet in the Grave*
*Butch Accountant and the Yuppie Kid*
*Canary Squad*
*Can't Cook, Won't Cook*
CARMMLT475
*Casablanca*
*Celebrity Chainsaw Ice-Sculpting Challenge*
Channel 2

Channel 72
*Charles Manson, the Early Years*
*Chicken Soup Machine Operative and a Gentleman, A*
*Chitty-Chitty Bang-Bang*
*Citizen Kane*
*Classic Androids*
*Come Jiving*
*Complete History of English Cricket, A*
*Coronation Street*
*Cosmoswide*
*Countdown*
*Current Affairs Programme, The*
*Dambusters, The*
*Darkness at Noon*
Dave
*Dave and Arn's Spacious Adventure*
*D-D-Don't Shoot*
*Decayed Flesh 5: The Zombies Take Manhattan*
*Del Monte*
*Dichotomy of Faith in a Post Materialistic Society, The*
*Die Screaming With Sharp Things in Your Head*
*Dirty Dozen*
*Doctor Who*
*Duel*
DVD
*Easy Rider*
*Flintstones, The*
*Four Funerals and Another One*
*Friday the 13th Part 1,649*
*Fugitive, The*
Geek Week
*GELFs Win Prizes*
*George of the Jungle*
*Go for the Burn!*
*God, I Love This War*
*Going for Chrome*
*Gone with the Wind*
*Good Morning Holograms*
*Great Railway Journeys of the World*
Groovy Channel 27
*Henry VIII*
*How Clean Is Your Cell?*
*I Jog Therefore I Am*
*Ishtar*
*It's a Wonderful Life*
*Jaws*
*King of Kings*
*Kookie Kola Bear News*
Krytie TV
*Lady With a Face, The*
*Life Styles of the Disgustingly Rich and Famous*
*Listers, The*
*Lunar Gonorrhea and You*
*Married With Robots*
*Marry Me My Darling*
*Mechanoids' Strip*
*Memento*
*Most Pathetic Dreams of Arnold Rimmer, Volume 1, The*
MTV
*Necrobics: Hologrammatic exercises for the dead*
*Neighbours*
*Now, Voyager*
*Oops, That's Groovy Channel 27 News!*
*Planet of the Apes*
*Press Gang*
*Ready Steady Stab*
*Rebel Without a Cause*
*Red Dwarf*
*Regional News*
*Revenge of the Mutant Splat Gore Monster*
*Revenge of the Surfboarding Killer Bikini Vampire Girls*
*Run for Your Wife*
Savalas TV
Ship's Log 1
*Simulants*
*Slightly More Complex Astro-Navigation and Invisible Numbers in Engineering Structure*
*Sons of Katie Elder, The*
*Space Cop Police Squad*
*St. Elsewhere*
*Star Trek*
*Starsky and Hutch*
*Student Prince, The*
*Tales of the Riverbank: The Next Generation*
*Tales of the Unexpected*
*Terminator, The*
test card
*That's My Chromosome*
*This City? What City?!*
*Titanic*
Tri-D Newsnet
*Vampire Bikini Girls Suck Paris*
*Victory South*
*Voterwatch Update*
*Wallpapering, Painting and Stippling—A DIY Guide*
*Watchdog: Shuttlecraft Special*
*West Side Story*
*What's My Fruit?*
*Whoops Vicar, There Goes My Groinal Socket*
*Whose Diode Is It Anyway?*
*Wild One, The*
*Willy Waffles*
*Wogan*
*Women's Shower Night*
*World Championship Risk*
*World Cops*
*World's Stupidest Stuntmen*
YouTube

## PHRASES, SAYINGS, SLANG AND SLOGANS

"001100111011000111100111001111 00"
"100% Mambo Ramp Jam"
"12-change-of-underwear trip"
"27th CRS"
"advanced mutual compatibility on the basis of a primary initial ident"
"Arnold—A Living Legend"
"Arnie Comes Out on Top"
"Arnie Does It Best"
"Arnie Has Had Lots of Girlfriends"
"Arnie Is Brave"
"Arnie Is Fab"
"Arnold on Top"
"Arnold's Tops With Us"
astro
Awooga Waltz
barge
black card
"*Blue Midget*—Jupiter Mining Corporation"
"brown trousers time"

“cat”
Catch-44
“Chameleonic Life Forms? No, Thanks”
“Chew on This”
“Coke Adds Life!”
“Cruise With Me for Awhile”
“Curiosity killed the human”
“Danger 2,000 Gigawatts”
“Danger Low Gravity No Leaping”
“Danger—Robots In Operation”
“D-D-Don’t Shoot”
“Denmark Forever”
“Dimension Invalid”
“Dloc Sknird”
“Do Not Engage Hyperdrive Inside Ship’s Gravity Field”
“Dog Market”
“Don’t stand around jabbering when you’re in mortal danger”
double-Polaroid
“dying”
E5:A9:O8:B7
“eh! wack”
“enig”
Eskimos
“etinoT eviL”
faberoo
“Fancy Dress Party 2nite”
feckles
“Fire Exit”
Five-Year Plan
“flamingoed up”
Game head
gar
“gazpacho soup”
Geldof
“Geronimo”
“Give Quiche a Chance”
gloop
“Go Ahead, Make My Day”
G.O.J.F.
“Gone Out”
“Greetings From-V Deck Broom Cupboard”
GROPE
“Guns ‘N Stuff”
hachum babow
Han hasset
hanaka
“Hate”
“Have a Fantastic Period”
hcanau
“Heaven This Way”
“hernunger”
“HolMem. Password override. The novels, Christie, Agatha.”
“Holograms Can Have Heart Attacks Too!”
“Home Sweet Home”
“I ♥ Flibble”
“I ♥ The Broom Cupboard”
“I ♥ Uranus”
“I am a fish”
“If you don’t gosub a program loop, you’ll never get a subroutine”
“If you lose a good friend, you can always get another; but if you lose your tail, things will always be drafty”
“If you’re gonna eat tuna, expect bones”
“I Like SKA”
“I Love Vindaloo”
“I Owe It All to Rimmer”
“It’s better to live one hour as a tiger than a whole lifetime as a worm”
“It’s Nearly Monday!”
“It’s Too Naughty!”
“I’ve Been to the Omni-Zone and Seen Infinity”
jozxyqk
“Just Say No to Smut”
“Kar nasa pinit”
“Kick Butts”
kinteteach
K.I.T.
“Klim”
“Lady Luck”
“Leave It to Rimmer”
“Lick Paws Before Knocking”
“Living It Up!!”
“Lucky 13”
lurve
“Make My Day”
masculinism
“Mike Butcher, What A Nice Guy!”
“Mimas Spaceport Welcomes Careful Drivers “
Monshoetree
“More Hate”
“Mummy, mummy”
“Mummy, of Mummyton, in the county of Mummyshire”
“Mutants Out”
“Mutant—We Love You”
“My Other Spaceship Is a *Red Dwarf*”
“Nodnol 871 Selim”
“No Entry”
“No Smoking”
“Now Irradiate Your Hands”
“nureek”
“Nylon Socks—They’re Really Cool!”
“Off Limits”
ogigon bachoo machwahah
one-armed bandit
Operation Khazi
Operation Sizzle
“Ourob Oros”
“Our Rob or Ross”
“Pinkle! Squirmy! Blip Blap Blap!”
Project Regen
Project *Wildflower*
“Psirens”
“Qw’k-Fytz”
“Rauchen Verboten!”
“Restore to Factory Settings”
Rimmer Directive 271
Rimmer Directive 483
Rimmer Directive, The
“Rimmer Does It Again”
Rimmermania
“Rock Music”
“Rock ‘N Roll”
“rotut”
rude alert
scatterbrained
“Season 29”
“Section 14 Maintenance Personnel”
“Set the Rozzers on the Prozzers”
sham glam
shiny thing
“Siwik Elur”
smeg
“Smoke me a kipper; I’ll be back for breakfast”
“Snappy Lover”
“So Long Smeeee Heees!!”

soul-sibling
"Souvenir of Titan"
"squelookle"
"Stoke me a clipper; I'll be back for Christmas"
Swirly Thing Alert
"Taking to Nearest Valid Reality"
"taranshula"
"Teacher in Space—NASA"
*tempus*
"Thank You for Not Smoking"
"thermonuclear megadeath"
"This Phone Will Not Accept Incoming Earth Calls"
"Tixe"
"Tomcat"
"Tomorrow Is the First Day of the Rest of Your Death"
"TopCats Brixton"
"To the Memory of the Memory of Lise Yates"
"Truncheons for Change"
Tueshoetree
"U=BTL"
"Unem"
"Wah twah morah!"
watunga
"We are all gonna die"
Wedshoetree
"What are you talking about, Dog-Breath?"
"While You Sleep, We're Probably Saving the Universe"
"While You Sleep, We're Probably Shaving Off Your Pubes and Gluing Them to Your Head"
white card
WOO
Yizox
"YJO s'diK"
"Ylhserf Tuc Sehciwdnas"
"You Are Now Leaving Existence"
"You Don't Have to Have a Rather Dry Sense of Humor to Live Here But It Certainly Helps"
"!ZN"
zoney

## *RED DWARF*: Components, Software, Systems and Technologies

179
184
200,000 MPH
32-12
8870t6
Abort Sequence X-1-X
auto-destruct system
AutoFOOD
Auto-Serve Dispensing Machine
bio-organic computer networking
black box recording
bypass unit
cadmium II
cadmium II coolant system
cadmium II core
Cam 5
Cameron Mackintosh 40-valve air-cooled diesel
carbon-carbon reinforced heat shields
central cargo pods
Chicken Soup Dispenser 14B
Circuit Board Epsilon 14598
Circuit Board Theta 29555
Class 40
Class A Emergency Awooga siren
Class Five
climate computer
comms unit
containment panels
cooling system
cremation tube
damage-report machine
Denti-bot
dream recorder
drive computer
drive plate
Embryo Refrigeration Unit
emergency battery power
Emergency Override Sequence Alpha-4-Alpha-9
engine core
Food Recycle Container
front cargo pods
garbage pod
General Assembly 4
grabber
Holly Hop Drive
hologram disk projection system
hologramic projection box
hologrammatic accessory computer
hologrammatic projection unit
hydro unit
hyper-drive
intruder alert
jet housings
JMC C-245
JMC onboard computer
landing bay interface
Little Monitor 2
medicomp
medicomputer
medi-scan
motivator
navicomp
oxygen recycler
porous circuit
quark-level matter-antimatter generator
ram scoop
recovery bed
Red Alert Bulb
scanner-scope
service dispenser
Ship Lib 5
ship rover
Shower Decon
solar panel
stasis field
vacuum shields
voice-recognition unit
waste disposal
waste grinder
Who's-Just-Sneaked-On-Board computer

## *RED DWARF*: Corridors, Decks, Rooms and Other Interior Areas

71
78
5A
A Deck
Admin level
air-conditioning complex

Red Corridor 357
*Red Dwarf* Central Line
*Red Dwarf* Waxwork Museum
refectory
reference library
refinery
research labs
roof bay doors
Room 1115
Scala, The
Scatter bar
Science Block
Science Department
Science Lab
Science Room
Sector 16
Sector P/4500000
secure visiting booth
Security Check
Security Deck
service elevator
Shuttle Bay 1
Shuttlebay Launch Suite
Sick Bay
Sleeping Quarter
sleeping quarters
Spud King
Stasis Booth 1344
stasis room
Status Room
storage bay
Stores
supervision field
Supplies
Supply Pipe 28
Tank, the
teaching room
technical library
Titan Taj Mahal
toilet block
toilet deck
transport decks
transport tubes
V Deck
Vacuum Storage
Vindaloovian Empire
waste-disposal bay
West 17/XC
White Corridor 159
White Corridor, Level Two
Women's Showers
Women's Wing
World's End Bar & Grill
XPress Lift
Xpress super lift
Z Deck
Zone 101

## RELIGION: Affiliations, Artifacts, Denominations, Terminology and Texts

14th Wednesday after Pentecost
15th Wednesday after Pentecost
Ascension Sunday
Asteroid of Turin
Bearth
Bible, The
Cat Bible, The
Chanski
Church of Judas, The
Clisterists
Cloisterists
crossed circuit
doughnut
Ecclesiastes
Electronic Bible, The
Elite, the
Frying Pantheist
Fuchal
Fuchal Day
Fuchal Diner, The
Fundamental Cloisterist
Fundamental Cloisterist priest collar
Fundamental Remonian
Ganymedian monastery
Gideons International, The
golden sausage
Holy Book, The
Holy Custard Stain
Holy Hydrant, The
Holy Mother, The
Holy Order of St. Geraldine
Holy, The
Jehovah's Witnesses
Last Supper, The
pantheist
Promised Land, the
Promised Planet, The
Sacred Gravy Marks
Sacred Hat, the
Sacred Laws, the
Sacred Writing, the
*Science and Health With Key to the Scriptures*
Seven Cat Commandments, the
Seventh-Day Advent Hoppists
Silicon Heaven
Silicon Hell
Suzdalism
Temple of Food
Virgin Birth, the
Wailing Wall

## SCIENCE: Ailments, Diseases, Viruses, Treatments and Other Medical

athlete's foot
athlete's hand
Brassica 2
castration therapy
"Coping With VD"
*Delecto quislibet*
dyslexia
Epideme virus
extreme nerdism therapy
*Felicitus populi*
gangrene
greed lift
Heimlich maneuver
holographic virus
holo-plague
holospasm
holovirus
*Ignotus venustas*
*Inflatus mentis*
KDNIUJVIURNVOENV984398404I-UFN98HR998SSJ
kidney stone
*Latin name*
libido shortening
lunar gonorrhea
mechaneumonia
mutated pneumonia
negative virus

nerdism
peritonitis
personality surgery
positive virus
programmable virus
psi-virus
reverse flu
roverostomy
selfishness tuck
sense of humor transplant
space madness
space mumps
space-crazy
temper tightening
yellow fever
Youngskin
ZCSBFD6577GJG93857JJJJJ-43767737837FHDKWOPIW53

## SCIENCE: Astronomy, Including Spatial Anomalies and Phenomena

astroglacier
Big Crunch, the
binary star
black hole
blue giant
gas nebula
hyperway
ion storm
Jupiter rise
meteor storm
neutrino-tachyon cloud
phasing comet
Pluto's Solstice
psi-moon
pulsar
quasar
reality minefield
rogue asteroid
S-3
stellar fog
S-type star
supergiant
temporal causeway
temporal rip
time hole
timezip
white hole
wormhole

## SCIENCE: Compounds, Drugs, Elements, Potions and Other Substances

agol
Android homebrew
Baquaii diamonds
barium hydrochlorate salad nicoise
Bliss
Boing
bri-nylon
cadmium II
cadmium-12
cesiumfrancolithicmyxialobidiumrixy-dexydixidoxidroxhide
cesiumfrancolithicmyxialobidiumrixy-dixydoxidexidroxhide
chloroform
corticoadrenaline
cryoplastic
cyberfoam
developing fluid
dilinium
dimanium
Eidetosol
Elastoplast
FLOB
fluid matrix
helium 3 isotopes de la maison
hex potion
Incinerex
Infinitol
IQ
learning drugs
Lemoplathinominecatholyrite
liquid oxygen
lithium carbonate
millennium oxide
MIT White
NeoProzak
nitroglycerine
oils of C'fadeert
Orodite
outrozone
plasma
psychotropic drug
smart drugs
Smarteez
Sodium Pentothal
strontium
stupid drugs
synaptic enhancer
synthiplast
tear gas
thorium-232
transparisteel
Ultimate Anti-Aging Cream
uranium-233
Zogothoniumeliumoxiixiexiphulmifhi-dikalidrihide

## SCIENCE: Hologrammic Technology and Terminology

Axis-syndrome hologram
bi-photonic monoprism
body-tailor
electronic aneurysm
H
hard light
hard light drive
hard light projection mode
hard light remote belt
holo exercise bike
holo-blaster
Holochamber
hologram
hologram box
hologram disc
hologram disk projection system
hologram projection suite
hologram simulation suite
hologramatic projection cage
hologramic projection box
hologrammatic accessory computer
hologrammatic projection unit
hologrammatic projection unit regeneration chamber
holographic projection device
Holographic Theory of the Brain
holographic virus
holo-knife
holo-lamp
holo-message

holo-plague
holoship
holo-slide
holospasm
holo-tracker
holovirus
holowhip
light bee
light bee remote
mind-patch
multi-spectrum SiC lens
personality chip
personality disk
physical data disc
projection unit
remote projection unit
resentment drain
soft light
soft light projection mode
Software Version RD93
Solidgram
solidogram
T-count

## SCIENCE: Miscellaneous

Aftering, the
ASC-2 code
Boyle's Fourth Law
brains
Burns-McDowell Law
Cartesian Principle, The
cartoonivore
Copernican Revolution
crylion spectro
CUTIE
cyberlake
cyber-psychologist
dibidollyhedecadodron
dimension jump (DJ)
dimension skid
Dimension Theory of Reality
dinosaur bowel movement frequency table
dividing
DynaTach
electromagnetic phasing frequency
electromagnetic radiation (EMR)
emo-field
ERRA-pert
evolution mode
fortnight
future echo
gee-gook
genome of DNA (G.O.D.)
glimbart
heuristic neural net
hexasexahedroadecon
hex vision
intelligence compression
Ionian nerve grip
L.S.
laser
mind enema
mind probe
mind scan
mind swap
mind-field
mind-patch
molecularization
moonquake
nanotek
nasal alert
phaser frequency 4-3-4
Plank constant, the
polydridocdecahooeyhedron
PSI
psi-proof chrysalis
Pythagorean theorem
relative time dilation
Shadow Time, the
Snake Diet
spaghettification
stasis leak
stasis seal
tachyon transmission
Tasha Yar Effect
temporal-displacement vortex
Theory of Relativity
Theta Delta Alpha Beta Gamma
thrust-to-input ratio
time traps
time-bend
transdimensional trace
transmogrification
unreality pocket
UO

## SPACE CORPS AND JMC: Directives, Divisions, Designations, Ranks and Regulations

00001
000-169
Admiral
Article 497
Article 5
Astronavigation Officer, Fourth Class
Console Officer
Deck Sergeant
Deck Swabber
Double-Rimmer
Emergency Regulation 479/B
Full-Rimmer
Half-Rimmer
Health and Safety Protocol 121
JMC Educational Exam Board
JMC Elevator Division
JMC Food Storage
JMC. RD. 431
JMC. RD. 432
JMC. RD. 433
JMC. RD. 434
JMC. RD. 435
JMC. RD. 436
Lift Maintenance
Lord of the Star Fleet
Mayday
metaphysical psychiatrist
military grey
navigation officer first class
ocean grey
Protocol 121
Protocol 175
RD 52 169
salvage leader
Space Corps anthem
Space Corps Directive 003
Space Corps Directive 112
Space Corps Directive 1138B, section 14, sub-paragraph M
Space Corps Directive 142
Space Corps Directive 147
Space Corps Directive 169
Space Corps Directive 1694
Space Corps Directive 1742

## SPACE CORPS AND JMC: Exams, Forms and Reports



## SPACESHIPS (GENERAL): Components, Software, Systems and Technologies



## SPACESHIPS (GENERAL): Corridors, Decks, Rooms and Other Interior Areas



## SPECIES: Fauna—Genetically Engineered

genetically engineered life form (GELF)
grizzly gerbil
Hniuplcxdewn
*Homo Rimmer*
*Homo Sapienoid*
jelly-finch
Kinitawowi
*Lupus aquaticus*
mutton vindaloo beast
not-a-cat
orang-u-rottweiler
Pleasure GELF
polymorph
Powersaur
Psiren
Snugiraffe
spiny dogeater
swanephant
symbi-morph
Tvcnkolphgkooq
Vidal Beast
Vindaloovian
werecod
whale-ipede
wildebeetroot

**SPECIES: Fauna—Non-engineered (Non-sentient)**

Alsatian
canary
cat
chicken
chimpanzee
cockroach
dog
dormouse
*Felis catus*
fish
frog
giant space weevil
hamster
iguana
Ionian bee
Iranian jird
leech
lemming
lobster
Mimian bladderfish
moose
ninja throwing squirrel
oysters
penguin
pigeon
shampooed rats
snake
space weevil
tarantula
trout
*Tyrannosaurus rex (T. rex)*
Venusian dogworm
Venusian fighting snail
war ferret

**SPECIES: Fauna—Non-engineered (Sentient)**

*Canis sapiens*
Cat People
cockroach
Dog People
*Felis erectus*
*Felis sapiens*
*Lapis sapiens*
man
*Mus sapiens*
*Rattus sapiens*

**SPECIES: Fauna—Other (Fictional, Hypothetical, Mutated, Etc.)**

dragon yak
Fire Belching William Shatner Pizza Beast
greenfly
laboratory mice
Lager Crab Thing
leaping mutton
litter bird
mermaid
ninja throwing squirrel
pan-dimensional liquid beast
Peperami
Quagaar
Rage of Innocence, the ("The Rage")
six-eyed carnivorous raging swamp beast
Space Monkeys
time fly
Venusian Orange creature
werewolf
Ziffed

**SPECIES: Flora—Plants and Vegetation**

Albert
apple
banana
Caesar Salad Monster
catangu nut
currant
freaky fungus
garlic nan tree
herring
lemon
orange
Potato People, the
singing potatoes
strawberry
Titan mushrooms
wildebeetroot

***STARBUG:* Components, Software, Systems and Technologies**

Analogue/Digital
autopilot
autopilot alert
auto-repair
auxiliary conductor nodes
auxiliary flight modulator
auxiliary power drives
backup boosters
caterpillar tracks
cloak
communication channels
CON 1
CON 2
damage-report machine
Data Threshhold
DataLoad
deep sleep unit
defensive shields

drive interface
drive module
Drive Output
emergency backup generator
Error Amp
Feedback/Input
flight recorder
Frequency Locked
fuel intake chambers
Fuel Pipe 9
fuel tanks
furry dice
generator
gravity unit
gyroscope
$H_2O$ Re-Cyc
Halogen Drive
handshake
hazard approach lights
HD-3500 homing device
heating system
Hubble telescope
hyperdrive
inertia rating
Inverting Input
landing jets
laser missile guidance control
lateral trimmers
Log/Antilog
long-long-long-range
long-long-range
long-range
magnetic coils
main fuel tanks
maneuvering thrusters
MCN
mediscan
mid-range
Modular Conduit
Non Inverting Input
override code
oxy-generation unit
Piledriver PN-14D Nuclear warhead firing device
pulse relays
Purple Alert
rear-thrust jets
refrigeration unit
retros
reverse thrust tube
safety harness
scanner table
security cameras
SEP scan
sewage processor
shields
solar batteries
Solenoid Prescaler
sonar scope
spectroscan
stabilizers
Start/Run
startup code
Synch/Inhibit Input
syscomp
Unit 1
Unit 2
Unit 5
waste compactor
Waste Disposal Unit 5
Waste Disposal Unit 8
weather computer
weather scan

**_STARBUG:_**
**Corridors, Decks, Rooms and Other Interior Areas**

Airlock 12
Airlock AZ-4
AR Suite
Artificial Reality Suite (ARS)
B Deck
C Deck
D Deck
E Deck
F Deck
Engine Bay 2
Engineering Deck
Engineering Supply Area
Landing Deck B
Log Recorder Suite
Obs Room
Supply Bunker 7
Supply Deck D
suspended animation booth
suspended animation suite
upper deck

**TOOLS, DEVICES AND TECHNOLOGY:**
**Medical and Scientific**

346
Admiral Nelson telescope
AI watch
artificial insemination syringe
B 53432 Modem Interface
bio-feedback catheter
bio-feedback sensors
Caleva
calibrator
catheter
colostomy bag
CX-114 Speaking Slide Rule
deep space probe
dimension cutter
Dinamap
DNA modifier
E-Accelerator
Emergency Death Pack
Emergency Ramp Seven
first aid box
hover stretcher
impulse valve
JMC "Scouter" Remote Drone
JMC scan probe
kidney bowl
laser bone-saw
laser scalpel
laser scalpel Mark II
Macro-Bollington
Martian power packs
medical shroud
medi-crates
medi-kit
mirror machine
molecular destabilizer
particle analyzer
Psi-scan
scalpel
self-gamete-mixing *in vitro* tube
solar accelerator
Spanner Scanner
sub-space conduits
teleporter
TI345
TI345xp

time matrix
Time Obelisk
time wand
transponder
triplicator
uterine simulator

### TOOLS, DEVICES AND TECHNOLOGY: Service and Repair

14B
14F
14-pound lump hammer
astro-stripper
bleeper
Brush-a-matic
Datanet
eco-accelerator rocket
grout gun
jet pack
Kirby XL
porta-trolley
smeg-hammer
sonic screwdriver
sonic super mop (SSM)
super deluxe vacuum cleaner
triple-bag easy-glide vac
volt meter
welding mallet

### TOOLS, DEVICES AND TECHNOLOGY: Miscellaneous

1952 Phase Four
20th-century telegraph poles
372
5517/W13 alpha-sim modem
599XRDP
Aerial Smog Sublimation (ASS)
alignment bracket
Artificial-Intelligence synthesizer
B47/7RF resistor
battleplan timetable
Betamax holo-recorder
BIOtrak Ident-chip
Blautechpunknicht
Canary Starter Pack
Chinese worry balls
computer slug
*Decree Nisi* Megadrive Chip
detachable power transfer adapter
dictopad
disintegrator
Encyclo implant chip
food bag
Heat 400
Holo-Flame Color Gas
homing device
Hover Rack 75
hypno-ring
Insta-Serve microwave
Javanese camphor-wood chest
Jovian boogle hoops
Justice Field
Keystone K-7 Deluxe
K-Tel Nose Hair Trimmer
laser chainsaw
mass compactor
Matter Paddle
Matter Transference device
memory machine
Mercurian boomerang spoon
Mimosian anti-matter chopsticks
mining laser
Model 75T
Model 7-6-80
morphing belt
multi purpose graph
neural interface helmet
No-Grav flying helmet
one-armed bandit
Palladium-core nano-torque sequencing unit
Pet Translator
polygraphic surveillance
portable walrus-polishing kit
psi-locator
psychic sub-ether enhancement implant
qik-pik
QNK base system
RE912 circuitry
reality scan
rechargeable absolute-zero unit
rejuvenation shower
returner remote
revision timetable
Sharp FNB-200
Sinclair ZX81
smug-o-meter
Snooper XL-7000
speaking clock
speaking slide-rule
Spoon of Destiny, the
Stations 1 to 4
steam-operated trouser press
suction beam
TH285 motion sensor
Time Retriever
timeslide
trouser press
Ultranet
universal translator (UT)
unoculars
Vid-E-Bone
video letter
VoxMod vocal disguise unit
wax-blaster
weather-blast goggles
Wilbur Weasel thermos flask
Z80012

### VEHICLES: Land, Air and Sea Vessels

277MJG
2G22394
882 FOP
Aston Martin
Bentley V8 convertible
C222 PFY
*Carbug*
Class D seeding ship
Cyberceptor
diving bell
E355 DPK
EYD 339C
Ferrari Testarossa
Ford Phallus
FSK 731
Gaz Mobile, the
GG 300
Harley-Peugeot "Le Hog Cosmique" space bike
Heinkel He 111
hopper

hover dinghy
hover-car
hover-limo
Jensen Interceptor
jet-cycle
JMC buggy
juggernaut
JVS-325
Lamborghini Sesto Elemento
lunar transport vehicle (LTV)
*Mary Celeste*
MFG-533
Mini Metro
Mole Tank
Morris Minor
motorized remote ore scoop
neutron tank
PG TIP
Reliant Robin
RG 211
*Rimmer One*
Rolls-Royce
sea buggy
*Seabug*
Series I E-Type Jaguar
space bike
ST4R B11G
T-72
terra buggy
Time copter
*Titanic*, RMS
Vauxhall Nova
voice-recognition unicycle
Volkswagen
VOTE 1
XHO274J
YB45 FND

**VEHICLES:**
**Spacecraft, Shuttles, Probes and Pods**

9000 SMG
Annihilator
*Apollo XIII*
*Arthur C. Clarke*
*Augustus*, SS
battle-class cruiser
*Beagle*
*Black Hole*
*Blue Midget*
Cat Ark
*Centauri*, SS
Class 3 transport ship
Class-A enforcement orb
colonization seeding ship
*Columbus 3*
Death Ship
Diva-Droid interstellar shuttle
Dog Arks
*Einstein*, SS
*Enlightenment*, SSS
escape pod
Escape Pod 1736
*Esperanto*, SSS
*FLIB-1*
Flight 261
Flight 578
*Gar Barge*
garbage tanker
GELF battle cruiser
GELF Transporter
*Gemini 12*
Genepool Biotech Corp BioSafe Genetic Waste Pod
*Hermes*, SS
*Hoarse Trojan*, SS
holoship
homing pod
*Howard Rimmer*, SS
JMC personnel shuttle
JMC159
Jupiter-class
*Lagos*
*Leif Erickson*, JMS
*Leviathan*
lightship
mail pod
*Manny Celeste*, SS
*Mayflower*
*McGovern, The*
*Midget 3*
nano-*Red Dwarf*
Nautical-Class seeding vessel
*Neutron Star*
*Neverdunroamin*
*Nostrilomo*
*Nova 5*
Nova-class scouting vessel
ocean seeding ship
ore sample pod
*Oregon*
*Pax Vert*
*Penhalagen*
*Pioneer*, SCS
*Playboy* Pleasure Cruiser
post pod
probe ship
Quantum Twister
*Red Dwarf*
*Red Dwarfski*
*Schellenberg*, SSS
*Scott Fitzgerald*
scouter
*Seabug*
search probe
Shuttlecraft 724
*Silverberg*, SSS
Simulant Death Ship
*Skylab*
Solar-class
Space Corps DJX-1 Prototype
Space Corps external enforcement vehicle
Space Corps external enforcement vehicle 5-Beta 3/2
Space Corps TTX-3 experimental craft
SpaceCondor
STA 7676-45-327-28V
*Starbug*
*Starbug 1*
*Starbug 2*
*Starbug 4*
Starhopper
stasis pod
survival pod
transdimensional homing beacon
*Trojan*, SS
*White Giant*
*White Midget*
*Wildfire*
*Wildfire One*
Zargon warship
zipper

**WEAPONS, ARMAMENTS, EXPLOSIVES AND TORTURE**

105 MM HOW HE FZ0 M5
A15 laser pistol
A30 laser cannon
agonize
AP-6
AR-16
argument-settler
Arre bubble
Ballbreaker Autofire Cannon
bazookoid MkI
bazookoid MkII
bazookoid pistol
biological explosives
blaster
C-180A Canary Rifle
Colt .45
crossbow
Death Wheel
deathagram
defensive micropedo
Emergency Ammo
Fast Charge
Fire and Forget
flare gun
garbage cannon
GeneStick pistol grip
genitometer
gonad electrocution kit
great fire of N'mjiuyhyes
groinal exploder
Heat 400
heat seeker
holo-blaster
holo-knife
holowhip
Hub of Pain
Incinerex
IR pistol
L24 E-carbine
laser
laser cannon
laser harpoon
laser lance
laser missile
laser-lancer
Lasex P-2
limpet mine
mini-grenades
missiles
Mr. Gun
munitions cabinet
nebulon missile
NeuroNet HUD sight
neutron tank
ninja throwing beret
ninja throwing squirrel
nipple-matic
Nova auto pistol
nuclear warhead
Oh God, Oh Crap (OGOC) missile
PAC-9000
particle accelerator cannon
Phlegm-Cannon
photon mutilator
plasmatic lacerator shell
Proton Cannon of Nakasami
pulse missile
Punisher Heavy Machine Gun (HMG)
rad pistol
reality mines
Reflec vest
RocketMan
rubber nuclear weapon
Smart But Casual Bomb
sound gun
Space Corps Penal System caseless round
spinal implant
Star Wars
Sword of Spite
T 27 electron harpoon
T-72
temporal ray
thermal grenade
thermonuclear device
throwing triangle
time gauntlet
Titan novelty nuclear warheads
Vindaloovian "Viper" Rifle
Volt Master
Wishbone Strike

# ABOUT THE AUTHOR

Paul C. Giachetti is the co-owner of Hasslein Books, a publishing company he launched with long-time friend Rich Handley in 2008. A magazine layout artist by trade, he is also Hasslein's graphic artist and layout designer, and has designed and produced all of the company's publications to date, as well as its marketing and promotional material. He lives on Long Island, New York.

Paul maintains a personal blog at paulanoma.blogspot.com, and occasionally contributes to Hasslein's blog, hassleinbooks.blogspot.com. A long-time fan of British comedy, he decided the time was right to compile this two-volume set—his debut publications for Hasslein Books—about his all-time-favorite franchise. Some of his other favorites include *Star Wars*, *Star Trek*, *Doctor Who*, *Babylon 5*, *Stargate*, *The Hitchhiker's Guide to the Galaxy* and *Farscape*. He is also an avid photographer, gamer and techie, and enjoys making fun of bad movies.

He can be followed at facebook.com/paulgiachetti.

# ABOUT HASSLEIN BOOKS

Hasslein Books (hassleinbooks.com) is a New York-based independent publisher of reference guides by geeks, for geeks. The company is named after Doctor Otto Hasslein, a physicist and time travel expert portrayed by actor Eric Braeden in the film *Escape from the Planet of the Apes*, and on the Hasslein Curve named in honor of his theories.

In addition to the *Red Dwarf Encyclopedia*, the company's lineup of unauthorized genre-based reference books includes *Timeline of the Planet of the Apes: The Definitive Chronology*, *Lexicon of the Planet of the Apes: The Comprehensive Encyclopedia*, *A Matter of Time: The Unauthorized Back to the Future Lexicon*, *Back in Time: The Unauthorized Back to the Future Chronology* and *Lost in Time and Space: An Unofficial Guide to the Uncharted Journeys of Doctor Who*, with future volumes slated to feature James Bond, *G.I. Joe*, *Alien vs. Predator*, *Battlestar Galactica*, *Ghostbusters*, *Universal Monsters* and *The Man From U.N.C.L.E.*

Follow Hasslein Books on Facebook (facebook.com/hassleinbooks) and Twitter (twitter.com/hassleinbooks), and at the Hasslein Blog (hassleinbooks.blogspot.com), to stay informed regarding upcoming projects.

Printed in Great Britain
by Amazon